READER'S DIGEST
CONDENSED BOOKS

www.readersdigest.co.uk

The Reader's Digest Association Limited 11 Westferry Circus Canary Wharf London E14 4HE

For information as to ownership of copyright in the material of this book, and acknowledgments, see last page.

Printed in France
ISBN 0 276 42662-2

READER'S DIGEST
CONDENSED BOOKS

*Selected and edited
by Reader's Digest*

CONDENSED BOOKS DIVISION

THE READER'S DIGEST ASSOCIATION LIMITED, LONDON

CONTENTS

With the Allies' plans for D-Day almost
finalised, a key Nazi communication centre
housed in the château of Sainte-Cécile must
be put out of action as a matter of extreme
urgency. The RAF has tried bombing it. The
French Resistance have tried a frontal assault
without success. Now it's up to SOE's best
agent, Felicity Clairet, to pull off their most
audacious plan to date. Ken Follett's legions
of fans will relish this lively new blockbuster.

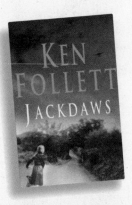

PUBLISHED BY MACMILLAN

Connor and Ed are smoke jumpers, elite
fire-fighters who parachute into blazing
forests to cut fire breaks. They are also
close friends, which causes problems when
Connor meets Ed's girlfriend, Julia, and
finds himself powerfully attracted to her.
From the best-selling author of *The Horse
Whisperer*, an epic novel of love, courage
and loyalty, set against the breathtaking
backdrop of Montana's wilderness.

PUBLISHED BY BANTAM PRESS

HOSTAGE
Robert Crais

page 293

LA hostage negotiator Jeff Talley has down-shifted to a quieter life as a police chief in one of California's small towns, only to find his old skills in demand again in the wake of a violent robbery. But this is a hostage situation like no other—even as he negotiates, Talley's wife and daughter are seized as bargaining chips to protect the interests of some very powerful men. High-tension action from a master of the suspense thriller.

PUBLISHED BY ORION

ON THE STREET WHERE YOU LIVE
Mary Higgins Clark

page 431

Seeking refuge from her troubled past, Manhattan attorney Emily Graham buys a house that once belonged to her ancestors in tranquil Spring Lake, New Jersey. When the skeletons of two women, murdered more than 100 years apart, are unearthed there, Emily is drawn into an investigation of the two deaths and becomes the target of a devious killer. A compelling mystery from a best-selling crime writer.

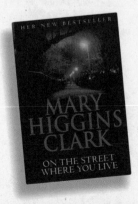

PUBLISHED BY SIMON & SCHUSTER

Jackdaws

KEN FOLLETT

With the hours to D-Day ticking away, and one of the Allies' key targets in northern France still not destroyed, Britain's Special Operations Executive decide on radical action.

Enter the 'Jackdaws'—a unique, all-female team that includes a one-time murderess, a safe-breaker and a most unusual telephone engineer . . .

THE FIRST DAY:
Sunday, May 28, 1944

One minute before the explosion, the square at Sainte-Cécile was at peace. The evening was warm, and a layer of still air covered the town like a blanket. The church bell tolled, a lazy beat calling worshippers to the service with little enthusiasm. To Felicity Clairet it sounded like a countdown.

The square was dominated by the seventeenth-century château. A small version of Versailles, it had a grand projecting front entrance, and wings on both sides that turned right angles and tailed off rearwards. There was a basement and two main floors topped by a tall roof with arched dormer windows.

Felicity, who was always called Flick, loved France. She enjoyed its graceful buildings, its mild weather, its leisurely lunches, its cultured people. She liked French paintings, French literature, and stylish French clothes. She had been speaking the language since she was six years old, and no one could tell she was a foreigner.

It angered her that the France she loved no longer existed. There was not enough food for leisurely lunches, the paintings had all been stolen by the Nazis, and only the whores had pretty clothes. Like most women, Flick was wearing a shapeless dress whose colours had long ago been washed to dullness. Her heart's desire was that the real France would come back. It might return soon, if she and people like her did what they were supposed to.

She might not live to see it—indeed, she might not survive the next

9

few minutes. She was no fatalist; she wanted to live. There were a hundred things she planned to do after the war: finish her doctorate, have a baby, see New York, drink champagne on the beach at Cannes. But if she were about to die, she was glad to be spending her last few moments in a sunlit square, looking at a beautiful old house, with the lilting sounds of the French language soft in her ears.

The château had been built here in the heart of the Champagne district as a home for the local aristocracy, but it now housed an important telephone exchange. Also in the building were the Gestapo regional headquarters. Four weeks ago they had been bombed by the Allies. Such precision bombing was new. The heavy four-engined Lancasters and Flying Fortresses that roared high over Europe every night were inaccurate—they sometimes missed an entire *city*—but the latest generation of fighter-bombers, the Lightnings and Thunderbolts, could sneak in by day and hit a small target, a bridge or a railway station. Much of the west wing of the château was now a heap of rubble. But the air raid had failed. Repairs were made quickly, and the phone service had been disrupted only as long as it took the Germans to install replacement switchboards. All the vital telephone equipment in the basement had escaped serious damage.

That was why Flick was here.

The château was on the north side of the square, surrounded by a high wall of stone pillars and iron railings, guarded by uniformed sentries. To the east was a small medieval church, and opposite the church, on the west side of the square, was the town hall. The south side was a row of shops and a bar called Café des Sports. Flick sat outside the bar, waiting for the church bell to stop. On the table in front of her was a glass of the local white wine, thin and light.

She was a British officer with the rank of major. Officially, she belonged to the First Aid Nursing Yeomanry, the all-female service inevitably called the FANYs. But that was a cover story. In fact, she worked for the Special Operations Executive, responsible for sabotage. At twenty-eight, she was a senior agent. This was not the first time she had felt herself close to death. She had learned to manage her fear, but all the same she felt a cold hand on her heart when she looked at the steel helmets and powerful rifles of the château guards.

Three years ago, her greatest ambition had been to become a professor of French literature in a British university. She had been working in the War Office, translating French documents, when she had been summoned to a mysterious interview and asked if she would be willing to do something dangerous. She had said yes without thinking much. All the boys she had been at Oxford with were risking their lives in the war, why shouldn't she? Two days after Christmas 1941 she had started her SOE training.

Six months later she was a courier, carrying messages from SOE headquarters at 64 Baker Street in London to Resistance groups in occupied France. She would parachute in, move around with her false identity papers, contact the Resistance, give them their orders and note their replies. For the return journey she would rendezvous with a small pick-up plane in a grassy field.

From courier work she had graduated to organising sabotage. The work was dangerous. Flick had survived because she was ruthless, quick, and careful about security to the point of paranoia.

Beside her today sat her husband, Michel, leader of the Resistance circuit codenamed Bollinger, which was based in the cathedral city of Reims, ten miles away. Although about to risk his life, Michel was sitting back in his chair, his right ankle resting on his left knee, holding a glass of watery wartime beer. His careless grin had won her heart when she was a student at the Sorbonne, writing a thesis that she had abandoned on the outbreak of war. He had been a dishevelled young philosophy lecturer with a legion of adoring students.

He was still the sexiest man she had ever met. He was tall, and dressed with careless elegance in rumpled suits and faded blue shirts. He had a come-to-bed voice and an intense blue-eyed gaze.

This mission had given Flick a welcome chance to spend a few days with her husband, but it had not been a happy time. They had not quarrelled exactly, but Michel's affection had seemed half-hearted. Instinct told her he was interested in someone else. He was only thirty-five, and his unkempt charm still worked on young women. It did not help that since their wedding they had been apart more than together, because of the war.

Flick still loved him. The morning mists of romantic love had lifted and in the clear daylight of married life she could see that he was vain, self-absorbed and unreliable. But when he chose to focus his attention on her, he could still make her feel unique and beautiful and cherished. His charm worked on men, too, and he was a great leader, courageous and charismatic.

He and Flick had figured out the battle plan together. Fifteen fighters from the Bollinger circuit would attack the château in two places, dividing the defenders, then regroup inside to penetrate the basement and blow up the main equipment room.

They had a floor plan of the building supplied by Antoinette Dupert, Michel's aunt, the supervisor of the group of local women who cleaned the château every evening. The cleaners started work at seven o'clock, the same time as Vespers, and Flick could see some of them now, presenting their special passes to the guard at the wrought-iron gate. Antoinette's sketch showed the entrance to the basement, but no further details, for it was a restricted area, open to Germans only, and cleaned by soldiers.

Michel's attack plan was based on reports from MI6, the British intelligence service, which said the château was guarded by a Waffen-SS detachment working in three shifts, each of twelve men. The fifteen attackers were now deployed either among the worshippers in the church, or posing as Sunday idlers around the square. If MI6 was right, the Resistance would outnumber the guards.

But a worry nagged at Flick's brain. When she had told Antoinette of MI6's estimate, Antoinette had frowned and said, 'It seems to me there are more.' There had been no time for further reconnaissance.

Flick looked around the square, picking out the people she knew, apparently innocent strollers who were in fact waiting to kill or be killed. The scene looked normal but for one element. Beside the church was parked an enormous, powerful sports car, a French-built Hispano-Suiza. It had a tall, arrogant-looking silver radiator, topped by the flying-stork mascot, and it was painted sky blue.

The car had arrived half an hour ago. The driver, a dark-haired handsome man of about forty, was wearing an elegant civilian suit, but he had to be a German officer—no one else would have the nerve to flaunt such a car. His companion, a tall, striking redhead in a green silk dress and high-heeled suede shoes, was too perfectly chic to be anything but French. The man had set up a camera on a tripod and was taking photographs of the château.

A few minutes ago, the man had scared Flick by asking her to take a picture of himself and his lady friend. He had spoken courteously, with only a trace of German accent. Flick had put on an expression of cold indifference and complied with the request.

The officer was obviously off duty. All the same he bothered Flick. There was a watchful alertness in his manner that was not appropriate for a tourist. His woman might be exactly what she seemed, his whore, but he was something else.

Before Flick could figure out what, the bell ceased to toll.

Flick and Michel stood up. Trying to look casual, they strolled to the café entrance and stood in the doorway, taking cover.

DIETER FRANCK had noticed the girl at the café table the moment he drove into the square. He always noticed beautiful women. This one was a pale blonde with light green eyes. Her small, slim body was wrapped in a dress like a sack, but she had added a bright yellow scarf, with a flair for style that he thought enchantingly French. When he spoke to her he had observed the initial flash of fear usual in a French person being approached by one of the German occupiers, but then he had seen on her face a look of ill-concealed defiance that had piqued his interest.

She was with an attractive man who was not very interested in her—probably her husband. Dieter had asked her to take a photo only because he wanted to talk to her. He had a wife and two pretty children in Cologne, and he shared his Paris apartment with Stéphanie, but that would not stop him making a play for another girl. French women were the most beautiful in the world. But everything French was beautiful: their bridges, their boulevards, their paintings, even their china tableware.

Dieter did not know where he had acquired such tastes. His father was a professor of music, but to Dieter, the dry academic life his father led seemed unbearably dull, and he had horrified his parents by becoming a policeman. By 1939, he was head of the criminal intelligence department of the Cologne police. In May 1940, when German tanks swept triumphantly through France, Dieter applied for a commission in the army. Because he spoke fluent French and adequate English, he was put to work interrogating prisoners. He had a talent for the work, and in North Africa his results had been noticed by Field Marshal Erwin Rommel himself.

Dieter was always willing to use torture when necessary, but he liked to persuade people by subtler means. That was how he had got Stéphanie. Poised, sensual and shrewd, she had owned a Paris boutique selling ladies' hats. But she had a Jewish grandmother. She had been on her way to a camp in Germany when Dieter rescued her.

He could have raped her. Instead, he had fed her, installed her in his apartment and treated her with gentle affection until one evening after dinner of *foie de veau*, he had seduced her deliciously on the couch in front of a blazing coal fire.

Today, though, she was part of his camouflage. He was working with Rommel again. The 'Desert Fox' was now Commander of Army Group B, defending northern France from an Allied invasion expected this summer. The British planned to slow Rommel's response by disrupting his communications.

Dieter's brief was to identify key communications targets and assess the ability of the Resistance to attack them. Today he was paying a surprise visit to a telephone exchange of enormous strategic importance. All telephone traffic from the High Command in Berlin to German forces in northern France passed through this building. The Allies obviously knew that and had tried to bomb the place, with limited success. It was the perfect candidate for a Resistance attack. Yet security was infuriatingly lax, by Dieter's standards. He had been here for half an hour, taking photographs of the place, his anger mounting as the men responsible for guarding the place continued to ignore him.

However, as the church bell stopped ringing, a Gestapo officer came strutting through the gates of the château. In bad French he shouted at Dieter, 'Give me that camera! It is forbidden to take photographs of the château.'

Dieter replied quietly in German, 'You took a damn long time to notice me.'

The man was taken aback. 'Who are you?'

'Major Dieter Franck, from Field Marshal Rommel's personal staff.'

'Franck!' said the man. 'I remember you.'

Dieter looked harder at him. 'My God,' he said as recognition dawned. 'Willi Weber.'

'Sturmbannführer Weber, at your service.' Like most senior Gestapo men, Weber held an SS rank, which he felt was more prestigious than his ordinary police rank. Weber and Dieter had been young policemen together in Cologne in the 1920s. Dieter had been a high-flier, Weber a failure. Weber resented Dieter's success.

Dieter had not seen the man for fifteen years, but he could guess the course of Weber's career: he had joined the Nazi party, applied for a job with the Gestapo citing his police training, and risen swiftly in that community of embittered second-raters. No wonder security at the château was slack.

Weber said, 'What are you doing here?'

'Checking your security, on behalf of the Field Marshal.'

Weber bristled. 'Our security is good.'

'Good enough for a sausage factory. Look around you.' Dieter waved a hand, indicating the town square. 'What if these people belonged to the Resistance? They could pick off your guards in seconds.' He pointed to a tall girl wearing a light summer coat over her dress. 'What if she had a gun under her coat? What if . . .'

He stopped. This was not just a fantasy he was weaving, he realised. His unconscious mind had realised that the people in the square were deploying in battle formation. The tiny blonde and her husband had taken cover in the bar. A tall girl in a summer coat, who had been staring into a shop window, was now standing in the shadow of Dieter's car. As Dieter looked, her coat flapped open, and he saw that she had a submachine gun. 'Get down!' he yelled.

Then there was a bang.

FLICK WAS IN THE DOORWAY of the Café des Sports, behind Michel, standing on tiptoe to look over his shoulder.

There were eight guards in sight: two at the gate checking passes, two just inside the gate, two patrolling the grounds inside the iron railings, and two at the top of the short flight of steps leading to the château's doorway. But Michel's main force would bypass the gate.

The long north side of the church formed part of the wall surrounding the château's grounds. The north transept jutted a few feet into the car park that had once been part of the ornamental garden. In the days of the *ancien régime,* the Comte de Sainte-Cécile had had his own personal entrance to the church, a little door in the transept wall. The doorway had been boarded up and plastered over more than a hundred years ago. But an hour ago, a retired quarryman called Gaston had entered the empty church and carefully placed plastic explosives at the foot of the blocked doorway. He had inserted detonators, and added a five-second fuse ignited by a thumb plunger. He had moved an old wooden bench in front of the doorway for concealment. Then he had knelt down to pray.

When the church bell had stopped ringing a few seconds ago, Gaston had got up from his pew, walked from the nave into the transept, depressed the plunger, and ducked back around the corner. The blast shook centuries of dust from the Gothic arches.

After the explosion, there was a long moment of silence in the square. Everyone froze: the guards at the château gate, the sentries patrolling the fence, the Gestapo major, and the well-dressed

German with the glamorous mistress. Flick, taut with apprehension, looked across the square and through the iron railings into the grounds. In the car park beside the château a soldier was filling the tank of one of the two black Citroëns of the Traction Avant type favoured by the Gestapo in France. Flick waited, holding her breath. Among the congregation in the church were ten armed men. At this moment, the ten would be rushing through the new hole in the wall.

At last they came into view round the end of the church, a motley army in old caps and worn-out shoes, running across the car park towards the grand entrance of the château, clutching their assorted weapons. They had not yet begun firing them, for they were trying to get as close as possible to the building before the shooting started.

Michel saw them at the same time. Now was the moment to distract the guards. Michel raised his rifle, drew a bead, then fired. At the gate, one of the guards cried out and fell.

Michel's shot was the signal for everyone else to open fire. In the church porch, seventeen-year-old Bertrand, the youngest member of the team, squeezed off two shots with his Colt automatic. He was too far from the guards for accuracy with a pistol, and he did not hit anyone. Beside him, Albert, another member of the Resistance team, pulled the ring of a grenade and hurled it high over the railing. From behind the parked sports car, Geneviève, a girl of twenty, opened up with her Sten gun. Another guard fell.

At last the Germans began to act. The guards took cover behind the stone pillars and brought their rifles to bear. The Gestapo major fumbled his pistol out of its holster. The redhead turned and ran, but her sexy shoes slipped on the cobblestones, and she fell. Her man lay on top of her, protecting her with his body.

The sentries opened fire. Almost immediately, Albert was hit. Flick saw him stagger and clutch his throat. A hand grenade he had been about to throw dropped from his grasp. Beside Albert, Bertrand saw the grenade roll across the stone step of the church porch. He hurled himself through the doorway as the grenade exploded. Flick waited for him to reappear, but he didn't.

In the car park, the team from the church stopped running, turned on the remaining sentries and opened up. The four guards near the gate were wiped out in seconds, leaving only the two on the château steps. Michel's plan was working, Flick thought with a surge of hope.

But the enemy troops inside the building now rushed to the windows and began to shoot, changing the odds again. Flick realised with dismay that there were many more guns in the château than she had expected. The men from the church, who should by now be inside the building, retreated to take cover behind the vehicles in the car park. Antoinette had been right, and MI6 wrong, about the number of troops stationed here.

From the upper floor of the château, a machine gun began to fire, causing horrible carnage among the Resistance in the car park. It was all over, Flick realised in despair. They were outnumbered.

'We can't take out that machine gunner from the ground!' Michel said. His gaze flew to the upper floor of the town hall. 'But if I could get into the mayor's office, I'd have a clear shot.'

'Wait.' Flick could not stop him risking his life, but she could improve the odds. She yelled: 'Geneviève! Cover Michel!'

Geneviève dashed out from behind the sports car, spraying bullets at the château windows. Michel sprinted across the square.

There was a flash on Flick's left. She glanced that way and saw the Gestapo major, flattened against the wall of the town hall, aiming his pistol at Michel.

She was under orders to observe and report back, and not to join the fighting under any circumstances, but now she thought: To hell with that. She reached into her shoulder bag and snatched out her personal weapon, a Browning automatic. She extended her arm and fired two hasty shots at the major. Her bullets chipped fragments of stone from the wall near his face and he ducked.

Michel ran on. He fired his rifle in the major's direction, but the shot went wild and the major fired back. This time, Michel went down and Flick let out a yell of fear.

Michel hit the ground, tried to get up, and collapsed. Flick thought fast. Geneviève's submachine-gun fire continued to draw the attention of the enemy inside the château. Flick had a chance of rescuing Michel. No orders could make her leave her husband bleeding on the ground. Besides, if he were captured and interrogated, it would be a catastrophe. As leader of the Bollinger circuit, Michel knew every name, every address, every code word.

She shot at the major again, forcing the man to take cover. She ran out of the bar into the square. The owner of the sports car was still protecting his mistress from gunfire by lying on top of her. Was he armed? If so, he could shoot Flick easily. But no bullets came.

She reached Michel and went down on one knee. She fired two wild shots to keep the major busy. Then she looked at her husband.

His eyes were open and he was breathing. He seemed to be bleeding from his left buttock. Her fear receded a little. She turned again towards the town hall.

The major had retreated to a shop doorway. Flick squeezed off four shots. The shop window exploded in a storm of glass, and the major staggered and fell.

Flick spoke to Michel in French. 'Try to get up,' she said. He rolled over, groaning in pain, and got to one knee, but he could not move his injured leg. 'Come on,' she said harshly. 'If you stay here, you'll be killed.' She grabbed him by the front of his shirt and heaved him upright with a mighty effort. He stood on his good leg, but he could not bear his own weight.

She glanced over to the major. He had blood on his face, but he did not seem badly injured. He might still be capable of shooting.

There was only one thing for it. She bent in front of Michel, grasped him round the thighs and eased him onto her shoulder in the classic fireman's lift. She staggered, but stayed upright.

Amid the continuing gunfire she made for the road leading out of the square to the south. She passed the German lying on top of the redhead, and for a startled moment she met his eye and saw an expression of surprise and wry admiration.

A moment later, she was round the corner and clear of the battle-field. Until now she had not thought where to go. Two getaway vehicles were waiting a couple of streets away, but she could not carry Michel that far. However, Antoinette Dupert lived on this street, just a few steps farther. She surely would not turn her nephew away.

Antoinette had a ground-floor apartment in a building with a courtyard. Flick hammered on her door, panting with effort. She heard a frightened voice say, 'What is it?'

Breathlessly, Flick said, 'Quickly! Your nephew is wounded.'

The door opened. Antoinette was a straight-backed woman of fifty wearing a faded cotton dress. She was pale with fear. 'Michel!'

Flick said impatiently, 'Let's get him inside.'

Together they carried him into the living room.

'Take care of him while I fetch the car,' Flick said.

She ran back out. The gunfire was dying down. She did not have long. She raced along the street and turned two corners. Outside a closed bakery, two vehicles were parked, engines running: a rusty Renault, stolen this morning, and a laundry van, borrowed from Bertrand's father. Flick decided to take the car, leaving the van for any survivors who might get away from the château.

She ran to the car, jumped in, and said, 'Let's go, quickly!'

At the wheel of the Renault was Gilberte, a nineteen-year-old girl with long dark hair, pretty but stupid. Flick did not know why she was in the Resistance—she was not the usual type. Instead of pulling away, Gilberte said, 'Where to?'

'I'll direct you—move!' Flick said. 'Left, then right.'

In the two minutes that followed, the full realisation of her failure hit her. Most of the Bollinger circuit was wiped out. Geneviève, Bertrand, and any others who survived would probably be tortured. And it was all for nothing. The telephone exchange was undamaged, and German communications were intact. What had she done wrong? Had it been a mistake to try a frontal attack? Not necessarily. The plan might have worked but for the inaccurate intelligence supplied by MI6. However, it would have been safer, she now thought, to get inside the building by some clandestine means.

Gilberte pulled up at the courtyard entrance. 'Turn the car round,' Flick said, and jumped out.

Michel was lying face down on Antoinette's sofa, trousers pulled down, looking undignified. Antoinette knelt beside him, holding a bloodstained towel, a pair of glasses perched on her nose, peering at his backside. 'The bleeding has slowed, but the bullet is still in there,' she said.

On the floor beside the sofa was her handbag. She had emptied the contents onto a small table, presumably while hurriedly searching for her spectacles. Flick's eye was caught by a little cardboard folder. It was the pass that permitted Antoinette to enter the château. In that moment, Flick had the glimmer of an idea.

'I've got a car outside,' Flick said.

Antoinette continued to study the wound. 'He shouldn't be moved.'

'If he stays here, the Boche will kill him.' Flick casually picked up Antoinette's pass and slipped it into her shoulder bag. Antoinette didn't notice. Flick said to her, 'Help me to get him up.'

The two women raised Michel to his feet. Antoinette pulled up his blue canvas trousers and fastened his worn leather belt.

'Stay inside,' Flick said to Antoinette. 'I don't want anyone to see you with us.'

Michel put his arm round Flick's shoulders and leaned heavily on her. She took his weight, and he hobbled out of the building into the street. Gilberte leapt out of the car and threw open the rear door. With her help, Flick bundled Michel onto the back seat. The two women jumped in the front.

'Let's get out of here,' said Flick.

DIETER WAS APPALLED. He had not thought the Resistance capable of such a well-planned attack. They had been bristling with guns and obviously not short of ammunition—unlike the German army. Worse, they had been courageous. Dieter had been impressed by the rifleman who had dashed across the square, by the girl with the Sten gun who had given him covering fire, and most of all by the little blonde who had picked up the wounded rifleman and had carried him to safety. These French Resistance people were fighters. But their defeat gave him a rare opportunity.

When he was sure the shooting had stopped, he got to his feet and helped Stéphanie up. Her cheeks were flushed. 'You made yourself a shield for me,' she said. Tears came to her eyes.

He brushed dirt from her hip. He was surprised by his own gallantry. The action had been instinctive. 'No harm should come to this perfect body,' he said.

He led her across the square and they entered the grounds of the château. The Waffen-SS troops had come out of the building and were disarming the attackers. Most were dead, but some were only wounded, and one or two appeared to have surrendered unhurt.

He shouted at a sergeant, 'You—get a doctor for these prisoners. I want to interrogate them. Don't let any die.'

Dieter took Stéphanie up the steps and through the stately doorway into the wide hall. It was a breathtaking sight: a pink marble floor, walls with Etruscan motifs in shades of pink and green, a ceiling painted with cherubs. Once, it had been filled with gorgeous furniture: high mirrors, dainty chairs with gilded legs, oil paintings, huge vases. All that was gone now. Instead there were rows of switchboards, each with its chair, and a snake's nest of floor cables.

Dieter sat Stéphanie at one of the switchboards, patted her shoulder and left her. He passed through double doors into the east wing. The château was laid out as a series of reception rooms, one leading into the next. The rooms were full of switchboards, but these had a more permanent look, the cables bundled into wooden trunking that disappeared through the floor into the cellar beneath.

At the end of the east wing was a stairwell. Dieter went down. At the foot of the staircase he passed through a steel door. A small desk and a chair stood just inside, and Dieter assumed the guard on duty had left his post to join in the fighting. Dieter entered unchallenged.

This was a different environment from that of the grand principal floors. Designed as storage and accommodation for the dozens of staff who would have serviced this house 300 years ago, the cellar had low ceilings, bare walls and stone floors. Dieter walked along a broad corridor. On his left, at the front of the building, was the complex equipment of a major telephone exchange: a generator, enormous batteries and rooms full of tangled cables. On his right, towards the back of the house, were the Gestapo's facilities: a photo lab, a large listening room for eavesdropping on the Resistance, and prison cells. The basement had been bombproofed: all windows were blocked, the walls sandbagged, the ceilings reinforced.

At the end of the corridor was a door marked INTERROGATION CENTRE. He went inside. The first room had white walls, bright lights, a cheap table, hard chairs. Dieter went through to the next room. Here the lights were less bright and the walls bare brick. There was a bloodstained pillar with hooks for tying people up; an umbrella stand holding a selection of wooden clubs and steel bars; an operating table with a head clamp and straps for wrists and ankles; an electric-shock machine. It was a torture chamber. Dieter had to remind himself that intelligence gathered in places such as this helped to save the lives of decent young German soldiers. All the same, the place gave him the creeps.

Dieter heard footsteps in the corridor. He returned to the interview room as the prisoners were brought in.

The first was the woman who had concealed a Sten gun beneath her coat. Dieter was pleased. It was useful to have a woman among the prisoners. Women could be as tough as men, but often the way to make a man talk was to beat a woman in front of him. This one was tall and sexy and seemed to be uninjured. Dieter spoke to the woman in French. 'What is your name?' he said in a friendly tone.

She looked at him with haughty eyes. 'Why should I tell you?'

He shrugged. This level of opposition was easy to overcome. He used an answer that had served him well a hundred times. 'Your relatives may enquire whether you are in custody. If we know your name, we may tell them.'

'I am Geneviève Delys.'

'A beautiful name for a beautiful woman.' He waved her on.

Next came a man in his sixties, bleeding from a head injury. Dieter said, 'You're a little old for this sort of thing, aren't you?'

The man looked proud. 'I set the charges,' he said defiantly.

'Name?'

'Gaston Lefèvre.'

'Just remember,' Dieter said in a kindly voice, 'the pain lasts as long as you choose. When you decide to end it, it will stop.'

Fear came into the man's eyes as he contemplated what faced him.

A youngster was next, no more than seventeen, Dieter guessed, a good-looking boy who was absolutely terrified. 'Name?'

He hesitated, seeming dazed by shock. 'Bertrand Bisset.'

'Good evening, Bertrand,' Dieter said pleasantly. 'Welcome to Hell.'

The boy looked as if he had been slapped. Dieter pushed him on.

Willi Weber appeared. 'How did you get in here?' he said rudely to Dieter.

'I walked in,' Dieter said. 'Your security stinks. I'm going to interview the prisoners.'

'That's the Gestapo's job.'

'Field Marshal Rommel has asked me, not the Gestapo, to limit the capacity of the Resistance to damage his communications. These prisoners can give me priceless information.'

'Not while they're in my custody. I shall interrogate them myself and send the results to the Field Marshal,' Weber said stubbornly.

'This means I'll have to go over your head.'

'If you can.'

'Of course I can, you damned fool,' Dieter said savagely. He turned on his heel and stalked out.

GILBERTE AND FLICK left the town of Sainte-Cécile behind, heading for Reims on a country back road. Their progress was slowed by many crossroads, but the number of junctions made it impossible for the Gestapo to block every route away from Sainte-Cécile. All the same, Flick gnawed her lip, worrying about the chance of being stopped by a patrol. She could not explain away a man in the back seat bleeding from a bullet wound.

Back in Sainte-Cécile, some of the team must have been taken. If the Gestapo were determined, they could make the strongest personality betray his or her dearest comrades. So Flick had to treat Michel's house as known to the enemy. She could not take him home. Where could she take him instead?

'How is he?' said Gilberte anxiously.

Flick glanced into the back seat. He had fallen into a sleep, but he was breathing normally. She looked at him fondly. He needed someone to take care of him, at least for a day or two. She turned to Gilberte, young and single. 'Where do you live?'

'On the outskirts of town, on the Route de Cernay.'

'On your own?'

For some reason, Gilberte looked scared. 'Yes, of course.'

'A house, an apartment, a bedsitter?'

Reluctantly, Gilberte said, 'An apartment, two rooms.'

'We'll go there. Is there a back entrance?'

'Yes, an alley that runs along the side of a little factory.'

'It sounds ideal.'

Flick was scheduled to return to London that night. She was to rendezvous with a plane outside the village of Chatelle, eight kilometres north of Reims. She wondered if the plane would make it. Navigating by the stars, it was extraordinarily difficult to find a specific field near a small village. She looked at the weather. A clear sky was darkening to the deep blue of evening. There would be moonlight, provided the weather held.

Her mind went to the comrades she had left behind. Was young Bertrand dead or alive? And Geneviève? Alive, they faced the agony of torture. Her heart convulsed with grief and she longed for a way to make sure their suffering was not in vain.

She thought about the pass she had stolen from Antoinette, and the possibility of getting into the château under cover. A team could enter disguised as civilian employees. She swiftly dismissed the idea of having them pose as telephone operators: it was a skilled job that took time to learn. But anyone could use a broom. And the Germans probably paid no attention to the women who mopped the floor.

SOE had a remarkable forgery department. They could quickly produce counterfeits of Antoinette's pass. Of course, all the cleaners were women, so the Resistance team that went in disguised as cleaners would have to be all-female. But then, Flick thought, why not?

It was dark when Gilberte pulled up near a low industrial building in the suburbs of Reims. Flick spoke sharply to Michel. 'Wake up! We have to get you indoors.'

He groaned as the two women helped him out of the car. But he put his arms over their shoulders, and they helped him along the narrow alley behind the factory and across the back yard of a small apartment building. They went in through a back door.

It was a block of cheap flats with five floors and no lift. Unfortunately, Gilberte's rooms were in the attic. Crossing their arms, they linked hands under Michel's thighs and took his weight. That way they carried him up eight flights.

They were breathing hard by the time they reached Gilberte's door. They stood Michel on his feet and he managed to limp inside, where he collapsed into an armchair.

Flick looked around. It was a girl's place, pretty and neat. Gilberte fussed about Michel, trying to make him comfortable with cushions, wiping his face gently with a towel, offering him aspirins.

'You need a doctor,' Flick said brusquely. 'What about Claude Bouler? He used to help us.'

'He's become scared since he got married,' Michel replied. 'But he'll come for me.'

Flick nodded. Lots of people would make exceptions for Michel. 'Gilberte, go and fetch Dr Bouler.'

'I'd rather stay with Michel.'

'Please do as I ask,' Flick said firmly. 'I need time alone with Michel before I return to London.'

'What about the curfew?'

'If you're stopped, say you're fetching a doctor.'

Gilberte looked troubled, but she pulled on a cardigan and left.

Flick sat on the arm of Michel's chair and kissed him. 'That was a catastrophe,' she said. 'I'll never trust those MI6 clowns again.'

He grunted. 'We lost Albert. I'll have to tell his wife.'

'I'm going back tonight. I'll get London to send you another radio operator.' She held his hand. 'How are you feeling?'

'Foolish. It's an undignified place for a bullet wound. And a little giddy.'

'You need something to drink. I wonder what she has.'

'Scotch would be nice.' Flick's friends in London had taught Michel to like whisky, before the war.

'That's a little strong.' The kitchen was in a corner of the living room. Flick opened a cupboard. To her surprise, she saw a bottle of Dewar's, an unlikely drink for a French girl. There was also an opened bottle of red wine. She poured half a glass and topped it up with water from the tap. Michel drank greedily.

Flick poked her nose into the bedroom. Michel said sharply, 'Where are you going?'

'Just looking around. I need the bathroom.'

'It's outside. Down the stairs and along the corridor.'

She followed his instructions. While she was in the bathroom she realised that something was bothering her, something about Gilberte's apartment. She thought hard. She never ignored her instincts: they had saved her life more than once. When she returned, she said to Michel, 'Something's wrong here. What is it?'

He shrugged, looking uncomfortable. 'I don't know.'

It had something to do with Gilberte's unease, with Michel's knowing where the bathroom was, with the whisky. She went into the bedroom, exploring. There was a doll on the counterpane. In the corner was a washbasin with a mirrored cabinet over it. Flick opened the cabinet door. Inside was a man's razor and shaving brush. They were a set, with polished bone handles. She recognised them. She had given them to Michel for his thirty-second birthday.

She was so shocked that for a moment she could not move.

She had suspected him of being interested in someone else, but she had not imagined it had gone this far. Shock turned to hurt. Then she became angry. She had been loyal and faithful, she had borne the loneliness of separation—but he had not.

She strode into the other room. 'You bastard. You lousy rotten bastard. How could you betray me for a nineteen-year-old nitwit?'

'It doesn't mean anything, she's just a pretty girl.'

'Do you think that makes it better?'

'Flick, my darling, let's not quarrel. Half our friends have just been killed. You're going back to England. We could both die soon.' He fixed Flick with his intense blue eyes. 'I plead guilty. I'm a louse. But I'm a louse who loves you, and I'm asking you to forgive me, this once in case I never see you again.'

It was hard to resist. Flick weighed five years of marriage against a fling with a popsy and gave in. She moved towards him. He put his arms round her legs and pressed his face into the worn cotton of her dress. She stroked his hair. 'All right,' she said. 'All right.'

The door opened and Gilberte came in with Claude Bouler. Flick gave a guilty start and released Michel's head from her embrace. Then she felt stupid. He was *her* husband, not Gilberte's.

Gilberte looked shocked to see her lover embracing his wife, but she recovered her composure.

Claude, a handsome young doctor, followed her in, looking anxious. He looked at Michel. 'How do you feel, old buddy?'

'I've got a bullet in my arse.'

'Then I'd better take it out.'

'I have another request,' Flick said. 'I'm meeting a plane at a quarter to midnight. I need you to drive us to Chatelle.'

Claude looked scared. Michel rolled over and sat upright. 'Claude, I'm begging you. Do it for me, will you?'

It was hard to say no to Michel. Claude sighed. 'When?'

THE VILLAGE OF CHATELLE consisted of three large houses, six cottages and a bakery clustered round a crossroads. Flick stood in a pasture two kilometres from the crossroads, holding a torch.

The field was almost a kilometre long—a Lysander needed 600 metres to land and take off. The ground beneath her feet was firm, and there was no slope. It was bordered by a pond, which was clearly visible from the air in the moonlight, providing a useful landmark for pilots.

Michel and Gilberte stood upwind of Flick in a straight line, also holding flashlights, and Claude stood a few metres to one side of Gilberte, making a flare path in the shape of an upside-down L to guide the pilot.

Waiting for the plane was always hell. If it did not arrive, Flick would face another twenty-four hours of danger before the next opportunity. But an agent never knew whether a plane would show up. The task of navigating by moonlight across hundreds of kilometres of country was monumentally difficult. The pilot used dead reckoning—calculating his position by direction, speed and elapsed time—and tried to verify the result by landmarks such as rivers, towns and railway lines. If there was cloud hiding the moon it was impossible. However, this was a fine night and Flick was hopeful.

Sure enough, a couple of minutes before midnight, she heard the sound of a single-engined plane, faint at first, then growing louder. She began to flash her light in the Morse letter X.

The plane circled once, then came down steeply. It touched down on Flick's right, braked, taxied back to Flick and turned into the wind again, completing a long oval and finishing up ready for takeoff.

The aircraft was a Westland Lysander, a small, high-winged monoplane, painted matt black. The pilot did not stop the engine. His aim was to remain on the ground no more than a few seconds.

Flick wanted to hug Michel and wish him well, but she also wanted to slap his face and tell him to keep his hands off other women. Perhaps it was just as well that she had no time for either. With a brief wave, she scrambled up the metal ladder, threw open the hatch and climbed aboard.

The pilot glanced behind. Flick gave him the thumbs-up. The little plane jerked forward, picked up speed, then rose into the air.

The Second Day:
Monday, May 29, 1944

Dieter Franck drove through the blacked-out streets of Paris in the big Hispano-Suiza, accompanied by his young assistant, Lieutenant Hans Hesse. Yesterday evening, Dieter had found a neat row of bullet holes stitched in the generous curve of the car's offside bumper, a souvenir of the skirmish in the square at Sainte-Cécile, but there was no mechanical damage, and he felt the holes added to the car's glamour.

Lieutenant Hesse removed the headlight covers when they got on the road to Normandy. They took turns at the wheel, two hours each. Dieter tried to picture his future. Would the Allies reconquer France? The thought of Germany defeated was dismal. He found it hard to imagine everyday life back in Cologne, with his wife and family, after the excitement of Paris and Stéphanie.

Before dawn they drove into the small medieval village of La Roche-Guyon, on the River Seine between Paris and Rouen. They went past silent, shuttered houses to a checkpoint at the gates of the ancient castle. At last they parked in the great cobbled courtyard and Dieter went inside. The castle was Rommel's headquarters.

In the hall, Dieter met Rommel's aide-de-camp, Major Walter Goedel, a cold personality with a formidable brain. They had spoken on the phone late last night. Dieter had outlined the problem he was having with the Gestapo and said he wanted to see Rommel as soon as possible. 'Be here at four,' Goedel had said. Rommel was always at his desk by four o'clock in the morning.

Now Goedel led Dieter along the hall.

Rommel's office was a grand room on the ground floor. Dieter noticed with envy a priceless Gobelin tapestry on one wall. Behind a huge antique desk sat a small man with receding sandy hair.

Goedel said, 'Major Franck is here, Field Marshal.'

Rommel continued reading for a few seconds, then looked up. The face was a boxer's face, with a flat nose and a broad chin and close-set eyes, and it was suffused with the naked aggression that had made Rommel a legendary commander.

'Sit down, Franck,' he said briskly. 'What's on your mind?'

Dieter had rehearsed this. 'On your instructions, I've been visiting key installations that might be vulnerable to attack by the Resistance, and upgrading their security. I've also been assessing the potential of the Resistance to hamper our response to an invasion. The situation is worse than we imagined.'

Rommel grunted with distaste. 'Reasons?'

Dieter recounted yesterday's attack at Sainte-Cécile: the imaginative planning, the plentiful weaponry, the bravery of the fighters.

'I was afraid of this,' Rommel said. He spoke quietly, almost to himself. 'I can beat off an invasion, even with the few troops I have, but if my communications fail, I'm lost.'

Dieter said, 'I believe we can turn the attack on the telephone exchange into an opportunity.'

Rommel turned to him with a wry smile. 'By God, I wish all my officers were like you. Go on, how will you do this?'

Dieter began to feel the meeting was going his way. 'If I can interrogate the captured prisoners, they may lead me to other groups. With luck, we might inflict a lot of damage on the Resistance. Unfortunately, the Gestapo is refusing me access to the prisoners.'

'They are such imbeciles.'

'I need you to intervene.'

'Of course.' Rommel looked at Goedel. 'Call Avenue Foch.' The Gestapo's French headquarters were at 84 Avenue Foch in Paris. 'Tell them that Major Franck will interrogate the prisoners in Sainte-Cécile today, or their next phone call will come from Berchtesgaden.' He was referring to Hitler's Bavarian fortress.

'Very good,' said Goedel.

'Keep me informed, please, Franck,' Rommel said, and returned his attention to his papers as Dieter left the room.

FLICK LANDED at RAF Tempsford, an airstrip fifty miles north of London. A young FANY corporal was waiting with a powerful Jaguar to drive her to London. 'I'm to take you directly to Orchard

Court,' the driver said. 'They're waiting to debrief you.'

Flick rubbed her eyes. 'God, do they think we don't need sleep?'

Dawn broke as the car sped south. Flick looked out at the modest houses, with vegetables growing in the front gardens, the country post offices where grumpy postmistresses resentfully doled out penny stamps, and the assorted pubs with their warm beer and battered pianos, and she felt profoundly grateful that the Nazis had not got this far. The feeling made her all the more determined to return to France. She wanted another chance to attack the château right away. It was a good thing she was to be debriefed immediately: she would have a chance to propose her new plan today.

Orchard Court was an apartment building in Portman Square. Flick went inside and made her way to SOE's flat. Agents were kept away from the headquarters on Baker Street so that they could not reveal its address under interrogation. Her spirits lifted when she saw Percy Thwaite. A balding man of fifty with a toothbrush moustache, he was paternally fond of Flick.

'I can tell by your face that it went badly,' Percy said.

His sympathetic tone of voice was too much for Flick to bear. The tragedy of what had happened overwhelmed her and she burst into tears. Percy put his arms round her and she buried her face in his old tweed jacket. 'Oh, God, I'm sorry to be such a girl.'

She sank into a sagging armchair and watched Percy as he made tea. He could be tough as well as compassionate. He would ask searching questions about her plan, but he would be open-minded.

He handed her a mug of tea with milk and sugar. 'There's a meeting later this morning,' he said. 'Hence the hurry.'

She sipped the sweet tea and told him what had happened at Sainte-Cécile. 'Based on Antoinette's misgivings about the intelligence, I should have postponed the raid,' she finished.

Percy shook his head sadly. 'This is no time for postponements. The invasion can't be more than a few days away. It had to be tried. The telephone exchange is too important.'

'Well, that's some consolation.' Flick was glad she did not have to believe Albert had died because she had made a tactical error.

'And Michel is all right?' Percy said.

'Mortified, but recovering.' When SOE had recruited Flick, she had not told them her husband was in the Resistance. If they had known, they might have steered her towards different work. But she had not really known it herself. In May 1940, she had been in

England, visiting her mother, and Michel had been in the French army. The fall of France had left them stranded in different countries. By the time she returned as a secret agent, and learned what role her husband was playing, she was already too useful to SOE for her to be fired on account of hypothetical emotional distractions.

Percy stood up. 'Well, you'd better get some sleep.'

'Not yet. First I want to know what we're going to do about the telephone exchange. We *have* to knock it out.'

He looked at her shrewdly. 'What have you got in mind?'

She took Antoinette's pass out of her bag. 'Here's a better way to get inside. It's used by the cleaners.'

Percy scrutinised the pass. 'Clever girl,' he said.

'I want to go back. I'll take a full team with me. We'll substitute for the cleaners in order to get into the château.'

'I take it the cleaners are women?'

'Yes. I'd need an all-female team.'

'Where would you find them?'

'Get approval for my plan and I'll find the women. I'll take SOE rejects, people who failed the training course, anybody. We must have a file of people who have dropped out for one reason or another.'

'Yes—because they were physically unfit, or couldn't keep their mouths shut, or lost their nerve in parachute training.'

'It doesn't matter,' Flick argued earnestly. 'This is the turning point, we have to throw everything at the enemy.'

'You couldn't use French Resistance women?'

Flick had already considered and rejected that idea. 'It would take too long to find them. Then we have to have a forged pass with a photo for each woman. That's hard to arrange over there. Here, we can do it in a day.'

'You're right, our people do work miracles in that department.'

Flick felt a surge of triumph. He was going to go for it.

Percy went on, 'But even assuming you can find enough French-speaking girls, don't the German guards know the cleaners?'

'It's probably not the same women every night—they must have days off. And men never notice who cleans up after them.'

'What about the French people inside? The telephone operators are local women, aren't they? Not every French person likes the Resistance. There are some who approve of the Nazis' ideas.'

Flick shook her head. 'The French have had four years of Nazi rule. Everyone over there is hoping desperately for the invasion. The switchboard girls will keep mum.'

'You hope. Look, I like this plan. I'm going to put it up to the boss. But I think he will reject it. No one but you could lead this team, but we can't send you back. You know too much. If you were captured, you could give away most of the Resistance circuits in northern France.'

'I know,' Flick said grimly. 'That's why I carry a suicide pill.'

GENERAL SIR BERNARD MONTGOMERY, commander of the 21st Army Group that was about to invade France, had set up improvised headquarters in west London, at a school whose pupils had been evacuated to the countryside. Meetings were held in the model room, and everyone sat on the schoolboys' hard wooden benches.

The Brits thought this was cute. Paul Chancellor from Boston, Massachusetts, thought it was bullshit. What would it have cost them to bring in a few chairs? He liked the British, but not when they were showing off about how eccentric they were.

Paul was on Monty's personal staff. His area of responsibility was intelligence. He was an organiser. He made sure the reports Monty needed were on his desk when he wanted them, chased those that came late, set up meetings with key people. He could think for himself and Monty had come to rely on him more and more.

He did have experience of clandestine work. He had been with the Office of Strategic Services, the American secret agency, and had served under cover in France and French-speaking North Africa. Then, six months ago, Paul had been wounded in a shoot-out with the Gestapo in Marseille. One bullet had taken off most of his left ear but harmed nothing other than his looks. Another smashed his right kneecap, which would never be the same again, and that was the reason he had a desk job.

The work was easy compared to living on the run in occupied territory. They were planning the invasion, and Paul was one of a few hundred people in the world who knew the date. In fact, there were three possible dates, based on the tides, the currents, the moon and the hours of daylight. These requirements left only a narrow window: the fleet could sail next Monday, June 5, or on the following Tuesday or Wednesday. The final decision would depend on the weather.

Paul was thrilled to be part of the team that was planning the greatest invasion of all time. With the thrill came anxiety, of course.

He knew that any error he made—a slip of the pen, a detail over-looked—could kill Allied troops.

Today at 10.00am, Paul had scheduled fifteen minutes on the French Resistance. It was Monty's idea. He was nothing if not a detail man.

At five to ten, Simon Fortescue came into the model room. Tall, in a pinstripe suit, he was one of the senior men at MI6. He was fol-lowed by John Graves, a nervous-looking civil servant from the Ministry of Economic Warfare, the department that oversaw SOE.

A moment later, Monty walked in, a small man with a pointed nose and receding hair. His face was deeply lined either side of his close-clipped moustache. He was fifty-six, but looked older.

Monty did not waste time. 'In the coming battle,' he said, 'the most dangerous moments will be the first. We will be hanging by our fin-gertips from a cliff edge. This will be the enemy's best opportunity. He has only to stamp on our fingers with the heel of his jackboot. Anything we can do to slow the enemy's response will be of crucial importance.' Monty looked at Graves.

'Well, SOE has more than a hundred agents in France, and thou-sands of French Resistance fighters,' Graves began. 'Over the last few weeks we have dropped them many hundreds of tons of guns, ammunition and explosives.'

Monty interrupted. 'How effective will they be?'

Graves hesitated and Fortescue jumped in. 'My expectations are modest. The performance of SOE is uneven.'

There was a subtext here, Paul knew. The old-time professional spies at MI6 hated the swashbuckling newcomers of SOE. Was that the game here? A bureaucratic spat between MI6 and SOE?

'Any *particular* reason for your pessimism,' Monty asked.

'Take last night's fiasco,' Fortescue replied. 'A Resistance group attacked a telephone exchange near Reims.'

'Who was in charge?' Monty asked.

'An SOE commander. Major Clairet. A woman.'

Paul had heard of Felicity Clairet. She was something of a legend among the small group who knew the secrets of the Allies' clandes-tine war. She had survived under cover in France longer than anyone. Her code name was Leopardess, and people said she moved around the streets of occupied France with the silent footsteps of a dangerous cat. They also said she was a pretty girl with a heart of stone. She had killed more than once.

'And what happened?' Monty said.

'Poor planning, an inexperienced commander and a lack of discipline among the men all played their part,' Fortescue replied.

'I'm not sure that's quite fair,' Graves protested feebly.

'We're not here to be fair to people,' Monty growled. He stood up. 'I think we've heard enough.'

Graves said, 'But what shall we do about the telephone exchange? SOE has come up with a new plan—'

'Bomb it,' said Monty.

'We've tried that,' Graves said. 'The damage was not sufficient to put the telephone exchange out of action for long.'

'Then bomb it again,' said Monty, and he walked out.

Graves threw a look of petulant fury at the man from MI6. 'Really, Fortescue,' he said. 'I mean to say . . . *really*.'

Fortescue did not respond.

They all left the room. In the hall outside, two people were waiting: a man of about fifty in a tweed jacket, and a short blonde woman wearing a worn blue cardigan over a cotton dress. The woman wore a bright yellow scarf tied with a touch of style that looked, to Paul Chancellor, distinctly French. Fortescue hurried past them, but Graves stopped. 'They turned you down,' he said. 'They're going to bomb it again.'

Paul guessed that the woman was the Leopardess, and he looked at her with interest. She was small and slim, with curly hair cut short, and rather lovely green eyes.

She reacted with indignation to Graves's statement. 'There's no point in bombing the place from the air, the basement is reinforced. For God's sake, why did they make that decision?'

'Perhaps you should ask this gentleman,' Graves said, turning to Paul. 'Major Chancellor, meet Major Clairet and Colonel Thwaite.'

Caught off guard, Paul replied with undiplomatic frankness. 'I don't see that there's much to explain. You screwed up and you're not being given a second chance.'

The woman glared up at him—she was a foot shorter than he—and spoke angrily. 'Screwed up?' she said. 'What the hell do you mean by that?'

'Maybe General Montgomery was misinformed, but wasn't this the first time you had commanded an action of this kind, Major?'

'Is *that* what you've been told? That it was my lack of experience?'

She was beautiful, he saw now. Anger made her eyes wide and her cheeks pink. But she was being very rude, so he decided to give it to her with both barrels. 'That and poor planning—'

'You arrogant pig!'

Paul took an involuntary step back. He had never been spoken to this way by a woman. She may be five feet nothing, he thought, but I bet she scares the damn Nazis.

Colonel Thwaite spoke for the first time. 'Calm down, Flick.' Turning to Paul, he went on, 'Let me guess—this account was given to you by Simon Fortescue of MI6, was it not?'

'That's correct,' Paul said stiffly.

'Did he mention that the attack plan was based on intelligence supplied by his organisation?'

'I don't believe he did.'

'I thought not,' said Thwaite. 'Thank you, Major.'

Paul did not feel the conversation was really over, but he had been dismissed by a senior officer, and he had no choice but to walk away.

He had obviously got caught in the crossfire of a turf war between MI6 and SOE. He felt most angry with Fortescue, who had used the meeting to score points. Had Monty made the right decision in choosing to bomb the telephone exchange rather than let SOE have another go at it? Paul was not sure.

He decided to ask some more questions.

DIETER HAD TOLD Rommel that the interrogation of the prisoners *might* enable him to cripple the Resistance before the invasion. Unfortunately, there was nothing guaranteed about an interrogation. Clever prisoners told lies that were impossible to check. Some found ingenious ways to kill themselves before the torture became unbearable. Worst of all, they might have been fed false information by the perfidious Allies, so that when they finally broke under torture, what they said was part of a deception plan.

As Lieutenant Hesse drove the sky-blue Hispano-Suiza towards Sainte-Cècile, Dieter began to put himself in the mood. He needed to be completely hard-hearted and calculating. He closed his eyes and felt a profound calm settle over him; a familiar bone-deep chill.

The car pulled into the grounds of the château. Workmen were repairing the smashed glass in the windows. In the ornate hall, the telephonists murmured into their microphones. Dieter, with Hans Hesse in tow, went down the stairs to the fortified basement. The sentry at the door to the interrogation centre saluted Dieter, who was in uniform, and made no attempt to detain him. In the outer room, Willi Weber sat at the table. Dieter barked, 'Heil Hitler!' and saluted, forcing Weber to stand.

'Where are the prisoners?'

Weber looked shifty. 'Two are in the cells.'

Dieter narrowed his eyes. 'And the third?'

Weber inclined his head towards the inner room. 'The third is under interrogation.'

Dieter opened the door. A Gestapo sergeant stood just inside the room. He was short and pudgy, with a fleshy face and close-cropped hair, and he was sweating and breathing hard, as if he had been taking vigorous exercise. He held a wooden club and was staring at a prisoner who was tied to a post.

Dieter's fears were confirmed. Despite his self-imposed calm, he grimaced with revulsion. The prisoner was the young woman, Geneviève, who had carried a Sten gun under her coat. She was naked, her face was swollen and one arm hung at an odd angle, apparently dislocated at the shoulder.

Dieter assumed a tone of authority. To the sergeant he said, 'I am Major Franck. Your name?'

The sergeant became deferential. 'Becker, sir, at your service.'

'What has she told you?'

Becker looked embarrassed. 'Nothing.'

Dieter nodded, suppressing his rage. It was as he had expected.

Weber was standing in the doorway, looking defiant. Dieter said, 'You were expressly told that I would conduct the interrogation.'

'We were ordered to give you access,' Weber replied. 'We were not prohibited from questioning the prisoners ourselves.'

'And are you satisfied with the results you have achieved?'

Weber did not answer.

Dieter said, 'Take me to the other two.'

Weber led the way along the corridor and stopped at a door with a peephole. Dieter slid back the panel and looked inside.

It was a bare room with a dirt floor. The only item of furniture was a bucket in the corner. Two men sat on the ground, staring into space. Dieter had seen both yesterday. The older one was Gaston, who had set the charges. He had a large bandage covering a scalp wound. The other, young Bertrand, had no visible injuries.

Dieter watched them for a while, taking time to think. He had to do this right. He could not afford to waste another captive. The kid would be scared, he foresaw, but might withstand a lot of pain. The other was too old for serious torture—he might die before he cracked—but he would be soft-hearted.

Dieter began to see a strategy for interrogating the two. He returned to the interview room. Dieter said, 'Sergeant Becker, untie the woman and put her in the cell with the other two.'

Becker went into the torture chamber and re-emerged carrying the broken body of Geneviève. Dieter said, 'Make sure the old man gets a good look at her, then bring him here.'

Becker went out. A short time later he returned with Gaston.

Dieter motioned the old man to a seat and offered him cigarettes and matches. Gaston took a cigarette and lit it with shaking hands.

Dieter spoke in French, using a friendly tone. 'I'm going to ask you some questions.'

'I don't know anything,' Gaston said.

'Oh, I think you do,' Dieter said. 'You're in your sixties, and you've probably lived in or around Reims all your life.' Gaston did not deny this. Dieter went on: 'I realise that the members of a Resistance cell use code names and give one another the minimum of personal information, as a security precaution.' Gaston gave a slight nod of agreement. 'But you've known most of these people for decades.'

'I can't tell you anything,' Gaston said in a near-whisper. He was scared, but he still had some courage left.

Dieter shrugged. It was to be the hard way, then. He spoke to Becker in German. 'Go back to the cell. Strip the boy and tie him to the pillar in the next room.' Then he turned back to Gaston. 'You're going to tell me the names and code names of all the men and women in your Resistance circuit.'

Gaston shook his head.

A moment later, Becker returned with Bertrand. Gaston stared as the naked boy was marched into the torture chamber.

Dieter stood up. 'Keep an eye on this old man,' he said to Lieutenant Hesse, who had taken a seat in the corner. Then Dieter followed Becker.

He was careful to leave the door a little ajar so that Gaston could hear everything.

Becker tied Bertrand to the pillar. Before Dieter could intervene, Becker punched Bertrand in the stomach. The young man groaned.

'No, no, no,' Dieter said. Becker's approach was completely unscientific. 'First, you blindfold him.' He produced a large bandana from his pocket and tied it over Bertrand's eyes. 'This way, every blow comes as a shock, and every moment between blows is an agony of anticipation.'

Becker picked up his wooden club and hit the side of the victim's head with a loud crack.

'No, no,' Dieter said again. 'Never hit the head. You may dislocate the jaw, preventing the subject from speaking. Worse, you may damage the brain, then nothing he says will be of any value.' He took the club from Becker and replaced it with a steel crowbar from the umbrella stand. 'Now, remember, the object is to inflict unbearable agony without endangering the subject's life or his ability to tell us what we need to know.'

A crafty look came over Becker's face. He walked round the pillar, then, taking careful aim, struck hard at Bertrand's elbow with the steel bar. The boy gave a scream of real agony.

'No more, please,' Bertrand implored, hysterical with pain. 'Please don't hit me again.'

Dieter went into the next room. Gaston sat where Dieter had left him, but he was a different man. He was bent over in his chair, face in his hands, sobbing and praying to God. Dieter knelt in front of him and said softly, 'Only you can make it stop.'

'Please, stop it, please,' Gaston moaned.

'Will you answer my questions?'

There was a pause. Bertrand screamed again. 'Yes!' Gaston yelled. 'Yes, yes, I'll tell you everything, if you just stop!'

Dieter called in German. 'Sergeant Becker! No more for now.'

'Yes, Major.' Becker sounded disappointed.

Dieter reverted to French. 'Now, Gaston, let's begin with the leader of the circuit. Name and code name. Who is he?'

'Michel Clairet. Code name Monet.'

The first name was the hardest. The rest would follow effortlessly.

FLICK'S HOME was an attic room in a big old house in Bayswater. There was little of her in the room: a photo of Michel playing a guitar, a shelf of Flaubert and Molière in French, a watercolour of Nice she had painted at the age of fifteen. The small chest had three drawers of clothing and one of guns and ammunition.

Now that her alternative plan had been rejected, she felt weary and depressed. She undressed, lay down on the bed, and tried looking through a magazine. But her mind kept returning to yesterday's failure. She reran the battle in her mind, imagining a dozen decisions she might have made differently. As well as losing the battle, she feared she might be losing her husband, and she wondered if there was a link: inadequate as a leader, inadequate as a wife. Perhaps there was some flaw deep in her character.

Eventually she drifted into an uneasy sleep. She was woken by someone banging on the door. 'Flick! Telephone!' The voice belonged to one of the girls in the flat below. She pulled on a dressing gown and ran downstairs to the phone in the hall.

Percy Thwaite's voice said, 'Can you come to Orchard Court? I need you to brief someone.'

She was always glad to hear Percy's voice. She had become very fond of him, and even though he constantly sent her into danger, Flick knew he would never take an unnecessary risk with her.

'I'll be there in a few minutes.' She dressed quickly.

Percy was waiting for her in the flat. 'I've found a radio operator to replace Albert. No experience, but he's done the training. I'm sending him to Reims tomorrow. We've heard nothing from Michel today. I need to know how much of the Bollinger circuit is left.'

Flick nodded. 'But what's the point?'

'Even if there's no one left but Michel and a couple of others, they can blow up railway lines, cut telephone wires, it all helps. But I can't direct them if I have no communication.'

Flick shrugged. 'I'll brief him, of course.'

Percy gave her a hard look. 'How was Michel—apart from his wound?'

'Fine.' Flick was silent for a moment. She could not deceive Percy, he knew her too well. 'There's a girl,' she said.

'I was afraid of that. I'm sorry.'

'It would help if I could tell myself that I'd made a sacrifice for a purpose, struck a magnificent blow for our side.'

'You've done more than most, over the last two years.'

'But there's no second prize in a war.' She stood up. She was grateful for Percy's fond sympathy, but it was making her maudlin. 'I'd better brief the new radio man.'

'Code name Helicopter. He's eager to see you.'

She frowned. 'Eager? Why?'

Percy gave a wry smile. 'Go and find out for yourself.'

Percy's secretary directed Flick to another room. Flick paused outside the door. This is how it is, she told herself: you pick yourself up and carry on, hoping that you will eventually forget.

Helicopter was a fair-skinned boy of about twenty-two, wearing a tweed suit. You could tell he was English from a mile away. Fortunately, before he got on the plane he would be kitted out in clothing that would look inconspicuous in a French town.

Flick introduced herself, and he said, 'Yes, we've met before, actually. You were at Oxford with my brother, Charles. You came to our house in Gloucestershire once.'

'Charlie Standish—of course!' Flick remembered another fair boy in tweeds, a weekend in a country house in the thirties, and a family with an amiable English father and a chic French mother. Charlie had had a kid brother, Brian, an awkward adolescent in shorts, very excited about his new camera. 'How is Charlie? I haven't seen him since we graduated.'

'He's dead, actually.' Brian looked suddenly grief-stricken. 'Died in forty-one. Killed in the b-b-bloody desert, actually.'

Flick was afraid he would cry. She took his hand, 'Brian, I'm so terribly sorry.'

He swallowed hard. 'I've seen you since then, just once. You gave a lecture to my SOE training group.'

'I hope my talk was useful.'

'You spoke about traitors within the Resistance and what to do about them. "It's quite simple," you said. "You put the barrel of your pistol to the back of the bastard's head and pull the trigger twice." Scared us all to death, actually.'

He was looking at her with something like hero worship, and she began to see what Percy had been hinting at. It looked as if Brian had a crush on her. She said, 'Well, we'd better begin. You know you're going to make contact with a Resistance circuit that has been largely wiped out.'

'Yes. I'm to find out how much of it is left and what it is still capable of doing, if anything.'

'Your contact in Reims is a woman codenamed Bourgeoise. Every day at three in the afternoon she goes to the crypt of the cathedral to pray. She'll be wearing odd shoes, one black and one brown. You say to her, "Pray for me." She replies, "I pray for peace." That's the code.'

He repeated the words. 'Easy enough to remember.'

'She'll take you to her house, then put you in touch with the head of the Bollinger circuit, whose code name is Monet. Don't mention the address or real name of Bourgeoise to other members of the circuit. It's better they don't know.' Flick herself had recruited Bourgeoise. Even Michel had not met the woman. 'Is there anything you want to ask me?'

'I'm sure there are a hundred things, but I can't think of any.'

'Well, good luck.' She stood up. 'Stay alive, Brian.'

She returned to Percy's room. 'He's not perfect secret agent material, Percy.'

Percy shrugged. 'He's brave, he speaks French like a Parisian and he can shoot straight.' He got up and went to the door. 'While I'm seeing him off, have a look at that rogues' gallery, will you?' He pointed to a pile of books and some scattered photos on his desk. 'Those are all the pictures that MI6 has of German officers. If the man you saw in the square at Sainte-Cécile should happen to be among them, I'd be interested to know his name.' He went out.

Flick picked up one of the books. It was a graduation yearbook from a military academy, showing stamp-sized photos of a couple of hundred fresh-faced young men. There were a dozen or more similar books, and several hundred loose photos.

The man in the square had looked about forty. He would have graduated at the age of twenty-two, roughly, or about 1926. None of the books was that old.

She turned her attention to the loose photographs. She recalled the man as tall and well dressed, with thick dark hair. She remembered dark eyes, a straight nose, a square chin . . . quite the matinée idol, in fact. She scanned the photos quickly, hesitating over each dark-haired man. None was as handsome as the one she recalled from the square. She passed over a photo of a man in police uniform, then went back to it. On a careful study she thought this was him.

She turned the photo over. Pasted to the back was a typewritten sheet. She read:

FRANCK, Dieter Wolfgang. Born Cologne June 3 1904; educ. Humboldt University of Berlin & Cologne Police Academy; mar. 1930 Waltraud Loewe, one son one dtr; Superintendent, Criminal Investigation Department, Cologne police, to 1940; Major, Intelligence Section, Afrika Korps, to ?
  A star of Rommel's intelligence staff, this officer is said to be a skilled interrogator and a ruthless torturer.

Flick shuddered. This was a frightening enemy.

Percy returned, and she handed him the picture. 'This is the man.'

'Dieter Franck!' said Percy. 'We know of him. How interesting.'

There was a tap at the door, and Percy's secretary looked in. 'There's a Major Chancellor to see you, Colonel Thwaite.'

Percy looked at Flick. She remembered the arrogant major who had been so rude to her this morning at Monty's headquarters. 'Oh God, him. What does he want?'

'Send him in,' said Percy.

Paul Chancellor walked with a limp that Flick had not noticed this morning. He had a pleasant American face, with a big nose and a jutting chin. Any chance he might have had of being handsome was spoiled by his left ear, or what remained of it. Flick assumed he had been wounded in action.

Chancellor saluted, 'Good evening, Colonel. Evening, Major.'

Percy said, 'We don't do a lot of saluting at SOE, Chancellor. Please sit down.'

Chancellor took a chair. 'I'm glad I caught you both,' he said. 'I've spent most of the day thinking about this morning's conversation.' He gave a self-effacing grin. 'Part of the time, I have to confess, I was composing wittily crushing remarks I could have made if only I had thought of them in time.'

Flick could not help smiling. She had done the same.

Chancellor went on. 'You hinted, Colonel, that MI6 might not have told the whole truth about the attack on the telephone exchange. So I sent for your report. When I read it, I realised the main reason for defeat was wrong intelligence.'

'Supplied by MI6!' Flick said indignantly.

'Yes,' Chancellor said.

'Obviously, MI6 was covering up its own incompetence. And they would never have got away with it if your boss had been at the meeting this morning to put SOE's side of the story. It seems too much of a coincidence that he was called away from it at the last minute.'

Percy looked dubious. 'He was summoned by the Prime Minister. I don't see how MI6 could have arranged that.'

'The meeting was not attended by Churchill. A Downing Street aide took the chair. And it *had* been arranged by MI6.'

'Those snakes!' Flick said angrily.

Chancellor said, 'I also looked at your plan, Major Clairet, for taking the château by stealth. It's risky but it could work.'

Did that mean it would be reconsidered? Flick hardly dared to ask.

Percy gave Chancellor a level look. 'So what are you going to do about all this?'

'I told Monty we had made a mistake.' He grimaced. 'Not easy with any general. But he's authorised your plan.'

'Thank God!' Flick jumped up. 'Another chance!'

Percy said, 'Splendid!'

Chancellor held up a warning hand. 'Two more things. The first one you may not like. He's put me in charge of the operation.'

'You?' Flick said.

'I'm sorry you seem dismayed. Monty has faith in me, even if you don't.'

Flick said, 'What's the other stipulation?'

'There's a time constraint. I can't tell you when the invasion will be. But if you haven't achieved the objective by midnight next Monday, it will probably be too late. We have exactly one week.'

The Third Day:
Tuesday, May 30, 1944

Flick left London at dawn, driving a motorcycle with a power-ful engine. The roads were deserted and she drove very fast. It was dangerous but exciting.

She felt the same about the mission, scared but eager. She had stayed up late last night with Percy and Paul, planning. There must be six women in the team, they had decided, as it was the unvarying number of cleaners on a shift. One had to be an explosives expert; another, a telephone engineer, to decide exactly where the charges should be placed. She wanted one good marksman and two tough soldiers. With herself, that would make six.

She had one day to find them. The team would need a minimum of two days' training. They would be dropped near Reims on Friday night, and enter the château on Saturday evening or Sunday. That left one spare day as a margin for error.

She took the road towards Canterbury. It was not yet six o'clock when she reached Somersholme, the country house of the barons of

Colefield. The baron himself, William, was in Italy, fighting his way towards Rome with the Eighth Army, Flick knew. His sister, the Honourable Diana Colefield, was the only member of the family living here now. The vast house, with its dozens of bedrooms, was being used as a convalescent home for wounded soldiers. The family now occupied only a small corner.

Flick parked the motorcycle on the gravel forecourt of the great house next to an ambulance and a scatter of Jeeps.

In the hall, nurses bustled about with cups of tea for the soldiers. Flick asked for Mrs Riley, the housekeeper, and was directed to the servants' quarters. She found her in the kitchen.

'Hello, Ma,' said Flick.

Her mother hugged her hard. 'I never know if you're alive until I see you. Come, I'll make you some breakfast.'

Flick had grown up in this house. She had played in the servants' hall, run wild in the woods, attended the village school. She had been extraordinarily privileged. Most women in her mother's position were forced to give up their jobs when they had a child. Ma had been allowed to stay because she was such a good housekeeper and the old baron had dreaded losing her. Flick's father had been butler, but he had died when she was six years old. Every February, Flick and her Ma had accompanied the family to their villa in Nice, which was where Flick had learned French.

The old baron, father of William and Diana, had encouraged Flick to study, even paying her school fees. He had been very proud when she won a scholarship to Oxford. When he died, soon after the start of the war, Flick had been heartbroken.

The family now occupied only a small corner of the house. The old butler's pantry was now the kitchen. Flick's mother put the kettle on. 'Just a piece of toast will be fine, Ma,' said Flick.

Her mother ignored her and started frying bacon. 'Well, I can see you're all right,' she said. 'How is that handsome husband?'

'Michel's alive,' Flick said. She sat at the kitchen table.

'Alive, is he? But not well, evidently. Wounded?'

'He got a bullet in his bum. It won't kill him.'

'You've seen him, then?'

Flick laughed. 'Ma, stop it! I'm not supposed to say.'

'Of course not. So, you're going back?'

Flick never ceased to be startled by the accuracy of her mother's intuition. 'I can't say.'

'Have you not done enough?'

'We haven't won the war yet, so no, I suppose I haven't.'

Ma put a plate of bacon and eggs in front of Flick. It probably represented a week's rations.

'You've got to win the war all on your own, of course,' she said with fond sarcasm as Flick tucked in hungrily. 'You were that way from a child—independent to a fault.'

'I don't know why. I was always looked after.'

'I encouraged you to be self-sufficient because you didn't have a father. Whenever you wanted me to do something for you, like fix a bicycle chain, or sew on a button, I used to say, "Try it yourself, and if you can't manage I'll help you."'

'A lot of the time, Mark used to help me.' Mark was Flick's older brother. He worked in the theatre as a stage manager, and lived with an actor called Steve. Ma had long known that Mark was 'not the marrying kind', as she put it.

Ma picked up Flick's empty plate and washed it. Flick stood up. Her mother smiled. 'It's lovely to see you. I worry about you.'

'I've got another reason for coming. I need to talk to Diana.'

'I hope you're not thinking of taking her to France with you.'

'Ma, hush! Who said anything about going to France?'

'She'll get you killed! She doesn't know what discipline is, why should she? She wasn't brought up that way. You'd be a fool to rely on her. She's had several war jobs, and been sacked from every one.'

'Yes, I know,' Flick said. But Diana was a crack shot, and Flick did not have time to be fussy. 'Where is Diana now, do you know?'

'In the woods,' Ma said. 'She went out early, after rabbits.'

Flick crossed the kitchen garden and entered the woods at the rear of the house. The trees were bright with new leaves. When she had gone a quarter of a mile she heard the report of a shotgun. She stopped, listened, and shouted, 'Diana!'

She heard, 'Over here, you noisy idiot, whoever you are!'

She came upon Diana in a clearing, sitting on the ground with her back against an oak tree, smoking a cigarette. A shotgun lay across her knees, and there were half a dozen dead rabbits beside her. 'Oh, it's you!' she said. 'You scared all the game away.'

'They'll come back tomorrow.' Flick studied her childhood companion. Diana was pretty in a boyish way, with dark hair cut short and freckles across her nose. She wore a shooting jacket and corduroy trousers. 'How are you, Diana?'

'Bored. Frustrated. Depressed. Otherwise fine.'

Flick sat on the grass beside her. This might be easier than she had thought. 'What's the matter?'

'I'm rotting away in the English countryside while my brother's conquering Italy, but no one will give me a proper job.'

'I might be able to help you there. You might not like it, though. I'm here to propose something difficult, and dangerous.'

'Don't tell me you're involved in cloak-and-dagger stuff.'

'I didn't get promoted to major by driving generals to meetings.'

'Good lord.' Against her will, Diana was impressed.

Flick had to get her positive agreement to volunteer. 'So—are you willing to do something that's quite likely to get you killed?'

Diana looked excited rather than discouraged. 'Of course.'

Diana was so keen that Flick decided to press her advantage. 'There's a condition, and you may find it worse than the danger. You're the baron's daughter, and I'm the housekeeper's brat. But I'm in charge of this operation. You'll have to defer to me. I'll be hard on you until you get used to it.'

'Yes, sir!'

'You won't need to call me sir, or ma'am. But we do enforce military discipline. In my work disobeying orders can get you killed.'

'Darling, how dramatic! But of course I understand.'

Flick was not at all sure Diana did understand, but she had done her best. She took a scratch pad from her blouse and wrote down an address. 'Pack a case for three days. This is where you need to go. Today.' Flick got to her feet. 'Your training starts at dawn.'

'I'll come back to the house with you and start packing.' Diana stood up. 'But tell me something? Why me?'

Flick nodded. 'I'll be blunt.' She looked at the rabbit corpses on the ground, then lifted her gaze to Diana's pretty face. 'You're a killer,' she said. 'And that's what I need.'

IN HIS SUITE at the Hôtel Frankfort in Reims, Dieter slept until ten. He woke with a headache, but otherwise felt good: excited, optimistic. Yesterday's interrogation of Gaston had given him a hot lead. The woman codenamed Bourgeoise, with her house in the rue du Bois, could be his way into the heart of the Resistance.

He took three aspirins, then went to the phone and called Lieutenant Hesse. 'Good morning, Hans, did you sleep well?'

'Yes, thank you, Major. Sir, I went to the town hall to check out the address in the rue du Bois. The house is owned and occupied by a Mademoiselle Jeanne Lemas. I also drove past, to have a look, and the place seemed quiet.'

'Be ready to leave in an hour. And, Hans—well done.'

Dieter hung up. He wondered what Mademoiselle Lemas was like. Gaston said no one in the Bollinger circuit had ever met her, and Dieter believed him: the house was a security cut-out. Incoming agents knew nothing more than where to contact the woman.

Dieter returned to the bedroom. Stéphanie had brushed her abundant red hair and was sitting up in bed. She looked tempting but he resisted the impulse to join her. 'Would you do something for me?' he said.

'I would do anything for you.'

'Come with me while I arrest a woman in the Resistance.'

Her face showed no emotion. 'Very well,' she said calmly.

'Thank you,' he said, and returned to the living room, where he placed a call to Willi Weber at the château at Sainte-Cécile. Mademoiselle Lemas might be alone, or the house could be crawling with Allied agents armed to the teeth. He needed some back-up.

'I'm going to raid a Resistance house,' he said when Weber came on the line. 'I may need some of your heavyweights. Will you send four men and a car to the Hôtel Frankfort?'

Weber was keen to have his men along on the operation. That way, the Gestapo could claim the credit for any success. He promised a car in half an hour.

Dieter dressed in a dark grey worsted suit, a fine cotton shirt, and a black tie with small white dots. He wore his Walther P38 automatic pistol in a shoulder holster beneath his jacket.

He sat down with a cup of coffee and watched Stéphanie dressing. The French made the most beautiful underwear in the world, he thought, as she stepped into silk camiknickers the colour of clotted cream. When she was ready, they left.

Hans Hesse was waiting outside with Dieter's Hispano-Suiza. Behind Dieter's car was a black Citroën Traction Avant containing four Gestapo men in plain clothes. Major Weber sat in the front passenger seat, wearing a green tweed suit that made him look like a farmer on his way to church. 'Follow me,' Dieter told him. 'When we get there, please stay in your car until I call you.'

Weber said, 'Where the hell did you get a car like that?'

'It was a bribe from a Jew. I helped him to escape to America.'

Weber grunted in disbelief, but in fact the story was true.

Bravado was the best attitude to take with men such as Weber. If Dieter had tried to keep Stéphanie hidden, Weber would have suspected that she was Jewish and might have investigated. But because Dieter flaunted her, the thought never crossed Weber's mind.

They headed for the rue du Bois.

There were few motor vehicles on the streets. Cars were used only by those on official business: the police, doctors, firemen and, of course, the Germans. The citizens went about by bicycle or on foot.

The rue du Bois was a pleasant, tree-lined street on the outskirts of town. Hans pulled up outside a tall house at the end of a row.

'Come if I wave to you,' Dieter said to Stéphanie as he got out of the car. Weber's Citroën drew up behind, but the Gestapo men stayed in the car, as instructed.

Dieter glanced into the courtyard beside the house. There was a garage. Beyond that, he saw a small garden with clipped hedges and rectangular flowerbeds. The owner had a tidy mind.

The woman who opened the door was about sixty. She had white hair tied up at the back. She wore a blue dress with a pattern of small white flowers. 'Good morning, monsieur.'

Dieter smiled. She was irreproachably genteel. Already he had thought of a way to torture her. 'Good morning . . . Mademoiselle Lemas?'

She heard the trace of a German accent. Fear came into her eyes. 'How may I help you?'

'Are you alone, Mademoiselle?' He watched her face carefully.

'Yes,' she said. 'Quite alone.'

He turned and beckoned Stéphanie. 'My colleague will join us.' He was not going to need Weber's men. 'I have some questions to ask you. May I come in?'

The front parlour was furnished with dark wood, highly polished. Dieter sat on a plush-upholstered couch. Stéphanie sat beside him, and Mademoiselle Lemas took an upright chair opposite. She was plump, Dieter observed. Food was her vice.

On a low table was a cigarette box. Dieter flipped the lid and saw that the box was full. 'Please feel free to smoke,' he said.

She looked mildly offended. 'I don't smoke.'

'Then who are these for?'

'Friends . . . neighbours . . .' She looked uncomfortable.

'And British spies.'

'That is absurd.'

Dieter gave her his most charming smile. 'I hope you will not be so foolish as to lie to me.'

'I shall tell you nothing,' she said.

Dieter feigned disappointment, but he was pleased. She had already abandoned the pretence that she did not know what he was talking about. That was as good as a confession. He stood up. 'Come with me, please.'

'Very well. Perhaps you will permit me to put on my hat.'

'Of course.' He nodded to Stéphanie. 'Go with Mademoiselle, please. Make sure she does not use the telephone or write anything down.' He did not want her to leave any kind of message.

He waited in the hall. When they returned, Mademoiselle Lemas wore a light coat and a cloche hat, and carried a tan leather handbag. The three of them went out through the front door.

The Gestapo Citroën followed Dieter's car to Sainte-Cécile. When they had parked in the grounds of the château, Dieter spoke to Weber. 'I'm going to take her upstairs and put her in an office.'

'Why? There are cells in the basement.'

'You'll see.'

Dieter led the prisoner up the stairs to the Gestapo offices. He picked the busiest, a combination typing pool and mail room occupied by young men and women in smart shirts and ties. Leaving Mademoiselle Lemas in the corridor, he closed the door and clapped his hands for attention. In a quiet voice he said, 'I'm going to bring a French woman in here. She is a prisoner, but I want you all to be friendly and polite to her. It's important that she feels respected.'

He brought her in, sat her at a table and, with a murmured apology, handcuffed her ankle to the table leg. He left Stéphanie with her and took Hesse outside. 'Go to the canteen and ask them to prepare lunch on a tray. Soup, a main course, a little wine, a bottle of mineral water and plenty of coffee.'

The lieutenant grinned admiringly. He had no idea what his boss was up to, but he felt sure it would be something clever.

A few minutes later he returned with a tray. Dieter carried it into the office and set it in front of Mademoiselle Lemas. 'Please,' he said. 'It's lunch time.'

'I couldn't eat anything, thank you.'

'Perhaps just a little soup.' He poured wine into her glass.

She added water to the wine and sipped it, then tried the soup.

'How is it?'

'Very good,' she admitted.

'French food is so refined. We Germans cannot imitate it.' Dieter talked nonsense to her, trying to relax her.

She refused the main course but drank all the coffee. Dieter was pleased. When she had finished, he began to question her. 'Where do you meet the Allied agents? How do they recognise you? What is the password?' She refused to answer.

He looked sadly at her. 'I am very sorry that you refuse to cooperate with me, after I have treated you kindly.'

She looked bewildered. 'I appreciate your kindness, but I cannot tell you anything.'

'Very well,' he said. He stood up as if to go.

'And now, monsieur,' said Mademoiselle Lemas. She looked embarrassed. 'I must ask to . . . visit the ladies' powder room.'

In a harsh voice, Dieter said, 'You want to go to the toilet?'

She reddened. 'In a word, yes.'

'I'm sorry,' Dieter said. 'That will not be possible.'

THE LAST THING Monty had said to Paul Chancellor, late on Monday night, had been, 'If you do only one thing in this war, make sure that telephone exchange is destroyed.'

Paul had woken this morning with that simple instruction echoing in his mind. If he could fulfil it, he would help to win the war.

He found Percy Thwaite in his office, staring at six boxes of files. He gestured to the files. 'Shall we get started?'

'What are these?'

'Records of people who were considered by us as possible agents, then rejected for some reason.'

They spent the morning going through the files together. The candidates were mostly in their early twenties, and they had only one other thing in common: they all spoke a foreign language with native fluency. By the time Percy and Paul had eliminated the men and women whose language was not French, they were left with only three names. Paul was disheartened. 'Four is the minimum number we need, even assuming that Flick recruits the woman she has gone to see this morning.'

'Diana Colefield.'

'And none of these is an explosives expert or a telephone engineer.'

Percy was more optimistic. 'They weren't, when SOE interviewed them, but they might be now. Women have learned to do all sorts of things.'

It took a while to track the three down. A further disappointment was that one was dead. The other two were in London. Ruby Romain, unfortunately, was in His Majesty's Prison for Women at Holloway, awaiting trial for murder. And Maude Valentine, whose file said simply 'psychologically unsuitable', was a FANY driver.

'We can't risk Flick's life with people like these!' Percy said.

Percy was desperate to protect Flick, Paul realised. The older man saw himself as Flick's guardian angel.

'We knew from the start we'd be looking at rejects,' Paul said.

Percy arranged for them to meet Maud Valentine at the Fenchurch Hotel, round the corner from SOE headquarters. She was a pretty girl with a flirtatious manner. Her uniform blouse was tight across the chest, and she wore her cap at a jaunty angle.

Paul spoke to her in French. 'What do you do in the FANYs?'

'I drive Monty.'

'Do you? I worked for Monty, but I don't recall seeing you.'

'Oh, it's not always Monty. I drive all the top generals.'

'Ah.' He poured her a cup of tea. Maude was enjoying the attention, Paul realised. While Percy asked questions, he studied the girl. She was petite, though not as tiny as Flick. She had a rosebud mouth and her dark hair was wavy.

'My family came to London when I was ten years old,' she said. 'My papa is the head pastry cook at Claridge's Hotel.'

'Very impressive.'

Maude's file was on the table. Percy moved it an inch closer to Paul. Paul's eye fell on a note made when Maude was first interviewed: *Father: Armand Valentin, 39, kitchen porter at Claridge's*.

When they had finished, they asked her to wait outside. 'She lives in a fantasy world,' Percy said as soon as she went out. 'She's promoted her father to chef, and changed her name to Valentine.'

Paul nodded. 'She told me she was Monty's driver—which I know she's not.'

'No doubt that was why she was rejected before.'

'But now we can't afford to be so particular,' Paul said.

'I suppose you're right,' Percy said reluctantly. 'And the ability to invent stories can be useful under interrogation.'

'All right. Let's get her on board.'

Paul called her back in. 'I'd like you to be part of a team that I'm setting up,' he told her. 'How would you feel about taking on some-thing dangerous?'

'Would we be going to Paris?' Maude said eagerly.

It was an odd response. Paul hesitated. 'Why do you ask?'

'I'd love to go to Paris. I've never been.'

'Wherever you go, you won't have time for sightseeing,' Percy said.

'How do you feel about the danger?' Paul persisted.

'That's all right,' Maude said airily. 'I'm not scared.'

PAUL WAS TO MEET Flick outside the prison where they would inter-view Ruby Romain together.

Percy drove him there. Flick was waiting at the entrance wearing her FANY uniform: a four-pocket tunic, a divided skirt and a little cap with a turned-up brim. The leather belt that was tightly cinched around her small waist emphasised her diminutive figure, and her fair curls spilled out from under the cap. For a moment she took Paul's breath away. 'She's such a pretty girl,' he said.

'She's married,' Percy remarked crisply. He hesitated, then added, 'You need to know this, I think. Her husband, Michel, is the leader of the Bollinger circuit.'

'Ah. Thanks.' Paul got out of the car and Percy drove away.

When Paul told Flick about Maude, she seemed cheerful. 'So, we have three team members, including me. Then we're halfway there.'

The entrance to Holloway Prison was guarded by stone monsters, massive winged griffins holding keys and shackles in their claws. Paul and Flick went in and were shown to the office of Miss Lindleigh, a barrel-shaped assistant governor with a hard face. 'I don't know why you wish to see Romain,' she said. 'Anyway, I must warn you that she is a violent prisoner. She was in here originally for drunkenness, then she killed another prisoner in a fight. She's await-ing trial for murder.'

'A tough customer,' Flick said with interest.

'Yes. She may seem reasonable at first, but she's easily riled.'

The assistant governor led them to an interview room.

Ruby Romain had nut-brown skin, straight dark hair and fierce black eyes. However, she was not a beauty: her nose was hooked and her chin curved up, giving her the look of a gnome.

Miss Lindleigh left them with a warder in the next room watching through a glazed door. Flick, Paul and the prisoner sat round a cheap table with a dirty ashtray on it. Paul put a pack of Lucky

Strikes on the table and said in French, 'Help yourself.' Ruby took two, putting one in her mouth and the other behind her ear.

Paul asked a few routine questions to break the ice. She replied clearly and politely but with a strong accent. 'My parents are travelling folk,' she said. 'When I was a girl, we went around France with a funfair. My father had a rifle range and my mother sold pancakes.'

'How did you come to England?'

'I fell in love with an English sailor I met in Calais. We got married and came to London. He was killed two years ago, his ship was sunk by a U-boat.' She shivered. 'A cold grave.'

'Tell us why you're in here,' Flick said.

'I got myself a little brazier and sold pancakes in the street. But the police kept harassing me. One night, I'd had some cognac—a weakness of mine, I admit—and, anyway, I got into a dispute with a copper. He shoved me and I knocked him down.'

Paul looked at her with a touch of amusement. She was no more than average height, and wiry, but she had big hands and muscular legs. He could imagine her flattening a London policeman.

Flick asked, 'What happened next?'

'His two mates came round the corner, and they took me in. I got fourteen days for drunk and disorderly.'

'And then you got into another fight.'

She gave Flick an appraising look. 'I don't know if I can explain to someone of your sort what it's like in here. Half the girls are mad, and they've all got weapons. You can file the edge of a spoon to make a blade. The warders never intervene in a fight between convicts. They like to watch us tear each other apart.'

Paul was shocked. Perhaps Ruby was exaggerating, but she seemed quietly sincere.

Flick said, 'What happened with the woman you killed?'

'She stole my soap. I took it back. She hit me over the head with a chair leg. I thought she was going to kill me. But I had a knife, a long sliver of glass. I'd wrapped the broad end in a length of bicycle tyre for a handle. I stuck it in her throat.'

Flick suppressed a shudder and said, 'It sounds like self-defence.'

'No. You've got to prove you couldn't possibly have run away. And I'd premeditated the murder by making a knife.'

Paul stood up. 'Wait here with the guard, please,' he said to Ruby. 'We'll just step outside.'

Ruby smiled at him. 'You're so polite,' she said appreciatively.

In the corridor, Paul said, 'What a dreadful story!'

'Remember, everyone in here says they're innocent,' Flick said guardedly. 'I think she's a killer.'

'So we reject her.'

'On the contrary,' said Flick. 'She's exactly what I want.'

They went back into the room. Flick said to Ruby, 'If you could get out of here, would you be willing to do dangerous war work?'

'Would we be going to France?'

Flick raised her eyebrows. 'What leads you to ask that?'

'You spoke French to me at the start.'

'Well, I can't tell you much about the job.'

'I bet it involves sabotage behind enemy lines.'

Paul was startled. Ruby was very quick on the uptake.

Seeing his surprise, Ruby went on, 'Look, at first I thought you might want me to do a bit of translation, but there's nothing dangerous about that. So we must be going to France. And what would the British army do there except blow up bridges and railway lines?' Ruby frowned. 'What I can't figure out is why would you be talking to me? You must be desperate. Well, if you want me, I'll do it.'

Flick said, 'You do understand that the job is dangerous.'

'Yeah,' said Ruby. 'But not as dangerous as being in this place.'

THEY TOOK THEIR LEAVE. When they got outside, they headed for the nearest Underground station. Flick was thoughtful.

'You turned Ruby from a tigress into a pussycat.'

'I wouldn't want a woman like that to dislike me.'

Flick laughed, and Paul was pleased that he had impressed her. But he was already looking ahead. 'By midnight, we should have half a team at the training centre in Hampshire.'

'We call it the Finishing School,' Flick said. 'Yes: Diana Colefield, Maude Valentine and Ruby Romain.'

Paul nodded grimly. 'An undisciplined aristocrat, a pretty flirt who can't tell fantasy from reality, and a murderess with a short temper. But we still don't have an explosives expert or a telephone engineer.'

Flick glanced at her wrist. 'It's still only four o'clock.'

Paul grinned. Flick's optimism was irresistible.

FLICK HAD ARRANGED to meet Percy back at Orchard Court. She found him in his office making tea.

He handed her a cup and sat behind his desk. 'Where's Paul?'

'Gone to arrange to get Ruby Romain out of jail.'

Percy gave her a quizzical glance. 'Do you like him?'

'More than I did initially.'

'How was Ruby Romain?'

'Terrifying. She slit someone's throat in a quarrel over a bar of soap.'

Percy shook his head. 'What the hell kind of a team are we putting together, Flick?'

'Dangerous. That's not the problem. My worry is that we don't have enough experts. There's no point taking a team of tough girls into France, then destroying the wrong cables.'

Percy drained his teacup. 'I know a woman explosives expert who speaks French. When I first thought of her, I dismissed her out of hand. She's about forty. SOE rarely uses anyone so old, especially on a parachute mission.'

Excited, Flick said, 'How did she become an explosives expert?'

Percy looked embarrassed. 'She's a safebreaker. I met her years ago when I was doing work in the East End.'

'I had no idea your past was so raffish. Where is she now?'

Percy looked at his watch. 'It's six o'clock. At this time of the evening, she'll be in the private bar of the White Swan pub.'

'Then let's go.'

Percy drove them to Stepney, not far from the docks. The bomb damage here was the worst Flick had seen. Whole streets were flattened. Percy parked outside the White Swan.

Geraldine Knight sat on a stool at the bar, looking as if she might own the place. She had vivid blonde hair and heavy make-up, expertly applied. Her plump figure had the apparent firmness that could only have come from a corset. It was hard to imagine anyone who looked less like a secret agent, Flick thought despondently.

'Percy Thwaite, as I live and breathe!' the woman said. She was obviously delighted to see him.

'Hello, Jelly, meet my friend Flick,' Percy said.

'Pleased to know you, I'm sure,' she said, shaking Flick's hand.

'Jelly?' Flick enquired.

'No one knows where I got that nickname.'

'Oh,' said Flick. 'Jelly Knight, gelignite.' Jelly ignored that. Flick spoke to her in French. 'Do you live in this part of London?'

'Since I was ten,' she replied, speaking French with a North American accent. 'I was born in Quebec.'

That was not so good, Flick thought. Germans might not notice the accent, but the French certainly would. Jelly would have to pose as a Canadian-born French citizen. It was a perfectly plausible history, but just unusual enough to attract curiosity. Damn. 'But you consider yourself British.'

'English, not British,' said Jelly with arch indignation. She switched back to the English language. 'I'm Church of England, I vote Conservative and I dislike foreigners, heathens and republicans.'

'I'm very glad to hear that you're so patriotic,' Flick said.

'And why would you be interested in such a thing, may I ask?'

'Because there's something you could do for your country.'

Percy put in, 'I told Flick about your . . . expertise, Jelly.'

She looked at her vermilion fingernails. 'Discretion, Percy, please.'

Flick said, 'I expect you know that there have been some fascinating recent developments in the field. Plastic explosives, I mean.'

'I try to keep up to date,' Jelly said. She looked shrewdly at Flick. 'If this is something to do with the war, count me in.'

'You'll be away for a few days. You might not come back.'

Jelly looked dismayed. 'Oh.' She swallowed. 'You want me to blow something up?'

Flick nodded silently.

'Oh, my gordon. You want me to go to France, don't you? Behind enemy lines! I'm too bloody old for that sort of thing. I'm . . .' She hesitated. 'I'm thirty-seven.'

She was about five years older than that, Flick thought, but she said, 'Well, I'm nearly thirty. We're not too old for adventure, are we?'

'Speak for yourself, dear.'

Percy said, 'Jelly, we're asking you to do a job that's really crucial for the war effort. And you're the only person in the country who can do it.'

'Get off,' she said sceptically.

'You're a female safebreaker who speaks French—how many others do you think there are? I'll tell you: none.'

She stared at him. 'You mean this, don't you?'

'I was never more serious in my life.'

'Bloody hell, Perce.' Jelly fell silent for a long moment. Flick held her breath. At last Jelly said, 'All right, I'll do it.'

HAVING LEFT JELLY in the pub, Percy and Flick parted company. Flick headed for the nearest Underground station, feeling jubilant. But on the train to Bayswater, her spirits fell again. She still did not have the most crucial member of the team. Without a telephone engineer, Jelly might place the explosives in the wrong location. They would do damage, but if the damage could be repaired in a day or two, the enormous effort and risk of death would have been in vain.

When she returned to her bedsitter, she found her brother Mark waiting there. She hugged and kissed him. 'What a nice surprise!'

'I've got a night off, so I thought I'd take you for a drink.'

Flick was tired, and her first inclination was to turn him down. Then she remembered that this could be the last time she ever saw her brother. 'How about the West End? We'll go to a nightclub.'

'Perfect!'

They left the house and walked arm-in-arm along the street. Flick said, 'I saw Ma this morning.'

'How is she?'

'All right.'

'How did you happen to see her?'

'I went down to Somersholme. It would take too long to explain.'

'Something hush-hush, I suppose.'

She smiled acknowledgment, then sighed as she remembered her problem.

'I don't suppose you happen to know a female telephone engineer who speaks French, do you?'

He stopped. 'Well,' he said, 'sort of.'

MADEMOISELLE LEMAS was in agony. She sat rigid on the hard upright chair, her face a mask of self-control. She clutched her sturdy leather handbag on her lap.

Around her, late-working clerks and secretaries in their well-pressed uniforms carried on typing and filing.

Dieter sat watching her. Mademoiselle Lemas's pain was not just physical, he knew. Even worse than her bursting bladder was the terror of soiling herself in a room full of polite, well-dressed people. For a respectable elderly lady, that was the worst of nightmares. He admired her fortitude, but he was becoming impatient. He decided to speed up the process. He sent Stéphanie for a bottle of beer and a glass. He opened the bottle, and poured the beer slowly in front of the prisoner. Tears of pain rolled down her plump cheeks. Dieter drank deeply. 'Your agony is almost over,' he said. 'You will answer my questions, then you will find ease.'

She closed her eyes.

'Where do you meet the British agents?' He paused. 'How do you recognise one another?' She said nothing. 'What is the password?'

He waited a moment, then said, 'Have the answers ready, so that when the time comes, you can tell me quickly. Then you can seek rapid release from your pain.'

He unlocked the cuffs that fastened her ankle to the table leg. He took her by the arm. 'Come with us, Stéphanie,' he said. 'We're going to the ladies' toilet.'

They left the room, Stéphanie leading the way, Dieter and Hans holding the prisoner, who hobbled along with difficulty, bent at the waist, biting her lip. They stopped at a door marked DAMEN. Mademoiselle Lemas groaned loudly when she saw it.

'Now,' said Dieter. 'Where do you meet the British agents?'

Mademoiselle Lemas began to cry. 'In the cathedral. In the crypt. Please let me go!'

Dieter breathed a long sigh of satisfaction. She had broken. 'When?'

'Three o'clock any afternoon, I go every day,' she sobbed.

'And how do you recognise one another?'

'I wear odd shoes, black and brown. Now can I go?'

'One more question. What is the password?'

'"Pray for me."'

'And your reply?'

'"I pray for peace", that's my reply. Oh, I beg you!'

'Thank you,' Dieter said, and released her.

She rushed inside. Stéphanie followed her in.

Dieter could not conceal his satisfaction. 'There, Hans, we make progress. When they come out, turn her over to the Gestapo. They'll arrange for her to disappear into a camp somewhere.'

He began to think about the best way to exploit the new information. The challenge was to capture agents without letting London know. Ideally, the next agent sent by London would go to the crypt of the cathedral and find Mademoiselle Lemas waiting there. She would take the agent home, and he would send a wireless message to London saying all was well. Then, when he was out of the house, Dieter could get hold of his code books. After that . . .

Willi Weber walked by. 'Well, Major, has the prisoner talked?'

'She has revealed the location of her rendezvous and the passwords.'

Weber looked interested. 'And where is the rendezvous?'

Dieter would have preferred not to tell Weber anything. But he needed the man's help. 'The cathedral crypt, afternoons at three.'

Dieter resumed thinking about his next step. The house in the rue du Bois was a cut-out. No one in the Bollinger circuit had met Mademoiselle Lemas. Agents coming in from London did not know what she looked like—hence the need for recognition signals and passwords. If he could get someone to impersonate her . . .

Stéphanie came out of the ladies' toilet with Mademoiselle Lemas.

She could do it. She was much younger than Mademoiselle Lemas, and looked completely different, but the agents would not know that. She was obviously French. All she had to do was take care of the agent for a day or so.

He took Stéphanie's arm. 'Hans will deal with the prisoner now. Come, let me buy you a glass of champagne.'

He walked her out of the château. In the square, soldiers had erected three stout wooden pillars for a firing squad. A handful of local people stood silent and watchful outside the church door.

Dieter and Stéphanie went into the café. Dieter ordered champagne. 'Thank you for helping me today,' he said. 'I appreciate it.'

'I love you,' she said. 'And you love me, I know, even though you never say it.'

'But how do you feel about what we did today? You're French, and you have that grandmother whose race we mustn't speak of.'

She shook her head violently. 'I no longer believe in nationality or race,' she said. 'When I was arrested by the Gestapo, no French people helped me. No Jews helped me. I was so cold in that prison.' She crossed her arms and shivered, although it was a warm evening. 'Not just cold on the outside. I felt cold in my heart and my bones.' She was silent for a long moment. Then she said, 'I'll never forget the warmth in your apartment. It made me human again. You saved me.'

He held her hand. 'There's something else you could do for me.'

'Anything.'

'I want you to impersonate Mademoiselle Lemas. Go to the cathedral crypt every afternoon at three, wearing one black shoe and one brown. When someone approaches you and says, "Pray for me," reply, "I pray for peace." Take the person to the house in the rue du Bois. Then call me.'

The champagne arrived and he poured two glasses. He decided to level with her. 'If the agent has met Mademoiselle Lemas before, you could be in danger. Will you take that chance?'

'Is it important to you?'

'It is.'

'Then I'll do it.'

In the square, there was a volley of gunfire. Through the window Dieter saw the three terrorists who had survived Sunday's skirmish. Their bodies, tied to the wooden pillars, were slumped in death.

WARTIME AUSTERITY had made little real difference to Soho, the red-light district in the heart of London's West End. The illuminated signs outside clubs and bars were switched off, because of the black-out. But the same groups of young men staggered through the streets, drunk on beer, though most of them were now in uniform. The same painted girls in tight dresses strolled along the pavements.

Mark and Flick arrived at the Criss-Cross Club at ten in the evening. The manager greeted Mark like a friend. Flick's spirits were high. Mark knew a female telephone engineer and Flick was about to meet her. Mark had not said much about her, except that her name was Greta.

The place was dimly lit and smoky. Flick could see a five-piece band on a low stage, a small dance floor, a scatter of tables. She had wondered if it would be the kind of place that catered to chaps like Mark who were 'not the marrying kind'.

Mark asked a waiter for a martini. Flick ordered Scotch.

A tall blonde in a red cocktail dress came swishing onto the stage to a burst of applause. 'This is Greta,' said Mark. 'She's a telephone engineer by day.'

Greta began to sing. She had a powerful, bluesy voice, but Flick noticed immediately that she had a German accent. Shouting into Mark's ear over the sound of the band, she said, 'I thought you said she was French.'

'She *speaks* French. But she's German.'

Flick was bitterly disappointed. Greta would have just as much of a German accent when she spoke French. The Gestapo might not notice, but the French police would. Still, did she have to pretend to be French? There were plenty of German women in France: officers' wives, drivers and typists. Flick began to feel excited again.

Greta finished her act with a hilariously suggestive blues number called 'Kitchen Man', full of *double entendres*. The audience loved it. She left the stage to rounds of applause.

Mark got up. 'We can talk to her in her dressing room.'

Flick followed him through a door set next to the stage, down a concrete corridor to a door that had a pink paper cut-out star fixed to it with drawing pins. Mark knocked on the door, then opened it without waiting for a reply.

The tiny room had a dressing table, a stool and a film poster of Greta Garbo. An elaborate blonde wig rested on a stand shaped like a head. The red dress Greta had worn on stage hung from a hook on the wall. Sitting on the stool in front of the mirror was a young man with a hairy chest.

Flick gasped. It was Greta, no question. The face was heavily made up with vivid lipstick and false eyelashes, and a layer of powder hid the shadow of a dark beard. The hair was cut short to accommodate the wig. The false bosom was presumably fixed inside the dress, but Greta still wore a half-slip, stockings and red high-heeled shoes.

Flick rounded on Mark. 'You didn't tell me!' she accused.

He laughed delightedly. 'Flick, meet Gerhard,' he said. 'He loves it when people don't realise.'

Flick saw that Gerhard was looking pleased. But she was angry with Mark. 'This was so mean of you!' she said. 'I thought you'd solved my problem, but you were just playing a joke.'

'It's not a joke,' Mark said. 'If you need a woman, take Greta.'

'I couldn't,' Flick said. It was a ridiculous idea. 'The top brass would never agree.'

'Don't tell them,' Mark suggested.

'Not tell them!' Flick was at first shocked, then intrigued. If Greta was to fool the Gestapo, she ought also to be able to fool SOE.

Gerhard said, 'Mark, sweetie, what is all this about?'

'I don't know,' Mark told him. 'My sister says it's hush-hush.'

'I'll explain,' Flick said. 'But first, tell me about yourself.'

'Well, sweetheart, where shall I begin?' Gerhard lit a cigarette. 'I'm from Hamburg. When I was sixteen, and an apprentice telephone engineer, it was a wonderful town, bars and nightclubs full of sailors. When I was eighteen I met Manfred, the love of my life.'

Tears came to Gerhard's eyes. 'Manfred loved me in drag, and he taught me how to do it right.'

'Why did you leave?'

'The bloody Nazis took Manfred away. He's probably dead, but I don't know for sure. So I came to London. My father was English. He died when I was two, so I never really knew him. As it turned out, I got out just in time. Happily, there's always work for a telephone engineer in any city. So here I am, the toast of London, the deviant diva. Now, why are you so interested in me, sweetheart?'

'I need a female telephone engineer. I can't tell you much about the job. One thing I can say is that you might get killed.'

'How absolutely chilling! But you can imagine that I'm not very good at rough stuff.'

'I've got all the tough soldiers I need. What I want from you is your expertise.'

'Would it mean a chance to hurt those bloody Nazis?'

'Absolutely.'

'Then, sweetheart, I'm your girl.'

The Fourth Day:
Wednesday, May 31, 1944

In the middle of the night, the roads of southern England were thronged with traffic. Great convoys of army trucks roared through the darkened towns, heading for the coast.

'My God,' said Greta. 'There really is going to be an invasion.'

She and Flick had left London shortly after midnight in a borrowed car. Greta wore one of her less eye-catching outfits, a simple black dress with a brunette wig. She would not be Gerhard again until the mission was over.

Flick hoped Greta was as expert as Mark had claimed. As they drove, Flick explained the mission, anxiously hoping the conversation would not reveal gaps in Greta's knowledge. 'The château contains a new automatic exchange put in by the Germans to handle their telephone and teleprinter traffic.'

At first Greta was sceptical about the plan. 'But, sweetheart, even if we succeed, what's to stop the Germans just rerouting calls around the network?'

'Volume of traffic. The system is overloaded. Now, imagine that the main automatic exchange is out of service and all the calls have to be made the old-fashioned way, by hello girls, taking ten times as long. Ninety per cent of them will never get through.'

'All right.' Greta was thoughtful. 'Well, we could destroy the common equipment racks. But the damage could be repaired. You need to knock out the manual exchange, the automatic exchange, the long-distance amplifiers, the telex exchange and the telex amplifiers—which are probably all in different rooms.'

'Remember, we can't carry a great quantity of explosives with us. There must be some equipment common to all the systems.'

'Yes, there is. The main distribution frame—the MDF. All the cables from outside come to one side of the frame; all the cables from the exchange come to the other; and they're connected by jumper links. Ideally, you'd want a fire hot enough to melt the copper in the cables.'

'How long would it take to reconnect the cables?'

'A couple of days. That assumes the repair men have the record cards that show how the cables are connected. If we burn them, too, it will take weeks of trial and error to figure out the connections.'

'This is sounding good. Now, listen. In the morning, when I explain our mission to the others, I'm going to tell them something completely different, a cover story. That way our mission won't be jeopardised if one of us is captured and interrogated. You're the only one who knows the true story, so keep it to yourself for now.'

They reached the Finishing School at three in the morning. The place was located in the grounds of Beaulieu, pronounced 'Bewly', a sprawling estate near the south coast. Hidden away in the woods were numerous large country houses that had been requisitioned by SOE and were used for training agents in security, wireless operation, map reading and dirtier skills such as burglary, sabotage, forgery and silent killing.

Flick drove down a rough track and pulled up in front of a large house. Coming here always felt like entering a fantasy world, one where deception and violence were talked of as commonplace. The house had an appropriate air of unreality. With its chimneys and dormer windows, hipped roofs and tile-hung bays, it was like an illustration in a children's novel.

The place was silent. The rest of the team were here, Flick knew, but they would be asleep. She found two vacant rooms in the attic, and she and Greta went gratefully to bed. Flick lay awake for a while, wondering how she would ever weld this bunch of misfits into a fighting unit, but she soon fell asleep.

She got up again at six and roused the others.

Percy and Paul were first to arrive in the big kitchen at the back of the house. The girls came down one by one, and before long they were all sitting round the big table eating eggs and bacon. Flick was startled by her first sight of Maude Valentine; neither Percy nor Paul had said how pretty she was. She appeared immaculately dressed and scented, her rosebud mouth accentuated by bright lipstick, looking as if she were off to lunch at the Savoy. She sat next to Paul and said with a suggestive air, 'Sleep well, Major?'

Flick was relieved to see the dark pirate face of Ruby Romain. She would not have been surprised if Ruby had run off in the night, never to be seen again. Of course, Ruby could then be rearrested for murder, but she might have decided to take the chance.

Jelly Knight looked her age, early in the morning. She sat beside Percy and gave him a fond smile. 'I suppose you slept like a top.'

'Clear conscience,' he replied.

She laughed. 'You haven't got a bloody conscience.'

When Greta came through the door, Flick held her breath.

She wore a pretty cotton dress with a small false bosom. A pink cardigan softened her shoulder line and a chiffon scarf concealed her masculine throat. She wore the short dark wig. By contrast with her sassy on-stage personality, today she was playing the part of a rather plain young woman who was perhaps a little embarrassed about being so tall. Flick introduced her and watched the reactions of the other women. They all smiled pleasantly, showing no sign that they saw anything wrong, and Flick breathed easier.

This is my team, Flick thought: one flirt, one murderess, one safebreaker, one female impersonator. There was someone missing, she realised: Diana. And it was now half past seven.

Flick said to Percy, 'You did tell Diana that reveille was at six?'

'I told everyone.'

'And I banged on her door at quarter past.' Flick stood up. 'I'd better check on her. Bedroom ten, right?'

She went upstairs and knocked at Diana's door. There was no response, so she went in. No Diana.

'She's disappeared,' she told the others with irritation, when she returned to the kitchen. 'We'll start without her.' She stood at the head of the table. 'We have two days' training in front of us. Then, on Friday night, we parachute into France. We're an all-female team because it is easier for women to move around occupied France—the Gestapo are less suspicious. Our mission is to blow up a railway tunnel near the village of Marle, not far from Reims.'

Flick glanced at Greta, who knew the story was false. She sat buttering toast and did not meet Flick's eye.

'The agent's course is normally three months,' Flick went on. 'But this tunnel has to be destroyed by Monday night. In two days, we hope to give you some basic security rules, teach you how to parachute, do some weapons training and show you how to kill people without making a noise.'

Maude looked pale. 'Kill people?'

Jelly gave a grunt of disgust. 'There is a war on, you know.'

Diana came in from the garden with bits of vegetation clinging to her corduroy trousers. 'I've been for a tramp in the woods,' she said enthusiastically. 'Marvellous.'

Flick said, 'Sit down, Diana, you're late for the briefing.'

'I'm sorry, darling, have I missed your lovely talk?'

'You're in the army now,' Flick said with exasperation. 'When you're told to be here by seven, it's not a suggestion.'

Diana sat down in silence, but she looked mutinous. Oh, hell, Flick thought, I didn't handle that very well.

The kitchen door opened with a bang and a small, muscular man of about forty came in. He had sergeant's chevrons on his uniform shirt. 'Good morning, girls!' he said heartily.

Flick said, 'This is Sergeant Bill Griffiths, one of the instructors. Sergeant, why don't you begin?'

He took her place at the head of the table. 'Landing with a parachute,' he began, 'is like jumping off a wall fourteen feet high.'

Flick heard Jelly say quietly, 'Oh, my gordon.'

'You cannot come down on your feet,' Bill continued. 'If you try, you will break your legs. The only safe way is to fall. So the first thing we're going to teach you is how to fall. We will assemble outside in three minutes.'

While the women were changing into overalls, Paul took his leave. 'We need a parachute training flight tomorrow, and they're going to tell me there are no planes available,' he said to Flick. 'I'm going to London to kick some butt. I'll be back tonight.'

In the garden was an old pine table, an ugly Victorian mahogany wardrobe, and a stepladder fourteen feet high. When they were all assembled, Bill said, 'First we're going to learn to fall from zero height. There are three ways: forwards, backwards and sideways.'

He demonstrated each method, dropping to the ground effortlessly and springing up again with a gymnast's agility. 'Keep your legs together. Do not throw out your arms to break your fall, but keep them at your sides.'

As Flick expected, the younger girls had no difficulty: Diana, Maude and Ruby were able to fall like athletes as soon as they were shown how. It was Jelly that Flick was worried about. She was a key member of the team, the only one who knew about explosives. But she had lost her girlish suppleness. However, she was game. She hit the ground with a grunt and was ready to try again.

To Flick's surprise, the worst student was Greta. 'I can't do this,' she said to Flick. 'I told you I'm no good at rough stuff.'

It was the first time Greta had spoken more than a couple of words, and Jelly frowned and muttered, 'Funny accent.'

'Let me help you,' Bill said to Greta. 'Stand still. Just relax.' He took her by the shoulders. Then, with a sudden strong motion, he threw her to the ground. She landed heavily and gave a gasp of pain, and began to cry. 'For God's sake,' Bill said disgustedly. 'What kind of people are they sending us?'

But Greta quickly gained confidence. When the others were jumping off the table, she joined in and landed perfectly. They gave her a round of applause.

AT THE TALL HOUSE in the rue du Bois, Dieter carried Stéphanie's suitcase up the stairs and into Mademoiselle Lemas's bedroom. He looked at the tightly made single bed, the prayer stool with the rosary on its lectern. 'It's not going to be easy to pretend this is your house,' he said.

'I'll say I've inherited it from a maiden aunt.'

'Clever. What will you do if the phone rings?'

Stéphanie thought for a minute. When she spoke, her voice was lower, and her Paris accent had been replaced by tones of provincial gentility. 'Yes, this is Mademoiselle Lemas. Who is calling, please?'

'Very good,' said Dieter. The impersonation might not fool a close friend or relative, but a casual caller would notice nothing.

They explored the house. There were four more bedrooms, each ready to receive a guest, the beds made up, a clean towel on each washstand. In the kitchen, they found a sack of rice that would have fed Mademoiselle Lemas for a year. In the cellar was half a case of Scotch whisky. The garage at the side of the house contained a bicycle and a little Simca Cinq, in good condition with a tank full of petrol. There was no way the authorities would have allowed

Mademoiselle Lemas to buy scarce petrol for a car to take her shopping. The vehicle must have been fuelled by the Resistance.

Stéphanie made lunch. They had shopped on the way. There was no meat or fish in the shops, but they had bought some mushrooms and a lettuce, and a loaf of bread. Stéphanie prepared a salad and a risotto, and they found some cheese in the larder.

'The war must have been the best thing that ever happened to her,' Dieter said as they ate. 'A woman alone, no husband, no family, her parents dead. Then into her life come all these young people, brave boys and girls on daredevil missions. She hides them in her house, gives them whisky and cigarettes, and sends them on their way. It was probably the most exciting time of her life.'

'Perhaps she would have preferred a peaceful life, shopping for hats with a woman friend, going to Paris once a year for a concert.'

'Nobody really prefers a peaceful life.' Dieter looked at his watch. It was almost three. 'Go to the crypt on your own,' he told Stéphanie. 'Use the little car in the garage. I'll be in the cathedral, though you may not see me.' He kissed her. Almost like a husband going to the office, he thought with grim amusement.

THE TEAM HAD GOT through the morning's instruction reasonably well, to Flick's relief. Everyone had learned the falling technique, which was the hardest part of parachuting. The map-reading session had been less successful. Ruby had never been to school and could barely read: a map was like a page of Chinese to her. Maude was baffled by directions such as north-northeast, and fluttered her eyelids prettily at the instructor. If the group got split up in France, Flick would not be able to rely on them finding their own way.

In the afternoon they moved on to the rough stuff. The weapons instructor was Captain Jim Cardwell, an easy-going man with a craggy face and a thick moustache. Ruby was comfortable with an automatic in her hand and could shoot accurately. Jelly, too, handled the firearms with relaxed familiarity. But Diana was the star of the session. Using a rifle, she hit the centre of the target with every shot. 'Very good!' Jim said in surprise. 'You can have my job.'

Greta was the only failure. Once again, she was more feminine than the real women. She jumped at every bang and closed her eyes in terror as she pulled the trigger. Jim worked with her patiently, but it was no good: she was too skittish ever to be a good shot. 'I'm just not cut out for this kind of thing!' she said in despair.

Jelly said, 'Then what the hell are you doing here?'

Flick interposed quickly. 'Greta's an engineer. She's going to tell you where to place the charges. Save your aggression for the next session. We're about to do hand-to-hand combat.' Bickering bothered her. She needed them to trust one another.

They returned to the garden of the house, where Bill Griffiths was waiting. He would demonstrate how an unarmed man could repel an attacker. He had a selection of weapons laid out on the old pine table: a wicked-looking SS knife, a Walther P38 automatic pistol, a French policeman's truncheon, a length of black and yellow electrical cord that he called a garotte, and a beer bottle with the neck snapped off.

'How to escape from a man who is pointing a gun at you,' he began. He handed the Walther to Maude. She pointed it at him. 'Sooner or later, your captor is going to want you to go somewhere.' He turned and put his hands in the air. 'Chances are, he'll follow close behind you, poking the gun in your back.' He walked round in a wide circle, with Maude behind. He quickened his pace slightly, forcing Maude to step out a little faster to keep up. As she did so, he moved sideways and back, caught her right wrist under his arm and hit her hand with a sharp, downward chop. She cried out and dropped the gun.

'At this point you can make a bad mistake,' he said as Maude rubbed her wrist. 'Do *not* run away. What you have to do is . . .' He picked up the pistol, pointed it at Maude, and pulled the trigger. There was a bang. Maude screamed, and so did Greta. 'This gun is loaded with blanks, of course,' Bill said.

Sometimes Flick wished Bill would not be quite so dramatic.

'We'll practise all these techniques on one another in a few minutes,' he went on. He picked up the electrical cord and turned to Greta. 'Put that round my neck. When I give the word, pull it as tight as you can.' He handed her the cord. 'Your Gestapo man could kill you with the cord, but he can't hold your weight with it. All right, Greta, strangle me.' Greta hesitated, then pulled the cord tight. Bill kicked out with both feet and fell to the ground, landing on his back. Greta lost her grip on the cord.

'Unfortunately,' Bill said, 'this leaves you lying on the ground with your enemy standing over you.' He got up. 'We'll do it again.' They resumed the position, and Greta pulled the cord tight. This time Bill grabbed her wrist, fell to the ground, pulling her forward and down.

As she fell on top of him, he bent one leg and kneed her viciously in the stomach.

She rolled off him and curled up, gasping for breath and retching. Flick said, 'For God's sake, Bill, that's a bit rough!'

He looked pleased. 'The Gestapo are a lot worse than me,' he said.

Bill picked his next victim, Ruby, and handed her the policeman's truncheon. There was a cunning look on Ruby's face, and Flick thought: If I were Bill I'd be careful with her.

Flick had seen Bill demonstrate this technique before. When Ruby raised her right hand to hit him with the truncheon, Bill was going to grab her arm, turn, and throw her over his shoulder.

'Right, girl,' Bill said. 'Hit me with the truncheon.'

Ruby lifted her arm, but when Bill reached for it, it was not there. The truncheon fell to the ground. Ruby moved close to Bill and brought her knee up hard into his groin. He gave a sharp cry of pain. She grabbed his shirt front, pulled him towards her sharply, and butted his nose. Then she kicked his shin. He fell to the ground, blood pouring from his nose.

'You bitch, you weren't supposed to do that!' he yelled.

'The Gestapo are a lot worse than me,' said Ruby.

IT WAS A MINUTE before three when Dieter parked and hurried across the cobbled square to the cathedral. It was almost too much to hope that an Allied agent would show up at the rendezvous the first day. On the other hand, if the invasion was really imminent, the Allies would be throwing in every last asset.

He passed through the great west door into the cool gloom of the interior. He looked for his assistant, Hans Hesse, and saw him sitting in the back row of pews. They nodded briefly to one another.

Dieter crossed to the south side of the building and walked up the long south aisle, his footsteps ringing on the stone floor. When he reached the transept, he saw the steps leading down to the crypt, which was below the high altar. Stéphanie was down there, he assumed, wearing one black shoe and one brown.

He knelt down and looked around. There was no service going on, but a handful of people were scattered around the pews in the side chapels. If an Allied agent showed up today, Dieter planned simply to watch and make sure nothing went wrong. Ideally Stéphanie would talk to the agent, exchange passwords and take him home to the rue du Bois.

After that, his plans were vaguer. Somehow the agent would then lead him to others.

He checked his watch. It was five past three. Probably no one would come today. He looked up. To his horror, he saw Willi Weber. What the hell was he doing here?

Weber was in plain clothes, wearing his green tweed suit. With him was a Gestapo man in a check jacket. They were walking towards Dieter from the east end of the church, though they had not seen him. They drew level with the crypt door and stopped.

Dieter cursed under his breath. This could ruin everything.

Looking along the south aisle, he saw a young man carrying a small suitcase. Dieter narrowed his eyes. The man was wearing a shabby blue suit of French cut, but he looked very English, with red hair, blue eyes and pale pink skin. He walked purposefully along the aisle, neither looking at the pillars like a tourist nor taking a seat like a worshipper. Dieter's heart beat faster. An agent on the first day! The case he carried was almost certainly a suitcase radio. That meant he had a code book, too. The agent passed Dieter and slowed his walk, obviously looking for the crypt.

Weber saw the man, gave him a hard look, then turned and pretended to study the fluting on a column.

The young man found the crypt gate and disappeared down the stone steps.

Weber looked across the south transept and gave a nod. Following his gaze, Dieter saw two more Gestapo men lurking beneath the organ loft. He wondered if he could speak to Weber, get him to call his men off. But there was no time. Almost immediately, Stéphanie came up from the crypt with the young man right behind her.

Weber stepped forward, took the agent by the arm and said something. Dieter's heart sank as he realised Weber was making an arrest. Stéphanie backed away, looking bewildered.

Dieter got up and walked quickly towards the group. Before he got close, the agent shook off Weber's hand and bolted.

Weber's companion in the check jacket reacted fast. He took two big strides, flung himself forward in a flying tackle, and threw his arms round the agent's knees. The agent fell headlong, his chunky body hitting the stone floor with a thwack. The suitcase went flying. The other two Gestapo men jumped on him. Weber came running up, looking pleased.

Dieter cursed. The mad fools were ruining everything. But maybe he could still save the situation. He reached into his jacket, drew his Walther P38, thumbed the safety catch and pointed it at the Gestapo. Speaking French, he yelled at the top of his voice, 'Get off him now, or I shoot!'

Weber said, 'Major, I—'

Dieter fired into the air, the report of the pistol crashed around the cathedral vaults, drowning Weber's giveaway words. 'Silence!' Dieter shouted in German. Weber looked scared and shut up. The Gestapo men stood up and backed away.

Dieter looked at Stéphanie. Calling her by Mademoiselle Lemas's name, he shouted, 'Jeanne! Go! Get away!' Stéphanie began to run for the west door.

The agent was scrambling to his feet. 'Go with her!' Dieter shouted at him. The man grabbed his suitcase, vaulted over the wooden choir stalls and ran down the nave.

Weber and his three associates looked bemused. 'Lie face down!' Dieter ordered them, reverting to German. As they obeyed, he backed away, still threatening them with the gun. Then he turned and ran after Stéphanie and the agent.

As the other two fled through the doorway, Dieter stopped and spoke to Hans, who stood near the back of the church. 'Talk to those damn fools. Explain what we're doing. Make sure they don't follow us.' Then he turned and ran outside.

The engine of the Simca was turning over. Dieter pushed the agent into the cramped back seat and got into the front passenger seat. Stéphanie stamped on the pedal and the little car shot forward.

As they raced out of the square, the agent said in French, 'I'm Helicopter. What the hell happened in there?'

Dieter realised that 'Helicopter' must be a code name. He recalled that Gaston had told him Mademoiselle Lemas's code name. 'This is Bourgeoise,' he said, indicating Stéphanie. 'And I'm Charenton,' he improvised. 'Bourgeoise has become suspicious, in the last few days, that the cathedral rendezvous might be watched, so she asked me to come with her.'

'You were brilliant!' Helicopter said. 'God, I was so scared, I thought I'd blown it on my first day.'

You have, Dieter thought silently. Helicopter now would trust Dieter in all things, being convinced Dieter had snatched him from the Gestapo. The challenge now was to make maximum use of Helicopter's trust.

They arrived at the rue du Bois and Stéphanie drove into Mademoiselle Lemas's garage. They entered the house by the back door and sat in the kitchen. Stéphanie got a bottle of Scotch from the cellar and poured them all a drink.

Dieter was anxious to confirm that Helicopter had a radio. He said, 'You'd better send a message to London right away.'

'I'm supposed to broadcast at eight o'clock and receive at eleven.'

Dieter made a mental note. 'But you need to tell them as soon as possible that the cathedral rendezvous is compromised.'

'Oh, my God, yes,' the young man said. 'I'll use the emergency frequency.' He lifted the suitcase onto the table and opened it.

Dieter hid a sigh of profound satisfaction. There it was.

The interior of the case was divided into four: two side compartments and, in the middle, one front and one back. Dieter could see immediately that the rear middle compartment contained the transmitter, with the Morse key in the lower right-hand corner, and the front middle was the receiver, with a socket for headphone connections. The right side compartment was the power supply, the left side held a selection of accessories and spare parts.

Dieter now had to learn the frequencies used, and the code.

Helicopter plugged a lead into an electrical outlet. Dieter said, 'I thought it was battery-operated?'

'Battery or mains power. If you lose the house current, you just have to reverse this plug and it switches to battery operation.'

Helicopter then took the aerial wire and asked Stéphanie to drape it over a tall cupboard. Dieter looked in the kitchen drawers and found a pencil and a notepad. 'You can use this to encode your message,' he said helpfully.

'First I'd better figure out what to say.' Helicopter scratched his head then began to write in English:

ARRIVED OK STOP CRYPT RENDEZVOUS UNSAFE STOP NABBED BY GESTAPO BUT GOT AWAY OVER.

Dieter said, 'We should give them a new rendezvous for future incomers. Say the Café de la Gare next to the railway station.'

Helicopter wrote it down. He took from the case a silk handkerchief printed with a complex table showing letters in pairs. He also took out a pad of a dozen or so sheets of paper printed with five-letter nonsense words. It was a one-time-pad encryption system, unbreakable unless you had the pad.

Over the words of his message, Helicopter wrote the five-letter groups from the pad; then he used the letters he had written to select columns of transpositions from the silk handkerchief.

When he had encrypted his message, Helicopter flicked the On/Off switch and turned a dial that bore three faint markings in yellow wax crayon. Helicopter had mistrusted his memory and had marked his broadcast positions. The setting he was using would be reserved for emergencies. Of the other two, one would be for transmission and the other for reception.

As Helicopter tapped out his message in Morse, Dieter watched, feeling elated. This was the spycatcher's dream: he had an agent in his hands and the agent did not know he had been captured.

When the message was sent, Helicopter shut down the radio quickly. In England, the message had to be transcribed, decoded, and passed to Helicopter's controller, which could take hours, so Helicopter would wait until the appointed hour for a response.

Now Dieter had to separate him from the wireless set and his coding materials. 'I presume you want to contact the Bollinger circuit now?' he said.

'Yes. London needs to know how much of it is left.'

'I'll drive you to Monet, the leader. He's in the centre of town.'

Monet, Michel Clairet, would not be at home. Dieter had checked. He had gone into hiding.

Dieter said, 'Does that radio battery need recharging?'

'Yes—in fact they tell us to plug it in at every opportunity.'

'So why don't you leave it where it is? We can come back for it.'

'Good idea.'

'Then let's go.' Dieter led the way to the garage and backed the Simca Cinq out. Then he said, 'Wait here a minute, I have to tell Bourgeoise something.'

He went back into the house. Stéphanie was in the kitchen, staring at the suitcase radio. Dieter took the one-time pad and the silk handkerchief from the accessories compartment. 'How long will it take you to copy these?' he said.

She made a face. 'All those gibberish letters? At least an hour.'

'Do it as fast as you can. I'll keep him out for an hour and a half.'

He returned to the car and drove Helicopter into the city centre. Dieter waited in the car while Helicopter went to Michel Clairet's door. After a few minutes, the agent came back. 'No answer.'

'You can try again in the morning,' Dieter said. 'Meanwhile, I know a bar used by the Resistance.' He knew no such thing. 'Let's go there and see if I recognise anyone.'

He picked a bar at random and the two of them sat drinking watery beer for an hour, then Dieter drove back to the rue du Bois. When they entered the kitchen, Stéphanie gave Dieter a slight nod. He took it to mean she had succeeded in copying everything. 'Now,' Dieter said to Helicopter, 'you'd probably like a bath, having spent a night in the open.'

'How kind you are.'

Dieter put him in an attic room farthest from the bathroom. As soon as he heard the man splashing in the bath, he went into the room and searched his clothes. In the jacket pockets were French cigarettes and matches and a wallet with half a million francs. The identity papers seemed impeccable, though they had to be forgeries.

There was also a photograph of Flick Clairet. Dieter stared at it in surprise. It was the woman he had seen in the square at Sainte-Cécile. She was wearing a swimsuit and smiling into the camera. Behind her and slightly out of focus, two young men in bathing trunks seemed about to dive into a river. The picture had obviously been taken at an innocent swimming party. But her seminakedness and the slight smile combined to make a sexually charged picture. Dieter could see why a young fellow would treasure it.

Agents were not supposed to carry photos with them into enemy territory—for very good reasons. Helicopter's passion for Flick Clairet might destroy her, and much of the French Resistance too.

Dieter slipped the photo into his pocket and left the room.

PAUL CHANCELLOR SPENT the day fighting the military bureaucracy. In the end, he got a plane for the team's parachute training. When he caught the train back to Hampshire, he found he was eager to see Flick again. He liked her a lot. She was smart, tough, and a pleasure to look at. He wished to hell she was single.

The train was delayed and he missed six o'clock dinner at the Finishing School. He found most of the team relaxing in the drawing room of the house. He sat on the sofa beside Flick and said quietly, 'How did it go today?'

'Better than we had a right to expect. But I don't know how much they're going to remember when they're in the field.'

Percy Thwaite and Jelly were playing poker for pennies. Jelly was a real character, Paul thought. How could a safebreaker consider herself a respectable English lady? 'How was Jelly?'

'She has more difficulty than the others with the physical training but she just gritted her teeth and got on with it. Her hostility to Greta is a problem though.'

'It's not surprising that an Englishwoman should hate Germans.'

'It's illogical, though—Greta's prepared to fight the Nazis.'

'People aren't logical about these things.'

Paul wanted to get Flick to himself so that they could talk more freely. 'Let's take a stroll round the garden.'

They stepped outside. The air was warm and there was an hour of daylight left. The house had several acres of lawn dotted with trees. Maude and Diana were sitting on a bench under a copper beech. Maude was listening avidly to something Diana was saying, looking into Diana's face almost with adoration. 'I wonder what Diana's saying?' Paul said. 'She's got Maude fascinated.'

'Maude likes to hear about the places she's been,' Flick said. 'The fashion shows, the balls, the ocean liners. I noticed her making a play for you. She's pretty.'

'Not my type, though. Not smart enough.'

'I'm glad,' Flick said. 'I would have thought less of you otherwise.'

He grinned. He could not help liking her, even when she was being condescending.

They walked in half-light under a canopy of leaves. Paul wanted to kiss her, but she was wearing a wedding ring.

When they had gone a bit farther he heard a low moan. Frowning, he looked and saw Ruby Romain with Jim Cardwell, the firearms instructor. Ruby had her back to a tree and they were kissing passionately. Paul looked at Flick. She had seen the same thing. She stared for a moment, then turned quickly away. Paul followed suit and they walked quietly back the way they had come.

Maude and Diana had gone from their seat under the copper beech. 'Let's sit here for a minute,' Paul said.

He sat sideways, looking at her, then took her hand and stroked her fingers. 'I know I shouldn't, but I really want to kiss you,' he said. She made no reply, but she did not pull her hand away. He took silence for assent and kissed her. Her mouth was soft and warm. He put his arms round her and pulled her to him, but she slipped out of his embrace and stood up. 'Enough,' she said, and turned towards the house.

He watched her go in the fading light. Her small, neat body suddenly seemed the most desirable thing in the world.

The Fifth Day:
Thursday, June 1, 1944

Dieter slept a few hours at the Hôtel Frankfort. He got up at 2.00am and drove to Sainte-Cécile, winding through the moonlit vineyards in his big car. He parked in front of the château and went to the photo lab in the basement. He had asked for two copies of Helicopter's picture of Flick Clairet, and his prints were there, pegged on a line to dry. He took them off the line and studied one. He pocketed the negative and picked up the original photo, which would have to be returned surreptitiously to Helicopter. He found an envelope and a sheet of paper and wrote Stéphanie a note:

> *My darling, while Helicopter is shaving, please put this in his inside jacket pocket, so that it will look as if it slipped out of his wallet. Thank you. D.*

He put the note and the picture in the envelope, sealed it, and wrote: 'Mlle Lemas' on the front. He would drop it off later.

He went upstairs. On the ground floor, the night shift operators were at their switchboards; above that were the Gestapo offices.

Dieter had not seen Weber since the fiasco in the cathedral. He was surprised to find him alone in his office, behind his desk.

Weber stood up. 'You pulled a gun on me yesterday,' he said. 'What the devil do you mean by threatening an officer? You could be court-martialled for what you did.'

'You were in the process of ruining a first-class counterintelligence coup,' Dieter said in exasperation. 'Don't you think a military court would take that into account?'

'I arrested a British terrorist spy.'

'And what's the point of that? He's just one. Left to go free, he will lead us to others. Fortunately for you, I saved you from a ghastly error.' Shaking his head in despair, Dieter went out.

He met Hans Hesse in the hall. They went to the back of the château, where Hans arranged to borrow a telephone van and a moped—a motorised bicycle. They put on overalls and drove away, with the moped in the back of the van.

They went to Reims and drove along the rue du Bois. In the faint light of dawn, Hans put the envelope containing the photo of Flick into the letterbox.

The sun was rising when they arrived outside Michel Clairet's house in the centre of town. Hans parked the van down the road and opened a manhole. He pretended to be working while watching the house. Dieter stayed in the van, keeping out of sight.

The town came slowly to life. First to appear were the women walking to the bakery opposite Michel's house. The shop was not yet open, but they stood patiently outside, waiting and talking. After that, the working men appeared in their boots and berets, each carrying a bag containing his lunch. Children were just setting out for school when Helicopter appeared, pedalling Jeanne Lemas's bicycle. Dieter sat upright. In the bicycle's basket was a rectangular object covered with a cloth: the suitcase radio, Dieter guessed.

Hans watched from beside the manhole as Helicopter went to Michel's door and knocked. There was no reply, of course.

Dieter had suggested to Helicopter what to do next. 'Go to Chez Régis, the bar along the street. Order coffee and rolls, and wait.' Dieter's hope was that the Resistance might be watching Michel's house, alert for an emissary from London. Before too long someone would show up and speak to Helicopter—and that person might lead Dieter to the heart of the Resistance.

A minute later Helicopter did as Dieter had suggested. He wheeled his bicycle along the street to the bar and sat at a pavement table. He ordered a cup of coffee. After twenty minutes or so he got another coffee and a newspaper from inside.

The morning wore on. Dieter began to wonder whether this was going to work. Eventually the time approached when Helicopter would have to order lunch to justify continuing to use the table. A waiter came out and spoke to him, then brought him a pastis. Dieter licked his lips; he would have liked a drink.

Another customer came and sat at the table next to Helicopter's. Dieter's hopes rose. The newcomer was a long-limbed man in his thirties. He wore a blue chambray shirt and navy canvas trousers, but he did not have the air of a working man. He was something else. Perhaps an artist? The man sat back in his chair and crossed his legs, resting his right ankle on his left knee, and the pose struck Dieter as familiar. Had he seen this man before?

The waiter came out and the newcomer ordered something. The

waiter brought a glass of pale beer on a tray. The man took a long pull, then spoke to Helicopter.

Dieter tensed. Could this be what he had been waiting for?

They exchanged a few casual words. Helicopter was smiling and talking with enthusiasm.

The newcomer drained his beer glass, and Dieter had a flash of recollection. He suddenly knew exactly who this man was. He had seen him in the square at Sainte-Cécile, at another café table, sitting with Flick Clairet, just before the skirmish. This was her husband, Michel himself.

Dieter thumped the dashboard with his fist in satisfaction. His strategy had been proved right. But now he had a dilemma. Should he arrest Michel right away? Or follow him, in the hope of catching even bigger fish?

Michel stood up, and Helicopter did the same.

Hans replaced the manhole cover and got into the van. 'Contact, sir?'

'Yes. Get the bike out, quick.'

Hans opened the back doors of the van and took out the moped.

The two men put money on the café tables and moved away. Dieter saw that Michel walked with a limp, and recalled that he had taken a bullet during the skirmish. He said to Hans, 'You follow them, I'll follow you.' He started the engine of the van.

Hans climbed on the moped and pedalled, which started the engine. He rode slowly along the street, keeping well behind his quarry. Dieter followed Hans.

Michel and Helicopter turned a corner. Following a minute later, Dieter saw that they had stopped to look in a shop window, a precaution against surveillance. As Dieter drove by, they turned and headed back the way they had come. They would be watching for a vehicle that made a U-turn, so Dieter could not pursue them. However, he saw Hans pull behind a truck and turn back keeping the two men in sight.

Dieter went round the block and caught up with them again. Michel and Helicopter were approaching the railway station. When they went inside, Hans left his moped and followed them. Dieter pulled up and did the same. If the two men went to the booking office, he would tell Hans to stand behind them in the queue and buy a ticket to the same destination.

Dieter entered the station just in time to see Hans go down a flight of steps to the tunnel beneath the lines that connected the platforms. On either side of the tunnel, steps led up to the platforms. Dieter followed Hans past all the platform entrances and quickened his pace as he mounted the stairs to the station's rear entrance. He caught up with Hans and they emerged together into the street.

Fear leapt in Dieter's chest. A hundred metres away, he saw Michel and Helicopter jumping into a black Renault Monaquatre, one of the most common cars in France. Dieter could not read its licence plate as the car pulled away and tore round a corner.

Dieter cursed. It was a simple ploy, but infallible. By entering the tunnel, they had forced their pursuers to abandon their vehicles; they had a car waiting at the other side, enabling them to escape.

Dieter had just one ray of hope. He knew Helicopter's times for radio contact, and the frequencies assigned to him. That information might yet be used to recapture him.

Would the British suspect that Helicopter had been found out? Helicopter would by now be giving Michel a full account of his adventures. Michel would question him closely about the arrest in the cathedral and subsequent escape. He would be particularly interested in the newcomer codenamed Charenton. However, he would have no reason to suspect that Mademoiselle Lemas was not who she claimed to be. Michel had never met her, so he would not be alerted even if Helicopter happened to mention that she was an attractive young redhead rather than a middle-aged spinster.

Perhaps, Dieter began to think, all was not yet lost.

THE FISHERMAN'S REST was a big pub that stood on the shore like a fort, with chimneys for gun turrets and smoked-glass windows instead of observation slits. Since SOE had moved into the neighbourhood, the pub had been busy every night; its lights blazing behind the blackout curtains, its piano loud, its bars crowded.

Flick and Paul took their team to the pub at the end of their two-day training course. Maude was prettier than ever in a pink summer frock. Ruby looked sultry in a borrowed black dress. Greta wore one of her stage outfits: an evening gown and red shoes. Even Diana was wearing a smart skirt instead of her usual country corduroys.

The team had been given the code name Jackdaws. They were going to parachute in near Reims, and Flick had remembered the legend of the Jackdaw of Reims, the bird that stole the bishop's ring. 'The monks couldn't figure out who had taken it, so the bishop cursed the unknown thief,' she explained to Paul as they both sipped Scotch. 'Next thing they knew the jackdaw appeared all bedraggled, and they realised he was suffering from the effects of the curse and must be the culprit. Sure enough, they found the ring in his nest.'

Paul nodded, smiling. Flick knew he would have nodded and smiled in exactly the same way no matter what she said. He just wanted to watch her.

She had got through the day on autopilot. Last night's kiss had shocked and thrilled her. She told herself that she did not want to have an affair, she wanted to win back the love of her faithless husband. But Paul had upended her priorities. She asked herself angrily why she should stand in line for Michel's affections when a man such as Paul was in love with her.

At other moments she was ashamed that she had kissed him. Worst of all, her feelings for Paul threatened to distract her from the job. She held in her hands the lives of five people, plus a crucial element in the invasion plan, and she really did not need to be thinking about whether his eyes were hazel or green.

'What are you thinking?' he asked.

She realised she must have been staring at him. 'Wondering whether we can pull this off,' she lied.

'We can, with a little luck.'

She looked round the room. Jelly and Percy were playing a gambling game. Percy was buying round after round of drinks. This was deliberate. Flick needed to know what the Jackdaws were like under the influence of booze. If any of them became rowdy, indiscreet or aggressive, she would have to take precautions in the field.

Ruby was drinking steadily, but Flick trusted her. She was a curious mixture. She could barely read or write, but she was the brightest and most intuitive of the group. Ruby gave Greta a hard look now and again, and she may have guessed that Greta was a man, but to her credit she had said nothing.

Greta was leaning on the piano with some pink cocktail in her hand, talking to three men who looked to be local residents. It seemed they had got over the shock of her German accent—no doubt she had told the story of her English father—and now she held them enthralled with tales about Hamburg nightclubs.

Flick stood up wearily. 'We'd better get the team to bed. This will be their last decent night's sleep for a while.'

Paul looked round the room. 'I don't see Diana and Maude.'

'They must have stepped out for a breath of air. I'll find them if you'll round up the rest.' Paul nodded and Flick went outside.

There was no sign of the two girls. Frowning, puzzled, Flick crossed the tarmac and went to the back of the pub. She came to a yard with old barrels and stacked crates. Across the yard was a small outbuilding with a wooden door that stood open. She went in.

Her eyes adjusted to the dim light. She was in a toolshed, and she saw Diana and Maude in a far corner. Maude was leaning against the wall and Diana was kissing her. Flick's jaw dropped. Maude saw her and met her eye. 'Have you had a good look?' she said saucily.

Diana jumped back from Maude. She turned round, and a look of horror came over her face. 'Oh, my *God*,' she said.

Flick stammered: 'I-I-I just came to say we're leaving.' Then she turned round and stumbled out.

WIRELESS OPERATORS were not quite invisible. They lived in a spirit world where their ghostly shapes could be dimly seen. Peering into the gloom, searching for them, were the men of the Gestapo's radio-detection teams. They had cars equipped with detection apparatus, and Dieter was now sitting in such a car, a long black Citroën parked on the outskirts of Reims. With him were three Gestapo men experienced in wireless detection. The car's receiver was tuned to Helicopter's frequency. It measured the strength, as well as the direction, of the broadcast, and Dieter would know he was getting nearer to the transmitter when the needle rose on the dial.

In addition, the Gestapo man sitting next to Dieter wore a receiver and an aerial concealed beneath his raincoat. On his wrist was a meter like a watch that showed the strength of the signal. When the search narrowed down to a particular street, city block, or building, the walker would take over. The Gestapo man in the front seat held a sledgehammer for breaking down doors.

Dieter had been hunting once. This was like lying in the hide in the early dawn, tense with anticipation, impatient for the deer to start moving. He was mortified to have lost Helicopter. He was so keen to recapture the man that he hardly minded having to rely on the help of Willi Weber.

Dieter checked his watch: one minute past eight. Helicopter was late coming on air. Perhaps he would not broadcast tonight—but that was unlikely. Today Helicopter had met up with Michel. He would want to report to his superiors.

Michel had phoned the house in the rue du Bois two hours ago. Dieter had been there. It was a tense moment. Stéphanie had answered, in her imitation of Mademoiselle Lemas's voice. Michel had given his code name, and asked whether 'Bourgeoise' remembered who he was. The question reassured Stéphanie. It indicated that Michel did not know Mademoiselle Lemas's voice very well and therefore would not realise this was an impersonator.

He had asked her about her new recruit, codenamed Charenton. 'He's my cousin,' Stéphanie had said gruffly. 'I've known him since we were children, I would trust him with my life.' Michel had told her she had no right to recruit people without at least discussing it with him, but he had appeared to believe her story.

All the same, Helicopter would know that the Gestapo would be listening and trying to find him. That was a risk he had to run: if he sent no messages home he was of no use.

The minutes ticked by. At five past eight, the receiver beeped. The driver set off immediately, driving south. The signal grew stronger. As they passed the cathedral in the centre of town, it fell back.

In the passenger seat, the Gestapo man talked into a short-wave radio. He was consulting with someone in a radio-detection truck two kilometres away. After a moment he said, 'Northwest quarter.' The driver immediately turned, and the signal began to strengthen.

'Got you,' Dieter breathed.

Back in Sainte-Cécile, a German radio operator had tuned to the same frequency and was taking down the coded message. Later, Dieter would decrypt it, using the one-time pad copied by Stéphanie. But the message was not as important as the messenger.

They entered a neighbourhood of large, decrepit old houses. The signal grew louder, then suddenly began to fade. 'Overshoot, overshoot!' said the Gestapo man in the front passenger seat. The driver braked. Dieter and the three Gestapo men sprang out. The one with the portable detection unit under his raincoat walked rapidly along the pavement, consulting his wrist dial constantly, and the others followed. He stopped and pointed to a derelict house. 'That one,' he said. 'But the transmission has ended.'

The Gestapo man carrying the sledgehammer broke the front door down with two blows. They all rushed in. The floors were bare and the place had a musty smell. Dieter threw a door open and looked into an empty room. He opened the door of the back room. It too was empty.

He ran up the stairs. On the next floor was a window overlooking a long back garden. Dieter saw Helicopter and Michel running across the grass, Helicopter carrying his suitcase. Dieter yelled, 'Back garden!' The Gestapo men ran and he followed.

They reached the next street just in time to see a black Renault disappearing round the corner. 'Hell!' Dieter said. For the second time in a day, Helicopter had slipped through his grasp.

WHEN THEY GOT BACK to the house, Flick went into the kitchen to make cocoa for the team. Paul stood watching her as she waited for the kettle to boil. She felt his eyes on her like a caress. She knew what he was going to say, and she had prepared her reply. It would have been easy to fall in love with Paul, but she was not going to betray the husband who was risking his life in occupied France.

His question surprised her. 'What will you do after the war?'

'I'm looking forward to being bored,' she said.

He laughed. 'You've had enough excitement.'

'Too much.' She thought for a moment. 'I want to be a teacher. I'd like to finish my doctorate, get at job at a university. Maybe write a guide book to France. What about you? What's your plan?'

'Oh, mine is simple. I want to marry you and have children.'

She stared at him. 'I already have a husband.'

'But you don't love him.'

'You have no right to say that!'

'I know, but I can't help it.'

She took the boiling kettle off the hob and poured water over the cocoa mixture in a big jug. 'Put some mugs on a tray,' she told Paul. 'A little housework might cure you of dreams of domesticity.'

In the living room they found Jelly and Greta having a row while the others looked on, half amused and half horrified.

Jelly was saying, 'You weren't using it!'

'I was resting my feet on it,' Greta replied.

'There aren't enough chairs.' Jelly was holding a small stuffed pouffe, and Flick guessed she had snatched it rudely from Greta.

Flick said, 'Ladies, please!'

They ignored her. Greta said, 'You only had to ask, sweetheart.'

'I don't have to ask permission from foreigners in my own country.'

'I'm not a foreigner, you fat bitch.'

'Oh!' Stung by the insult, Jelly reached out and pulled Greta's hair. Greta's brunette wig came off in her hand.

With her head of close-cropped dark hair exposed, Greta suddenly looked unmistakably like a man. Diana said, 'Good God!' and Maude gave a little scream of fright.

Jelly was the first of them to recover her wits. 'A pervert!' she said triumphantly. 'It's a foreign pervert! I bet she's a spy!'

Flick said, 'Shut up, Jelly. She's not a spy. I knew she was a man.'

Greta was in tears. Flick said, 'Greta, please. Sit down. Jelly, give me the damn wig.'

Jelly handed it to Flick, who put it back on Greta's head.

'Now listen to me, all of you,' said Flick. 'Greta is an engineer. We need her and we need her to be a woman. So get used to it.'

Jelly gave a contemptuous grunt.

'There's something else I ought to explain,' Flick said. She looked hard at Jelly. 'You were all commissioned as officers, yesterday, after tea. That means you're under military discipline. I'll fire anyone I have to from this team and you'll spend the rest of the war at some remote base in Scotland, with no leave. You all know too much.'

'So we're prisoners?' Diana said.

'You're in the army,' Flick said. 'It's much the same thing. Now drink your cocoa and then go to bed.'

They drifted off one by one until only Diana was left. Flick had been expecting this. Seeing her and Maude in a clinch had been a real shock. Flick recalled that at school some of the girls had developed crushes on one another, but Flick had never known a grown woman who desired other women.

Did it matter? Not in everyday life. But would Diana's relationship with Maude affect the mission? Flick had decided to leave well enough alone. But Diana wanted to talk.

'It's not what it seems,' Diana said without preamble. 'You've got to believe me. It was just a stupid thing, a joke—'

Flick said, 'Calm down. The world is not going to come to an end simply because you kissed Maude.'

'I suppose that's the end of the mission for us.'

'It most certainly is not. I still need you.'

Diana took out a handkerchief and blew her nose. Flick went to the window, giving her time to recover her composure. After a minute, she said, 'Go to bed, Diana. And if I were you . . .'

'What?'

'I'd go to bed with Maude. It may be your last chance.'

'Thank you,' Diana whispered. 'Good night.'

After Diana left the room Flick turned and looked out at the garden. The moon was three-quarters full. In a few days' time it would be full, and the Allies would invade France.

She ought to get some sleep. She left the room and climbed the stairs. She thought of what she had said to Diana: *It may be your last chance.* She hesitated outside Paul's door. It was different for Diana—she was single. Flick was married.

But it might be her last chance.

She knocked at the door and stepped inside.

SUNK IN GLOOM, Dieter returned to the château at Sainte-Cécile. He went to the listening room in the basement. Willi Weber was there.

'You have the message he sent?' Dieter asked.

Weber handed him a carbon copy of the typed message. 'It has already been sent to the cryptanalysis office in Berlin.'

Dieter looked at the meaningless strings of letters. 'They won't be able to decode it. He's using a one-time pad.' He folded the sheet and slipped it into his pocket.

'What can you do with it?' Weber said.

'I have a copy of his code book,' Dieter said. 'He's scheduled to receive a reply at eleven o'clock.' Dieter looked at his watch. It was a few minutes before eleven. 'I will decrypt the two together.'

Weber left. Dieter waited in the windowless room. On the dot of eleven, a receiver tuned to Helicopter's listening frequency began to chatter with the long-and-short beeps of Morse. An operator wrote the letters down, then typed out what he had on his notepad. He gave Dieter a carbon copy.

The two messages could be everything or nothing, Dieter thought as he got behind the wheel of his own car. The moon was bright as he followed the twisting road through the vineyards to Reims and parked in the rue du Bois. It was good weather for an invasion.

Stéphanie was waiting for him in the kitchen of Mademoiselle Lemas's house. He put the coded messages on the table and took out the copies Stéphanie had made of the pad and the silk handkerchief. He rubbed his eyes and began to decode the first message, the one Helicopter had sent. Stéphanie looked over his shoulder for a while, then began to decode the second message herself.

Dieter's decrypt gave a concise account of the incident at the cathedral, naming Dieter as Charenton and saying he had been recruited by Bourgeoise. It said Monet (Michel) had taken the unusual step of phoning Bourgeoise to confirm that Charenton was trustworthy. It listed the code names of the survivors of the Bollinger circuit. There were only four.

Dieter drank coffee while he waited for Stéphanie to finish her decoding. When he read it, he could hardly believe his luck. It said:

> PREPARE RECEIVE GROUP OF SIX PARACHUTISTS CODENAMED
> JACKDAWS LEADER LEOPARDESS ARRIVING ELEVEN PIP EMMA
> FRIDAY FIRST JUNE CHAMP DE PIERRE.

'My God,' he whispered.

Champ de Pierre was a code name, but Gaston had told him what it meant. It was a drop zone in a pasture outside Chatelle, a small village eight kilometres from Reims. Dieter now knew exactly where Helicopter and Michel would be tomorrow night, and could pick them up. He could also capture six more Allied agents as they parachuted to earth. And one of them was Leopardess: Flick Clairet. The woman who, under torture, would give him the information he needed to break the back of the Resistance.

The Sixth Day:
Friday, June 2, 1944

Dieter had decided to hold his briefing in the ballroom of the château at Sainte-Cécile. On the blackboard he had chalked a neat map of the village of Chatelle, including, to the east, a large cow pasture, bordered by a broad pond.

'The parachutists will aim to land in the pasture,' Dieter said. He paused. 'The most important thing for everyone here to remember is that *we want these parachutists to land*. We must avoid any action that might betray our presence. We will arrive at the village at twenty hundred hours. All the residents will be brought to the largest of the three big houses and held there until it is all over.

'We will watch the parachutists land and wait for the reception committee to round them up. *Not until this process has been completed will we arrest anyone!* No one is to fire on the enemy—is that clear? We want to interrogate these parachutists, not kill them.'

AT TWO IN THE AFTERNOON the Jackdaws arrived at a large mansion called Tempsford House. Flick had been here before: it was the assembly point for nearby Tempsford Airfield.

They had tea and sandwiches in the dining room and afterwards met in the library. The room looked more like the wardrobe of a film studio. There were racks of coats and dresses, boxes of hats and shoes, and several sewing machines.

In charge of the operation was Madame Guillemin, a slim woman of about fifty with spectacles on the end of her nose and a tape measure round her neck. She spoke to them in perfect French. 'As you know, French clothes are distinctively different from British clothes. I won't say they are more stylish, but, you know, they are . . . more stylish.' She gave a French shrug, and the girls laughed.

Flick said, 'We need clothes that are fairly expensive, but well worn. I want us to look like respectable women.' When they needed to pose as cleaners, they could quickly downgrade their appearance by taking off their hats, gloves and belts.

Madame Guillemin began with Ruby, picking a navy dress and a tan raincoat. 'Try those. It's a man's coat, but in France today no one can afford to be particular.' She pointed across the room. 'You can change behind that screen if you wish. For the very shy there is a little anteroom behind the desk.'

The seamstress looked hard at Greta, then moved on, saying, 'I'll come back to you.' She picked outfits for Jelly, Diana and Maude, and they went behind the screen. Then she turned to Greta. 'You're a man,' she said. 'You might fool a lot of people, but not me. The shoulders are too broad, the hips too narrow, the legs too muscular.'

Flick said irritably, 'She has to be a woman for this mission. Dress her as best you can.'

The seamstress turned to Greta. 'I'll give you a contrasting skirt and blouse, to reduce your height, and a three-quarter-length coat.' She handed the clothes to Greta, who viewed them with disapproval.

Finally, Madame gave Flick an apple-green dress with a matching coat. 'The colour shows off your eyes,' she said. The dress was loose and looked like a tent on Flick, but she put on a leather belt to give it a waist. 'You are so chic,' said Madame Guillemin.

They all put on their new clothes and paraded round the room, preening and giggling. Greta came out of the anteroom looking surprisingly glamorous. Flick studied her with interest. She had turned up the collar of the plain white blouse so that it looked stylish, and wore the shapeless coat draped over her shoulders cloak-style.

Flick's dress had to be shortened. While that was being done she studied the coat, anxiously checking the details. She showed Madame Guillemin her lapel knife. It was only three inches long, with a thin blade, but it was wickedly sharp. It had a small handle and no hilt. It came in a slim leather sheath pierced with holes for thread. She asked Madame to sew it to the coat under the lapel.

Madame gave them each a little pile of underwear, two of everything, all French. Finally she produced an assortment of travel bags, each containing a French toothbrush, toothpaste, face powder, shoe polish, cigarettes and matches.

'Remember,' Flick said, 'you may not take with you anything that you have not been given this afternoon. Your life depends on that. Now, please go to your rooms and change into your French outfits including underwear. Then we'll meet downstairs for dinner.'

THEIR LAST MEAL in England was a banquet by wartime standards, and the women tucked in with relish. When they had finished, it was time to go to Tempsford Airfield. They returned to their rooms to collect their bags, then boarded a bus which took them along a country lane towards a cluster of buildings beside a large, flat field.

They stepped down from the bus and went into what looked like a cowshed, where they found a uniformed RAF officer standing guard over steel racks of equipment. Paul distributed their identity cards, ration cards and clothing coupons. Each woman was given 100,000 French francs, mostly in grubby 1,000-franc notes. They also got weapons: .45 calibre Colt automatic pistols and sharp double-bladed Commando knives. Flick declined both. She took her personal gun, a Browning automatic, which she preferred to the SOE Colt because it had thirteen rounds in the clip instead of seven. She had her lapel knife instead of the more cumbersome Commando knife.

In addition there was a rifle for Diana and a submachine gun with silencer for Flick.

The plastic explosive Jelly would need was distributed around the six women so that even if one or two bags were lost there would still be enough to do the job.

Maude said, 'It might blow me up!'

Jelly explained that it was extraordinarily safe.

They were given grenades and each Jackdaw got a fountain pen with a hollow cap containing a suicide pill.

Finally they put on their flying suits, donned helmet and goggles and shrugged into their parachute harnesses.

Paul asked Flick to step outside for a moment. He had held back the all-important special passes which would enable the women to enter the château as cleaners. For safety, he gave all the passes to Flick, to be distributed at the last minute.

Then he kissed her. 'Don't get killed,' he said into her ear.

They were interrupted by a discreet cough. Flick smelt Percy's pipe. She broke the clinch.

Percy said to Paul, 'The pilot is waiting for a word with you.'

Paul nodded and moved away.

Percy looked grim, and Flick had a bad feeling. 'What's wrong?'

He took a sheet of paper from his jacket pocket and handed it to her. 'This came from Brian Standish last night.'

Flick looked at the paper. Its contents hit her like a punch in the stomach. 'Brian has been in the hands of the Gestapo!'

'Only for a few seconds.'

Flick took a deep breath. 'Any agent who is captured by the enemy, *whatever the circumstances*, must immediately return to London for debriefing. We'll have no wireless operator. And what about this Charenton? All recruits are supposed to be vetted by London.'

'You know that rule has never been followed. Besides, Michel is satisfied.'

She sighed. 'I don't like it. But we have to take the risk. There's no time for precautions. If we don't disable the telephone exchange in the next three days it will be too late.'

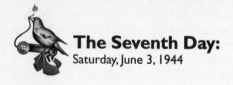

The Seventh Day:
Saturday, June 3, 1944

The plane the Jackdaws boarded was an American-made twin-engined Hudson light bomber borrowed by SOE from the RAF. At the back was a slide like a water chute, down which the parachutists would glide into space. There were no seats inside, and the six women and their dispatcher lay on the metal floor. They shared the space with a dozen metal containers, each equipped with a parachute harness, all containing—Flick presumed—guns and ammunition for some other Resistance circuit. After dropping the Jackdaws at Chatelle, the Hudson would fly on to another destination before heading back to Tempsford. Takeoff had been delayed by a faulty altimeter which had to be replaced, so it was one o'clock in the morning when they left the English coastline behind.

The navigator was constantly busy with his maps, calculating the plane's position by dead reckoning and trying to confirm it by landmarks. The moon was waxing, and only three days from full, so large towns were easily visible, despite the blackout. However, they generally had antiaircraft batteries, and so had to be avoided, as did army camps and military sites, for the same reason.

As they approached Chatelle, Flick spotted the pond that bordered the cow pasture, and pointed it out to the navigator. They flew over it at 300 feet. Flick could see the flare path; four weak, flickering lights in an L shape, with the torch at the toe of the L flashing the prearranged code. The pilot climbed towards 600 feet, the ideal altitude for a parachute drop: any higher, and the wind could blow the parachutists away from the drop zone; lower, and the chutes might not have time to open fully.

'Ready when you are,' said the pilot.

'I'm not ready,' Flick said. 'Something's wrong.' She pointed west, to the village. 'Look, no lights.'

'That surprises you? There's a blackout. And it's after three o'clock in the morning.'

Flick shook her head. 'This is the countryside, they're careless about the blackout. And there's always someone up: a mother with a new baby, an insomniac. I've never seen it completely dark.'

What should she do? She could hardly abort the mission just because the villagers were obeying the blackout rules for once.

The plane overflew the field and banked to turn. The pilot said anxiously, 'Remember, each time we overfly increases the risk. Someone in that village might call the police.'

'Exactly!' she said. 'We must have awakened the entire place. Yet no one has switched on a light! This is peculiar.'

Suddenly it came to her. 'The baker should have lit his oven. You can normally see the glow from the air. This is like a ghost town!'

'Then let's get out of here.'

It was as if someone had rounded up the villagers, including the baker, and locked them away—which was probably what the

Gestapo would have done if they were lying in wait for her.

Suddenly she remembered the containers of supplies in the passenger cabin. 'What's your next destination?'

'A field north of Chartres.'

That meant the Vestryman Resistance circuit. 'I know them,' Flick said with mounting excitement. 'You could drop us with the containers. By train we could be in Paris this afternoon, Reims by tomorrow morning.'

He reached for the joystick. 'I can drop you there, no problem. The tactical decision is yours.'

Flick considered. She would need to get a message to Michel via Brian's radio, saying that although her landing had been aborted, she was still on her way. She could write a brief radio signal for the pilot to take back to Percy. Brian would have it in a couple of hours.

She would also have to change the arrangements for picking up the Jackdaws after the mission. Diverting to Chartres meant the mission would take an extra day, so the pick-up flight would have to come on Monday. But landing at Chatelle could mean the entire mission failed and all the Jackdaws ended up in Gestapo hands. It was no contest. 'Go to Chartres,' she said to the pilot.

DIETER LAY BENEATH A HEDGE and watched, bewildered, while the British plane banked, turned, and roared away to the south. He was mortified. Flick Clairet had evaded him—in front of Willi Weber and twenty Gestapo men.

What had gone wrong? As the drone of the plane's engines receded, Dieter could hear shouts of indignation in French. The Resistance seemed as perplexed as he was.

Dieter considered briefly. There were four Resistance people here: Michel the leader, still limping from his bullet wound; Helicopter, the radio operator; a Frenchman Dieter did not recognise, and a young woman. He had to get something out of tonight's fiasco.

He brought the mouthpiece of the short-wave radio to his lips and said softly, 'All units, this is Major Franck. Action, I repeat, action.' Then he got to his feet.

Searchlights concealed in the trees blazed into life, lighting up the four terrorists in the middle of the field. Dieter called out in French, 'You are surrounded! Raise your hands!'

One of the men in the field started to run. Dieter swore. It was Helicopter, stupid boy.

'Shoot him,' Dieter said. The Gestapo riflemen fired. Helicopter ran another two paces, then fell.

Dieter looked at the other three. Slowly, they raised their hands.

'Move in. Secure the prisoners,' Dieter ordered.

He walked over to where Helicopter lay. The body was still. He knelt beside it and felt for a pulse, but there was none. He closed the eyes. Then he stood up and looked over at the other three as they were disarmed and fettered. Michel would resist interrogation well. Dieter had seen him in action, and he had courage. A Gestapo man searched the other man and showed Dieter a pass which permitted Dr Claude Bouler to be out after curfew. Under arrest he looked pale but composed. He, too, would be a difficult subject.

The girl was the most promising. She was about nineteen, and pretty, with long dark hair and big eyes, but she had a vacant look. Her papers showed that she was Gilberte Duval. Dieter knew from his interrogation of Gaston that Gilberte was the lover of Michel. Handled correctly, she might prove easy to turn.

The prisoners went to Sainte-Cécile in a truck with the Gestapo men. Dieter was driven in Weber's Mercedes. By the time they reached the château, his interrogation strategy was fully formed.

He ordered Lieutenant Hesse to prepare Michel by tying him to a chair in the torture chamber. 'Show him the instrument used for pulling out fingernails,' he said. 'Leave it on the table in front of him.' While that was being done, he got a pen, a bottle of ink and a pad of letter paper from the offices on the upper floor. He also located a copy of *Madame Bovary*.

Dieter studied Michel for a few moments. The Resistance leader looked scared but determined.

Dieter put the pen, ink and paper on the table next to the fingernail pliers, to show that they were alternatives. 'Untie his hands,' he said. 'I will take samples of his handwriting.' To Michel he said, 'Copy out chapter nine.'

Michel hesitated. It seemed a harmless request. He suspected a trick, Dieter could tell, but he could not see what it was. He began writing. When Michel had finished two pages, Dieter stopped him. He told Hans to return Michel to his cell and to bring Gilberte.

Dieter tore one page very carefully to leave only certain words.

Gilberte came in looking terrified but defiant.

'You're a lovely woman. I don't believe you are a murderer.'

'No, I'm not!' she said gratefully.

'A woman does things for love, doesn't she?'

She looked at him with surprise. 'You understand.'

'I know all about you. You are in love with Michel. A married man, of course. This is regrettable. But you love him. And that's why you help the Resistance. Out of love, not hate. Am I right?'

She bowed her head. 'Yes,' she whispered.

'But you have been misguided, my dear. I'm afraid he doesn't really love you. He loves his wife.'

Tears came to her eyes, and she said, 'I don't believe you.'

'He writes to her, you know. I imagine he gets the couriers to take his letters back to England. He sends her love letters, saying how much he misses her. He was carrying one when we arrested all of you.' Dieter took from his pocket the sheet he had torn and handed it to her. Gilberte read it slowly, moving her lips: *I think of you constantly. The memory of you drives me to despair.*

She threw down the paper with a sob.

Dieter took the white linen handkerchief from the breast pocket of his suit and handed it to her. She buried her face in it.

'I suppose Michel has been living with you since Flick left.'

'Longer than that,' she said indignantly.

'Wasn't it difficult to have Helicopter living with you as well, in a small place?'

'No. Michel found him a place, an empty room over the old bookshop in the rue Molière.'

'Didn't he leave his stuff at your place when you went to Chatelle to meet the plane?'

'No, he took it to the room.'

'Ah.' Dieter had what he wanted. Helicopter's radio set was in that room. 'I've finished with this stupid cow,' he said to Hans in German. 'Turn her over to Becker.'

Dieter's own car, the blue Hispano-Suiza, was parked in front of the château. With Hans Hesse beside him, he drove fast to Reims and quickly found the bookshop in the rue Molière. They broke the door down and climbed a bare wooden staircase to the room over the shop. On the floor beside a rough bed stood a bottle of whisky, a bag containing toiletries, and the small suitcase.

Dieter opened it to show Hans the radio. 'With this,' Dieter said triumphantly, 'I can become Helicopter.'

On the way back to Sainte-Cécile, they discussed what message to send. 'First, Helicopter would want to know why the parachutists did not drop,' Dieter said. 'Then he would want to know what he should do next, so he will ask for further instructions.'

They reached the château and went to the wireless listening-room in the basement. A middle-aged operator called Joachim plugged the set in and tuned it to Helicopter's emergency frequency, while Dieter scribbled the agreed message. He carefully showed Joachim how to encode it, including the security tags.

Joachim began to tap out the letters.

Dieter and Hans went to the kitchen for breakfast. It was daylight when a young woman in SS uniform came to tell them that the reply had come in and Joachim had almost finished typing it.

They hurried downstairs. Weber was already there. Joachim handed the typed message to him and a carbon copy to Dieter. It read:

JACKDAWS ABORTED DROP BUT HAVE LANDED ELSEWHERE AWAIT
CONTACT FROM LEOPARDESS

Dieter was jubilant. 'Leopardess is in France—and I have a picture of her!' He pulled the photos of Flick Clairet from his pocket and handed one to Weber. 'Have a thousand copies printed. I want to see that picture all over Reims. Hans, get my car ready.'

'Where are you going?'

'To Paris, with the other photograph, to do the same thing there. I've got her now!'

THE PARACHUTE DROP went smoothly. The containers were pushed out first, then the Jackdaws took turns to sit on the top of the slide and slither down into space.

Flick went last. She landed perfectly, with her knees bent and her arms tucked into her sides. She lay still for a moment, then stood up. In the moonlight, she could see half a dozen Resistance people carrying away the containers.

She struggled out of her parachute harness, helmet and flying suit. A young man ran up to her and said in breathless French, 'We weren't expecting any personnel, just supplies!'

'A change of plan,' she said. 'Find Anton quickly, please.' Anton was the code name of the leader of the Vestryman circuit. 'Tell him Leopardess is here. We have six people who need transport.'

'Very good.' He hurried away.

The Jackdaws, riding in the back of a builder's van, entered Chartres just as the sun came up.

Flick was planning ahead. 'From now on, we split up into pairs,' she said. The teams had been decided back at the Finishing School. Flick had put Diana with Maude, for otherwise Diana would make a fuss. Flick paired herself with Ruby, because she wanted to be able to discuss problems with someone, and Ruby was the cleverest Jackdaw. That left Greta with Jelly, who had objected at first, until Flick said, 'This is a military operation. You do what you're told.'

Now Flick said, 'We'll have to modify our cover stories, to explain the train trip. Any ideas?'

Greta said, 'I'm the wife of Major Remmer, a German officer working in Paris. I'm returning from a visit to the cathedral at Chartres with my French maid.'

'Good enough. Diana?'

'Maude and I are secretaries working for the electric company in Reims. We've been to Chartres because . . . Maude has lost contact with her fiancé and we thought he might be here.'

Flick nodded, satisfied. 'And I went to Chartres to fetch my orphaned cousin and bring her to live with me in Reims.' She spoke to the driver. 'Look for a quiet spot to let us out. We can find the station on our own.'

A couple of minutes later the Jackdaws found themselves in a narrow alley with high houses on either side.

Flick reminded them of the plan. 'Go to the station, buy one-way tickets to Paris, and get the first train. Each pair will pretend not to know the others. We regroup in Paris; you have the address.' They were going to a dosshouse called Hôtel de la Chapelle.

'Diana and Maude first, off you go, quick! Jelly and Greta next, more slowly.' They went off, looking scared. After a few minutes Flick and Ruby walked out of the alley.

The first few steps in a French town were always the worst. Flick felt as if she had a sign on her back saying: 'British Agent!' But a couple of German officers walked by as if she were nobody special, and her pulse began to return to normal.

At the station, there was a queue at the ticket window. That meant local people were optimistic there would be a train soon. Greta and Jelly were in the queue, Diana and Maude already on the platform.

They bought their tickets without incident. On the way to the platform they had to pass a Gestapo checkpoint, and Flick's pulse beat faster. Greta and Jelly were ahead of them in line. This would be their first encounter with the enemy.

Greta spoke to the Gestapo men in German. Flick could clearly hear her giving her cover story. 'I know a Major Remmer,' said one of the men, a sergeant. 'Is he an engineer?'

'No, he's in intelligence,' Greta replied.

'You must like cathedrals,' he said conversationally. 'There's nothing else to see in this dump.' He turned to Jelly's papers and began to speak French, 'You travel everywhere with Frau Remmer?'

'Yes, she's very kind to me,' Jelly replied. Flick heard the tremor in her voice and knew that she was terrified.

The sergeant handed back their papers. 'I hope you won't have to wait too long for a train,' he said.

Greta and Jelly walked on, and Flick breathed again.

When she and Ruby got to the head of the line, it was Flick's turn to tell her story to the Gestapo.

'You're cousins?' the sergeant said, looking from her to Ruby and back again.

'Not much resemblance, is there?' Flick said with a cheerful air. 'Her mother came from Naples.'

He shrugged and addressed Ruby. 'How did your parents die?'

'In a train derailed by Resistance saboteurs,' she said.

'My sympathies, young lady. Those people are animals.'

He handed the papers back and they walked on.

Diana and Maude had gone to the bar and were drinking champagne. Flick felt cross. Diana should realise they needed their wits about them.

Greta and Jelly were sitting on a bench, and Flick and Ruby found another bench some distance away and sat down to wait.

It was eleven o'clock when a train pulled in. The coaches were full, so Flick and Ruby had to stand. Greta and Jelly did, too, but Diana and Maude managed to get seats in a six-person compartment with two middle-aged women and two gendarmes.

The gendarmes worried Flick. She managed to squeeze into a place right outside the compartment, where she could look through the glass. Fortunately, the combination of a restless night and the champagne they had drunk at the station put Diana and Maude to sleep as soon as the train pulled out.

They chugged through woods and rolling fields. An hour later the two middle-aged French women got off the train, and Flick and Ruby quickly slid into the vacated seats. The gendarmes immediately struck up a conversation.

Their names were Christian and Jean-Marie. Both appeared to be in their twenties. Christian, the talkative one, was in the middle seat, and Ruby sat next to him. Flick was on the opposite banquette, with Maude beside her, slumped the other way with her head on Diana's shoulder.

The gendarmes were travelling to Paris to pick up a prisoner, they said. It was nothing to do with the war. He was a local man who had murdered his wife and stepson, then fled to Paris, where he had been caught. Christian reached into his tunic pocket and pulled out the handcuffs they would put on him, as if to prove that he was not boasting.

As the train entered the outskirts of Paris, Diana woke up and said loudly, in English, 'Good God, my head hurts, what bloody time is it?' A moment later she saw the gendarmes and realised instantly what she had done—but it was too late.

'She spoke English!' said Christian.

Flick saw Ruby reach for her gun.

'You're British!' he said to Diana. He looked at Maude. 'You, too!' His gaze went round the compartment. 'All of you!'

Flick reached across and grabbed Ruby's wrist as her gun was halfway out of her raincoat pocket. Christian saw what Ruby had in her hand, and said, 'And armed!'

Flick waited on tenterhooks to see what he would do. Several frozen seconds passed. Then Christian smiled. 'Good luck!' he said, lowering his voice. 'Your secret is safe with us!'

Flick slumped with relief. 'Thank you,' she said. 'I'm so glad you are on our side.'

'I have always been against the Germans.' Christian puffed himself up a little. 'In my job, I have been able to render some useful services to the Resistance, in a discreet way.'

Flick did not believe him for a second. However, he could see which way the wind was blowing, and he was not going to turn Allied agents over to the Gestapo a few days before the invasion.

The train slowed, and Flick saw that they were coming into the Gare d'Orsay station. She stood up. Christian kissed her hand. 'You are a brave woman. Good luck!'

She left the carriage first. As she stepped onto the platform, she saw a workman pasting up a poster of her.

Her heart stopped. She had never seen it before, and she had no recollection of ever having had her photograph taken in a swimsuit.

The poster gave her name and said she was a murderess. The workman was finishing his task. He picked up his bucket of paste and a stack of posters and moved on.

Flick realised her picture must be all over Paris. She stood frozen on the platform. Then she got hold of herself. Her first problem was how to get out of the station. She looked along the platform and saw a checkpoint manned by Gestapo officers. They must have seen the picture. How could she get past them?

She turned round. Ruby, Diana and Maude had got off the train. Christian and Jean-Marie were about to follow. Then Flick remembered the handcuffs in Christian's pocket. She pushed Christian back into the carriage and climbed in after him.

He smiled anxiously. 'What's the matter?'

'Look,' she said. 'There's a poster of me on the wall. You must help me get through the checkpoint,' she said. 'They won't be suspicious of police officers in uniform. Put the handcuffs on me. Pretend you have captured me. Tell them you're taking me to eighty-four Avenue Foch.' It was the address of Gestapo headquarters.

Christian looked terrified. Flick could tell that he wanted to back out. But he hardly could, after his big talk about the Resistance.

Jean-Marie was calmer. 'It will work,' he said.

Ruby climbed back into the carriage. 'Flick! That poster—'

'I know. The gendarmes are going to march me through the checkpoint and release me later. If things go wrong, you're in charge of the mission.' She switched to English. 'Forget the railway tunnel, that's a cover story. The real target is the telephone exchange at Sainte-Cécile. But don't tell the others until the last minute. Now get them back in here, quickly.'

A few moments later they were all crowded into the carriage. Flick told them the plan. Then she said, 'If this doesn't work, and I get arrested, remember, the mission comes first. Abandon me, regroup at the hotel, and carry on. Ruby will be in command.' She turned to Christian. 'The handcuffs. The rest of you, get going.'

Christian handcuffed Flick's right hand to Jean-Marie's left, then they stepped down from the train and marched along the platform three abreast, Christian carrying Flick's suitcase and her shoulder bag with the automatic pistol in it. There was a queue at the checkpoint. Jean-Marie said loudly, 'Stand aside, there. Coming through.' They went straight to the head of the line. Both gendarmes saluted the Gestapo officers.

The captain in charge of the checkpoint looked hard at Flick. 'She's the one on the poster.'

Jean-Marie answered. 'Yes, captain. Our orders are to deliver her to Avenue Foch.'

The captain nodded. 'These British, They send little girls to do their fighting for them.' He shook his head in disbelief. 'Carry on.'

Flick and the gendarmes marched through the checkpoint and out into the sunshine.

PAUL CHANCELLOR had been violently angry with Percy Thwaite, when he found out about the message from Brian Standish. 'You deceived me!' Paul had shouted. 'You made sure I was out of the way before you showed it to Flick!'

'I thought you would have aborted the flight.'

'Perhaps I would have—maybe I should have.'

'But you would have done it for love of Flick, not because it was right operationally.'

There Percy had touched Paul's weak spot, which made him even more angry.

The two men had stayed at the airfield all night, smoking and pacing and worrying about the woman they both, in different ways, loved. Paul had, in his shirt pocket, the wooden French toothbrush he and Flick had shared on Friday morning, after their night together. He was not normally superstitious, but he kept touching it, as if he were touching her, making sure she was OK.

When the plane returned, and the pilot told them how Flick had become suspicious at Chatelle, and had eventually dropped near Chartres, Paul had been so relieved he almost wept.

Minutes later, Percy had had a call from SOE headquarters in London and had learned of Brian Standish's message demanding to know what had gone wrong. Paul had decided to respond by sending the reply drafted by Flick and brought home by her pilot: that the Jackdaws had landed and would contact him.

Still no one was sure what had happened out there. The uncertainty was unbearable. Flick had to go to Reims, but she might be walking into a trap. There must be a way to check whether Brian's transmissions were genuine?

There were subtle methods of checking, Percy said, but they depended on the girls at the listening station. So Paul had gone there.

Grendon Underwood was another grand country house vacated

by the owners and taken over by the military. It was a home to 400 wireless operators and coders, most of them young women in the FANYs. On its extensive grounds were radio aerials grouped in great arcs, listening to messages from all over Europe.

Paul was shown around by a supervisor, Jean Bevins, a heavy woman with spectacles. She took him to the transmitting room, where a hundred or so girls sat. A big board showed agents' code names and scheduled times and frequencies for transmission.

Jean introduced Paul to Lucy Briggs, a pretty blonde girl with a strong Yorkshire accent. 'Helicopter?' she said. 'Aye, I know Helicopter—he's new.'

'Would you recognise his "fist"?'

She looked dubious. 'He's only broadcast three times. On Wednesday he was a bit nervous, probably because it was his first, but his pace was steady, as if he knew he had plenty of time.'

'What about his second broadcast?'

'That was Thursday, and he was rushed. When they're in a hurry, it can be difficult to be sure what they mean—you know, was that two dots run together, or a short dash? Wherever he was sending from, he wanted to get out of there fast.'

'And then?'

'He came on the air on Saturday morning, just before dawn. It was an emergency message, but he didn't sound panicky, in fact I remember thinking to myself, "He's getting the hang of this."'

'Could it have been someone else using his transmitter that time?'

She looked thoughtful. 'I suppose. And if it was a German, pretending to be him, they would sound nice and steady, wouldn't they, because they'd have nothing to fear?'

Jean had disappeared, and returned now with a sheaf of papers. 'I've brought the decrypts of the three signals received from Helicopter,' she said.

Her quiet efficiency pleased Paul. The first message read:

ARRIVED OK STOP CRYT RENDEVOUS UNSAFE STOP NABBED BY GESTAPO BUT GOT AWAY STOP IN FUTURE RENDEVOUS AT CAFE DE LA GARE OVER

'He can't spell for nuts,' Paul commented.

'It's not his spelling,' Jean said. 'They always make errors in the Morse. We order the decoders to leave them in the decrypt, in case there's some significance.'

Brian's second transmission was longer:

ACTIV AGENTS NUMBER FIVE AS FOLOWS STOP MONET WHO IS WOUNED STOP COMTESSE OK STOP CHEVAL HELPS OCASIONLY STOP BOURGEOISE STILL IM PLACE STOP PLUS MY RESCUER CODNAME CHARENTON STOP

There was more of the second message, mainly a detailed account of the incident at the cathedral. Paul went on to the third:

WHAT THE DEVIL HAPPENED QUERY SEND INSTRUCTIONS STOP REPLY IMEDIATELY OVER

'He's improving,' Paul said. 'Only one mistake.'

'I thought he was more relaxed,' Lucy said. 'Either that, or someone else sent the signal.' Suddenly, Paul thought he saw a way to find out. 'Lucy, do you ever make mistakes in transmission?'

'Hardly ever. There should never be any mistakes—the agents have enough problems to cope with.'

Paul turned to Jean. 'If I draft a message, would you encode it exactly as it is? It would be a kind of test.'

'Of course. When he calls in at eight, we'll just tell him to stand by to receive an emergency message immediately.'

Paul sat down, thought for a moment, then wrote on a pad:

GIVE YOUR ARMS HOW MAN AUTOMATS HOW MY STENS ALSO AMMO HOW MNY ROUNDS ECH PLUS GREDANES REPLY IMMEDIATELY

He considered it for a moment. It was an unreasonable request, phrased in a high-handed tone, and it appeared to be carelessly encoded and transmitted. He showed it to Jean. She frowned. 'That's a terrible message. I'd be ashamed of it.'

'What do you think an agent's reaction would be?'

'He would send an angry reply with a few swear words in it.'

'Please encode it exactly as it is and send it to Helicopter.'

She looked troubled. 'If that's what you wish.'

THE RED-LIGHT DISTRICT of Paris was a neighbourhood of narrow, dirty streets on a low hill behind the rue de la Chapelle, not far from the Gare du Nord. At its heart was the rue de la Charbonnière. On the north side of the street stood a convent where eight nuns dedicated their lives to helping the poor. Next door to the convent stood the Hôtel de la Chapelle. It was not exactly a brothel, but when the place was not full of guests, the proprietress was willing to rent rooms by the hour.

Flick walked through the door with a mighty sense of relief. The gendarmes had dropped her off 800 metres away. She had seen two copies of her 'Wanted' poster on the way. Christian had given her his handkerchief, a clean cotton square, red with white dots, and she had tied it over her head in an attempt to hide her blonde hair, but anyone who looked hard would recognise her from the poster.

The proprietress was a friendly, overweight woman wearing a pink silk bathrobe. Flick had stayed at the place before, but the proprietress did not appear to remember her. She took Flick's money and gave her a room key without asking any questions.

Flick was about to go upstairs to her room when Diana and Maude arrived. 'Good God, what a dump,' said Diana when she walked in. 'Perhaps we can eat out.'

'Don't even think about it,' Flick said crossly. 'We're going to lie low here, then go to the Gare de l'Est at first light.'

Maude looked accusingly at Diana. 'You promised to take me to the Ritz.'

Flick controlled her temper. 'What world are you living in?' she hissed at Maude. 'Nobody leaves! Is that understood? One of us will go out and buy food later. I have to get out of sight now. Diana, you wait here for the others while Maude checks into your room.'

Climbing the stairs, Flick passed a Negro girl in a tight red dress and noticed that she had a full head of straight black hair. 'Wait,' Flick said to her. 'Will you sell me your wig?'

'I can't work without it, honey.' She looked Flick up and down, taking her for an amateur hooker. 'Frankly, I'd say you need more than a wig.'

Flick handed her a 1,000-franc note. 'Buy yourself another.'

The girl looked at Flick with new eyes, realising she had too much money to be a prostitute. With a shrug, she accepted the money and handed the wig over. 'Well, I guess this is my night off.'

Flick found her room. There was a mirror over a basin. She combed her short blonde hair back and pinned it with hair clips. She put the wig on. The black hair altered her appearance radically. However, her fair eyebrows now looked peculiar. She took the eyebrow pencil from her make-up kit and darkened them. Much better.

Next she took her identity papers from her jacket pocket and with great care retouched the photograph, using the eyebrow pencil to draw faint lines of dark hair and narrow dark eyebrows.

She lay on the bed, closed her eyes and dropped off to sleep within seconds.

She was woken by a knock at the door. It was getting dark; she had slept for several hours. 'Who is it?'

'Ruby.'

She let her in. 'Is everything all right?'

'I'm not sure. Everyone has checked in. But Diana and Maude are not in their room and I can't find them anywhere.'

'The bloody fools,' Flick said in dismay. 'They've gone out.'

'Where would they have gone?'

'Maude wanted to go to the Ritz.'

Ruby was incredulous. 'They can't be that stupid!'

'Diana's in love,' Flick said. 'She'll do anything Maude asks. Come on. We've got to get them out of there—if we're not too late.'

Flick put her wig on. Ruby said, 'I wondered why your eyebrows had gone dark. It's effective, you look like someone else.'

'Good. Get your gun.'

In the lobby, the proprietress handed Flick a note. It was addressed in Diana's handwriting. Flick read: *We're going to a better hotel. We'll meet you at the Gare de l'Est at 5am. Don't worry!*

She showed it to Ruby, then ripped it to shreds.

DIETER WAS EXHAUSTED. He had not slept the previous night. His nerves were jangled, he had a headache and his temper was short.

But a feeling of peace descended on him as soon as he entered the grand apartment overlooking the Bois de Boulogne. Getting this place had taken a lot of bribery and bullying. It had been worth it. He loved the dark mahogany panelling, the heavy curtains, the high ceilings, the eighteenth-century silver on the sideboard.

He washed his face and neck. Then he put on a clean white shirt, inserted gold links in the French cuffs, and chose a silver-grey tie.

He now had to wait for someone to spot Felicity Clairet. He looked at the phone on his desk, contemplating trying to call his home in Cologne. It was difficult to get through: the French phone system was overloaded, and military traffic had priority. All the same, he felt a sudden longing to hear the voices of his children.

The phone rang before he touched it. He picked it up. 'Major Franck here.'

'This is Lieutenant Hesse.'

Dieter's pulse quickened. 'You have found Felicity Clairet?'

'No. But something almost as good.'

THE LOBBY OF THE RITZ Hotel on the Place Vendôme was bright with light, and the bars on either side were full of men in evening dress or uniform. The buzz of conversation clicked and whirred with German consonants.

While Ruby held back, Flick went up to the desk. A concierge looked down his nose at her. Judging her to be neither a German nor a wealthy French woman, he said coldly, 'What is it?'

'Check whether Mademoiselle Legrand is in her room,' Flick said peremptorily. She assumed that Diana must be using the false name on her papers. 'I am Madame Martigny, her employee.'

'Very good. In fact, Mademoiselle is in the rear dining room.'

Flick and Ruby crossed the lobby and entered the restaurant. It was a picture of elegant living: white tablecloths, silver cutlery, candles, and waiters in black gliding round the room with dishes of food.

Pausing on the threshold, Flick saw Diana and Maude at a small table on the far side of the room, drinking wine.

She started to walk to the table, but the head waiter stood in her way. Pointedly looking at her creased coat, he said, 'Yes, madame?'

'Good evening,' she said. 'I must speak with that lady over there.'

'I will tell her that you are here. The name?'

'I am Madame Martigny,' Flick said. 'Tell her I must speak to her immediately.'

'Very well. If madame would care to wait here.'

The head waiter spoke to Diana, then beckoned Flick.

Flick said to Ruby, 'You'd better wait here—one is less conspicuous than two.' Then she started across to Diana's table.

There was a commotion behind her. Flick turned round and gasped. Standing in the entrance was the well-dressed German officer she had last seen in the square at Sainte-Cécile. She quickly turned away, heart pounding, and prayed that he had not noticed her.

His name came back to her from Percy Thwaite's files: Dieter Franck, a star of Rommel's intelligence staff. Flick did not believe in coincidence. There was a reason he was here at the same time as she.

She soon found out what it was. He strode straight to Diana's table, with four Gestapo types trailing him.

The whole place suddenly became quiet. Flick walked back to

where Ruby stood. Ruby whispered, 'He's going to arrest them.'

'There's nothing we can do. We might take on him and four Gestapo men, but we're surrounded by German officers.'

Franck was questioning Diana and Maude. He must have asked for their papers, because the two women simultaneously reached for their handbags, on the floor beside their chairs. Franck shifted his position so that he was to one side of Diana and slightly behind her. Suddenly Flick knew what was going to happen next.

Maude took out her identity papers, but Diana pulled a gun. A shot rang out, and one of the uniformed Gestapo men doubled over. The restaurant erupted. Women screamed, men dived for cover. There was a second shot, and another Gestapo man cried out.

Diana's gun hand moved towards a third Gestapo man. But she did not fire. Dieter Franck had kept a cool head. He seized Diana's right forearm and banged her wrist on the edge of the table. She screamed with pain and the gun fell from her grasp.

Flick said to Ruby, 'Let's get out of here.'

There was a crush at the doorway, panicky men and women all trying to flee. They forced their way through the crowd, shoving ruthlessly, then burst out into the lobby and ran with everyone else.

Cars were parked in a line along the kerb. Chauffeurs were hurrying towards the hotel to see what was happening. Flick picked a black Mercedes 230 sedan. The key was in it. 'Get in!' she yelled at Ruby. She got behind the wheel, pulled the self-starter and accelerated away from the Ritz.

Flick dumped the car in the rue de la Chapelle. She and Ruby walked quickly to the dosshouse. Ruby rounded up Greta and Jelly and Flick told them what had happened.

'Diana and Maude will be questioned straightaway,' she said, 'then sent to the camps. So we have to assume they will tell everything they know—including this address. We have to leave now. We'll hide in the convent next door. I've hidden there before. Fortunately, I have a spare set of papers for all of us, using the same photographs but different identities. We'll go to the station about ten o'clock when it should be busy.'

Ruby said, 'Diana will also tell them what our mission is.'

'She'll tell them we're going to blow up the railway tunnel at Marle. Fortunately, that's not our real mission. It's a cover story.'

Jelly said admiringly, 'Flick, you think of everything.'

'Yes,' she said grimly. 'That's why I'm still alive.'

PAUL SAT at Grendon Underwood, brooding anxiously about Flick. He was beginning to believe that Brian Standish had been compromised. The incident in the cathedral, and the unnatural correctness of the third radio message, pointed in that direction.

At last, Jean Bevins handed him Helicopter's reply. She looked annoyed. 'I can't understand this,' she said. Paul read it quickly.

TWO STENS WITH SIX MAGAZINES FOR EACH STOP ONE LEE ENFELD RIFLE WITH TEN CLIPS STOP SIX COLT AUTOMATICS WITH ABOUT ONE HUNDRED ROUNDS STOP NO GRENADES OVER

'I expected him to be furious,' Jean said. 'He doesn't complain at all, just answers your questions, as nice as pie.'

'Exactly,' said Paul. 'That's because it's not him.' This message did not come from a harassed agent in the field who had been presented with a sudden unreasonable request by his bureaucratic superiors. The reply had been drafted by a Gestapo officer desperate to maintain the appearance of normality. The only spelling mistake was 'Enfeld'' instead of 'Enfield,' and even that suggested a German, for *feld* was German for 'field'.

There was no longer any doubt. Flick was in terrible danger.

He dialled Percy's office. 'This is Paul. I'm convinced Brian has been captured. His radio is being operated by the Gestapo.'

'Oh, hell,' Percy said. 'And without the radio, we have no way to warn Flick.'

'Yes, we do,' said Paul. 'Get me a plane. I'm going to Reims.'

The Eighth Day:
Sunday, June 4, 1944

The Avenue Foch seemed to have been built for the richest people in the world. The wide road, running from the Arc de Triomphe to the Bois de Boulogne, had ornamental gardens on both sides flanked by palatial houses. Number 84 was a residence with five storeys of charming rooms. The Gestapo had turned it into a house of torture.

Dieter sat in a perfectly proportioned drawing room, preparing himself for the interrogation. He had to sharpen his wits and at the same time numb his feelings. He closed his eyes.

Some men enjoyed torturing prisoners. Dieter loathed it.

Now he imagined himself closing doors in his soul, shutting his emotions away. He thought of the two women as pieces of machinery that would disgorge information as soon as he figured out how to switch them on. He felt a familiar coldness settle over him like a blanket of snow. He was ready. 'Bring the older one,' he said.

Lieutenant Hesse went to fetch her.

Dieter watched her carefully as she came in and sat in the chair. She had short hair and broad shoulders and wore a tailored man's suit. Her right hand hung limply, and she was supporting the swollen forearm with her left hand: Dieter had broken her wrist.

He spoke to her in French. 'To begin with, tell me where is the London headquarters of the Special Operations Executive.'

'Eighty-one Regent Street,' she said.

He nodded. 'Let me explain something. I will ask you many questions to which I already know the answers. This way I will know whether you are lying to me. Where is the London headquarters?'

'Carlton House Terrace.'

He slapped her face hard. She cried out in pain but looked defiantly at him. 'Is that how German officers treat ladies?'

She spoke French with the accent of the upper classes. 'Ladies?' he said scornfully. 'You have just shot and killed two policemen. No, this is not how we treat ladies, it's how we treat murderers.'

She looked away. He had scored a hit. He said, 'How well do you know Flick Clairet?'

Her eyes widened in an involuntary expression of surprise. But she recovered her composure and said, 'I don't know anyone of that name.'

He reached down and knocked her left hand away. She cried out in pain as her broken wrist lost its support and sagged. He took her right hand and jerked it. She screamed.

'Why were you having dinner at the Ritz?'

She caught her breath. 'I like the food there.'

She was even tougher than he had thought. 'Take her away. Bring the other one.'

The younger girl was quite pretty. She had put up no resistance when arrested, so she still looked presentable. She appeared much more frightened than her colleague. 'Why were you having dinner at the Ritz?'

'I've always wanted to go there,' she replied.

He could hardly believe his ears. 'Weren't you afraid it might be dangerous?'

'I thought Diana would look after me.'

So the other one's name was Diana. 'What's your name?'

'Maude.'

This was suspiciously easy. 'How long have you known Felicity Clairet?'

'Do you mean Flick? Only a few days. She's awfully bossy. She was right, though—we shouldn't have gone to the Ritz.' She began to cry. 'I never meant to do anything wrong. I just wanted to have a good time and see places.'

'What's your team's code name?'

'The Blackbirds,' she said in English. 'It's because of some poem, "The Blackbird of Reims", I think. No, "The Jackdaw of Reims", that's it.'

'Where do you think Flick is now?'

Maude thought for a long moment then said, 'I really don't know.'

Dieter sighed in frustration. One prisoner was too tough to talk, the other too stupid to know anything useful. This was going to take longer than he had hoped.

There might be a way of shortening the process. He was curious about the relationship between these two. Why had the dominant, mannish older woman risked her life to take the pretty, empty-headed girl to dinner at the Ritz?

'Take her away,' he said in German. 'Bring the older one again.'

When Diana was brought in the second time, he had her tied to the chair. Then he said, 'Prepare the electrical machinery.' He waited. Every minute was taking Flick Clairet further away from him.

When everything was ready, he seized Diana by the hair. Holding her head still, he attached two crocodile clips to her lower lip. He turned the power on for ten seconds. Diana screamed.

When her sobbing began to ease he said, 'That was less than half power.' It was true. 'Are you willing to answer my questions?'

She groaned, but she did not say yes.

Dieter said, 'Bring the other one.'

Lieutenant Hesse brought Maude in and tied her to a chair. She was wearing a light summer blouse. Dieter tore it open. He took the crocodile clips from Diana's mouth and approached Maude.

'All right,' Diana said quietly. 'I'll tell you everything.'

DIETER ARRANGED for the railway tunnel at Marle to be heavily guarded. If the Jackdaws got that far, they would find it almost impossible to enter the tunnel. He felt confident that Flick would not now achieve her objective. But that was secondary. His burning ambition was to capture and interrogate her. In a few hours he could break the back of the French Resistance—if he could get Flick. He needed only the list of names and addresses that she had in her head. Instead of the massive uprising that the Allies were no doubt hoping for to aid their invasion, there would be calm and order, enabling the Germans to push the invaders back into the sea.

He had sent a Gestapo team to raid the Hôtel de la Chapelle, but that was a matter of form. He was certain Flick and the other three would be gone. Where was Flick now? Reims was the natural jumping-off point for an attack on the tunnel at Marle. Dieter thought it likely that Flick would still pass through that city. It was on the road and rail routes to Marle, and there was probably some kind of help she needed from the remnants of the Bollinger circuit.

He called Weber and explained the situation. For once Weber was not obstructive. He agreed to send two Gestapo men to keep an eye on Michel's town house, two more to watch Gilberte's building and two to the rue du Bois to guard Stéphanie.

Finally, Dieter called Stéphanie. 'The British terrorists are on their way to Reims. I'm sending two men to guard you.'

She was as calm as ever. 'Thank you.'

'It's important that you continue to go to the rendezvous. But remember, we changed the location. It's not the cathedral crypt any more, it's the Café de la Gare. If anyone shows up, just drive them back to the house. The Gestapo can take over from that point.'

'OK.'

'I'll get a few hours' sleep and leave here in the morning.'

'I love you,' she said.

The words *I love you, too,* came to his lips, but he hesitated, reluctant from old habit to say them, and then there was a click as Stéphanie hung up.

IN THE EARLY HOURS of Sunday morning, Paul Chancellor parachuted into a potato field near the village of Laroque, west of Reims, without the benefit—or the risk—of a reception committee. The landing gave him a tremendous jolt of pain in his wounded knee. He gritted his teeth and lay motionless on the ground. When the pain eased he struggled to his feet and got out of his parachute harness. He found the road, orientated himself by the stars, and started walking, but he was limping badly and progress was slow.

His identity, cobbled together by Percy Thwaite, was that of a schoolteacher from Epernay, a few kilometres west. He was hitch-hiking to Reims to visit his father, who was ill. Percy had got him all the necessary papers, some of them hastily forged last night. Getting here was the simple part. Now he had to find Flick. His only hope was that part of the Bollinger circuit was left intact. Once in Reims, he would have to contact Mademoiselle Lemas.

He thumbed a lift from a lad on a tractor, who dropped him off on the outskirts, and he limped on into town. The rendezvous had changed, but the time was the same, three o'clock. He had hours to kill. He went into the Café de la Gare to get breakfast and reconnoitre, then spent the morning dozing through services in the cathedral.

He went back into the café at one thirty for lunch. The place emptied out at around two thirty, and he stayed drinking ersatz coffee.

At exactly three o'clock a tall, attractive woman came in, dressed with unobtrusive elegance in a green frock and a straw hat. She wore odd shoes: one black, one brown. This must be Bourgeoise.

Paul had expected an older woman although Flick had never actually described her. All the same, he was not yet ready to trust her. He got up and left the café.

He walked to the railway station and stood in the entrance, watching the café. Paul began to believe that this was not a Gestapo trap. There was no one in sight who looked remotely dangerous.

At three thirty, Bourgeoise left the café. She walked along the pavement away from the station. Paul followed. She got into a small black car, a Simca Cinq, and started the engine. It was time for Paul to decide. At some point, risks had to be taken.

He went up to the car on the passenger side and opened the door. 'Pray for me,' he said.

She looked coolly at him. 'I pray for peace.'

Paul got into the car. Giving himself a code name, he said, 'I am Danton.'

She pulled away. 'Why didn't you speak to me in the café?'

'I wanted to be sure this wasn't a trap.'

She glanced at him. 'You heard what happened to Helicopter?'

'Yes. Where's your friend who rescued him, Charenton?'

She headed south, driving fast. 'He's working today.'

'On Sunday? What does he do?'

'Fireman. He's on duty.'

That explained that. 'Where's Helicopter?'

She shook her head. 'No idea.'

'Have you heard from Leopardess?'

'No.'

Paul brooded as the car threaded through the suburbs. Eventually she pulled into a courtyard alongside a tall house.

'Come inside and get cleaned up,' she said.

He got out of the car. Everything seemed to be in order. On the other hand, Bourgeoise had given him no useful information. As she led him to the front door and opened it, he touched the wooden toothbrush in his shirt pocket: it was French-made, so he had been permitted to bring it with him. Now an impulse seized him. As Bourgeoise stepped into the house, he slipped the toothbrush from his pocket and dropped it on the ground just in front of the door.

He followed her inside. She opened a door and stood aside for him to go first. 'Come into the kitchen.'

He stepped inside and saw two men in uniform. Both held automatic pistols. And both guns were pointed at Paul.

DIETER'S CAR SUFFERED a puncture on the road from Paris. A bent nail was stuck in the tyre. The delay irritated him, and he paced the roadside restlessly as Lieutenant Hesse jacked the car up and changed the wheel. He wanted be in Reims. He had set a trap for Flick Clairet, and he needed to be there when she fell into it.

As the big Hispano-Suiza flew along an arrow-straight road he also worried about his mistress. He cursed himself for involving Stéphanie so closely in his mission and leaving her so exposed. Resistance fighters did not take prisoners. Being in constant peril themselves, they had no scruples about killing French people who collaborated with the enemy.

The thought that Stéphanie might be killed made his chest tighten. He could hardly contemplate life without her, and he realised he must be in love with her. He wished all the more that he was already in Reims at her side.

A second puncture occurred, another bent nail. Dieter wanted to scream with frustration. Did French people deliberately drop their old nails on the road, knowing that nine vehicles out of ten were driven by the occupying forces?

The car did not have a second spare, so the tyre had to be mended before they could drive on. They left the car and walked. After a couple of kilometres, they found a farmhouse. Dieter bullied the farmer into hitching up his horse and cart and driving them into the next town, where a surly mechanic was persuaded to fire up an ancient truck and drive off with Hans beside him.

Dieter sat in the living room of the mechanic's house while the mechanic's wife bustled about in the kitchen.

He thought of Stéphanie again. There was a phone in the hallway. He looked into the kitchen. 'May I make a call?' he asked politely. 'I will pay you, of course.'

She gave him a hostile glare, but nodded.

Stéphanie answered immediately, imitating Mademoiselle Lemas. His heart gladdened with relief. 'Is everything all right?'

'My darling,' she said. 'I've captured another agent for you.'

'My God . . . well done! How did it happen?'

'I picked him up in the Café de la Gare and brought him here. I was about to call Sainte-Cécile and have him picked up.'

'Don't do that. Lock him in the cellar. I want to talk to him. I should be with you in an hour or two. How do you feel?'

'How do I *feel*?' She paused. 'That's a question you don't usually ask.'

Dieter hesitated. 'I don't usually involve you in capturing terrorists. I don't want to lose you.'

Her voice softened. 'I feel fine. Don't worry about me.'

There was an odd sound at the other end. He realised she was crying. He felt choked up himself. 'I'll be with you soon,' he said.

'I love you,' she said.

He glanced at the mechanic's wife. She was staring at him. To hell with her, he thought. 'I love you, too,' he said, then hung up.

IT TOOK THE JACKDAWS most of the day to get from Paris to Reims. They passed through all the checkpoints without incident. Their new fake identities worked as well as the old, and no one noticed that Flick's photo had been retouched with eyebrow pencil.

But their train was delayed repeatedly, stopping for an hour at a time in the middle of nowhere. Flick sat in the hot carriage fuming with impatience as the precious minutes leaked away uselessly.

They arrived in Reims a few minutes after four on Sunday afternoon. That meant it was too late to carry out their mission the same evening. It also meant finding a place to spend the night.

Flick knew of three possible hide-outs: Michel's town house, Gilberte's apartment, and Mademoiselle Lemas's house in the rue du Bois. Any of them might be under surveillance, depending on how deeply the Gestapo had penetrated the Bollinger circuit.

There was nothing for it but to go and look. 'We must split up into pairs again,' she told the others. 'Four women together is too conspicuous. Ruby and I will go first. Greta and Jelly, follow a hundred metres behind us.'

They walked to Michel's place, not far from the station. It was Flick's marital home, but she always thought of it as his house. It was in a busy street with several shops. Outside the baker's shop was a black Citroën Traction Avant with two men sitting in the front.

Flick tensed. She was wearing her dark wig, so she felt sure they would not recognise her as the girl on the 'Wanted' poster. All the same her pulse beat faster and she hurried past them. Her fears had been justified. Michel's house was no use to her.

She considered the other two possibilities. Gilberte's apartment building was a tiny place, and four overnight guests might be noticed, so the obvious place for them was the house in the rue du Bois. Flick had been there twice. It was big, with lots of bedrooms, and a mile or so from the centre of town. The four women set out to walk there, still in pairs a hundred metres apart.

They arrived half an hour later. The rue du Bois was a quiet suburban street. Flick and Ruby took a preliminary walk past Mademoiselle Lemas's house. It looked the same as always. Her Simca Cinq stood in the courtyard. Flick slowed her pace and surreptitiously looked in at the parlour window. She saw no one.

As she passed the door, her eye was caught by something on the ground. It was a wooden toothbrush. Without pausing in her stride, she stooped and picked it up.

'This looks like Paul's,' she told Ruby.

'Why would he have come to France?'

'I don't know. To warn us of danger, perhaps.'

They walked on round the block. Before approaching the house again, Flick let Greta and Jelly catch up. 'You knock on the front door,' Flick told them. 'Ruby and I will go round to the back, as a precaution. Don't say anything about us; just wait for us to appear.'

Flick and Ruby went into the courtyard and past the Simca Cinq and crept round to the back. The kitchen ran almost the whole width of the house at the rear. Flick waited until she heard the doorbell, then risked a peep through a window. Her heart stopped.

There were three people in the kitchen: two men in Gestapo uniform, and a tall woman with luxuriant red hair who was definitely not the middle-aged Mademoiselle Lemas. In a fraction of a second, Flick noted that all three were looking away from the windows, reflexively turning in the direction of the front door. She thought fast. The woman must be posing as Mademoiselle Lemas. The safe house had been betrayed and the place was now a trap for Allied agents. Flick drew her pistol. Ruby did the same.

'Three people,' she told Ruby in a low voice. 'Two men and a woman.' She took a deep breath. 'We're going to kill the men.'

Ruby nodded.

'I'd prefer to keep the woman alive for questioning, but we'll shoot her if she seems likely to escape. The men are at the left-hand end of the kitchen. The woman will probably go to the door. You take this window, I'll take the far one. Aim at the man nearest to you. Shoot when I shoot.'

Flick crept across the width of the house and crouched under the other window. Her heart was beating like a steam hammer. She straightened up and looked in through the window.

The two men were standing facing the door to the hall. Both had pistols drawn. Flick levelled her gun at the one nearest her.

The woman had gone, but as Flick looked she returned, holding the kitchen door open. Greta and Jelly walked in ahead of her, all unsuspecting; then they saw the Gestapo men. Greta gave a small scream of fear.

The fake Mademoiselle Lemas walked into the kitchen behind them. Seeing her full-face, Flick felt the shock of recognition. She had seen her before. The woman had been in the square at Sainte-Cécile last Sunday with Dieter Franck.

A moment later the woman saw Flick's face at the window. Her eyes widened, and she lifted her hand to point at what she'd seen. The two men began to turn.

Flick pulled the trigger. The bang of the gun seemed simultaneous with the crash of breaking glass. Holding the gun level and steady, she fired twice more. A second later, Ruby fired. Both men fell to the ground and lay still.

Flick threw the back door open and stepped inside.

The young woman had already turned away. She was making a

dash for the front door. Jelly threw herself after her and brought her down on the tiled floor of the hall.

The woman was wearing odd shoes, one black and one brown.

Flick said, 'Jelly, keep the woman covered. Greta, find some string and tie her to a chair. Ruby, go upstairs and make sure there's no one else in the house. I'll check the basement.'

She ran down the stairs to the cellar. There on the dirt floor she saw Paul, tied up and gagged. She pulled the gag from his mouth, and gave him a long, passionate kiss. 'Welcome to France.'

He grinned. 'Best welcome I ever had.'

'I've got your toothbrush.'

'It was a last-second thing. I wasn't sure of the redhead.'

She took the sharp little knife from its sheath under her lapel and began to cut the cords that bound him. 'Why are you here?'

'I parachuted in last night. Brian's radio is being operated by the Gestapo. I wanted to warn you.'

She threw her arms round him in a burst of affection. 'I'm so glad you're here!'

They went upstairs. 'Look who I found in the cellar,' Flick said.

They were all waiting for instructions. She thought for a moment. They had to be out of here as soon as possible. She turned her attention to the fake Mademoiselle Lemas, now tied to a kitchen chair. She knew what had to be done, and her heart sank at the prospect. 'What is your name?'

'Stéphanie Vinson.'

'You're the mistress of Dieter Franck.'

She was as pale as a sheet but looked defiant. 'He saved my life.'

So that was how Franck had won her loyalty. It made no difference: a traitor was a traitor. 'You brought Helicopter to this house to be captured. Is he alive or dead?'

'I don't know.'

Flick pointed to Paul. 'You brought him here, too.'

Stéphanie lowered her gaze.

Flick walked behind the chair and drew her gun. The others, seeing what was coming, stood aside, out of the line of fire.

Stéphanie sensed what was happening. She whispered, 'What are you going to do with me?'

'If we leave you here now, you will tell Dieter Franck about us, and help him to capture us.' Flick pointed the gun at the back of Stéphanie's head. 'Do you have any excuse for helping the enemy?'

'I did what I had to. Doesn't everyone?'

'Exactly,' Flick said, and she pulled the trigger twice.

They were all silent for a moment. Then Flick said. 'Let's get out of here.'

IT WAS SIX O'CLOCK in the evening when Dieter parked outside the house in the rue du Bois. He noticed that Mademoiselle Lemas's Simca Cinq was gone. Was Stéphanie using the car? She should be waiting here for him.

He strode up to the door and pulled the bell rope. The ring of the bell died away, leaving the house strangely silent. He rang again. There was no response.

He walked round to the rear. Two windows were broken and the back door stood open. Fear grew in his heart. He stepped inside.

At first he did not understand what he was looking at. Then he let out a howl of anguish and sank slowly to his knees, sobbing.

She was gone. She would not throw him that proud glance again. Her style and her wit, her fears and her desires, were all wiped out, ended. He felt as if *he* had been shot, had lost part of himself.

Then he heard a voice behind him: a wordless grunt. He leapt to his feet, turned round and for the first time noticed two men on the floor, Stéphanie's Gestapo bodyguards. One lay still, but the other was trying to speak. He was young, nineteen or twenty.

Dieter knelt and put his ear to the man's mouth.

'Who was it?' he said.

'Four women,' the man said hoarsely. 'Two at the front . . . two at the back.'

'The Jackdaws,' Dieter said bitterly. 'Who killed Stéphanie?'

'The small one,' said the Gestapo man.

'Flick,' said Dieter, and his heart raged for revenge.

The man whispered: 'I'm sorry, Major . . .' Then his lips were still and his breathing stopped.

IT WAS A STRUGGLE to fit five people into the Simca Cinq. Ruby and Jelly sat on the back seat. Paul drove. Greta took the front passenger seat, and Flick sat on Greta's lap.

Ordinarily they would have giggled about it, but they were in sombre mood. They had nothing on their minds but survival.

Flick guided Paul to Gilberte's street. Flick remembered coming here with her wounded husband exactly seven days ago. Parked in the street was a black Citroën Traction Avant with two men sitting in the front. This was bad news, Flick thought despairingly. Someone had talked, and Dieter Franck had painstakingly followed the trail first to Mademoiselle Lemas, then to Brian, and finally to Gilberte. And Michel? Was he in custody? It seemed all too probable.

'No good,' she said. 'The Gestapo are watching.'

'Hell,' Paul said. 'Where do we go now?'

'I know of one more place to try,' said Flick. 'First drive to the station. We'll dump the car there.'

'Good idea,' Paul said. 'Maybe they'll think we've left town.'

They reached the railway station without incident. Paul parked and they all got out and hurried away from the vehicle.

'I'll have to do this alone,' Flick said. 'The rest of you had better go to the cathedral and wait for me there.'

She returned to the street where Michel lived. A hundred metres from his house was the bar Chez Régis. Flick went in. The proprietor, Alexandre Régis, gave her a nod of recognition but said nothing.

She went through the door marked 'Toilettes.' She walked along a short passage, then opened what looked like a cupboard door. It led to a steep staircase going up. At the top was a heavy door with a peephole. Flick banged on it and stood where her face could be seen. A moment later the door was opened by Mémé Régis, the mother of the proprietor.

Flick entered a large room with blacked-out windows. At one end was a roulette wheel. Around a large circular table a group of men were playing cards. There was a bar in one corner. This was an illegal gambling club.

Michel liked to play poker for high stakes, and he occasionally came here for an evening. Flick never played, but she sometimes sat and watched. It was a good place to hide from the Gestapo, and Flick had been hoping she might find him here.

She went to the bar and sat on a stool. The barmaid, a middle-aged woman with bright-red lipstick, was Yvette Régis, the wife of Alexandre. 'I'm looking for Michel,' Flick said.

'I haven't seen him for a week or so,' Yvette said.

Flick ordered a Scotch. 'I'll wait a while, in case he shows up.'

DIETER WAS DESPERATE. Flick had evaded his trap. She was somewhere in the city of Reims, but he had no way of finding her. He had Michel's house and Gilberte's flat under surveillance, but he felt sure that Flick was too wily to let herself be seen by the average Gestapo flatfoot. There were posters of her all over town, but she must have changed her appearance by now for no one had reported seeing her. She had outwitted him at every step.

He needed a stroke of genius. And he had come up with one.

He sat on a bicycle at the roadside in the centre of town. He wore a beret, goggles, and a rough cotton sweater, and his trousers were tucked into his socks. No one would suspect him.

He stared west along the street, looking for a black Citroën. He checked his watch: any minute now.

On the other side of the road, Hans was at the wheel of a wheezy old Peugeot, disguised in sunglasses and a cap, and wearing a shabby suit and down-at-heel shoes.

Dieter had no idea whether his scheme would work, but he was desperate. Monday was the night of the full moon. He felt sure the Allies were about to invade. Flick was worth a great deal of risk.

But winning the war was no longer what most occupied his mind. Flick Clairet had ruined his life; she had murdered Stéphanie. He wanted to capture her and take her to the basement of the château. There he would taste the satisfaction of revenge.

In the distance he saw a black Citroën, the two-door model used for transporting prisoners. He saw four people inside, and he recognised the handsome face of Michel in the back, guarded by a uniformed Gestapo man.

As the Citroën came level with Dieter, Hans suddenly pulled away from the kerb in the old Peugeot. The car smashed straight into the front of the Citroën. There were sounds of crumpling metal and breaking glass. The two Gestapo men leaped out of the front of the Citroën and began yelling at Hans in bad French—seeming not to notice that their colleague in the back appeared to have banged his head and was slumped, unconscious, beside his prisoner. This was the critical moment, Dieter thought. Would Michel take the bait?

Michel seemed to come to. He reached over the front seats, fumbled at the door, pushed down the front seat, and scrambled out. He glanced at the two Gestapo men still arguing with Hans. They had their backs to him. He turned and walked quickly away.

Dieter's heart leapt with triumph. His plan was working. He followed Michel. Hans followed Dieter on foot.

To Dieter's surprise, Michel headed for his house near the cathedral. Surely he must suspect that his home was under surveillance?

However, he did not go to his own place but entered a bar across the street called Chez Régis.

Dieter leaned his bicycle against the wall of the next building, a vacant store with a faded 'Charcuterie' sign. He waited a few minutes. When it was clear Michel was staying a while, Dieter went in, relying on his goggles and beret to conceal his identity.

Michel was nowhere in sight. Puzzled, Dieter hesitated.

The barman said, 'Yes, sir?'

'Beer,' said Dieter. 'Draft.' He hoped that if he kept his conversation to a minimum the barman would not notice his slight German accent.

'Coming up.'

'Where's the toilet?'

The barman directed Dieter to a door in the corner. Michel was not in the men's room or the ladies'. He opened what looked like a cupboard door. It led to a staircase. At the top was a heavy door with a peephole. He knocked, but there was no answer. He felt sure there was someone looking at him through the peephole. He scratched his head, shrugged, and went back down the stairs.

He took his glass to a table. The beer was tasteless, but he forced himself to finish it, then went out.

'He's in a private room upstairs,' Dieter told Hans. 'I don't want to burst in on him before he's led us to someone worthwhile.'

Hans nodded, understanding the dilemma.

'When he comes out, I'll follow him. Then you raid the place.' Dieter pointed to two Gestapo men in a Citroën keeping watch on Michel's house. 'Get them to help you.'

UNTIL THE MOMENT Michel walked in, Flick was feeling pessimistic.

She sat at the bar in the makeshift casino, making desultory conversation with Yvette. If she did not find Michel, she was in trouble. The other Jackdaws were in the cathedral, but they could not stay there all night. They also needed transport. If they could not get a car or van from the Bollinger circuit, they would have to steal one.

There was another reason for her gloom: the image of Stéphanie Vinson kept coming back to her. It was the first time Flick had killed a bound, helpless captive, and the first time she had shot a woman.

She drained her whisky. Then Michel came through the door. Relief flooded her. Michel would be able to help her. Suddenly the mission seemed possible again.

She felt a wry affection as she took in the lanky figure in a rumpled jacket. As he came closer, she saw that he was not looking so good. His face seemed to have new lines. Exhaustion and fear showed in his expression, and he might have been fifty rather than thirty-five, she thought anxiously.

He was visibly delighted to see her. 'Flick!' he cried. 'I knew you would get here!'

'I was afraid the Gestapo had captured you.'

'They did!' He turned so that no one could see, and showed her his hands, bound at the wrists with stout rope.

She drew the little knife from its sheath under her lapel and discreetly cut through his bonds as he told how he had escaped.

'I was so lucky!' he finished.

Flick nodded. 'Too lucky, perhaps. It could be a trick. Could you have been followed here?'

He was indignant, no doubt resenting the implication that he was gullible. 'No,' he said firmly. 'I checked, of course.'

She was uneasy, but she let it go. 'So Brian Standish is dead, and three others are in custody—Mademoiselle Lemas, Gilberte and Dr Bouler.'

'The rest are dead. The Germans released the bodies of those killed in the skirmish. The survivors were shot by a firing squad.'

'Dear God.'

Michel asked for a beer. He drank half in a single draught and wiped his lips. 'I presume you've come back for another attempt on the château.'

She nodded. 'We need somewhere to stay the night.'

He thought for a moment. 'Joseph Laperrière's cellar.'

Laperrière was a champagne maker. 'Is he one of us?'

'A sympathiser.' He gave a sour grin. 'Everyone is a sympathiser now.'

'Fine. The other thing I need is a vehicle for tomorrow.'

'To drive to Sainte-Cécile?'

'And afterwards, to meet our pick-up plane, if we're still alive.'

'You realise that you can't use the drop zone at Chatelle, don't you? The Gestapo know about it—it's where I was picked up.'

'Yes. The plane is coming to the field at Laroque. The vehicle?'

'Philippe Moulier has a van. He delivers meat to the Germans.'

'Good. Bring the van to the cellar at ten in the morning.'

He touched her cheek. 'Can't we spend the night together?'

She felt a familiar stirring inside, but it was like the memory of an old desire. She wanted to tell him the truth, for she hated to be less than honest. But she needed his cooperation. 'No,' she said.

He looked crestfallen. 'Is it because of Gilberte?'

She could not lie. She said, 'Well, partly.'

He looked vulnerable, almost scared. 'Have you got someone else?'

She could not bring herself to hurt him. 'No,' she lied.

He looked hard at her. 'Good,' he said at last. 'I'm glad.' He finished his beer and got off his stool. 'Laperrière's place is in the chemin de la Carrière. It will take you thirty minutes to walk there. I'd better go and see Moulier about the van.' He kissed her lips.

She felt dreadful. Kissing Michel seemed so disloyal to Paul. She closed her eyes and waited passively until he broke away.

He could not fail to notice her lack of enthusiasm. He looked thoughtfully at her for a moment. 'I'll see you at ten,' he said, then left.

She decided to wait five minutes before following him out. She asked Yvette for another Scotch. While she was sipping it, a red light began to flash over the door.

No one spoke, but everyone in the room moved at once. The croupier stopped the roulette wheel and turned it upside-down so that it looked like a normal table top. The card players swept up their stakes and put their jackets on. 'Police raid,' Yvette said. 'Alexandre downstairs has given us the warning. Get going, quickly!' She pointed across the room to where Mémé Régis was stepping into what looked like a cupboard. As she watched, Mémé shoved aside a couple of old coats and the gamblers began to leave by the hidden door.

The red light went out, and a banging began on the main door. Flick joined the men pushing through the cupboard. She followed the crowd down some stairs and found herself in a disused delicatessen. The blind in the front window was down. They all went through the back door, which led to an alley. When they reached the street at the end of the alley, the men went in different directions.

Flick soon found herself alone. Breathing hard, she reorientated herself and headed for the cathedral, where the other Jackdaws were waiting. 'My God,' she whispered to herself, 'that was close.'

As she got her breath back, she began to see the raid on the gambling club in a different light. It had happened just minutes after Michel had left. The more she thought about it, the more convinced she became that whoever was banging on the door had been looking for her.

The story of Michel's escape had aroused her suspicions from the start. His escape must have been faked, like the 'rescue' of Brian Standish. She saw the sly brain of Dieter Franck behind this. Someone had followed Michel to the café.

In that case, Michel was still under surveillance. He would be trailed to Philippe Moulier's house tonight, and in the morning, driving the van, he would be followed to the champagne cellar where the Jackdaws were hiding.

And what the hell, Flick thought, am I going to do about that?

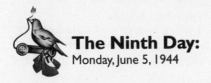

The Ninth Day:
Monday, June 5, 1944

Dieter woke before daylight in his room at the Hôtel Frankfort. As he began to shave, he ran over the events of the previous evening, asking himself if he had done everything possible.

Leaving Lieutenant Hesse outside Chez Régis, he had followed Michel Clairet to the premises of Philippe Moulier, a meat supplier. Dieter had watched the place for an hour, but no one had come out.

Deciding that Michel intended to spend the night there, Dieter had found a bar and phoned Hans Hesse. Hans had got on a motorcycle and joined him outside the Moulier place. The lieutenant told Dieter the story of the inexplicably empty room above Chez Régis. 'There's some early-warning system,' Dieter speculated. 'The barman downstairs sounds the alarm if anyone comes looking. Did you arrest the barman?'

'I arrested everyone in the place. They're at the château now.'

Dieter had left Hans watching the Moulier property and had driven to Sainte-Cécile. There he questioned the terrified proprietor, Alexandre Régis, and learned within minutes that Michel Clairet had met his wife there. It was another maddeningly near miss.

Now, he got dressed, begged half a dozen warm croissants from the hotel kitchen, and phoned the château to order a car with a driver and two Gestapo men to pick him up.

At the Moulier place he found Hans lurking in a warehouse doorway fifty metres along the street. No one had come or gone all night,

Hans said, so Michel must still be inside. Dieter stood with Hans, sharing the croissants and watching the sun rise over the city. Today, perhaps, he would be led into the very heart of the Resistance.

It was after nine o'clock when the front door opened.

'At last,' Dieter breathed.

Michel came out. In the yard, a black van was parked. White lettering on the side read MOULIER & FILS—VIANDES. Michel got in.

Dieter was electrified. 'Let's go!' he said.

Hans hurried to his motorcycle, and followed as Michel drove out of the yard and headed away. Dieter jumped into the waiting Gestapo car and ordered the driver to follow Hans.

They headed east. Eventually the van slowed and pulled into the yard of a champagne house called Laperrière. Hans drove past and turned the next corner. Dieter's driver followed. They pulled up and Dieter leapt out.

'I think the Jackdaws hid out there overnight,' Dieter said.

They walked to the corner and watched the Laperrière place. There was a tall, elegant house, a courtyard full of barrels, and a low industrial building. Dieter's pulse was racing. Any moment now, Michel would reappear with Flick and the other Jackdaws.

As they watched, Michel came out of the low building. He wore a frown and he stood indecisively in the yard, looking perplexed. Hans said, 'What's the matter with him?'

Dieter's heart sank. 'Something he didn't expect.' It seemed the Jackdaws were not here.

Dieter cursed as he watched Michel get into the van. He said to Hans, 'We'll do the same as last night, only this time *you* follow Michel and I'll raid the place.'

Dieter watched Michel drive away, followed by Hans on his motorcycle. He summoned the three Gestapo men with a wave and walked quickly to the Laperrière house. He pointed at two of the men. 'Check the house. Make sure no one leaves.' Nodding at the third man, he said, 'You and I will search the winery.'

He led the way into the low building. On the ground floor there was a large grape press and three enormous vats. Dieter found the stairs and ran down. In the cool underground chamber he searched room after room of racks of champagne. But there were no women.

In an alcove at the far end of the last tunnel, Dieter found crumbs of bread, cigarette ends and a hair clip. The Jackdaws had spent the night here. But they had escaped.

Dieter was furious. He went to the house, where he ordered everyone inside arrested. As he was leaving, the phone rang in the hall. Dieter picked it up.

'Lieutenant Hesse here, Major. I'm at the station. Michel parked the van and bought a ticket to Marle. The train is about to leave.'

It was as Dieter had thought: the Jackdaws had gone ahead and left instructions for Michel to join them. They were still planning to blow up the railway tunnel. 'Get on the train,' he said to Hans. 'Stay with him. I'll meet you at Marle.'

In the Café de la Gare near the railway station, Flick and Paul had a breakfast of ersatz coffee and black bread. Ruby, Jelly and Greta sat at a separate table, not acknowledging them. Flick kept an eye on the street outside.

She knew that Michel was in terrible danger. She had contemplated going to warn him, but that could have played into the hands of the Gestapo, who must be following him in the hope that he would lead them to her. Instead, she had left a message for him with Madame Laperrière. It read:

Michel, I am sure you are under surveillance. The place we were at last night was raided after you left. You have probably been followed this morning. We will leave before you get here and wait in the town centre. Park the van near the station and leave the key under the driver's seat. Get a train to Marle. Shake off your shadow and come back. Now burn this.

She waited all morning to see whether it would work. Then, at eleven o'clock, she saw a black van draw up and park. Michel got out and walked into the station. He was carrying out her plan.

She looked to see who might be following him, but it was impossible. People arrived at the station constantly. Any of them might have been shadowing Michel.

She remained in the café, keeping an eye on the van, but she did not spot anyone who might have been watching it. After fifteen minutes, she nodded. They picked up their cases and walked out.

Flick opened the van door and got into the driving seat. Paul got in the other side. Ruby, Jelly and Greta came out of the café and got in the back. Ruby pulled the doors shut.

'We did it!' Jelly said. 'Thank gordon.'

Flick smiled thinly. The hard part was still ahead.

She drove out of town on the road to Sainte-Cécile. She watched for Gestapo Citroëns, but she felt fairly safe for the moment.

Soon after midday they reached Sainte-Cécile. Flick drove to Antoinette's building. A pair of tall wooden doors, half-open, led to the inner courtyard. Paul leapt out of the van and opened the doors, Flick drove in and Paul closed the doors behind her. Now the van could not be seen from the street.

Flick went to Antoinette's door. The last time she had knocked on this door, eight days and a lifetime ago, Michel's aunt Antoinette had hesitated to answer, jumpy on account of the gunfire from the square, but today she came right away. She opened the door and looked blankly at Flick, who still had the dark wig on. Then recognition dawned. 'You!' she said. A look of panic came over her face. 'What do you want?'

Flick called the others, then pushed Antoinette back inside. 'Don't worry,' she said. 'I'll explain in a moment.'

The others came in and Ruby closed the apartment door. They went into Antoinette's kitchen. A meal was laid out on the table: black bread, a salad of shredded carrots, a heel of cheese. Antoinette said shakily, 'What is this?'

'It's very simple,' Flick said. 'You and your ladies are not going to clean the château tonight . . . we are.'

She looked baffled. 'How will that happen?'

'We're going to send notes to each of the women on duty tonight, telling them to come here and see you before they go to work. When they arrive, we will tie all of you up so the Germans will think we forced you. Then we will go to the château.'

'You can't, you don't have passes.'

'Yes, we do.'

'How . . . ?' Antoinette gasped. 'You stole my pass! Last Sunday. I thought I had lost it.'

'I'm sorry if you got into trouble.'

'But this will be worse—you're going to blow the place up!' Antoinette began to moan. 'They'll blame me. We'll all be tortured. We might be killed.'

Flick hardened her heart. 'That's why it's called a war,' she said.

MARLE IS A SMALL town to the east of Reims. The tunnel through the mountains, which begins just beyond the town, carried a constant stream of supplies to the German forces occupying France.

The destruction of the tunnel would starve Rommel of ammunition.

The town itself looks Bavarian, with half-timbered houses painted in bright colours. The local Gestapo chief had taken over the mayor's office opposite the railway station, and now stood poring over a map with Dieter Franck and a Captain Bern, who was in charge of the military guard on the tunnel.

'I have twenty men at each end of the tunnel and another group patrolling the mountain,' said Bern. 'So far we have seen nothing suspicious.'

Bern was short and slight and wore spectacles with thick lenses. He struck Dieter as an intelligent and efficient young officer.

Dieter said, 'How vulnerable is the tunnel to explosives?'

'It goes through solid rock. They would need a truckload of dynamite. And they need to get it here without our seeing it.'

Dieter turned to the Gestapo chief. 'Have you received any reports of strange vehicles, or a group of people arriving in the town?'

'None at all. My men have seen nothing unusual.'

Captain Bern said, 'Is it conceivable, Major, that the report you received, of an attack on the tunnel, was some kind of diversion to draw your attention away from the real target?'

That infuriating possibility had already begun to dawn on Dieter. Had Flick Clairet fooled him again? The thought was too humiliating to contemplate. 'You could be right. It's possible our informant had been misinformed, deliberately, as a precaution.'

Bern cocked his head and said, 'A train is coming.'

The Gestapo chief went to the window. 'This is a westbound train,' he said. 'Your man is eastbound, I think you said.'

Dieter nodded.

Bern said, 'In fact there are two trains approaching, one from either direction.'

The three men went out and walked to the station entrance.

The westbound train came in first. While its passengers were still unloading their bags and stepping onto the platform, the eastbound train chugged in. A Gestapo checkpoint stood next to the ticket barrier. The Gestapo chief waited there. Captain Bern leaned on a pillar to one side. Dieter returned to his car and sat in the back, watching the station.

What would he do if Captain Bern was right, and the tunnel was a diversion? He would have to consider alternatives. He could interrogate Michel right now, as soon as he got off the train, but would

Michel know the truth? Dieter would do better just to follow him until he met up with Flick. She knew the real target.

Dieter waited impatiently while papers were carefully checked and passengers trickled through. A whistle blew, and the westbound train pulled out. The eastbound train left. Then Hans Hesse emerged from the station. He looked round the square, saw the Citroën, and ran towards it.

Dieter jumped out of the car.

Hans said, 'What happened? Where is he?'

'What do you mean?' Dieter shouted. 'You're following him!'

'I did! He got off the train. I lost sight of him in the queue for the checkpoint.'

'Could he have got on the other train?'

Hans's mouth dropped open. 'I lost sight of him about the time we were passing the end of the Reims platform . . .'

'Hell!' said Dieter. 'He's on his way back to Reims. He's a decoy. This whole trip was a diversion.' He was furious that he had fallen for it. 'We'll catch up with the train and you can follow him again. Get in the car. Let's go!'

FLICK COULD HARDLY BELIEVE she had got this far. Four of the original six Jackdaws had evaded capture. They were now in Antoinette's kitchen, a few steps from the château, right under the noses of the Gestapo.

Antoinette and the other five cleaners were firmly tied to kitchen chairs. Paul had gagged all but Antoinette. Each cleaner had arrived carrying a little shopping basket or canvas bag containing food and drink for their 9.30 break. Now the Jackdaws were hastily emptying the bags and reloading them with the things they needed to carry into the château: electric torches, guns, ammunition and sticks of yellow plastic explosive.

Flick quickly realised that the cleaners' bags were not big enough. She herself had a Sten submachine gun with a silencer, disassembled into three parts each about a foot long. Jelly had sixteen detonators in a shockproof can, an incendiary thermite bomb and a chemical block that produced oxygen for setting fires in enclosed spaces. After loading their ordnance into the bags, they had to conceal it with packets of food. There was not enough room.

In Antoinette's pantry Flick found a large basket made of woven reeds, but she needed three more.

'Where did you get your basket?' she asked Antoinette.

'At the little shop across the street.'

Flick turned to Ruby. 'Go and buy three more baskets, quickly. If you can, get different shapes and colours.'

'Right.' Ruby went out.

Flick gave cleaners' passes to Jelly and Greta. With Ruby's pass in her hand, she went to the window.

Ruby was coming out of the store carrying three shopping baskets. Flick was relieved. It was two minutes to seven.

Then disaster struck. As Ruby was about to cross the road, she was accosted by a man in the uniform of the Milice, the security militia that did the dirty work of the regime. 'Oh, no!' Flick said.

Paul came and looked. 'Hell, it's a frigging Militian.'

Flick's mind raced. Was this a chance encounter, or part of an organised security sweep directed at the Jackdaws?

The cop started to question Ruby aggressively. Ruby took out her papers. The man examined them, then continued to question her.

Paul drew his pistol.

'Put it away,' Flick commanded. 'If we have a shoot-out now, we're finished.'

The conversation between Ruby and the Militian became heated. The man grabbed Ruby's left shoulder, obviously arresting her.

Ruby moved fast. She dropped the baskets. Her right hand came out of her coat pocket holding a knife. She swung it up from hip level with great force, sticking the blade through his uniform shirt just below the ribs. The man gave a scream that quickly died off.

Flick was thinking ahead. If she could get the body out of sight quickly, they might get away with this. Had anyone seen the stabbing? Flick leaned out of the window. To her left, the rue du Château was deserted. Looking the other way she saw, coming along the pavement, two men and a woman in Gestapo uniforms.

The Militian fell to the pavement. Before Flick could open her mouth to warn her, the two Gestapo men sprang forward and grabbed Ruby. One banged her right hand against the shop wall until she dropped the knife. The woman ran off, back in the direction of the château, presumably to get help. The two men frog-marched Ruby in the same direction.

Flick said, 'Paul—go and get the baskets Ruby dropped.'

Paul did not hesitate. He crossed the road, swiftly picked up the three baskets, and came back.

'Let's move quickly,' Flick said as Paul came into the kitchen. 'I want us to pass through that checkpoint while the guards are still excited about Ruby.' She stuffed one of the baskets with a powerful torch, her disassembled Sten gun, six 32-round magazines, and her share of the plastic explosive. Her pistol and knife were in her pockets. She covered the weapons in the basket with a cloth and put in a slice of vegetable terrine wrapped in baking paper.

The church bell in the town square struck seven.

Flick said to Paul, 'Someone is sure to notice there are only three cleaners instead of the usual six. If anyone shows up here to ask Antoinette what's gone wrong, you'll just have to shoot him.'

She kissed Paul, then went out, with Jelly and Greta following.

The three turned towards the square. Ahead, Flick could see Ruby and her two captors passing through the gates of the château. Well, Flick thought, at least Ruby is inside.

Two guards from the château came across the square at a run, carrying their rifles, no doubt heading for the wounded Militian. They took no notice of the little group of cleaning women.

Flick reached the gate. This was the first really dangerous moment.

One guard was left. He kept looking past Flick at his comrades running across the square. He glanced at Flick's pass and waved her in. Greta came next, and the guard did the same. Flick thought they were home free, but when he had checked Jelly's pass he glanced into her basket. 'Something smells good,' he said.

'Sausage for my supper,' Jelly said. 'You can smell the garlic.'

He waved her on and the three Jackdaws walked up the short drive, mounted the steps, and at last entered the château.

DIETER SPENT the afternoon shadowing Michel's train, stopping at every sleepy country halt in case Michel got off. But Michel rode the train all the way back to Reims.

A sense of impending failure overwhelmed Dieter as he sat in the car near Reims station waiting for Michel to emerge. What if following Michel led nowhere? At some point, Dieter would have to cut his losses and interrogate the man. But how much time did he have? Tonight was the night of the full moon. The English Channel was stormy, but the Allies might decide to take their chances.

Dieter considered how to interrogate Michel. The man's weak point was probably Gilberte. Right now she was in a cell at the château. She would stay there until Dieter was finished with her, then she would be executed or sent to a camp in Germany. The thought of the camps gave Dieter an idea. Leaning forward, he said to his driver, 'When the Gestapo send prisoners to Germany, you put them in railway cars used for transporting livestock?'

'Cattle trucks, yes, sir. They board right here in Reims.'

'And how often do those trains run?'

'There's one most days. It leaves Paris late in the afternoon and stops here around eight in the evening, if it's on time.'

Before he could progress his idea further, Dieter saw Michel emerge from the station. Behind him in the crowd was Hans Hesse. Michel turned into the alley alongside the Café de la Gare. Hans quickened his pace and turned the same corner a minute later.

Dieter frowned. Was Michel trying to shake off his tail?

Hans re-emerged from the alley and looked up and down the street with a worried frown.

Dieter groaned aloud. Hans had lost Michel again.

As Dieter stared despondently at the mouth of the alley, Michel emerged from the front entrance of the café. He crossed the road, breaking into a run, and headed back the way he had come—towards Dieter in the car.

Dieter thought fast. The surveillance was over. It was time to seize Michel. He opened the car door. As Michel drew level, running awkwardly because of his bullet wound, Dieter got out, narrowing the available pavement by holding the door wide. Michel swerved, Dieter stuck out his leg, Michel tripped and went flying. He fell heavily on the pavement.

Dieter drew his pistol and touched the barrel of the gun to Michel's temple. 'Don't get up,' he said in French.

The driver got a pair of handcuffs from the boot, secured Michel's wrists and bundled him into the back of the car.

Hans reappeared, looking dismayed. 'What happened?'

'He went in through the back door of the Café de la Gare and came out of the front.' Dieter turned to the driver. 'Keep a close watch on this man. If he tries to escape, shoot him in the legs.'

Dieter and Hans walked briskly into the station. Dieter quickly found the stationmaster.

'What can I do for you?' the man said with a nervous smile. He was frightened by this visit from a high-powered German.

'Are you expecting a train from Paris with prisoners tonight?'

'Yes, at eight o'clock, as usual.'

'When it comes, hold it here until you hear from me. I have a special prisoner I want to board.' Dieter turned to Hans. 'I want you to take Michel Clairet to the Reims police station, then return here and make sure my orders are carried out.'

'Of course, Major.'

Dieter called Weber at the château. 'There's a woman in the cells called Gilberte. Please send her to the railway station in Reims. Lieutenant Hesse is here, he will take charge of her.'

'Very well,' said Weber. 'By the way, I have some news for you. I have captured an Allied agent.'

'What?' Dieter said. This was a lucky break. 'When?'

'A few minutes ago. She attacked a Militian, and three of my bright young people happened to witness it. They captured the culprit. She was armed with a Colt automatic.'

'Did you say "she"? The agent is a woman?'

That settled it. The Jackdaws were in Sainte-Cécile. The château was their target.

Dieter said, 'Weber, listen to me. I think she is part of a team of saboteurs intending to attack the château.'

'They tried that before,' Weber said. 'We gave them a hiding.'

'Indeed you did, so they may be more sly this time. May I suggest a security alert? Double the guards, search the château, and question all non-German personnel in the building. I will return to Sainte-Cécile immediately. I need to interrogate the new prisoner.'

'I have already begun. Sergeant Becker is softening her up.'

'For God's sake! I want her sane and able to speak.'

'Very well, Franck. I will make sure he doesn't overdo it.'

FLICK PAUSED at the entrance to the great hall of the château. Her pulse was racing. She was in the lions' den.

She surveyed the palatial room rapidly. Telephone switchboards had been installed in precise parade-ground rows. There was a hubbub of chatter from forty operators. Those nearest glanced at the new arrivals. The operators were all from the surrounding area and would realise the Jackdaws were strangers. But Flick was gambling that they would say nothing to the Germans.

She orientated herself quickly, bringing to mind the plan Antoinette had drawn. She turned right and led Greta and Jelly through a pair of tall panelled doors into the east wing. One room led to another, each room full of equipment. In the third room, a supervisor in German uniform called out, 'Where is Antoinette?'

Flick answered without pausing in her stride. 'She's coming.'

The woman glanced up at the clock. 'You're late.'

'Very sorry, madame, we'll get started right away.' Flick hurried into the next room, with Greta and Jelly close behind.

At the end of the east wing the Jackdaws turned left and moved into the service wing. Following Antoinette's directions, they found a small room where cleaning materials were stored: mops, buckets, brooms and rubbish bins, plus the cleaners' brown cotton overall coats. Flick closed the door.

'So far, so good,' said Jelly.

Greta said, 'I'm so scared! I don't think I can go on.'

Flick gave her a reassuring smile. 'You'll be fine. Let's get on with it. Put your ordnance into these cleaning buckets.'

They did as she said. Flick assembled her submachine gun without its rifle butt, reducing the length by a foot to make it easier to conceal. She fitted the noise suppressor and flicked the switch for single-shot firing as required when using the silencer. She pushed the weapon under her leather belt, then put on an overall. It covered the gun. She left the buttons undone for quick access. The other two also put on overalls, concealing the guns and ammunition in their pockets.

They were headed for the basement. However, it was a high-security area and French personnel were not allowed in. Before entering, the Jackdaws were going to create a little confusion.

They were about to leave the small room when the door opened and a Gestapo lieutenant looked in. 'Passes!' he barked.

Flick tensed. The Gestapo must have guessed that Ruby was an Allied agent and it made sense for them to take extra precautions at the château. She took out her pass. He looked at it carefully, comparing the picture with her face, and handed it back. He did the same with Jelly and Greta. 'I must search you,' he said.

Behind his back, Flick drew the Sten gun from under her overall, disengaged the cocking lever of her gun from the safety slot and shot him in the back. He jerked and fell.

Flick ejected the cartridge, then reloaded the chamber and put the gun back under her overall.

Jelly dragged the body to the wall and shoved it behind the door.

'Let's get out of here,' said Flick.

Jelly went out. Greta stood frozen, staring at the dead officer.

Flick said, 'Greta. We have a job to do. Let's go.'

They went into the canteen, where Jelly began to sweep the floor.

Greta took a deep breath, straightened her back, and together she and Flick entered the kitchen.

The fuse boxes for the building were in a cupboard beside the large electric oven. There was a young German at the kitchen range. Flick gave him a sexy smile. 'What have you got to offer a hungry girl?'

He grinned at her. Behind his back, Greta took out a stout pair of pliers with rubberised handles, then opened the cupboard door.

AT THE CHÂTEAU GATE, Dieter noticed four guards instead of the usual two. Although he was in a Gestapo car, the sergeant carefully examined his pass and his driver's before waving the car in. Dieter was pleased: Weber had taken seriously the need for extra security.

He walked to the grand entrance. Seeing the women at their switchboards, it occurred to him that the Jackdaws might try to enter the château disguised as telephonists. He spoke to the supervisor. 'Have any of these women joined in the last few days?'

'No, Major,' she said, which put paid to his theory.

At the end of the east wing he took the staircase down. The door to the basement stood open, as usual, but there were two soldiers instead of the usual one standing inside. Weber had doubled the guard. The corporal saluted and the sergeant asked for his pass.

Dieter entered the basement corridor. He could hear the rumble of the diesel-fuelled generator that supplied electricity to the phone system. He passed the doors of the equipment rooms and came to the interview room. He hoped to find the new prisoner here, but the room was empty. Puzzled, he stepped inside. From the inner chamber came a long scream of utter agony. He threw open the door.

Becker stood at the electric-shock machine. Weber sat on a chair nearby. A young woman lay on the operating table with her wrists and ankles strapped and her head clamped in the head restraint of the machine.

Weber said, 'Hello, Franck. Join us, please. She hasn't said anything yet, but we've only just started. Give her another shock, Sergeant. Turn the voltage up this time.'

Then the lights went out.

THERE WAS A BLUE flash and a bang from behind the oven. The lights went out, and the kitchen was filled with the smell of scorched insulation. The young cook said, 'What's going on?'

Flick ran out of the door and through the canteen with Jelly and Greta at her heels. They followed a short corridor to the top of the basement stairs. Flick held her submachine gun concealed under the flap of her coat and they ran down the stairs. The daylight coming from the ground-floor windows faded rapidly as they descended to the entrance to the basement.

There were two soldiers standing just inside the door. One said, 'Don't worry, ladies, it's only a power cut.'

Flick shot him in the chest, then shot the other.

The three Jackdaws stepped through the doorway. Flick held her gun in her right hand and her torch in her left. She could hear a low rumble of machinery and several voices shouting in German from distant rooms. She saw the flicker of a match at the far end of the corridor. About thirty seconds had passed since Greta had cut off the power. It would not be long before the Germans found torches. She had only a minute, maybe less, to get out of sight.

She tried the nearest door. It was locked. She guessed, from the position of the room at the front of the château, under a corner of the car park, that the room beyond contained the fuel tanks.

She moved along the corridor and opened the next door. The rumble of machinery became louder. She flashed her torch and saw an electricity generator. 'Drag the bodies in here!'

Jelly and Greta pulled the dead guards across the floor. Flick returned to the basement entrance, slammed the steel door shut and bolted it. Now the corridor was in total darkness. She returned to the generator room, closed the door and turned on her torch.

There was a mass of pipes and cables in the room, all colour-coded with German efficiency. Flick directed her torch at the brown fuel line to the generator. 'Later, if we have time, I want you to blow a hole in that,' she told Jelly. 'Now, put your hand on my shoulder and follow me. Greta, you follow Jelly the same way.'

Flick turned off her torch and opened the door. Now they had to explore the basement blind. Using the wall as a guide, she began to walk, heading further inside. She reached another door, opened it and flashed her torch again. Greta whispered, 'Battery room. Go to the next door.'

An authoritative voice said in German: 'Was that a flashlight? Bring it over here!'

'Just coming,' said Greta in German, in a man's voice, but the three Jackdaws walked in the opposite direction.

Flick came to the next room, led the other two inside, and closed the door before shining her torch. It was a long chamber with floor-to-ceiling racks of equipment along both walls. One pair of racks was bristling with thousands of terminals in tidy rows. Flick looked at Greta. 'Well?'

Greta was examining the equipment by the light of her own torch, a fascinated expression on her face. 'This is the main distribution frame.' Greta swung her torch. 'Over there are the amplifiers and carrier circuit equipment for the long-distance lines.'

'Good,' Flick said briskly. 'Show Jelly where to place the charges.'

The three of them went to work. Greta unwrapped the waxed-paper packets of yellow plastic explosive while Flick cut the fuse cord into lengths. It burned at a rate of one centimetre per second. 'I'll make all the fuses three metres long,' Flick said. 'That will give us five minutes to get out.'

Flick held a torch while Greta moulded the charges to the frames and Jelly stuck the firing cap into the soft explosive. They worked fast. In five minutes all the equipment was covered with charges. The fuse cords led to a common source where they were loosely twisted together, so that one light would serve to ignite them all.

Jelly took out a thermite bomb, a black can containing finely powdered aluminium oxide and iron oxide. It would burn with intense heat. She took off the lid to reveal two fuses, then placed it behind the MDF. Then she placed an oxygen-generating pack on the floor at the blind end of the room. 'This will make the fire hotter,' she said. 'With this, the copper cables should melt.'

Everything was ready. Jelly took out a cigarette lighter.

Flick said, 'You two, make your way outside the building. Jelly, on your way, go into the generating room and blow a hole in the fuel line. We meet up at Antoinette's.'

Greta said anxiously, 'Where are *you* going?'

'To find Ruby.'

Jelly nodded. 'You have five minutes.' She lit the fuse.

WHEN DIETER PASSED from the darkness of the basement into the half-light of the stairwell, he noticed that the guards had gone from the entrance. Had they been taken away at gunpoint? Was an attack on the château already under way?

He ran up the stairs heading for the maintenance workshops, but on the way there he looked into the kitchen and found three soldiers staring at a fuse box. 'There's a power cut in the basement,' he said.

'I know,' said one of the men. 'All these wires have been cut.'

'Then get your tools out and reconnect them, you damn fool!'

A worried-looking young cook said, 'They were cleaning behind the oven, and there was a bang . . .'

'Who? Who was cleaning?'

'I don't know, sir. Just a cleaner.'

Dieter did not know what to think. Clearly the château was under attack. But where were the enemy? He left the kitchen, went to the stairwell, and ran up towards the offices on the upper floor. Something caught his eye and he looked back. A tall woman in a cleaner's overall was coming up from the basement, carrying a mop and a bucket.

He froze, staring at her, his mind racing. She should not have been there. Only Germans were allowed into the basement. And the cook had blamed a cleaner for the power cut. He came back down the stairs. 'Why were you in the basement?' he asked her in French.

'I went there to clean, but the lights are out.'

Dieter frowned. 'You're not supposed to go there.'

'Yes, the soldier told me that they clean it themselves. I didn't know.'

'Come with me.' He took her arm and led her to the kitchen.

Dieter spoke to the cook. 'Do you recognise this woman?'

'Yes, sir. She's the one who was cleaning behind the oven.'

'I'm very sorry if I damaged something,' she said.

Dieter recognised her accent. 'You're German,' he said. 'You filthy traitor. You're going to tell me everything.'

FLICK OPENED THE DOOR marked 'Interview Room,' stepped inside, closed the door behind her and swept the room with her torch. The room was empty of people. She was puzzled. But Ruby had to be here somewhere.

Then she saw a door leading, presumably, to an inner chamber.

She opened the door and stepped through. She saw Ruby strapped to a table.

She stepped to the table. 'Ruby, can you hear me?'

Ruby groaned. Flick's heart leaped: she was still alive. She put her Sten gun down on the table and undid the straps that bound Ruby.

'Flick,' Ruby moaned. 'Behind you.'

Flick jumped to one side. Something heavy brushed her ear and thumped her left shoulder hard. She cried out in pain, dropped her torch and fell. She scrabbled on the floor for her torch. Before she found it, the lights came on.

She blinked and saw a squat, stocky man with a round head and close-cropped hair. Behind him stood Ruby. In the dark she had picked up what looked like a steel bar, and now she brought it down on his head. The man slumped to the floor and lay still.

'Meet Sergeant Becker,' Ruby said.

'Are you all right?' Flick said as she got up.

'I'm in bloody agony, but I'm going to get my own back on this bastard.' Grasping the front of Becker's tunic, Ruby heaved him upright, then onto the operating table. She strapped him in by his wrists and ankles, then tightened the head restraint. She took a terminal from the shock machine and stuffed it into his mouth. Then she went to the machine and fumbled with the switch.

The man on the table let out a strangled scream.

They went out, leaving him there, and stepped out into the corridor. The confusion had died down. Flick checked her watch. Two minutes had passed since Jelly lit the fuses. Then she glimpsed the tall figure of Dieter Franck approaching, followed by two or three other people she could not clearly see. She opened the nearest door. It was marked 'Wireless Room'. The room was empty. They stepped inside.

A moment later, Franck's footsteps passed. Flick waited, listening. A door slammed. She peeped out. Franck had disappeared.

'Let's go,' she said to Ruby. They walked to the stairs.

DIETER TIED the prisoner to a chair. He looked at the woman for a moment, wondering how much time he had. One agent had been arrested in the street outside the château. This one, if she was an agent, had been caught coming up from the basement. Were others waiting somewhere to be let in? Or were they in the building?

Dieter began with the traditional slap in the face, sudden and demoralising. 'Where are your friends?' he asked the woman. Her cheek reddened, but what he saw in her face mystified him. She looked happy. 'You're in the basement of the château,' he told her. 'Through that door is the torture chamber. Beyond that partition wall is the telephone switchboard gear. If your friends blow up the building, you and I will surely die here.'

Her expression did not change.

Perhaps the château was not about to blow up, Dieter thought.

But then what was the mission? 'You're German,' he said. 'Why are you helping your country's enemies?'

At last she spoke. 'I'll tell you.' She spoke German with a Hamburg accent. 'Some years ago, I had a lover. His name was Manfred. Your Nazis arrested him and sent him to a camp.' She paused, swallowing. After a moment she went on. 'When they took him away from me, I swore I would have my revenge—and this is it.' She smiled happily. 'Your foul regime is almost finished. And I've helped to destroy it.'

There was something wrong here. She spoke as if the deed was already done. A dreadful suspicion dawned on Dieter. 'Why are you telling me this? Are you trying to keep me occupied while your friends get away? Are you sacrificing your life to ensure the success of the mission?'

She just smiled.

Dieter's train of thought was broken by a faint noise coming from the next room. He sprang up and went into the torture chamber. On the table he recognised the squat figure of Sergeant Becker.

UPSTAIRS, ALL WAS NORMAL. Flick and Ruby walked quickly through the ranks of telephone operators, all busy at their switchboards, murmuring into their headsets as they plugged jacks into sockets, connecting decision-makers in Berlin, Paris and Normandy. Flick checked her watch. In exactly two minutes all those connections would be destroyed and the military machine would fall apart.

They passed out of the building without incident. But, in the courtyard, they met Jelly—coming back.

'Where's Greta?' she said.

'She left with you!' Flick replied.

'I stopped to set a charge on the diesel fuel line in the generator room, like you said. Greta went on ahead of me. But she never reached Antoinette's place. I came back to look for her.'

Flick looked at her watch. 'We have less than two minutes.'

They ran back inside. The switchboard girls stared at them as they raced through the rooms. Flick was already having second thoughts. In attempting to save one of her team, was she about to sacrifice two more—and herself?

As they reached the stairwell, a voice from above said, 'What's going on here?'

Flick froze. She looked over her shoulder. On the staircase coming down from the top floor stood four men. One, pointing a pistol at her, was Major Weber.

'What do you want with us?' Flick said. 'We're the cleaners.'

'Perhaps you are,' he said. 'But there is a team of female enemy agents in the district. Raise your hands in the air.'

As she lifted her wrist past her face, Flick checked her watch.

Thirty seconds left.

'Down the stairs,' said Weber.

Reluctantly, Flick went down into the basement. Ruby and Jelly went with her, followed by the four men.

She stopped at the foot of the stairs. Twenty seconds.

'Keep moving,' said Weber.

Five seconds.

They passed through the basement door.

There was a tremendous bang.

At the far end of the corridor, the partition walls of the equipment chamber exploded outwards. Flames billowed over the debris. Flick was knocked down. She got up on one knee, pulled the submachine gun out from under her overall and spun round. Jelly and Ruby were either side of her. Weber and the other three men had also fallen. Flick pulled the trigger.

Of the Germans, only Weber had kept his presence of mind. As Flick sprayed bullets, Weber fired his pistol. Jelly, struggling to her feet, cried out and fell. Flick hit Weber in the chest and he went down.

Ruby bent over Jelly, feeling for a pulse. After a moment she looked up. 'Dead,' she said.

Flick looked towards the far end of the corridor, where Greta was. Flames were billowing out from the equipment chamber, but the wall of the interview room seemed intact.

She ran towards the inferno.

DIETER FOUND himself lying on the floor without knowing how he had got there. He heard the roaring of flames and smelt smoke. He struggled to his feet and looked into the interview room.

He realised immediately that the brick walls of the torture chamber had saved his life. The partition between the interview room and the equipment chamber had disappeared. The few pieces of furniture in the interview room had been thrown up against the wall. The prisoner had suffered the same fate and lay on the ground, still tied to the chair, neck broken. She was dead. The equipment chamber was aflame and the fire was spreading rapidly.

The door to the interview room opened and Flick Clairet stood there holding a submachine gun. She wore a dark wig that had fallen askew to reveal her own blonde hair beneath.

If he had had a gun in his hand at that moment, he would have mowed her down in blind rage. But she had the gun.

At first she did not see Dieter, but stared at the body of her comrade. Then she lifted her gaze and met his eyes. He saw the thirst for revenge in the twist of her mouth. She raised the Sten gun.

Dieter ducked back into the torture chamber as her bullets chipped fragments of brick off the wall. He drew his pistol and waited for Flick to come through. When she did not appear he risked a look. Flick had gone. He dashed across the burning interrogation room, threw open the door and stepped into the corridor. Flick and another woman were running towards the far end. As he raised his gun, a hot pain burnt his arm. He cried out and dropped his gun. He saw that his sleeve was on fire. He tore off his jacket.

When he looked up again, the women had gone.

Dieter picked up his pistol and went after them. As he ran, he smelt fuel. Perhaps the saboteurs had holed a pipe. Any second now, the basement would explode like a giant bomb.

FLICK AND RUBY RACED through the switchboard rooms, reached the front entrance and ran down the steps. In the square, they could see Moulier's meat van, backed up to the château gates with its engine running and its rear doors open. Paul stood beside it, staring anxiously through the iron railings.

Flick and Ruby ran for the gates. Paul jumped into the front of the van. Flick and Ruby threw themselves into the back.

As the van pulled away, Flick saw Dieter run towards the car park.

At that moment, the fire reached the basement fuel tanks.

There was a deep underground boom. The car park erupted, gravel and earth and slabs of concrete flying into the air. Half the cars parked there were overturned. Huge stones and chunks of brickwork rained down on the rest. Dieter was thrown back across the steps. Then the van left the square, and Flick could see no more.

DIETER PICKED HIMSELF up off the ground and stared at the carnage. The Jackdaws had succeeded in their mission. But they were still in France. And if he could capture and interrogate Flick Clairet, he could yet turn defeat into victory. Some time tonight, she must be planning to meet a small plane, in a field not far from Reims. He had to find out where and when.

And he knew who would tell him. Her husband.

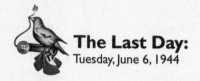

The Last Day:
Tuesday, June 6, 1944

Dieter sat on the platform at Reims station, his heart full of rage. The prison train was hours late, but he had to wait. He had no other cards to play.

The train rolled in a few minutes after midnight.

He noticed the stink even before it came to a halt. The livestock wagons had sides of wooden slats. The prisoners put their arms through the slats, begging for something to eat, for water.

He had two Waffen-SS corporals with him, both good marksmen. He turned to them now and said, 'Bring Michel Clairet.'

The corporals went away and reappeared with Michel between them. His ankles were hobbled so that he could not run. He was trying to maintain an air of bravado, but the attempt was a failure.

Dieter took Michel's arm and walked him closer to the train. 'I need some information,' he said.

Michel shook his head. 'Put me on the train.'

'Tell me where the Jackdaws' plane will land—and when.'

Michel stared at him. 'You haven't caught them,' he said. Hope came back into his face. 'They've blown up the château, haven't they? They succeeded.'

Dieter made Michel walk the length of the train, slowly. At the women's car Michel bowed his head, refusing to look.

Dieter beckoned. Hans Hesse walked out of the shadows, escorting a young woman. Her face was white, her hair greasy, and she had sores on her lips. She walked with difficulty. It was Gilberte.

Michel gasped.

Dieter repeated his question. 'Where will the plane land, and when?'

Michel said nothing.

Dieter said, 'Put her on the train.'

A guard opened the gate of a cattle car and pushed Gilberte into the car. 'No,' she cried. 'No, please!'

The guard was about to close the gate, but Dieter said, 'Wait.' He looked at Michel. Tears were pouring down the man's face.

Gilberte said, 'Please, Michel, I beg you.'

'The time and place,' Dieter said.

Michel nodded. 'The potato field east of Laroque, at two a.m.'

Dieter looked at his watch. It was twelve fifteen. 'Show me.'

FIVE KILOMETRES from Laroque, Moulier's meat van was parked next to a barn. In the deep moon-shadow, the surviving Jackdaws sat waiting.

'What are you looking forward to?' said Ruby.

Paul said, 'A steak.'

Flick said, 'A soft bed with clean sheets. How about you?'

'Seeing Jim.'

Flick recalled that Ruby had had a fling with the firearms instructor.

'What about you two?' Ruby asked.

Paul said, 'I'm single.' He looked at Flick.

She shook her head. 'I intended to ask Michel for a divorce . . . but how could I, in the middle of an operation?'

'So we'll wait until after the war to get married,' Paul said.

Typical man, Flick thought. He slips marriage into the conversation like a minor detail. So much for romance. But she was pleased.

She looked at her watch. It was one thirty. 'Time to go,' she said.

DIETER'S LIMOUSINE was parked at the edge of the vineyard next to the potato field at Laroque, camouflaged with leafy vines. Michel and Gilberte were in the back seat, bound hand and foot, guarded by Hans. Dieter and the two corporals, each armed with a rifle, stood by the car.

Dieter said, 'The terrorists will be here in the next few minutes. Remember, I must have them alive—especially the leader, the small woman. Shoot to wound, not kill.'

They fell silent. A motor vehicle was approaching. They all knelt, invisible against the dark mass of the vines.

A van with its lights off pulled up by the gate to the potato field. Two women and a man got out.

'Quiet now,' Dieter whispered.

Suddenly the hush was shattered by the blare of a car horn.

Dieter jumped and cursed. It came from the limousine. He leapt to his feet and ran to the driver's door. He saw immediately what had happened. Michel had sprung forward, leaning across the front seat, and before Hans could stop him he had pressed on the horn with his bound hands. Hans, in the front passenger seat, was trying to pull out his pistol, but Gilberte had joined in, and she was lying half over Hans, hampering his movements.

The horn continued to sound a deafening warning.

Dieter fumbled for his gun.

Michel found the light switch, and the car's headlamps came on. Dieter looked up. The riflemen were hideously exposed in the glare. There was a rattle of machine-gun fire from the field. One rifleman clutched his belly and fell; then the other was shot in the head. A sharp pain stung Dieter's left arm, and he let out a yell.

Then there was a shot from within the car, and Michel cried out. Hans had at last flung Gilberte off himself and got his pistol out. He fired again, and Michel slumped, but Michel's hand was still on the horn and it continued to blare. Gilberte threw herself at Hans again, grabbing at his gun arm with her manacled hands. Dieter had his gun out but could not shoot her for fear of hitting Hans.

There was another shot. It was Hans's gun again, but now it was somehow pointing upwards, and he shot himself, the bullet hitting him under the chin. He slumped back against the door.

Dieter took aim and shot Gilberte in the head.

He shoved the corpse of Michel away from the steering wheel. The horn was silenced. He killed the headlamps.

He looked across the field. He listened. He was alone.

FLICK CRAWLED through the vineyard on her hands and knees, heading for Dieter Franck's car. She wished for a cloud to shade the moon, but for the moment the sky was clear.

She had firmly instructed Paul and Ruby to stay behind near the van. Three people made three times the noise, and she did not want a companion to betray her presence. As she crawled, she listened for the incoming plane. She had to locate any remaining enemy and kill them before the plane arrived. The Jackdaws could not stand in the field to guide the pilot with torches while armed troops were aiming at them. And if they did not hold torches, the plane would return to England without touching down. The thought was unbearable.

She was five rows of vines from Dieter Franck's car. She would approach from behind. With the submachine gun in her right hand, she crawled across the rows of vines. She saw moonlight glint off the car's rear window. She grew ultracautious as she approached the car, but she saw no one. She thought she could make out two motionless bodies in uniform. How many were there in total? The limousine could easily carry six.

She crept closer. Eventually she crawled right up to the car.

The doors were wide open, and the interior seemed full of bodies. She looked in the front and recognised Michel. She choked back a sob. She guessed he had been the one to sound the horn. If so, he had died saving her life.

Next to Michel lay a lieutenant who had been shot in the throat. There were more bodies in the back. One was that of a woman. She gasped: it was Gilberte.

She leaned over Gilberte to look at the fourth corpse. It rose up from the floor in a swift motion, grabbed her by the hair and thrust the barrel of a gun into the soft flesh of her throat.

'Drop the gun,' Dieter Franck said in French.

She had no choice: she dropped it.

'Back away.'

As she stepped back, he followed her, getting out of the car, keeping the gun at her throat. She wished she had not been so fierce in ordering Paul and Ruby to wait in hiding. There was now no chance they would come to her rescue. 'You're so small,' he said, looking her up and down. 'And you've done so much damage. Don't look pleased. Now you're going to damage the Resistance. You're going to give me all the names and addresses in your head.'

She thought of the suicide pill concealed in the hollow cap of her fountain pen. Would she have a chance to take it?

'I wonder what will break you?' he said. He touched her face. 'The loss of your looks, perhaps.'

Flick felt sick, but she maintained a stony expression.

Keeping the pistol on her he reached into his pocket with his other hand and drew out a pair of handcuffs. 'Give me your hands.'

Helpless, she raised her hands.

As he closed one cuff over her left wrist she made her last desperate move. She struck sideways with her handcuffed left hand, knocking his gun away from her shoulder. At the same time she used her right hand to draw the small knife from its hidden sheath behind the lapel of her jacket. She lunged and thrust the knife directly into his left eye. He screamed in agony and fired his gun, but the shots went into the air.

He staggered, fell backwards and hit the ground, dropping his gun. Flick grabbed it and aimed it at Franck. But he was still.

She heard footsteps. Paul rushed up. 'Flick! Are you all right?'

She nodded. She was still pointing the Walther at Dieter Franck.

'I don't think that will be necessary,' Paul said softly. He gently took the gun from her and engaged the safety catch.

Ruby appeared. 'Listen!' she cried. 'Listen!'

Flick heard the drone of an aeroplane.

'Let's get moving,' Paul said.

They ran out into the field to signal the plane that would take them home.

THEY CROSSED the English Channel in strong winds and intermittent rain. During a quiet spell, the navigator said, 'You might want to take a look outside.'

Flick, Ruby and Paul were dozing, exhausted. Flick was wrapped in Paul's arms and she did not want to move.

The navigator pressed them. 'You'll never see anything like this again if you live to be a hundred.'

Curiosity overcame Flick's tiredness. She got up and staggered to the small window. Ruby did the same. The pilot dipped a wing.

The moon was full and she could see clearly. At first she could hardly believe her eyes. Immediately below the plane was a grey-painted warship bristling with guns. Alongside it was a small ocean liner, its paintwork gleaming white in the moonlight. Beyond them were troop transports, battered tankers and shallow-draught landing ships. There were ships as far as Flick could see, hundreds of them spread out over the sea like a carpet.

'Paul, look at this!' she cried. 'It's the invasion!'

He came and stood beside her. 'Jeepers!' he said.

The navigator said, 'I'd give a lot to be part of that, wouldn't you?'

Flick looked at Paul and Ruby, and they all smiled. 'Oh, we are,' she said. 'We're part of it, all right.'

KEN FOLLETT

It was a highly original thriller about the Second World War that catapulted Ken Follett to worldwide fame back in 1978, when he was twenty-seven. *Eye of the Needle*, which told of the hunt for an elusive and ruthless Nazi agent, was made into a successful film starring Donald Sutherland and Kate Nelligan. The success of the book enabled Follett to give up his job at a London publishing house and turn to writing full-time.

Since then, the Cardiff-born author has written a stream of best sellers, many of them thrillers. *The Key to Rebecca* and *Night Over Water* were also set during the Second World War, the period that provides the vivid backdrop for *Jackdaws*.

Although wholly fictional, Follett's latest novel is inspired by the true-life exploits of the many women who were sent into occupied Europe by Britain's Special Operations Executive. When he began researching *Jackdaws*, he already knew about the most extraordinary women agents—Odette Churchill and Violette Szabo, for example, whose stories became widely known through the films *Odette* and *Carve Her Name with Pride*—but he was not aware just how many of them there had been. 'I came across a statistic that intrigues me. There were fifty women secret agents sent into occupied France during the Second World War, principally by SOE . . . That's quite a lot. Something like a third of them were captured by the Nazis. And if they were captured they would automatically be tortured for information. So they were tremendously heroic.'

Ken Follett publishes a book approximately every two years. The first year is spent doing research and working out the plot, while the second is devoted to writing. 'People say I'm very self-disciplined, but it's no effort for me to sit down and work,' he says. 'When I wake up in the morning that's what's on my mind. It's what I want to do.'

THE
SMOKE
JUMPER

NICHOLAS
EVANS

AS FIRE BURNS ITS WAY ACROSS
SNAKE MOUNTAIN, SMOKE JUMPER
CONNOR FORD RISKS HIS LIFE TO
SAVE THE WOMAN THAT HIS
LIFELONG FRIEND ED TULLY
INTENDS TO MARRY. WHILE HE
BATTLES THE FLAMES, CONNOR
KNOWS HE MUST ALSO FIGHT THE
PASSION FOR JULIA THAT IS
BURNING IN HIS HEART.

FOR HOW CAN HE POSSIBLY
RECONCILE HIS LOVE FOR HER
WITH HIS LOYALTY TO HIS
GREATEST FRIEND?

PART ONE
CHAPTER ONE

The important things in life always happened by accident. At fifteen she didn't know much—in fact, with each passing year she was a lot less clear about most things. But this much she did know. You could worry yourself sick trying to be a better person, spend sleepless nights figuring out how to live clean and decent and honest. You could make a plan and bolt it in place, kneel by your bed every night and swear to God you'd stick to it—and then, out of the black beyond, some nameless catastrophe would swoop into your life and turn everything upside-down and inside out for ever.

It all started in a real low-key kind of way when those two women came sashaying into the bar. She didn't know who they were but what they were was plain for all the world. They both wore tight little tops, one red, one silver, and the woman in front, who had long black hair and breasts propped up like melons on a shelf, had a skirt so short she needn't have bothered.

The men they were with were close behind them and obscured. Both wore cowboy hats and from the corner booth where Skye and her friends were sitting, she couldn't make out their faces.

She watched them mostly because she was bored, which was kind of sad, too, considering it was her birthday. Jed and Calvin were slumped stoned and speechless beside her, Roxy was crying into her hands at something Craig had said, and Craig was cussing about his goddamn heap of a car. Another great night in fun city, Skye said to herself and took a swig of her beer. Happy birthday to me.

The bar was a godforsaken dump so close to the railroad that the bottles shook whenever a train went by. The cops left the place alone and the staff turned a blind eye to underage drinking, so much of the clientele was around the same age as Skye. A lot younger for sure than the four who had just walked in. They were at the bar now, with their backs to her, and Skye again found herself staring at them.

She watched the tall man's hands moving on the black-haired woman's hips and saw him lean in close, nuzzling her neck. He must have whispered something dirty because the woman suddenly threw back her head, laughed raucously and made a playful attempt to slap him. The man laughed too and swivelled to avoid her and his hat fell off and for the first time Skye could see his face.

It was her stepfather. She saw him recognise her and his face clouded and became the one she feared and loathed, the one she saw when he came back in the early hours to the trailer, seething with drink and fury, and called her mother a squaw bitch and beat her until she howled for mercy and then turned his attention upon Skye.

He straightened up and put his hat on the bar and headed towards the booth. Skye squashed out her cigarette and stood up.

'Let's go,' she said quietly.

But she was trapped in the booth. On one side Roxy was sobbing into Craig's shoulder and hadn't heard and on the other Calvin and Jed were still out of it. Her stepfather reached the table.

'What the fuck are you doing in here?'

'Come on, it's my birthday.'

'Don't give me that shit. You're just fifteen years old!'

'Aw, give her a break, man. We're only having a little fun.' It was Jed, who had resurfaced. Skye's stepfather leaned across and grabbed him by the throat, hauling him halfway across the table.

'You dare talk to me like that, you little slice of shit.'

Craig was on his feet now, but Skye's stepfather twisted himself round and punched the boy full in the face. Roxy screamed.

'For God's sake,' Skye shouted. 'Stop it! Stop it!'

Everyone in the bar was staring at them. One of the waiters was coming over along with the man her stepfather had arrived with.

'Hey, folks, let's cool it here, shall we?' the waiter said.

Skye's stepfather shoved Jed into his seat and turned his dark, narrowed eyes on the waiter.

'Did you serve alcohol to these kids?'

'They said they were twenty-one. Sir, could we talk about this—?'

Skye stood up and pushed her way out of the booth. 'Look, we're going, OK? We're going!'

Her stepfather spun round and lifted his hand to hit her and although all her instincts told her to cower, somehow she managed not to and instead stood her ground, glaring at him.

'Don't you dare lay a finger on me.' It was little more than a whisper but it stopped him. He lowered his hand.

'Get your ass home, you little Indian whore. I'll see to you later.'

'The only whores in here are the two you came in with.'

He made a lunge for her, but she ducked out of his reach and ran for the door. His friend and the waiter grabbed his arms to stop him coming after her. She burst into the night and started to run.

The air hung hot and humid and she could feel the tears on her cheeks. A freight train was going by and she ran alongside it. Had it been travelling more slowly she would have climbed on board and let it bear her wherever in the world it was headed. She ran until her lungs could take no more, and as she stopped, the train's last wagon passed by and she stood slumped with her hands on her knees, gasping and watching its taillights grow smaller.

'Never mind. You can catch the next one.'

The voice startled her. It was male and close at hand. Skye scanned the darkness around her. She couldn't see him.

'Over here.'

He was sitting on the ground, leaning against a stack of fence posts. He was a white boy, eighteen or nineteen maybe and very thin. He was wearing torn jeans and a T-shirt emblazoned with a roaring dragon. A duffle bag lay on the ground beside him. He was rolling a joint.

'Why are you crying?'

'I'm not. What's it to you anyhow?'

He shrugged. For a while neither of them spoke. Skye knew she should probably walk away. But something within her, some hapless craving for comfort or company, made her stay. She looked at him again. He lit the joint and took a draw. He held it out to her. 'Here.'

'I don't do drugs.'

'Sure.'

THE CAR THEY STOLE belonged to somebody with small kids. There were little seats fitted in the back and the floor was littered with toys and picture books and sweet papers. It took the boy only a couple of minutes to pop the door lock and get the engine going.

He said his name was Sean and she told him hers and that was all they knew about each other except for some common hurt or longing that didn't need uttering.

They drove north until they hit the interstate, then headed west with the dawn rearing in a widening red scar over the plains behind them. They pulled off the interstate to get gas. There was a diner just opening and they bought coffee and muffins and sat at a table by the window. While they ate he asked her how old she was and she lied and told him she was seventeen. She said she'd been born in South Dakota and was half Oglala Sioux, on her mother's side, and he said that was cool, but she told him that she didn't think it was.

He said he came from Detroit and that his parents were in jail. When he was fourteen he had taken off and for the last three years had been travelling.

Skye asked why he had come to Montana and he said it was because he wanted to meet a grizzly bear in the wild. He said that he had been a bear in another life. She laughed and asked him how he planned to go about finding a grizzly. He figured they should head for Glacier National Park, which he'd been told was a good place to look.

Skye nodded, trying to look serious. 'Right,' she said.

'You got a better idea?'

She could think of about a hundred. 'Whatever,' she said.

They drove the rest of the day, while the sun swung over them, heading for the mountains. She saw the police car before he did. Something made her look back and as she did so the cop turned on his flashing lights. Sean looked in the rearview mirror and said nothing. He slowed and pulled onto the shoulder and the police car behind did the same.

The cop got out of his car and walked slowly towards them. Sean lowered the window, watching him in the side mirror all the way. As he came alongside, the cop bent so that he could get a look at Skye. He was young, in his mid-twenties maybe, with friendly blue eyes.

'Howdy. Where you folks headed?'

'Glacier,' Sean said, not looking at him.

'This your vehicle?'

'Belongs to a friend.'

'Uh-huh. OK. Well, I'd like to see your driver's licence, registration and insurance, please.'

Sean turned to reach for his bag. Skye suddenly had a bad feeling that he had a gun in there and that he was going to do something dumb and dreadful. But he turned back to the cop.

'I forgot. All that stuff got stolen.'

Something shifted and hardened in the cop's eyes. 'Would you mind stepping out of the vehicle, please, sir?'

He straightened up and reached for the door handle and in the same moment Sean gunned the engine. The cop yanked the door open and tried to grab Sean's shoulder, but the car was already moving and he lost his balance and fell, and in the fall his arm went down behind Sean's seat and twisted and got trapped. He cried out.

'Stop!' Skye shouted. 'Stop!'

But Sean just hit the gas pedal harder so that the tyres squealed and smoked, and the car snaked its way back onto the highway, dragging the cop beside it yelling and shrieking. Skye screamed.

'Are you crazy? Stop the car! For God's sake, stop!'

She screamed again and started to hit the boy and he struck her hard in the mouth. She felt a tooth break and blood start to flow and with all her strength and anger she lashed at him until finally he punched her so hard she felt something give in her head and she slumped in her seat watching the world twirl away from her in a red benumbing mist.

THE DAY THAT EDWARD TULLY met the love of his life began badly. Snow had been falling all week, but in the early hours of Friday morning it turned to rain, and by daybreak Boston was knee-deep in grey sludge. It was raining indoors too. Around midmorning the heating and water for the whole apartment building went off. When Ed went to investigate he found the elevators out of action and water cascading down the stairwell.

The building was being renovated and this morning, it emerged, a carpenter had severed a power cable and a water pipe in one surgical flourish of his power drill.

Ed had been working most of the night on the second act of his new musical, the one that was going to make him famous. It was going well, though he was increasingly aware of how the construction work was infusing both music and lyrics with a dark, menacing tone. When he squelched into his apartment he found there had been a more literal infusion. The ceiling had sprung a leak directly above the piano. The piano itself seemed undamaged, but the stack of music

153

sheets that lay upon it, Ed's entire night's work, was sodden.

Then the mail arrived, returning to him, with thanks, not one but two rejected scripts and demo tapes of his last musical, the one that clearly wasn't going to make him famous.

Since finishing college three years ago, Ed made enough money to keep on composing by teaching piano to precocious ten-year-olds. During the winter his only other source of income was from playing every Friday night in a downtown bar, which, despite being paid little money and less attention, he still enjoyed.

The bar was called Ralff's, and it stood near the waterfront on the fringe of a jauntily revamped tourist area. Apart from Ralff's the only reason for going there was the movie theatre just across the street, which was good for business but bad for parking. Tonight, however, Ed was in luck.

As he came round the corner, he could see a Jeep pulling out of a space outside the bar. He signalled right and stopped to let it leave. The car behind hooted. He looked in his mirror and saw a beaten-up white VW bug. Ed shook his head. What a moron. The Jeep vacated the space and Ed moved forward so he could reverse into it. As he shifted into reverse and turned in his seat he saw the VW nip sharply into his space. He couldn't believe it. He switched on his hazard lights and got out.

Two people were getting out of the VW. The driver was a young woman wearing a red ski jacket with the hood turned up, and as Ed stomped towards her she flashed him a dazzling smile. The passenger was a man, taller and broader than Ed, and Ed noticed through his rain-streaked glasses that the guy was grinning.

'Excuse me,' Ed said in a level voice. 'That's my space.'

The woman looked at her car then looked back at him with that same infuriating butter-wouldn't-melt smile. 'No. It's ours.'

She locked the car and zipped up her jacket. Even with steam coming out of his ears, Ed recognised that he was confronting an extraordinarily good-looking woman. She was olive-skinned, with a wide mouth and perfect teeth. Her eyes were big and dark and flashing now with amusement. And this served only to fuel Ed's rage.

'Listen, you knew darn well what I was doing, and you snuck in behind me. You can't do that, damn it!'

The woman's boyfriend came ambling round the back of the car towards them. 'Hey, man, I'm sorry. But life's a jungle. In a few thousand years the only drivers will be those whose ancestors first learned how to nip into other people's parking spaces. It's called survival of the fittest. Now, please excuse us or we'll be late for the movie.'

And, with a smile, he took the woman's arm and steered her across the street. Ed trudged back to his car and got in and dried his glasses. He had to cruise the area for twenty minutes before he found a space just a few cars along the street from the VW. As he walked back past it he had the idea.

He went into Ralff's and apologised to Bryan, the manager, for being late. He went behind the bar and found a piece of paper and a pen. He scrawled something on the paper, found some wrap and sealed it so the rain wouldn't get to it. Then he headed for the door.

Outside, the movie theatre crowds had disappeared. Ed went straight to the VW and disengaged the wipers. He inserted his note under one of the arms. He stood back with a satisfied smile. Vengeance, he concluded, sticking the wipers into his coat pocket, was a dish best eaten wet. He turned and headed back to the bar.

In a few thousand years, the note said, *the only drivers will be those who learned how to steal the wipers of the parking space thieves. It's called survival of the fittest.*

DESPITE THE DAMPNESS of his clothes and the miserable day he'd had, he played well that night. Around ten, the place started to fill. One of the tables applauded every number and it caught on with the others. He racked his brain for songs about rain and they went down well. 'Stormy Weather' even got calls for an encore.

Every time the door opened he was gratified to see that it was still raining. He kept imagining the woman coming back to her car and finding the note and he wished he could be there to see her face.

But he was wrong. He had just taken a fifteen-minute break before his last set. He'd settled back at the piano and was taking a drink, when he saw her. It was the red ski jacket he noticed and had he looked a moment later he might not have recognised her, for she was just taking it off. Under it she was wearing a cream sweater. While her boyfriend was ordering drinks she sat on her stool, looking around the room. Ed watched her.

She dragged her hands back through her thick, dark hair in a gesture that presumably had some practical purpose, such as untangling it, and another woman might have made it look like preening. But with her it seemed entirely without vanity. And one of the sexiest things Ed had ever seen.

Suddenly he realised that she was staring right back at him and a slow smile of recognition spread across her face. And, in what he would later call a moment of pure genius, Ed started to play a number from his last (never performed) musical. It was a smoochy, late-night love song called 'Your Place or Mine'. The chorus went:

> 'We've finished the whiskey,
> Let's finish the wine.
> I feel kinda frisky,
> Is it your place or mine?'

He kept his eyes on her while he sang. Her boyfriend didn't seem to mind, he was enjoying the joke too. Ed went on with the set, playing any song he could think of that was vaguely relevant, changing a lyric here and there to make her laugh. He played '(You've) Gotta Get Out of This Place' and 'Somewhere' (there's a place for [You]) from *West Side Story*. He was playing only for her, so he was more than a little disappointed when he was just halfway through 'Lovely Rita, Meter Maid', to see her stand up and start putting on her ski jacket. Then he saw they were coming towards him.

They waited on the far side of the piano until he'd finished. While the applause rippled around them he nodded at her.

'That was funny,' she said. 'You're good.'

'It's true, I admit it. Thank you.'

'Listen, I'm really sorry about what happened. I don't know what came over me. I've never done anything like that before in my life.'

'It was my fault,' the boyfriend cut in. 'I made her do it. It's just, we were late for the movie and, well, anyhow, we're . . . sorry.'

Ed nodded without looking at him. He couldn't take his eyes off the woman. God, she was gorgeous. 'Well, thanks,' he said.

His coat was hanging on the back of his chair and he reached into the damp pocket, found the wipers and held them out to her. 'Here.'

She frowned.

'You haven't been back to your car yet?'

'No.'

'Well, I think you'll find you need these.'

She gave him a wry smile and took them. The boyfriend laughed. 'Quits?' Ed said.

She narrowed her eyes at him. 'Well, we'll have to see about that.'

'I tell you if you didn't have such a big boyfriend, you'd have really been in trouble.'

'This is my cousin David.'

They were the sweetest words Ed had heard all day. He held ou
hand. 'Edward Tully. Pleased to meet you.'

David said he was pleased to meet him too. The guy had a hand-
shake like a steam press. Ed turned to the woman with whom he was
already in love and offered his hand and she took it in hers.

'Julia Bishop,' she said. Her hand felt cool and delicious.

She smiled and said sorry again and then they all said goodbye
and she and her cousin headed for the door. Ed started to play a
John Lennon song he hadn't played in years. But if she knew it, Julia
showed no sign of recognition. She simply walked out into the night
with her cousin and didn't once look back.

> 'Half of what I say is meaningless,
> But I say it just to reach you, Julia.'

When Ed got to his car half an hour later, still cursing himself that
he hadn't had the sense to get her phone number, he found his wipers
had been removed and a note tucked under one of the arms. 'I
learned,' it said on one side. On the other side was a phone number.

It had stopped raining.

IT WAS NIGH ON NOON when the smoke jumpers came. They plum-
meted in pairs on each pass of the plane, their bodies jolting as the
parachutes cracked open and filled and left them floating like
medusas in an ocean of sky.

They were a crew of six men and two women and every one of
them landed safely in the jump spot, a clearing not forty yards wide.
They shed their parachutes and jumpsuits and stowed them, then
unpacked their chainsaws, pulaskis—with an axe blade on one side
and pickaxe on the other—and shovels from bags dropped separately, and were soon ready to start cutting a fire line.

The peak that watched over them was called Iron Mountain. The
fire had been spotted by a ranger that morning and, fanned by a
strengthening westerly, had already taken out more than 100 acres. If
it continued to head east or switched to the north there was little
risk. But to the south and west there were ranches and cabins and if
the wind shifted they would be in danger, which was why the call had
come for the smoke jumpers.

They cut their line along a limestone ridge that ran along its southern flank. The line was a yard wide and half a mile long. They

worked in waves, sawyers first, then the swampers to clear the felled trees and branches, then the diggers. They cleared the ground so that when the fire arrived it would be starved of fuel. By the time it was done, they were soaked in sweat and their flameproof yellow shirts and green trousers were blotched with earth and ash and debris.

Now they were resting, some squatting, some standing, strung along the ridge like weary infantry. Last in line stood a tall, lean young man with tangled, straw-coloured hair. His ash-covered face was striped black where the sweat had run and his pale blue eyes looked somehow feral. He had set his pack on a slab of rock and was wiping clean the steel head of his pulaski. When he had it gleaming he leaned the shaft against the pack and unhitched his canteen.

He was twenty-six years old and his name was Connor Ford. It was his first jump of the season, and though he was tired and dirty and his lungs were sore from the smoke that shrouded the mountainside, there was nowhere in the world he would rather have been.

The water in his canteen tasted warm and metallic. It was only the end of May but the temperature was well into the nineties. It had barely rained all year and if things kept on this way it was going to be one hell of a summer for fires. Back at the base in Missoula, some of the jumpers were already fantasising about how they were going to spend the overtime and hazard pay. He'd called Ed in Boston two nights ago and told him to put down a deposit on the new car he'd been promising himself. Ed and that fabulous girlfriend he'd been going on about for months were arriving in Montana at the weekend. It was the first time ever he'd missed the start of a fire season, which showed what a sorry effect a woman could have on a man.

From above him up the slope now he heard Hank Thomas, the incident commander, give the word to move on. Connor fastened and stowed his canteen and was about to shoulder his pack when he heard a strange sound. It was faint, like a strangled cry, and seemed to come from over the ridge where the fire was. He looked and saw what at first he took to be a flaming branch rise above the spine of rock. It took him several seconds to recognise that it was no branch.

It was a large bull elk. Every hair of its coat had been burned and its skin was charred black. Its great rack of antlers flamed like a torch. The animal scrambled up onto the ridge, dislodging a clatter of falling stone, and just as it found its footing it saw him.

For a long moment the two of them stood quite still, staring at each other. Connor felt the sweat chill on his neck. Slowly he reached for the small Leica that he kept in his pocket and at the same time felt the wind around him lift, and he saw the flames on the elk's antlers fan sideways and he heard the fire beyond it bellow.

The animal was in his viewfinder now and it raised its muzzle proudly as if posing for a portrait. Connor pressed the button and at the sound of the shutter the elk turned and vanished. Distantly he heard a voice calling him.

'Hey, Connor! We got a fire to fight here.'

He picked up his pack and swung it over his shoulder.

THAT NIGHT THEY SNATCHED a couple of hours' sleep in a sheltered shoulder of the mountain through which the fire had already passed. They worked shifts, checking for hot spots where the fire still smouldered in roots and stumps and crevices. The beams of their headlamps sent shadows jagging on the blackened earth as they made their slow patrol among the charred scrub. And all the while the fire kept up its muffled roar around the corner of the mountain.

Connor woke around one o'clock, feeling hungry and cold. He pulled his sleeping-bag around his shoulders and lay on his back.

The image of the burning elk had haunted him all night. He wondered if the elk had lived and if so what lonely vigil it now kept and where. Then he cussed himself for allowing it such rampant access to his thoughts.

It was with relief that he heard Hank Thomas starting to wake those who were still asleep. Connor sat up and rubbed his eyes. He fitted his headlamp and switched it on, then hauled himself out of his sleeping-bag and set about organising his gear.

'How you doing, cowboy?' Hank called.

'OK. I could handle a steak and a beer.'

'I'll get on the radio right away.'

Others chimed in with their fantasy orders while they packed their gear. Ice cream, pizza, chocolate milk shakes.

'So when's that lazy good-for-nothing musician friend of yours going to grace us with his presence?' Hank asked.

'Flies in Saturday.'

'I hear he's in love.'

'I figure he must be. He's bringing her with him.'

'Is she a fire-fighter or what?'

'Got enough on her hands fighting Ed off,' said Donna Kiamoto, a 'snookie', or second-season jumper, from Wisconsin.

'No,' Connor said. 'She's going to be working on some wilderness programme. Kids who've got into trouble with the law.'

'I know it,' Hank said. 'Out of Helena. They're a good outfit.'

Hank's radio squawked into life and everyone hushed to listen. A helicopter was on its way to make a water drop on the flank of the fire nearest to them. Hank reported that they were moving out to cut another line. Soon they were all packed and ready to hike.

'OK, boys and girls,' Hank said. 'Unless anyone wants a shower from that helicopter, I suggest we get our backsides out of here.'

BY THE TIME they got back to the base it was just before midnight on Friday. Driving back into town Connor was so tired he almost fell asleep at the wheel of his truck. He collapsed on his bed still wearing his clothes and boots and slept for twelve hours.

He and Ed were renting the same two-bedroom apartment they'd taken the previous summer. It was on the top floor of a ramshackle pale blue clapboard house on the east side of town.

He opened his eyes just past noon and showered, shaved and dressed in blue jeans and a white T-shirt. And after he'd made himself some coffee and then cooked a brunch of ham and eggs and fried potatoes, it was getting on for two o'clock. He just had time to go to the studio and process the roll of film he'd shot on the mountain before Ed and Julia flew in.

Outside, the heat was shimmering off the sidewalks. He walked along Front Street, hugging the shade where he could find it. The darkroom he used was tucked among some garages in a backstreet off North Higgins. It was one narrow room with a studio at one end and the darkroom area boxed off at the other. The place belonged to a friend who worked for the local newspaper. She had given him a key to the studio so that he could use it whenever he liked.

Connor let himself in and switched on the lights. The air was hot and dank and smelt of chemicals and he left the door open until he'd got the air conditioning going. When everything was ready, he shut the door, turned out the main lights and took the film from his pocket. He worked carefully, taking his time.

He had taken pictures ever since he was a child, and in his late teens and early twenties he made a few dollars here and there selling skiing and climbing pictures to one or two magazines who liked his work. But it was smoke jumping that gave him his first big break.

It had happened three years ago, his and Ed's rookie season. It turned into one of the driest summers on record and forest fires became big news, especially the ones sweeping through Yellowstone Park. Connor always took a pocket camera with him. And one day, almost by accident, he took this breathtaking picture of Ed, alone on a ridge, swinging his pulaski, silhouetted against a wall of flames.

He got in touch with a photo agency in New York and the picture was printed on the front page of the *New York Times* and in newspapers and magazines all over the world. It earned Connor more money than he'd ever seen, and with it he paid off all the debts that had accumulated on his mother's ranch and still had enough to buy some new cameras and lenses. Back in Boston that fall, Ed had the Yellowstone photograph of his silhouette blown up five feet wide and hung it on his wall.

The two of them had met some years earlier when Ed was a freshman at the university in Missoula and Connor was wondering if he was going to be a ranch hand all his life. Every summer, throughout the West, the Forest Service took on casual 'pounders' to fight back-country fires. Pounding was a lot less glamorous than smoke jumping but you had to do it for several seasons before you could even apply to be a jumper. Connor and Ed had found themselves side by side, cutting line on the same crew, and Connor, who already had a season of pounding under his belt, had gone along with the tradition of giving the college-kid rookies a hard time.

In the macho world of fire-fighting, Edward Cavendish Tully was an easy target. He was from a wealthy family in Lexington, Kentucky, and was studying music and, at first, for both these facts, along with his slight southern drawl, the round gold-rimmed spectacles and aristocratic good looks, he was mercilessly teased. But he was as fit and tough as the best of them and took the taunts with such good humour that soon he was liked by the whole crew. On top of all this, it turned out that this classical music scholar also played lead guitar in a college band and could do a more than passable impression of Jimi Hendrix.

Connor was even more impressed when he found out that since the age of six Ed had been diabetic and needed to inject himself with insulin before every meal. Ed had something of a struggle persuading those in charge of selection at the Missoula base that his diabetes wasn't going to be a problem. But he excelled himself in training and managed to convince them that his condition would in no way interfere with his ability to do the job.

It was an attraction of opposites: Ed the extrovert intellectual, always ready with a joke or a story or an opinion on anything, and Connor the level, laconic one. What they shared was a passion for the outdoors. On their days off they would go climbing or fly-fishing or canoeing. The fires they fought that first summer forged a deep and durable friendship. They even invented their own private ritual. It came about when they were cutting line one day and the wind changed and the fire blew up and they suddenly found themselves, just the two of them, surrounded by flame.

'Hey, man!' Ed called. 'We're in the heart of the fire!'

And for some weird reason, without any rehearsal, they had both put their clenched right fists to their chests and solemnly declaimed 'Hearts of fire!' and then given each other a high-five. It was only a kind of mock macho joke and they laughed about it afterwards. But they'd done it ever since before every fire they'd fought.

After he graduated, Ed had moved to Boston, where he'd stayed ever since. Yet every summer he managed to come back to Montana and the two of them would spend some months together, fighting fires and having fun. Ed loved to help out on the ranch. It was only a small spread and since Connor's father died, twelve years earlier, mother and son had had to handle pretty much everything on their own.

From the roll of film that he was processing now, Connor was only really interested in one frame. His heart had beaten a little faster as soon as he held the negative up to the light and saw that it was there. The moment the negative was dry enough he had gone straight for a ten-by-eight print. It was in the tray now and as he rocked it, letting the developer swill slowly to and fro across the paper, he could see the elk starting to appear, as if through a haze of smoke, just as it had on the mountain.

In that fraction of a moment when he had taken the picture, the animal had lifted its head and turned it to a three-quarter profile and in so doing had sent the flames leaping from its antlers in a furious jagged swirl. But it wasn't this, nor the ripple of flames along its charred back, that made Connor shiver again. It was the look in the animal's eye. The message it conveyed was not of fear itself but rather of some fearful admonition.

ONE OF THE MANY THINGS she admired about Ed was the effortless way he fell asleep. No matter where he was, no matter how much chaos was going on around him, he could close his eyes and rest his head and before you could count to twenty he was away. On this occasion, the resting place was Julia's shoulder. Ed had insisted she take the window seat so she would have the better view of Montana when they flew over.

It was more than four months now since Ed had called to claim his wipers, and Julia was shocked at how quickly the two of them had become what her mother, with a disparaging tone, called 'an item'.

Since breaking off her engagement to Michael the previous spring, Julia hadn't dated anyone and was enjoying a life free from romantic complication. Michael was at Harvard Law School and was handsome, blond, brilliant and seriously rich. If not dazzled by all this, Julia had, for a while at least, been sufficiently distracted so as not to notice another of Michael's attributes. He was boring.

Her best friend and room-mate, Linda Rosner, had pointed this out the very first time she laid eyes on Michael, and had broken open the champagne when Julia broke off the engagement. The whole experience probably accounted for why the next man in Julia's life should be a passionate musician from the South who liked to parachute onto forest fires.

The effect of Ed playing those songs just for her had been devastating. She was an instant pushover. Well, almost instant. They had gone to bed on their third date, though had he asked—and had Linda not been sitting there all eyes and ears—Julia would have happily succumbed when he showed up for his wipers.

Like Julia, Linda was a New Yorker, though from a much wealthier family. They had met at art college where Linda was a member of the Neo-Gothic Radicals, which seemed to involve wearing a lot of black lipstick and dressing up like a distant cousin of the Addams family. After two years as a struggling artist, she'd dumped the weird clothes and black lipstick and gone to law school.

The moment Ed stepped into the apartment that night, Julia knew he had Linda's seal of approval. They opened a bottle of wine and then another and sat talking until two in the morning. Ed had them both helpless with laughter about the flood at his apartment, and when he told them that as well as being a musician and composer he was also a smoke jumper, Julia thought Linda was going to swoon.

Now, four months later, Ed and Julia were still at that stage where it was hard to keep their hands off each other, and the idea of being apart for the summer didn't appeal to either of them. Ed had therefore suggested that she should try to fix a vacation job in Montana.

When Julia was at art college she used to spend June to September working in Colorado with an organisation called WAY, Wilderness and Youth. The kids who went there were young offenders, sent by the courts as a last chance. In groups of up to a dozen they were taken out into the back country for two months. They were given a pair of hiking boots, a sleeping-bag, a waterproof poncho and a tarpaulin. With the support and supervision of four field staff—of which Julia was one—they had to learn how to survive in the wild.

Until then Julia had always assumed that she was going to try to make a living as a painter. But what she witnessed during those three summers, the transformation of some of those kids from apparent no-hopers into confident, social young adults, had such a profound effect on her that she changed her mind. She went on to get a master's degree in educational psychology and ever since had been working as an art therapist at a school in Boston for children with special needs.

Two years ago WAY had started a second centre, in Helena, Montana, and in one simple phone call Julia managed to get herself hired for the summer. WAY's Colorado field director, Glen Nielsen, had moved up there to run it and, when she called him, he said he was thrilled to have her back.

How much she and Ed would see of each other she didn't know. The WAY staff rotated in shifts. You did eight days with your group and then another team took over while you took a six-day break. Ed would get either Fridays and Saturdays off or Sundays and Mondays.

She felt his head stir now on her shoulder.

'Are we there yet?' he said like a drowsy child.

'We're on our way home. You slept the whole summer.'

He kissed her cheek then put on his glasses and leaned over her to look out of the window as the plane descended towards Missoula.

On arrival at the airport, when they stepped out of the plane, the air was laced with the smell of fuel and sun-baked asphalt. Even so, Ed filled his lungs with it as if it were the sweetest he'd ever breathed. He put his arm round her and they walked to the arrivals gate.

'There he is.'

Ed waved and through the glass of the arrivals lounge Julia saw a tall young man with long blond hair waving a cowboy hat at them. The crowd of passengers moved slowly and it took a long time to get to the gate. At last they reached him.

'Excuse me,' Ed said. 'Is this the way to the fire?'

'Too late, man. We already put 'em all out.'

Ed opened his arms and they gave each other one of those funny man-to-man hugs that involve slapping each other's backs.

'Hey, old buddy,' Ed said. 'How's it going?'

'Good. Better for seeing you.' He turned to Julia and held out his hand. 'You must be the famous Julia. Welcome to Montana.'

'Thank you.'

His hand was hard and calloused and he was fixing her with his pale blue eyes in such a direct and steady way that it made her feel almost shy, as if he could somehow see inside her head.

On the way to the baggage hall and while they waited by the carousel, Ed bombarded Connor with questions. He wanted to know who was jumping this summer, what fires they'd fought so far and where, what the weather forecasters were saying and so on.

Their bags arrived and they wheeled everything on a trolley out to the parking lot. They dumped the bags in the back of Connor's old pale blue Chevy pick-up and climbed into the cab, where they sat three abreast with Julia in the middle. On the way into town Connor asked about her job with WAY and she told him what she knew about it from her time in Colorado.

They ate that night at a little upstairs diner just across the Clark Fork River and afterwards strolled back over the bridge. When they got back to the apartment, Connor made some coffee and they sat round the kitchen table talking. Ed asked how the photography was going and Connor said he'd had a couple of commissions lately but on the whole things were quiet. He went across the room and came back with a large brown envelope, pulling a picture from it which he said he'd printed only that afternoon. He handed it first to Ed, who was sitting across the table from Julia, so only he could see it. His eyes widened.

'Wow. What on earth is that? Is it an elk?'

'Yeah. He just stepped out of the fire.'

'What happened next?'

'I don't know. One moment he was there and the next he was gone.'

'Connor, man, that's one hell of a picture.'

Ed handed it to Julia. It took her a moment to focus and when she saw what it was she took a sudden sharp breath.

'It's terrible.'

Ed laughed. 'So much for compliments.'

But Connor wasn't laughing. He was staring at her as if he knew exactly what she meant. She handed him the picture.

'I'm sorry, but I can't look at that.'

Connor took it from her without a word, and slid it into its envelope. Ed made a joke about Julia being a tough critic of his music too but she was too shocked by what she'd seen to catch it. She stood up. Ed looked suddenly worried.

'Julia? Are you OK?'

'I'm sorry, I'm just so tired. I'll leave you guys to it.'

She kissed Ed on the top of his head. He said he wouldn't be long.

'Good night, Connor.'

''Night, Julia.'

She brushed her teeth in the bathroom, then went to their bedroom and undressed. Connor had given them the bigger room and thoughtfully pushed the two single beds together.

She got into bed and pulled the covers up over her shoulders against the chill she'd felt within her since seeing Connor's photograph. She couldn't get the image out of her head. Ed had called it 'one hell of a picture' without realising that was literally what it was. But Connor had understood.

 CHAPTER TWO

The eagle rose in languid circles on the thermal, its shadow sliding across the canyon wall that glowed like baked ochre in the afternoon sun. Every so often the eagle called and the sound wafted away down the canyon in an echoing lament. What, if anything, the bird made of the straggled band of beings many hundred feet below was impossible to tell, but the woe of its cry was never more apt. They came trudging along a steep trail that wound beside the bed of a dried-up creek. Their heads were bowed, their shoulders slumped, their faces caked with dirt and sweat.

They were passing through a tangle of dead pines that had been ripped from their roots by a torrent of snowmelt. And here they halted while one of their number stumbled away from the trail and hid herself behind a clump of willow scrub.

'Let's hear the call, Skye!' There was a pause. 'Come on, Skye. You've gotta call your number!'

Behind the screen of scrub, Skye McReedie, half-breed, cop killer and all-round no-hoper, squatted with her teeth clenched and her trousers hitched around her knees, peeing into the dust. She was damned if she'd play their dumbass kids' games.

'Skye, if you don't call it, we'll have to come looking.'

Skye closed her eyes to contain her anger. It was so humiliating. You couldn't even take a piss without them being on top of you. That stuck-up little missy-prissy Julia, the one yelling at her right now, was the worst of all. She was always so goddamn nice. You'd think she'd understand how tough it was for her. There were ten kids on this chain gang and Skye was the only girl.

'OK, sorry, Skye, but I'm coming in there!'

'Fuck you,' Skye muttered. She angrily hauled up her trousers and fastened them. 'Seven!' she shouted.

'Keep calling it, Skye.'

'Seven! Seven! Seven! Seven!'

She stomped out from behind the bushes and kept shouting her number all the way back to the others, until she was standing right in front of Julia and shouting it a foot away from her nose.

'Seven! Seven! Seven! OK? Is that OK now?'

'Yes, Skye. That's fine. Thank you.'

Mitch, the self-appointed bigmouth of the group, made some smart remark about how pissed Skye was and she wheeled round and told him to shut up or she'd kick his face in.

'OK, OK, everybody,' Julia said. 'Let's circle up, right now.'

There were groans, but the other staff—Scott, Katie and Laura—started marshalling everyone and soon, for the umpteenth time that day, they were all standing in a circle looking at each other in silence.

'OK,' Julia said calmly. 'We all know by now what happens when someone uses abusive or inappropriate language. So, Skye, when you're ready, we'd like to hear twenty alternatives to what you just said. And then we'll have twenty alternatives from Mitch.'

Mitch gawped with offended innocence and there was a ripple of laughter. At seventeen he was the oldest in the group. He was tall and dark and muscular and knew exactly how good-looking and smart he was. Skye couldn't stand him. They all fell silent again. Everyone was staring at Skye and she was still staring at the ground.

'Well, Skye,' Julia said. 'There are no deadlines here. We've got all the time in the world, so all we're going to be late for is supper.'

Skye sighed. 'OK,' she said. 'Like, I could have said: "Oh please, dear Mitch, please don't make jokes about poor little me."'

'Good. That's one. Let's try and steer clear of sarcasm, though.'

It took another half-hour for her to come up with the other nineteen. And then almost as long again for Mitch to do his twenty. And at last, after they'd all taken a drink from their water bottles, they shouldered their packs and set off again up the trail.

When the judge had told her he was going to send her on this programme Skye hadn't had any idea what it might involve. All she knew was that it sure sounded better than being sent to jail like that maniac Sean. And for the first month it had been a breeze.

They'd lived in a disused barracks just outside Helena and although it was a pain being the only girl in the group, and you had to get up at the crack of dawn and do all kinds of dumb things like jogging twice a day and hoisting the flag every morning, the rest of the time all you had to do was sit around and be 'evaluated', which meant answering the same boring questions she had been asked a million times before by probation officers and case managers and social workers and shrinks.

After a month at the barracks, suddenly, one night last week, they were given this big spaghetti meal, handed a sleeping-bag and a few other things, bundled onto a bus and, four hours later, dumped in the middle of nowhere. For two days, with barely a bite to eat, they had hiked thirty miles through the mountains, which Skye figured was supposed to shock them or break them, and because of that she kept her head down and just did it.

On the third night they arrived at a clearing and there was Glen, the programme director, to meet them and some other staff, all smiling and joking and saying how well they'd all done.

On that first evening, as they sat round the campfire, Glen told them that they were going to have to learn how to make fires with a bow drill, like Native Americans did. Glen looked like some old hippie with his long blond hair in a ponytail and wispy beard.

All of the group, he went on, would have to master the bow-drill technique. Each night it would be somebody's turn to make the fire, and if he or she couldn't do it, then that night no one would get hot food. Which was fine for him because the next morning he got in his truck and went home, leaving Julia in charge.

They all had to make their own little bow-drill set after combing the forest for the right bits of wood and, in the five days that had since passed, all but two of the group had learned how to use them. The only two who hadn't were Skye and a kid called Lester whose head was cooked from all the crack he'd done. Skye figured she could make a bow-drill fire easily enough, but she was damned if she was going to try. Last night it had been her turn and everyone had to eat cold food. She wasn't popular, but who gave a shit?

The hiking since that first forced march had been easier. No one told them where they were or where they were headed, and whenever anyone asked, Julia just smiled that annoying, cute little smile of hers and said it was the journey that mattered, not the destination.

Skye was one of Julia's 'primaries', which meant that Skye was supposed to go to her for help, cry on her shoulder and confide her innermost secrets. Yeah, right. Julia was walking behind her now as they made their way up the canyon. In front was Byron, a boy from Great Falls, who'd stabbed someone in a robbery. He had straggly red hair and his skin was as pale as an albino's. Skye liked him. He tried to act tough like the others, but you sometimes got a glimpse of the sweet kid he really was. He was the only boy in the group who was at all friendly towards her.

The light in the canyon was fading. For half a mile the trail grew steep and treacherous with rocks that slipped beneath their boots. Then, as they rounded a ridge, the land fell away before them and opened into a meadow with a lake at its centre. Far beyond it, the mountains they had glimpsed throughout the day were still catching the last rays of the sun and their reflection shone pink and unruffled on the surface of the lake. The group stopped and stood in silence, gathering their breath and taking in the view.

'Is this where we camp?' Byron asked.

'That's right,' Julia said.

'Cool.'

'Pretty enough for you, Skye?'

Skye shrugged and fiddled with the strap of her pack though it didn't need fixing. 'Why should I care?'

THEY SAT IN A CIRCLE round the fire, warming their feet against the flames. This was Lester's fire, started with his own bow and drill without help. And the pride he felt was plain for all to see. He sat straight, with his head held high and a permanent lopsided smile. The sight of him made Julia feel warm inside.

Lester was fifteen years old and most of those years had been spent in institutions. Two years ago he had overdosed and spent three days in a coma that had left him permanently damaged. He was sitting between Mitch and Katie, a bouncy and slightly irritating

PE student from Montana State University, Billings.

Skye was sitting between Byron and Scott and was staring into the fire as if she wished it would consume her. Scott was a philosophy graduate from Denver and had done three seasons with WAY in Colorado. He had a wise and gentle manner that the kids related to. During supper he had been quietly trying to engage Skye in the conversation. But she was having none of it. She looked so sad that Julia had to fight an urge to go over and hug her. When Lester succeeded in making his fire, Julia had seen on Skye's face the realisation that she was now the only obstacle between the group and a hot meal every night.

FOR THREE DAYS there was rain without pause and it moistened both land and air enough to give the Missoula smoke jumpers a few days' calm. Not that calm was ever too welcome. Rain meant fewer fires and fewer fires meant less overtime, less hazard pay and a lot less fun. A smoke jumper's definition of what constituted a 'good' summer bore little resemblance to anyone else's. During a 'normal' summer, the Missoula base got five or six fire calls a week, whereas a 'good' summer could bring that many each day.

Until the heavens opened, ten days ago, this summer had been looking good. Since the rain stopped there had only been four calls, all to minor fires that were quickly put out. But the skies had cleared, humidity was falling and the new heat wave looked set to stay. And as the barometer and fire risk rose, so did the jumpers' mood.

The smoke-jumper base lay in a long and shallow valley just south of Missoula Airport. It was a cluster of mundane white buildings and an airstrip where planes stood ready to roll at a moment's notice. Looming to one side were the towers and platforms and high-wire rigging of the training units.

The epicentre of the base was known as 'the loft', a warren of interconnecting rooms where the jumpers worked when they weren't on a fire. At its hub was the lounge, a long room with a linoleum floor and low armchairs set against whitewashed walls. It was here, every morning, that the jumpers gathered for roll call. Leading off it were the operations room, the loadmaster's where the fire-fighting gear and supplies were sorted and the ready room where every jumper had a bin. Then there was the manufacturing room, where parachutes and jumpsuits were made and repaired. And, finally, the tower, where parachutes were hoisted for inspection after every jump.

On this particular July morning, five Missoula smoke jumpers, all male, were sitting demurely at sewing machines in the manufacturing room. Ed was between Connor and Hank Thomas. Next to Hank was a rookie called Phil Wheatley, whom Hank had already nick-named Pee-Wee, and Chuck Hamer, a snookie who looked like a bear with a crew cut.

It was a tradition that jumpers made and repaired much of their own clothing and gear. Ed was stitching the last seam of a new red waterproof top. The siren sounded just as he snipped the thread.

'We have a jump request at the Lolo National Forest. The jumpers will be Tully, Ford, Hamer . . .'

Chuck Hamer let out a whoop and the sound of the loudspeaker was drowned for a moment as everyone headed for the door. They didn't have to listen for they all knew who was on the jump list.

'. . . Schneider, Lennox, Pfeffer . . .'

The routine was that those who weren't scheduled to jump helped those who were. Within seconds they were all in the ready room and by the time Ed got to his bin Donna Kiamoto was there holding out his jumpsuit for him to climb into. The suits were padded and made of Kevlar.

'There you go, soldier.'

'Thanks.'

It was Donna's birthday in two days' time and she was throwing a party. Ed and three friends he used to have a band with had promised to play.

'If you're not back by Friday night, Tully, you're dead meat.'

'Well, if it goes that long I'll be in overtime, so at least I'll be rich dead meat.'

Everyone laughed. Donna helped Ed fasten his suit and then he reached into his bin for his boots. Connor was already suited and booted and in his harness. He bent forward while someone attached his parachute, then clipped on his reserve chute and personal gear bag and picked up his helmet, ready to roll.

'Come on, you tired-ass bunch of slowpokes, what's keeping you? We've got a plane to catch.'

FROM THE WINDOW of the Twin Otter, the fire looked a halfhearted affair, six or seven acres at most. And with little wind, it didn't seem to be going anywhere in a hurry. Then again, you never could tell.

The plane made another pass over the fire while the spotter and assistant spotter squatted by the open door, hooked in for safety, trying to figure out a likely jump spot.

They were flying at about 110 miles an hour at 1,500 feet and the spotter had to yell to make himself heard over the noise of the engines when he showed them the jump spot, a thin clearing that ran down the mountainside in a crooked green scar. They passed over it three more times, dropping a pair of crepe-paper streamers on each pass to measure the wind drift. The streamers were pink and blue and yellow and weighted with sand and Ed watched them snake and flutter away below him towards the trees.

'Looks like we've got about three hundred yards of wind drift,' the spotter shouted. 'Everybody see the spot? OK, let's do it.'

The jumpers were all putting on their gloves and helmets and personal gear bags and going through their final checks. Ed and Connor were jumping first stick, which meant that Ed was going to be the first man out of the plane. Once they'd landed, that made him the incident commander. He could feel the adrenalin begin to course through his veins and he took some long deep breaths to calm himself. Connor stepped close so that their helmets touched.

Ed turned to face him and they put their fists to their chests and looked each other in the eye.

'Hearts of fire!'

They said it together then gave each other a high-five.

'OK, fellas,' the spotter yelled. 'We're going to come around on final now. Get in the door!'

Ed stepped forward and squatted in the door, grasping the sides of the doorway with both hands. He felt the plane tilt and watched the forest rotate below him as the plane came around and steadied into its final approach.

'OK, we're on final!' the spotter yelled. 'Get ready!'

Ed felt a sharp slap on his left shoulder from the spotter and he launched himself with all his might through the doorway and out into the thin blue air.

'One-one-thousand . . . two-one-thousand . . .'

The rush of air seemed to suck the words from his head.

'Three-one-thousand . . . four-one-thousand . . .'

He braced himself and an instant later he heard a whoosh and a crack and he was jerked like a fish on a line. His body skewed and straightened and he looked up and saw the white, blue and yellow dome of his canopy billowing above him. And there was Connor, higher and to his right, the lines of his chute streaming out and then the chute filling. And the plane was gone and the only sound was the whisper and flutter of the two parachutes.

Ed could see the pale green brush of the clearing revealing itself before him now, but he didn't think he was going to clear the final line of trees. He toggled hard to the left surfing the treetops and then he was out and clear and over the trees and floating down into the pale green calm of the clearing. He hit the ground with both feet and rolled and was standing again before his chute had time to settle. He felt like taking a bow. He took off his harness and was just climbing out of his jumpsuit when he heard Connor's voice.

'Shit! Ow! *Ow!* Goddamn it!'

There was a loud cracking and splintering of timber and then Connor's boots appeared through the branches of one of the big lodgepole pines, followed by the rest of him. For a bad moment Ed thought he was going to fall all the way down. But after about ten feet his lines snagged and held and Connor hung there, swinging gently to and fro about seventy feet above the ground.

Ed stood looking up at him and Connor lifted his face guard and hung there, looking down. Ed was trying to keep a straight face.

'Hi,' he said. 'You OK?'

'Yeah, I'm terrific.'

'I bet the view's really great up there, huh? Need any help?'

'Not from you, asshole.'

Ed laughed and started gathering his chute. Connor found a foothold on a branch then he reached into his pants pocket for his letdown rope and tied himself off to the tree. The Twin Otter passed overhead and a few moments later Chuck Hamer and Phil Wheatley came gliding into the jump spot. Both made perfect landings.

'Hey, Connor,' Chuck said. 'You picking apples up there? You're out of luck, man, that there's a pine tree.'

Connor didn't reply. He was trying to disentangle his chute. By the time he was ready to lower himself out of the tree, he had a full audience. All the other seven jumpers had hit the spot and every one of them made some smart remark. As Connor slid down the rope they all cheered. He waved a finger at them.

'Thank you. Thank you all so much.'

When he was only three feet from the ground he let go of the rope and jumped, and as he hit the ground his right leg buckled and he cried out and fell. Ed ran over.

'What happened?'

'My ankle. I landed on a rock or something. Shit.' He sat up and hoisted the bottom of his jumpsuit. He undid his bootlaces and pulled down his sock. Ed saw that the leg was already swelling fast.

'Hell, Connor. You're such a goddamn attention-seeker.'

'I know. I just want to be loved.'

They radioed for a helicopter and Connor was lifted out and the seven remaining jumpers set about putting out the fire. They got the tail under control first, then cut line along the north and south flanks. The wind dropped and with the night came air that was cool and moist and the fire lay down like a lamb. The following day they starved the head with a burnout. The lines held and the night was spent mopping up. By the second dawn it was done and dusted.

Ed and his friends played at Donna Kiamoto's party and played so well they weren't allowed to stop. 'Great Balls of Fire' got three encores. He hadn't expected Julia to be there, but it was her staff changeover day and she'd managed to slip away early. Ed kept his eyes locked on her while he sang. She danced with just about everyone, except poor old Connor, who sat watching and drinking too many beers, his bandaged leg propped up on a chair. The ankle had turned out not to be broken, just sprained, but badly enough to stop him jumping for a while.

Connor was finding it hard to take his eyes off Julia. He'd found it hard since the moment they'd met. There was something about her that just hauled you in. Her laugh, her dark brown eyes and how they creased up when she smiled—Connor stopped himself, ashamed that he should even notice such things. This was his best friend's girlfriend, for heaven's sake.

Ed and Julia helped him home, one on either side, his arms draped round their shoulders and Ed carrying his crutches. It was nearly dawn. Connor was singing 'Great Balls of Fire', while Ed and Julia laughed and teased him. They helped him up the stairs and he was going on about what a beautiful couple they made. He said they were the most beautiful couple in the whole world.

'It's true,' he slurred. 'You're just . . . beautiful. Julia, you're . . . beautiful. I don't mean like, to look at . . .'

'Hey, thanks, Connor.'

'No, I mean . . . You are, of course you are. God, you *are*. But you know what I mean. Ed, you're real lucky to have a woman like this. And, Julia, you're lucky too, to have this . . . ugly old sonofabitch.'

They lowered him onto his bed and Ed pulled the boot off his left foot. Connor held up his bandaged foot which had no boot and Julia began to laugh again so that she had to sit down on the bed.

'You're not wearing one on that foot,' Ed said.

'What? Oh.'

'You go to sleep now.'

Connor suddenly reached out and held on to them both. He'd lifted his head off the pillow and there was a sad urgency in those pale blue eyes that Ed had never seen before and didn't understand.

'I love you guys. I really love you, you know?'

Ed ruffled his hair and Julia leaned over him and gently kissed his forehead. 'We love you too, cowboy,' Ed said. 'Now sleep.'

 # CHAPTER THREE

Julia was lying on her back in her sleeping-bag, looking at the moon and listening. For the fifth time in half an hour, she looked at her watch. It was twenty past three. He was late.

Julia was lying between Byron and Skye and, by the sound of their breathing, both seemed to be asleep, though with Skye you never could tell. Sometimes Julia would wake in the night and find her staring into space, tears rolling down her cheeks. The first time she had reached out and touched Skye on the shoulder and asked if she was all right and Skye had quickly turned her back without replying.

There was something about the girl that moved Julia more than any child she had ever worked with. One of the basic ideas of the programme was to let peer pressure work on hostile and uncooperative attitudes. Those who caused difficulty for the others soon learned the consequences of their actions. Many of these children had been so assaulted by the world in which they had grown up that simply to survive they had built walls around themselves. And to watch these walls crumble and to witness instead a dawning of empathy and trust was almost magical. And it was happening with this group already. Even Mitch, the one who considered himself so hard, even he was showing signs of softening.

But not Skye. For more than six weeks now the girl had kept her defences in place, even strengthened them. She seemed to have figured out the minimum level of cooperation and stuck to it. She spoke only when spoken to and with no elaboration. Her face was locked into a mask of haughty indifference. Only on those rare occasions when she looked you in the eye could you glimpse the pain.

At the heart of the programme was the nightly campfire. Julia had seen it cast its spell upon group after group, infecting the students with light and warmth. It was where they ate and laughed and told stories, where they discussed what had happened during the day and where even the hardest kids seemed able to open their hearts. But on every night that it was Skye's turn to make the fire, the group sat in darkness, ate their cold cornmeal or oatmeal in silence and turned in early. They resented it, some of them deeply, but they had grown tired of telling her so. Apart from the staff, the only friend she had was Byron. Skye had rejected him many times but still he stuck by her and defended her.

Julia had spent many hours discussing Skye with the programme therapy team. They agreed that it was time for something radical. They would take Skye on a 'quest'.

The quest was the programme's ultimate tool, used only when there was some sort of deadlock. The student was removed from the group and taken by two staff members on a two-day journey that was both physically and psychologically gruelling. Its effects could be dramatic and so, deliberately, was its initiation. Which was why Glen was coming out now, at the dead of night, to join them.

At least, he was supposed to be. He'd said he would be there at three and it was now after three thirty. Then Julia heard the snap of a branch down by the creek and she peered through the shadows and saw a figure. She eased herself silently out of her sleeping-bag, put on her boots and made her way down the slope towards him.

'Hey, I'm sorry. I got lost.'

' "Wilderness Director Gets Lost." That's a good story.'

'Tell a soul and you're fired.'

They stood awhile, talking in whispers. Julia was feeling nervous.

'Boy, I hope this doesn't freak her out.'

'It will, a little. And that's good. Are you ready?'

'SKYE? SKYE! IT'S ME, Julia. And Glen.'

Skye sat up, rubbing her eyes. 'What's going on?' She looked around her. The other kids were sitting up and looking at her.

'We're going to do something special,' Glen said. 'Can we have some light here?'

Julia had a flashlight and Katie, Laura and Scott switched theirs on too. Skye shielded her eyes. Her head was still swirling with dreams and she felt bewildered by all these people.

'What's going on? What time is it?'

'OK, everybody,' Glen announced. 'I'd like everyone to circle up here, please. Quick as you can.'

There were murmurs and groans, but in a minute everyone was standing in a circle. At night they all had to hand in their boots and pants to deter them from running away, so some, like Skye, now stood with their sleeping-bags around them and some were just bare-legged. When everyone was silent, Glen went on.

'OK. I'm sorry to wake you up like this, but I've come out here tonight for a very important reason. Can anyone guess what that reason might be?'

Mitch put up a hand. 'Skye. It's gotta be something to do with Skye.'

'Good. That's right. I'm here because of Skye.'

Skye stared at the ground. She was shocked, but damned if she was going to show it.

Then Glen announced that he and Julia were going to take Skye away on a 'quest' and he asked if anyone had any idea what that might be. Another boy, Wayne, put up a finger.

'Like, looking for something? Like *Dragon Quest* or something.' There was laughter. Wayne grinned at Mitch. 'It's a video game. You have to find, like, this sacred key.'

'Uh-huh,' Glen nodded. 'That's exactly it. We're going on a journey of our own for a couple of days to help Skye find a key.'

Skye raised her eyes to the stars. These guys never knew when to quit. It was all so embarrassing and stupid.

'A *key*?' she said. 'A key to what?'

'What do *you* think?' Glen asked.

'I haven't the faintest idea. And you know what? Tell you the truth, I don't give a—' She looked down. 'I don't care.'

Glen nodded thoughtfully. 'OK, Skye. Then, we'll have to try and find the key to that too. So, if you and Julia would get dressed and gather all your gear, we'll be setting off in five minutes. Thank you all. I'm sorry we've disturbed your sleep, but this is an important moment for Skye. Maybe you would like to wish her well.'

The only ones who did were Byron and the staff. The rest just shuffled their feet and muttered.

Skye got dressed, pulled on her boots and got her stuff together.

Her heart was beating hard and her head was whirling. She felt proud and scared and defiant all at the same time. If they thought they could break her, they had another think coming.

They hiked in single file, Glen leading the way with his headlamp and Julia behind. They walked in silence, just the crunch of their boots on the pine needles. It surprised her that neither of them spoke, because she had expected them to start banging on at her right away, but maybe that wasn't the idea.

She had no wristwatch and no notion of how long they hiked, but it was many hours. It began to get light as they headed downhill and out of the trees and into a meadow filled with wild flowers. They came to a narrow creek of tumbling foam and dark swirling pools. By one of the pools there was a shelf of rock and here they stopped and put down their packs. They gathered wood and Glen lit a fire and cooked oatmeal and raisins, on which they sprinkled cinnamon and brown sugar.

As they ate, Skye looked up along the valley and in the far, far distance saw a mountain shaped like a pyramid. Glen saw her gazing at it and told her that was where they were headed.

Then he started telling one of those dumb stories the staff always told when they wanted to teach you some great lesson. This particular story was called 'The Wolf and the Rock' and it was about a little wolf cub called Nooshka-Lalooshka. One day this wolf cub was chasing a chipmunk and ran into a rock and really hurt himself, and all the other wolves laughed at him.

'The chipmunk got away and Nooshka-Lalooshka felt embarrassed and he told the others that he'd meant to crash into the rock and it hadn't hurt a bit. So they said, OK, if it didn't hurt, do it again. And he did. And this time it hurt even more and he got this big bloody bruise on his chest, but the other wolves roared with laughter and said how funny he was and how tough he must be.'

No prizes for guessing who this is supposed to be, Skye thought.

'And from then on whenever the wolves got bored, they'd say, hey, Nooshka-Lalooshka, do your rock trick for us! And if he said he didn't want to, they'd tell him he was chicken, so to prove he wasn't he'd crash into the rock again. His wound never had time to heal and as he grew older it got worse and infected his leg, until one day he found he couldn't run at all and could only collapse onto the rock instead of crashing into it. The other wolves got bored and said it wasn't fun to watch any more. They told him he was of no use to the pack and they banished him, and Nooshka-Lalooshka limped off, alone and forlorn, into the wilderness.

'Well, he got thinner and thinner and sadder and sadder and soon he didn't want to go on living. So he found a cave and he lay down in it and waited to die. But the next morning he woke up and there was this little pile of nuts right in front of him. He had just enough strength to eat them and they tasted good. And he felt a little better and slept all day. And when he woke up there was another pile of nuts and he ate them, wondering who had put them there. The next morning he pretended to be asleep but kept his eyes open just enough to keep watch.

'And after a while he saw a little old chipmunk, staggering along, carrying a great armful of nuts and dumping them down in front of him. And Nooshka-Lalooshka said, hey! And the chipmunk nearly jumped out of its skin and said, please, please don't eat me! And Nooshka-Lalooshka asked the chipmunk why would he be so kind to a wolf when everybody knows that wolves eat chipmunks? And the chipmunk said it was because once, long ago, a wolf had been very kind to him, and instead of eating him had let him go and crashed into a rock, just to make some other wolves laugh.'

Glen smiled, and for a moment or two nobody said anything.

'Is that it?' Skye said.

'Unless you want to take it any further,' Julia said.

'Like, the wolf grabs the chipmunk and bites his head off.'

'If that's how you want it to go.'

Skye looked away. There was another silence.

'So I guess I'm supposed to "identify" with someone in that story?'

'Well, do you?' Glen asked.

Skye shrugged. 'Yeah. I'm one of the nuts.'

Julia burst out laughing and then Glen started laughing too. Skye looked at them in amazement. Hell, it wasn't that funny. But Julia's shoulders were shaking helplessly and the more she laughed the more Glen laughed. Skye tried to keep her own face stony straight, but soon she just couldn't hold out any longer and she felt her lips begin to twitch and soon she was laughing too. And it felt so strange, as if some alien power had taken her over and was shaking her insides around, unlocking something there.

Then something even stranger happened. Although Skye was still laughing, she felt a heaving in her chest, like ocean waves breaking and shaking her whole body. And she felt tears begin to sluice down her cheeks and she heard her own laughter turn itself into a kind of convulsive animal howl. She cried for herself and for her whole life and the mess she'd made of it and for her mother and all that they both had suffered and for her long-lost father and for all the terrible things she'd done. For all this, she tilted her streaming face to the sky and wept and howled.

She felt their arms slip round her and hug her. It was the first loving touch of another human being that Skye had felt for a long time, and she had neither the strength nor the will to resist. She could tell that they were weeping too, and although it struck her as strange that these two people she barely knew should shed tears for her, she didn't doubt them. And for a long time the three of them clung together and wept.

HENRY'S WAS A MURKY CORRIDOR of a bar at the far end of North Higgins. Along the left-hand wall was a row of tall wooden tables where you could lean or perch precariously on stools. And it was at one of these, this particular summer's night, that Connor Ford sat staring morosely up at the TV news.

There were helicopter shots of a blazing mountainside and a plane flying in low. 'Fire-fighters from all over California have been unable to put out the blaze that has now been burning for five days,' the reporter was saying. 'And so today saw the arrival at Redding Airfield of sixteen smoke jumpers from Missoula, Montana.'

There was a raucous cheer from the bar. And there they were, stepping down from the plane, and Ed was among them. He had on his best movie-star face, a kind of shy but resolute grin.

Connor had done his best to persuade the personnel officer that his ankle was good enough for him to go with them. It was ten days since his fall and the swelling was almost gone, but yesterday he'd taken the mandatory PT test at the base, which involved running one and half miles in eleven minutes, and when the foreman saw him hobbling off he called him back and said sorry, there was no way he was going to Redding.

The news moved on to another story and Connor took the last swig from his bottle of soda. He hadn't touched alcohol since the night of Donna's party and still felt embarrassed that he'd made a fool of himself. He stood up and put on his hat.

Outside, the night air was balmy and the street was deserted. Connor strolled down towards the bridge, looking idly into the store windows. There was a little place that sold secondhand books and magazines and never seemed to shut, and on impulse Connor went inside. The guy who ran it knew him and said hello.

He spent about ten minutes browsing the shelves and finding nothing and was about to leave when a book caught his eye. It was about a British photographer called Larry Burrows, who had taken some of the most powerful pictures of the Vietnam War and had lost his life doing so. Connor bought the book for five dollars.

The apartment seemed oddly quiet without Ed, who was always yacking or singing. Connor undressed and took a glass of milk and the Burrows book to bed.

He didn't know much about Burrows except that he'd taken many extraordinary pictures for *Life* magazine and that he'd died when a helicopter in which he was travelling was shot down in Laos. Connor read the book from cover to cover in a couple of hours and was greatly moved.

Long after he had put the book down and turned out the light, Connor lay wondering whether he himself could summon the kind of courage that Burrows must have had to look horror in the face again and again. And somehow, for the first time, he knew with absolute clarity that one day he would find out.

ANOTHER WEEK WENT BY and Connor spent most of it doing odd jobs around the base. Ed was still down in Redding, but on Tuesday evening he called to say the fire was under control and the word was that they'd be back for the weekend. He asked how Connor's ankle was and Connor told him it was OK and Ed said good because he had a plan which he'd already talked over with Julia: a canoe trip in Idaho, on a stretch of the Salmon River that he and Connor had done a couple of times before. Ed said he'd try to hitch a ride with a fire crew from Boise who were heading home on Friday.

By the time Julia got back to Missoula on Thursday evening Connor had it all sorted out. He'd borrowed a pair of canoes and a second tent, got the camping gear ready and bought food. Julia was tired but in good spirits and he poured her a glass of wine and made her sit down while he cooked supper. And while he busied himself in the kitchen area, she sat on the couch and told him all that had happened, about the quest and how Skye had broken down, and then the walk to the mountain and how Skye had made her first bow-drill fire. And how Skye had talked and talked, as if a dam had broken inside the girl and sixteen years of repressed pain had flooded forth.

Julia's face was tanned and dirty from all her hiking and her hair had gone all straggly and she'd tied it up with a pale green bandanna. Connor had never seen her looking so lovely.

He'd bought a fillet of salmon and panfried it and they ate it with salad and some baby potatoes. Then they had blueberries and cream and coffee and sat talking for a long time.

The Larry Burrows book was on the table and Julia picked it up and flicked slowly through the pictures. She stopped at one in which a young girl was crouched over the body of her mother, howling distraught at the camera.

'Do you think it's heartless to take a picture like that?' she said.

'You mean rather than help her?'

Julia nodded, still staring at the child.

'No. A picture never tells what happened next. A lot of photographers help people when they can. But the most important thing, I guess, is to show the world what's going on.'

'I guess.'

She asked if she could borrow the book and Connor said sure, and then the phone rang and Julia reached for it. It was Ed.

Connor stood up and started clearing the dishes. He listened to her telling Ed some of the same things and found himself trying to detect some greater intimacy in her tone of voice, but he couldn't.

Julia handed him the phone and said she was going to have a bath. Connor listened while Ed told him about the fire. Finally they talked about the arrangements for the following day. The idea was to put the canoes in the river at a little town called Stanley. One of the Idaho fire-fighters with whom Ed had grown friendly lived near there and was going to give him a lift from Boise Airport. He figured they would get to Stanley around two o'clock.

As he undressed in his room, Connor could hear Julia in the bathroom and he could hear the splash of the water as she washed herself in the tub and he had to try hard to censor his thoughts. He heard her opening the bathroom door and switching off the light.

'Connor?'

'Yeah?'

'Thanks for a great supper.'

'You're welcome.'

'Good night.'

'Good night.'

STANLEY WAS A FIVE-HOUR drive from Missoula and they arrived an hour early and pulled up close by the Salmon River and unloaded the canoes and all the gear onto the grassy bank. The camping gear and food were stowed in black waterproof duffle bags.

Julia settled herself on the grass while Connor took the truck to the parking lot behind the Mountain Village Mercantile where they had arranged to meet Ed.

Connor was wearing only shorts and a grey T-shirt, but in the thin mountain air the midday sun felt hot. The heat shimmered on the tarmac as he walked towards the front of the store. Going inside was like stepping into an age gone by. There were old guns and an axe hanging on the wall and the place seemed to sell anything a man might need, from a pair of pants to a pastrami sandwich. What Connor needed now was a couple of cold sodas.

The woman behind the counter served him with a smile and asked where he was headed and Connor said they were going to canoe down to Challis. She had just baked some chocolate-chip cookies and Connor bought some and some oranges too and thanked her.

When he got back to the river he saw Julia was wearing sunglasses and had taken off her sandals and rolled up her shorts.

Connor sat down beside her and they drank the sodas and ate the cookies and watched the sun spangle on the water. She said what a beautiful place it was, and Connor pointed out some of the peaks he and Ed had climbed over the years.

Two o'clock came and went and Ed hadn't arrived. They'd agreed that he would call the Mercantile if there were any problems and Connor walked over there a couple of times but there were no messages. Though she tried not to show it, Connor could tell Julia was worried. He went over to the payphone and called the smoke-jumper base in Missoula. The operations office told him that the California fire had flared up again overnight and that Ed and the others were still needed. As soon as Connor hung up, the woman came out of the store and said there was a call for him inside.

'Connor?'

'Hey, Ed. I just called the base and heard.'

'Man, I'm so sorry. I'd have called sooner but things have gone crazy down here.'

'You OK?'

'Yeah, I'm fine. Just pissed as hell I can't come with you guys.'

'Well, the river isn't going anyplace. We'll do it another time.'

'Are you kidding? Do it. You'll have a ball. Julia'll love it.'

Connor hesitated. He wasn't sure she would want to if it was going to be just the two of them. 'Listen, Ed. Talk to Julia, she's right here.'

He handed over the phone and while they talked he wandered round the store, pretending to look at things but really just listening.

'You bet we're going to do it,' she said, before saying goodbye.

They were on the river within half an hour. They put the spare canoe and gear on the truck and the woman at the Mercantile said she would keep an eye on it until they came back on the bus on Sunday night. They bought a bag of cherries and the last of her cookies and headed for the river.

They put on their life vests and took off their shoes and stowed the duffle bags between the two seats. Then Julia climbed in and took the forward seat and Connor pointed the canoe out into the stream and pushed off and stepped aboard. They slipped slowly out into the body of the river and let the current take them.

The water was clear and cool and swifter than it had looked from the bank. Dark shapes of fish darted and skewed away in panic as the canoe slid by. The sun had lost its brazen heat and as it angled lower it turned to gold the clouds of flies pirouetting above the water.

They had talked for many hours and it was good now to be silent and to listen to the swoosh of the paddles and the sounds of the wilderness around them. Julia had tied up her hair again with the bandanna, and no matter where Connor looked his eyes kept coming back to the nape of her neck and a little brown smudge of a birthmark that showed above the sunbleached red of her life vest.

As the river twisted west they saw the setting sun, and the water before them turned to molten gold. They came to a place where the river ran in a long curve. There was a bench of rock along the southern bank some ten feet above the water and Connor recognised it as a place he and Ed had camped before. They dragged the canoe from the water and hauled the bags up to the bench, and while Julia gathered wood and made a fire Connor took his fishing rod and waded into the shallows.

There were fish rising all around him and on only his second cast he hooked one and Julia, watching from above, let out a whoop and he looked up at her and grinned. It was a fine trout of around two pounds and they cooked it over the fire. Its flesh was as pink as the gathering night sky and tasted pure as the river itself.

They ate the rest of the cookies and some cherries and sat by the fire, watching the light fade on the river. Connor had brought both tents and he offered now to put one up for her. But Julia said if anyone was used to sleeping in the open she was, and on a night like this that was the only way to go. So they spread their sleeping-bags by the fire and Connor bear-bagged the food and went off to hang it in the trees.

The fire burned low and they lay looking at the stars. There were two falling stars in quick succession and Julia said they must both make secret wishes and Connor didn't make the one he truly wanted but simply wished that the three of them would all be happy. They were silent awhile. Then Julia spoke again.

'That book of yours, about the war photographer?'

'Larry Burrows.'

'Uh-huh. Is that the kind of work you want to do?'

He wondered how she knew what he had scarcely admitted to himself. 'Maybe part of me does, yeah.'

There was a long pause. 'Connor?'

Something earnest in her tone made him turn to look at her and in the dying glow of the fire he saw her dark eyes were fixed on him.

'What?' he said.

'Don't. Please don't.'

THE FIRE ON SNAKE MOUNTAIN that was to change so many lives started with a single shaft of lightning. It struck high on a ridge of pale rock, where a dead lodgepole pine, stripped of bark and bleached by several summers, tilted over fathoms of forest. In the fractured moment of the flash the tree stood frozen in a negative of neon bone against the black of the night. Tiny tongues of flame licked and flickered along its stem and the only hint of what had taken place and what was to come was the curl of smoke that issued briefly from the charred cleft of the pine.

The sun rose on a world that seemed unchanged. It climbed vast and red from behind the mountain and as the light crept across the land a pair of ravens flew in from the north. Skye heard their croaking and looked up and watched them pass overhead.

'That's what I'm going to come back as.'

Julia was standing beside her, watching them too. 'As a raven?'

'Yeah. Wouldn't it be cool? Next time around, that's me.'

Julia shrugged. 'I don't know. That's what I was last time. The flying's good but the food's terrible. All that rotten meat. Yuck.'

Skye laughed and looked at her. 'You're funny.'

The weather had reverted to the remorseless dry heat of the early summer, and Julia had changed their routine to allow for it. The group rose early now and hiked while there was still a trace of cool in the air. By eleven, when it was too hot to go on, they would find a sheltered spot and stay there until around four when the heat began to subside. They spent the time reading and writing in their journals or doing construction or art projects that involved the whole group.

Today they had settled in the shade of some old cottonwoods that grew along the banks of a dried-out creek and they ate a late breakfast. The creek bed was lined with rocks of strange shapes and colours and the banks were littered with dead wood and Julia suggested they use the rocks and the wood to make a sculpture.

They found a tree limb shaped like a horse's body and head and Skye said why didn't they make a statue of Crazy Horse, the great Oglala warrior. They all seemed to think it was a good idea and they propped the horse on four stacks of flat rocks for its legs, then went off scouring the creek and its banks for more materials.

Skye wandered along the creek in search of something to make a war bonnet. They weren't supposed to go out of sight of the staff, but as she got to a bend in the creek she spotted something just beyond it, up among the rocks, and without thinking made her way towards it. It was the bloody remains of a bird, some kind of grouse. She plucked its tail feathers and picked some stems of dried grass and sat on a rock, braiding them to make a band for the feathers.

'Hey, look what you found. Cool.' She looked up and saw Mitch grinning down at her. 'Can I help?'

She thought of saying no because she couldn't stand the guy, but since the quest she had resolved to be friendly to everyone. He sat down beside her, picked up some of the grass and made a futile attempt at braiding it.

'Look,' she said. 'I'll show you.' She put down her own grass and took his and got the braid started. 'You gotta keep it tight, otherwise the feathers will just fall out.'

She handed it back to him and because she didn't want to lose the tension in the braid, she kept her fingers on it while he took hold of it. As he did so their hands touched.

'Your skin feels real good,' he said.

'What?' She snatched her hand away.

The braid uncoiled in his hands and he stared at it for a short while then slowly looked up at her and smiled and shrugged.

'It does,' he said. 'It feels beautiful.'

Looking her in the eye, he reached up and ran the backs of his fingers down the bare skin of her upper arm. Skye froze. She could feel her heart pounding. He was looking at her in the same slow-eyed way her stepfather did when he came home late reeking of drink.

'Come on, it's OK,' he coaxed, glancing over her shoulder. 'No one will know, we can go up there behind the rocks.'

Skye knew they were out of sight of the others. Mitch touched her breast and something exploded inside her and she swung at him with the back of her hand and hit him hard in the face.

'Jesus!'

He staggered to his feet, clutching his nose. 'You little bitch!'

'If you ever lay a finger on me again, I'll kill you.'

She too was on her feet now and she grabbed the feathers and turned and headed back along the creek. She thought he might come after her and she wanted to run but something told her not to, so she just walked as fast as she could and didn't once look back.

IT WAS MORE than two weeks since the canoe trip and Julia had spent much of that time replaying it in her head and wondering how she could have allowed it to unsettle her so. She had lain awake at night and chastised herself as a fickle, shameful creature for letting such thoughts into her head about her lover's best friend.

Not that Connor had done or said anything to prompt all this. He had behaved impeccably. She could imagine how shocked he would be to know that she harboured such feelings for him. But the truth was that ever since she had first laid eyes on him, that evening at the airport, something inside her had turned.

She repeated to herself, again and again like a mantra, that it was Ed she loved—and she did, she really did. But on the river that weekend she hadn't been able to take her eyes off Connor. Lying next to him by the fire, with their bodies only a few inches apart, she had kept imagining what it would be like to kiss him and she'd felt a physical longing for him that shocked her.

Ed had flown back to Missoula on Sunday and was there in the apartment to greet them when they returned. He had supper waiting for them and gave them such a warm welcome and it was wonderful to see him again. And when they made love that night, she told him again and again how much she loved him and realised that it wasn't Ed she was trying to convince but herself.

She had hoped that coming back to the group would bring some relief from all this mental turmoil. But if anything it had grown worse and was in danger of marring what should otherwise have been a time of great fulfilment. For Skye's transformation had transformed the whole group. Since her quest she had become its centre, joyous and vibrant and considerate to everyone.

So, now, as soon as Skye arrived back with the feathers, Julia knew something was wrong. The face was locked in its old frown. When Julia asked her if she was all right, she just gave a curt nod and didn't reply. A few minutes later, Mitch walked in. Julia could see his nose had been bleeding and when she asked him what had happened he said he'd slipped and knocked his head on a tree.

By now the sculpture was looking magnificent, but Skye seemed to have lost interest. Instead, Byron had taken the lead. He got everyone to contribute something coloured, a bandanna or even just some strips of paper, and these were all tied to Crazy Horse's body. Skye sat to one side, staring off into the distance. Every so often Julia would try to involve her but it was no good. When the sculpture was nearly done and the others were busy making final touches, Julia walked over and sat down beside her.

'So what do you think? Not bad, huh?'

Skye looked across at the sculpture. 'Yeah. It looks great.'

Her voice was lifeless and little and Julia looked her squarely in the face and saw there were tears in her eyes.

'OK. Tell me what happened.'

Skye shook her head. And the tears started to roll and she wiped them viciously away. Julia reached out and gently put her arm round her shoulders, half expecting to be shrugged off, but instead Skye turned to her and put her head on Julia's chest and put her arms round her and sobbed. Julia stroked her hair and held her.

'It's OK, sweetheart, let it go. Just let it go.'

Skye murmured something.

'What, honey?'

'I just get everything wrong.'

Julia tried again to find out what had happened but Skye wouldn't say and soon she stopped crying and gathered herself. And by four o'clock, after they had eaten and set out on the trail again, leaving Crazy Horse behind them proudly guarding the creek, she seemed almost back to normal.

They made camp that night in a rocky bowl on the east side of Snake Mountain. While supper was being prepared, Julia made the usual evening radio call back to base to let Glen know their position. They talked about routine things and Glen said that because of the hot, dry weather the Forest Service had upped the fire risk warning and that the group should take extra care with their campfires.

As they sat round the fire that evening, Julia kept alert for any sign of tension between Mitch and Skye, who was sitting beside her, but if anything was going on, neither of them was showing it. After they put out the fire, Katie and Laura and Scott collected everyone's pants and boots, as usual, and they settled down for the night. Julia and Katie lay either side of Skye. She said she was tired and wanted to go to sleep. She gave Julia a brave little smile.

'Thank you,' she said softly.

'What for?'

'For believing in me.'

Julia reached out and stroked her hair. 'You're a wonderful person, Skye. And the way you've been handling things is awesome.'

'Maybe.'

'Believe me.'

They said good night. Julia watched her for a long time, staring blankly at the sky. Only when Julia was certain Skye was asleep did she allow herself to think of other things. And thinking, by habit now, of Connor, she drifted into sleep herself.

WHEN JULIA SMELT the smoke, her first thought was that they had failed to kill the campfire, and with a pang of panic she sat up in her sleeping-bag and peered towards the place where they had sat last night. All was still with not even a wisp of smoke to be seen.

Everyone around her was still asleep. Skye was buried deep in her sleeping-bag, as she often slept, with the top pulled right over her head. Julia looked at her watch. It was a little after five thirty. She slipped from her sleeping-bag and stood up. She took her shorts and boots from the locked duffle bag she used for a pillow, put them on and then headed off up through the trees.

She followed a narrow deer trail for about half a mile, with the smell of smoke growing stronger. She came to a clearing, and as she stepped out of the trees she got her first clear view of the sky and of Snake Mountain rearing above her, the sun just catching its eastern tip and lighting the cloud that was drifting away behind it. Julia was just thinking how beautiful it looked when she noticed that this wasn't a normal cloud, but a wind-blown column of smoke.

She ran back down through the trees as fast as she could safely go. When she reached camp nobody had stirred. Holding her finger to her lips, she gently woke Katie and Laura and Scott. Julia told them in a whisper that there was a forest fire and that they should get everyone up and dressed as fast as they could.

'It's on the other side of the mountain. If we hike out the way we came, we'll be fine. Any questions? OK. You get everyone moving. I'm going to call Glen.'

She took out the radio and was walking away from them, adjusting the controls, when Katie came running after her.

'Julia! Julia!'

Julia turned and waited for her to come close. Katie was still wearing the T-shirt and underpants she slept in.

'Skye's gone.'

'*What?*'

'She must have slipped away in the night. She stuffed her pack into her sleeping-bag. She's taken my boots and trousers and gone.'

IT WAS KATIE who found Skye's footprints. She recognised the tread pattern of her own boots in the dust at the start of the trail that Julia had taken earlier up towards the ridge. While Katie put on Skye's trousers and boots, Julia grabbed a day pack and quickly put together what they might need: some food and water, a map of the mountain, a compass and a pair of binoculars. Now the two of them were following Skye's tracks up through the trees.

In a series of radio conversations, Glen and Julia had worked out a plan: Scott and Laura would hike out south with the rest of the students while Julia and Katie began searching for Skye. The Forest Service and the police had already been alerted. A planeload of smoke jumpers was on its way from Missoula.

Katie was going on about how guilty she felt for not stowing her boots and trousers securely. Julia had told her three times already that she shouldn't be too hard on herself and that it could happen to any of them. But as they followed Skye's footprints up the trail and came out into the clearing, she lost patience and stopped.

'Listen, Katie. You feel bad, I feel bad. I should have seen it coming. So let's just take it as read that we both feel guilty and get on with the job of finding her.'

It sounded sharper than she had intended. Katie looked chastened and just nodded and they didn't speak again for a long while.

What Julia had said about her own feelings of guilt wasn't the half of it. Although she still didn't know what had happened yesterday between Skye and Mitch, she knew it was her fault that they had been allowed to wander out of sight. If she had been more vigilant, none of this would have happened.

As they walked the last few steps to the ridge, the other side of the mountain revealed itself and for the first time Julia saw the fire itself and the damage it had already done. For perhaps 1,000 feet below where they stood, the land was a smoking wasteland, the trees burnt to charred spikes that still smouldered in the wind. Below that, beyond one of the rocky spines that traversed the mountain, the forest was as yet untouched. The fire had been driven north and east across the mountain by the wind. Julia could see it about half a mile away, a tall front of flame moving steadily away from her.

Julia turned and saw that Katie was transfixed by the fire. She looked very frightened.

'Katie, we're safe here. Ed always says it's like with money: if you're in the black, you're OK. Everything around here is black and burnt. We're safe.'

Katie nodded. Julia got out her map and worked out exactly where they were. 'So if you were Skye, standing here, where would you go?'

Katie looked at the map and then pointed to her left down the southern section of the mountain face where the unburnt gullies funnelled down towards the river. 'Down there, I guess.'

'Me too. I'd head for the river. Come on, let's go.'

 CHAPTER FOUR

They had made radio contact with Julia on their first pass across the mountain. It was only Hank Thomas who got to hear her voice, but he relayed what she said and Ed felt a great rush of relief that she was safe. Connor grinned and gave him a pat on the back. Julia told Hank where on the mountain she was and on the next pass everyone peered out of the windows and saw two tiny figures 1,500 feet below, standing on a strip of white rock and waving frantically.

The jump spot was a patch of grass and sliprock below the tail of the fire. Ed and Connor were jumping last stick and by the time they reached it, the others had stowed their jumpsuits and parachutes. Everyone gathered round Hank Thomas. He was talking with Julia on the radio and looking at the map, while she gave him the map reference of where she and Katie were.

'What's the girl's name?' Hank asked her.

'Skye. Skye McReedie.'

Hank asked her if she'd seen any sign of the helicopter search-and-rescue team that was on its way. Julia hadn't and Hank said he would radio to see what was keeping it. Meanwhile he would send three of his jumpers to help her and Katie look for the girl.

'Julia, one more thing. You see those thunderheads over to the northwest? There's a cold front coming in and the wind's going to blow stronger. This old fire could start moving any which way. We don't want anyone taking any risks. Do you copy?'

'Copy.'

He signed off. Hank named Ed, Connor and Chuck Hamer as the three he was sending to help in the search. Hank and the other four jumpers would cut a line round the fire's eastern flank.

IT TOOK THE THREE of them twenty minutes to hike across to where Julia was. They headed up along one of the strange spines of rock that they had seen from the air. This one had acted as a natural fire line. The mountainside above it was black, with the charred trees still smoking, while the forest below remained unburnt.

They walked in single file with Connor in the lead until they spotted Julia up ahead sitting on a platform of rock with Katie. He called and they waved and came running down towards them. Ed ran ahead to meet them and he and Julia flung their arms round each other and held each other while Connor and Chuck walked towards them.

Julia turned to Connor as he came near and hugged him too and he held her tight and was almost overwhelmed by the feel of her. They stepped apart and she smiled bravely and looked away and he could see the tension in her face. She said hello to Chuck and introduced Katie, who promptly burst into tears and hugged Chuck.

'Hell,' he said. 'Why can't I always have that effect on women?'

They spread the map on the rock and Julia showed them the route she thought Skye might be taking. She suggested they fan out across the slope and move down the mountainside in a line, keeping radio contact. Katie was the only one without a radio and Connor suggested that she should team up with Chuck. As they were about to move out, Hank came on the radio and said the rescue helicopter had lost radio contact and no one knew where it was. For the time being, he said, they were on their own.

Ed was going to take the northern end of the line, nearest the fire, Julia next, then Connor, with Chuck and Katie taking the southern end. Ed stayed where he was and wished them luck, as Connor and the others set off to take up their positions.

Chuck and Katie hiked on. Connor walked beside Julia.

'Oh, Connor,' she said quietly. 'If anything happens to her, I'll never forgive myself. It's all my fault.'

He put a hand gently on her shoulder and she pressed her hand on his hand but still didn't look at him.

'We'll find her,' he said. He wondered what had happened to make Skye run, but it didn't seem the time to ask.

SKYE WATCHED THE CLOUDS moving ever nearer. They were the colour of gunmetal seamed with a sickly yellow, and as they came they seethed and merged and lightning flickered from their joined belly like the tongues of angry serpents.

The land was tilting and sending her towards a vast curving valley of grass and boulders, which seemed the best way down to the river. The valley was fringed on both sides by unburnt forest. She stopped to catch her breath. Her blisters hurt and her knees ached from hiking downhill for so long.

She wasn't scared any more. Not like she'd been when she first came over the ridge and saw the fire. She'd stood watching it a while, wondering if she should go back and warn the others, then deciding not to and telling herself there was nothing to be scared of. The worst that could happen was that she might die, and what was the big deal about dying? It was just bang and then nothing. It sounded like bliss. Still, after she'd set off down the mountain, the fire kept on scaring her, the sound of it more than the sight.

But now she was OK. She was even starting to think how good it was to be on the run again. For a while, these last two or three weeks, she thought she'd found somewhere she belonged. But it had turned bad, just like everything always did, and the best thing was to get the hell out of it.

She was thirsty and reached for the knotted red T-shirt that she was using for a bag. All she had in it were her water bottle and Katie's headlamp. The water bottle was almost empty, and she drained it in one swig and threw it away and still felt thirsty. Her own grey T-shirt was sweaty and torn, so she untied the knots in Katie's red one and put it on instead and threw hers and the headlamp into the bushes.

The fire was hidden from her now by a low shoulder of the mountain. Oddly, the sound of it seemed louder and for the first time in a long while she could smell smoke. It didn't occur to Skye that this was something she should worry about, for by now she was surely far enough down the mountain to be out of danger. Directly below her there was a steep slope of loose rocks and she considered going down it, but the slope looked too dangerous. Instead, she would stay high and cross over to join the valley at the top where the gullies linked up. The decision seemed to fuel her resolve and she set off again at a jog.

IT WAS ED who saw her first. Down the mountainside and away to his left, he caught a glimpse of red. He reached into his personal gear bag for the small pair of binoculars he always carried, but when he looked through them all he could see was trees and smoke drifting across them towards that huge valley that funnelled down to the river. Then he saw another flash of red and this time he saw it was a figure, maybe a mile or more away. He reached for his radio.

'Julia, this is Ed.'

For a few moments there was no reply. Then, 'This is Julia.'

'Is Skye wearing red?'

'No. Grey T-shirt, blue trousers.'

'Ed. This is Chuck. The girl took Katie's red T-shirt. She might be wearing it.'

Ed didn't have a map and it was tricky describing exactly where it was that he had seen her. He got Julia to study the map for him and while they were talking, Skye dropped out of sight again. But Ed was sure she must be heading across to the top of the valley. Presumably because it was an easier route, Skye was staying above the trees. Maybe if he were to take a short cut diagonally down through the forest, he would be able to drop into the valley below her and cut her off. Julia checked the map and said that there was a creek he would have to cross, but it certainly looked possible. She and the others would head down towards the top of the valley.

When he reached the edge of the forest, Ed could see why Skye had chosen the higher route. The land fell away steeply down to the trees in a 600-foot run of broken shale. But he had run scree slopes as a boy and could remember the thrill, and without further hesitation he launched himself off the edge.

With his first stride, it all came back to him. The rocks slid with your boots and you had to be fearless and trust the slide and go with it. He tilted himself forward and soon he was striding like a giant, each step taking him another twenty or thirty feet. Then, about halfway down, his foot caught in a clump of sage and he went head over heels and slithered the rest of the way on his back.

He came to rest at the edge of the forest and stood up gingerly. He seemed to be in one piece and glanced around him to get his bearings. He looked up at the treetops and was just registering how low and black the clouds above them seemed, when the air around him cracked asunder in a searing flash of white light. Ed dived to the ground. And there he stayed until the shock subsided and his heart started beating again. He sat up.

'Holy shit,' he said.

It was the nearest he had ever come to being struck by lightning and he threw back his head and laughed out loud in relief that he was still alive. Where exactly it had struck, he couldn't see.

He had just got to his feet when he heard Julia calling his name on the radio. He tried to reply but she obviously couldn't hear him because she kept saying 'Ed, do you copy?' over and over again. Maybe he'd damaged his radio when he fell. He holstered the radio, checked his compass and walked into the forest.

The going was tougher than he'd hoped and sometimes he had to take detours from the direction he knew he should stick to. And all the while the wind whooshed above him. There was a smell of smoke, but he thought it was the smoke from the fire across the mountain. Then he heard a sound that told him it wasn't.

It started in a low roar and grew steadily louder, like a train thundering towards him through a tunnel. And Ed knew at once what it was and he felt a first jab of pure fear. He peered to his right through the trees and saw nothing, not even smoke. Then he heard the first tree explode and then another, and he felt the fire's heat and knew that it was close and coming closer at great speed. He started to run.

JULIA DIDN'T SEE the lightning strike, but she heard its hellish crack and its echo rolling across the mountain. Then, as she climbed out of the gully that she was following and got her first full view of the forest, she saw a patch of fire among the treetops that even while she watched began to spread. She was already having to fight hard to keep panic at bay. And when she saw the fire and realised that Ed was somewhere near it or, heaven forbid, beneath it, the animal in her almost won. She could scarcely believe it was happening.

She tried calling Ed again on the radio and could hear Connor and Chuck trying too. But still there was no reply. She called Connor.

'Connor, do you see the fire down there?'

'Yeah, I see it.'

'That's where Ed is.'

'Yeah. Don't worry. He knows what to do.'

His voice was calm. He asked her how far she was from the head of the valley and she told him that it would take her about five minutes to get there. Connor said he should be there in ten. Neither of them could see into the valley yet, nor could they see Skye. Julia signed off and started to run.

As soon as Connor saw the valley open up below him and saw the fire away to the right moving steadily towards it through the forest, he knew why this place made him feel so uneasy.

On August 5, 1949, at Mann Gulch, just 100 miles from where they now were, thirteen smoke jumpers had died when a fire chased them up a drainage very like the one Connor was now looking at. Just like here, there had been a river at the bottom of the drainage and the geography had conspired to create its own wind so that the valley acted like an immense chimney, sucking the fire up it faster than any man or beast could ever run.

Connor called Hank and told him what was happening and Hank sent out an emergency call for helicopters to evacuate them. He told Connor to get everyone away from the drainage and back up into the black where the earlier fire had passed through, or, if that wasn't possible, into rocky terrain where the fire would have less fuel.

There was Julia below him now, heading down into the valley and there, way below her, was Skye, her red T-shirt vivid against the flaxen grass. The fire was to the girl's right and Connor guessed it would take fifteen minutes to reach the valley, maybe less. And somewhere, in that burning forest, was his best friend.

Connor scrambled down the slope as fast as he could. He pulled out his radio and kept going as he spoke.

'Julia, this is Connor. You mustn't go down there. Turn around and get out of the valley.'

'What are you talking about? I can see her. She's right below me.'

'Julia, this is Chuck.'

'I hear you, Chuck.'

'Connor's right. Don't go down there. Once the fire gets in there, it'll come racing up towards you. I'm getting Katie out right now.'

Julia was staring back up the mountain at Connor. Then she looked down the valley again and above the rush of the wind he could just hear her calling Skye's name, again and again. But if the girl heard, she gave no sign. She just kept hiking down the valley. Once more Julia looked back at him and he knew she was deciding and knew also which way it would go. And, sure enough, she turned and started to run down the valley, calling to Skye as she went.

Connor yelled for her to stop and said the same, as calmly as he could, over the radio. But she paid no attention. And now he was running, leaping over scrub and rock, with stone and debris avalanching with him, his eyes darting from where he trod to Julia and Skye and from them to the advancing fire.

ED'S FIRST THOUGHT was to head downhill and get below the fire. But the forest floor seemed to flatten and the fire seemed to be spreading as fast in that direction as it was elsewhere. Instead, he turned south again and ran as fast as he could towards the creek that Julia had told him about.

He could hear the fire rampaging behind him and by the time he reached the creek he could see the flames only fifty yards behind him and could feel its heat, raw and intense.

It was both more than a creek and less than one. What water there normally was had long dried. But its northern bank was a sheer cliff of about forty feet upon whose rim Ed was now standing, aware that each second he hesitated might be the one that cost him his life.

His first thought was to clamber down it, but the cliff face looked loose and treacherous and the rocks below unforgiving. Ed had a rope and, though it wasn't long enough to get him all the way to the bottom, he figured that he'd be able to jump the rest. He pulled the rope from his bag and looked for the best place to tie it.

All but one of the trees stood back too far from the edge. That one leaned perilously from the very edge of the cliff with half its roots exposed to the air, but when Ed leaned against the trunk it seemed stable enough. He threw the rope around it, made it fast and manoeuvred himself out over the edge.

He had barely begun to rappel down when he heard the crash. It was directly above him and as he looked up he was showered in sparks and flying embers. He managed to keep his grip on the rope and when he looked again he saw that the base of the tree was wreathed in flames. The rope was already burning. He loosened his grip and let it run through his bare hands and felt it searing his flesh as he spiralled down, flaming fragments falling with him.

But before he was halfway down, the rope snapped. Ed lunged and clawed with both hands at the cliff face, but the rocks crumbled under his fingernails and all he succeeded in doing was to flip himself over so that now he was flying face down like a chuteless skydiver.

The fall lasted no more than two or three seconds, but it seemed stretched to a small eternity. He watched the ground swirl slowly into focus below him. He heard his radio crackle and Connor calling his name again. And the last thing that he saw and would ever see was a red butterfly lifting from the rocks and fluttering away.

JULIA WAS RUNNING as fast as she could down through the long white grass. She kept shouting Skye's name and her voice was cracking and she knew that it was pointless, because even as each cry left her lips it was swept away on the wind and lost. Above the unburnt trees that topped the right-hand ridge of the valley a column of smoke reared like a writhing black dragon, its belly undulating and mottled with the orange glow of the fire. Skye, not more than 400 yards below her now and running too, kept glancing up at it, and once in doing so she tripped on one of the smaller boulders and fell headlong, but scrambled to her feet and kept running.

'Skye! Skye!'

So far the girl hadn't once looked back and she didn't now. But suddenly she stopped in her tracks. All as one, with a boom that seemed to shake the whole mountainside, the trees along the right-hand ridge exploded into flames. Julia also stopped, and for a few moments the two of them stood transfixed. Connor was calling her on the radio.

'Julia, stop! Turn around. You haven't got time.'

She looked back up the slope and saw him hurtling down towards her in long strides. He was 100 yards away and gaining fast. She turned back and saw that Skye had at last seen her. Julia waved to her, signalling to her to come back up the slope, and Skye stared at her for a moment then turned to look back at the burning trees.

'Come on, Skye! For God's sake, come on!'

Above them now the crowns of two flaming trees, and then a third, lifted off and flew like comets down into the middle of the valley. They came to earth only twenty yards below Skye and cartwheeled as they landed, sending showers of sparks into the grass.

Skye took one look and immediately turned and started back up the slope. At last, Julia thought. At last, thank God.

EVEN AS HE RAN, Connor knew there was no way they could get out of the valley in time. He could see the wind whipping the fire that had been started by the flying crowns, driving it up the valley towards them. The place was exactly like Mann Gulch, he thought, just one enormous chimney. The girl was going to die. But there was a chance, just a chance, that he could save Julia.

She was only twenty yards ahead of him but, damn it, now she was off again, running down towards Skye. The slope was steep and the poor girl, 300 yards below, maybe more, was stumbling as she tried to retrace her steps. Behind her now the three fires had become one and, sucked by the wind, the flames were raging through the grass and closing on her fast. Connor knew there was no hope for her and none for any of them if they tried to help her.

'Julia!'

At last he caught up with her and as his hand closed on her shoulder she wheeled round to face him.

'Julia, listen! You can't go down there!'

'Look at her! We've got to help her!'

'No! She's not going to make it. And if we go to her, neither are we.'

She tried to break free but he twisted his hand in the shoulder of her T-shirt and hooked his other arm round her waist.

'Let me go, damn you!'

She lashed out at him and he ducked, and as she leaned over him he came up again and hoisted her off the ground on his shoulder. She was screaming at him but he set off back up the slope.

'Don't look back,' he said. 'Don't look at her.'

'You bastard! You fucking bastard!'

Connor pictured Skye behind, watching them desert her. The flames must be licking at her heels by now, ready to devour her. He pulled a shutter down in his mind.

'Let me go! Let me go!'

One man had survived the Mann Gulch fire: the only one who

hadn't tried to outrun it. Connor had already chosen the spot. On his way down he had run past a cluster of boulders and decided that it was the only place where they stood a chance. It was about twenty yards up the slope, but with Julia putting up such a struggle it was hard to move fast. The smoke was thick and rolling around them now. He reached into his pocket for a fusee to have ready for when they reached the boulders.

Fifteen yards to go. Twelve. Ten . . .

Julia gave a terrible scream and kept on screaming and he knew that the flames had caught up with the girl and engulfed her and that Julia was watching her die.

'Don't look, Julia. For Christ's sake, don't look.'

The scream turned to a wail and he felt her body writhe and convulse on his shoulder as if something inside her were dying too.

And now they were there and Connor lowered her so that she stood propped against the nearest boulder. She slid slowly down the rock and crumpled to the ground.

Connor left her there and lit the fusee and it flared brightly in his hand. There were three large boulders and a few smaller ones and they formed a triangle two yards across. Connor lit the grass between them. It caught fire with a rush and burned fast and fiercely and the wind whipped it through the gaps between the boulders and soon the slope above was on fire too. Connor watched it go and only hoped that by now Chuck and Katie were well clear.

He peered through the smoke below and saw the whole valley was alight. A low wall of flame was rushing up towards them. The grass between the boulders had finished burning, and he walked into its smouldering remains and stamped it out. He could hear Julia moaning on the downhill side of the boulder, where he had left her, and with the fusee still flaring in one hand he ran round and found her slumped there, sobbing. With his free hand he grabbed her wrist and dragged her a few yards down the slope, and then he lit the grass between himself and the boulders and waited until it had burned.

The boulders now stood in a patch of smoking black some fifteen yards across. Connor threw the fusee uphill beyond the boulders and then knelt beside Julia and gathered her in his arms. She thrashed at his face and chest with her fists as he lifted her.

'You bastard! You let her die! Why did you let her die?'

Connor didn't answer. He just let her hit him and carried her between the boulders and set her down on the blackened earth. He took out his water bottle. 'OK, I'm going to pour this over you.'

'Fuck you.'

He pulled a bandanna from his pocket and wet it, then he drenched Julia's head and shoulders and emptied the rest over his own and threw the bottle away. The thick smoke stung his eyes and he figured the fire was about thirty yards away.

He took out his fire shelter and shook it open. It was a small tubed tent of aluminium foil. He laid it out on the ground and opened it up. The wind rattled the foil.

'Julia, stand up.'

She didn't move, so he hoisted her to her feet and leaned her against him, supporting her with one arm, for she seemed unable to stand. She was still crying, but silently now. The shelters were designed for one person, but Connor figured there was just enough room for them both. He managed to lift it above them and pulled it over their heads and slid it down over their bodies so that they were cocooned. Then he put his arms round her and lowered her gently until they were lying on the ground. He handed her the wet bandanna.

'Put this over your face.'

She wouldn't, so he did it for her. Their bodies were pressed tightly together and he could feel the shudder of her sobs. And as the roar of the closing fire grew louder and louder, he circled her with his arms and held her against his chest, and waited.

PART TWO
CHAPTER FIVE

Lexington lay shrouded in a layer of cloud and, when the plane dropped below it, all Connor could see through the rain-streaked window was sodden pasture and a highway jammed with cars.

He wondered if she would be there to meet him.

It was late February, and in the six months since the fire he hadn't seen her once. When Ed's condition had stabilised, she had flown back with him to Kentucky and had stayed with his parents while he was in the hospital. Now that he was convalescing at home, Julia spent her weekdays working in Boston and came back here every weekend—except the two when Connor had come to stay. On both occasions she had stayed in Boston, allegedly because of work.

At first he had kept on trying to phone her. In Boston all he ever got was her answering machine and she never returned his calls. Twice she picked up the phone at Ed's parents' house and was polite and distant, relating Ed's progress in a voice devoid of emotion. Yes, the burns were healing fine; yes, the broken hip too; in fact, he was walking almost without a limp now, and, no, there was still no progress with his eyesight.

In his fall, Ed had suffered retinal haemorrhages in both eyes. The doctors said that it was somehow connected with his diabetes. He'd apparently had some recent eye trouble that he hadn't disclosed in case they stopped him from jumping. Connor didn't ask too much about the medical details. All that mattered was that his friend was blind and seemed almost certain to stay that way.

Connor spoke with Ed on the phone two or three times a week and his mood was rarely less than ebullient. Once his hip had mended he spent a month at a rehabilitation centre for the blind and came back with hilarious accounts of mishaps and mischief. Last week he had been going on about all the new computer gear he was getting to help him in his composing.

Connor didn't push to find out what was going on behind this brave face. He knew that both Ed and Julia had been having some kind of post-traumatic therapy. It had been offered to Connor too, back in Missoula, but he hadn't followed it up. The strange thing was, he and Ed hadn't yet really talked about the fire.

Ed had sounded thrilled when Connor asked if he could come to see him in Kentucky again. He promised that this time he'd be at the airport to meet him. Connor wasn't counting on Julia being with him. She would probably make another excuse and stay in Boston.

But he was wrong. As he came through the gate, with his old leather duffle bag slung on his shoulder, he saw her, though if Ed hadn't been standing next to her, Connor might not have recognised her. Her hair was cut short and she was pale and much thinner. There were dark rings under her eyes and she looked beautiful and tragic. She saw him and waved and he saw her whisper to Ed, telling him which direction to face, and Ed dutifully lined up and beamed and waved too.

'Hey, cowboy! Over here!'

Ed was wearing dark glasses and an old yellow ski jacket. He too had lost weight, but the burn scars on his face had calmed and looked a lot better. Connor walked over.

'Hey, old buddy,' he said, putting down his bag. He took Ed by the shoulders and the two of them stood there hugging each other for a long time. 'Hey, man, it's good to see you,' Connor said softly.

'It's good to see you too, man.' Ed laughed and held Connor at arm's length as if inspecting him. 'And see? I still say "see" and I'm not going to stop. Anyhow, in my head I can see you. And you're still an ugly sonofabitch.'

Connor laughed and turned to Julia. 'Hi, Julia.'

'Connor.' She nodded. 'How're you doing?'

'Good. How are you?'

'I'm fine. Thanks.'

Neither of them seemed to know what to say or do next, whether to kiss or hug or even shake hands. Connor took the plunge. He stepped closer and put his arms around her and kissed her cheek, and the smell of her came back to him in a rush. She didn't hug him back, just briefly touched his shoulders. He let her go and looked into her eyes, but she looked away almost at once.

'You had your hair cut,' he said dumbly.

'Yeah. Well, it was all singed and frazzled, you know . . .'

Connor felt dumber still.

'Suits her, doesn't it?' Ed said, grinning. He ran his hand up the back of her head and ruffled her hair, and Julia dutifully smiled.

'Yes, it does,' Connor said.

There was another beat of awkward silence.

'So. Did you check any luggage in or anything?' Julia said.

'No, this is it.' He picked up his bag.

'Well, what the hell are we waiting for?' Ed said. 'Let's go get this cowboy a beer!'

They walked slowly across the concourse, Ed in the middle, his arm linked in Julia's, while people scurried past. They stepped out into the gloom of the afternoon and Julia went off to fetch the car, leaving Connor and Ed standing in the shelter of the pick-up zone.

'How do you think she looks?' Ed said.

'She looks great. A little tired maybe.'

'Yeah. She works too hard. She's been incredible. You know, man, she feels so bad about what she said to you.'

Connor knew what he meant but felt he should pretend not to. 'What do you mean?'

Ed sighed. 'Well, she told me how she swore at you and said it was your fault that the girl . . . you know.'

'Hell, I never thought she meant it.'

'That's good. Because she knows you saved her life and that you had no choice about the girl.'

'Well, maybe.'

Ed fumbled for Connor's arm and grasped it tightly. 'You had no choice, man. Any of us would have done what you did. Or tried to. The truth is, most of us would have failed and died.'

The official inquiry into what happened hadn't published its final report yet, but Connor already knew that this would be its verdict too. It didn't make anything feel any better.

After what seemed a long time, a black Jaguar slid up to the kerb, and through the tinted glass Connor saw Julia lean across and open the passenger door. She too was wearing sunglasses now which, given that it was almost dark, struck him as strange.

'Here she is,' he said, and steered Ed gently towards the car.

DINNER AT GRASSLAND—or Château Tully, as Ed called it—was at seven thirty prompt and it was considered bad form to be late. It was already twenty past and Julia was still soaking in the bath, trying to summon the strength to face Connor again.

Ed had first brought her to Grassland on their way to Montana the previous spring to meet his parents. And from the moment they had landed at the airport, culture shock had set in. Raoul, Ed's father's driver, met them at the airport, ushering them into the back of a spacious Mercedes. When they turned off the highway, a pair of enormous wrought-iron gates whirred open and the car purred up a driveway that wound through parkland to this pillared palace. There were fountains and peacocks and a whole army of servants.

Now Grassland felt like her second home. And the more she got to know Ed's parents, the more she liked them. The accident had drawn the three of them close and Julia could tell that they adored her.

Susan Tully's bravery over what had happened was almost as daunting as Ed's. The shock and sorrow of seeing a son blinded and burned were more than Julia could imagine, but Susan had kept her grief well hidden. Outwardly, from the start, she had been strong, practical and cheerful. Julia had drawn on this and tried to emulate it and, most of the time, succeeded. No one, not even the trauma therapist she had been seeing in Boston, knew what was going on inside her; of the terrible dreams she had, of the demons that came to visit her in the night, of the burden of guilt she now carried.

The water in the bathtub was cooling now and she hoisted herself out and dried herself, thinking about Connor and wishing she'd stayed in Boston for the weekend.

She had done her best to conceal how much she wanted to avoid him. Ed had only sensed it the last time Connor came to Kentucky when again she had made herself absent. He asked her why and she told him it was because she was ashamed of how she had behaved on the day of the fire. It was the truth, but not the whole of it.

Secretly Julia was more ashamed of what she had felt for him last summer and of what, if she were to allow herself, she still felt for him. Even before the fire, these feelings had seemed like a betrayal of Ed. Now they seemed monstrous. Julia knew where her duty lay and so long as Connor was out of sight and many miles away she could bury her feelings for him and get on with looking after Ed.

But at the airport it had all come flooding back. The sight of him walking towards her, the way he'd looked at her with those pale blue eyes, the sound of his voice. She had hoped to God that he wouldn't hug or kiss her and when he did and put his arms round her, she felt something break inside her and it was all she could do not to collapse and cling to him and cry on his shoulder. She managed to hold back the tears until she went off to get the car. In the parking lot she'd sat with her head bowed on the steering wheel, sobbing.

At least now she felt a little stronger. She dried her hair and dressed in a pair of black velvet trousers and a green cashmere sweater. As she was making herself up in the bedroom mirror, she heard Ed's special little knock on the door, the one he used when he came to her room at night after everyone had gone to bed.

'Milady's presence is eagerly anticipated in the banqueting hall.'

'I'm coming.'

He was practising using his cane and she heard him tapping his way across the bedroom and saw him appear in the mirror behind her. He had nicked himself shaving and there was a dried trickle of blood on one cheek. She turned and went to him and he took hold of her and kissed the side of her neck.

'You smell so good, I could eat you.'

She smiled then reached up and dabbed the blood from his cheek.

'Damn, did I cut myself?'

'Just a little. There. All gone. Come on, let's go downstairs. Have you told him yet?'

'No. I thought we'd tell him after dinner.'

THE OTHERS WERE all at the table when Ed and Julia came into the dining room. He heard the scraping of chairs and knew his father and Connor had stood up.

'Sorry we're late,' he said. 'It's my fault. I nearly cut my head off shaving.'

'Why don't you use that electric shaver I got you?' his mother said.

'I like to live dangerously.'

There was a moment of silence. Julia steered him to his chair and took her place beside him.

'Come on, let's eat,' his father said. 'Connor here is about to die of starvation.'

While they ate, Ed's father asked Connor about his flight from Montana and then launched into a tedious monologue on the merits of various airlines. He asked Julia which airline she used from Boston and Julia replied politely. For a while everyone was silent. Then Ed's father spoke up again.

'So, Connor. What do you think about this pair of lovebirds here getting hitched and all?'

Ed felt like kicking him under the table. But it was too late.

'I'm sorry, Mr Tully?' Connor said.

'These two . . . Hell, Ed, haven't you even told your best friend yet?'

'You guys are getting married?' Connor asked.

'We were keeping it as a surprise for later. Thanks, Dad.' Ed reached for Julia's hand and felt a tension there that surprised him.

'Yes. I picked my moment, got her exceedingly drunk, popped the question and, incredible as it may seem, she said yes.'

He leaned towards her and they kissed each other on the lips.

'Well,' Connor said. 'That's great. Congratulations.'

'Thanks, man.'

'I think you should propose a toast, Jim,' Ed's mother said. 'Before you put your foot in it again.'

'You bet.'

Ed could hear them all picking up their glasses.

'To Julia and Ed.'

CONNOR WATCHED HER sitting on the rug in front of the great fire-place in the den. He and Ed were sitting in high-backed leather arm-chairs, facing one another across the hearth, each cradling a glass of Jim Tully's finest brandy. Julia had her back propped against Ed's legs and was staring into the fire.

Ed's parents had gone to bed, so now it was just the three of them. Suddenly there was silence and Connor realised that Ed had asked him a question.

'Sorry, man, I was just thinking about something. What was that?'

'I said, we're really sorry about the way you found out. We wanted to tell you ourselves.'

'Hey, that's OK. I'm happy for you both. When's the wedding?'

'The last Saturday in June. I need to get a little fitter first. You know, for the honeymoon.' He laughed and Julia pulled a face and tapped him on the knee like a schoolmarm. 'I've asked all my friends but nobody seems to want to be my best man, so I wondered if you'd do it.'

'I'll have to see if I'm available. Where's it going to be?'

'Here. We wanted to do it in Montana, but until we've found a place, we figured it was simpler to do it here.'

'Found a place? You mean you're coming to live in Montana?'

'Hey, pal, it's a free country.'

'That's great.' Connor tried to sound enthusiastic. 'Where?'

'Oh, somewhere around Missoula, if we can find the right place. Listen, sorry, guys, I've got to go take a leak. I'll be right back.'

He put down his glass, found his cane and stood up. Julia looked into the fire while the tapping of Ed's cane faded across the hallway.

'Julia? Are you OK?'

She shook her head. 'Not really. But I'm getting there.'

He held out his hand and she hesitated, then took it and held it in both of hers. Her skin felt cold.

'I'm sorry I never returned your calls. I guess I just didn't know what to say. I was so ashamed about what I said to you that day. I didn't mean it.'

'I know. It's OK.'

'You saved my life. And I know I should . . .' She swallowed and shook her head and looked away into the fire.

'Tell me.'

'I just . . . sometimes wish you hadn't.' Tears broke from her eyes.

Connor leaned forward and clasped both her hands in his. 'Julia, what happened wasn't your fault.'

Out in the hallway a door clicked and again they heard the tap of the cane. Julia took her hands away and wiped away her tears. Connor's voice was low and urgent now.

'You mustn't think that. You did all you could.'

She gave a wry little smile. 'Sure.'

Ed came into the room and Connor watched him find his way without falter to his chair. Silence hung over them like a shroud.

'OK,' Ed said. 'So either you're asleep or you were talking about me—which is fine. What better subject is there?'

'Don't flatter yourself,' Julia said. Her voice was instantly, startlingly cheerful. The only hint of what had just passed was the smudged mascara under her left eye. 'Anyhow, we've been talking about you all evening. You haven't asked Connor a single thing about what he's up to.'

'True. So what's hot in Montana? How's the photo business?'

'Oh, pretty much the same as ever. It's OK, I guess. I've sold a few pictures. Truth is, it's time I moved on.'

He took a sip of brandy. They waited for him to continue.

'I'm going to travel a little. Europe first, then Africa maybe.'

'That's great. To take pictures?'

'Uh-huh.'

'So, where in Europe exactly?'

Connor knew Julia was staring at him. He was avoiding her eyes.

'I'm going to Bosnia.'

'Wow. You got, like, an assignment or something?'

'No, I figured I'd just go.'

'What, you can go to a war zone, just like that?'

Connor shrugged. 'I guess I'll find out. I'm going to play it by ear.'

'Wow! Well, good for you, man. When do you go?'

'Well, I was figuring on leaving pretty soon. Now I guess I'll have to kick my heels till after this darned wedding of yours.'

He had made it all sound more definite than it was, or at least, than it had been. He'd been thinking about the trip for some time and had done his research. But it wasn't until just now, hearing that the woman he loved was to be married, that he knew for certain that he would go. Julia hadn't said a word, nor taken her eyes off him. And at last he looked at her and smiled, but she didn't smile back.

Had he thought about it, and had Ed been able to see, he would never have done what he then did. Quite on impulse, he leaned forward and wiped the mascara from Julia's cheek. And she closed her eyes at his touch and silently bowed her head.

THE HOUSE THAT THEY FOUND in Montana stood above a rocky bend of the Bitterroot River, with the forest rising steeply behind it. It was on two floors, built of logs and had an acre and a half of land. There were apple trees and pear trees and the side of the house that looked down on the river had tall glass doors and a verandah and a yellow rambling rose running riot. The place had been built nine years ago by a couple who were sculptors, and there was a long barn that they had used as a studio.

Ed's parents had given him a new piano as a wedding present, a sleek black Yamaha baby grand. He had positioned it near the glass doors that led out onto the verandah. He made it the centre of what he called NASA control—the complex of keyboards, screens and computer equipment that did indeed look capable of launching a small missile. On the piano's lid, among the stacks of braille sheets, stood the silver-framed black and white picture that Connor had taken of them at the wedding. In it Ed was laughing, the Kentucky sun flaring like a starburst in his sunglasses, while Julia kissed him on the cheek. It still struck Julia as odd that Ed had never seen nor ever would see how they had looked that day.

They had moved into the house at the end of September, and those first few months had been hectic. The local Blind and Low Vision Services had sent rehab counsellors to help them. They adapted the kitchen, marking the food containers with rubber dots and magnets so that Ed could figure things out. They pruned the rose and the fruit trees so that he wouldn't catch his face on them, and erected posts with a rope strung between them all the way from the verandah down to the river and along the bank, so that he could safely go there by himself.

It was Julia's first Montana winter. The early snow came in October and kept topping itself up like an overattentive waiter. Far from feeling trapped by it, as she had feared she might, Julia loved it. They wrapped up warm and went for long walks. Their evenings were spent cocooned together on the couch by the big log fire, reading and listening to music or, if Ed insisted, watching a favourite old western or musical on TV. He would make her give a running commentary about what was happening. Sometimes she would tease him by inventing characters or pieces of action, but he knew most of the movies so well that he would cotton on right away.

Thanks to the generosity of Ed's father and to the smoke-jumper insurance money, they had few financial worries. Julia hadn't worked since giving up her job in Boston the previous spring and, although she intended to find a new job, she was still relishing the freedom to read and potter and to get back to some serious painting, which she did most mornings in the barn studio. Ed, however, was keen to demonstrate that he could support himself. The long-term plan was still, of course, to make it as a composer, but meanwhile he was determined to go on giving piano lessons.

Back in the fall he'd put an ad into *The Missoulian* and it had conjured over a dozen pupils. Word-of-mouth soon conjured more. Nearly all were children who came to the house after school. And having them around the place and seeing how much fun Ed had with them, Julia knew it wouldn't be long before he raised the subject of having children of their own.

It happened on the night after Thanksgiving. They had made love on the couch beside the fire and were lying in each other's arms. Julia was watching the snow fall in slow, fat flakes outside on the verandah.

'So, what do you think?' he said.

'You mean out of ten? Mmm, I'd give you a four, maybe five.'

He dug his fingers under her arms. 'You know what I mean.'

She did, though quite how was a mystery. She often seemed able to read his thoughts and only hoped it wasn't mutual.

'Isn't it a little early? I mean, shouldn't we get a little more settled?'

'I don't know. I feel pretty settled.'

'Well, so do I, but . . .'

'Listen, if you're not sure, that's cool. We'll wait.'

She thought about it all night and all the next day. She wanted children just as much as he did. What was the point in waiting? They had always used condoms and the next time they made love, she silently stopped him as he reached for one. Neither of them said another word about it, as if by some tacit accord that to do so might jeopardise their efforts.

More than four months later, Julia still hadn't conceived. And although she knew that these things took time and that some couples could spend years trying, an irrational voice had started to nag her that there was something wrong. Having started unsure, by now she could feel herself becoming almost obsessed with having a child. Without telling Ed, she went to see her doctor and had him run some tests. When she went to find out the results he told her she was in great shape. He went through the details with her but Julia was too elated to pay much attention.

'Of course, it takes two to tango,' he said, almost, it seemed, as an afterthought. 'And if it still isn't happening, maybe Ed should come in and we could run a few tests on him too.'

CHAPTER SIX

They saw the smoke from a long way off, rising like a tilting black tower from behind the ridge at the head of the valley. The road that was leading them there was narrow and pitted with tank tracks.

They had the windows down and the fraying cloth sunroof rolled right back and the air that gusted in was blowing Sylvie's dyed blonde hair over her face. All the way she had kept asking Connor to light cigarettes for her. She had several cartons of Marlboros stowed under their camera gear and flak jackets on the back seat so that she could hand them out at roadblocks. Three times in the last hour they had been stopped by hatchet-faced Serb militiamen and she had joked with them in her husky Parisian voice, then handed out packets of cigarettes and in no time at all they were being waved through.

Sylvie Guillard was pushing forty and had been photographing wars while Connor was still in fourth grade. She was with the famous Magnum agency and her fearlessness was as legendary as her talent. Connor had been aware of her since he arrived in Bosnia in the fall. She was little and skinny and something of a fantasy figure among the male journalists in Sarajevo. She was known as a loner, which made it all the more surprising that lately she had taken Connor under her wing. He hadn't so far managed to sell many pictures, but had it not been for Sylvie's help he wouldn't have sold any.

At three o'clock that morning Sylvie had knocked on his door at the Holiday Inn and told him to get his gear together. She had received a call on her satellite phone from one of her many mysterious contacts, telling her that the Red Cobras, one of the most feared Serb paramilitary groups, were moving in on Muslim enclaves in these hills. The informant said she should get out here fast.

With roadblocks and diversions, the trip from Sarajevo had taken nearly five hours, and during that time Sylvie had told him about the Cobras. Their leader was a charismatic fascist called Grujo, a meat wholesaler with a penchant for expensive cars.

As they neared the end of the valley now, they passed a string of houses that had been burnt, but there was no sign among them of either life or death. At the valley's end the road grew steep, and they started to climb through the forest in a slow zigzag of bends.

They could smell what had happened before they saw it. Even as the road levelled and they emerged from the trees into the sunlight they knew from the sour charnel waft in the air that more had burned here than houses. It was—or had been—more a hamlet than a village. Just a cluster of a dozen small dwellings and barns in a shallow bowl of meadow filled with spring flowers.

Sylvie stopped the car 100 yards short of the first building and switched off the engine, and they sat awhile, staring ahead and listening, but all they could hear was the hum of insects. A white dog ran across the road, then disappeared behind a stone wall into a small orchard. There were two dark shapes among the blossom and, though they were partly concealed, Connor knew what they were.

Still without speaking, they reached into the back of the VW for their camera bags. Then they got out and walked slowly side by side along the road towards the blackened buildings, taking pictures.

There were charred mounds lying in the grass beside the road with flies busy around them, and it took Connor a moment to realise that they were cattle with the remains of torched tyres round their necks.

The first human bodies were a little further along the road, lying outside what had once been their home. While Sylvie photographed them, Connor walked across the road and into the little orchard.

There were two of them there, hanging by their wrists from the bough of an apple tree. A mother and daughter, Connor guessed.

In the past months he had taken pictures of enough corpses to haunt a small gallery, and he no longer wanted to be sick when he saw them through the camera's eye. He still felt both pity and revulsion and hoped that he always would. But as he went about his business, he kept these feelings, if not capped, like a lens, then at least filtered. And what he mostly now felt was a sense of wonder that human beings were capable of such casual, even gleeful, atrocity.

At first, it had bothered him that he could do it. That he could look upon some child's father or some mother's child with the warmth of life still ebbing from them and at the same time scroll through the myriad tiny calculations that would make the image good or bad; the choice of lens, of exposure, of composition. But he concluded, like so many before him, that these were the very distractions that made it possible to document the horror laid before him.

The sunlight dappling on the blossom around the woman's head had a terrible beauty to it, and Connor took more pictures than perhaps he should have. Sylvie joined him but shot only a few frames and then moved away up the street.

They counted fifteen bodies in all. The last two were sitting side by side, a small boy and an old man. Above their heads, in splashed red paint, someone had written *BALIJE*, an insulting term for Muslims, and a coiled cobra, its head reared and ready to strike.

They were photographing this when they heard the trucks.

'Give me your film,' Sylvie said. She was unscrewing the cap to the centre stem of the telescopic aluminium tripod she always carried. 'Quick, come on. All of it.'

He handed her the rolls he'd shot and she slid them roll by roll along with her own inside the hollow tubing. She capped it again and then quickly fished half a dozen rolls from her bag and handed them to him. They were tail in, as if exposed.

'Put them in your bag.'

They could see the trucks now, coming towards them across the meadows. They loaded more film into their cameras and started taking pictures of them. There were two Jeeps, an armoured car and a big open-backed farm truck. There were twenty or thirty men, bristling with AK-47s and RPGs.

The convoy pulled up about twenty yards away from where they stood and the men scrambled out. Most of them were dressed in black fatigues and wore forage caps with the Red Cobra insignia painted on them. At least half a dozen were heading towards them.

From the way he looked and walked it was clear which of them was in charge. He was a man of about Connor's age, thickly muscled and taller than the others. As he came up to them Sylvie greeted him warmly in Serbo-Croat. He stopped close in front of them, looking down at her with contempt, and when he spoke it was in English.

'Who are you? What are you doing here?'

Sylvie answered in Serbo-Croat and though she spoke too fast for Connor to understand much, he heard her mention the name Grujo a couple of times, dropping it casually, as if they were friends. The man didn't seem impressed.

'Give me your papers.'

They handed him their passports and Connor got out his UN press card, the only other official-looking document he possessed and about as useful as a ticket to a cancelled ball game.

'You're American?'

'Yes.'

'What newspaper?'

Connor shrugged. 'Any that's interested. Mostly none.'

The man nodded towards the bodies of the old man and the boy. 'The American people, they are interested in this?'

'Hell, I don't know. I am.'

'So, what is it you find interesting?'

Connor held the man's gaze without flinching. 'I guess what mostly interests me is what kind of man it takes to murder and torture women and children and defenceless old men.'

The man looked at him and Connor searched for the eyes behind the sunglasses, but all he could see were his own staring back at him.

'Give us your film,' he said.

Sylvie started speaking, calmly but forcefully, telling him she wasn't going to. He kept telling her to hand it over and at last reached for her camera bag and Sylvie swore at him in several languages and he shouted a command and all hell broke loose.

They grabbed them both and shoved guns into their faces and pinned their arms behind their backs. Then they ripped off their cameras and their bags and took out every roll of film and smashed the cassettes under their boots and unravelled the film to the light and then opened their cameras and did the same again. And all the while Sylvie screamed and spat abuse at them.

Then, at the man's command, they were marched off down the road with guns at the back of their necks, and with every step Connor felt more convinced that they were going to be taken behind a building and shot.

But they were only taking them to the VW.

The soldiers searched the car for more film, but found none. They helped themselves to the cigarettes and gave Sylvie and Connor back their papers and their camera gear, including the tripod, and told them to get in and go. Sylvie turned the car round, keeping up her torrent of abuse. By now the men were all laughing and jeering.

As they dropped out of sight into the forest, she slapped the steering wheel with the palms of her hands and threw her head back and started to laugh. Connor smiled but said nothing. He would have liked to share her exhilaration but he couldn't. He was in shock.

In his head he was still walking down that road, certain that in a few moments he too would be dead. And what shocked him was the discovery that he hadn't cared.

THE LAB SYLVIE USED was a short walk from the hotel, or rather, a short duck and run across three streets surveyed by Serb snipers. The place was cramped and Connor perched himself in a corner and let Sylvie do most of the work.

She dried the negatives with a hair dryer and laid them out on the light box. When she got to one of the black and white rolls that Connor had shot in the orchard, Sylvie let out a low whistle.

'Which one,' she said. 'Tell me.'

'The best shot, you mean?'

She nodded and stood back to let him study them. Connor said he didn't think there was a lot to choose between them, but she said he was wrong and told him to make some test prints.

Even as the image was coming through on the paper Connor knew which one she meant. You could see the girl was naked but, apart from their faces and arms, both she and the woman were discreetly veiled by shadow and somehow this made what they had suffered all the more appalling. The sunlight on the blossom behind them and above them where their wrists were tied was exquisite and shocking.

'That is the picture of the day,' she said. 'Maybe even of the year.'

'I don't know about that.'

'Please don't think I would bother to flatter you.'

He looked at her and smiled. He lifted the print out and placed it in the fixer tray and started tidying things up.

'OK,' she said. 'Now let's go earn you some money.'

THE PICTURE OF THE WOMEN in the blossom found its way onto the front page of newspapers all over the world. Sylvie flew home to Paris the following week and then was sent at once to Africa. Connor didn't see her again until August, when she came back to Sarajevo. The following week Connor caught a piece of shrapnel in the back of his right leg and was flown in a UN Hercules to a hospital on the Croatian coast. Sylvie had gone north for a few days and he never got to say goodbye. It was only a flesh wound, but the doctors suggested he should go home to recuperate.

New York was hot and humid and everyone seemed miserable. When he hobbled into the offices of his agency, they greeted him like a war hero. He wished he could have felt like one, but all he felt was empty. One of the editors, Harry Turney, took him to lunch in the smartest place he had ever eaten. Connor ate like a starved wolf and still felt hungry. As the coffee was being served, Turney said he was sorry to hear about Sylvie. Connor asked him what he meant.

'You haven't heard?'

'Heard what?'

'It was in yesterday's *Times*. She was with a Reuters reporter some-where up north, near the border. They drove over a land mine. Both killed outright.'

JULIA TOOK THE STEAKS and the chicken legs out of the barbecue marinade and put them on the big wooden tray along with the salad and all the relishes. Donna Kiamoto had already ferried the rest of the food out onto the verandah where they had set up the table. Julia could hear Ed out there, making sure everyone knew the plan.

'So, we're all hiding out here, Donna's behind the drapes, the front door's open, the place looks deserted. As he comes into the living room, Donna gives the signal and I start to play. Hank and Phil, you guys unroll the banner—and make sure it's the right way up, OK? He may not be bright, but he can read.'

'Julia, how do you manage to live with this guy?' Hank Thomas asked her as she came out onto the verandah with the tray.

'Ear plugs.'

Ed was now fiddling with the amplifier for his electric guitar. Julia watched him for a moment and had to smile. He was in full buzz mode, happy as a puppy, and looked boyish and cute in his baggy shorts and Hawaiian shirt. He had wanted to frizz his hair into a Jimi Hendrix Afro but she'd talked him out of it. He'd settled instead for purple shades and a bandanna.

Poor Connor. He thought he was just coming over for a quiet supper with the two of them, but Ed had insisted they lay on this surprise welcome-home party. There were twenty guests, mostly Connor's old smoke-jumping buddies and their assorted spouses and lovers. All had been instructed to arrive early and park next door so that Connor wouldn't see the cars.

At least he was going to see the place at its best. It was a perfect September evening, balmy and clear. There were apples on the trees and the rambling rose above the verandah was a blaze of yellow. Julia had cleaned the house from top to bottom, put flowers in every room and spent far too much time and money getting the food and drink. She had even bought a new dress in a shade of pale blue that flattered her tan.

There was one tray of food left in the kitchen, and while Julia was on her way to fetch it, Donna came running through the front door. Ed had posted her at the end of the driveway to keep watch.

'Does he still drive that old Chevy?' she said.

'I guess. A pick-up, pale blue.'

'That's it. He's coming.'

Donna ran out and told everyone and Julia followed with the tray and helped her hide behind the drapes. She went to stand beside Ed.

'Where's my guitar, Julia?'

She handed it to him and he looped the strap over his shoulder, touching the strings to make a final check on the amplifier.

'OK, smoke jumpers. Stand ready.'

They all froze and after a few moments heard Connor's truck pulling up in the driveway, then the clunk of the car door and foot-steps on the gravel.

There was a knock on the front door and a long pause. 'Hello?'

At the sound of his voice, Julia felt something quicken within her. 'Ed? Julia?'

Donna nodded from her spyhole and Julia touched Ed on the shoulder. And on cue he made the guitar howl and launched into the Jimi Hendrix version of 'The Star-Spangled Banner'. Hank and Phil, on chairs either side of the doorway, unfurled the banner. Julia had written WELCOME HOME CONNOR on it in red and blue glitter-paint and dotted it with silver stars. And suddenly there he was below it, wearing his old cowboy hat and giving everyone that slow grin of his. His eyes scanned the faces and found hers and stayed.

Ed stopped playing and everyone cheered and gathered round Connor.

'Hey, Chuck, how're you doing? Hank, Donna . . .' He shook hands and hugged everyone, leaving Ed and Julia until last. Finally he came smiling towards them. She noticed he was limping a little.

'Julia, who *is* this weird dude you're standing next to?'

'My man.' Ed put his fist to chest.

'Hearts of fire!' They high-fived and Connor took off his hat and the two friends hugged each other.

Connor planted his hat on Ed's head and turned at last to Julia. She knew there was something different about his face but she couldn't work out what. He was thinner and his eyes seemed deeper set.

'Hi, Connor. Welcome home.'

'Hell, it's not as if I've been gone that long.'

'It just seems like it.'

They put their arms round each other and she felt his hands grip her back and hold her firmly for a moment, and all the breath seemed to leave her lungs. She worried that her feelings might be obvious to the others and quickly let him go and hooked her arm under Ed's.

'Just look at the pair of you,' Connor said. 'And look at all this.' He gave a sweep of his arm. 'You got your own little Garden of Eden here.'

'Julia as Eve, I can buy,' Hank Thomas said. 'But if that's Adam . . .'

'In those shades he looks more like the serpent,' Donna said.

'Here, Donna,' Ed said. 'Have an apple.'

The banter went on and grew cruder and Julia dragged Chuck away to the barbecue and told him to get the meat going and then went inside to fetch the champagne. When she came out again they were all teasing Connor about his 'war wound', but he was giving as good as he got, spinning a story that seemed to involve him single-handedly taking on the entire Serbian army. Ed opened the champagne and when all their glasses were charged he proposed a toast. And as Julia drank his health with the rest of them, Connor's eyes again settled on hers and stayed, and she had to look away.

CONNOR WATCHED HER as she walked ahead of him up the stairs, watched the way her hips moved inside her dress and how she trailed her left hand with its plain gold wedding band on the banister. The light outside was fading and the skin of her shoulders was dark against the pale blue of the dress.

Ed had put some Bob Marley on the stereo in the hope that people might start dancing, but everyone was enjoying sitting and chatting out on the verandah and on the grass below. Julia had lit candles out there in glass sleeves and set some more in the trees and everything looked magical. Connor had asked if he could take a look at the house and so she was giving him the tour.

As she reached the top of the stairs, she turned to look at him. He hoped that she hadn't caught him looking at her hips that way.

'It's a great place,' he said clumsily.

'Yeah. It works real well for us. Though it'd be easier for Ed if we lived in town.'

'Why's that?'

'Oh, you know, he could be more independent, find his own way around more. He has a map of Missoula in his head, whereas out here it's all new and . . . well, riskier. Not that it stops him doing things, mind. Did he tell you his latest plan?'

'Nope.'

'Rock climbing. He took this course down in Colorado where they teach blind people to climb. When your leg's better he wants the three of us to go climbing together.'

'Sounds great. Give me a week and I'm up for it.'

She cocked her head to one side and put her hands on her hips.

'You know what? You're as bad as he is.'

They smiled at each other for a moment. 'Come on,' Julia said. 'I'll show you the rest.'

There were three bedrooms and a bathroom. One of the bedrooms was decorated with yellow wallpaper and Julia said this was where he would be sleeping tonight, if that was OK. He said he hadn't figured on staying over and she looked genuinely upset so he said he would, if she was sure it was convenient. She gave him one of her school-marm looks.

'Connor, it's convenient. OK?'

'Ed told me you're teaching again,' he said.

'Yeah. It's great. Only part-time, you know. I do three days a week at this little elementary school in Missoula.'

'Teaching art?'

'Uh-huh. But mostly wiping noses and hosing them down after they've thrown paint all over each other.'

'Sounds like fun.'

'It is.'

They stood without speaking for a moment.

'He was really worried about you, you know?' she said. 'We'd hear about all those awful things going on out there, not knowing where you were and we—Ed, I mean, he just got a little worried.'

'You didn't get my cards?'

She laughed. 'Oh yeah, "Weather terrible, wish you were here."'

'I'm sorry.'

They stared at each other for a moment. Then, suddenly, she gave a little smile, a distancing kind of smile, like a shutter coming down.

'I'd better go and see if everyone's OK out there.'

'SO ARE THE SNIPERS always there watching?' Ed asked. 'Just waiting for somebody to cross?'

'You don't know until the bullet hits you. Some of the side streets off Snipers' Alley, you can go for days without a shot being fired. Then, bam, somebody gets killed.'

They were lying in the grass down by the river, just the two of them. Above the babble of the water, they could hear the others talking and laughing up at the house.

'How's the music going?'

'Oh, you know.'

'Well, if I did, I wouldn't ask.'

Ed smiled. He didn't want to talk about it, but it seemed unfair not to after the interrogation he'd just given Connor. He sighed.

'Well, to be honest, it's not going at all.'

'Julia says you play all the time.'

'Oh, sure. I play. I've even done a couple of gigs in a bar in town. But I haven't written anything in over a year. Anything worth keeping, anyhow. I just seem to have . . . I don't know. Lost it.'

'It'll come back. You've had to learn a whole new way of doing it.'

'Oh, sure, but that's not it. I've got the best equipment money can buy and I know my way around it. It's not that. I guess I've just had to accept that I haven't . . . got the talent.'

'Man, you've got more talent than anyone I know.'

'Well, that's nice of you to say it, but you know as much about music as I know about photography.'

'I know you're good.'

'Connor, do you know how many goddamn musicals I've written?'

'No.'

'Eleven. And God knows how many other bits and pieces. And every one of them has been rejected, lots of times. I haven't had a thing performed since I left college. And there comes a point when you have to get real. It's not going to happen.'

He could tell from Connor's silence that the poor guy didn't know what to say. He reached out and found his friend's shoulder.

'Do you know how proud I've been of you, just going out there and making a go of things? Man, I was proud. That picture of the women? I know it. I know what it looks like. I had Julia describe every single little detail of it and I know how extraordinary it is and I was so proud. And you know what? I was jealous as hell.'

'Ed, I just got lucky. Like I did that time at Yellowstone. I stumbled across a moment and took one good picture. What you're trying to pull off is a hell of a lot more difficult.'

'Hey, please. Don't patronise me.'

'Patronise you? Jesus.'

They sat silent for a while. Ed could imagine Connor shaking his head and staring out across the river. He felt like kicking himself for saying that. It was the first time in ages that he'd allowed himself to be hijacked by self-pity. He reached out and found Connor's shoulder again. After a moment Connor put his own hand on Ed's and said he was sorry if that's how it had sounded.

'No, man. I'm sorry. I just find it hard sometimes to hold it all together, you know? Hell, I've got so much to be thankful for. I've got Julia, this fantastic place. And you know what? I'm a great piano teacher. I used to find teaching a real drag, but now I really enjoy it.'

'That's good.'

'Yeah. It is.' He paused. He hadn't intended telling anyone the true cause of his low spirits. But sitting here with his best friend, he suddenly wanted to share it. He swallowed.

'Did Julia tell you we've been trying to have a kid?'

'No. Hey, that's great.'

'Yeah. In theory. We've been trying for almost a year and nothing's happened.'

'Well, I'm no expert. But that's not so long, is it?'

'Well, maybe. Anyhow, last month I had this minor problem with my diabetes. No big deal, it turned out that I just needed to increase my insulin a little. But when I was having it checked out, the doctor asked me if we were going to have children. And I told him we'd been trying but it hadn't happened yet. Then he asked me if I'd ever had any immuno-suppressant treatment. And I said hell, I don't know, I was only a little kid at the time, why? And he said that some of the drugs they used in those days had been found to have an adverse effect on fertility.

'So right away I call my mom and sure enough she says yeah, I had a blitz course of these immunosuppressant things. Seems the doctors thought they might be able to knock the diabetes on the head. So I go back to my doctor here, he runs the tests, and you know what? Zilch. Blanks, man. I fire blanks.'

'Can they do anything about it?'

'Not a thing.'

'Have you told Julia?'

'Not yet. I only found out at the end of last week. I just haven't had the balls to do it yet. So to speak.'

He laughed and felt Connor's hand grasp his shoulder.

'I mean, I know we can adopt and all, but . . . I guess it's just the shock, you know.' He paused. 'Well, hey! There's a party-pooper if ever there was one. I'm sorry, man. I shouldn't have—'

'Don't be sorry. I'm glad you told me.'

Julia stood back and watched them, marvelling at how such a small number of six-year-olds could make such a vast volume of noise. They were spread out along the back wall of the playground, all wearing their red and blue painting smocks. There was more chalk on their faces and smocks than was on the wall. It wasn't every day that law-abiding junior citizens were given licence to deface state property and they were sure making the most of it.

The outside of the school was being redecorated and Julia had asked Mrs Leitner, the principal, if her first-grade class could do a little decorating of their own before the painters got there. They had spent the previous week talking about it and today the kids were let loose on the playground wall.

While Julia watched, half her mind returned to what had been pre-occupying her all morning and all through the night. She thought about Ed and his astonishing suggestion.

They had spent the previous evening with Connor at The Karmic Moose, where Ed occasionally played piano and sang. It was a Thursday evening and there weren't too many people there but Ed played all his best numbers, from Cole Porter to Dolly Parton, and by the end the crowd had grown and was calling for more.

The two weeks since Connor's party had been an emotional roller-coaster ride. Ed had told her about his sterility immediately after Connor left that Sunday evening, and they had spent that night and almost every waking hour since talking about it. Together they went to see Ed's doctor, who confirmed the diagnosis, and when they got home Ed broke down and cried. Since then, however, he had been strong and positive and so had Julia. It was sad, she told herself, more than sad. But the solution was simple. They would adopt.

Ed had intended to cancel his gig at The Karmic Moose, but when the time came their feelings had calmed and they agreed that a night out would do them both good. They called Connor. He drove over from his mother's ranch in Augusta. Montana, and after the gig took them both round the corner for supper at The Depot.

It was almost like old times. Connor was in good spirits. He looked less strung out and said that his leg was as good as mended. He said he was ready to do that climb whenever they wanted. Flushed and happy, they said goodbye to Connor in the parking lot and agreed that, weather permitting, they would do the climb a week this coming Saturday.

For the first few miles of the drive back home, Ed didn't speak, then, out of the blue, he said it.

'How would you feel if we asked Connor if he'd be prepared to father a child for us.'

Julia almost drove off the road in shock.

'What?! You're kidding. Are you serious?'

One look at him told her that he was.

'Jesus, Ed.'

'No, hang on a minute. Listen. Stop the car here.'

'I think I'd better.'

She pulled off the road and turned off the engine but left the headlights on. Ed reached for her hand and held it in both of his.

'Just listen to me for a moment. I've thought about it a lot and—'

'Great. Well, don't waste any more time on it, OK?' She pulled her hand away and folded her arms.

'Julia, will you just shut up and let me speak? We've got a choice here. We both want a child, right? So. We can either adopt, the child of two total strangers. And—don't get me wrong—if that's what you want, that's fine. Or we could have a child who is much more truly ours, a child who'd at least have the genes of one of us.' He lifted his hand and stroked her face. 'Yours.'

Julia sighed and looked away along the empty road ahead.

'And this is a child who could grow inside you. We could share all that and watch him, or her, grow. It'd be our child, Julia. In a way an adopted child could never be. Don't you see that?'

She didn't reply. She was too shocked to think straight.

Ed went on, calmly. 'And then the only question is, who would be the biological father?'

'And you want it to be Connor. Jesus, Ed! Have you and Connor talked about this?'

'Of course not. What do you think I am?'

'Ed, drop it. The answer's no, OK?' She started the engine again.

'Fine.'

She pulled out onto the highway and drove for a while in silence.

'Sorry,' he said at last. 'Let's just forget it. It was a bad idea.'

They didn't speak again, not even after they reached home and went upstairs to bed, not even to say good night. Julia slept, but it was a fitful, skimming semi-sleep in which Connor and Ed and the knowing faces of unborn infants flitted like phantoms.

They were still flitting in her head while she drove wide awake to work and still there now despite the renewed din of the children.

At last the bell rang to signal the end of school.

When the kids had dumped their smocks and disappeared, Julia returned to the playground to clear up the chalk.

As she drove home, she tried to figure out why she had reacted with such vehemence to Ed's proposal. It was clearly something to do with her feelings for Connor, which seemed to grow stronger every time she saw him and which she still considered a shameful betrayal of Ed.

But to have Connor's child . . . Would that not seal the betrayal in blood, make it many times worse? Or was it simply that she didn't trust herself, that she feared the world might change if she were to have his seed within her, to feel it stir, to give it life and bring it forth into the world and nourish and protect it? Julia started to shake.

She was approaching the place where she and Ed had stopped to talk last night and now she stopped again. She got out and crossed the road and stood for a long time staring down at the river. And slowly, all the doubts and fears in her head stilled and dispelled and she knew, calmly and with utter clarity, what she wanted.

She couldn't have Connor, but she could, if he agreed, have his child. A child that would be part him, part her and, for Ed, the greatest gift imaginable.

CONNOR SCRAMBLED UP onto the ledge and secured himself to the anchor point. 'Taking in!' he called.

He peered down into the chimney and saw Ed on a thinner ledge some thirty feet below taking the rope from his belay system and saw Julia a little lower and to one side watching him too. Connor began hauling in the loose rope hand over hand until he felt it go tight.

'That's me!' Ed called. 'Climbing!'

'OK!' Connor began to take in the slack, watching Ed in awed silence. No stranger would ever have guessed that he was blind. He was feeling his way and only twice had they had to help him. And now they had just one more pitch to the summit.

It was one of those perfect early fall days, the sky vast and cloudless and the air blood-warm without a whisper of wind to chill it. The green ocean of the forest was dotted with islands of amber and rust and here and there a yellow splash of cottonwood or quakin' asp. The higher peaks had their first sprinkling of snow.

Half an hour later they reached the top. And watching Ed's beaming face as he stepped up onto the platform of rock, Connor felt greatly moved. He hugged him and congratulated him and they did their 'Hearts of Fire' routine. Ed asked him to take him over to a little pinnacle and he placed his palms on it, then turned and stood with his back pressed to the rock as if surveying the horizon. Connor looked at Julia. She was watching Ed and wiping away tears and grinning all at the same time.

'Pictures!' Ed said. 'We gotta take pictures!'

He made a joke about how honoured they were to have such a big-shot photographer on hand and Connor played the role and lined them up, bossing them around and making pretentious observations about the light. Then, Julia propped her camera on some rocks and set the timer and ran to get into the picture.

'Now I have to take one of you two,' Ed said.

Connor handed him the Leica and helped him position himself. Julia watched him walking back towards her and as he came near she reached out and put her arm round his waist and drew him close. He put his round her shoulders and she looked up at him.

'Am I pointing the right way?' Ed called.

'Down a little,' Connor said. 'And a little to your right.'

'OK?'

'Perfect.'

'Man, you're going to be mad when my picture's better than yours. OK, big smiles now . . .'

They sat in the sun and ate their picnic and afterwards Ed made Julia describe the view to him in all its detail. And when she had finished he sat in silence, picturing it all in his mind's eye.

'Connor?' Ed said and put his arm round Julia's shoulders. 'Julia and I have something to ask you.'

Connor could see in their faces that it was something that mattered and he told him to go ahead. Ed swallowed and started talking in a rambling way. He said how fond he and Julia were of him, how he was their best friend and how much they'd all shared. And how they'd been trying to have kids and how they'd discovered that this wasn't going to be possible and how they'd been talking about adoption—which was probably, in the end, what they were going to do—except . . . Except there was this other crazy idea they'd discussed . . .

And Connor suddenly got it. A full twenty seconds before Ed

actually found the words. And while he waited for him to utter them it was like hearing a train coming towards him through a tunnel, the rush of air getting louder and louder in his head.

'And we just wondered if you . . . I mean, we feel kind of embarrassed asking. If you think it's a terrible idea, all you have to do is say no. But we wondered if you would be . . . if you would consider being, the father—the biological father—of our child.'

Connor took a deep breath. 'Well. I don't—'

'Really, man. It's a hell of a thing to ask and the chances are you won't want to. And that's OK by us. Isn't that right, honey?'

'Absolutely.'

Ed kissed her cheek and she gave an embarrassed smile. Connor had been staring at her. She was still avoiding his eyes. At last she seemed to find the courage to look at him and the connection set something reeling inside him.

'I mean, listen, man,' Ed went on. 'It was just an idea, you know?'

'Ed,' Connor said. 'Will you just stop talking a moment?'

Connor was too stunned to think straight. He found himself saying that Ed sure knew how to shock the hell out of a man and they all laughed in a kind of nervous release. Then he told them he was moved and honoured that they should ask this of him, but bringing a child into the world, he said, was no small matter, and he asked if he could take a while to think about it. They said in unison that he should take as long as he liked.

Coming down the mountain took almost as long as going up. They had to concentrate hard on the rappels, guiding Ed precisely so that he didn't injure himself. Connor was grateful that there was no time for small talk, which would have seemed phoney after what had been said at the summit. On the journey back to the house, with night closing in, Ed did his best to lift the atmosphere but things between the three of them seemed a little forced. They asked Connor to stay over, but he made a lame excuse about having to get back to his mother's.

Julia kissed him goodbye and went into the house and he knew she was doing it so that he and Ed could be alone. He got into the truck and rolled down the window. Ed put his hands on the sill.

'Listen,' Ed said. 'I just want to say again. Whatever you decide is fine. I really mean that. It's a hell of a thing to lay on you like that.'

'Tell me one thing. Is Julia as sure about this as you are?'

'Completely.'

Connor didn't say anything for a moment. Ed reached into the car and put his hand on Connor's shoulder. 'Take your time, you hear?'

'I'll call you.'

THE FIRST TIME he'd seen it he thought it was smoke, but now he could usually tell the difference. You would see it swirling in a black cloud above the canopy of palm and eucalyptus. And then you would get a little closer and start to hear the cries, and that was when you realised that the cloud was a living thing consisting entirely of birds. Vultures and kites and crows mostly. But by the time you were that close, you had no need of sight or sound, for the smell alone told you where the bodies were.

For three days now he had been with this same contingent of the Rwandan Patriotic Front, pushing steadily south and west. And although he still photographed the bodies they came across, he had long ago stopped counting. He had seen them hacked in their hundreds in ditches and marshes and around their ransacked homes. He had seen them stacked by the roadside and he had seen garbage trucks collecting them. And he had photographed them all and sent the pictures from his scanner spinning home across the heavens.

Now it was night and the village was throbbing with its new population of relief-agency workers, journalists, human-rights monitors and assorted bureaucrats. Connor and some of the other journalists were gathered round the young RPF lieutenant who had been assigned to brief them. The lieutenant said they had so far counted 209 bodies, all Tutsis.

Connor walked out of the village past where the soldiers were camped. He followed a dirt track that led away from the road and meandered through the banana groves until it broadened into a grassy clearing. There were some rocks there and he sat down on one of them and listened to the pulsing clamour of the insects and frogs. And then he thought, as he did every day and every night, of Julia and of his child that was in her womb.

He hadn't spoken to Ed and Julia since Christmas. He'd phoned them from Nairobi where he had gone after things became too dangerous in Somalia. Ed told him that Julia was two months pregnant. She had conceived after the first insemination from the deposit Connor had left at the clinic before he flew out to Africa.

'It's like it was meant to be,' Ed said.

They had written him a letter via his agency telling him but, like much of the mail forwarded to him, Connor had never received it. Then Julia came on the line and wished him a merry Christmas and he could tell from both their voices, how full of joy they were. And he tried to sound that way too, and only hoped that it sounded more convincing to them than it did to him. The truth was that even now, after months of thinking about it, he still didn't know what he felt.

He was happy that his gift had brought them such joy. And there were times when he drew strength from it. Walking among the dead, as he had almost every day, he would force himself to think of this new life so many thousand miles away and it gave him hope and courage. But in his heart there was also a hollowing sense of loss.

JULIA LAY STILL, watching in wonder as the dome of her belly shifted shape and moved from one side of the bathtub to the other.

'Whoa there!'

Ed was standing naked at the basin beside her, shaving.

'On the move again?'

'Big time. We're training for the Olympics here.'

He put down his razor and knelt beside the bath. He put his hands on her belly and they waited for another movement.

'He's gone all shy,' Ed said.

'No she hasn't.'

'Come on, Tadpole. One more time for Daddy.'

At her last scan they'd shown her a picture of the foetus and asked her if she wanted to know what it was going to be and she said it was OK, thanks, she already knew—it was going to be a baby. They all laughed and left it at that but, actually, even though she didn't want to be told, she did know. It was going to be a girl.

Quite how she knew, Julia wasn't sure, except that it had something to do with Skye. She didn't think about her so much any more. For about a year after the fire, Skye had been there all the time in the corner of her mind, but, with time, the image had faded and now appeared only when summoned in Julia's prayers or darkly magnified in those treacherous, sleepless recesses of the night.

It wasn't that the guilt had diminished. She had come to the conclusion that guilt was made of some imperishable matter upon which time and happiness had not the slightest corrosive effect. It was a fact and you lived with it and dealt with the consequences, a kind of contract under which your actions led to inevitable obligations. Those to Ed, she was already fulfilling, by devoting her life to him. Now it was

Skye's turn. Julia was responsible for the loss to the world of a young female life and therefore she must restore one. And although she knew it wasn't rational, this was why she had convinced herself that the baby, now seven months grown in her womb, was a girl.

Ed had different ideas. The Montana wing of the Tully dynasty, he grandly declared, needed—and would have, damn it—a male heir.

He still had his hands on her belly. 'He's gone to sleep.'

'No . . . Here we go again.'

'Wow! Look at him go. That's my boy!'

She watched Ed grinning, his eyes flickering a little as they did nowadays. She wondered sometimes, when he had his hands upon her like this and felt the baby stir, whether the joy it so clearly gave him was tinged in any way by the fact that the child wasn't truly his.

It was something they had never discussed. Almost from the start, Ed had been incredible. After Connor called to give them his decision, and while they were waiting for the first insemination, Ed had seemed troubled and she had half expected him to change his mind. But when she asked him if he was still sure about it, he told her of course he was, so she never asked again.

They spoke of Connor often, wondering where he might be and what he might be doing. At Ed's insistence, a photograph of the three of them—the one taken by timer on the climb last fall—had been blown up and now hung framed on the living-room wall. Ed said he wanted it to be there for Tadpole to see, right from the start, so he would know the set-up: Mom, Dad and Bio-Dad. He said that Connor had the better title; Bio-Dad sounded like a superhero. Julia said she thought it sounded more like a detergent.

The bathwater was growing cold now and the baby had finished her workout or maybe just got bored. And so had Ed's hands. They were wandering up towards her breasts, which were now enormous. She slapped his hand.

'Hey,' she said. 'Cut it out. I'll be late for work.'

 CHAPTER EIGHT

When Connor checked into the Norfolk Hotel in Nairobi they handed him the mail they had been keeping for him. He thumbed through it while he followed the boy carrying his bag to the room, and found what he was looking for, a white envelope from Missoula,

Montana, addressed to him in Julia's broad, elegant handwriting.

He didn't know why, but he didn't want to open it right away, so he showered and washed his hair, sluicing away the smell of death. And only when he had put on some fresh clothes and settled in a chair by the window, with the evening sky glowing pink and orange above the silhouetted palms, did he open it.

There was a letter and a photograph of Julia sitting up and smiling in a hospital bed with Ed perched grinning beside her and the baby wrapped and pink and crumple-faced in her arms.

The letter said that she had been born on July 5, weighing in at seven pounds and twelve ounces. After debate, they had settled on calling her Amy. Her middle name was to be Constance, which was as near to Connor as they could think of. Julia hoped that was OK. They wanted him to be the child's godfather and were going to wait until he next came home before having her baptised.

A six-figure salary and a fancy new Manhattan lifestyle didn't seem to have altered Linda Rosner at all. In fact, from the black clothes she had been wearing all weekend, Amy's newly recruited godmother appeared to be revisiting the Land of the Neo-Gothics. Nor did her lawyerly qualifications seem to have instilled in her any verbal restraint. In church yesterday she had taken one look at Connor and *sotto voce* to Julia adjudged him as fine a piece of ass as she'd seen in years. The only discernible change was that instead of rolling her own cigarettes, she now bought them ready-made. She had one dangling from her lips now while she stacked the dishwasher. Across the kitchen Julia was making coffee.

The christening, for which Linda had flown in on Friday, had evolved into a weekend party marathon and this was the last lap: Sunday supper for what Ed called 'Amy's inner circle—parents real, godly and grand'. Assembled round the candlelit table outside on the verandah were Ed and his parents, Connor and his mother, and Julia's mother, Maria. By the sound of it, they still hadn't run short of conversation. Amy was upstairs, asleep in her crib.

'Well,' Linda said, dropping her voice. 'All I can say, babe, is that you sure picked some good genes there. I mean, I tell you, in your shoes, I wouldn't have bothered with all that clinic shit. I'd have insisted on first-hand delivery.'

'Linda. That is so out of order.'

Linda held up her hands. 'I know. I'm sorry.'

There was a pause. The last of the coffee gurgled through the machine and Julia lifted the pot and put it on the tray with the cups.

'Didn't you even think about it though? Be honest.'

'Linda!'

'Sorry, sorry.'

Julia felt herself blushing and saw Linda register this. On cue, as if to rescue her, Amy started to cry upstairs. Julia asked Linda to take the tray out to the verandah and hurried up to the bedroom.

Amy had her own room, but had been evicted for the weekend. Only her godparents were staying at the house, Linda in Amy's room, Connor in the guest room. Everyone else was at the Red Lion in town. Amy's crib was temporarily parked in the corner of Julia and Ed's room, and as soon as Julia appeared above it the baby stopped crying and gave a burbling, gummy grin.

'You little monkey. You just wanted company, didn't you, huh?'

She lifted her out and snuggled her and breathed the wonderful, sweet milky smell of her. She carried her over to the window and stood there in the dark, looking down at the table on the verandah where everyone sat talking, while Linda poured the coffee.

She couldn't hear what anyone was saying and she found herself staring at Connor. It was exactly a year since they had last seen him. He was tanned and his hair, which he wore shorter now, was bleached almost white. There were lines around his eyes and Julia wondered if this was only from squinting in the African sun or from what he'd had to squint at.

As if hearing her thoughts, he suddenly looked up and, even though she had thought herself invisible in the darkness, he saw her and smiled. And no one but she saw him do so, just the two of them together in that moment. She smiled back and felt something quicken within her, which she hastily repressed. And she turned away and sat on the bed and uncovered her breast to feed Amy and soon, in the streaming intimacy, found calm and comfort.

ED FOUND JULIA in their bedroom, trying to settle Amy who sounded as if being settled was the last thing she had in mind.

'Did you feed her already?'

'Yeah. She's wide awake.'

'Bring her down. It's her party after all.'

Ed carried Amy out onto the verandah and all the women started oohing and aahing and competing to hold her, and Ed said he was going to have to organise some kind of ticketing system. He held Amy's face to his ear as if she were whispering something to him.

'Really? OK, you're the boss. You know whose knee she says she wants to sit on?' He started humming the theme tune from *The Godfather* and handed her to Connor.

'I made her an offer she couldn't refuse,' Connor said.

Ed cuffed him over the head, harder than he should have. 'Hey, pal, that's my line. If you're not careful, you'll be sleeping with the fishes tonight.'

The joke didn't come out well either. His voice had a harsh edge to it. He reached for his wineglass. It wasn't where he had left it.

'Hey, did someone move my glass?'

Nobody heard him. He asked again, more loudly, and Linda said she had moved it. She apologised and filled it and handed it to him then went right back to talking with Amy and Connor.

Everyone was talking, but nobody was talking to him, and suddenly he felt isolated and grouchy. He sat back in his chair and drained his glass in two gulps.

Suddenly he felt Julia's arms reaching from behind him around his neck and felt her face nuzzling his. She kissed him on the cheek and asked quietly if he was OK.

'Me? Yeah, I'm fine. Why, what's the matter? Don't I look fine?'

'Of course you do.'

'Then why ask?'

'It's OK. I'm sorry.'

She removed her arms and he could hear her footsteps going away, and immediately he felt guilty for being so unpleasant. He heard Connor talking to Amy and—again he couldn't help it—but it made him feel . . . what? Angry? Not exactly. More like . . . jealous.

There was no point lying to himself about it. He felt jealous. And to be honest, he'd felt that way all weekend, whenever Connor was around Amy. He resented the fact that Connor could *see* her. And that he could see Julia too. It was insane, Ed knew, but it made him feel excluded. Even now he could picture Amy sitting happily on Connor's knee and people looking at them both and knowing that he was her real father. And then glancing over at poor old Ed sitting all alone at the end of the table and thinking, *Poor guy, what a pity he couldn't do it himself, but isn't it all just lovely?* Well, it wasn't.

Amy started to cry and Connor handed her to Julia in whose arms, as always, she again became calm. And after a couple more glasses of wine, Ed stopped feeling sorry for himself, although he knew that the evening never quite recovered.

The next thing he knew, Julia was undressing him and putting him to bed. And the last thing he remembered was her kissing him on the forehead and saying good night and telling him that she loved him.

CONNOR DIDN'T KNOW how long he had been lying awake, but it was certainly hours. After all the others had left, he'd helped Julia lift Ed out of his chair, where he'd fallen asleep, and haul him up to bed. Then they finished tidying up in the kitchen, while Linda sat perched on the worktop, doing her best to entertain them. But they were all tired and soon went up to their separate rooms.

Some time ago he had heard Amy crying, but the house was now quiet again. There was a dull and restless aching in his chest that had been there ever since he lay down. He'd gone over the weekend in his mind and still couldn't figure out why such a happy time had left him feeling so low. Whatever it was, he knew that something had shifted between the three of them and that it could never be the same again.

He felt it most strongly with Ed. They hadn't had a decent talk all weekend, and when they had managed a few words there was something forced about it. The reason, of course, was Amy. Before he arrived, Connor had tried to prepare himself for the moment he first laid eyes on her. But there was no way he could have predicted the effect she would have on him. His own flesh and blood joined with Julia's, living and breathing and cooing up at him from her crib. And the thought hit him there and then, like the blast of a bomb, that neither child nor mother was his or would ever be his. And he thought, how could he have been so dumb to have done this? And yet, seeing the child, how could he not have?

He looked at his watch. It was three o'clock and he was wide awake. He got out of bed and went over to the window. Maybe he would just go outside and get some air. He pulled on his jeans and T-shirt and quietly opened the bedroom door. He could hear Ed snoring across the landing, but otherwise all was quiet. He walked in his bare feet to the top of the stairs.

He saw her as he came through the living room. She was sitting outside on the steps of the verandah. She was wearing a white shift of a nightgown and was looking out towards the river. She heard him and turned as he came onto the verandah.

'Did Amy wake you?'

'No.' He sat down beside her.

'I can't wait till she sleeps through. I wasn't cut out for this three-times-a-night wake-up thing. I walk around all day like a zombie.'

'Well, you look pretty good on it.'

'I wish. I feel fat and frazzled.'

He wanted to tell her how lovely she looked, but didn't trust himself, and they sat awhile in silence looking out into the grey night.

'I'm sorry about Ed,' she said.

'He just had a glass too many, that's all.'

'No. I think he's finding it all a little harder than he expected. It's the first time you've been around Amy and . . . well, you know.'

He did but he didn't know what to say.

'She's beautiful,' he said simply.

'Of course she is.'

'And the way Ed is with her. He's a great father.'

'Yep. He's amazing.'

They were silent again. Julia was staring at her bare feet.

'Oh God,' she sighed. Suddenly she stood up and stretched her arms high above her. 'Will you walk to the river with me?'

'Sure.'

They walked side by side through cool damp grass, following the rail of rope to the riverbank where there was a wooden bench. Julia sat down at one end of it and he at the other and they looked out at the river and for a long while said nothing.

'So how does it make you feel?' she said quietly.

What was he to say? That it almost broke his heart? That he sometimes wished he had never laid eyes on Julia, for only then would he be whole again and not some empty shadow of a man.

'It's OK,' she said. 'You don't have to say if you don't want to.'

'I'm just real happy for the both of you.'

She looked at him for a long time. 'But?'

'No buts. That's how it is.'

'Connor, you're such a poor liar.'

He smiled. She was still staring at him and he held her gaze for a while but then had to look away.

'I was thinking just now about the first time we met,' she said. 'Do you remember? When you came to collect us at the airport?'

'I remember.'

'It's weird, but it wasn't like meeting you. More like recognising you. As if we somehow already knew each other.'

'I felt the same.'

'You know how some people say things are "meant to be", like it's written in the stars or something. Do you think that?'

'I don't know. I never used to. But now I think it might just be.'

'With me it's the other way round.' She paused and looked away across the river. 'I remember Skye saying one time how all the important things in life happened by accident. And I said no, I didn't think so, that in my view life was all mapped out and decided and just got revealed to us as we went along. But I don't think that any more. I think there are accidents and then we have to make choices.'

Connor didn't reply.

'But you now think it's all mapped out?' she said.

'No. I think you're right. There are choices. It's just that sometimes the important ones aren't ours to make.'

'Well, you've sure made some pretty big ones lately. Look at Amy. Look at this new career of yours. Going off to all these dangerous places, risking your life. They don't get much bigger than that.'

He laughed.

'What? What's so funny?'

'Well, it's just that I don't see it that way. I do what I do because someone else made the big choice. Not me.'

She frowned at him. 'What choice? Tell me. Who?'

He looked at her and because already in his heart he knew that this was the last time he would see her, he went ahead and told her.

'You,' he said simply. 'You chose Ed.'

She stared at him in silence and he could see her face slowly fill with sadness as she understood.

'Oh, Connor,' she whispered. 'I had no idea.'

'Then I'm a better liar than we both thought.'

'Oh, Connor.'

He smiled sadly at her.

'I've loved you from the very first moment I saw you,' he said.

'Don't. Don't say any more.'

'I'm sorry. I should never have told you. And I promise I'll never say it again. But that's just how it is. And hell, I'm a lucky guy. I'm part of Amy and she's part of you. And whatever happens to me, she'll have you for ever.'

'Oh, Connor. Oh God.'

She closed her eyes and started to sob, and the sound was so deep and harrowing that it seemed to come from some dark netherworld of long-forgotten sorrows. With her eyes tight shut she slowly opened her arms to him and he moved towards her and held her and held her head to his chest and felt her tears wet against him and felt tears of his own begin to run. She lifted her face and kissed him and said that she loved him too and had always loved him and she kissed him again and kissed his tears and Connor kissed hers.

How long they stayed like that, he didn't know. All he could think of was that these moments were all he would ever have of her and that he must live them and feel them with every particle of his being. And then store them away and treasure them for the rest of his life.

PART THREE
CHAPTER NINE

Amy Constance Tully was an angel. She even had the wings to prove it. As the daughter of the composer and musical director of the school's Christmas show, she had been able to pick her part—at least, among the supporting cast, for bigger stars with better agents from the fourth and fifth grades had bagged the leads. Six weeks ago she had unequivocally declared that she wanted to be an angel.

Of course, seeing as the school was a multicultural and altogether right-on kind of a place, this naturally didn't mean angel as in hovering-over-the-baby-Jesus-in-his-manger sort of angel. No, the angels were much more of the avenging, in-your-face variety and by the end of the show they had disposed of several evil loggers and an oil slick called Mr Gloop.

Now Amy was tucked up in bed looking every inch a regular angel and happy to be one. Her cheeks glowed pink from her bath and her mop of blonde curls was brushed as neatly as it ever allowed. The colour was clearly from Connor, but nobody had a clue where the curls came from. Her eyes were dark brown like Julia's and she had the same olive tone to her skin. Yet, if asked, as occasionally she was, to say which of her parents, in character, Amy most resembled, Julia would reply without a moment's hesitation that it was Ed.

She was boisterous and funny and quick-witted and naturally musical. She had picked up Ed's habit of singing to herself when she was doing something and when she pulled out the stops, her voice could be exquisite. Long before she was out of nappies, Ed was teaching her songs and sitting her on his lap at the piano, which by now, at seven years old, she played as proficiently as some of his pupils three years her senior.

Julia was lying on the covers beside her now in the cluttered cavern of Amy's room. Together they were reading Amy's favourite Dr Seuss, *The Butter Battle Book*. As usual, Julia was doing most of the reading. Amy liked the different funny voices that Julia put on for the Zooks and the Yooks as they escalated their crazy war over which way bread should be eaten: butter side up or butter side down.

It intrigued Julia that this was Amy's favourite Dr Seuss, for it wasn't his funniest. In fact, it was downright chilling, telling, as it did, of a world sliding towards apocalypse because of a fatuous disagreement. Buying the book, about two years ago, had prompted a long discussion about war and why people sometimes hated and wanted to kill each other. Julia reassured her that hardly anyone nowadays expected the kind of world war that was depicted in the book. But there were wars, she said, smaller ones, that were always going on in different parts of the world. She found herself telling Amy that her biological father often went to these places and took pictures.

When Amy was still a baby, Ed and Julia had discussed at what age they would tell Amy about various things. They wanted her to know about having two fathers right away. But they hadn't felt that way about the fire. They worried that it might traumatise the child and agreed that they would tell her when she was, say, twelve years old. But at the age of four and a half, Amy asked Ed how he came to be blind and the story came pouring out. And instead of upsetting her, it seemed to make her proud of them all, especially of her two superhero fathers who jumped out of the sky to rescue mom.

Amy didn't talk about Connor so much any more. It was hard to keep a memory alive when there were only photographs and stories and the occasional letter to feed it with. He still wrote to Amy and sent exotic gifts from far-flung corners of the world. But never once, since the christening, had he come again to see her.

During the first year, Julia had written several letters to Connor but destroyed them all. In those days she had thought about him all the time. Barely a waking hour went by without her replaying in her mind that last image of him, sitting beside her in the cold moonlight, confessing his love and then holding her and kissing her tears.

Before he left the following day, she had slipped a photograph into his packed bag. It was the one that Ed had taken of the two of them that last day they climbed together.

She kept track of him as best she could. One way or another—mostly through the eagle-eyed Linda—she would hear about some magazine that had used his latest photographs. She noticed that he now often wrote the accompanying stories, whereas at first the words had always been someone else's. The pieces that moved her most were about a little-reported war which had been going on for years in northern Uganda. Connor seemed to return there often. His most recent piece was about a rehabilitation centre for children who'd been abducted from their homes and forced to serve as soldiers in the rebel army. The pictures had made Julia weep.

Only once had she and Ed drawn near to speaking the truth about why Connor had stayed away. A brown paper package, mailed from Kampala, had arrived on Amy's fourth birthday. It contained a little dress—just the right size—and a shawl, both in a vivid African fabric. Amy was thrilled. She wore the outfit for a week.

Ed was furious. Once Amy was safely out of earshot, he exploded.

'Goddamn presents!' he said. 'What does he say on the card? "Say hi to your mom and dad"? Terrific. Maybe one day he'll come say it himself. Or even pick up the phone and say it. She's never heard his voice! He was my best friend, for God's sake!'

'Maybe he thinks it's fairer to stay away.'

'Fairer? How the hell do you work that one out?'

'Well, I don't know. Maybe he thinks you might find it hard.'

'What, like, I'd be jealous of him and Amy or something?'

'No, not exactly. Please, Ed, let's just drop it, OK?'

'No, I'm interested. That's obviously what you think. That he's staying away because he thinks I'm threatened by him being Amy's biological father. Is that right?'

'Well. Maybe a little. The way you were at the christening—'

'What do you mean? Like I was hostile to him or something?'

'A little, yes.'

He stood there in silence for a moment, still and inscrutable behind his dark glasses. It was as though he were staring into her head with something more powerful than vision and it unsettled her.

'Wow,' he said quietly. He shook his head sadly. 'Oh boy.'

And Julia at once regretted saying it, and tried to soften it by saying that it probably wasn't that after all and that maybe Connor had found it hard seeing Amy and felt it better to keep his contact with her at a distance in case he grew too attached. She babbled on for a while, but she could tell Ed wasn't listening. He was thoughtful for days and since that day had never criticised Connor again.

When Julia reflected on why Connor stayed away, she suspected that both of the things she had said were true. Probably he had sensed Ed's jealousy and concluded that the best he could do for his friend was to keep clear. And probably he did find the prospect too painful of seeing his daughter growing up as someone else's. If he couldn't have all of Amy, then perhaps it was better to have none. This, Julia had little doubt, was what he also felt about her. And if she were honest with herself, this was how she preferred it to be. If not all of him, then none.

KAY NEUMARK TOLD the chipmunks for the third time to quit fooling around and trying to trip the angels. Still, a first full rehearsal was always a test of nerves, and so far it was going all right.

Kay was going to be credited as the director and co-writer with Ed. She taught history and English by all accounts with the same gusto and good humour that she had brought to the show. From Julia's description of her, Ed knew that she was in her mid-thirties, had cropped silvery hair and a penchant for baggy striped sweaters. Ed knew her more for her booming voice.

'All right,' she was calling out now. 'Let's do that one more time. And this time, Mr Gloop, more menace. Know what I mean? Yeah, just like that. Here we go. Positions, please. Julia, are you ready back there?'

Julia was assistant stage manager and somewhere behind the partially painted scenery was marshalling the troops. She shouted that she was as ready as she ever would be.

'OK, maestro,' Kay called.

Ed was sitting ready at the piano which, apart from a few taped sound effects, was all the accompaniment there was. The show had turned out to involve a lot more work than Ed had expected, and nowadays, since he'd been on dialysis, he didn't have the stamina he'd once had. In fact, lately he felt tired more often than he didn't. Maybe he was just getting old. He took a deep breath.

'OK, one more time,' he called. 'Gloop and Loggers, from the top!' And off they went again.

Ed had been on dialysis for a little over two years now. His annual diabetes checkup had revealed that he had abnormally high levels of potassium and protein waste products in his blood. His kidneys weren't doing a good enough job cleaning it. So now, three mornings a week, he had to go into Missoula and get hooked up to a damn machine to do it instead. He'd been there four long hours this morning. He hated the whole process with a vengeance.

All in all, the rehearsal went well and everyone went away in high spirits. Ed closed his eyes, thinking about the show. How ironic it was, he thought, that this was where all his grand ambitions had led. Ten years ago it had been so clear. He'd had his entire career mapped out: first there would be the little off-Broadway gem that got rave reviews, then Broadway itself, then he was going to reinvent the Hollywood musical for a whole new generation. And now here he was, nearly thirty-six years old, a blind piano teacher in a little western town, busting his ass over his daughter's elementary-school show. Surprisingly, he didn't feel one little bit cheated or bitter about it. Other things were more important in life.

What was particularly ironic was that of the two of them, it should be Connor who'd ended up famous. Only the other day Julia read that he had just been awarded some major photojournalism prize. He even had an exhibition coming up at a fancy New York gallery. Yet he had never once struck Ed as even slightly ambitious.

He still missed Connor badly. He'd never had a friend so close, nor probably ever would again. At first he had felt angry, until three years ago, when Julia told him what she believed to be the reason for Connor's estrangement. Ed had written him a long letter via the photo agency, apologising for his behaviour at the christening. Connor never replied. For a while Ed worried that the letter had gone astray and wondered if he should write again.

But he never did. And as time went by he began to think that maybe it was all for the best. Ed hadn't exactly admitted his jealousy in the letter, but the more he thought about it, the more certain he became that Connor knew about it. Ed hated himself for feeling jealous. It was unreasonable and ungrateful, but he couldn't help it. The harsh truth was that Ed feared that Connor was more of a father to Amy than he was, or ever would be, and that maybe Julia felt that way too. If Connor had been constantly around these past years, the paranoia would no doubt have festered, making Ed ever more twisted and resentful. It was sad to admit it, but estrangement had probably been the only course.

Poor old Connor. How he missed him. What a mess it all was.

CONNOR ASKED THE CABDRIVER to pull up across the street from the gallery and handed him a twenty-dollar bill, then climbed out into the freezing night air.

The street was narrow and the buildings on both sides were tall and grim. He stood in the shadows and shivered, then looked across at the big plate-glass window of the gallery. There were maybe twenty or thirty people in there, sipping champagne and chatting. One or two were even looking at his photographs.

He was an hour late and almost hadn't come at all. Why he had ever let himself be talked into it, he couldn't imagine. Eloise, the gallery owner, was a friend of his editor, dear old Harry Turney, and it was hard to figure out who was doing whom a favour. Eloise had lots of fancy media connections and some of them were going to be there tonight. He took a deep breath and headed across the street.

Eloise Martin was one of those black-garbed New York women, thin and chic and sharp. Harry Turney had it on good authority that she was pushing sixty, but you would never have guessed. She divided her time, according to Harry, between art and philanthropy.

Connor's exhibition fell into the latter category. Several of the photographs were from his most recent trip to northern Uganda, where he had spent two weeks at St Mary of the Angels, a rehabilitation centre for child soldiers. He had been there several times before and regularly sent them money. The proceeds from any pictures sold from the exhibition would be going there too.

Eloise came to greet him while he was still checking in his coat.

'Connor, darling. You're such a naughty boy. There are so many people dying to meet you.'

'I'm sorry, the traffic was terrible.'

'Of course. Have some champagne. Don't the pictures look simply marvellous?'

'Yeah, you did a great job.'

She summoned one of the waiters and Connor took a glass and drained half of it in one gulp. Eloise went off to find 'someone important' whom she wanted him to meet. His heart sank lower. Harry sidled up and put a consoling hand on his shoulder.

'Don't worry,' he said quietly. 'You don't have to stay long.'

Eloise came back with a tall young woman, so mesmerisingly beautiful that Connor didn't concentrate on Eloise's introduction. All he caught was her first name, Beatrice, and that she worked for *Vanity Fair*. Eloise led Harry away, leaving the two of them alone.

Beatrice asked him if he would give her a guided tour of his photographs and, although he didn't want to, he agreed.

It had been hard enough selecting the photographs and printing them, so he had left the hanging to Eloise. This was the first time he had seen them together. They covered pretty much his whole career and were hung chronologically, starting with his picture of Ed silhouetted against the Yellowstone fire. He had also included the shot of the elk with its flaming antlers. He hadn't looked at it for many years and out of superstition had never had it published.

Sometimes she stopped and asked a question, but mostly she just looked. Walking behind her, studying them in sequence, it was as if he were taking a tour of his life. And as he moved from one image to the next, and saw the pain and the loss and the horror in the eyes of those before whom he had stood, he felt a cold sorrow well within him. The women hanging in the blossom; a little girl in Snipers' Alley, howling over her mother's body; a young Liberian rebel kneeling bound before his executioners. One face after another, staring in silence as Connor passed, watching him walk his own private catacomb, the dead and the dying and the cold-eyed killers.

At last they reached the final picture. It was of Thomas, one of the children Connor had photographed at St Mary of the Angels. At the age of ten, he and his twin brother had been kidnapped by rebels who called themselves the Warriors for God. To seal the boys' loyalty, they were forced to take part in the burning of their own village and the massacre of their own people. Many months later, Thomas had either escaped or been discarded to die. A government border patrol found him wandering in the bush, shrivelled and skeletal.

Connor stood in front of the picture for a long time, staring at it and then staring through it, at the vision of himself that was on display here and in all the other pictures. Something seemed to be expanding inside his chest, squeezing his lungs, making it hard for him to breathe. He felt himself sway and his shoulders start to shake.

'What were you looking for?'

He turned and saw Beatrice staring at the picture too, as if she had addressed the question to the boy. Connor didn't know if he could trust his own voice. 'In this picture, you mean?'

'In all of them.'

It was a question so uncannily close to his own thoughts that his instinct was to brush it off. But instead, as if it sprang from nowhere, he gave a different answer. 'Hope.'

It was a shock to hear himself say it. He couldn't stop shaking. Beatrice was looking at him now, assessing what he had just said. He shrugged and went on, trying to make light of it. 'Maybe not. Who knows? Hell, I don't think I'm looking for anything.'

'Oh yes. I think you are. But I don't think it's hope.'

Connor forced a little laugh but it sounded odd.

'So OK, what is it I'm looking for?' he said sharply.

She looked at him for a moment and saw his anger. She smiled politely. 'I'm sorry. It's none of my business.'

'No, please. You'd be doing me a favour. Feel free, go right ahead and tell me. What am I looking for?'

Beatrice paused again and then said quietly and simply, 'I think you're looking for a mirror of your own sadness.'

Connor stood staring at her and then nodded.

'Well, thanks. Now I know. Beatrice, it's been a pleasure.'

He turned abruptly and walked towards the door. He felt tears coming. What the hell was going on? He heard Eloise calling after him but he didn't turn, just rummaged for his coat among the others.

'Connor? Where are you going? What happened?'

'I'm sorry, Eloise. I've got to go. I'm sorry.'

He found his coat and launched himself out into the street. He took a gulp of the frozen, pungent air and tried to gather himself. His heart was thumping like a jackhammer and he thought for a moment that he must be having a heart attack. But no, he was OK.

How far he walked or where, he never knew. But by the time he got back to his apartment, the East Side skyline was streaked with crimson. The apartment was as cold as outside. The heating didn't work and he hadn't bothered to get it fixed. It was six years since he'd bought the place, but the only thing he'd spent money on was converting the bedroom into a state-of-the-art darkroom. He slept instead in the long living room which, with all his camera gear stacked in cases around it, looked more like a left-luggage place than a home. The bed was at one end; at the other was a big table littered with papers and photographs. There was a small, drab bathroom and a smaller, drabber kitchen. Apart from a TV, a phone and an armchair, the only gestures to comfort were a couple of rugs and a handful of carved figures he'd brought back from his travels.

He didn't switch on the lights but went directly to the bed and lay down on his back, still wrapped in his coat, his breath rising in a cold fog above him. He stared without blinking at the ceiling, watching the reflected lights of the traffic move across it, yellow and red and fading, as another day came bleeding through the blinds.

A mirror of his own sadness.

He realised that the reason he had reacted so harshly to what Beatrice said was that she was right. She had seen something in him that he thought he kept concealed.

He wondered if he would still have ended up this way if he hadn't made that choice seven years ago when Amy was born. But at the time it hadn't seemed like a choice. It was simply how it had to be, for all of their sakes. Having made his decision, he should have allowed himself to move on. He had always believed that happiness was a matter of choice. You could either wallow in regret, even drown in it, or you could choose not to. But he had underestimated the power of habit. Because once you'd started wallowing, pretty soon that's all you were fit for. The daunting truth, which Beatrice had glimpsed at the gallery, was that Connor now knew no other way to be.

In the first two or three years there had been many times when he almost changed his mind about staying away. But by the time Ed's letter arrived, apologising for how he had been at the christening, it was too late. He had made his decision and he would stick to it.

The letters that arrived two or three times a year from Amy were still the closest that he ever came to happiness. He had her picture on his bedside table, next to the one of him and Julia that Julia had slipped into his bag seven years ago. He had made smaller copies of them and laminated them so that he could take them with him wherever he travelled. In the one of him and Julia, their faces were almost touching. Anyone who didn't know the truth would assume they were a couple. And Connor would lie there and stare at it and think of how, in another, more forgiving world, they might have been.

 CHAPTER TEN

There were only three and a half hours to go until curtain-up time and Ed still had a hundred things to do. He'd even skipped his appointment at the hospital this morning. It was no big deal. He'd missed a couple of dialysis sessions before with no serious consequences, so he knew he'd be fine. These medics always played it safe, he reasoned. All he prayed was that Julia didn't find out, as she had the last time he'd played truant. She'd given him hell for days.

Kay Neumark was coming to pick him up at four and he still hadn't finished half of what he'd hoped to get done. Ed was just putting on his headphones when the phone rang. It was Julia, calling from the school with bad news. The chief logger, clearly taking theatrical tradition too literally, had fallen over in the snow and broken his leg. Kay wanted to come and pick Ed up earlier so that they could all work out what to do. She was on her way right now.

FROM THE WINGS Julia watched Amy standing centre stage in the dazzle of the lights, singing her socks off. The socks, like all the chief logger's costume, were several sizes too large for her, but what she lacked in stature she more than made up for in sheer pizzazz. It was the chief logger's big number and she was giving it all she'd got.

Julia was astonished that the girl had agreed to do it. It had been Ed's idea and made perfect sense because Amy had lived and breathed the show for the best part of four months and knew everybody's lines by heart. She had half an hour's rehearsal, going through some of the moves she wasn't so familiar with and now here she was, belting out the chief logger's lines as if she'd rehearsed them for weeks. Julia had never been more proud of her and from the grin on Ed's face at the piano she could see he felt the same.

The auditorium was packed. Probably 200 people, Julia estimated, with more standing at the back. Kay, who was sitting beside Ed to cue him, had announced at the start that the part of the chief logger would tonight be played by 'Miss Amy Tully' who had 'agreed to stand in at only a moment's notice'. Naturally, the whole audience was rooting for her. When she finished her song, the cheers and applause must have sent the snow sliding off the roof.

'That's done it,' Julia said to one of the other teachers who was helping her backstage. 'The poor kid'll be stage-struck for ever.'

An hour later the show was over and was adjudged by one and all a roaring success. Amy got a standing ovation and stood there in the spotlights, squinting and grinning and a little dazed. Kay Neumark dragged Ed up onto the stage and he got a standing ovation too.

Julia watched him from the wings with tears streaming down her face, clapping so hard that her hands hurt. He stood there in his smart black shirt, smiling and bowing and spreading his arms to include the whole cast in the applause, cameras flashing in the lenses of his sunglasses. The cast was applauding him too.

What a guy, Julia thought. What an amazing guy I married.

WELL, IT MIGHT not be Broadway, Ed thought, but it still felt pretty wonderful all the same. They wouldn't stop clapping. He reached out and called for Amy and felt her hot little hand find his and everybody cheered even louder. He bent down and kissed her.

'What a star,' he whispered.

'Did I do OK?'

'Yeah. You did OK.'

It took at least another hour before they could even think of going home. Ed felt himself in danger of being kissed to death, but it wasn't a bad way to go. Everybody wanted to congratulate him.

Now, at last, the auditorium was almost clear, and while Julia helped the last few kids into their coats and sent them off with their parents, Ed and Kay sat on the front of the stage, going over a few things that needed fixing for tomorrow's performance.

Now that he was allowed to, Ed was starting to wilt. Before the show Julia had made sure that he had his insulin shot and had sent out for some steak sandwiches and milk shakes. During the show he'd had this odd, dull ache in his chest and it was still there now. It was probably just indigestion. The show had used up a lot of his energy and he knew that he should eat something because he was finding it hard to concentrate on what Kay was saying. He'd found a candy bar in his bag but was having trouble unwrapping it.

'Want me to help with that?' Kay said at last.

'Oh, yeah. Thanks. I'm all fingers and thumbs.'

'Are you feeling all right?'

'Just a little tired.'

'Listen, we can talk about this in the morning.'

'Maybe that'd be better.'

She went to fetch his coat, and when Ed stood up to put it on he felt weak at the knees and swayed a little.

'Whoa there,' Kay said, supporting him. 'You sure you're all right?'

'I'm fine. It's been a long day.'

By the time Julia and Amy came to find him, he felt steadier.

Outside it was snowing again. Julia said the parking lot was icy and treacherous and she made him wait just inside the door with Amy while she went to get the Jeep. They stood holding hands, saying good night to the last few parents and children who came past. The indigestion was still there in his chest and even after eating the candy bar he still felt a little weird. Kind of fuddled and detached. Maybe he was getting the flu or something.

'Daddy, your hand's so cold!' Amy said.

'Well, you know what they say—cold hand, warm heart.'

'Mine's hot. Does that mean I've got a cold heart?'

'No. Doesn't work that way. Hey, you were so good tonight. You sang like an angel.'

'Come on, here's Mommy.'

The snow was indeed treacherous. He slipped and almost fell while Amy led him the few yards to the Jeep. Julia got out and came hurrying round to help him. She didn't often treat him like an invalid, but when she did it annoyed the hell out of him.

'I don't need help.'

'It's slippy. You nearly fell. Ed? Look at me.'

'I'm OK.'

'You don't look it. What's going on? Ed, talk to me.'

'Don't fuss. I'm tired, that's all. Let's just get Shirley Temple here back to her bed.'

'Who's Shirley Temple?' Amy asked.

He was just starting to tell her when suddenly the pain in his chest exploded. It was as if someone had jabbed him with a cattle prod. He reeled backwards and heard Amy cry out in alarm.

He must have blacked out for a few moments, because the next thing he knew, Julia was shaking him by his coat lapels and slapping his face and yelling at him. The pain in his chest wasn't so bad now. Just a weird flooding feeling. He seemed to be lying on his back in the snow, because he could feel it all cold on the back of his head and could feel the flakes landing on his face. Man, did he feel sleepy.

Julia was calling him from somewhere far away. He could only just hear her. And he could hear Amy crying and Julia shouting for her to go and get help, and suddenly there were several pairs of hands grabbing him and he was being dragged backwards, his feet trailing after him through the snow. He tried to call out, but he couldn't find his voice. What the hell were they playing at? It was all such a pain in the ass. All he wanted to do was sleep. If they would just leave him alone and let him sleep, he'd be fine.

THEY DIDN'T HAVE to say it. Julia already knew. She knew he was dead even before the ambulance pulled up outside the hospital and the emergency-team medics came running out into the snow to meet them. Huddled in the corner of the ambulance, she'd watched the paramedics battling to start his heart, thumping his chest and injecting him and yelling instructions to each other over his limp body, and his face fading beneath the oxygen mask. She'd told them about his diabetes and dialysis as soon as they'd arrived at the school, and in the ambulance they'd fired questions at her which she did her best to answer in a steady voice.

Kay Neumark had arrived with Amy just as they were wheeling him in through the doors, and Julia ran and gathered Amy up and hugged her and told her, stupidly, not to worry, Daddy was going to be all right, he'd be all right.

Julia had wanted to follow the stretcher into the emergency room, but one of the nurses had stopped her and said it would be better if she waited here with Amy, and so they'd sat with Kay and several strangers in the cold fluorescent light, holding on to each other and watching the green figures moving behind the frosted glass doors.

And now one of the medics had emerged and was speaking to the nurse at the desk and she nodded towards Julia and Amy. He turned and started to walk towards them. And Julia stood up and made Amy wait with Kay and she walked towards him.

He was sorry, he said. They'd done all they could. He was so sorry.

THEY BURIED HIM the Tuesday before Christmas on a crisp and clear morning. More than 200 people came, crowding shoulder to shoulder into the little white clapboard church with the sun streaming in upon them through the windows.

Ed's parents and brothers and their wives and children had all flown in from Kentucky, and there were doctors, nurses, smoke jumpers, old college friends, pupils and their parents and many others Julia didn't recognise. Almost everyone who loved him. Except Connor.

She had tried to reach him and left messages everywhere she could think of, asking him to call. No one seemed to know where he was or how to contact him, not even his own mother, who was here now, sitting next to Ed's parents. Julia had called the photo agency and was put through to a man with a kind voice who told her that he had no idea where Connor was. He was a law unto himself these days, the man said with a sigh, always secretive about his projects. There was no way of contacting him, for he had long ago ditched his satellite phone and scanner; often he went missing for months.

Listening to this, Julia felt a confusion of anger and guilt rise within her. How could Connor have become like this? How could she—how could they all—have allowed this to happen? And when the man finally asked if there was any message, if he did happen to call in, she let her feelings spill.

'Just tell him his best friend died.'

The service started with everyone singing 'Silent Night', Ed's favourite carol. Then Amy and a choir of others from the school show sang the angels' song unaccompanied.

Julia watched her daughter's face and marvelled at her strength and courage, for she herself felt neither. Linda, sitting beside her, was squeezing her hand hard and both of them were trying not to cry. Julia knew that if she started she wouldn't be able to stop. There had been enough crying already and, anyhow, she knew from Ed's letter that he wanted a celebration not a mourning.

The letter had arrived from his lawyer in Missoula three days ago. The lawyer explained that Ed had lodged it with him last fall with instructions that it be given to her in the event of his death. Julia made sure that she was alone when she opened it.

My darling Julia,

It may strike you as strange that I should have done this, but life is a tightrope and you never know when you're going to topple off. I didn't want to hit the floor without saying a few things that need to be said. And, although it sounds dumb, I guess what I feel most needs saying is: Thank You.

Thank you for being my eyes, for being my guardian angel, for being the light of my life and the inspiration of my every good thought. For being the wondrous mother of a wondrous child. For being beautiful and loving and sexy and for being so big-hearted and generous and forgiving and patient and so full of energy.

I guess what I'm saying is, simply, thank you for being who you are and for allowing me to share your life.

So those are the thankyous.

That just leaves the things I want to say sorry for. So here goes.

I'm sorry for being such a pain in the ass, so impatient and grouchy and for getting mad at you for fussing when all you were trying to do was keep this poor ungrateful jerk alive.

Most of all, I'm sorry I wasn't able to give you all those children we should have had. But maybe the fact that I couldn't has made Amy even more special. (As if that were possible!)

While we're on the subject, I'm sorry that I deprived you of

Connor. I know you loved him and probably still do. I may be blind, but not to that. I always knew. I tried so hard not to be jealous, but jealousy is such a tenacious creature. And I'm sorry that I wasn't able to be a bigger man and to get my head round it, for all of us have lost out through my driving him away.

If it's not too late, and if it makes you and Amy happy, perhaps you and Connor will find each other again one day. If so, you have my blessing. Your happiness—and Amy's—is all I pray for.

I love you so much, Julia.

Ed

Amy had finished singing now and, when she came back, Julia kissed her and settled her between herself and Linda, and they all held hands while the preacher spoke about Ed. He told the congregation that Ed was one of the finest, bravest souls that he'd ever had the honour of knowing, and that he had touched the lives of all he met with light and joy.

And then it was Julia's turn. She walked to the lectern at the front of the church and unfolded the sheet of paper that had been enclosed with Ed's letter. She raised her head and looked out at all the faces watching and waiting, half lit by the angling sun. There was perfect silence. She cleared her throat and began.

'If I be the first of us to die,
Let grief not blacken long your sky.
Be bold yet modest in your grieving.
There is a change but not a leaving.
For just as death is part of life,
The dead live on for ever in the living.'

JULIA PUT ON the leather gauntlets, lowered the visor of her hard hat and picked up the chainsaw.

'OK, buddy. Keep that rope taut, do you hear?'

Amy nodded. She was standing about twelve feet away, holding on to the other end of the rope that was attached to the post that Julia was about to cut down. She took the strain and grinned.

'What are you smirking at?' Julia said.

'You. You look so funny.'

'I think I look pretty darned cool.'

'You look hot. You're all sweaty and yucky.'

'Well, thank you, Missy Prissy. OK, get ready.'

She yanked the cord and the chainsaw spluttered and roared into life. It was a hot August afternoon and she was indeed all sweaty and yucky. They were removing the posts of the old rope rail that Ed had always used to find his way to the river, and they had worked their way up from the river to the house. The post through which Julia was sawing now was the last. The symbolic significance of the job wasn't lost on either of them.

The first six months had been a matter of plain survival for both of them. When the shock wave of Ed's death subsided, it had left Julia feeling oddly separate from everyone and everything but Amy. They clung to each other like abandoned creatures in a nest, and when Julia peeped out at the world it was as if she saw it through a cold haze.

During those first cold months, it hadn't occurred to her to start removing or rearranging his things. It was crazy, she knew, but it seemed perfectly possible that one day he might reappear, as if nothing had happened. So his clothes stayed in the closet, his shaving things in the bathroom cabinet, his sheets of music stacked on the piano, which Amy rarely played any more. Julia understood why and didn't push her, hoping that in time she would come back to it.

On the night Ed died, Amy had slept in Julia's bed and she'd slept there since. Julia worried that this might somehow hamper the child's independence, but the truth was, they both enjoyed the comfort and the company. At weekends they would have breakfast in bed and lounge there half the morning, reading books and chatting. And it was while doing that this morning that Julia had floated the idea of removing the rope rail.

'Would we get a man in to do it?'

'A *man*? Are you kidding? This is no job for a man. You and me, sister. The gals is gonna do it.'

Amy grinned. 'Cool.'

'You don't think it matters that it was, well, Daddy's thing?'

'No. He'd say it was the right thing to do.'

Now, six hours later, the chainsaw was almost through the last post. 'OK!' Julia yelled. 'Get ready. Here she goes!'

'Timber!'

The post toppled slowly and, as it landed on the grass with a thump, they both cheered.

A week later Julia gathered Ed's clothes and shoes and gave them to a charity store in town. She cleared his things from the bathroom cabinet and boxed all the sheets of music. And she gave his computer equipment to the local chapter of the Association for the Blind.

School started again for both of them and Julia tried to fire herself with a new enthusiasm for her work but found she couldn't. The prospect of another winter and another school year depressed her.

She loved Montana, and if Ed were still alive she would have been content to go on calling it home. But it had always been more his place than hers. She couldn't see herself spending the rest of her life there. Of course, it was Amy's place too, the only home she had ever known. But the girl was young and bright and secure enough to adapt anywhere. As the days drew shorter, so Julia grew more restless and convinced that it was time for some sort of new beginning.

In her new mode of tidying and clearing, Julia had found some boxes of photographs that for years she had promised herself to sift through and stick into albums. It was just the job for a cold, gloomy weekend and Amy was excited by the idea. They went into Missoula to buy six smart albums, came home and lit the fire, and then settled in front of it on the floor with the photos spread around them.

In one of the boxes there were photos that Julia had taken as reference for her painting; among them were those she had shot on a trip to Kenya, the summer before she met Ed. Amy was transfixed. She wanted to know the story behind every picture and about everything else that Julia had seen and done while she was there. One of the pictures was of some lions lazing in a tree.

'Did you really get that close?'

'Uh-huh. We were in a truck, so, you know, we were safe.'

'Can we go to Africa one day?'

'I don't see why not. One day.'

Not long afterwards, Julia was sorting through some old magazines and came across the one with Connor's article about St Mary of the Angels, the rehabilitation centre for child soldiers in Uganda. She put it aside and took it to bed that night and, with Amy snuggled asleep beside her, read the article again.

Connor wrote that the centre was mostly funded by a charitable organisation based in Geneva, but that its resources were sorely stretched and that there was a constant need for 'both financial and practical help'. The next sentence quoted Sister Emily, the centre director, saying that she was always short of 'properly trained and qualified staff'. It set Julia's mind whirring.

That was precisely her field. She thought of what Amy had said about wanting to go to Africa. She put the magazine down, switched off the light, but couldn't switch off her head. She lay awake almost the entire night thinking about it.

For days she didn't mention it to anyone. It was an absurd idea. How could she uproot them both, take Amy out of school and go waltzing off with her to Africa? What about the danger and disease? It was out of the question.

But try as she might, she couldn't shake the idea that somehow it was meant to be. What an extraordinary experience for a child it would be, to see another continent, to get to know another culture and another people. And it wasn't as if it was going to be for ever. A few months, a year at the most. She wouldn't even have to give up her job at the school; she would be able to take a sabbatical, she was sure. They could rent out the house, which would pay for the trip. And they would both come home with their lives enriched.

She agonised about how best to broach the subject with Amy. In the end she came right out with it. They were having supper at the kitchen table, eating spaghetti with pesto sauce.

'Do you remember how you said you'd like to go to Africa? Did you really mean that?'

'Sure I did. Why?'

'Well, I've been thinking about it. Maybe we should.'

'You mean, like, a vacation?'

'Well, yeah. We could do a safari, see all the animals.'

'Hey, Mom! Are you serious? Wow!'

'But I was also thinking that maybe I could work there for a few months, maybe.'

'Where?'

Julia had the magazine ready and pushed it across the table. Amy glanced at it and went on eating her spaghetti.

'I already saw that. Is that where you'd work?'

'If they'd have me. Did you read it?'

'Sure. I always read Connor's stuff. Is that where he lives?'

Julia laughed. 'Oh, no. I think he was just visiting. I don't know where he is right now. Where was the last postcard he sent you from?'

Amy frowned. 'I think it was . . . India. Is Uganda like Kenya?'

'It's right next door. People say it's even more beautiful. They call it the Pearl of Africa. So, what do you think about you and me going to help these children in Uganda?'

Amy shrugged. 'Cool.'

'You mean you'd like to?'

'Sure. May I have some more spaghetti?'

Julia found the phone number of the charity in Geneva and called them. An efficient-sounding woman said yes, they did indeed need qualified counsellors at St Mary's. She told Julia that the organisation had an office in New York and gave her the number.

Julia called Linda in New York to get her reaction, half expecting to be told she was insane. Instead, Linda asked a couple of questions, weighed things up for about a second and said, 'Go for it, girl.' Why not bring Amy to New York for Thanksgiving, she suggested. Julia could visit the charity's office and check things out.

Julia wrote to the charity's New York office, enclosing a résumé, and a woman called her two days later. She said she hoped that Julia understood that St Mary's was, technically, in a war zone (although for more than a year things had, in fact, been peaceful), that the food and accommodation were basic and that the pay was somewhat less than basic, in other words, none.

Julia asked about the possibility of bringing Amy, and the woman said it was unusual but not unheard of. However, she must understand that the organisation could not in any way be held responsible for the girl. Julia said fine. They arranged the interview.

They flew into New York on the Wednesday evening and after putting Amy to bed in Linda's apartment, Julia joined Linda on the big leather couch. Linda poured them a Jack Daniel's and they sat talking until long past midnight. About family and friends and work and, finally, men. In particular, Linda's apparently endless quest for one with whom she could bear to spend so much as a year, let alone a lifetime. Then, as if out of the blue, she asked about Connor and whether Julia had heard from him lately.

'Not for a long time. Amy had a postcard from India a few months ago. But since then nothing. He even forgot her birthday this year. First time ever.'

Linda took another drink, staring at her over the rim of the glass.

'What? What's with the meaningful look?'

Linda shrugged. 'Well, one didn't exactly need a degree in telepathy to figure out what you two felt about each other.'

'Don't be ridiculous. You were the one who was smitten.'

'I don't deny it. Who wouldn't be?'

'Well, me, for one. He was my husband's best friend for heaven's sake! How could you even think such a thing?'

'Hey, all I asked was had you heard from him.'

'Well, I haven't.'

'Well, fine.'

There was a lengthy pause. Linda lit another of her long cigarettes and leaned her head against the back of the couch.

'Is he the reason you want to go to Africa?'

Julia erupted. 'Linda, for crying out loud, what's got into you tonight? Of course he isn't. How could you even think that?'

'Whoa, babe. Sor-ry!'

'I mean, really, Linda. Sometimes . . .'

They changed the subject but the conversation never quite recovered. Julia went to bed feeling rather foolish for having over-reacted so. The truth was, Connor was an issue that she had long ago trained herself to handle by denial. When Linda had challenged her so directly about her feelings for him, it was like someone poking the scar of an old wound.

And as she lay there, with Amy asleep beside her, Julia admitted to herself that her friend was right. Deep down she knew that this urge to go to Africa was connected with Connor. She knew full well that they wouldn't find him there, but she wanted to see what he had seen, to take their child to a place that had moved him. And even though he was now a stranger, and must long ago have stopped loving her, at least she might yet share this part of him.

 CHAPTER ELEVEN

Connor woke with a start, and for a moment couldn't figure out where he was. He lay still and listened, staring up into the folds of his mosquito net dimly paled by the first hint of dawn. Then he heard orders being barked and soldiers running across the dirt compound outside, and he remembered.

He could hear an engine making its way up from the lower camp beside the river and he quickly got up and unrolled his jeans and shirt that he used for a pillow. By the time the vehicle roared to a halt outside, with its lights slicing in through the hut's open doorway, he was dressed and had picked up his camera bag.

'*Muzungu!* Wake up! You must come!'

It was Okello, the arrogant young colonel who had been his chaperon for the past twelve long days of waiting. He knew Connor's name but always called him *muzungu*, the Swahili for 'white man'.

'*Muzungu!* Get up! Get dressed!'

He yelled at the young guard, who sat all night outside Connor's hut. According to Okello, the guard was there for protection, but Connor knew that the real purpose was to stop him sneaking down into the camp to talk to the abducted child soldiers.

Okello ducked into the doorway and stood peering in. He was maybe twenty-five years old, about six foot three inches tall and powerfully built. His eyes were always screened by a pair of wrap-around sunglasses.

'You must come! Now!'

'What's going on? Is it Makuma? Is he here?' Connor asked.

'You will see. Come, hurry!'

The compound was thronged with soldiers, some still pulling on their clothes as they ran, while those of higher rank yelled at them. In the back of Okello's Jeep sat two of his henchmen, one cradling an M16 and the other a rocket launcher. Connor swung himself up into the passenger seat while Okello climbed behind the wheel. He rammed the Jeep into gear and sent it hurtling through the crowd.

In the dusty purple half-light, they followed the rutted trail that climbed in a long meander to the plateau, their headlights bouncing and jagging across eucalyptus thickets and the threadbare backs of the soldiers going the same way on foot.

Half an hour later the soldiers were lined up on the plateau of baked earth and grass, rank upon rank of them, maybe 2,000, Connor figured. He scanned the rows of faces, searching for the one that was the cause of his coming here, but there were too many of them and the light was still too dim.

Nevertheless, he could see just how young many of them were. Those in front wore ragged fatigues. The clothes of those behind looked as though they had been salvaged from a garbage dump, torn and dirty T-shirts and pyjama tops and trousers that were frayed and caked with filth. Some had boots and others sandals made from tyres, but many more stood barefoot. The soldiers were mostly boys, but there were girls among them, too, and many more behind, huddled with the women who were kidnapped to cook and carry and to serve as sex slaves to the older soldiers.

Connor didn't need to ask again what was going on. There could be only one reason for everyone to be gathered here: Daniel Makuma, The Blessed One, mystic, prophet and supreme spiritual leader of the

Warriors for God, was about to descend from the heavens.

Makuma's followers claimed that he had been instructed in a vision to continue the holy war against the 'great evil' that governed the country. To that end, for more than a decade, he had bolstered the delinquent rabble of his rebel army with abducted children, and from bases such as this, in southern Sudan, sent them forth in God's name over the border to burn and rape and murder and pillage their way across the land he claimed to love and sought to save.

Until now Makuma had never once granted access to a Western journalist or photographer, and it had taken every atom of guile and persistence that Connor possessed to find his way through the maze of secrecy and paranoia that surrounded The Blessed One.

Now, with the sun flaring up behind the mountains, a murmur spread across the waiting crowd. One of Okello's henchmen called out and pointed and Connor looked away to the north and saw the lights of a plane lowering towards the plateau.

With a nod from Okello, he started to photograph the plane which was making its final approach from the east. The plane touched down, then slowed and turned and began to taxi back. Okello called for Connor to follow and set off towards the plane with a little reception committee of senior officers shambling after him.

The plane stopped, and a moment later the door opened and steps unfolded to the ground. Then a small figure, dressed all in white, stepped into the sunlight and a great cheer went up from all the soldiers. Makuma stood at the top of the steps with both his arms aloft, and Connor zoomed in on his smiling face.

Through the lens he saw a handsome man with delicate features. His eyes and his smile were beatific. He came carefully down the steps, followed by a small group of advisers and bodyguards.

Okello walked forward in welcome and Makuma opened his arms and the two of them embraced. A pretty teenaged girl was waiting with a garland of flowers, and on a sign from Okello she stepped forward to place it round Makuma's neck. As he lowered his head he glanced sideways at Connor, and in that brief moment Connor caught a glimpse of something cold and daunting in the man's eyes.

Okello was about to lead the party off on a tour of inspection, when Makuma turned and walked towards Connor. Connor lowered his camera and shook the hand that Makuma offered.

'I am sorry that you have had to wait so long.' His voice was gentle and his English meticulous.

'No problem. Colonel Okello and I had a lot of laughs.'

'I am glad. There will be time later to answer your questions.'

'I sure hope so. I've got a real important one for you.'

THE SUMMONS CAME at sunset. Two of Okello's sidekicks picked him up and drove him along the ridge trail above the camp that Connor had been forbidden to visit. Through the eucalyptus trees he caught glimpses of crumbling mud huts and improvised tents and shelters. All was veiled in a blue drift of smoke from campfires, and the smell of cooking rose on the golden air.

Sheltered among the trees at the end of the ridge was the officers' camp. As the Jeep pulled up, Okello came out to meet him.

'The Blessed One is tired. You have twenty minutes, no more.'

Connor didn't bother to argue. Okello led him through a labyrinth of avenues between the tents and huts to an earth-floored yard where two of Makuma's bodyguards stood outside a hut far grander than the rest. Okello left him there and the guards checked his camera bag and frisked him, and then one of them nodded for him to enter.

It was dark inside and in the furthest corner Connor could see a doorway with a dim light spilling at the edges. Quietly, he stepped closer, and through the gap he saw Makuma kneeling in prayer at an alcoved shrine upon which stood a gold cross and two candles. Connor quickly headed back to the centre of the room and turned in time to see Makuma emerge holding a small, black leather Bible.

'How much do you know of the spiritual beliefs of my people, Mr Ford?'

'The Acholi people? Not much I'm afraid.'

Makuma put his Bible down on the table. He gestured at one of the canvas chairs and took another for himself and they both sat.

'Do you believe in God, Mr Ford?'

'It seems to me that many things exist, both good and evil, whether there's a God who wants them to or not. Is it OK if I record this?'

'If you wish.'

Connor took his recorder from his pocket and set it beside the Bible.

'So, you don't believe in God, but you do believe in good and evil?'

'I know that men are capable of both.'

'And you believe that you can distinguish between them?'

'Between good and evil? Yes, I do.'

'But if there is no God, how can that be possible?'

In answer to Makuma's question, Connor opened his camera bag and pulled out the photograph. It was the one he had taken of Thomas, the boy at St Mary's. He held it out to Makuma, who took it.

'I have seen this before. I read the article and the lies you told.'

He handed the picture back, but Connor wouldn't take it.

'You asked me how I can tell good from evil. What was done to this boy was evil. Your soldiers murdered his mother and his father, abducted him, then forced him to go back and murder the rest of his family and friends and burn down his own village. Then they left him in the bush to die. Tell me, does that sound like evil to you?'

Makuma laid the photograph on the table. He gently put his palms together as if in prayer and raised his fingertips to his chin.

'Whoever told you these things was telling lies,' he said quietly. 'We do not abduct the children who fight for our cause. They flock in their hundreds to join us. Why? Because they want to help purge our land of the great evil that has seized it. It is the government who tortures and kills my people and who burns our villages and then pretends to the world that we are to blame.'

'I've seen it with my own eyes.'

'Then your eyes deceive you. Tell me, did you come here, all this way, to interview me or to insult me?'

Connor took a deep breath and pulled out a sheet of paper from his pocket and held it out to Makuma.

'This is a list of some of the children who have been kidnapped by your soldiers from the Karingoa area. There are seventy-three of them. The last name on the list, Lawrence Nyeko, is the twin brother of Thomas, the boy in the picture there. Please, take it.'

Makuma didn't move, so Connor leaned forward and put the list on the table in front of him.

'Now, I'm all set to do an interview with you and to take your picture and all. And you can say whatever the heck you like, correct all those lies you say I told about you, whatever. I'll make sure it gets printed. But what I'm really here for is to make you an offer.'

He paused and pointed at the list.

'I don't know what you think these children are worth. If they're in anything like the shape of those I've met, who escaped, my guess is they're not a whole lot of use to you. And maybe some of them aren't here. But those who are, I'd like to buy.'

Makuma looked at him, plainly astonished. Then he laughed.

'How is it that Americans always think everything is for sale?'

'All I'm trying to buy is their freedom.'

'With whose money?'

'My own.'

Makuma laughed in scorn.

'You don't have to believe me. But the cash is ready and waiting in an account in Nairobi. I'll give you two thousand US dollars for every child on that list. Payment on delivery, however you want.'

Makuma looked at his watch. 'Go now,' he said. 'We will talk again in the morning.'

CONNOR WAS WOKEN by the roar of Okello's Jeep pulling up outside the hut. And a moment later the man himself was in the doorway and yelling, '*Muzungu! Muzungu!*'

As he stepped out of the doorway, Okello gave him a shove between his shoulder blades. Connor turned on him. 'What the hell was that for?'

'Get in.'

The two henchmen in the back were grinning, and seemed to be privy to some joke that no one had told him yet. They drove down the winding trail that led to the lower camp. Connor looked over his shoulder and saw that another Jeep was right behind with Makuma in the front passenger seat. They drove through the camp and stopped at the edge of a mud clearing, where a group of the youngest soldiers Connor had yet seen stood waiting on parade. He estimated that there were about forty of them and their ages ranged from maybe nine or ten to about sixteen. All but a handful were boys. On command, as Makuma alighted from his Jeep, they snapped to attention. Everyone else got out of the Jeeps, too, and Connor stood by the hood, watching Makuma come sauntering towards him.

'These are your so-called "abducted" children. There are forty-two of them. Nineteen of the others on your list are serving with active units. The other twelve names on the list we know nothing about. Probably they were taken or killed by government forces.'

'Is it OK if I take some pictures?'

'No.'

'A photograph would at least let their parents know they're alive. I've never seen these children. I need some way to identify them.'

Makuma nodded to Okello, who on cue held up the list and started shouting out the names. One by one the young soldiers piped up in answer. Connor watched, shaking his head. He had little doubt that this was a set-up. The last name that Okello called was Thomas's brother, Lawrence Nyeko.

'Let me talk to him,' Connor said.

Makuma nodded to Okello and the boy was called forth.

Connor could see the likeness in this boy's face when he was still twenty yards away. He halted before them and gave Okello a brave salute. His eyes flicked nervously from Makuma to Okello and on to Connor. Connor smiled at him.

'Lawrence?' Connor held out his hand. '*Jambo. Jina langu ni Connor.*'

'He does not speak Swahili,' Okello said. 'Nor English. Only Acholi.'

Lawrence looked at the hand and then at Okello, who nodded permission to shake it. The boy's little hand felt cold and limp and bony. Connor showed him the picture of Thomas. Lawrence looked at it briefly then looked up again at Okello to check how he should react.

'Ask him who this is.'

Okello did so and Connor heard the name Thomas in the boy's reply but couldn't understand the rest. Okello translated.

'He says it is his brother, Thomas, who died a traitor.'

'Tell him that's not true. Tell him his brother is alive.'

Okello glanced at Makuma and Connor told the boy himself in Swahili, but he could see that he didn't understand. The boy's eyes were darting with fear. Okello spoke to him again, and when he replied his little voice cracked.

'He says you are lying,' Okello said.

Connor had had enough. 'I don't know what the hell either one of you is saying, but any damn fool can see this poor kid's terrified.'

'I think it is you he fears,' Makuma said. He spoke to Lawrence again and the boy listened, then shook his head violently.

'What did you say to him?'

'That you had come to buy him. I asked if he wants to be sold.'

Connor shook his head and looked away. What a fool he was to think this could ever have worked.

'I will ask all of them the same question.'

'Yeah, right. I bet you will.'

Makuma spoke for about a minute and from the tone of his voice Connor had a clear enough idea of what he was saying. The speech ended with what was clearly a question and all of the children stood silent, too terrified even to look at each other. Makuma turned and smiled at Connor with smug regret.

'I asked if any of them want to be sold to you. And you see? Not one.'

'Tell them that I will take them home. They will be with their families again. Tell them that.'

Makuma spoke again, but Connor knew damn well that he wasn't saying that and so he began to shout it out himself in Swahili. At once Okello turned on him and yelled for him to stop and when Connor didn't he struck him across the shoulder with his stick. Connor lunged at him but Okello's two henchmen grabbed him from behind by his arms and Okello struck him again hard across the face and punched him in the stomach, knocking the air from his lungs.

Connor sank to his knees, gasping for breath, and Okello kicked him in the chest and sent him sprawling backwards. Connor lay there and the last thing he heard, before the blow that delivered him to darkness, was Makuma calling out the Warriors for God battle cry and the shrill automaton chant of the children in response.

THE TOWN OF KARINGOA was a single street of terraced stores with a church at one end and a police station at the other. In the distant days before the war it had been a sleepy, unassuming place of only a few thousand people. Now, however, the population had grown fifty-fold while homesteads and villages for many miles around lay plundered, burnt and deserted.

The Ugandan government had set up 'protected' camps to which they urged the dispossessed to move, but many resisted, for the camps were far away and even there the rebels still came at night to steal their children. So, instead, large numbers had flocked to Karingoa's squalid shanty camp. At least, from here, those who were brave enough could from time to time sneak back to their villages to plant or gather crops. And often, when they did, they found children who had escaped from the rebels or been cast aside, wandering the ruins of their homes, searching for their families.

The rehabilitation centre of St Mary of the Angels, where many of these children were eventually brought, stood in the southern outskirts of Karingoa's shantytown. The old convent building was three broad storeys tall and stood square and stalwart at the foot of a red-dirt driveway lined with flame trees and, beyond them on either side, palms and giant mango trees colonised by fruit bats. Both the convent and the chapel alongside it were whitewashed and garlanded with crimson bougainvillea. Behind the main building was a straggle of smaller buildings that serviced the centre's needs. The kitchens stood around a low-walled compound where scrawny chickens and ducks scrabbled in the dust for scraps. A vast, open-sided tent served as the centre's dining room. There were storerooms, a medical clinic, a workshop and a garage, where a motley collection of vehicles stood in various states of disrepair. Towering over them was a red double-decker bus that had been driven a decade ago on an epic fund-raising trip all the way from England. It was called Gertrude and, thanks to the loving attention of George, the centre's gardener and mechanic, was still in good working order. Beside it was a red dirt field patched with dried grass where now, in the late-afternoon sunshine, the children were playing soccer and basketball. Finally, beyond it all, lay twelve acres of garden, an overgrown eden of orange, banana, mango and avocado.

Surveying this scene from her second-floor window, Julia remembered how alien everything had seemed when they arrived here three months ago, and how quickly they had come to feel at home.

She and Amy had just had their daily Acholi lesson with Sister Emily and, as usual, Amy had put her mother to shame. The girl was almost fluent by now, while Julia still sometimes faltered over simple sentences. After the lesson, Amy had run outside to play basketball.

The room they shared was spartan but spacious. There were two metal-framed beds pushed together under one big mosquito net, a wooden desk with drawers, a couple of chairs and a giant closet.

Julia checked her watch. She had half an hour before the voluntary English class that she had recently started teaching every evening before supper. She sat at the desk and finished a letter to Linda.

In her last letter to Julia, Linda had asked about Connor and whether the people at St Mary's knew where he was. They didn't. But Sister Emily had more recent news than anyone. About six months ago he had called from Nairobi and asked her for a list of local children known to have been abducted by the Warriors for God. She assumed it must be for an article he was writing.

It was clear from the way that she and the other nuns and counsellors at St Mary's talked about him that Connor was greatly loved. Julia gathered that he regularly sent money and great packages of clothing and shoes, and that on his last visit he had brought them a new video and stereo system. Julia had mentioned that he was Amy's godfather, but not that he was also her father.

On hearing Sister Emily's news, she had felt such a surge of relief that she had almost burst into tears. Connor was alive. At least he was alive. But swiftly afterwards came feelings of hurt that he hadn't contacted them for so long. She presumed that he still didn't know about Ed's death, for surely, if he did, he would have been in touch.

There were forty-two children at St Mary's, two-thirds of whom were boys. Of the nine counsellors who worked with them, all but three were nuns who had been at the convent when it was a school. The other two counsellors were a jovial, middle-aged Swiss divorcée called Françoise, and Peter Pringle, a sweet and slightly intense young Scotsman, who doubled as the centre's physician.

Julia finished her letter and gathered the props that she needed for her class. She always liked to have a theme and this evening's was a visit to the market. She had collected a basketload of items that the children could pretend to buy and sell and haggle over, from oranges and bananas to clothespegs and combs, along with several boxes of matches to use for money.

The class went well. There was a record attendance of fifteen children. The biggest surprise was to see Thomas there, the boy in Connor's photograph. He had put on a little weight since the time of the photograph, but he was still thin and frail.

Throughout this evening's English class he sat watching from the back of the room and when it was his turn to come to the front and buy something from the market stall, he just shook his head. Julia picked up a few items and took them to him and eventually succeeded in getting him to point to a comb and pay for it with five matches. Everybody cheered and he gave a rare shy smile.

How much English anyone ended up learning, Julia wasn't sure, but they all had a good laugh, which was probably more important. She ended up thoroughly exhausted and was relieved when the bell rang for supper.

As she came out into the corridor she was surprised to see two soldiers standing in the hallway, talking with Sister Emily. From their uniforms Julia could tell they were members of the Uganda People's Defence Force, the government army who had a base at the northern end of town. As Julia walked towards them, she heard one of the soldiers say the name 'Makuma', but then he saw her and stopped talking until she was out of earshot.

They were all outside in the dining tent, and halfway through supper, when Sister Emily joined them. She was a tall, graceful woman in her late thirties. Her official position was Director of the

Rehabilitation Programme, but to the children she was the mother that many of them had lost and that's what they called her.

The staff ate at a separate table from the children, though everyone always ate the same meal. They had left a place for Sister Emily and, as she sat down among them, one of the kitchen maids put a plate of food in front of her. Since the beginning of supper, all they had talked about was the soldiers and why they might have come, and now everyone fell silent, waiting for her to tell them. She looked up at all the expectant faces and smiled. 'All right,' she said. 'It's nothing. Just rumours. They have had intelligence reports that Makuma has been gathering a big force across the border and that he is planning some new offensive. They want to station some soldiers with us as a precaution, to set up a camp here in the garden.'

'And what did you say?' Pringle asked.

'I said no, of course. How would it be for the children to have soldiers tramping all over the place? We have our own guards on the gates. It is enough.' Sister Emily took a mouthful of food. 'Julia, the stew is good, no? I bet you don't have stew as good as this in America.' It was a signal that the subject of the war was closed.

Julia smiled and shook her head. 'Nowhere near as good.'

After supper was ended, the staff and children usually convened in the recreation room and played music or a game of some sort or watched a video. Tonight they were watching one of the tapes that Julia and Amy had brought with them, *The Lion King*. Julia told Amy that she was going up to their room to read.

Walking through the darkened hallway to the stairs, she saw Sister Emily sitting writing by lamplight at her desk in her office near the front doors. She heard Julia's footsteps and looked up and smiled.

'Julia, do you have a moment?'

'Of course.'

She walked into the office and Sister Emily gestured for her to sit.

'We are all so busy that sometimes we don't get a chance to talk. I just wanted to hear if everything is all right, you know, with your work and so on.'

'Well, yes. Absolutely. I love every minute of it.'

'I hear your English classes are a great success.'

'Yeah, the kids are doing great. I just wish I could learn their language as fast as they learn mine.'

'Oh, but you speak Acholi well now.'

'I wish! Amy's the one who's got the hang of it.'

'The children love having her here. It is very good for them. She is a beautiful child. She is very like her father.'

Julia frowned. 'You mean . . .'

'I'm sorry, I mean her . . . what is it she says? Her "biological" father.'

'Amy told you about Connor?'

'Yes. Was she not supposed to?'

'No. I mean, yes. It's fine. I just didn't know she had.'

'She is very proud of him. And so she should be. He is a fine man.'

'Yes. Yes, I know.'

She couldn't think why, but the issue made her feel uncomfortable. She decided to change the subject.

'So you don't think the war is going to flare up again?'

'I don't believe so. Karingoa has never been an important place for the rebels.'

A few days later, Peter Pringle had to drive down to Entebbe Airport to collect some medical supplies. He returned with the sobering news that there were reliable reports that Makuma and his army were moving south towards the border.

On his drive back north, Pringle told them, he had followed great convoys of government troops and, as he drew near to Karingoa, he had seen a first trickle of refugees heading on foot in the opposite direction with their children and their bundled belongings.

THEY HAD TAKEN AWAY his watch, so he always waited for the day to show its face before he allowed himself to count it. And when at last it came seeping through the slit of the window, he would feel with one hand under the grass matting of his bed and find the shard of rock, and then he would hoist the mosquito net and carefully etch another small vertical line on the hut's mud wall. Fifty-six days.

He still didn't know what Makuma had in mind for him. Okello had taken pictures of him on the first day of his imprisonment, before confiscating all his camera gear along with his recorder and his notebooks and pens.

The only clue about what they intended to do with him had come from Makuma himself. Lying in the dust after the beating, just as he was coming round, he had heard the man make some smart remark about being able to get a better price for an American photographer than for a few bony children. But that was the last anyone had said about it. In all these weeks he hadn't seen Makuma again.

At the start they had kept him cooped up in his hut. The beating had left him with two cracked ribs, and for those first few days the pain had been so intense that he kept passing out. They slid his food and water under the door, and it took all his strength to crawl to it or to the bucket that they gave him as a toilet. Then one morning Okello came with an officer he hadn't seen before, who had obviously had some medical training. The officer examined him and was visibly shocked by what he saw. He obviously had status, too, for Connor could hear him outside afterwards yelling at Okello.

From that day on, things improved dramatically. The food got better; he was given clean water, enough to wash himself and his clothes, and twice a day he was allowed outside for exercise. The medical officer came several more times to check on him and seemed pleased with Connor's recovery. He brought him some antimalarial pills, and some iodine to purify the water, and the last time he came he brought a Bible and an oil lamp to read it by.

There was still always an armed guard outside the hut and they all seemed to have been instructed not to talk or become friendly. Only one of them, a tall young man called Vincent, who regularly did the night shift, seemed prepared to take the risk. He spoke a little English and, when he was sure nobody else was around, he would ask Connor questions about America and teach him a little Acholi.

This evening, when he took his walk, the guard who accompanied him was new and nervous. He kept shouting at him not to walk too far ahead. Instead of letting him sit outside to eat his supper and watch the sun go down, as Vincent and most of the other guards now let him, this tyro tyrant shoved him inside and locked the door.

As darkness crowded in, Connor sat brooding and feeling cheated and bitter and sorry for himself. He undressed and lay on his bed mat in the dark, closer to despair than he had been for many weeks. Finally he fell into a troubled sleep.

He woke in the middle of the night and knew something was going on outside. He opened his mosquito net and looked across the hut. He saw a shadow move across a slatted square of moonlight on the mud floor, and heard voices outside. Connor got up and walked naked to the door and peered out through the slats.

The guard was standing before a soldier much smaller than himself, prodding him in the chest with his rifle and haranguing him. Then Connor saw a third figure step from the shadows behind the guard and move silently towards him. He was as tall as the guard and had a machete in his right hand. The man raised it and brought it down towards the back of the guard's neck. The guard crumpled to the ground.

The two others took his rifle and his knife and hurried towards the hut. The taller one had a bag slung over his shoulder. Connor ran to the bed and unrolled his jeans and shirt and quickly dressed. He could hear the rattle of the key in the padlock. Then the door swung open and the taller one stepped in, and as his face turned it caught the moonlight and Connor saw that it was Vincent.

'Put on your boots, quick,' he said. 'Get your things.'

Connor didn't ask any questions. He found his boots and pulled them on, then bundled his few belongings in his spare T-shirt. Vincent had hauled the guard's body towards the hut and Connor helped him drag it inside. The short one had been kicking dust over the blood and now he came towards them and Connor saw that it was Lawrence Nyeko. The boy looked very frightened. He said something in Acholi and Vincent nodded and turned to Connor.

'He asks if it is true that his brother is alive?'

Connor told him that it was. Lawrence gave a little nod.

'Stay close and be quiet,' Vincent said. 'If they see us, they kill us all.'

They ran across the compound and into the shadow of the trees along the ridge that overlooked the camp. Vincent went first, with Lawrence close behind and Connor at the rear. Vincent had the guard's AK-47 in his hand, and sometimes he would hold it up as a signal for them to stop and they would all stand as if frozen, peering into the dappled shadow and barely daring to draw breath.

How long they walked, he couldn't tell. Maybe two or three hours. When they came to a small clearing of pale grass and a first glimmer of dawn brightened the horizon ahead, Vincent stopped. He pulled a piece of paper from his pocket and handed it to Connor. There was enough light to see that it was a crude map drawn in charcoal.

'Follow the river east, but do not go too close to it,' Vincent said. 'Stay in the high ground, in the trees. And travel only at night.'

'How far is it to Karingoa?'

'I don't know. Maybe sixty, seventy miles south of here. But you must not go south. Between here and the border there are more camps. Many, many soldiers. They prepare a great war. You must go east. Three, maybe four days. Only there is it safe to cross.'

'You're not coming with us?'

'I can't. Take this.' He unslung the bag from his shoulder and gave it to Connor. 'There is a little food and water.'

Then he held out the rifle. Connor shook his head.

'Take it!'

'I feel safer without it.'

Vincent clearly considered this crazy and insisted that they should at least take the machete. Vincent laid a hand on Lawrence's shoulder and said something in Acholi. The boy nodded and murmured a few words in reply, of which Connor understood just enough to know that he was offering his thanks.

Connor held out his hand and Vincent shook it.

'Thank you,' Connor said.

Vincent nodded. 'Go now. Take the boy to his brother.'

They went their separate ways and Connor didn't look back until he and Lawrence had reached the far side of the clearing. But when he did, Vincent had already vanished into the trees.

THEY DID AS BIDDEN and travelled only at night. The map was of little use, but the sky was mostly cloudless, and Connor steered by the stars and by the passage of the moon. As they hiked higher into the mountains the air grew thinner and the going more treacherous. When they were forced into the lower land they kept when they could, in the cover of the trees, and in the elephant grass, and always away from any road or trail they came across, for many of these were mined and monitored.

When the sky began to pale, they would start looking for a place to shelter for the day, some shaded enclave in the rocks or jungle glade where they could rest in safety. The food and water that Vincent had given them lasted two days. They shared the water, but Connor made the boy eat most of the food and he used the iodine to treat the open sores on his bony arms and his bare and swollen feet.

Most of the drainages they passed were dry, but they found just enough water to get by. At the camp the children had tried to supplement their meagre rations by scavenging in the bush, and Lawrence had learned which trees and plants had leaves that were edible. When they came across one, he would point it out and the two of them would stop and force themselves to eat.

As dawn approached on the sixth day, they found themselves walking along the side of a winding wooded valley. Their night's journey had been hard and they were weary and weak from hunger.

As they dropped deeper into the valley bed, they heard the rush and tumble of a stream and soon caught sight of it down between the trees. There was a waterfall and a dark pool below, half rimmed with rock. They made their way down, and by the time they had drunk their fill and washed themselves and rinsed their clothes, the sun had almost risen. They found a place to lie up and spread their clothes on the bushes, and then settled in the grass to sleep.

Connor woke with the feeling that an insect had landed on his neck. Without opening his eyes, he lazily lifted a hand to brush the bug away, and it was then that he felt the cold edge of the blade.

He opened his eyes and saw the figure standing over him, silhouetted by the flaring sun behind. Then he saw it was a man and that the blade now poking hard into his throat belonged to a spear. The man was tall and broad and his eyes were fierce. Connor saw there were half a dozen others with him, all armed with spears and machetes.

The men made them both get to their feet and were yelling so excitedly that it took Connor a while to figure out that they were speaking a kind of Swahili. He understood enough to know that he and Lawrence were suspected of belonging to the rebels. Connor kept his eyes fixed on the one who appeared to be their leader and who still had his spear poking at his chest. Connor greeted him in Swahili and told him as calmly as he could that they were not Makuma's spies, but his captives, and that they had escaped.

There was a gabbled conference and from the little Connor understood, it seemed that he had sown enough doubt to avoid being murdered on the spot. The leader turned to Connor and said that they must put on their clothes and come with them.

They were marched for maybe an hour down the valley, with spears at their backs, until they saw a cluster of mud and grass huts in a clearing above the river, sheltered by acacia and borassus palms. They were made to sit on the ground in the shade of the palms, with two of their captors standing guard. A short while later a woman brought them a pot of water and two bowls filled with a thick porridge, which they both ate hungrily.

In the late afternoon some soldiers arrived and from the drift of their questions Connor gathered that they belonged to the Sudan People's Liberation Army, the SPLA. Their commander wanted to know all about Makuma's camp, how many men were there and how well armed. Connor and Lawrence told him what they knew.

At dusk they were taken to a bare hut and fed again. Lawrence sat slumped and forlorn against the wall, staring at the ground. Connor settled himself beside him and put his arm round his shoulders. The boy fell asleep with his head resting on Connor's chest.

The soldiers woke them at dawn and marched them from the camp. It soon became clear that they were heading south, following the course of the river. The valley was thickly forested and the going hard, and by the time they stopped to rest, the sun had climbed high and their clothes were soaked with sweat. They cooled themselves in the river and drank.

The commander told Connor that they were close to the Ugandan border now and that he had sent men ahead to make contact with the Ugandan government forces who patrolled it. Half an hour later the men returned with a sergeant in the UPDF and two younger soldiers. The sergeant greeted Connor solemnly and asked the same questions that they had answered many times already. The SPLA commander led his soldiers off without another word.

Once across the border they were met by a Land Rover and driven south for many miles along dirt roads and then across dry savannah, until at dusk they arrived at an army barracks. There they were separated and Connor was led to a room with a dirty cement floor and bare walls with barred windows. There was a table and two chairs and he sat waiting for a long time, until a young major in a smartly pressed shirt came in and sat in the other chair on the other side of the table, and in precise English asked all the same questions again, and more besides.

Afterwards Connor was led across the compound to some sort of detention block, where he found Lawrence already in the cell waiting for him. The boy looked relieved to see him.

The cell had two narrow bunks. It was the first time in almost three months that Connor had slept in anything like a proper bed and, even though the mattress was hard and full of lumps and the blanket mangy, it felt like five-star luxury.

The next morning he was summoned once more to see the major, and this time the man's manner was friendlier. He said he had made a number of calls, including one to the US embassy in Kampala. Someone there had managed to get hold of Harry Turney at the agency in New York and even tracked his mother down in Montana.

'Everybody thought you were dead. You have been missing for a long time, much longer than you told me.'

'I was travelling.'

He didn't elaborate and the major didn't press the point.

'You and the boy will be taken today to Kampala.'

'We have to get to Karingoa.'

'That is impossible. The rebels have made a great push south. There is much bad fighting. The army has sealed off that whole section of the country. You cannot even get to Gulu.'

Connor asked if he could call St Mary's to tell them about Lawrence, but the major said this too was impossible. All communications with Karingoa had been cut.

CONNOR SAT ON THE BED looking out over the hotel gardens and waiting for the operator to call him back. It was late afternoon and he felt weary after the frantic activity of the past hours. He had spent the day so far shuttling around Kampala, talking to government officials and aid agencies and people at the US embassy and trying to figure out what to do about Lawrence. The embassy people were going to fix Connor a new passport and they let him use the phone to call his bank in Nairobi to arrange for some money to be wired. Meanwhile, so that he could buy them both some new clothes, he had borrowed money from the only real friend he had in Kampala.

Geoffrey Odong was a journalist he had met on his first ever visit here before going into Rwanda. Both he and his wife Elizabeth were Acholis and it was they who had first made Connor aware of what was going on in the north and about the extraordinary work being done at St Mary of the Angels. They lived with their three daughters in a modest house at the foot of one of the city's seven green hills.

Connor had called them the previous night as soon as he and Lawrence arrived in the city. Geoffrey came to collect them and insisted they stay the night. Elizabeth fed them until Connor thought the boy was going to burst. Their eldest daughter was Lawrence's age, and after a shy start the two of them were getting along well. The place was small and Connor felt bad that the girls had been ousted to the living room so that he could have their bedroom. After heavy protest, Elizabeth had reluctantly conceded that he should move to the Sheraton, but only on condition that Lawrence stay on.

Connor had asked the concierge for a razor and shaving foam and after showering for twenty minutes he had slowly scraped off his scraggly beard. He sat now with a towel wrapped round his waist and another over his shoulders, wondering if the operator had forgotten about the call he had placed. At last the phone rang. The operator said she had New York on the line and told him to go ahead. Connor asked for Harry Turney and waited.

'Connor! Where the fuck have you been?'

'You know, I don't think I ever heard you swear till now.'

'Yeah? Well, you save it for when you need it. I mean, Jesus, Connor, how can you do that? If you want to go get yourself kidnapped and killed, that's your business, but you might have the sense or decency to let someone know where the hell you're doing it.'

'Harry, I'm sorry.'

'So you damn well should be. Have you called your mother?'

'I'm just about to.'

'What's the matter with you? Get off the phone and do it now. I'll call you back. What's your number?'

Connor told him and hung up, smiling to himself guiltily. He called the operator to give her his mother's number, and while he waited for the call to come through he got dressed.

His mother was a lot more forgiving. She said that she had long ago got used to his vanishing acts and she hadn't been worried. Connor didn't believe her for a moment.

'You heard about Ed, of course,' she asked.

'What about him?'

There was a long pause. 'Son, Ed died. Christmas before last. I forgot how long you've been gone.'

Connor was stunned. She told him what had happened and what a shock it had been and he sat on the bed and listened in a muted daze.

'How are Julia and Amy?'

'Well, heck, they're right out there where you are. She's gone to work with those poor kids you photographed, you know, the ones they turn into soldiers. Taken Amy with her.'

'In Karingoa? St Mary of the Angels?'

'That's the place. I had a postcard about a month ago.'

There was a pause.

'Connor? Are you there?'

'Yeah.'

But he was too choked with emotion to go on speaking. In little more than a whisper he promised his mother that he would call again later and hung up.

An hour later he was pacing back and forth across Geoffrey Odong's cubicle of an office at the newspaper. For the past twenty minutes Geoffrey had been on the phone to an old college friend who was now a senior UPDF officer.

Connor could hear only one side of the conversation but he had already got the drift. At last Geoffrey hung up. He gave Connor a gloomy look and shook his head.

'There's no way. There are roadblocks on every route into the area. They're not letting anyone near the place, least of all any journalists.'

'What's happening in Karingoa?'

'He said the rebel advance has been checked, but I don't think I believe it. He said many people have already left. He claims that the situation is under control, but it sounds to me as if the government has greatly underestimated the rebels' strength.'

'Geoffrey, I have to get to them.'

'There is no way. And they may have already been evacuated.'

'If I know Sister Emily, they'll be the last to leave.' Connor turned to face him. 'Do you know someone who would fly me up there?'

THREE TIMES NOW the government soldiers had come to advise them to leave and every time Sister Emily had refused. St Mary of the Angels had stood firm against Makuma's threats and thieving raids for more than a decade and she wasn't about to yield to him now.

At first the calm and confidence she displayed had been infectious. She told children and staff that there was nothing to fear. If things got bad, she said, they could all pile into Gertrude, the double-decker bus, and be away in minutes. Everyone seemed reassured.

Yet as the days went by and the boom of the guns grew nightly nearer, it became apparent that this was more than another 'thieving raid'. On the road beyond the convent gates the trickle of refugees was swelling to a steady flood.

Though Julia did her best to allay any worries the children voiced, she had secretly begun to share them. It wasn't for herself that she worried but for Amy. Perhaps they should go before it was too late.

Last night, after the soldiers' third visit and all the children had gone to bed, Sister Emily asked Julia, Françoise and Peter Pringle to convene in her office and announced quietly that they should consider themselves free to leave.

'I still refuse to believe there is any cause for concern. But, Julia, if you are concerned about Amy, then you should go. We would understand.' She turned to Peter Pringle and Françoise. 'The same goes for both of you. We would miss you, of course, but we can manage.'

There was a short silence. Pringle cleared his throat.

'Well, I can only speak for myself,' he said. 'But as long as you and the children are here, I'm not going anywhere.'

His little declaration made Julia feel ashamed. That night, for the first time in a week, there was no sound of shell fire. Julia lay scolding herself for being weak and foolish. How could she, even for one moment, consider abandoning everyone? Wasn't that what she had done all those years ago with Skye? Once was enough.

She woke in the morning with a new resolve.

But it lasted only a few hours. As they were sitting down for supper in the tent, a white Land Rover came roaring round the side of the building and two people, a man and a woman, climbed quickly out. Julia recognised them. They were Danish aid workers who sometimes came here to eat.

They reached the staff table and Sister Emily and all of them stood and gathered around. The man was breathing heavily and trying to conceal his alarm. In a low voice he told them that Makuma had broken through and that the government forces were retreating in disarray before him. The rebels were less than ten miles away and moving steadily towards the northern outskirts of the town, looting and burning all before them.

 CHAPTER TWELVE

The man sat with his bare elbows on the table either side of his beer, his pale blue eyes fixed unblinking on Connor.

It had taken Geoffrey just three phone calls to find the kind of person Connor needed. Johannes Kriel ran a small aviation company and was rumoured to be involved in smuggling, gunrunning and many darker deeds beside. Connor was told to go to the Parkside Inn next to the old taxi park and find a table out on the balcony. Kriel would join him there.

When he did, the man neither said hello nor offered his hand. In a South African accent he told the waiter to bring him a Nile Special and then he sat down and told Connor to say what he wanted. As Connor told it all, Kriel listened.

'Did anyone tell you there's a war going on up there?'

'Just get me as near as you safely can.'

He took a drink of his beer. 'When were you thinking of doing this?'

'Right now.'

'Tonight? You think I'm going to land in the bush in the middle of the fucking night?'

'You wouldn't have to. I'll jump. Can you find me a parachute?'

'Maybe.' He grinned. 'Whether it'll open is another matter.'

'I'll give you two thousand dollars.'

The man laughed and looked away and took another drink. 'For ten I might think about it.'

They settled on six.

Kriel had a black Range Rover parked outside with a driver waiting, and they climbed in and headed out of the city to a small private airstrip. It was heavily fenced and there were armed guards at the gate who let the vehicle pass as soon as they saw Kriel's face.

There was a small office with a flickering fluorescent strip and a colony of mosquitoes. Kriel asked for the name of his bank and dialled the number to make sure it was the real thing. Then he handed Connor the phone and wrote down his own bank details and loomed over him while Connor arranged for the transfer.

When it was done he went round to the storeroom at the back of the building to dig out the parachute. While he was gone, Connor called Geoffrey and asked him to let Lawrence know that he would come back for him as soon as he could and if for some reason he couldn't, to make sure that the boy was reunited with his brother. Geoffrey promised.

'I remember you talking about this woman when we first met all those years ago. You must still love her very much.'

'Always have and always will,' Connor said simply.

Kriel reappeared carrying a stained canvas bag. When he dumped it on the floor it sent up a cloud of dust.

He grinned. 'Been a long time since anyone had call to use it.'

Connor asked for a flashlight and when Kriel found him one he carried the bag outside and unpacked it. He hooked the end of the parachute to the wall and stretched it out to examine it. It wasn't great but it was good enough.

While Connor carefully repacked the chute, Kriel appeared with a 9mm automatic holstered at his hip and was carrying a black nylon jacket which he tossed to Connor.

'Put that on. You'd be hard to miss wearing that shirt.'

Twenty minutes later they were taxiing along the runway in an unmarked Cessna 206. There was a cargo door at the rear of the starboard side, so jumping out wasn't going to be as tricky as Connor had expected.

They took off to the south with the black expanse of Lake

Victoria stretching away to nothing below them. Then they circled round and headed north with the lights of Kampala to their right. It was the first moment of stillness that Connor had allowed himself since the phone call to his mother, and he realised that in his obsession to reach Julia and Amy, he hadn't yet spared proper thought for his lost friend Ed. And as the little Cessna nosed its way north into the ominous night, he felt sorrow surge within him and settle like a leaden weight in the hollow of his chest.

THE BRANCHES of the flame trees scraped against the top of the bus as it passed beneath them on its way up the driveway, and the noise was so loud and shocking that some of the children sitting on the upper deck cried out in fright.

Julia was sitting with her arm round Amy in the rearmost seat at the top of the stairway. When she looked back she could see Peter Pringle's determined face at the wheel of the truck behind. Most of the children and staff were on the bus, but the rest sat crammed in the open back of Pringle's truck. Behind that were two smaller trucks with all the cooks and maids and kitchen boys. The centre's four security guards had been allocated one to each vehicle.

When the bus reached the convent gates it had to stop, for the road outside was a seething river of panic and confusion. Most of the refugees were walking or running, and there were cars and trucks and vans weaving among them with their horns blaring and people clinging desperately to their sides and roofs. Oblivious to all, and thundering past through the pall of illumined red dust that swirled above the chaos came the retreating army trucks packed with soldiers, the weary and the wounded, the shell-shocked and the dead.

When the crowd caught sight of the St Mary's convoy, a score or more came running and yelling and waving their arms, and as the bus started to move out into the road they screamed and hammered on its sides, and Julia could hear the security guard and Sister Emily below fending them off and telling them again and again that there was no room. Amy was quaking with fear.

'Mommy!'

'It's all right, honey. It's all right.'

It wasn't, of course, and perhaps it never would be, but there was nothing else to say. Julia stroked her hair and felt her burrow deeper and cling more tightly.

The bus was on the road now and George the gardener was steering Gertrude south through the parting waves of people. Julia looked back again and saw the other trucks following. And beyond them now, for the first time, she saw the flash of exploding shells.

There was a clatter of footsteps on the stairway and Sister Emily emerged, beaming as if they were all on some exotic school outing. She looked round at Julia and saw Amy sheltering under her arm.

'Amy, we need a song. What do you think we should sing?'

Amy gave a small shrug. Sister Emily persisted.

'How about one of those English songs you taught us all? From your *Lion* film. No? Then what about the Purple Submarine?'

'Yellow.'

Sister Emily frowned. 'Are you sure? I think it was purple.'

'It was yellow!'

'Oh well, maybe you are right. Anyway, how about that one?'

Sister Emily had clearly forgotten the tune, and she looked at Julia to give a lead. And because Julia's singing talents had always been a favourite source of mirth and mockery for her daughter, she had only to sing a few bars before Amy began to grin and then to giggle. Then Thomas sitting nearby started to giggle too, not just at Julia but at Sister Emily who had the hang of the tune but not of the lyrics. On every chorus she gave the submarine a different colour, and this made Amy sing ever more loudly to correct her, until gradually, row by row, the other children joined in.

Even as she sang, Julia was aware that their contrived merriment was a kind of denial, but as she watched the singing lift the children's spirits she began to feel stronger herself. When the song was done they sang another, and when she looked over her shoulder Julia could see that Pringle and his passengers were singing too.

It would be all right, she told herself. They would all get through.

THEY FLEW WITHOUT lights and for the first hour kept high with the land unfurling far below. They sat side by side, with Connor on the right and the lights of the instruments glowing between them. They wore headsets so that they could talk above the roar of the engine, but they rarely did.

They were some seventy miles south of Karingoa when they got their first glimpse of the war. Through a gap in the clouds they saw the lights of trucks on a road. Kriel banked away west and started to climb. The next time they saw the road it seemed much more crowded and the lights were moving more slowly. They climbed higher and saw to the north a dim red glow, which, as they flew nearer, seemed to spread and intensify. And from his days as a smoke jumper Connor knew what it was.

Soon the canopy of cloud glowed like a vast red cauldron before them and Kriel nosed the Cessna further to the west to skirt it. A moment later the clouds parted and they saw the town of Karingoa and the swath of flame that fringed it to the north.

'I'll come around once more and then I'm out of here. If you're going to bail out, you better get back there.'

Connor unbuckled his seat belt and took off the headset. As he got up from his seat, Kriel held up his right hand.

'Good luck, bro.'

Connor grasped the hand and thanked him.

'Now get the fuck out of here,' Kriel said.

Connor made his faltering way back to the cargo door as the plane banked and juddered through the cloud. He checked his harness, then squatted down beside the door and took hold of the handle. 'OK!' he yelled. 'I'm opening up!'

Without looking back, Kriel gave him a thumbs up.

The door ripped open and a moment later Kriel nosed the plane below the line of the clouds and Connor got a first murky view of the terrain he was going to be landing in.

'OK,' Kriel yelled. 'We're at fourteen-fifty. I'll take you down to twelve hundred but that's as low as I go. Get in the door!'

Connor manoeuvred himself into the doorway so that he was squatting with the toes of his boots poking out into the void.

'Twelve-fifty!'

Connor fisted his right hand and pressed it to his chest.

'Hey, old friend,' he whispered in the wind. 'Hearts of fire.'

'Twelve hundred! Jump, you crazy bastard!'

Connor launched himself into the night with all the power he had. He felt the warm air rushing past.

'One-one-thousand . . .'

He was twisting as he fell and looking up he saw the belly of the Cessna tilt sharply away and climb towards the clouds. The air was laced with smoke. It tasted thick and acrid in his mouth and stung his eyes and nostrils.

When he was still some eighty feet from the ground, the smoke seemed suddenly to clear. Somewhere away to his left he heard men shouting and then caught a glimpse of figures running towards him, maybe 300 yards away. He looked down and saw the dark tops of some giant palm trees racing up towards him. The next thing he knew, he was being dragged chest-high through the clattering palm fronds, then dropping fast beyond them. His boots hit the ground hard and he rolled and somersaulted and came to rest on his back in time to see the canopy floating down over him.

Connor felt a jab of pain in his right shoulder, but his legs were fine, and that was what mattered. He could hear the voices, though how close he couldn't tell. In a few moments, however, he was free from the chute and he ran as fast as he could for cover.

How far he travelled through the bush he had no way of knowing. Every so often through the fringe of the trees he would catch sight of the burning town, and at last he saw the water tower that stood near the marketplace and was able to get his bearings from it and adjust his course. In the confusion he could only guess, but it seemed as if the rebels had almost succeeded in taking the town, with the government forces putting up some last resistance in its southern enclaves.

As Connor headed yet further south, Karingoa became obscured by trees and soon all he could see of it was the rising glow of fire above them. At last, through the darkness, he saw what he had been searching for: a pale horizontal band with the black shapes of trees beyond. It was the rear wall of the convent gardens. He jumped the ditch before it and then clambered over the wall and hoisted himself into the garden.

The convent was burning and so was the chapel. From the shelter of the orange trees he could see the flames licking hungrily from the upstairs windows. He was expecting to see soldiers, but the place seemed deserted. There was no sound of gunfire now, only the crackle of the burning building.

He walked across the playing field through flaming scraps of debris, past the looted kitchens and the smouldering shreds and poles of the dining tent and then round the side of the chapel to the driveway. As he drew near to the gates he saw that the road outside was blocked by two overturned trucks, both in flames. A moment later he heard the rattle of a heavy machine gun and ducked in among the mango trees and almost at once tripped over a soldier.

The man was lying in the grass under cover of the wall, with his assault rifle trained on the gate. From his uniform Connor was almost certain that he was UPDF. There were others too, six or seven of them, all lying there. Connor got to his knees but they yelled at him to get down and no sooner had he hit the ground when a grenade went off between the gates.

'Come! Come! Come!'

Suddenly they were all up and running across the driveway, and without a moment's thought Connor got up and ran with them. As they crossed the gateway through the clearing smoke of the grenade, the machine gun opened up again and Connor heard the bullets thwack against the stucco columns. They ran ducking and dodging among the bushes, and when they got to the side wall of the convent grounds they helped one another and Connor to scramble up and over and down into the scrub beyond. One of them had a sergeant's stripes on his sleeve. He grabbed hold of Connor's shoulder.

'You are a teacher here?'

'Yes,' Connor answered.

'Come now. We must go quick.'

About a mile down the road they reached a small convoy of trucks that stood waiting for them under cover of some tall eucalyptus trees.

Connor was the only civilian and foreigner among them, but nobody asked who he was or what he was doing there, so he stayed close to the sergeant and climbed into the open back of one of the trucks with the men. As each truck filled, so it was waved out onto the road, and soon Connor's too was heading off through the choking dust with the flames of St Mary of the Angels lighting the sky behind.

The rebels seemed to have circled the town in an attempt to cut the valley road, for along the hilltops on either side there were sporadic flashes and booms, and in the headlights of the truck behind them he could see the road was cratered with shell holes and strewn with the debris of evacuation. There were bodies too, and as they went by Connor scanned them with a growing sense of foreboding, telling himself again and again with fading conviction that the two he loved most in all the world were somewhere safe.

How long he slept he didn't know, but when he woke, the sky was washed with dawn. The clouds were low and leaden and the air was damp. Most of the soldiers in the truck were still asleep. Connor looked back along the road, idly watching the dimming lights of the truck behind them in the convoy as it slowed to manoeuvre round some burnt-out vehicles.

And that was when he saw it. The convent's ancient double-decker bus.

He leapt to his feet and yelled for the driver to stop, and the soldiers around him woke and some of them grumbled or shouted at him to sit down. He scrambled forward over the soldiers' legs until he reached the driver's cab, then he hammered on its rear windows.

'Stop! You gotta stop!'

The driver didn't look pleased and yelled something back at him, but Connor couldn't hear what it was and just kept on shouting until the truck slowed, and even before it came to a halt he had hoisted himself over the side and jumped down onto the road. The driver climbed down from the cab, haranguing him, and many of the soldiers in the back were doing the same, but Connor didn't care.

'The bus! That's the convent bus! My family!'

He turned and started to run. The truck coming towards him blasted its horn at him but he ignored it and ran past. Gertrude lay askew with one wheel in the ditch and tilting perilously as though a mere touch might topple her. Long before he got there, Connor could see that she had been burned out. In the driver's cab, hunched and curled, as if even now in death he sought to protect himself, was a body burned beyond recognition.

Connor braced himself to find more bodies inside. But he checked both decks and found none. The young sergeant and two of his men had arrived now to bring him back.

'We must not stop here,' the sergeant said. 'You must come. It is dangerous.'

'They might be here. Somewhere.'

'Where? Look, there's no one.'

Another truck roared by along the road, sounding its horn as it passed. Connor turned away in anguish and looked up at the seamless dark green jungle of the hillside. He felt a slow, churning sense of loss and desperation rise within him, and he walked in faltering steps into the scrub at the side of the road and howled at the sky.

'*Julia!*'

The sound echoed along the valley and he called her name again and again. And when the last echo faded he stood and scoured the hillside for any sign of movement, but nothing stirred.

Then the rain began to fall, slowly at first, in heavy drops that slapped upon the ground and upon his face and shoulders and quickly filled the air with the smell of thirsting dust.

'Come,' the sergeant said gently. 'Perhaps you find them in one of the camps.'

Connor nodded and bowed his head. The others waiting in the back of the truck were calling impatiently.

'Come now,' the sergeant said. He put a hand on Connor's shoulder and Connor let himself be steered back towards the truck.

When they were halfway there the calling of the soldiers suddenly seemed different, as if they were no longer chiding him. And the sergeant beside him glanced back towards the bus and then stopped.

'Look,' he said.

Connor turned. The rain was so heavy now, and his eyes so brimmed with tears, that at first he saw nothing. And then the figure standing in the scrub at the side of the road moved and he saw her.

'Connor?' Through the rain her voice sounded small and frail and full of disbelief. 'Connor? Is that really you?'

He started to walk back along the road and his legs felt so weak that he almost stumbled. She was stepping onto the road now and walking towards him through the pale curtain of the rain.

'Julia?'

They stopped a little way apart and stood staring at each other as if they were seeing each other's ghost. Her cotton dress was ripped, her face filthy and her short hair bedraggled. Even in all his years of dreaming she had never looked more beautiful.

'Why are you . . .?' she said. 'What are you . . .?'

'I heard you were here. I had to find you.'

She shook her head slightly and then her face crumpled and he stepped towards her and took hold of her and he could feel her whole body begin to shake. And he tried to say what was in his heart but he couldn't find the words nor even the voice to utter them. She slowly lifted her arms and put them round him and clung to him. She tried to say something but couldn't and just started to sob until he thought she would break.

Over her shoulder he saw the others now, emerging from the trees. He saw Pringle, the doctor, and Sister Emily holding the hands of two children, and others following, ushered by the nuns. And hurrying past them now onto the road and running through the rain towards her mother came Amy, the daughter he hadn't held since she was a baby and who was now this tall, fine girl.

'Mommy?'

Julia gathered her in her arms and started to explain who Connor was, but somehow the child already knew and tentatively reached out to him and took his hand. And with the rain beating down upon them and turning the road around them into a river, the three of them stood clinging to one another as if the world and whatever it might bring would never be allowed to part them.

 # CHAPTER THIRTEEN

It was one of those crystalline Montana mornings, when the freshly fallen snow glinted in the sun like sequinned satin and the mountains stood so bold against the blue of the sky that you could count every frosted crevice. Julia followed the dogs out onto the pristine planks of the new porch and closed the kitchen door behind her.

She came down the steps and stopped again and shielded her eyes from the glare of the snow. The only trace of the horses were the twin tracks that led from the barn and out past the corral and then up across the hillside and into the trees. She guessed that they would probably be coming back their usual way so she turned up her collar and headed down towards the creek.

The house that they had built stood in a low fold of the hills some dozen miles east of the massive limestone wall of the Rocky Mountain Front. The building was low and modest and made of wood and, with the smoke curling from its stone chimney, it already looked as if it belonged. It had taken them more than a year to build. And with each beam and nail, each rafter and strut, so too the new construction of their lives had slowly taken shape.

THEIR HOMECOMING had been hard.

In those few days that they spent in Kampala before flying home, Julia and Amy had stayed cocooned in their hotel room while Connor rushed round the city organising things. He wanted to help Sister Emily to start looking for a new home for the children of St Mary's and then he had to reunite Thomas and Lawrence Nyeko who had both now been adopted by Connor's friends the Odongs. He even helped arrange the funeral of poor George, the gardener, who had been the sole casualty of the flight from Karingoa. The result was that Julia and Connor had scarcely had a moment to themselves. Even the airline conspired against them. There weren't three seats together, so Connor sat separately.

After his astonishing quest to find them, Julia had assumed that everything was resolved and that, once they got back to Montana, she and Connor would be together. But it wasn't to be like that.

While they were away in Africa, the house in Missoula had been rented out to some students. They were friends of friends and had left it clean and tidy and done no damage, but they had left the place smelling so utterly different that Amy promptly burst into tears. It no longer felt like home, she said.

Once she had found her old toys and books and made contact again with friends, she soon felt better. And whether it faded or they just got used to it, they soon forgot about the smell. But there was something more potent in the air that no amount of freshening could banish. The memory of Ed was everywhere, like an almost palpable presence in every room.

Julia knew that Connor must sense it even more sharply than she did. She tried to view it as benign, to convince herself that they had Ed's blessing, but she couldn't make the mental leap. She knew that she and Connor should talk about it, but it was too vast a subject.

He stayed for a couple of days to help them settle in and get organised. But Julia could tell how awkward he felt. On the third morning Connor left to go to his mother's ranch, and perhaps she imagined it, but he looked relieved to be going. When he kissed her goodbye, it was on the cheek, like a friend.

In the weeks that followed, Connor phoned every day and came often to see them. And at weekends she and Amy would drive over to stay with him and his mother at the ranch. It was the cusp of spring and Connor would take Amy riding, and when the weather grew warmer, the three of them would sometimes go hiking.

Connor had a way with Amy that was altogether different from Ed's. Amy's relationship with Ed had been full of exuberant banter; they were both great talkers and extroverts. Connor talked too, but mostly he just listened, fixing her with those pale blue eyes and smiling and nodding.

Watching the two of them grow steadily closer, Julia felt happy for them both. But she couldn't quite suppress a twinge of envy. For her own relationship with Connor seemed becalmed in a kind of sibling friendship. There were moments, the occasional look or touch, when she felt sure that he wanted her as much she wanted him. But neither of them seemed willing or able to step across the line.

By early June, Amy seemed to have recovered most of her former confidence. At supper one evening she announced that the coming weekend her friend Molly was having a sleepover birthday party.

'Is it OK if I go?' she asked tentatively.

'Is it "OK"? I think that's terrific.'

'You're sure you don't mind?'

'Heck, I might even have a sleepover myself!'

'With Connor?'

Julia gulped. She laughed too loudly and felt herself blushing. 'Well, no, honey. That's not what I meant. I just said it as a joke.'

'It's OK, you know. I don't mind.'

Julia didn't know where to look or what to say.

Amy went on, 'I mean, I thought we were all going to live together.'

'Is that what you want?'

'Of course I do! I love him. He's not my daddy but he is my father.'

That did it. Julia got up and went to her and they grabbed hold of each other, crying and laughing at the same time.

Julia called Connor that same evening and asked him bluntly what he was doing on Friday night.

'Well, I've got a date.'

'Oh.' Julia was floored.

'With you and Amy. Aren't you coming over this weekend?'

'Amy's got a birthday party.' She swallowed. 'It's a sleepover. So, I just wondered if you'd like to come over and I could cook us something nice to eat. Maybe cook outside if it stays dry.'

'Just the two of us.'

'Yes.'

There was a silence. Was he teasing her? She couldn't tell.

'What time?'

'I have to drop her off at six.'

'I'll be there at seven.'

Friday was slow in coming, but at last it did, and Julia spent most of it feeling like a high-school kid preparing for a prom. She went into town to buy the food and to get her hair cut. When she came back Amy said how nice she looked and Julia tried to act all casual and said, well, you know, it was summer and short hair was cooler.

Julia dropped Amy at Molly's house in Missoula ten minutes early and nearly got caught speeding on the way home. The weather was clear and warm and so she had decided that they would eat outside. She set the table and put candles all round the rail of the verandah and in the trees. They were going to have tuna steaks and salad and then raspberries and cream. She lit the barbecue and hurried inside.

She showered and dried off and smoothed herself all over with some fifty-dollar moisturiser that Linda had given her. She put on the old pale blue dress that she had bought all those years ago for Connor's surprise homecoming party. It looked great. A little eye-shadow and mascara, no lipstick.

It was five past seven when she heard Connor's truck turn into the driveway. She took a last look at herself in the hallway mirror, then stood perfectly still for a moment with her eyes closed.

'Ed?' she whispered. 'It's OK. Isn't it? Tell me it's OK.'

She took his silence as a yes.

Connor was wearing a salmon-coloured denim shirt with white snap buttons and his old blue jeans looked as if they'd come straight from the laundry. He had on his best boots too and his best hat, which he removed as he walked towards her across the gravel, never once taking his eyes off her. In his other hand he had a bottle of champagne and there was a bunch of blue cornflowers tucked under his arm. When he was still a short way off he stopped and stood looking at her, smiling his slow smile.

'I remember that dress. You look so darn beautiful, I don't know where else to look.'

Julia swallowed and smiled and held his gaze. 'Well, why don't you just keep on looking.'

He stepped towards her and handed her the flowers.

'Thank you.'

Her voice was so small she could hardly hear it herself. She tried to stop herself trembling but couldn't. He stepped still closer until they were almost touching and she could smell his clean soapy smell and saw him take a deep breath of her scent and lower his eyes to her lips. She opened her mouth a little, and moved it slowly up towards his, and as their lips touched everything went still.

Their hands were too full of flowers and hats and bottles so all that touched were their mouths. Then, without a word, she turned and led him into the house. And though it wasn't what she'd planned, she led him up the stairs and into her bedroom. She dropped the flowers on the bedside table and he laid the champagne and his hat on the chair and turned to face her, and they stood close, looking into each other's eyes. He traced down the outside of her arms with his fingertips and then took her by the shoulders and bent his head and kissed her neck and beneath her chin and along the line of her jaw.

'Oh, Connor, I've wanted you for so long.'

'I've wanted you too. I dreamed of you like this.'

'I dreamed of you. Promise you'll never go away again.'

'I promise.'

THERE WAS ALMOST A FOOT of new snow and it scrunched and squeaked beneath her boots. The collies ran ahead, chasing each other among the trees. The banks of the creek were plated with jutting overhangs of ice and the water between them curled with steam.

She followed the dogs along the bank, and on and up and around the bend until the land flattened and opened and she could see all the way up the valley. And there they were, still a good half-mile away, coming at an easy walk along the creek towards her.

They were too wrapped up in their talking to have spotted her, and she stood at the edge of the cottonwoods and watched them ride slowly towards her.

The dogs blew Julia's cover. They went racing away towards the horses and as soon as Connor saw them he looked beyond them and saw her and waved and so did Amy. Julia waved back and watched them quicken the horses to a trot and then to a lope, kicking snow over the dogs at their heels.

They slowed the horses as they drew near and reined them to a halt.

'Hey, Mrs Ford, I thought you were supposed to stay in bed.'

'On a day like this? Give me a break.'

He put his hand on the great dome of her stomach and kissed her on the lips.

'Do you want to ride sidesaddle?' he said. 'I can lift you.'

'Sure, if you want me to have the baby right here and now.'

'I don't think so,' Amy said.

Julia was eight months pregnant. They already knew it was a girl. They even knew what they were going to call her. Her first name would be Emily and the middle name Skye.

Amy rode on ahead now, letting her horse splash through the icy shallows. Connor put his arm around Julia and walked her back towards the house with the horse blowing softly behind.

She wondered sometimes what would or wouldn't have happened if Amy hadn't taken the initiative and gone to that sleepover party. The important things in life never happened by accident. But even with those things that were meant to be, sometimes you had to wait awhile and then maybe give them a little nudge.

NICHOLAS EVANS

The idea for *The Smoke Jumper* came to Nicholas Evans when he was in the middle of researching his second novel, *The Loop*. He was driving back to his hotel, after a weekend spent radio-tracking wolves in the Nine Mile Valley north of Missoula, when he spotted a sign saying 'Smoke Jumpers' on the side of the road. 'I was so intrigued by the sign that I didn't notice a police car pulling up in front of me. I swerved to overtake him and almost clipped his wing mirror. He gave me a ticket for "making an improper pass". I have it framed on my wall and so I know the exact day when I first started thinking about *The Smoke Jumper*! That road sign brought to mind a powerful image of somebody jumping into flames . . . It became the central image of the novel.'

He researched the book by hanging out for a few weeks with smoke jumpers in Montana during the long, hot summer of 2000, when some terrible fires broke out across America. 'I got to know two smoke jumpers in Missoula really well, and spent a lot of time with them, asking them millions of questions and watching the way they work. It seems to me that the world is short of heroes and smoke jumpers are people who can genuinely be described as heroes.'

Nicholas Evans's first novel, *The Horse Whisperer*, was a spectacular success when it was published in 1995, selling over 14 million copies around the world. Like *The Loop* and *The Smoke Jumper* it was set mostly in Montana, a part of the American West that Evans has been obsessed with ever since childhood, when he would watch Westerns on television for hours on end. When he got to visit Montana, in order to research *The Horse Whisperer*, he was overwhelmed by the sheer size and beauty of the place and fell for it completely. 'It felt like coming home,' he says. 'You really are in the wild and I love that. I'm never happier than when I'm there.'

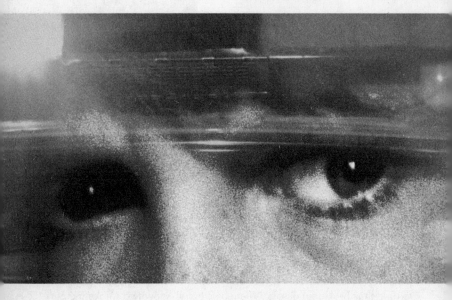

ROBERT CRAIS

HOSTAGE

Dennis and Kevin Rooney, and their new friend Mars, are only out to steal a few dollars. A simple convenience-store robbery—that's all they're planning. But from the moment Dennis steps through the door and shows his gun, events start to spiral way out of control and the three teenagers find themselves involved in far more than they ever bargained for . . .

PROLOGUE

The man in the house was going to kill himself. When the man threw his phone into the yard, Talley knew that he had accepted his own death. After six years as a crisis negotiator with the Los Angeles Police Department's SWAT team, Sergeant Jeff Talley knew that people in crisis often spoke in symbols. This symbol was clear: Talk was over. Talley feared that the man would die by his own hand, or do something to force the police to kill him. It was called suicide by cop. Talley believed it to be his fault.

'Did they find his wife yet?'

'Not yet. They're still looking.'

'Looking doesn't help, Murray. I gotta have something to give this guy after what happened.'

'That's not your fault.'

'It is my fault. I blew it, and now this guy is circling the drain.'

Talley crouched behind an armoured vehicle with the SWAT commander, Murray Leifitz. From this position, Talley had spoken to George Malik through a dedicated crisis phone that had been cut into the house line. Now that Malik had thrown his phone into the yard, Talley could use the public address megaphone or do it face to face. He hated the megaphone, which made his voice harsh and depersonalised the contact. The illusion of a personal relationship was important; the illusion of trust was everything. Talley strapped on a Kevlar vest.

Malik shouted through the broken window, his voice high and strained. 'I'm going to kill this dog! I'm going to kill it!'

Leifitz leaned past Talley to peek at the house. This was the first time Malik had mentioned a dog. 'What the hell? Does he have a dog in there?'

'How do I know? I've got to try to undo some of the damage here, OK? Ask the neighbours about the dog. Get me a name.'

Leifitz scuttled backwards to speak with Malik's neighbours.

George Malik was an unemployed housepainter with too much debt, an unfaithful wife who flaunted her affairs, and prostate cancer. Fourteen hours earlier, at two twelve that morning, he had fired one shot above the heads of police officers who had come to his door in response to a disturbance complaint. He barricaded the door and threatened to kill himself unless his wife agreed to speak to him. The officers ascertained from neighbours that Malik's wife, Elena, had left with their only child, a nine-year-old boy named Brendan. As detectives set about locating her, Malik threatened suicide with greater frequency until Talley was convinced that Malik was nearing the terminal point. When the detectives reported what they believed to be a solid location obtained from the wife's sister, Talley took a chance. He told Malik that his wife had been found. That was his mistake. He had violated a cardinal rule of crisis negotiation: he had lied, and been caught. He had destroyed the illusion of trust that he had been building.

'I'm gonna kill this friggin' dog, goddammit! This is her damned dog, and I'm gonna shoot this sonofabitch, she don't start talkin' to me!'

Talley stepped out from behind the vehicle. He had been on the scene for eleven hours. His skin was greased with sweat, his head throbbed and his stomach was cramping from too much coffee and stress. He made his voice conversational, yet concerned. 'George, it's me, Jeff. Don't kill anything, OK? We don't want to hear a gun go off.'

'You liar! You said my wife was gonna talk to me!'

It was a small stucco house. Drapes had been pulled across the windows. The window on the left was broken from the phone. Eight feet to the right of the porch, a five-member SWAT Tactical Team hunkered against the wall, waiting to breach the door. Malik could not be seen.

'George, listen, I said that we'd found her, and I want to explain that. I was wrong. We got our wires crossed out here, and they gave me bad information. But we're still looking, and when we find her, we'll have her talk to you.'

'You lied before, you bastard, and now you're lying again. You're lying to protect that bitch, and I won't have it. I'm gonna shoot her dog and then I'm gonna blow my brains out.'

Talley waited. It was important that he appear calm and give Malik the room to cool. People burned off stress when they talked. If he could reduce Malik's level of stress, they could still climb out of this.

'Don't shoot the dog, George. Whatever's between you and your wife, let's not take it out on the dog. Is it your dog, too?'

'I don't know whose damn dog it is. She lied about everything else, so she probably lied about the dog. She's a natural-born liar. Like you.'

'George, c'mon. I was wrong, but I didn't lie. I made a mistake. Now, I'm a dog guy myself. What kind of dog you got in there?'

'I don't believe you. You know right where she is, and unless you make her talk to me, I'm gonna shoot this dog.'

'Don't give up, George. I'm sure that she'll talk to you.'

'Then why won't she open her mouth? Why won't the bitch just say something, that's all she's gotta do?'

'We'll work it out.'

'Say something, goddammit!'

'I said we'll work it out.'

'Say something or I'm gonna shoot this damned dog!'

Talley took a breath, thinking. Malik's choice of words left him confused. Talley had spoken clearly, yet Malik acted as if he hadn't heard.

Talley saw Leifitz return to the rear of the vehicle. They were close, only a few feet apart, Leifitz under cover, Talley exposed.

Talley spoke under his breath. 'What's the dog's name?'

Leifitz shook his head. 'They say he doesn't have a dog.'

Something hard pounded in the centre of Talley's head. He suddenly realised that illusions worked both ways. The detectives hadn't found Malik's wife because Malik's wife was inside. The neighbours were wrong. She had been inside the entire time. The wife and the boy.

'Murray, launch the team!' Talley shouted at Murray Leifitz just as a loud whipcrack echoed from the house. A second shot popped even as the tactical team breached the front door.

Talley ran forward. Later, he would not remember entering through the door. Malik's lifeless body was pinned to the floor, his hands being cuffed behind his back even though he was already dead. Malik's wife was sprawled on the living-room sofa where she had been dead for over fourteen hours. Two officers in the SWAT tactical team were trying to stop the geyser of arterial blood that spurted from the neck of Malik's nine-year-old son. One of them screamed for the paramedics. The boy's eyes were wide, searching the room as if trying to find a reason for all this. His mouth opened and closed. His eyes found Talley, who knelt and rested a hand on the boy's leg. Talley never broke eye contact.

He didn't allow himself to blink. He let Brendan Malik have that comfort as he watched the boy die.

After a while, Talley went out to sit on the porch. He lit a cigarette, then replayed the past eleven hours, looking for clues that should have told him what was real. He had blown it. The boy had been here the entire time, curled at the feet of his murdered mother like a faithful dog.

Jeff Talley had been a Los Angeles SWAT officer for thirteen years, serving as a Crisis Response Team negotiator for six. Today was his third crisis call in five days. He tried to recall the boy's eyes, but had already forgotten if they were brown or blue.

Talley crushed his cigarette, walked down the street to his car and went home. He had an eleven-year-old daughter named Amanda. He wanted to check her eyes. He couldn't remember their colour and was scared that he no longer cared.

PART ONE

Bristo Camino, California

Friday, 2:47pm. It was one of those high-desert days in the suburban communities north of Los Angeles with the air so dry it was like breathing sand; the sun licked their skin with fire. They were riding in Dennis's truck, a red Nissan pick-up he'd bought for $600; Dennis Rooney driving, twenty-two years old and eleven days out of the Antelope Valley Correctional Facility, what the inmates called the Ant Farm; his younger brother, Kevin, wedged in the middle; and a guy named Mars filling the shotgun seat.

Later, in the coming hours when Dennis would frantically reconsider his actions, he would decide that it hadn't been the saw-toothed heat that had put him in the mood to do crime; it was fear. Fear that something special was waiting for him that he would never find, and that this special thing would disappear round some curve in his life, and with it his one shot at being more than nothing.

Dennis decided that they should rob the minimart. 'Hey, I know. Let's rob that minimart, the one on the other side of Bristo.'

'I thought we were going to the movie.' That being Kevin, wearing his chickenshit face: eyebrows crawling over the top of his head, darting eyeballs and quivering lips. In the movie of Dennis's life, he saw himself as the brooding outsider all the cheerleaders wanted; his brother was the geekass cripple holding him back.

'This is a better idea. We'll go to the movie after.'

'You just got back from the Farm, Dennis. You want to go back?'

Dennis flicked his cigarette out of the window as he considered himself in the Nissan's sideview. By his own estimation, he had moody deep-set eyes, dramatic cheekbones and sensuous lips.

He adjusted the .32-calibre automatic wedged in his jeans, then glanced past Kevin to Mars. Mars was a big guy, heavy across the shoulders. He had a tattoo on the back of his shaved head that said BURN IT. Dennis had met him at the construction site where he and Kevin were pulling day work for a cement contractor.

'What do you think, dude?'

'I think let's go see.'

That was all it took.

THE MINIMART WAS on Flanders Road, a rural boulevard that linked several expensive housing tracts. Four pump islands framed a bunker-like market that sold booze and convenience items. Dennis pulled up behind the building so they couldn't be seen from inside.

'Look at this, man. The place is dead. It's perfect.'

'C'mon, Dennis, this is stupid. We'll get caught.'

'I'm just gonna see, is all.'

The parking lot was empty except for a black Beemer at the pumps and two bicycles by the front door. Dennis's heart was pounding, his underarms clammy. He was nervous. Fresh off the Farm, he didn't want to go back, but he didn't see how they could get caught.

Dennis pushed inside. Two kids were at the magazine rack by the door. A fat Chinaman was hunkered down behind the counter.

The minimart was two aisles and a cold cabinet packed with beer. Dennis went to the cold cabinet, then along the rear wall to make sure no one was in the aisles. As he was walking back to the truck, the Beemer pulled away. He went to the passenger window. To Mars.

'There's nothing but two kids and a Chinaman in there.'

Kevin squirmed. 'Dennis, please. What are we going to get here, a couple of hundred bucks? Jesus, let's go to the movie.'

Mars was watching. Dennis felt himself flush, and wondered if Mars was judging him. Mars was a boulder of a guy; dense and quiet, watchful with the patience of a rock.

'Mars, we're gonna do this. We're robbing this store.'

Mars climbed out of the truck. 'Let's do it.'

Kevin didn't move. The two kids pedalled away.

'*No one's here, Kevin!* All you have to do is stand by the door and watch. This fat gook will cough right up with the cash. They're insured, so they just hand over the cash. They get fired if they don't.'

Dennis grabbed his brother's T-shirt. The Lemonheads, for chrissake. Mars was already halfway to the door.

'Get out of the truck. You're making us look bad.'

Kevin wilted and slid out like a baby.

JUNIOR KIM, JR, knew a cheese dip when he saw one.

Junior, a second-generation Korean-American, had put in sixteen years behind a minimart counter in the Newton area of Los Angeles. Down in Shootin' Newton (as the LAPD called it), Junior had been beaten, mugged, stabbed, shot at, clubbed and robbed. Enough was enough. After sixteen years of that, Junior moved north to the far less dangerous demographic of suburbia.

Junior was not naive. A minimart, by its nature, draws cheese dips like bad meat draws flies. Even here in Bristo Camino, you had your shoplifters, your hookers passing counterfeit currency (driven up from LA by their pimps) and your drunks. Lightweight stuff compared to LA, but Junior believed in being prepared. After sixteen years of hard-won inner-city lessons, Junior kept 'a little something' under the counter for anyone who got out of hand.

When three cheese dips walked in that Friday afternoon, Junior leaned forward so that his chest touched the counter and his hands were hidden. 'May I help you?'

A skinny kid in a Lemonheads T-shirt stayed by the door. An older kid in a faded black shirt and a large man with a shaved head walked towards him, the older kid raising his shirt to show the ugly black grip of a pistol. 'Two packs of Marlboros for my friend here and all the cash you got in that box, you gook bastard.'

Junior Kim fished under the counter for his 9mm Glock. He found it just as the cheese dip launched himself over the counter. Junior lurched to his feet, bringing up the Glock as the black-shirted dip crashed into him. Junior hadn't expected him to jump over the counter, and hadn't been able to thumb off the safety.

The larger man shouted, 'He's got a gun!'

The black shirt tried to twist away Junior's gun. The big guy reached across the counter, also grabbing for the gun.

Then the safety slipped free, and the Glock went off.

Junior felt the most incredible pain in his chest. He stumbled back into the soft drinks' machine as the blood spilled out of his chest and spread across his shirt. Then he slid to the floor.

The last thing Junior heard was the cheese dip by the door, shouting, 'Dennis! Hurry up! Somebody's outside!'

Outside at the second pump island, Margaret Hammond heard a car backfire as she climbed from her Lexus.

Margaret saw three young white males run out of the minimart and get into a red Nissan pick-up truck, which lurched away with the jumpy acceleration that tells you the clutch is shot.

Margaret locked the pump nozzle to fill her tank, then went into the minimart to buy a Nestlé's Crunch chocolate bar.

Less than ten seconds later, by her own estimation, Margaret Hammond ran back into the parking lot. The red Nissan had disappeared. Margaret used her cellphone to call 911, who patched her through to the Bristo Camino Police Department.

THEIR VOICES OVERLAPPED, Kevin grabbing Dennis's arm, making the truck swerve. 'You killed that guy! You *shot* him!'

Dennis punched him away. 'I don't know if he's dead or what! He had a gun! I didn't know he would have a gun! It just went off!'

Mars sat quietly in the shotgun seat, as calm as if he had just woken from a trance. He was holding the Chinaman's gun.

'Shit! Throw it out, dude! We might get stopped.'

Mars pushed the gun into his waistband. 'We might need it.'

Dennis upshifted hard, ignoring the clash of gears as he threw the Nissan towards the freeway. At least four people had seen the truck. Even these dumb Bristo cops would be able to put two and two together if they had witnesses who could tie them to the truck.

Kevin's eyes were like dinner plates. 'We gotta turn ourselves in.'

'No one's turning themselves in! We can get outta this! We just gotta figure out what to do!' Dennis pushed harder on the accelerator, felt the transmission lag, and then a loud BANG came from under the truck. The transmission let go and the truck lost power, bucking as Dennis guided it off the road. Even before it lurched to a stop, Dennis shoved open the door, desperate to run. Kevin caught his arm, holding him back.

'There's nothing we can do, Dennis. We're only making it worse.'

Dennis shook off his brother's hand and slid out of the truck. He searched up and down the road. Flanders Road cut through an area of affluent housing developments. Most of the communities were hidden from the road by hedges that masked heavy stone walls. Dennis wondered if escape lay beyond them.

It was like Mars read his mind. 'Let's steal a car.'

OFFICER MIKE WELCH was rolling code seven to the doughnut shop on the west side of Bristo Camino when he got the call.

'Unit four, base.'

'Four.'

'Armed robbery, Kim's Minimart on Flanders Road, shots fired. Three white males driving a red Nissan pick-up last seen on Flanders Road. Get over there and see about Junior.'

Welch went code three, hitting the lights and siren.

'I'm on Flanders now. Is Junior shot?'

'That's affirm. Ambulance is inbound.'

Welch floored it. He was past the red truck parked on the opposite side of the road before he realised that it matched the description of the getaway vehicle.

Welch shut his siren and pulled off onto the shoulder. He stared back up the street. He couldn't see anyone in or around the truck, but there it was, a red Nissan pick-up. Welch swung round and drove back, pulling off behind the Nissan. He keyed his shoulder mike.

'Base, four. I'm a mile and a half east of Kim's on Flanders. Got a red Nissan pick-up, licence Three-Kilo-Lima-Mike-Four-Two-Nine. It appears abandoned. Can you send someone else to Kim's?'

'Ah, we can.'

'I'm gonna check it out.'

Welch climbed out of his car and rested his right hand on the butt of his Browning Hi-Power. He walked up along the passenger side of the truck, glanced underneath, then walked round the front. The engine was still ticking and the hood was warm.

'Base, four. Area's clear. Vehicle is abandoned.'

'Rog.'

Welch couldn't be sure this was the getaway vehicle, but his heart was hammering with excitement. He looked up and down the road, wondering why they had abandoned the truck and where they had gone. He stared at the hedges. He squatted, trying to see under the low branches, but saw nothing except a wall. Welch drew his gun, then approached the hedges, looking more closely. Several branches were broken. He glanced back at the truck, thinking it through, imagining three suspects pushing through the hedges, going over the wall. On the other side was a development called York Estates. Welch knew from his patrol route that there were only two streets out unless they went over the wall again. They would be running like hell out the back side of the development, trying to get away.

Welch listened to the Nissan's ticking engine, and decided that he was no more than a few minutes behind them. He made his decision.

Welch burned rubber as he swung out onto the road, intent on cutting them off before they escaped the development.

DENNIS DROPPED from the wall into a different world, hidden behind lush ferns and orange trees. His impulse was to keep running. The siren was right on top of them. And then the siren stopped.

They were in a dense garden surrounding a tennis court. A swimming pool was directly in front of them with the main house beyond the pool, a big two-storey house with lots of windows and doors, and one of the doors was open. If people were home, there would be a car. A Sony boom box beside the pool was playing music. There wouldn't be music if no one was home.

SIXTY FEET AWAY through the open door, Jennifer Smith was thoroughly pissed off about the state of her life. Her father was behind closed doors at the front of the house, working. He was an accountant, and often worked at home. Her mother was in Florida visiting their Aunt Kate. With her mom in Florida and her dad working, Jen was forced to ride herd all the time on her ten-year-old brother, Thomas. Jennifer Smith was sixteen years old. Having Thomas grafted to her like this was wrecking her summer.

Jen had been out by the pool, but she had come in to make tuna fish sandwiches. Thomas was playing Nintendo in the family room.

When the three young men stepped inside, Jen's first thought was that they were gardeners. Her second thought was that maybe they were older kids from school, but that didn't feel right either.

Jennifer said, 'May I help you?'

The first one pointed at Thomas. 'Mars, get the troll.'

The biggest one ran at Thomas, as the first one charged into the kitchen. Jennifer screamed just as the first boy covered her mouth so tightly that she thought her face would break. Thomas tried to shout, but the bigger boy mashed his face into the carpet.

The third one was younger. He hung back near the door, crying, talking in a loud stage whisper. 'Dennis, let's go! This is crazy!'

'Shut up, Kevin! We're here. Deal with it.'

Jennifer fought hard until she saw the gun. The bigger boy was holding a black pistol to Thomas's head. Jennifer stopped fighting.

The one holding her, the one she now knew as Dennis, said, 'I'm going to take my hand away, but you better not yell. Understand?' Dennis took away his hand, but kept it close, ready to clamp her mouth again. His voice was a whisper. 'Who else is here?'

'My father.'

'Is there anyone else?'

'No.'

'Where is he?'

'In his office.'

'Is there a car?'

Her voice failed. All she could do was nod.

'Where's his office?'

She pointed towards the entry. Dennis laced his fingers through her hair and pushed her towards the hall. He followed so closely that his body brushed hers, reminding her that she was wearing only shorts and a bikini top.

Her father's office was off the entry hall. Dennis pulled open the door, and the big one, Mars, carried in Thomas, the gun still at his head. Dennis pushed her onto the floor, then ran across the room, pointing his gun at her father, a slender man with a receding hairline and glasses. Her father was working at his computer.

Dennis aimed his gun with both hands, shouting, 'Don't move!'

What her father said made no sense to her. 'Who sent you?'

Dennis shoved Kevin with his free hand. 'Kevin, close the windows!' Kevin went to the windows and closed the shutters.

Dennis waved his gun at Mars. 'Keep him covered, dude.'

Mars pushed Thomas onto the floor with Jennifer, then aimed at her father. Dennis put his own gun in the waistband of his jeans, then snatched a lamp from the corner of her father's desk. He jerked the plug from the wall, then the electrical cord from the lamp.

'Don't go psycho and everything will be fine. I'm gonna tie you up so you can't call the cops, and I'm gonna take your car. I don't want to hurt you.'

Her father looked confused. 'That's what you want, the car?'

'Am I talking Russian here or what? *Do you have a car?*'

Her father raised his hands, placating.

'In the garage. The keys are on the wall by the garage door.'

'Kevin, go get the keys, then come help tie these bastards up so we can get outta here.'

Kevin, still by the windows, said, 'There's a cop coming.'

Jennifer saw the police car through the gaps in the shutters. A policeman got out. He looked around, then came towards their house.

Dennis grabbed her hair again. 'Don't say a word.'

'Please don't hurt my children.'

'*Shut up.* Mars, you be ready! Mars!'

Jennifer watched the policeman come up the walk. He disappeared past the edge of the window, then their doorbell rang.

Jennifer wanted to scream. Her father stared at her, his eyes locked onto hers, slowly shaking his head. She didn't know if he was telling her not to scream, or even if he realised that he was doing it.

The cop walked past the windows towards the side of the house.

Dennis went to the window. He peered through the shutters, then rushed back to Jennifer and grabbed her by the hair again. 'Get up.'

As near as Officer Mike Welch could figure, the people from the red Nissan had jumped the wall into these people's back yard. He suspected that they were blocks away by now, but he hoped that someone had seen them and could provide a direction of flight.

When no one answered the door, Welch went to the side gate and called out. He was turning away to try the neighbour when the heavy front door opened and a pretty teenage girl looked out. She was pale. Her eyes were rimmed red.

Welch gave his best professional smile. 'Miss, I'm Officer Mike Welch. Did you happen to see three men running through the area?'

'No.' Her voice was so soft he could barely hear her.

'It would've been five or ten minutes ago. I have reason to believe that they jumped the wall into your back yard.'

'No.' The red-rimmed eyes filled.

Welch watched her eyes blur, watched twin tears roll in slow motion down her cheeks, and knew that they were in the house with her. They were probably right on the other side of the door.

'OK, miss, like I said, I was just checking. You have a good day.'

He quietly unsnapped the release on his holster and rested his hand on his gun. He shifted his eyes pointedly to the door, then mouthed a silent question, asking if anyone was there.

Inside, someone that Mike Welch could not see shouted, 'He's going for his gun!'

Loud explosions blew through the door and window. Something hit Mike Welch in the chest, knocking him backwards. His Kevlar vest stopped the first bullet, but another punched into his belly below the vest, and a third slipped over the top of his vest to lodge high in his chest. He tried to keep his feet under him, but they fell away.

Mike Welch found himself flat on his back. He could no longer hold his gun. It was all he could do to key his shoulder mike.

'Officer down. Officer down. Jesus, I've been shot.'

Friday, 3:24pm. Two miles from York Estates, Jeff Talley was parked in an avocado orchard, talking to his daughter on his cellphone. He often left his office in the afternoon and came to this orchard, which he had discovered not long after he had taken the job as chief of Bristo Camino's fourteen-member police department. Rows of trees, standing in the clean desert air like a chorus of silent witnesses. He found peace in the sameness of it.

His daughter, Amanda, now fourteen, broke that peace. 'Why can't I bring Derek? At least I would have someone to hang with.'

Her voice reeked of coldness. He had called Amanda because today was Friday; she would be coming up for the weekend.

'I thought we would go to a movie together.'

'We can still go to the movies. We'll just bring Derek.'

'Maybe another time.'

She made an exaggerated sigh that left him feeling defensive.

'Mandy? It's OK if you bring friends. But I enjoy our alone time, too. I want us to talk about things.'

She didn't answer.

'I love you, Amanda.'

'You always say you want to talk, but then we go sit in a movie so we can't talk. Here's Mom.'

Jane Talley came on the line. They had separated five months after he resigned from the Los Angeles Police Department, took up residence on their couch, and stared at the television for twenty hours a day until neither of them could take it any more and he had moved out. That was two years ago.

'Hey, Chief. She's not in the greatest mood. How you doing?'

Talley thought about it. 'She's not liking me very much.'

'She's still trying to understand.'

'I try to talk to her.' He could hear the frustration in his own voice.

'Jeffrey, you've been trying to talk for two years, but nothing comes out. You have this new life up there and she's making a new life down here. You understand that, don't you?'

Talley didn't say anything, because he didn't know what to say. Every day since he moved to Bristo Camino he told himself that he would ask them to join him, but he hadn't been able to do it. He knew that Jane had spent the past two years waiting for him.

Jane finally broke the silence. 'Do you want me to drop her at your house or at the office?'

'The house would be fine.'

'Six o'clock?'

'Six. We can have dinner, maybe.'

'I won't be staying.'

IN THOSE FIRST WEEKS, Brendan Malik's eyes watched him from every shadow. He saw the light in them die over and over.

Talley resigned from the LAPD, then sat on his couch for almost a year, first in his home and later in the cheap apartment he rented after Jane threw him out. The incorporated township of Bristo Camino was looking for a chief of police and they were glad to have him. They liked it that he was SWAT, even though the job was no more demanding than writing traffic citations and speaking at local schools. He told himself that it was a good place to heal. Jane had been willing to wait for the healing, but the healing never quite seemed to happen. Talley believed that it never would.

Talley started the car and eased out of the orchard onto a gravel road, following it down to the state highway. When he reached the highway, he turned up his radio and heard Sarah Weinman, the BCPD dispatch officer, shouting frantically over the link.

'... *Welch is down. We have a man down in York Estates* ...'

Other voices were crackling back at her, Officers Larry Anders and Kenn Jorgenson talking over each other in a mad rush.

Talley punched the command freq button that linked him to dispatch on a dedicated frequency.

'Sarah, one. What do you mean, Mike's down?'

'Chief? He's been shot. The paramedics from Sierra Rock Fire are on the way. Jorgy and Larry are rolling from the east.'

In the nine months that Talley had been in Bristo, there had been only three felonies, two for nonviolent burglaries and once when a woman had tried to run down her husband with the family car.

'Are you saying that he was *intentionally* shot?'

'Junior Kim's been shot, too! Three white males driving a red Nissan pick-up. Mike called in the truck, then called a forty-one fourteen at one-eight Castle Way in York Estates, and the next thing I know he said he'd been shot. I haven't been able to raise him since.'

Forty-one fourteen. Welch had intended to approach the residence.

Talley turned on his lights and siren. York Estates was six minutes away. 'I'm six out and rolling. Fill me in on the way.'

WHEN MARS AND DENNIS started shooting, Jennifer screamed. Dennis slammed the front door, pulled her backwards to the office, then pushed her down. She grabbed Thomas and held tight. Her father wrapped them in his arms.

When the shooting was done, Dennis sucked air like a bellows, his face white. 'We're screwed! That cop is *down!*'

Mars went to the entry. He didn't hurry or seem scared; he *strolled*.

'Let's get the car before more of them get here.'

Kevin was on the floor beside her father's desk, shaking. His face was milky. 'You shot a cop. You shot a cop, Dennis!'

'Didn't you hear Mars? He was going for his gun!'

Jennifer heard a siren approaching behind the shouting.

Mars spoke from the entry, his voice as calm as still water.

'Let's take the man's car, Dennis. We have to go.'

Then the siren suddenly seemed to be in the house, and it was too late. Tyres screeched outside. The shooting started again.

YORK ESTATES WAS a development of twenty-eight homes on one-to three-acre sites in a pattern of winding streets and cul-de-sacs surrounded by a stone wall. Talley cut his siren as he entered, but kept the lights flashing. Jorgenson and Anders were shouting that they were under fire.

When he turned into Castle Way, Talley saw Jorgenson and Anders crouched behind their car with their weapons out. Two women were in the open door of the house behind them and a teenaged boy was standing near the cul-de-sac's mouth. Talley hit the public-address key on his mike as he sped up the street.

'You people take cover. Get inside your homes *now!*'

Talley hit the brakes hard, stopping behind Jorgenson's unit. Two shots pinged from the house, one snapping past overhead, the other thumping dully into Talley's windshield. He rolled out of the door and pulled himself into a tight ball behind the front wheel, using the hub as cover. Mike Welch lay crumpled on the front lawn of a large Tudor home less than forty feet away.

Anders shouted, 'Welch is down! They shot him!'

'Are all three subjects inside?'

'I don't know! We haven't seen anyone!'

'Are civilians in the house?'

'I don't know!'

More sirens were coming from the east. Talley knew that would be Dreyer and Mikkelson in unit six with the ambulance. He called to Welch from behind the car. 'Mike! Can you hear me?'

Welch didn't respond.

Talley keyed his transceiver mike. 'Six, one. Who's on?'

Dreyer's voice came back. 'We're one minute out, Chief.'

'Where's the ambulance?'

'Right behind us.'

'OK. You guys set up on Flanders by the truck in case these guys go back over the wall. Send the ambulance in, but tell them to wait at Castle and Tower. I'll bring Welch to them.'

Talley broke the connection. 'Larry, did you guys fire on the house?'

'No, sir.'

'Stay down. Don't fire at the house.'

Talley climbed back into his car, keeping his head low and the driver's door open. He backed up, then powered into the yard, manoeuvring to a stop between Welch and the house. Another shot popped the passenger-side window. He rolled out of the car, opened the rear door, then dragged Welch to the car. Welch moaned. He was alive. Talley propped him upright in the open door, then lifted for all he was worth to fold Welch onto the back seat. He slammed the door, then saw Welch's gun on the grass. He went back for it. He returned to the car and floored the accelerator, fishtailing across the slick grass as he cut across the yard and into the street. He sped back along the cul-de-sac to the corner where the ambulance was waiting. Two paramedics pulled Welch from the rear and pushed a compress to his chest.

Talley keyed the mike again to call his dispatcher. He had four units on duty and another five officers off. He would need them all.

'Chief, I pulled Dreyer and Mikkelson off the minimart. We've got no one on the scene now. It's totally unsecured.'

'Call the California Highway Patrol and the Sheriffs. Tell them what's going on and request a full crisis team. Tell them we've got two men down and we have a possible hostage situation.'

Talley remembered Welch's gun. He sniffed the muzzle, then checked the magazine. Welch had returned fire, which meant that he might have wounded someone in the house. Maybe even an innocent.

JENNIFER FELT her father sigh before he spoke. He slowly pushed to his knees. 'None of you are going to get out of this.'

Dennis said, 'Shut up! Kevin, go through the house and lock all the windows. Lock the doors, then watch the back yard.'

Kevin disappeared towards the rear through the entry.

Her father stood up. Dennis and Mars aimed their guns at him.

Her father raised his hands. 'I just want to go to my desk.'

Dennis extended his gun. 'You're not going anywhere!'

'Just take it easy, son.' Her father went behind his desk, carefully placing two computer disks in a black leather disk case as he spoke.

Dennis followed along beside him, shouting for him to stop, shouting that he shouldn't take another step, and pointing the gun at his head. 'I'm warning you, goddammit!'

'I'm going to open my desk.'

'*I'll kill you!*'

Jennifer's father held up a single finger as if to show them that one tiny finger could do them no harm, then used it to slide open the drawer. He took out a thick booklet.

'This is a list of every criminal lawyer in California. If you give up right now, I'll help you get the best lawyer in the state.'

Dennis slapped the book aside. 'Screw you! We just killed a cop! We killed that Chinaman! We'll get the death penalty!'

'I'm telling you that you won't, not if you let me help you. But if you stay in this house, I can promise you this: You'll die.'

'*Shut up!*' Dennis swung his gun hard and hit her father in the temple with a wet thud. He fell sideways like a sack that had been dropped to the floor.

'*No!*' Jennifer lunged forward, then dropped to her knees beside her father. The gun had cut an ugly gouge behind his right eye at the hairline. The gouge pulsed blood and was already swelling.

'Daddy? Daddy, wake up!'

He didn't respond.

Friday, 3:51pm. Talley requested a second ambulance to stand by, then once more drove into the cul-de-sac. He slipped out of his car and hunkered behind the front wheel again, calling over to Anders and Jorgenson.

'Larry, Jorgy, listen up.'

They were young guys. Men who had never seen anything like what was now developing on Castle Way.

'We've got to evacuate these houses and seal the neighbourhood. I want all the streets coming in here blocked.'

Anders nodded vigorously. 'Just the cul-de-sac?'

'All the streets. Use Welch's unit to get back to the corner, then go from house to house here on the cul-de-sac through the back yards. Climb the walls if you have to, and move everyone out the same way. Don't expose yourself or anyone else to this house.'

'Right, Chief.'

'Find out who lives here. We need to know.'

'OK.'

'One more thing. We might have one or more perps still on the loose. Have the other guys start a house-to-house.'

Crouching, Anders moved to the first car in the line, then swung it round in a tight turn and accelerated out of the cul-de-sac.

Talley keyed his mike to talk to his other cars.

'This is Talley. Clear the freq and listen. Jorgenson and I are currently in front of the house at one-eight Castle Way in York Estates. Anders is evacuating the residents of the surrounding houses. Dreyer and Mikkelson are at the rear of the property on Flanders Road near a red Nissan pick-up. We believe that one or more of the people who shot Junior Kim and Mike Welch are in the house. They are armed. We need an ID. Did Welch run the plates on that truck?'

Mikkelson came back. 'Chief, two. The truck is registered to Dennis James Rooney, white male, age twenty-two.'

Talley pulled out his pad and scratched down Rooney's name.

His radio popped again. 'Chief, Anders. I'm with one of the neighbours. She says the people in the house are named Smith, Walter and Pamela Smith. They've got two kids. Jennifer and Thomas. The girl is about fifteen and the boy is younger.'

'Does she know if they're in the house?'

Talley could hear Anders talking with the neighbour.

'She says the wife is in Florida visiting a sister, but she believes that the rest of the family is at home. She says the husband works there.'

Talley took a deep breath to gather himself, then keyed his public-address system so that he could speak to the house. Three killers, three possible hostages. In the next moment the negotiation would begin. Talley had sworn that he would never again be in this place. He had turned his life inside out to avoid it, yet here he was.

'My name is Jeff Talley. Is anyone in the house hurt?'

His voice echoed through the neighbourhood.

'Everyone in the house relax. We're not in a hurry here. If you've got wounded, let's get them tended to. We can work this out.'

No one answered. Talley knew that if you gave the subjects time to calm down and think about their situation, sometimes they realised their only way out was to surrender. Then all you had to do was give them an excuse to give up. Talley had been taught these things at the FBI's Crisis Management School, and it had worked that way every time until George Malik had shot his own son in the neck.

JENNIFER'S FATHER'S EYES flickered as if he were dreaming. He made a soft whimpering sound, but his eyes didn't open. His wound pulsed steadily, but the bleeding had almost stopped, the clotted blood and injured flesh swelling into an ugly purple volcano.

Jennifer stood, and faced Dennis. 'I'm getting some ice. He's hurt.'

Dennis glanced at Mars, then at her father. Finally, he turned back to the shutters. 'Mars, take her into the kitchen.'

Jennifer left without waiting for Mars, and went to the kitchen. She saw Kevin hiding behind the couch in the family room so that he could see the French doors that opened onto the back yard. She found a cloth, then went to the freezer. She pulled it open, then scooped ice into the cloth. Most of it spilled onto the floor.

'I need a bowl.'

'So get one.' Mars walked away as she got the bowl. He went into the family room.

Jennifer chose a green Tupperware bowl, then saw the paring knife on the counter, left from when she diced a slice of onion for the tuna. Mars came back to the kitchen. Without thinking about it, she pushed the knife behind the food processor on the counter.

Mars went to the refrigerator and pulled it open. He took out a beer, twisted off the cap, and drank. He took a second bottle.

She followed him back to the office, where Mars gave the second beer to Dennis at the shutters. Jennifer joined Thomas beside their father. She scooped ice from the bowl into the cloth, then made an ice pack and pressed it to her father's wound. He moaned.

The phone rang.

Dennis stalked to the desk, scooped up the phone, then slammed it down. The ringing stopped. Dennis went back to the shutters.

The phone rang again.

The public-address voice from the street echoed through the house.

'Answer the phone, Dennis Rooney. It's the police.'

HUNKERED BEHIND the front wheel of his radio car, Talley listened to the ringing in his ear as a helicopter appeared. It spiralled down for a closer look until Talley could see that it was from one of the Los Angeles television stations. If the helicopters were here, the vans and reporters would be close behind. Talley covered the phone and twisted round to see Jorgenson.

'Tell Sarah to call the phone company. Get a list of all the lines to the house and have them blocked except through my cell number. I don't want these guys talking with anyone on the outside except us.'

Tally was still giving orders when the phone stopped ringing and a male voice answered.

'Hello?'

Talley took a breath to centre himself. He did not want his voice to reveal his fear. 'Is this Dennis Rooney?'

'Who are *you*?'

'My name is Jeff Talley. I'm with the Bristo Police Department, out here behind the car in front of you. Is this Dennis Rooney?'

Talley specifically did not identify himself as the chief of police. He wanted to appear to have a certain degree of power, but he also did not want to be seen as the final authority. The negotiator was always the man in the middle. If Rooney made demands, Talley wanted to be able to stall by telling him that he had to check with his boss. That way Talley remained the good guy. He could build a bond with Rooney through their mutual adversity.

'That cop was going for his gun. That Chinaman pulled a gun, too. No one wanted to shoot him. It was an accident.'

'Is this Dennis Rooney? I want to know with whom I'm speaking.'

'Yeah. I'm Rooney.'

Talley felt himself relax. Rooney wasn't a lunatic; he didn't start off by screaming that he was going to murder everyone in the house.

Talley made his voice firm, but relaxed.

'Well, Dennis, I need to know whether or not anyone in there needs a doctor. There was an awful lot of shooting.'

'We're cool.'

'Everyone out here is concerned about who's in there with you, Dennis. Do you have some people in there with you?'

Talley could hear breathing, then a muffled sound as if Rooney had covered the phone. Talley knew that thinking things through logically would be hard for Rooney during these next few minutes. Rooney would be pumping on adrenaline, frantic and scared. Finally, he came back on the line.

'I got this family. That isn't kidnapping, is it? I mean, they were already here. We didn't grab 'em and take 'em someplace.'

Rooney's answer was a good sign; by showing concern for the future, he revealed that he did not want to die and feared the consequences of his actions.

'Can you identify them for me, Dennis?'

'You don't need to know that. I've told you enough.'

Talley let that slide. 'OK, you're not going to tell me their names right now. I hear that. Will you at least tell me how they're doing?'

'They're fine.'

'How about your two friends? You don't have a man dying on you, do you?'

'They're fine.'

Talley had got Rooney to admit that all three gunmen were in the house. He muted the phone and turned to Jorgenson.

'All three subjects are in the house. Tell Larry to call off the house-to-house.'

Jorgenson radioed his call as Talley returned to Rooney.

Talley said, 'OK, Dennis, I want to explain your situation.'

'I didn't shoot that Chinaman. He pulled a gun and we were wrestling and his own gun went off. That Chinaman shot himself.'

'I understand, Dennis. There'll probably be a security camera. We'll be able to see what happened.'

'What I want to know is, that Chinaman, is he OK?'

'Mr Kim didn't make it, Dennis. He died.'

Rooney didn't respond, but Talley knew that images of shooting his way out and possibly even of suicide would be kaleidoscoping through his head. Talley had to give him a vent for the pressure.

'I won't lie to you, Dennis; you guys are in trouble. But if what you said about the struggle is true, that could be a mitigating circumstance. Don't make things worse than they already are.'

Kim having pulled a gun would mitigate nothing. Under California law, any death occurring during the commission of a felony was murder, but Talley needed to give Rooney some measure of hope.

Rooney said, 'What about the cop? He went for his gun, too.'

'He's still alive. You caught a break there, Dennis.'

'Don't you forget I've got these people in here. Don't you guys try to rush the house.'

'Dennis, I'm going to ask you right now to let those people go.'

'No way. They're the only thing keeping you from blowing us away. You'll kill us for shooting that cop.'

'I know you're feeling that way right now, Dennis, but I'm going to give you my word about something. We're not going to storm the house. But I want you to know what you're facing out here. We have officers surrounding the house, and this neighbourhood is locked down. You can't escape, Dennis; that just isn't going to happen. The reason I'm out here talking to you is that I want to get out of this thing without you or the people in that house getting hurt. That's my goal here. Do you understand that?'

'I understand.'

'The best thing you can do to help yourself is to let those people go, Dennis. Let them go, then surrender. If you're cooperative now, it will look better for the judge later. Do you see that?'

Rooney didn't respond, which Talley took as a positive sign. Rooney wasn't arguing. He was thinking. Talley decided to terminate the contact and let Rooney consider his options.

'I don't know about you, Dennis, but I could use a break. You think about what I said. I'll call back in twenty minutes. If you want to talk before that, just shout, and I'll phone you again.'

Talley closed the phone. His hands were shaking so badly that he dropped it. He took another deep breath and then another.

Jorgenson said, 'Chief? You OK?'

Talley waved that he was fine. He put the phone in his pocket, told Jorgenson to call if anything changed, then backed his car out of the cul-de-sac. One conversation with a scared twenty-two-year-old kid, and Talley wanted to vomit. Larry Anders was waiting at the intersection along with two more of his officers: Scott Campbell and Leigh Metzger. Campbell was a retired Bakersfield security officer who signed on with Bristo to supplement his pension. Metzger was a single mother who had spent eight years on the San Bernardino Police Department as an instructional officer. She had almost no street time. Seeing them gave Talley no confidence.

'Jesus, Larry, are the goddamned Sheriffs coming here on foot? Where are they?'

'Sarah's been on the phone with them, Chief. She says you should call.'

Talley felt his stomach clench. 'What's wrong?'

'I don't know. She also says that the newspeople want to know what's happening. They're on their way here.'

'When the newspeople get here, let them into the development, but don't let them come here to the cul-de-sac.'

'There's an empty lot by King and Lady. Can I put them there?'

'Perfect. I'll get over there in a few minutes and make a statement.'

Talley went to his car, opened the door and radioed his office.

'Give me some good news, Sarah. I need it.'

'The Highway Patrol is sending six patrol units. They should be about ten minutes out, and inbound now.'

Patrol units. 'What about a tactical squad and the negotiation team? We need to get those people deployed.'

'I'm sorry, Chief. Their response team is hung up in Pico Rivera. They said they'll get here as soon as possible.'

'That's just great! What are we supposed to do until then?'

'They said you'll have to handle it yourself.'

Talley pulled the door shut, started the engine and turned on the air conditioner. He turned the vents so they blew the cold air into his face. Talley shook so badly that he pushed his hands under his legs, feeling frightened and ashamed. He told himself that he was no longer a negotiator, that the lives of the people in the house did not rest with him. He only had to hang on until the Sheriffs took over, and then he could go back to his orchard and the perfect peace of its stillness. He told himself that, but he didn't believe it.

Friday, 4:22pm. Dennis slapped down the phone, livid with anger.

Talley thought he was an idiot, all that shit about wanting a peaceful resolution and promising not to storm the house. Dennis knew the score when it came to cops: A cop was down, so somebody had to pay. The bastards would probably assassinate him the first chance they got without ever giving him a chance to stand trial.

Mars said, 'What did they want?'

'What do you think they want? They want us to give up.'

Mars shrugged, his expression simple. 'I'm not giving up.'

Dennis stalked out of the office. He crossed through the kitchen, found the keys on a peg-board just like the man had said, and shoved open the door to the garage. A gleaming Jaguar and Range Rover were waiting. Dennis checked the gas in the Jaguar, and found the tank full. If they had driven away only five minutes sooner . . .

Dennis smashed his fist into the steering wheel, shouting, '*Shit!*'

He closed his eyes.

'Dennis?'

Dennis opened his eyes and saw Kevin in the door.

'I need to talk to you. Where's Mars?'

'He's watching the front like you're supposed to be watching the back. Get out of here.'

Dennis shut his eyes tight. The cops were watching the front and back of the house, but it was a big house; there had to be a window or door that the cops couldn't see. The house was surrounded by trees and bushes and walls, all of which blended and merged with the heavy cover of the surrounding houses.

'Dennis? It's about Mars. We've got to talk about what happened.'

Kevin wore the don't-kick-me expression that made Dennis want to punch him. Dennis hated the suffocating weight of having to carry his younger brother through life. He didn't need the prison shrink to tell him why: Kevin was their past; he was their ineffectual mother who brought home a steady procession of strange men, who drank too much and abandoned them, their brutal, meth-head father who beat them, their pathetic and embarrassing place in life. Kevin was the shadow of their future failure, and Dennis hated him for it.

'What we've got to do, Kevin, is find a way out of here.'

Dennis pushed past his brother, unable even to look at him. Kevin followed along behind. They went through the kitchen, then along a wide hall to a den with leather couches and a copper bar.

They reached the master bedroom at the rear of the house. It was a huge room with sliding glass doors that looked out on the pool.

Kevin plucked at Dennis's arm. 'Dennis, *listen*. Mars lied about that cop who came to the door. He put his hand on his gun, but he didn't pull it. I'm telling you that cop never drew.'

Dennis didn't know what to say. 'You just didn't see, is all.'

'I was *there*. Mars lied.'

'Why would he do that?'

'Something's wrong with him. He *wanted* to shoot that cop.'

'You don't know what you're talking about. We're surrounded by

315

cops and we're looking at a homicide charge. We've got to find a way out of this, so just *stop*.'

Three doors opened off the bedroom. Dennis thought they might lead to closets or bathrooms with maybe a window on the side of the house, but that isn't what he found.

Clothes hung on racks like any other large closet, but this room had something more: a bank of small black and white televisions filled the near wall; Mars and the two kids could be seen on one of the screens; another showed the cop car sitting out front; every room, bathroom and hall inside the house was visible, as well as views of the outside, the garage, the pool and even the area behind the poolhouse. Every inch of the property seemed to be watched.

'Kevin?'

Kevin came up behind him, and made a hissing sound.

'What is this?'

'It's a security system. Jesus, look at this stuff.'

Dennis studied the view of the master bedroom. The camera appeared to be looking from the upper left ceiling corner above the door through which he had just entered. Dennis went out and looked up into the corner. He saw nothing.

Still inside the room, Kevin said, 'Hey, I can see you.'

Dennis rejoined his brother. The monitors were above a long keyboard set with button pads, and red and green lights. Right now, all of the lights glowed green. Rows of buttons were lined along the right side of the keyboard, the buttons labelled MOTION SENSORS, INFRARED, UPSTAIRS LOCKS, DOWNSTAIRS LOCKS and ALARMS. Dennis turned back to the door and slowly pushed it. The door swung easily, but with a feeling of weight and density. Dennis rapped on the door with his knuckles. Steel. He turned back to his brother. 'What the hell is going on here? They've got this place stitched up like a bank.'

Kevin was on his knees at the back of the closet, partially buried by a wall of hanging clothes. He slowly rocked back on his heels, then turned round holding a white cardboard box about the size of a shoe box. Dennis saw that the wall behind the clothes was like a small metal garage door that could be raised or lowered. It was raised, and more white boxes were stacked behind it.

Kevin held out the box. 'Look.'

The box was filled with $100 bills. Kevin pulled out a second box, then a third. They bulged with money.

JENNIFER WAS WORRIED. Her father's breathing was raspy. His eyes jerked spastically beneath their lids like eyes do when someone is having bad dreams. She placed a cushion from his couch beneath his head, and sat beside him, holding the ice to his head. The bleeding had stopped, but the wound was red and inflamed, and an ugly bruise was spreading across his face. She was scared that her father needed a doctor, and might get worse without medical attention.

The phone on her father's desk rang. Mars glanced over, but made no move to answer it. The phone stopped ringing just as Dennis and Kevin reappeared from the rear of the house. Dennis walked over and stared down at her father, then her. He squatted beside her.

'Your old man, what's he do for a living?'

'He's an accountant.'

'He does taxes for other rich people, handles their money, what?'

'Duh. That's what accountants do.' Jennifer knew she was taunting him, and she was ready for his anger.

Dennis seemed to consider her. 'What's your name?'

'Jennifer.'

'What's your last name?'

'Smith.'

'OK, Jennifer Smith. And your old man?'

'Walter Smith.'

Dennis looked at Thomas. 'How about you, fat boy?'

Thomas blurted out his name. 'Thomas!'

Dennis smiled at Jennifer and lowered his voice.

'We're going to be here a while, Jennifer. Where's your bedroom?'

Jennifer blushed furiously, and Dennis smiled wider.

'Now don't think nasty thoughts on me, Jennifer. I didn't mean it like that. You look cold, wearing just the bikini top. I'll bring you a shirt. Cover up that fine body.'

She averted her eyes and blushed harder. 'It's upstairs.'

'OK. I'll bring you something.'

Dennis told Mars to come with him, and then the two of them left.

Kevin went to the window. The phone rang again, but Kevin ignored it. The ringing went on for ever.

Thomas nudged Jennifer's knee, wanting to say something.

Jennifer made sure that Kevin wasn't watching them, then mouthed the word more than spoke it. 'What?'

Thomas leaned close and lowered his voice even more. 'I know where Daddy has a gun.'

Friday, 5:10pm. Glen Howell closed his cellphone after fifteen rings. He didn't like that. He was expected, and he knew that this person always answered his phone, and was irritated that now, him running late like this, the sonofabitch would pick *now* not to answer.

Howell didn't know why the streets leading into York Estates were blocked, but the traffic was at a standstill. He figured it had to be a broken gas line or something like that.

The window on his big S-class Mercedes slid down without a sound. Glen craned out his head, trying to see the reason for the delay. A lone cop was working the intersection, waving some cars away. He let a television news van through. Glen raised the window again, the heavy tint cutting the glare. He took the .40-calibre Smith & Wesson from his pocket and put it in the glove box. He had a valid California Concealed Weapon Permit, but thought it best not to draw attention to himself if he had to get out of the car.

Three of the cars ahead of him turned away, one car was let through, and then it was his turn. The cop was a young guy, with a protruding Adam's apple.

Glen lowered the window. The heat ballooned in, making him wish he was back in Palm Springs, instead of being an errand boy. He tried to look professional and superior.

'What's going on, Officer? Why the roadblock?'

The cop looked uncertain. 'Do you live here in the neighbourhood, sir?'

'I have a business appointment. My associate is expecting me.'

'We've got a problem in the neighbourhood, so we've had to close the area. We're only admitting residents.'

'What kind of problem?'

'Do you have family in the development, sir?'

'Just my friends. You're making me worried about them, Officer.'

The cop frowned, and glanced back along the row of cars behind Glen. 'Well, what it is, we've got robbery suspects in one of the houses. We've had to evacuate several of the homes, and close off the development until we can secure the area. It could take a while.'

Glen nodded, trying to look reasonable. 'Listen, my client is expecting me, Officer. I just need a few minutes, then I'm gone.'

'Can't let you in, sir, I'm sorry. Maybe you could phone your party and have them come and meet you, if they're still inside.'

Glen worked on staying calm. He smiled, and stared past the patrol car like he was thinking. 'OK. Can I park over here to call?'

'Sure.'

Glen pulled his car to the side, then called the number again. He let it ring fifteen times, but still didn't get an answer. Glen figured the guy must've been evacuated, in which case he would probably call Palm Springs to arrange another meet location, and Palm Springs would phone Glen.

He wheeled round in a slow U and headed back up the street. He saw that another television news van had joined the line. Glen lowered his window when he reached the van. The driver was a balding guy. A trim Asian woman with pouty lips perched in the passenger seat. Glen guessed her for the on-air talent.

Glen said, 'Excuse me. They wouldn't tell me what's going on. Do you guys know anything about this?'

The woman twisted in her seat and leaned forward to see past the driver. 'We don't have anything confirmed, but it looks like three men were fleeing the scene of a robbery and took a family hostage.'

'No shit. That's terrible.'

'Do you live in the neighbourhood?'

Glen knew that she was angling for something and began to relax. If she thought he had something that she wanted, she might be willing to get him inside.

'I don't live here, but I have friends in there. Why?'

The reporter flipped through a yellow pad. 'We've got reports that there are children involved, but we can't get anyone to tell us anything about the family. It's a family named Smith.'

The big Mercedes sensed the heat. The air conditioner blew harder. Glen didn't feel it. 'What was the name again?'

'Mr and Mrs Walter Smith. We've heard they have two children.'

'They're being held hostage? These three guys have the Smiths?'

'That's right. Do you know them?'

'I don't know them. Sorry.' Glen rolled up the window and pulled away. He had the strange sensation of being removed from his body, as if the world had receded and he was no longer a part of it. Walter Smith. Three assholes had crashed into Walter Smith's home, and now the place was surrounded by cops and cameras.

Three blocks later, Glen pulled into a parking lot. He took his gun from the glove box and put it back in his pocket. He felt safer that way. He opened his phone again, and dialled another number. This time, his call was answered on the first ring.

Glen spoke four words. 'We have a problem.'

Palm Springs, California

Friday, 5:26pm. Sonny Benza stood in the games room of his mansion perched on a ridge above Palm Springs. Outside, his two kids, Chris and Gina, home from school, were splashing in the pool. Inside, Phil Tuzee and Charles 'Sally' Salvetti pulled an extra television, a 36-inch Sony, next to the big screen. They were anxious to get the set on. Between the big-screen projection TV with the picture-in-picture function and the Sony, they could watch all three major Los Angeles television stations. Two showed aerial views of Walter Smith's house, the third some talking head outside a gas station.

Sonny Benza still refused to believe it.

'What do we know for *sure*? Maybe it's a different Walter Smith.'

Salvetti wiped the sweat from his forehead. 'Glen Howell called it in. He's at the house, Sonny. It's *our* Walter Smith.'

Tuzee made a patting motion with his hands, trying to play the cooler. 'Let's everybody take it easy. Let's relax and walk through this a step at a time. The Feds aren't knocking on the door.'

Benza said, 'OK. What exactly are we dealing with here? What does Smith have in the house?'

'It's tax time, Sonny. He has our records.'

'You're sure? Glen hadn't made the pick-up?'

'He was on his way to do that.'

Sonny Benza's legitimate business holdings included sixteen bars, eight restaurants and 32,000 acres of vineyards in California. These businesses were profitable in their own right, but they were also used to launder the $90 million generated every year by drug trafficking, hijackings, and shipping stolen automobiles out of the country. Walter Smith's job was to create false but reasonable profit records for Sonny's legitimate holdings which Benza would present to his 'real' accountants. Those accountants would then file the appropriate tax returns, never knowing that the records had been falsified. Benza would pay the appropriate taxes, then be able to openly bank, spend, or invest the after-tax cash. To do this, Walter Smith held the income records of all Benza businesses, both legal and illegal. These records were in his computer. In his house. Surrounded by cops.

Sonny went over to the big glass wall that gave him a breathtaking view of Palm Springs on the desert floor below.

Phil Tuzee followed him, trying to be upbeat.

'Hey, look, it's just three kids, Sonny. They're gonna get tired and come out. Smith knows what to do. He'll hide the stuff. These kids will walk out and the cops will arrest them, and that's that. There won't be any reason for the cops to search the house.'

Sonny Benza looked over his shoulder at his friend. 'The records don't just show our business, Phil. They show our split with the families back east. If the cops get those records, we won't be the only ones who fall. The East Coast will take a hit, too.'

Sonny turned back to the others. 'OK. Three kids like this, they'll see that the only way out is to give up. Two hours tops, they'll walk out, hands up, then everybody goes to the station. But that's a best-case scenario. Worst case, it's a blood bath. When it's over, the detectives go in for forensic evidence and come out with Smith's computer. If that happens, we go to jail for the rest of our lives.' He looked at each man. 'If we live long enough to stand trial.'

Salvetti and Tuzee traded a look. They knew it was true. The East Coast families would kill them.

Tuzee said, 'Maybe we should warn them. Call old man Castellano to let 'em know. That might take off some of the edge.'

Salvetti raised his hands. 'No way! They'll be all over us out here.'

Sonny agreed. 'Sally's right. This problem with Smith, we've got to solve it before those bastards back in Manhattan find out.'

Sonny looked back at the televisions and thought it through. Control and containment. 'Who's the controlling authority? LAPD?'

Salvetti grunted. Salvetti, like Phil Tuzee, was a graduate of University of South Carolina Law School. He knew criminal law. 'Bristo is an incorporated township up by Canyon Country. They have their own police force, something like ten, fifteen guys. We're talking a pimple on LA's ass.'

Tuzee shook his head. 'If the locals can't handle this, they'll call in the Sheriffs or even the Feds. Either way, there'll be more than a few hick cops to deal with.'

'That's true, Phil, but it will all be processed back through the Bristo PD office because it's their jurisdiction. They've got a chief of police up there. It's his crime scene even if he turns over control.'

Sonny turned back to the televisions. 'This chief, what's his name?'

Salvetti glanced at his notes. 'Talley. I saw him being interviewed.'

'Put our people on the scene. When the Feds and Sheriffs come in, I want to know who's running their act, and whether they've ever worked OC.' If they had experience working Organised Crime, he would have to be careful who he deployed to the area.

'It's already happening, Sonny. I've got people on the way, clean guys, not anyone they would recognise.'

Benza nodded.

'Everything that comes out of that house, I want to know it, Phil.'

'I'm on it. We'll know.'

'I want to know about this guy Talley. Find out everything there is to know about him, and every way we can hurt him. By the end of the day, I want to own him.'

PART TWO

Friday, 6:17pm. Two of Talley's night-shift duty officers, Fred Cooper and Joycelyn Frost, rolled up in their personal cars. They joined Campbell and Anders in the street. Talley sat motionless in his car.

When Talley rolled to a hostage situation with SWAT, his crisis team had included a tactical team, a negotiating team, a traffic control team, a communications team, and the supervisors to coordinate their actions. The negotiating team alone included a supervisor, an intelligence officer to gather facts, a primary negotiator to deal with the subject, a secondary negotiator to assist the primary by taking notes and maintaining records, and a psychologist to evaluate the subject's personality and recommend negotiating techniques. Now Talley had only himself and a handful of untrained officers.

Talley knew he was in the beginning moments of panic. He forced himself to concentrate on the three things that he needed to do: secure the environment, gather information and keep Rooney cool.

Sarah called him over his radio. 'Chief? Mikkelson and Dreyer got the security tape from the minimart. They said you can see these guys plain as a zit on your nose.'

'They inbound?'

'Five minutes out. Maybe less.'

Talley felt himself relax. The tape was something concrete and focused. Seeing Dennis Rooney and the other subjects would make it easier to read the emotional content in Rooney's voice.

Talley climbed out of his car. They needed a house in which to view the tape. Talley set Metzger to that, then divided more tasks among the others. Someone had to locate Mrs Smith in Florida. The

Sheriffs would need a floor plan of the Smith house and information on any security systems involved; if none were available from the permit office, neighbours should sketch the layout from memory.

Mikkelson and Dreyer arrived with the tape. Talley met them at a large Mediterranean-style home owned by a Mrs Peña. Talley identified himself as the chief of police and thanked her for her cooperation. She led them to the television in a large family room, where Mikkelson loaded the videotape.

'Did you pull up anything on Rooney from traffic or warrants?'

'Yes, sir.' Dreyer opened his citation pad.

Talley saw that notes had been scrawled across a citation.

'Dennis Rooney has a younger brother, Kevin, aged nineteen. They live together in Agua Dulce. Dennis just pulled thirty days at the Ant Farm for burglary. He's got multiple offences, including car theft, shoplifting and drug possession.'

'I want you to talk to their landlord. Find out if they've ever threatened him. Find out if they have jobs. If they work, ask their employers to come talk to me.'

Mikkelson stepped away from the video. 'We're ready, Chief.'

As the tape engaged, the bright colour image of a daytime Spanish-language soap opera was replaced by the soundless black and white security picture of Junior Kim's minimart. The camera showed Junior Kim and a small portion of the area behind the counter. It gave a partial view of the rest of the store.

Mikkelson said, 'OK. Here they come.'

A sharp-featured white male matching Dennis Rooney's description opened the door and walked directly to Junior Kim. A larger white male with a broad face and body entered with him. The second man's hair was shaved down to his scalp. A third white male stepped inside. Talley knew the third man was Rooney's brother from the resemblance. Kevin waited by the door.

Talley studied their expressions and the way they carried themselves. Rooney was a good-looking kid, with eyes that were hard but uncertain. He walked with an arrogant, rolling gait. Kevin Rooney shuffled from foot to foot, his eyes flicking from Dennis to the pump islands outside the store. He was clearly terrified. The larger man had a wide flat face and expressionless eyes.

The events in Kim's Minimart happened quickly: Rooney lifted his shirt to expose a gun, then vaulted over the counter. Kim stood with a gun of his own. Talley was relieved that Rooney had told the truth about Kim having a gun. It wouldn't help Rooney in court, but Talley could use what he was seeing to play on Rooney's sense of being the victim of bad luck.

The struggle between Rooney and Junior Kim lasted only seconds, then Kim staggered backwards, dropped his pistol and slumped against the soft drinks' machine. Rooney jumped back over the counter and ran to the door. Junior Kim's pistol had landed on the counter. The larger man tucked it into his waistband, then leaned over the counter, resting his weight on his left hand.

Mikkelson said, 'What's he doing?'

'He's watching Kim die.'

The big man's pasty Pillsbury Doughboy face creased.

Mikkelson said, 'Jesus, he's smiling.'

Talley's back and chest prickled. He stopped the tape, then rewound it until the unknown subject leaned forward on his hand.

'We need to confirm that the younger guy is Kevin Rooney, and we need to ID the third subject. Make hard-copy prints from the tape. Show them to Rooney's landlord, his neighbours, and the people at his job. We might get a fast ID on the third guy that way.'

Talley pointed out the unknown subject's hand resting on the counter. He turned to Cooper and Frost. 'See where he put his hand? I want you to meet the Sheriff's homicide team at Kim's, and tell them about this. They'll be able to lift a good set of prints.'

Talley headed back out to the street and climbed into his car. He checked his watch. It was time. He opened his phone and punched the redial button. The phone in Smith's house rang. On the tenth ring, Rooney still hadn't answered. Talley radioed Jorgenson. 'Who's on with the CHiPs?'

The California Highway Patrol officers had been used to supplement his own people on the perimeter of the house. They worked off their own communication frequency.

'I am.'

'Tell them to advance to the property lines. I don't want them exposed to fire, but I want Rooney to see them.'

'Rog. I'll take care of it.'

If Rooney wouldn't answer the phone, Talley would force him to call.

DENNIS BROUGHT MARS to the closet, letting him see the boxes of cash that crowded the closet floor. 'There's gotta be a million dollars here. Maybe more. Look at it, Mars! This place is a bank!'

Mars barely glanced at the money. He went to the back of the little room, looking at the ceiling and the floor, tapping the walls, then studied the monitors. He pushed the boxes aside with his feet.

'It's a safety room. Steel door, reinforced walls, all the security; it's like a bunker. If anyone breaks into your house, you can hide.'

Dennis was irritated that Mars showed so little interest in the cash. 'Who gives a shit, Mars? Check out this *cash*. We're rich.'

'We're trapped in a house.'

Dennis was getting pissed off. This was the life-altering event that Dennis had always known was waiting for him. This house, this money, here and now—this was his destiny and his fate; the moment that had plucked at him to take chances and commit outrageous acts—all along it had been pulling him forward to the here and now, and Mars was harshing his mellow. He shoved a packet of cash into his pocket and stood.

'Mars, listen, we're going to take this with us. We'll put it in some-thing. They must have suitcases or plastic bags.'

'You can't run with a suitcase. It's going to be heavy.'

Dennis was getting more pissed off. He told Mars to go back to the office to make sure Kevin wasn't screwing up. When Mars left, Dennis searched through the other closets in the bedroom until he found a suitcase. He filled it with packs of hundreds; worn bills that had seen a lot of use. When the suitcase was full, Dennis wheeled it into the bedroom. Mars was right: he didn't know how he was going to get out of here lugging that case, but he refused to believe that he had come this close to his destiny to let it slip away.

Dennis returned to the office and found Mars watching the TV.

'It's on every channel, dude. You're a star.'

Dennis saw himself on television. The newspeople had cut one of Dennis's old arrest photos into the upper right corner of the screen.

The picture changed to an aerial view of the house they were in. Dennis saw police cars parked in the street and two cops hunkered behind the wheels. A hot newschick was saying how Dennis had recently been released from the Ant Farm. Dennis found himself grinning. He had arrived. He felt real.

The phone rang, spoiling the magic of the television. That would be Talley. Dennis ignored it, and returned to the television. Everyone was here because of him. It was *The Dennis Rooney Show*.

Then Kevin screamed from his position by the French doors.

'Dennis! There's cops all over the place out here! *They're coming!*'

TALLEY WAS in the cul-de-sac, waiting behind his car, when Dennis began shouting from the house. Talley let him rant, then opened his phone and called.

Dennis answered on the first ring. 'You bastard! You tell those cops to move back! I don't like 'em this close!'

'Take it easy, Dennis.'

'If these bastards try to come in here, everybody's gonna die!'

'No one is going to hurt you, Dennis. I told you that before. Now I can't see them from behind my car. Where are they?'

Talley heard muffling sounds, as if Rooney was moving with the phone. Talley wondered if it was a cordless. Like all hostage negotiators, he hated cordless and cellphones because they didn't anchor the subject. If you launched a tactical breach, knowing the subject's location could save lives.

Rooney said, 'All the way around, goddammit! They're right on the wall! You make them get back!'

Talley hit the mute button, counted to fifty, then opened the cell line again. 'Dennis, we got a little problem here. Those officers are Highway Patrolmen, Dennis. I'm with the Bristo Camino Police Department. They don't work for me.'

'Bullshit!'

'I can tell you what they're going to say.'

'If they come over that wall, people are going to die!'

'If I tell these guys you're being cooperative, they'll be more inclined to cooperate with you. Everyone out here is concerned that the civilians in there are OK. Let me speak with Mr Smith.'

'*I told you they're fine.*'

Talley sensed that everything inside wasn't as Rooney claimed. Most hostage takers agreed to let their hostages say a few words because they enjoyed taunting the police with their control of the hostage. If Rooney wouldn't let the Smiths talk, then he must be frightened of what they might say. 'Tell me what's wrong, Dennis.'

'Nothing's wrong! I'll let the sonofabitch talk when I get good and goddamned ready. I'm in charge of this shit, not you!'

Dennis sounded so stressed that Talley backed off. If anything was wrong in the house, he didn't want to make the situation worse. But having pressed Rooney for a concession, he had to get something or lose credibility. 'OK, Dennis, fair enough for now, but you've still got to give me something if you want the patrolmen to back off. So how about this: You tell me who you have in there. Just their names.'

'If I tell you, will you get these assholes to back off?'

'Dennis, I just got word from their commander. He'll go along.'

Rooney hesitated, but then he answered. 'Walter Smith, Jennifer Smith and Thomas Smith. There's no one else in here.'

Talley muted the phone. 'Jorgy, tell the CHiPs to back off.'

Talley waited as Jorgenson spoke into his mike, then he went back to his phone. 'Dennis, what do you see?'

'They're pulling back.'

'OK. We made it work, me and you. We did something here, Dennis. Way to go.' Talley wanted Rooney to feel as if they had accomplished something together. Like they were a team.

'Just keep them away. I don't like them that close. They come over that wall, people are going to die in here. Do you understand?'

'I'll give you my word about that right now. We won't come over that wall unless we think you're hurting someone.'

'You want these people, Talley? You want them right now?'

Talley knew that Rooney was about to make his first demand. It could be as innocent as a pack of cigarettes or as outrageous as a phone call from the President. 'You know that I do.'

'I want a helicopter with a full tank of gas to take us to Mexico. If I get the helicopter, you get these people.'

During his time with SWAT, Talley had been asked for helicopters, jet aircraft, limousines, buses, cars and, once, a flying saucer. All negotiators were trained that certain demands were non-negotiable: firearms, ammunition, narcotics, alcohol and transportation. You never allowed a subject the hope of escape. You kept him isolated. That was how you broke him down.

Talley responded without hesitation, making his voice reasonable but firm, letting his tone assure Rooney the refusal wasn't the end of the world, and wasn't confrontational. 'Can't do that, Dennis.'

Rooney's voice came back strained. 'I've got these people.'

'The Sheriffs won't trade for a helicopter. They have their rules about these things.'

Talley wanted to change the subject. Rooney would brood about the helicopter now, but Talley thought he could give him something else to think about. 'I saw the security tape from the minimart.'

'Did you see that Chinaman pull a gun? Did you see that?'

'It played out just the way you said.'

'None of this would've happened if he hadn't pulled that gun.'

'Then none of this was premeditated. That's what you're saying, right?' Rooney wanted to be seen as the victim, so Talley was sending the subtle message that he sympathised with Rooney's situation.

'We just wanted to rob the place. I'll admit that. But, hell, here comes the Chinaman pulling a gun. I had to defend myself, right? I wasn't trying to shoot him. I was just trying to get the gun away so he couldn't shoot *me*. It was an accident.'

The adversarial edge disappeared from Rooney's voice. This was the first indication that Rooney was beginning to see Talley as a collaborator. Talley lowered his voice, sending a subtle cue that this was just between them. 'Can the other two guys hear me?'

'Why do you want to know that?'

'I understand that they might be there with you, so you don't have to respond to what I'm about to say, Dennis. Just listen.'

'What are you talking about?'

'I know you're worried about what will happen to you because the officer was shot. I've been thinking about that, so I've got a question. Was anyone else in there shooting besides you?'

Talley already knew the answer from Jorgenson and Anders.

'Yes.'

'Then maybe it wasn't your bullets that hit the officer.'

Talley had suggested that Rooney could beat the rap by shifting the blame to one of the other subjects. He had given Rooney a doorway out. Now, he had to back off and let Rooney brood over whether or not to step through. 'Dennis, I want to give you my cellphone number. That way you can reach me whenever you want to talk. You won't have to shout out the window.'

Talley gave him the number, told Rooney that he was going to take another break, then once more backed his car out of the cul-de-sac. Leigh Metzger was waiting for him on the street outside Mrs Peña's home. Talley's wife and daughter were with her.

Talley felt embarrassed and angry with himself. He had been so consumed that he had forgotten about Jane and Amanda.

Talley kissed his daughter, who was as responsive as a wet towel.

'Sarah told us that there are men with guns barricaded in a house! Where are they?'

Talley pointed. 'Just around the corner and up that street.'

Rather than stand outside, Talley brought them into the house. He introduced them to Mrs Peña, then led them into the family room. The TV was playing live coverage of the scene.

Amanda went to the television. 'Sarah said they have hostages.'

'A father and two children. One of them is a girl about your age.'

'This is *so* cool. Can we go see the house?'

'No, we can't go up there.'

'But you're the chief of police. Why not?'

Jane said, 'It's a crime scene, Mandy. It's dangerous.'

Talley turned to his wife. 'I should've called, Jane. This thing broke just after we spoke, then everything was happening so fast that I didn't even think of it. I'm sorry.'

Jane touched his arm. 'How are *you* doing?'

'I think the guy's going to come around.'

'I'm not asking about the situation, Chief. I mean *you*.' She glanced at her hand on his arm, then looked at him again. 'You're shaking.'

Talley stepped away just enough so that her hand fell.

'The Sheriffs are taking over as soon as they get here.'

'But they're not here. You are. I know what this does to you.'

'I'm the chief of police, Jane. That's it.' He looked away. It hurt to see her concern.

'You guys should have dinner up here before you head back. Let some of the traffic bleed out. Maybe that Thai place you like?'

Jane nodded. 'We could do that. I don't want to just drop her off at your place so she has to sit there all alone, so how about she and I go eat, then we'll both stay over. We'll rent a movie.'

Talley noticed that Jane had dyed her hair. She had coloured it the same rich chestnut for as long as Talley could remember, but now it was a deep red so dark that it was almost black. Her hair was cut shorter, too, almost a boy cut. Talley realised then that this woman deserved more than he would ever be able to give her. He had to set her free, not curse her with a man whose heart had died.

He looked away again. 'You and I need to talk.'

She stared up at him. He could tell that she was frightened.

'All right, Jeff.'

Friday, 7:02pm. Glen Howell didn't have to warn his people to keep their voices down; they were surrounded by middle-class vanilla families in Chili's Restaurant, six miles west of Bristo Camino. Howell had called in each of them himself, running each name past Sonny Benza personally. They were longtime associates who could do what needed to be done without drawing attention to themselves.

Ken Seymore, who had spent the past two hours pretending to be a reporter from the *Los Angeles Times*, was saying, 'They requested a full crisis response team from the Sheriff's Department. The Sheriffs are on the way, but there's been some problem, so they've been delayed.'

Duane Manelli fired off a question. 'How many people in the Sheriff's team?' Duane Manelli had spent twelve years in the army. He currently ran the best hijack crew in Sonny Benza's operation.

Seymore found his notes. 'We're looking at about thirty-five new bodies on the scene.'

LJ Ruiz leaned forward on his elbows, frowning. Ruiz was a quiet, thoughtful man who worked for Howell as an enforcer. 'When will the Sheriffs arrive?'

'Cop I talked to said they'll be here in three hours, four tops.'

Howell nodded at Gayle Devarona, one of the two women at the table. Like Seymore, she had pretended to be a news reporter in order to openly ask questions.

'What's up with the local cops?'

'We got fourteen police officers and two office people.' Devarona tore a single sheet from a yellow legal pad and passed it to Howell. 'I got their names from the Bristo police office. The addresses and phones I got from a contact at the phone company.'

Howell scanned a neatly hand-printed list. Talley's name was at the top, along with his address and two phone numbers. 'You get any background on Talley?' Sonny Benza had specifically told him to zero in on Talley. You cut off the head, the body dies.

She said, 'Single. He was on LAPD thirteen years, then he resigned. The woman I talked to didn't want to say, but I'd make him for a stress release. Something's hinky about why he hung it up.'

Howell made a note to pass that up to Palm Springs. He knew that Benza had people on the Los Angeles Police Department. If they turned something rotten on Talley, they might be able to use it as leverage. He considered the sixteen names on Devarona's list.

'OK, divide up the names and start digging. Gayle, you're on credit and finances. We get lucky, one of these clowns is gonna be in so deep that he's drowning. Maybe we can toss him a life preserver. Duane, Ruiz, find out where these people play. Some married doof is gonna keep a whore on the side. Shovel dirt and find the skeletons. Ken, you're back at the house with the reporters. If anything breaks, I want to know about it before God.'

Ken Seymore leaned forward, and lowered his voice. 'If things get wet, we're going to need people who can handle that end.'

Wet work was blood work. Howell had already thought of that and had already made the call. 'The right people are on their way.'

Howell copied Talley's address and phone numbers on the bottom of the sheet. He tore off his copy, then stood. He put Talley's address in his pocket as he walked out to his car. Not just anyone would murder a chief of police with an army of cameras and newspeople around. He needed someone special for a job like that.

Friday, 7:39pm. His name was Marion Clewes. He was in a doughnut shop in Newhall, California, twelve miles west of Bristo Camino. He took a seat at a table facing the door to wait for Glen Howell. Marion was used to meeting Howell in places like this. Howell was never comfortable with him, and probably didn't even like him, but that was OK. They paid him well for doing what he enjoyed, and he did these things with a merciless dependability.

Headlights flashed across the glass. Marion glanced up to see Howell's Mercedes pull to a stop. He watched Howell get out of the car and come inside. Howell took a seat opposite him.

Howell spoke softly, getting down to business. He placed a slip of yellow paper on the table in front of Marion. 'Talley lives here. Here's the drill: We have to own this guy and we don't have a lot of time. I need you to find something we can use to twist him.'

Marion put the address away. He knew what was needed. He would search for pornography and drugs, old love letters and sex toys, prescription medications and computer files. Maybe a lab report from a personal physician describing heart disease or phone records to another man's wife. There was always something.

'Is he there now?'

'Don't you listen to the news?'

Marion shook his head.

'He's not home, but I can't tell you when he'll get back there.'

'What if he walks in on me?'

'We don't want him dead, but if he's got you, kill him.' Howell got up without another word.

Marion watched the Mercedes slide away into the deepening twilight, then left to do his job.

Friday, 7:40pm. The helicopters over York Estates switched on their lights to become brilliant stars. Talley didn't like losing the sun. The creeping darkness changed the psychology of hostage takers and police officers alike. Subjects felt safer in the dark, hidden and more powerful, the night allowing them fantasies of escape. Perimeter guards knew this, so their stress level would rise as their efficiency decayed. Night laid the foundation for overreaction and death.

Talley stood by his car, sipping Diet Coke as his officers reported. Rooney's employer, who believed that he could identify the unknown subject, had been located and was inbound; Walter Smith's wife had not yet been found; ten large pizzas (half veggie, half meat) had just been delivered from Domino's.

Barry Peters and Earl Robb trotted up the street from their car.

'We're set with the phone company, Chief. PacBell shows six hard lines into the house, four listed, two unlisted. They blocked all six in and out like you wanted. No one else can call in on those numbers, and the only number they can reach calling out is your cell.'

Talley felt relief; now he didn't have to worry that someone would get the Smiths' number and convince Rooney to murder his hostages.

Peters turned on his Maglite, lighting two floor-plan sketches.

'I worked these out with the neighbours, Chief. This is the upstairs, this is the downstairs.'

Talley grunted. He wasn't confident they were accurate; details like window placement and closet location could be critical if a forced entry was required. Talley asked about architectural drawings.

'There wasn't anything at the building commission.'

'There should be. This is a planned community. Get hold of someone from the mayor's office or one of the council people. Tell them we need access to the permit office. Pull the permits you find and check the contractors. Somebody had to keep a set of file plans.'

As Peters hustled away, Larry Anders's car pulled to a stop beside Talley. A slim, nervous man climbed from the passenger side.

'Chief, this is Brad Dill, Rooney's employer.'

'Thanks for coming, Mr Dill.' Talley knew that Dill owned a small cement-contracting business. 'You know what's going on here?'

Dill glanced up the street. 'The officer told me.'

'Mr Dill, I'm hoping you can help me understand them, but before we get into that, I want you to identify these guys. Let's look at the pictures. Larry, do you have them?'

Anders returned to the car and brought back the two eight-by-ten prints that had been made from the security tape.

'OK, Mr Dill. Let's take a look. Can you identify these people?'

'Sure. That's Dennis. And that one is Kevin, Dennis's kid brother.'

'And Officer Anders says you also know the third man?'

'That would be Mars Krupchek. He come on the job about a month ago. Him, I don't know so well.'

Anders nodded. 'I called Krupchek in to Sarah on the drive, Chief. She's running his name through the Department of Motor Vehicles and the National Crime Information Center.'

Talley questioned Dill about how Dennis behaved on the job. Dill described a temperamental personality with a penchant for drama. Talley grew convinced that his original impression was correct: Rooney was an aggressive narcissist with esteem problems. Kevin, on the other hand, was a passive personality who would take his cues from the stronger personalities in his sphere of influence.

'What can you tell me about Krupchek?'

'Not so much. He showed up one day looking for work when I needed a guy. He was well spoken and polite. He's big and strong, you know, so I gave him a try.'

'You know what he did before this?'

'No, sir. Nope.'

'Mr Dill, do you have an address for Krupchek?'

Dill pulled a tiny address book from his back pocket and read off an address and phone number. Anders copied them.

Talley thanked Brad Dill for his help, told him that Anders would bring him home, then took Anders aside out of earshot.

'Check that Krupchek's address matches with the billing address listed with the phone. If it does, call the Palmdale City Attorney's office and ask for a telephonic search warrant, then head to his residence and see what you find. Take someone with you.'

DENNIS TRIED not to look at Mars after his conversation with Talley, but he couldn't help himself. He thought about what Kevin had told him, about Mars wanting to shoot the cop, about Mars lying that the cop had pulled his weapon and Mars firing first. Maybe Talley had something; maybe Dennis could beat the rap if it was Mars who shot the officer, and not him. If Kevin backed him up, they might be able to cut a deal with the prosecutor for their testimony against Mars. Dennis felt a desperate hope, but then he remembered the money. He wasn't ready to give up the cash.

Kevin looked at him anxiously. 'Are they giving us the helicopter?'

'No. We gotta find another way out of here. Let's start looking.'

The girl and her fat brother were still kneeling beside their father.

Mars lumbered to his feet, large and gross. 'We should tie them up so we don't have to worry about them.'

Dennis spoke to Kevin. 'Mars is right. Find something to tie 'em up with, and take them upstairs.'

'What do I use to tie them?'

'Look in the garage. Look in the kitchen. Mars, you find something, OK? You know what we need.'

MARS OPENED the door to Jennifer's room, then stepped aside so that she and Kevin could enter. He had come back from the garage with extension cords, duct tape, a hammer and nails. He gave two extension cords to Kevin. 'Tie her to the chair, and tie her feet. I'll take care of the windows and door when I finish with the boy.'

Mars pulled Thomas away as Kevin brought Jennifer into the room. The lights were on because she never turned them off. The shades had been pulled.

Kevin dragged her desk chair into the middle of the floor. Nervous, he avoided her eyes. 'Sit here and put your hands behind the chair.'

Jennifer perched on the chair, tense and wary. She cringed when Kevin touched her, but he didn't treat her roughly or twist her arms. When he'd finished with her wrists, he moved around in front of her to tie her ankles to the legs of the chair.

A shadow moved behind Kevin. Mars stood in the doorway, staring at them. He went to the windows. He hammered heavy nails into the sills so that the windows wouldn't open, then came back to stand in front of Jennifer. He tore a strip of wide grey duct tape off the roll. He pressed it hard over her mouth. 'Go downstairs, Kevin.'

Kevin hesitated at the door. 'Aren't you coming?'

'I'll be along. Go.'

Jennifer looked at Kevin, pleading with him not to leave her alone with Mars. Kevin left.

Mars straightened. 'I want to show you something.'

He pulled off his shirt. Tattooed across his flabby chest in flowing script was: *A Mother's Son.*

'You see? It cost two hundred and forty dollars. That's how much I love my mom.'

His chest and belly were specked with small grey knots as if he were diseased. She thought they might be warts.

He touched one of them, a hard grey knot, and the corner of his mouth curled into a smile. 'My mom burned me with cigarettes.'

334

Jennifer felt sick. They weren't warts; they were scars.

Mars pulled on his shirt, then went to the door. He turned off the lights, stepped out, then pulled the door closed. The sound of his hammer was as loud as thunder, but not so loud as her fearful heart.

DENNIS WAS at the window, watching the police, when one of the patrol cars out front fired up. The lead car swung round in a tight arc, roaring away as a new Highway Patrol car arrived. He couldn't tell if Talley was still outside or not. The cops were up to something, which made Dennis feel queasy and scared.

Mars settled onto the couch by Walter Smith. 'They didn't give you the helicopter because they don't believe you're serious.'

Dennis paced away from the window, irritated. 'You don't know what you're talking about. They've got rules about this stuff.'

Mars stroked Smith's head as if he was probing the contours of his skull. Dennis thought it was weird.

'You don't understand the power we have, Dennis. The police will only take us seriously if they're scared we'll kill these people.'

'OK, dude. Mars, you're creeping me out.'

'The police have no reason to deal with us unless they take us seriously. All they have to do is wait until we get tired, and then we'll give up. They know that, Dennis. They're counting on it.'

Dennis felt his chest expand against a tight pressure that filled the room. 'So how do we convince them?'

'Tell them we're going to let the fat boy go as a sign of good faith.'

Dennis didn't move. He could see Kevin from the corner of his eye, and knew that Kevin was feeling the same awful pressure.

'We send the fat boy out the front door. We wait until he's about halfway across the yard, then we shoot him. Then they'll know we mean business, and we'll have something to trade.'

Dennis tried to tell himself that Mars was kidding, but he knew that Mars was serious. Mars meant every word.

'Mars. We couldn't do something like that.'

Mars looked curious. 'I could. I'll do it, if you want.'

'I don't think so, dude.'

The bright intensity in Mars's eyes faded like a candle losing its flame, and Mars shrugged. Dennis felt relieved. He told them to watch out for the cops, then once more walked through the house, checking each window to see if he could use it to sneak out, but all of the windows were in plain view of the cops. He went into the garage.

He hoped to find some kind of side door, but instead came to a small utility bathroom at the end of a workshop off the garage. A sliding window with frosted glass was let into the wall above the sink. Dennis opened it, and saw the heavy leaves of an oleander bush thick against the dusty fly screen. He pressed his face to the screen and peered out, but it was impossible to see much in the growing darkness. Excited, Dennis quietly pushed out the screen. He opened the window wider and leaned out. The ground was four feet below. He worked his shoulders through the window. The row of oleanders followed the wall. He pushed himself back into the house, then turned round so he could step through feet first, one leg and then another. He lowered himself to the ground. He was outside the house.

Dennis crouched on the ground beneath the oleander, his back pressed to the wall, listening. He could hear the police radios from the cars parked at the front of the house. He caught tiny glimpses of the two cars through the leaves. The cops would be watching the front of the house, not the row of shrubs along the side wall. Dennis lay down at the base of the wall and inched along its length. The oleanders were thinner in some places, but the police didn't see him. He came to the end of the wall and saw that the oleanders continued into the neighbour's front yard. Dennis grew more excited. They could bag the cash, drag it along behind the oleanders, then slip away while the cops were watching the house, right under their noses!

Dennis worked his way back to the window and climbed into the house. He ran back to the office to tell Kevin and Mars that he had found the way out.

THE STARS WERE NOT yet out, but the planet Venus hung low in the blackening western sky. Talley's condominium was one of forty-eight units spread over four buildings, arranged like the letter H. Each unit had a small fenced patio at ground level, and small, unprotected parking lots were on either side of each building.

Marion Clewes circled the building with Talley's unit. Because the buildings were older, the gas and electric meters, and junction boxes for both telephones and cable TV were clustered together at an out-of-the-way spot opposite the parking lots. Marion was pleased to see that the building had no alarms.

Marion found Talley's unit, let himself through the gate to the front door. The patio and door were hidden by a six-foot privacy fence. He couldn't have asked for anything easier. He rang the bell twice, then knocked, already knowing that no one was home; the house was dark. He pulled on latex gloves, took out his crowbar and pick, then set to work. Four minutes later, the deadbolt slipped. Eighty seconds after that, he let himself in.

'Hello?' He didn't expect an answer, and none came. Marion shut the door behind him, but did not lock it.

The kitchen was to the left, a small dining room to the right. Sliding glass doors offered a view of the patio. Directly ahead was a large living room. He unlatched the glass doors, then crossed the living room to open the largest window. He would relock everything if he left at his leisure, but for now he arranged fast exits.

Marion climbed steep stairs to a landing with doors leading to a bathroom and two other rooms, the room to his right the master bedroom. He turned on the light. Marion expected to search every closet and drawer in the house for something that could be used as leverage, but there it was as soon as he entered, right there, waiting.

A desk rested against the far wall, scattered with papers and bills and receipts, but that isn't what caught Marion's eye. Five photographs waited at the back of the desk, Talley with a woman and girl, the woman and Talley always the same, the girl at different ages.

Marion knelt, brought the frame to his face. A woman. A girl. A wife. A daughter. Marion considered the possibilities.

Friday, 8:06pm. The Los Angeles County Sheriff's Department Crisis Response Team came round the corner like a military convoy. A plain Sheriff's sedan led the file, followed by a bulky Mobile Command Post vehicle. The Sheriffs wouldn't need Mrs Peña's home; the van contained its own power generator, a bathroom, uplinks for the intelligence officer's computers, and a communications centre for command and control coordination. It also had a coffee machine. The Sheriff's SWAT team, geared out in dark green tactical uniforms, followed in two large GMC Suburbans with a second van containing their weapons and gear. As the convoy stopped, the SWAT cops hustled to the second van, where a sergeant-supervisor passed out radios and firearms. Four radio cars followed the tactical vehicles with uniformed deputies who clustered around their own sergeant-supervisor. Talley heard a change in the helicopters' rotor turbulence as they repositioned to broadcast the Sheriffs' arrival. Talley hurried to the lead car.

A tall, slender African-American officer climbed out from behind the wheel as a blond officer with thinning hair climbed from the passenger side.

Talley put out his hand. 'Jeff Talley. I'm the chief here. Are you the team commander?'

The tall man flashed a relaxed smile. 'Will Maddox. I'll be the primary negotiator. This is Chuck Ellison, my secondary. The commander would be Captain Martin. She's back in the van.'

The energy on the street changed dramatically; Talley had felt that he was hanging from a ledge by his fingers, but now an organised military weight was settling over York Estates. Talley no longer felt alone.

He said, 'Mr Maddox, I am damned glad to see you here.'

Talley walked with them back towards the control van to find the captain. He knew from his own experience that Maddox and Ellison would want a virtual replay of his conversations with Rooney.

'Are the innocents under an immediate threat?' asked Maddox.

'I don't believe so. Last contact I had with Rooney was twenty minutes ago. Way I left it, he's in there thinking he has outs both for Kim's murder and the attempt on the officer. You know about that?'

While inbound, the Sheriffs had received a radio briefing on the events leading up to the barricade situation. Maddox confirmed that they knew the bare bones. 'Has he made any demands?'

Talley told him about Rooney demanding that the perimeter be pulled back and the deal they'd made, the hostage names for the pullback. Getting the first concession was often the most difficult, and how it was got could set the tone for everything that was to follow.

'Good job, Chief. Sounds like we're in pretty good shape. You used to be with LAPD SWAT, didn't you?'

Talley looked closely at Maddox. 'That's right. Have we met?'

'I was on LAPD as a uniform before I went with the Sheriffs, which put us there about the same time. When we got the call here today, your name rang a bell.'

Talley said nothing. Maddox seemed to sense his discomfort, and dropped the subject.

When they reached the command van, a woman wearing a green uniform stepped from among a knot of sergeants. She had a cut jaw, smart black eyes and short blonde hair.

'Is this Chief Talley?'

Maddox nodded. 'This is him.'

She put out her hand. She had a tough grip. 'Laura Martin. Captain. I'm the field commander in charge of the Crisis Response

Team. Do you have a perimeter in place around the house?'

'Yes, ma'am.'

'How many men?'

'Eleven. A mix of my people and the Highway Patrol.'

As Talley spoke, Martin didn't seem to be paying attention. She glanced both ways along the street, leading Talley to think that she was sizing up his officers. He found himself irritated. The command van was being repositioned further down the block over an access point to the underground phone lines.

'I'll get my supervisors together so you can brief everyone at once. I want to rotate my tactical people into the perimeter as soon as we've stabilised the situation.'

Talley felt another flash of irritation; it was clear that the scene was stable. As Martin called her people together under a streetlight, Talley radioed Metzger for copies of the floor plan. He passed them out as everyone assembled, and gave a fast overview of his conversations with Rooney.

Martin stood next to him, arms crossed tightly. 'Have you cut the power and phones?'

'We blocked the phones. I didn't see any reason to cut the power.'

Martin told her intelligence officer to have someone from the utility companies standing by if they needed to pull the plug.

Metzger pointed up the street. 'They're already standing by. See that guy in the Duke cap? That's him.'

Martin turned to her tactical team supervisor, a veteran sergeant named Carl Hicks. 'Float two men around the perimeter to find out exactly what we're dealing with. Let's make sure this place is secure.'

Talley said, 'Captain, be advised that he's hinky about the perimeter. I pulled back the line to start the negotiation. That was part of the deal.'

Martin stepped away to stare up the street. 'I understand that, Chief. Thank you. Now, will you be ready to hand off the phone to Maddox and Ellison as soon as we're in place?'

Maddox's face was tight. Talley thought he was probably irritated with her manner, also. 'I'd like to spend some time going over the Chief's prior conversations with these guys.'

Martin checked her watch, impatient. 'You can do that while we rotate into the perimeter; I want to get the show on the road. Chief Talley, I have seven minutes after the hour. Do I now have command of the scene?'

'Yes, ma'am. It's yours.'

'Then log it. I now have command and control.' Martin trotted away into the milling SWAT officers.

Maddox stared after her for a moment, then looked at Talley. 'She's wound kinda tight.'

Talley nodded, but said nothing. He had thought that he would feel relieved when he turned over command of the scene. He didn't.

ALONE IN HIS DARK ROOM, Thomas was spread-eagled on his lower bunk, face up, his wrists and ankles tied to the corner bedposts. After Mars had finished tying him, he had taped over his mouth. Then Mars turned off the lights, and left, pulling the door closed. Thomas set about working his way free.

Thomas was good at working his way free. He was also good at moving through his home without being seen, because he had changed some of the camera angles. Just a bit, so that his mom and dad couldn't see *everything*. He knew that most people didn't live in houses where every room was watched by a closed-circuit television system. His father explained that they had such a system because he handled other people's financial records and someone might want to steal them. It was a big responsibility, his father had said, and so they had to protect those records as best they could.

The wire holding his left wrist was slack. When Mars was tying Thomas's right wrist to the post, Thomas had scrunched away just enough so that now the cord held a little bit of play. He worked at it, pulling the knots tighter but creating enough slack to touch the knot that held him to the post. The knot was *tight*. Thomas dug at it so hard that the pain in his fingertips brought tears, but then the knot loosened. He worked frantically, terrified that Mars or one of the others would throw open the door, and then the knot gave and his left hand was free. The tape hurt coming off his mouth. He untied his right hand, then his feet, and then he was free.

Thomas stayed on the bed, listening. Nothing.

I know where Daddy has a gun.

Thomas slipped to the floor and crawled along the wall towards his closet, passing under his desk.

In *The Lion, the Witch and the Wardrobe*, the children found a secret door at the rear of their wardrobe that let them escape into the magical land of Narnia. Thomas had his own secret door at the back of his closet: an access hatch to the attic crawl space that ran beneath the steep pitch of the roof, through which he could move along the eaves to the other access hatches dotted around the house.

Thomas pulled open the hatch and wiggled into the crawl space. He found the flashlight that he kept just inside the hatch, turned it on, then pulled the hatch closed.

THE LITTLE BATHROOM off the garage was as dark as a cave when Dennis showed them the window, telling Mars and Kevin that they could work their way into the neighbour's yard to slip past the cops.

Mars seemed thoughtful. 'This could work.'

'Damn right, it could work.'

'But you never know what the police are doing or where they might be. We have to give them something to think about besides us.'

Kevin said, 'I don't like any of it. We should give up.'

Mars went into the garage, his face lit by the dim light from the kitchen. 'If you want to get away, we should burn the house.'

Dennis had been thinking of putting the kids in the Jaguar and opening the garage door with the remote as a diversion, but a fire made better sense. 'That's not a bad idea. We could start a fire on the other side of the house.'

Kevin raised his hands. 'You guys are crazy. That adds arson to the charges against us.'

'It makes sense, Kevin. All the cops will be watching the fire. They won't be looking at the neighbour's yard.'

'But what about the Smiths?'

Dennis was about to answer when Mars did. 'They'll burn.'

The back of Dennis's neck tingled as if Mars had raked a nail across a blackboard. 'Jesus, Mars, nobody has to burn. We can put 'em here in the garage before we take off. We'll figure somethin' out.'

They decided to use gasoline to start the fire. Mars used the plastic air hose from the family's aquarium to siphon gas from the Jaguar. He filled a two-gallon gas can, then a large plastic bucket that was stained by detergent. They were carrying the gasoline into the house when they heard the helicopters change pitch and more cars pull into the cul-de-sac.

Dennis stopped with the bucket, listening, when suddenly the front of the house was bathed in light, framing the huge garage door and spilling into the bathroom window even through the oleanders.

'What the hell?! What's going on?'

They hurried to the front of the house, gasoline splashing.

'Kevin! Watch the French doors!'

Dennis and Mars left the gasoline in the entry, then ran into the office where Walter Smith still twitched on the couch. Spears of light cut through the shutters, painting them with zebra stripes. Dennis opened the shutters and saw two more police cars. All four cars had trained their spotlights on the house and a great pool of light from the helicopters burned brilliantly on the front yard.

The television showed the LA County Sheriffs rolling through the dark streets of York Estates. Dennis watched a SWAT group trot through an oval of helicopter light as they deployed through the neighbourhood. Snipers: stone-cold killers dressed in ninja suits with rifles equipped with night-vision scopes and laser sights.

Dennis peeked out of the shutters again, but so many floodlights had been set up in the street that the glare was blinding; a thousand cops could be standing sixty feet away, and he wouldn't know.

Everything had once more changed. One minute he had a great plan to slip away, but now all sides of the house were lit up like the sun and an army of cops was filling the streets. Sneaking through the adjoining neighbour's yard would now be impossible.

Dennis went to the door. 'I'm going to check the windows again, OK? I gotta make sure Kevin isn't falling asleep. Mars, you keep an eye on the TV. If anything happens, yell.'

Mars, leaning against the wall with his face to the shutters, didn't respond. Dennis trotted back to the family room to find Kevin.

'What's going on? Aren't we leaving?'

'The Sheriffs are here. They're crawling all over the goddamned neighbourhood. They got *snipers* out there!'

'What are we going to do?'

'I don't know! They got so many lights out there I can't see a damn thing. Maybe I can see better on those TVs in the safety room.'

Dennis left Kevin at the mouth of the hall, then trotted back to the master bedroom, and into the safety room.

He hadn't checked the monitors since the sky was rimmed with red. Now he saw Mars standing by the shutters; and the girl tied to a chair in her upstairs room. He couldn't see the boy, but didn't think twice about it; Dennis searched the monitors for angles outside the house, but those views were shadowed and unreadable. 'Shit!'

He considered the buttons and switches beneath the monitors. Nothing was labelled, but he didn't have anything to lose. If it was up, he pushed it down; if it was out, he pushed it in. Suddenly a monitor that had shown nothing but shadows on the wall at the rear of the property beyond the pool was bathed in light. Two SWAT cops with rifles were climbing over the wall.

'*Shit!!!*' Dennis sprinted back through the house, shouting. '*They're coming!!! Kev, Mars!!! They're coming!*'

Dennis raced to the French doors in the dark beyond the kitchen. He couldn't see the cops past the blinding outside lights, but he knew they were there, and he knew they were coming. He fired two shots into the darkness, not even thinking about it, just pulling the trigger, *bam bam*. Two glass panes in the French doors shattered.

Dennis thought his world was about to explode: They would fire tear gas, then crash through the doors. They were probably rushing the house right now with battering rams.

'Mars! Kev, we gotta get those kids!'

Dennis ran for the stairs, Kevin behind him.

THREE MINUTES before Dennis Rooney saw the SWAT officers and fired two rounds, Thomas lowered himself through the ceiling into the laundry room. He let himself down on top of the hot-water heater, felt with his toe to find the washing machine, then slid to the floor.

He held still, listening to Kevin and Dennis. He could hear them talking, though he couldn't understand what they were saying, and then the voices stopped. Thomas crept through the laundry room to his father's tiny hobby room at the end opposite the kitchen. Both rooms were at the rear of the garage.

When Thomas reached the hobby room, he eased the door closed, then turned on his flashlight. His father's hobby was building plastic models of rocket ships from the early days of the space programme. He bought kits, built and painted them at a little workbench, then put them on shelves above the bench. His father also had a Sig Sauer 9mm pistol in a metal box on the top shelf. His dad used to keep it under the front seat of the Jaguar, but his mom raised such a stink that his father had taken it out of the car and put it in the box. Thomas could use the stool to climb onto the bench, and, from there, he could probably reach the box.

He climbed. He stretched up onto his toes. His fingers grazed the box just enough for him to work it towards the edge of the shelf.

That's when he heard Dennis.

'*They're coming!!! Kev, Mars!!! They're coming!*'

Thomas jumped down from the bench and ran to the laundry as

two gunshots exploded in the house, so loud they made his ears ring.

He wasn't thinking about Jennifer's bag. It was on the table by the door to the garage, that convenient place where everyone in the family dropped their stuff when they came in from the garage. Jennifer's bag was there. Thomas grabbed it. He scrambled up into the crawl space. The last thing he heard before closing the hatch was Dennis shouting that they had to get the kids.

HANDING OFF the role of primary negotiator was never easy. Talley had forged a bond with Rooney, and now would pull away, replacing himself with Maddox. Rooney might resist, but the subject was never given a choice. Having a choice was having power, and the subject was never given power.

Talley brought Maddox and Ellison into the cul-de-sac where they hunkered behind their car. Talley wanted to go over his earlier conversations with Rooney in greater detail so that Maddox would have something with which to work, but they didn't have time. The gunshots from the house cracked through the summer air: *poppop*.

Almost instantly, a storm of transmissions crackled over their radios: '*Shots fired! Shots fired! We are under fire from the house, west rear at the wall! Advise on response!*'

All three of them knew what had happened the instant they heard the calls.

'Damnit, she moved in too close! Rooney thinks he's being breached!'

Talley felt sick; this is the way it went bad, this is how people got dead, just this fast. He dialled the tactical team's frequency into his own transceiver. 'Pull back, pull back! Do NOT return fire!'

Talley had his cellphone out. He punched redial to call the house, praying that Rooney would answer, then ran to Jorgenson's car, still there in the street, and turned on the public-address system.

THOMAS SCRAMBLED across the joists like a spider. He scurried past the access hatch in Jennifer's closet, past their bathrooms and then to the access hatch in his closet, scrambled through the hatch and ran to his bed. He wanted to retie himself. He pulled the ropes back over his ankles, as footsteps pounded towards him through the hall.

He looped the ropes and slipped his hands through, realised in a flash of fear that he had forgotten the tape that had covered his mouth, but then it was too late.

DENNIS THREW open the door. He saw that the boy had damn near untied himself, but he didn't care. He pulled the boy from his bed, hooked an arm round his neck, and dragged him back towards the stairs. If the cops crashed through the front door, he would hold his gun to the kid's head and threaten to kill him. He would hide behind the kid and make the cops back down. He had a chance.

'Hurry up, Kevin! Bring the girl!'

Dennis dragged the boy down the stairs and into the office where Mars was waiting calmly by the window.

MARTIN AND HICKS ran into the cul-de-sac without waiting for a cover vehicle. As Martin hit the ground beside Talley, she shouted, 'What do you think you're doing, interfering with my deployment?'

'He's shooting at your people because he thinks they're assaulting the house, Martin. You're violating my agreement with him.'

'This scene now belongs to me. You handed off control.'

'Pull back your people, Martin. Nothing is going on in there.'

Talley keyed the PA mike.

'Dennis, take it easy in there. Please. Just pick up the phone.'

'Hicks!'

Hicks leaned into the car past Talley and jerked the mike plug from its jack.

Talley's head was throbbing. He felt caught in a vice.

'Let me talk to him, Captain. Order your people to stand down, and let me talk to him. If it's too far gone you can breach, but right now let me try. Tell her, Maddox.'

Martin glared at Maddox, who looked embarrassed. 'He's right, Captain. Let's not get too aggressive here. If Talley made a deal, we have to honour it or this guy isn't going to trust me.'

Martin glared at him. She glanced at Hicks, then bit out the words. 'Pull back.'

Hicks, looking uncomfortable, plugged the PA plug back into its jack, then mumbled orders into his tactical mike.

Talley turned back to the house. 'Pick up the phone, Dennis. Talk to me.' Talley held the cellphone to his ear, counting the rings.

Finally, Rooney answered, screaming. 'You bastard! You lied to me! I've got a friggin' gun to this kid's head right here! We've got these people! We'll kill 'em, you bastard!'

Talley spoke over him, his voice loud and forceful so that Rooney would hear him, but not strident. It was important to appear in control even when you weren't. 'They're pulling back. They are pulling back, Dennis. Look. You see the officers pulling back?'

The sounds of movement came over the phone. Talley guessed that Rooney had a cordless and was watching the tactical team at the rear of the property.

'Yeah. I guess. They're going back over the wall.'

'I didn't lie to you, Dennis. It's over now, OK? Don't hurt anyone.'

'We'll burn this place down, you try to come in here. We've got gasoline all good to go, Talley.'

Talley locked eyes with Maddox. If Rooney was creating a situation dangerous to the hostages, it could justify a pre-emptive breach of the house.

'Don't do anything to endanger yourself or those children, Dennis. For your own sake and for the sake of the innocents in there. This kind of thing can create problems.'

'Then stay on the other side of that wall. You try to come get us and this place is gonna burn.'

Talley muted the phone to warn Maddox about the gasoline. If Rooney was telling the truth, firing tear gas or flash-bang grenades into the house could ignite an inferno.

'No one is coming in. We screwed up. Some new guys came out and we got our wires crossed, but I didn't lie to you. I wouldn't do that.'

'You damn well *did* screw up, dude! Jesus!'

The tension lessened in Rooney's voice, and, with it, Talley felt the vice ease its grip. If Rooney was talking, he wouldn't shoot.

'What's the status in there, Dennis? You didn't hurt anyone, did you?'

'Not yet.'

'No one needs a doctor?'

'*You're* gonna need a doctor, you try this again.'

Talley glanced at Martin and muted the receiver again. 'He's calming down. I think now would be a good time for the handoff.'

Martin glanced at Maddox. 'You ready?'

'I'm ready.'

Martin nodded at Talley. 'Go.'

Talley uncovered his phone. 'Dennis, can I tell you something of a personal nature?'

'What?'

'I gotta piss real bad.'

Rooney laughed. Just like that, and Talley knew that the handoff would work. He made his voice relaxed, putting a friendly spin on it, indicating that everything that was about to happen was the most natural thing in the world and beyond all objection.

'Dennis, I'm going to take a break out here. I'm going to put an officer named Will Maddox on the line. You scared me so bad that I've gotta go clean my shorts, you know? So Maddox will be here on the line if you want to talk or if you need anything.'

'You're a funny guy, Talley.'

'Here he is, Dennis. You stay cool in there.'

'I'm cool.'

Talley handed the phone to Maddox, who introduced himself with a warm, mellow voice. 'Hey, Dennis. You should've seen ol' Jeff out here. I think he crapped his pants.'

Talley didn't listen to any more. The rest of it would be up to Maddox. He slumped down onto the street and leaned against the car, feeling drained.

AFTER THE SCREAMING, after those frantic moments when Thomas thought that Dennis would shoot him in the head as he was threatening, Jennifer went to their father.

Mars returned from elsewhere in the house, his arms filled with big white candles. He lit one, dripped wax on the television, seated the base in the wax. He moved to the bookcase, did it again.

Dennis finally noticed. 'What the hell are you doing?'

Mars answered as he lit another candle. 'They might cut the power. Here, take this.' He tossed a flashlight to Dennis.

Soon, the office looked like an altar.

Dennis suddenly said, 'We should stack pots and pans under the windows in case they try to sneak in, things that will fall, so we'll hear. Mars, do that, OK? Set up some booby traps.'

Jennifer said, 'What about my father? He needs a doctor!'

'Kevin, take 'em back upstairs. *Please.*'

'Do you want me to tie them again?'

Dennis squinched his face, thinking. 'It took too long to cut all that shit off, you and Mars tying them like a couple of mummies. Just make sure they're locked in real good.'

Mars finished with the candles.

'I can take care of that. Bring them up.'

Kevin brought them, holding Jennifer's arm, Thomas walking in front. They waited at the top of the stairs until Mars rejoined them, now with a hammer and screwdriver. He led them to Thomas's room first. Mars pushed him inside, then knelt by the knob, the one Thomas would use to get out. He hammered the screwdriver under the base, popped it off, unfastened three screws, then pulled the knob free, leaving only a square hole. He looked at Jennifer.

'You see? That's how you keep a child in its room.'

They left Thomas like that, pulling the door, then hammering the door closed. Thomas listened until he heard the crash of Jennifer's knob coming free and her door being nailed, and then he scrambled for his closet. He was thinking only of the gun, but as soon as he turned on his flashlight he saw Jennifer's bag. He had dropped it just inside the hatch when he scrambled back into the room. He clawed it open and upended it. Out fell her cellphone.

Palm Springs, California

Friday, 8:32pm. The three of them had Glen Howell on the speaker, Benza, Tuzee and Salvetti, the TVs muted so they could hear.

Sitting in his car somewhere in the dark, Howell said, 'He's got a wife and kid, a daughter. They're separated or something. The wife and kid live down in LA, but he sees the kid every two weeks or so. He's seeing them this weekend. We got that from his office, an older woman there who likes to talk, you know, how sad it is and all because the Chief's such a nice man.'

'Where are they now, the family I mean?'

'That, I don't know. I got people on that. They're due up tonight, though. That part I know for sure.'

Benza nodded. 'We've gotta think about this.'

Howell said, 'There's more. They're looking at the building permits.'

'Why?'

'Something like this happens, some asshole barricades himself in a building, they want the floor plans. So now they're trying to find the people who built the house so they can get the plans.'

'Shit.' Benza sighed and leaned back. He owned the construction companies that built the house and installed the security systems. He didn't like where this was going. He stood. 'I'm going to walk, so if you can't hear me just say, OK?'

'Sure, Sonny.'

'First things first. Our records. I'm looking at this house on the television right now. There's a ring of cops around it, but let me ask you something. Could we get our people in there?'

'No. I've got good people, Sonny, the best, but we can't get in right now. Not the way it stands now. We'd have to own the cops to do that. You give me a day, two days, I could probably do it.'

'Could we get close? Now. Not owning the cops, but now?'

Howell thought about it. 'We could probably get close.'

Benza looked at Tuzee and Salvetti. 'How about we burn it down? Right now, tonight. Get some guys in there with some accelerant, torch the place, burn it to the ground.'

Salvetti shrugged, unimpressed. 'No way to know the disks would be destroyed. Not for sure. If Smith has any of that stuff in his security room, it isn't gonna burn. Why don't we just call 'em? Talk to these kids ourselves, cut a deal.'

Howell's voice hissed from the speaker. 'The lines are blocked. The cops did that.'

Benza caught Tuzee looking at him, resigned. 'What, Phil?'

Tuzee slumped in his chair. 'Talley's family.'

'You know where that ends, don't you?'

'You're the guy just suggested we burn the house down, six people inside, the whole world watching.'

'I know.'

'We can't just sit. We came damned close with what just happened with the Sheriffs, and now they're looking at the building permits and God knows what else. That's bad enough, but I'm worried about New York. I'm thinking, how long can we keep the lid on this?'

'We've got the lid on. I trust the guys we have on the scene.'

'I trust our guys too, but old man Castellano is going to find out sooner or later. It's bound to happen.'

'It's only been a few hours.'

'However long it's been, we need to get a handle on things before they find out. By the time that old man hears, we've gotta be able to tell him that we're no longer a threat to him. We've gotta laugh about this over schnapps and cigars, else he'll hand us our asses.'

Benza felt tired in his heart, but relieved, too. Comfort came with the decision. 'Glen, if we move on Talley like this, you got a man there who can do whatever needs to be done? All the way?'

'Yes, Sonny. Can and will. I can handle the rest.'

Benza glanced at Phil Tuzee, Tuzee nodding, then Salvetti, Salvetti ducking his head one time.

'OK, Glen. Get it done.'

New York City

Friday, 11:40pm, Eastern time. 8:40pm, Pacific time. His wife was a light sleeper, so Vittorio 'Vic' Castellano left their bedroom to take the call. He put on a bathrobe, and shuffled alongside Jamie Beldone to the kitchen. Beldone held a cellphone. On the other end of it was a man they employed to keep an eye on things in California.

Vic, seventy-eight years old and two weeks away from a hip replacement, poured a small glass of water.

'You sure it's this bad?'

'The police have the house locked down with all Benza's records inside, including the books that link to us.'

'That sonofabitch. What's in his records?'

'They show how much he kicks to us. If the Feds recover this, it will help them build an IRS case against you.'

'It's been how long this is goin' on?'

'About five hours now.'

Castellano checked the time. 'Does Benza know that we know?'

'No, sir.'

'That sonofabitch. Heaven forbid he call to warn me like a real man. He'd rather let me get caught cold than have time to prepare. What's he doin' about it?'

'He sent in a team. You know Glen Howell?'

'No.'

'Benza's fixer. He's good.'

'Do we have our own guy there?'

Beldone tipped the phone, nodding. 'He's on the line now. I have to tell him what to do.'

Vic drank the water, then sighed. It was going to be a long night. 'I can't believe Benza hasn't called me. What's he thinking back there?'

'He's thinking that if it goes south, he's going to run. He's probably more afraid of you than the Feds.'

'He should be.' Vic sighed again, then went to the door. Forty years as the boss of the most powerful crime family on the East Coast had taught him to worry about the things he could control, and let other people worry about the things he couldn't.

He stopped in the doorway and turned back to Jamie Beldone. 'If it goes south, Sonny Benza isn't goin' anywhere. You understand?'

'Yes, sir.'

Vic Castellano shuffled back to his bed, but could not sleep.

Friday, 8:43pm. Talley was in Mrs Peña's home with the Sheriffs, sipping her coffee. They were watching the security tape.

Talley pointed at the television with his cup. 'The first one inside is Rooney, this next guy is Krupchek. Kevin comes in last.'

He told them what he had learned from Brad Dill about Krupchek and the Rooney brothers, then filled them in on having dispatched Mikkelson and Dreyer to locate landlords and neighbours.

Ellison said, 'These guys have any family we can bring out? We had a guy once, he backed us off for twelve hours until his mama gets there. She gets on the phone, tells him to get his ass out of that house, the guy comes out crying like a baby.'

Talley had worked with subjects like that, too. 'If we can find their landlords or friends, we might get a line on the families.'

Maddox nodded, his face creased with attention. 'I might want to talk to Dill and those people myself.'

As the new primary negotiator, Maddox had the responsibility to form his own opinions on the behaviour characteristics of a subject. Talley would have done the same thing.

Leigh Metzger came up behind Talley and touched his arm.

'Chief, see you a second?'

Talley followed Metzger into the adjoining room. Metzger glanced back at the Sheriffs, then lowered her voice. 'Sarah wants you to call her right away. She's says it's *important*. You're supposed to call on your office line, not use a radio.'

Talley took out his cellphone, hitting the autodial for his office.

Sarah answered on the first ring.

'It's me, Sarah. What's up?'

'Oh, thank God. There's a little boy on the phone. He says that his name is Thomas Smith, and that he's calling from inside the house.'

'It's a crank. Forget it.'

Warren Kenner, Talley's personnel supervisor, came on the line.

'Chief, I checked the phone number the boy says he's calling from with the cell company. It's registered to the Smiths, all right.'

'Did you talk with the boy, or just Sarah?'

'No, I talked to him. He sounds real, saying things about the three guys in that house, and his sister and father. He says his dad's hurt in there, that he got knocked out.'

'Is he still on the phone?'

'Yes, sir. Sarah's talking to him right now on another line. They locked him in his room. He says he's on his sister's cellphone.'

'Stand by.' Talley went to the door; several officers and Highway Patrolmen were milling near Mrs Peña's kitchen, drinking coffee. He called Martin, Maddox and Ellison into the room, then led them as far from the others as possible. 'I think we've got something. Kid on the phone, saying he's Thomas Smith from inside the house.'

Martin's face tightened. 'Is this bogus or real?'

Talley went back to the phone. 'Warren? Who else knows about this?'

'Just us, Chief. Me and Sarah, and now you.'

'If this turns out to be real, I don't want the press finding out about this. Tell Sarah. That means you don't talk about this with anyone, not even the other police, not even off the record.'

Talley looked at Martin as he spoke. She nodded, agreeing.

'If Rooney and those other guys see the press talking about some-one in the house calling out, I don't know what they might do.'

'I understand, Chief. I'll tell Sarah.'

'Put him on.'

A boy came on the line, his voice low and careful, but not fright-ened. 'Hello? Is this the Chief?'

'This is Chief Talley. Tell me your name, son.'

'Thomas Smith. I'm in the house that's on TV. Dennis hit my dad and now he won't wake up. You gotta come get him.'

'I have a couple of questions for you first, Thomas. Who's in the house with you?'

'These three guys, Dennis, Kevin and Mars.'

'Besides them.'

'My father and sister.'

The boy could have got all of this information off the news, but so far as Talley knew, no one had as yet reported, or knew, the where-abouts of the mother. They were still trying to locate her.

'What about your mother?'

'She's in Florida with my Aunt Kate.'

Talley made a scribbling gesture with his hand. Martin glanced at Ellison, who fumbled out his spiral notepad and a pen.

'What's your aunt's name, bud?'

'Kate Toepfer. She has blonde hair.'

Talley repeated it, watching Ellison write. 'Where does she live?'

'West Palm Beach.'

Talley didn't bother to cover the phone. 'We got the boy. Get a number for this woman, Kate Toepfer in West Palm Beach, that's where the mother is.'

Talley went back to the boy. Martin stepped close, pulling at his arm to tip the phone so that she could hear.

'Where you are now, son? Could they catch you talking to me?'

'They locked me in my room. I'm on my sister's cellphone.'

'Where's that, your room?'

'Upstairs.'

'OK. Where's your dad and sister?'

'My sister's locked in her room. My dad's down in the office. He needs a doctor.'

'Was he shot?'

'Dennis hit him, and now he won't wake up.'

'Is he bleeding?'

'Not any more. He just won't wake up. I'm really scared.'

'OK, Thomas, we're going to get you out of there as fast as we can, but I want to ask something. Could you let yourself out of your window if we were down below to catch you?'

'They've got the windows nailed shut. But even if they didn't, they could see me.'

'They could see you climbing out of the window even though you're alone?'

'We have security cameras. They could see on the monitors in my folks' room if they were looking.'

'OK, son, one more thing. Dennis told me that he had set up the house to burn with gasoline. Is that true?'

'They've got a bucket of gas in the entry hall. I saw it when they brought me downstairs. It really stinks.'

The boy's voice dropped. 'They're coming.' Then he hung up.

Martin took a deep breath. 'You think they caught him?'

Talley closed the phone. 'I don't think so. He didn't sound panicked when he shut the phone; he just had to end the call.'

Martin's expression was grim. 'If the father is in imminent danger, we might have to risk a breach.'

'The boy didn't say anyone is dying, he just said the man is hurt.'

Talley repeated Thomas's description of Walter Smith's condition.

Martin nodded. 'So we've got a possible concussion, but we can't be sure. We can't ask Rooney about the father. He might get it in his head that one of those kids is calling out.'

Maddox agreed. 'When I talk with Rooney again I'll push him to find out how everyone's doing. Maybe I can kick free some information about the father.'

Martin looked back at Talley. 'If the boy calls again, he'll call through your office.'

'I would guess so. He must've gotten the department's number from information.'

Talley knew what she wanted. 'I'll have someone in my office around the clock. If he calls, they'll page me and I'll bring you in.'

Martin looked at Maddox. 'I want you and Ellison set up in front of that house so we can start breaking these guys down.'

Talley knew what that meant: they would maintain a high noise-level profile, phoning Rooney periodically throughout the night to keep him awake. They would try to wear him down by depriving him of sleep. Sometimes, if you got them tired enough, they gave up.

Martin turned back to Talley. She put out her hand, and Talley took it. 'I appreciate your help, Chief. You've done a good job keeping this situation under control.'

'Thanks, Captain.'

'You want to relieve your people now, that's fine. I'd like four of your officers for liaison with the locals, but past that, we've got it.'

'It's yours, Captain. You have my numbers. If you need me, call. Otherwise, I'll grab a few hours' sleep and see you in the morning.'

Talley thanked Mrs Peña for her help, then went to his car. He wondered if Jane and Amanda were still at dinner or waiting at home.

KEN SEYMORE was sitting in his car, near the gate. He told the two cops there, who had asked him what he was doing, that he was waiting for a pool photographer to arrive from Los Angeles. Going to snap some shots of the guys guarding the development, he had said. That had been enough. They'd left him alone.

When Seymore saw Talley drive out, he picked up his phone.

'He's leaving.' That was all he needed to say.

Friday, 8:46pm. 'Earth to Mom?'

Jane Talley focused on her daughter. 'Sorry.'

'What were you thinking?'

'If your father likes my new hair colour.'

Amanda's face darkened. 'Like you should care. Please.'

'All right. I was wondering if that mess is going to blow up in his face. Is that better?'

They had stopped at *Le Chine*, a Vietnamese-Thai place in a mall near the freeway. They ate there often, sometimes with Jeff.

Jane had toyed with the plain white rice, but that was it. She put down her fork. 'Let me tell you something.'

'Can't we go home? I don't want to be here, anyway. I told him that.'

'Don't say "him". He's your father.'

'Whatever.'

'He's having a hard time.'

'A year ago it was a hard time, now it's just boring.'

Jane was so tired of keeping all the balls in the air, of being the supportive nurturing mother, of waiting for Jeff to come to his senses, that she wanted to scream. A flash of anger shook her.

'Let me tell you something. This has been hard on everybody; on you, on me, on him. He's not like this. It was that goddamned job.'

'Here we go with the job.'

Jane called for the bill, so livid that she didn't trust herself to look at her daughter. As always, the owner, who knew they were Talley's family, insisted that there was no charge. As always, Jane paid, this time quickly, in cash, not waiting for change.

'Let's go.' Jane walked out to the parking lot, still not looking at Amanda. She got behind the wheel but did not start the car. Amanda slid in beside her, pulling the door.

When Jane figured out what she needed to say, she said it.

'I am scared to death that your father is finally going to give up and call it quits. I could see it in him tonight. Your father knows what this is doing to us, he's not stupid. We talk, Amanda; he says he's empty, I don't know how to fill him; he says he's dead, I don't know how to bring him to life. You think I don't try? Here we are, split apart, time passing, him wallowing in his damn depression; your father will end it just to spare us. Well, miss, let me tell you something: I don't want to be spared. I *choose* not to be spared. Your father used to be filled with life and strength, and I fell in love with that special man more deeply than you can know. If you think I'm a loser by waiting for him, tough. I could have other men; I don't want them. I don't even know if he still loves me, but I love him, I want this marriage, and I damn well care whether or not he likes my hair.'

Jane, crying, saw that Amanda was crying too. She slumped back in the seat, bouncing her head on the headrest.

Sharp rapping on the window startled her.

'Ma'am? Are you all right?'

Jane rolled down the window, just an inch, two. The man seemed embarrassed, leaning forward, one hand on the roof, the other on her door, his expression asking if there was anything he could do.

'I'm sorry, I know it's not my business. I heard crying.'

'That's all right. We're fine. Thank you.'

She was reaching for the key when he jerked open the door, pushing her sideways into Amanda.

Later, she would know that his name was Marion Clewes.

Friday, 9:12pm. Talley turned off his command radio. It wasn't his show any more, so he didn't need the radio. He needed to think.

Stretched out ahead and curving between the mountains, the street was bright with headlights rushing towards him. The past six hours had flicked past, one moment overtaking the next with an intensity of experience that Talley hadn't known in a long time; part fear, part elation. Talley found himself working through the events of the day, and realised that he was enjoying himself. That surprised him. It was as if some dormant part of himself was waking.

Talley turned onto the condominium grounds. He found Jane's car parked in the first of the two spaces that were his, and pulled in beside it. Stepping from his car, he noticed that the parking lot was darker than usual; both security lights were out. Talley was locking his car as a woman stepped from the path that led to his building.

'Chief Talley? Could I have a word with you?'

Talley thought she might be one of his neighbours. Most of the people in the complex knew he was the chief of police, often coming to him with complaints and problems.

'It's pretty late. Could this keep until tomorrow?'

She was attractive, but not pretty, with a clean, businesslike expression, and hair that cupped her face. He did not recognise her.

'I wish it could, Chief, but we have to discuss this tonight.'

Talley heard a single footstep behind him, the *shush* of shoe on grit, then an arm hooked his throat from behind, lifting him backwards and off his feet. Someone held a gun before his face and he stopped struggling.

'That's better. We're only going to talk, that's all, but I will kill you if I have to.'

They lowered him, gave him his feet again. Someone opened his car as someone else felt beneath his jacket and round his waist.

'Where's your gun?'

'I don't carry it.'

'Bullshit. Where is it?'

The hands went to his ankles.

'I don't carry it. I'm the Chief. I don't have to.'

They pushed him behind the wheel. Talley saw shapes; he wasn't sure how many; maybe three. Someone in the back seat smashed the ceiling light with the gun, then pushed the gun hard to his neck.

'Start the car. Back up. We're just going to talk to you.'

'Who are you?'

Talley tried to turn, but strong hands shoved his face forward. Two men wearing black knit ski masks and gloves were in the back seat.

'The car. Back up.'

Talley did as he was told, his headlights swinging across the path. The woman was gone. Red taillights waited at the far end of the parking lot.

'See that car? Follow it. We won't go far.'

Talley pulled in tight on the car. It was a green Ford Mustang with California plates. Talley worked at remembering the number, 2KLX561, then glanced in the mirror as a second car tucked in behind his.

'Is this about what's happening?'

'Just drive. Don't worry about it.'

The Mustang drove back to the street, then out along Flanders Road to a minimall less than a mile away. All the shops were closed, the parking lot empty. Talley followed the Mustang into the alley behind the shops, where it stopped beside a Dumpster.

'Pull up closer. Closer. Bumper to bumper.'

He bumped the Mustang.

'Turn off the ignition.'

Talley had known a kind of fear when he had worked the tactical teams on SWAT; but that was an impersonal fear, a going-into-combat fear. This was different, up close and personal. Men were assassinated like this, their bodies left in Dumpsters.

He turned off the ignition. The second car came up so close that it was inches from his own, blocking him in.

The passenger door opened. A third man slipped inside, also wearing a mask and gloves. He was wearing a black jacket over a grey T-shirt and jeans. When his left sleeve hiked up, a gold Rolex flashed. He wasn't large, about Talley's size, trim. The skin around his mouth and eyes was tanned. He held a cellphone.

'OK, Chief, I know you're scared, but trust me, unless you do something stupid, we're not here to hurt you. Do you understand?'

Talley tried to recall the Mustang's licence number.

'Don't just stare at me, Chief. We've got to make some headway.'

'What do you want?'

The third man gestured to the back seat, giving Talley another glimpse of the watch. Talley thought of him as the Watchman.

'The man behind you is going to reach round and get hold of you. Don't freak out. OK? He's just going to hold you.'

The arm looped round his neck again; a hand took his left wrist, twisted it behind his back; another took his right; the second man in the back was helping.

Talley could barely breathe. 'What is this?'

'Listen.' The Watchman put the phone to Talley's ear. 'Say hello.'

The phone was cold against Talley's ear. 'Who is this?'

Jane's voice, shaky and frightened. 'Jeff? Is that you?'

Talley tried to buck away from the arm crossing his throat; he strained to pull his arms free, but couldn't. Seconds passed before Talley realised the Watchman was talking to him.

'Take it easy, Chief. She's all right. Your kid, she's all right, too. Now just remember: from this point on, you control what happens to them. You want to talk to her again, see that she's OK?'

Talley nodded against the pressure of the arm, finally managed to croak, 'You sonofabitch.'

The Watchman held the phone to Talley's ear again.

'Jane?'

'What's going on, Jeff? Who are these people?'

'I don't know. Are you all right? Is Mandy?'

'Jeff, I'm scared.' Jane was crying.

The Watchman took back the phone. 'That's enough.'

'Who the hell are you?'

'Can we let you go and you won't do something stupid?'

'You can let go.'

The Watchman glanced at the back seat, and Talley was released. 'Walter Smith has two computer disks in his house that belong to us. We want them, and you're going to see that we get them.'

Talley didn't know what the Watchman was talking about; he shook his head. 'What does that mean? What?'

'You're going to control the scene.'

'The Sheriffs control the scene.'

'Not any more. It's your scene. You'll take it back or whatever it is you have to do, because no one—let me repeat that—*no one* is going into that house until *my* people go in that house.'

'You don't know what you're talking about. I can't control that.'

'I know exactly what I'm talking about. You have a coordinated mixed scene now with your people—the Bristo Police Department—and the Sheriffs. In just over a couple of hours, a group of my people are going to arrive at York Estates. You will tell everyone involved that they are an FBI tactical team. They'll look the part.'

'I don't have any idea what you're talking about. I can't control any of this. I can't control what happens in that house.'

'You'd better get up to speed fast, then. Your wife and kid are counting on you.'

'What do you want me to do?'

'You get my people set up, then you wait to hear from me.'

The Watchman handed Talley the cellphone. 'When this phone rings, you answer. It'll be me. I'll tell you what to do. When it comes time to go in the house, my people will be the first in. Nothing will be removed from that house except by my people. Do you get that?'

Talley gripped the phone with both hands. 'OK. All right.'

'You're going to be thinking about calling the FBI or bringing the Sheriffs in, about getting me before something happens to your wife and child, but, Chief, think about this: I have people right there in York Estates, reporting everything that happens. If you bring anyone in, if you do *anything* other than what I am telling you to do, you'll get your wife and kid back in the mail. Are we clear on that?'

'Yes.'

'When I have what I want, your wife and daughter will be released. We're cool with that.'

'What is it you want? Disks? Like computer disks? Where are they, where in the house?'

'Two disks, bigger than normal disks. They're called Zip disks, labelled Disk One and Disk Two. We won't know where they are until we find them, but Smith will know.' The Watchman opened the door, his glance flicking to the phone. 'Answer when it rings, Chief.'

Doors opened, closed, and the Mustang pulled away. The second car roared away.

Talley started his car and spun the wheel hard, flooring it, fishtailing gravel. He hit his lights and siren, blasting straight back to his condo, never bothered to pull into a space, just left the car like that in the parking lot, lights popping, and ran inside.

The condo was empty. He went upstairs to the little desk in his bedroom where he stared at the photographs. Jane and Amanda, much younger then, stared back in a picture taken at Disneyland. Talley choked a sob in his chest. He went to his closet for the blue nylon gym bag on the top shelf, and brought the bag to his bed. He took out the pistol that he had carried during his SWAT days, a Colt .45 Model 1911.

Talley ejected the empty magazine, filled it with seven bullets, then reseated it. He dug through the gym bag for the black ballistic nylon holster. He took off his uniform, then put on blue jeans and tennis shoes. He fitted the holster onto his belt at his side, then covered it with a black sweatshirt. He clipped his badge to his belt.

The cellphone that the Watchman gave him was sitting on his desk. Talley stared at it, thinking he should go directly to the FBI. That was what he would have done except that he believed that the Watchman was telling the truth about having someone at York Estates, and would kill his family.

Talley put the cellphone in his pocket and drove to his office.

The Bristo Camino Police Department was a two-storey space in the mall that used to be a toy store. Talley left his car at the kerb.

Warren Kenner, sitting at the front desk, raised his eyebrows in surprise when Talley entered. 'Hey, Chief. I thought you went off duty.'

'I've got more to do.'

Sarah waved from the communications bay. Talley nodded at her, but didn't stop to chat the way he ordinarily would. He went straight to the National Law Enforcement Telecommunication System computer, typed in the Mustang's licence number and requested a California Department of Motor Vehicles search.

The DMV search came back, showing that licence plate 2KLX561 was unregistered. Next, he typed in the name *Walter Smith* and ran it through the National Crime Information Center, limiting the search to white males in the southwest within a five-year time frame. The NCIC search kicked back thirty-one hits. He skimmed the results. Twenty-two of the thirty-two arrestees were currently incarcerated, and the remaining ten were too young. As far as the law enforcement computer network knew, the Walter Smith who lived in York Estates was just another upstanding American with something in his house that men were willing to kill for.

Talley deleted the screen, then tried to recall as many details as possible about the three men and the woman who kidnapped him. The woman: short dark hair that cupped her face, five foot five, slender, light-coloured blouse and skirt; it had been too dark to see any more. The three men had worn nicely tailored jackets, gloves and masks; he had noticed no identifying characteristics. He tried to remember background noise from when he spoke with Jane, some sound that could identify her location, but there had been none.

Talley took out the Watchman's phone, wondering if a print could be lifted. It was a new black Nokia. *Think*. It was his link to the people who had Jane and Amanda, a link that might lead back to them. If the Watchman had called Jane's location, that number would be in the memory. Talley pressed redial. No number came up. He checked the phone's stored memory. No numbers were listed. *Think!* Someone had paid for the phone and was paying for its service. Talley turned off the phone, then turned it back on. As the view screen lit, the phone's number appeared. He copied the number, his only lead.

Then Talley realised he had another lead: Walter Smith. Smith could identify these people, Smith had what they wanted, and Smith might even be able to tell him where they had taken Jane and Amanda. Smith had answers. All Talley had to do was reach him.

TALLEY CALLED Larry Anders when he was five minutes from the development, saying to meet him inside the south entrance, and to wait there alone. A long line of gawkers made the going slow once Talley turned off Flanders Road. He burped his siren to make them pull to the side, then waved himself through the blockade.

Anders was parked on the side of the road. Talley pulled up behind him and flicked his lights.

Anders walked back to Talley's window, looking nervous. 'Chief?'

'Get in.' Talley waited as Anders walked round the front of the car and climbed in. Anders wasn't the oldest person on his department, but he was the senior officer in years served, and Talley respected him. He thought again that the man in the ski mask had someone here, and wondered if that person was Larry Anders.

Anders squirmed. 'Chief, why are you staring at me like that?'

'I have something for you to do. You're not to tell anyone else what you're doing, not Metzger, not the other guys, not the Sheriffs, no one; just tell them that I want you to run down some background info, but don't tell them what. You understand me, Larry?'

Anders replied slowly, 'This isn't something illegal, is it, Chief?'

'It's police work, the real thing. I want you to find out as much as you can about Walter Smith.'

'The guy in the house?'

'I believe he's involved in illegal activity or associates with people who are. I need to find out what that is. Talk to the neighbours, but don't be obvious about it. Don't tell anyone what you suspect. Try to find out whatever you can about him, his business, his clients, anything that will give us a handle on him. When you've finished here, go back to the office and run him through the FBI and the NLETS database. I went back five years, but you go back twenty.'

'What's the problem with telling our guys? I mean, why not?'

'Because that's the way I want it, Larry. I have a good reason, I just can't tell you right now, but I'm trusting that you'll keep your word.'

'I will, Chief. Yes, sir, I will.'

Talley gave him the Nokia's cellphone number on a slip of paper. 'Before you do that, I want you to trace this cellphone number. Find out who it's billed to. If you need a court order, call the Palmdale District Court. They have a judge on page for night work.'

'The judge, he'll want to know why, won't he?'

'Tell him we believe this number will provide life-or-death information about one of the men in the house.' Talley thought, trying to remember if there was something else, something that might give him a line to find out who he was dealing with. 'When you get back to the office, run a DMV stolen-vehicle search for a green Mustang, this year's model. It would be a recent theft, maybe even today.'

Anders took out his pad to make notes. 'Ah, you got a number?'

'It's running a dead plate. If you get a hit, note where it was stolen. Who was checking into the building permits?'

'Ah, that was Cooper.'

'I want you to find out who built that house. Update me with everything you find out, whatever time it is. Don't use the radio. Call my cell. Get to it.'

Talley watched Anders drive away. He parked outside Mrs Peña's house and went to the Sheriff's command van. The back gate was open. Martin, Hicks and the intelligence officer were clumped round the coffee machine.

Talley rapped on the side of the van as he climbed inside.

Martin glanced over. 'I thought you left.'

'I'm taking back command of the scene.'

Martin's brow furrowed. 'I don't understand. *You* requested our help. You couldn't wait to hand off to me.'

Talley had readied the lie. 'I know I did, Captain, but it's a liability issue. The city supervisors want a representative of Bristo to be in charge. I'm sorry, but that's the way it has to be. As of now, I'm resuming command of the scene.'

Hicks put his fists on his hips. 'What kind of half-assed hicktown crap is this?'

Talley pointedly looked at Hicks. 'No tactical action is to be taken without my approval. Is that clear?'

Martin stalked across the van, stopping only inches away. 'Outside. I want to talk about this.'

Talley didn't move. He knew that the Sheriffs regularly worked under local restraints when they functioned in advisory and support roles; Martin would still be in direct control of her people, though Talley would command the operation. Martin would go along.

'There's nothing to talk about, Captain. I'm not going to tell you how to do your job; I need you, and I appreciate your being here. But I have to sign off on any action we take, and right now I'm saying that there will be no tactical action.'

Martin started to say something, then stopped. She seemed to search his eyes. Talley wondered if she could see that he was lying.

He stepped back. He wanted to get out of the van. 'I want to talk to Maddox. Is he still at the house?'

Martin lowered her voice. 'What's wrong, Chief? You look like something's bothering you.'

'It has to be this way, that's all. I want to see Maddox.'

'He's in the cul-de-sac. I'll tell him you're on the way.'

Talley found Maddox and Ellison waiting at their car.

Ellison looked curious. 'Can't get too much of a good thing, Chief?'

'Guess not. Has he made any more demands?'

Maddox shook his head. 'Nothing.'

'All right. I want to move up by the house.'

Maddox opened his driver's-side door. 'You taking back the phone?'

'That's it. Let's go.'

They eased the car into the cul-de-sac and returned to the house.

WHEN HER DOOR OPENED, Jennifer saw Mars framed in dim light.

Mars said, 'We're hungry. You're going to cook.'

'I'm not going to cook for you. You're out of your mind.'

'You'll cook.' He pushed her through the door, along the hall and down the stairs. Two frozen pizzas were sitting on the counter. 'Heat the pizza.'

Mars went to the refrigerator. Jennifer remembered the paring knife, pushed behind the food processor when they first invaded her home. She glanced towards it. When she looked back at Mars, he was watching her, holding a carton of eggs.

'I want scrambled eggs and hot dogs on mine.'

Jennifer got a frying pan and the other things she would need, broke nine eggs into a glass bowl, then put the frying pan on to heat. Mars stood in the family room, staring at her.

'Stop watching me. I'm going to burn the eggs.'

Mars went to the French doors. Jennifer beat the eggs, sprayed the pan with cooking spray, then poured in the eggs. She glanced over at Mars, expecting that he would be watching her, but he had moved deeper into the family room. The paring knife was sticking out from behind the food processor, directly beneath the cabinet with the plates. She glanced at Mars again. She couldn't see his face, only the shadow of his bulk. He might have been looking at her, but she couldn't tell. She walked directly to the cabinet, took down some plates and picked up the knife. She fought the urge to glance at Mars. She pushed the knife under her shirt into the waist of her shorts horizontally so that it lay against the flat of her belly.

'What are you doing?'

'Getting plates.'

'You're burning the eggs. I can smell 'em.'

She brought the plates to the stove, feeling the hard shape of the knife low on her belly.

Across the house in the office, the telephone rang.

Friday, 11:02pm. The Sheriffs had set up a dedicated phone for Maddox and Ellison. It was looped by a cell link from Maddox's car to the command van, where it was hard-wired into the Smiths' phone line. It provided the negotiators with freedom of movement while allowing conversations to be recorded in the van. Martin, Hicks and everyone else in the van would be listening to every word. Talley didn't want that.

He took out his cellphone, but he had forgotten Smith's number and had to ask for it.

Maddox, watching him, said, 'We've got the hard line.'

'I'm more comfortable with this. You got the number?'

Unless the Sheriffs had changed the phone block, the Smiths' phone should still accept Talley's calls. Ellison read off the number as Maddox watched Talley. Talley knew they thought this was odd, but he didn't care.

'Why are you doing this?'

'What?'

'Out of the blue, you're back, you're calling the house. Every call has to have a point. Why?'

Talley stopped dialling the number and tried to order his thoughts. He wanted Smith. Smith was his link to the people who had his wife and daughter. He needed to say something that would bring Maddox onto his side.

'I'm scared that Smith is dead. I think I can push Rooney into telling us without tipping him off that the boy called.'

'If he's dead, the boy would've told us.'

'So what do we do, Maddox? You want to breach the house?'

Maddox held his gaze, then nodded. 'All right, then.'

Talley redialled the number. The phone rang, Rooney picked up.

'That you, Talley? I saw you come back.'

For the space of three heartbeats, Talley said nothing. It took that time for Talley to push aside the anxiety that he knew would be in his voice. He could have nothing weak in his voice. Nothing that might warn Rooney or put him on guard.

'Hello, Dennis. You there in the office, watching us?'

The shutters flicked open, then closed.

'I guess you are. Did you miss me?'

'I don't like that new guy, Maddox. He thinks I'm stupid, calling every fifteen minutes, pretending he wants to make sure we're all right, but it's to keep us awake. I'm not stupid.'

Talley felt himself grow calm now he was back on the phone. He had hated it earlier today, but now felt a confidence he hadn't known in years, a sense that he could control this world if not the larger one.

'I came back tonight because we've got a big problem out here.'

Talley knew that what he was about to say would surprise Maddox and Ellison, so he glanced at them and touched his lips. Then he firmed his voice to show that he was serious and concerned.

'I need you to let me talk to Mr Smith.'

'We been through that, Talley. Forget it.'

'I can't forget it this time, Dennis. These people out here, the Sheriffs, they think you won't let me talk to Mr Smith or his children because they're dead. They think you've murdered them.'

'That's bullshit!'

'If you don't let me speak with Mr Smith, they are going to assume that he's dead, and they are going to breach the house.'

Rooney started cursing and shouting that everyone was going to die and that the house would burn. Talley let him vent.

Maddox gripped Talley's arm. 'You can't say somethin' like that!'

Talley held up a hand, telling him to back off. He waited for a break in Dennis's rant.

'Dennis, I believe you, but they don't. This isn't up to me, son. I believe you. But unless you give me something to convince them, they're going in. Let me speak to him, Dennis.'

Talley's hope was that Smith was unconscious. If Rooney would admit his condition, Talley had a shot at getting Smith released.

Rooney screamed, '*Shit!*'

Talley could hear the frustration in Rooney's voice. He waited. Rooney was silent and that meant he was thinking; he couldn't put Smith on the phone, but he was scared to admit that Smith was injured. Talley softened his voice, made it understanding and sympathetic. *We're both in this together, pal.*

'Is something wrong in there, Dennis? Is there a reason you can't put Smith on the phone?'

'He got knocked out. He won't wake up.'

Talley knew better than to ask how; it would put Rooney on the defensive, and Talley didn't want to do that. He had Smith's situation out in the open, so now he could try to get Smith.

'So you're saying that Mr Smith is unconscious. OK. That explains things. Now we can deal with it.'

'They better not try to come in here.'

They, not *you*.

'Are we talking about a head injury here, Dennis? I'm not asking how this happened, but is that what's wrong with him?'

'It was an accident.'

'Dennis, now I understand why you couldn't put him on, but you've got a guy in there who needs to be in the hospital. Let me come get him.'

'Screw that! I know you bastards, you'll rush the house.'

'No. No, we wouldn't do that.' Talley could have suggested sending in a paramedic or a doctor, but he didn't want anyone going in; he wanted Walter Smith coming out. 'If you won't let us come in, all you have to do is put him outside the front door.'

'I'm not stupid! I'm not gonna walk out the door with all the snipers you have out there!'

'No one is going to shoot you. Just put him outside and we'll come get him. If you save his life, it will help you when you get to court.'

Rooney's voice rose. 'No!' He slammed down the phone.

KEVIN WENT to the couch and stared down at Walter Smith. 'We should let them have him. I think he's having seizures.'

Smith would be still as a corpse, then he would suddenly jerk, his whole body twitching. Dennis couldn't look at him.

Dennis went to the shutters. Nothing had changed since he'd looked the time before, but he was scared. He was hungry and tired. His pockets bulged with the money he had stuffed in them.

Kevin came over to him. 'Dennis, it's bad enough we got the Chinaman and that cop; this guy dies they'll add another murder charge.'

'Shut up, Kevin. I'm working on it.'

Walter Smith twitched and trembled again. It looked like he was freezing to death, the way you'd shiver if you were sleeping on a block of ice.

Mars and the girl came in with the pizzas, but when the girl saw her father, she dropped the pizza and ran straight to her father.

'What's wrong with him? *Daddy?!*'

She dropped to her knees, leaning over her father.

'Why is he shaking like this? Aren't you going to do something?'

Kevin picked up the phone. 'Call them. Let them have him.'

'No.'

'They'll like it that you're trying to help. They might even cut us some slack. Think about it, Dennis. *Think.*'

Kevin stepped closer, his whisper more than a plea. 'If those SWAT guys come in here, you'll never keep the money.'

Dennis wanted the money. He took the phone and punched in Talley's number.

TALLEY WAS CHARGING his phone off the cigarette lighter in Maddox's car when the phone rang. He tensed, a jag of fear jolting him because he thought it was the Watchman's Nokia.

He opened his phone. 'Talley.'

It was Rooney.

'OK, Talley. If you want him, come get him. But just you.'

Talley had thought it was over, thought he had completely blown any chance at getting to Smith, but here was Rooney delivering him. He had a chance at Jane and Amanda!

He muted the phone to hiss at Maddox. 'Ambulance. He's coming out.'

Maddox went on the hard line as Talley un-muted his phone.

'OK, Dennis. I'm here. I'm with you. Let's figure this out.'

'There's nothing to figure out, goddammit. Come get him. But you better keep SWAT outta here. That's the deal.'

'I can't carry him by myself. I'll have to bring someone else.'

'Liar! You're going to try to kill me!'

'That won't happen, Dennis. You can trust me. Me and one other person and a stretcher. That's it.'

'All right! You and one other guy, but that's it! You gotta strip down! I want you stripped! I gotta know you aren't carrying guns!'

'OK, Dennis. If that's what you want, that's what we'll do.'

'If those bastards try something these kids are gonna die! Everybody's gonna die.'

The connection popped in Talley's ear. Rooney was gone.

Maddox stared at him, and Ellison smiled.

'Sonofa*bitch*. You kicked one free. That was great work, man.'

Talley left them without a word. He climbed into the back seat, stripped off his clothes except for his underwear and shoes, and waited for the ambulance. In an earlier life Talley would have felt proud, but now he wasn't. He hadn't done it for Walter Smith. He was risking Smith's life, his own, and possibly the children's in the house. He had done it for himself, and for Amanda and Jane.

Friday, 11:19pm. Martin buzzed around him like an angry wasp. She had ridden up in the ambulance with an ER doctor named Klaus from Canyon Country Emergency. 'Wear a bulletproof vest. Just strap it over your chest, he'll be able to see you're not armed.'

'The deal was that we'd be stripped. I don't want to spook him.'

One of the paramedics, an overweight man named Bigelow, volunteered to go with Talley. Here was Bigelow, walking over from the ambulance, wearing only striped boxers with his clunky paramedic shoes and black socks up to his knees. Bigelow's partner, a woman named Colby, brought the stretcher.

Talley called the house on his cellphone. Rooney answered.

'OK, Dennis. Put him outside. We're stripped, so you can see we're unarmed. We'll wait in the drive. We won't approach the house until after you've closed the door.'

Rooney hung up without answering.

Talley glanced at Bigelow. 'Here we go. I'll walk in front of you going up to the door. Once we have him on the stretcher, I'll take the rear position coming out. OK?'

Talley and Bigelow went round the car and stepped in front of the lights. It was like passing into a world of glare.

Talley watched the house. First, the shutters opened like a narrowed eye. That would be Rooney, looking them over for weapons. Smith's front door opened. Kevin Rooney and Mars Krupchek waddled out with Smith between them, put him on the front entry about six feet from the door, then returned to the house.

'OK, let's do it.' Talley went directly to Smith. The contusion on the side of his head was visible even from the mouth of the drive.

Bigelow said, 'Let me set down by his head.'

Talley stepped away, letting the paramedic open the stretcher. Talley watched Smith. Smith trembled from the centre of his body, and Talley grew frightened that the man might be in a coma.

Bigelow fingered Smith's neck, probing for a cervical injury, and seemed satisfied by what he found. 'OK. We don't need a brace. I'll support his head and shoulders. You lift beneath his hips and knees.'

They slid Smith onto the stretcher and moved straight down the drive to the street and into the lights, where they were immediately surrounded by Hicks's tactical team.

Colby took over from Talley to help Bigelow. Ellison brought over Talley's clothes, and Talley pulled on his jeans while they loaded Smith into the ambulance. Talley followed Klaus inside.

'I have to talk to him.'

Klaus peeled back Smith's eyelid and flashed a penlight in his eye. He did the same with the other eye. 'We've got unequal pupilation. At best it's a concussion, but it could mean brain damage. We'll have to do plates and a CT scan at the hospital to know for sure.'

'Wake him. I need to talk to him.'

Klaus checked Smith's pulse. 'I'm not going to wake this man.'

'I just need him for a few minutes. That's why I got him.'

Klaus pressed his stethoscope to Smith's neck. 'He's going to the hospital. He could have an intracranial haematoma or a fracture, or both. You get a pressure build-up in the brain, it can be bad.'

Talley took Smith by the face and shook him. 'Smith! Wake up!'

Klaus grabbed Talley's hand, trying to pull it away. 'What the hell are you doing? Get away from him!'

Talley shook Smith harder. 'Wake up, dammit!'

Smith's eyes fluttered, one open more than the other.

Talley said, 'Who are you?'

Klaus pushed at him now. 'Let go of him. I'll have you brought up on charges, you sonofabitch.'

Smith's eyes lost their focus and closed.

Talley took Klaus by the arm, trying to make him see. 'Use smelling salts, give him a shot, whatever. I just need a minute.'

Colby cranked the engine, and Talley slapped at the wall, shouting. '*Don't move this van!*'

Klaus and Bigelow both stared at him.

Klaus slowly looked at Talley's hand gripping his arm. 'I'm not going to wake him. I don't even know that I can. Now let go of me.'

'We're talking about lives here. Innocent lives. I just need to ask him a few questions.'

'Let go of me, goddammit. We're taking this man to the hospital.'

Martin was watching him from the door, Metzger behind her.

Talley released the doctor's arm. 'When is he going to wake up?'

'I don't know if he'll ever wake up. You get bleeding between the skull and brain, the pressure can build to such a degree that brain death can result. Now stay in or get out, but just let us go.'

Talley climbed out of the ambulance and pulled Metzger aside. 'Who's still here? Which of our guys is still here?'

'Jorgy. I think Campbell is still—'

'Then Jorgenson stays here. I want you waiting in this guy's lap. I want to know the second, and I mean the *second*, that he wakes up.'

He turned away and saw Martin watching him. He didn't care.

DENNIS TURNED to the girl. 'Your old man's out. You happy now?'

'Thank you.'

'I'm starving. Go back in the kitchen and fix something else. This time don't throw it on the floor.'

Mars took the girl back to the kitchen.

When they were gone, Dennis noticed that Kevin was staring at him. 'What?'

'We're not going to get out of here. Mars and I don't care about the money. You won't let go of it and that's why we're still here. There's no way to get away with it, Dennis. We're surrounded. We're on frigging television. We're *screwed*.'

Dennis pushed out of the chair so quickly that Kevin jumped back. He was sick of dealing with their negativity.

'We're screwed until we think of a way out. Then we're not screwed, we're rich.'

Dennis went to the den. He wanted a drink, and the den was his favourite room. The dark wood panelling and leather furniture made Dennis feel rich, like he was in the lobby of a fine hotel. And the bar was beautiful: bright beaten copper that looked a thousand years old, and stainless-steel fixtures gleaming with the overhead light. Dennis selected a bottle of vodka, then found ice in a small refrigerator and glasses on a shelf. He poured a short one, then went round the bar to sit on a stool. Dennis peeled a $100 bill from the roll in his pocket and tossed it on the bar. 'Keep the change, m'man.'

Dennis drank most of the vodka, a stiff belt that pushed its way into his head. He refilled his glass. The clean cold vodka made his eyes water. He rubbed his eyes, but couldn't make the water stop.

'Dennis?'

Dennis cleared his eyes, then slid off the bar stool. 'Be quiet, Kevin. I'm not leaving here until I can take that cash.'

Dennis went back to the office and unplugged the phone. There was no point in talking to the cops until he knew what to say.

THE CHANNEL EIGHT news van was parked at the edge of the empty lot. The reporter was a pretty boy, couldn't have been twenty-five. The reporter pool complained because there were no toilets; Seymore asked the guy if it would be all right to step behind their van, take the lizard for a walk. The pretty boy laughed, sure, but watch where you step, they got a regular lizard trail back there.

Seymore stepped behind the van. Coming out he saw the reporter conferring with his producer and cameraman. They looked excited.

Seymore said, 'Thanks, buddy.'

'No problem. You hear? They're getting one out of the house.'

Seymore stopped. 'They are?'

'I think it's the father. He's hurt.'

A siren spooled up, and they all knew it was the ambulance. Every camera crew in the lot hustled to the street in hopes of a shot.

Seymore's phone rang as the siren Dopplered away. He answered as he walked off, lowering his voice but unable to hide his irritation. He knew who it was; he started right in.

'Why the hell I gotta hear this from a *reporter*?'

'Do you think I can get to a phone any time I want? I'm right out front in this; I have to be careful.'

'All right. So was he talking? The guy here says he was hurt.'
'I don't know. I couldn't get close enough.'
'Did he have the disks? Maybe he had the disks.'
'I don't know.'
Seymore felt himself losing it. 'If anyone should know, it's *you*, goddammit. What the hell are we paying you for?'
'They're taking him to Canyon Country Hospital.'
The line went dead. Seymore called Glen Howell.

PART THREE

Pearblossom, California

Friday, 11:36pm. Mikkelson and Dreyer found Mars Krupchek's trailer at the end of a paved road in Pearblossom, a farm community of orchards and day workers in the low foothills at the base of the Antelope Valley.

Dreyer swivelled the passenger-side floodlight and lit up the place. Krupchek's road ran the gut of a shallow canyon between two low ridges. No streetlights, no cable TV, no nothing out here; they had phone service and power, but that was about it.

Mikkelson, tall and athletic, got out first. Dreyer, short and square, came up beside her, the rocky soil crunching.

They approached the trailer. Mikkelson rapped on the door with her Maglite, calling, 'Anyone in there? This is the police.'

She did that twice, getting no answer, then tried the door. It was locked.

Mikkelson got the tyre iron from their trunk, wedged it in the jamb by the knob, and popped the door.

A smell like simmering mustard greens rolled out at them.

Mikkelson stepped inside and found the light switch. The interior of the trailer was dingy and cramped with tattered furniture.

Dreyer turned to the kitchen. 'Jesus, look at *that*.'

Five or six boxes, and Mikkelson would have laughed, but the overwhelming sight of so many screamed insanity. Later, the Sheriff's forensics people would count: 716 Count Chocula boxes, empty, flattened and folded, neatly bound with cord, stacked against

372

the walls and on the kitchen counters in great teetering towers, each box mutilated in exactly the same way, a single cigarette burn, charred and black, on the point of Count Chocula's nose.

Dreyer, not getting the same creepy read as Mikkelson, went for the joke. 'You think he got something good for all these box tops?'

'Put on your gloves. Let's be careful here.'

'It's cereal, for chrissake.'

'Just put on the gloves.'

'You think he eats it? Maybe he just scrounges for the boxes. There must be a giveaway, you know, a contest.'

The caravan was cut into three, the kitchen to their right, the living room where they entered, the bedroom to their left, all of it cramped and claustrophobic, littered with clothes and beer cans.

Mikkelson moved left to the bedroom, pulling on the disposable gloves, wondering about the smell. At the door, she lit up the bed with her Maglite torch, saw stained sheets in a rumpled mess, clothes on the floor, and the jars. 'Dreyer. I think we should call.'

Dreyer stepped up behind. 'Shit. What is that?'

Mikkelson stepped in, holding out her light. Gallon-sized glass jars lined the walls. Shapes floated in the jars, suspended in yellow fluid. Some of the jars were so jammed with fleshy shapes there was almost no fluid.

Mikkelson squatted for a better look, wanting to cover her mouth, maybe put on a gas mask or something so she wouldn't have to breathe the fetid air. 'Shit, it's squirrels. He's got squirrels in here.'

Dreyer left, keying his radio as he fled to the safer night air.

Mikkelson backed out of the room. She knew she should go through Krupchek's things, look for information, things that might help Talley at the scene. She went back to the kitchen, looking for the phone, found herself standing at the refrigerator.

Outside, Dreyer called, 'You coming out? The Sheriffs are sending detectives.'

The refrigerator came open without effort: empty and strangely clean against the squalor of the trailer, no soda, no beer, no leftovers, just white enamel that had been lovingly polished.

A thin metal door was set in the top of the box; the freezer. Mikkelson's hand had a mind of its own, reaching out, pulling the door. Her first thought was that it was a cabbage, wrapped in foil and clingfilm. She stared at it, stared hard, then closed the doors, never once, not once, tempted to touch that thing in the freezer.

Mikkelson left the trailer to wait with Dreyer in the hot night air, the two of them saying nothing, waiting for the Sheriffs, Mikkelson thinking, *Let them touch it.*

Santa Clarita, California

Friday, 11:40pm. Glen Howell took three rooms in the Comfort Inn, all at the rear of the motel with outside entrances. Marion Clewes had the woman and the girl bound hand and foot in one room, tape over their eyes and mouths.

Howell was sitting on his bed when he received the call from Ken Seymore, and heard that Walter Smith had been removed from the house.

'He just walked out?'

'They carried him. One of the pricks in there must've beaten him. They took him out in an ambulance.'

Howell sat silent for a moment, thinking. Smith in the hospital where they'd pop him full of dope, get him high, that was a problem.

Howell used his cellphone to call Palm Springs.

Phil Tuzee answered. Howell filled him in, then waited as Tuzee talked it over with the others.

Sonny Benza came back on the line. 'This is bad, Glen.'

'I know.'

'Find out if he has the disks and see if he's been talking to anyone. That won't be good if he's talking. His kids are still in that house?'

'Yeah.'

'Sonofabitch.'

Howell knew they were all thinking the same thing; a man desperate to save his kids might say anything. Howell tried to sound hopeful. 'If he's unconscious he can't be talking. The press pool out there is talking a concussion with possible brain injury. They make it sound like the guy's in a coma.'

'That's why those pricks let him out? Maybe we'll get lucky and the bastard will die.'

'Talley talked them into letting him out.'

'You know something, Glen? That sounds like the damn wheels are comin' off. Do I have to come out there myself?'

'No way, Sonny. I got it.'

'I don't want Smith talking, not to anyone, you understand?'

'I understand.'

'OK.' Benza hung up. It was their call; they had made it.

Howell picked up the hotel phone and called two rooms down. 'Come over here. I got something for you to do.'

Friday, 11:52pm. Talley paced the mouth of the cul-de-sac. When the phone rang he again thought it was the Watchman's Nokia, but it was his private line.

Larry Anders's voice was low, as if he were trying to keep his words private. 'I'm with Cooper here in the city planner's office.'

Talley took out his notepad. 'First tell me about the cell number.'

'The number is registered to Bakmanifelsu and Associates. It's a jewellery company in Beverly Hills. You want me to contact them?'

'Forget it. It's a dead end.' Talley knew without hearing more that the number had been cloned and stolen. 'What about the Mustang?'

'There's nothing, Chief. We got sixteen hits for cars that were still unrecovered, but nothing green came up.'

'OK. What about the building permits?'

'We can't find any of that, but the planner knew the developer, a man named Clive Briggs. I just got off the phone with him. He says the contractor who built the house is probably at Terminal Island.'

Terminal Island was the federal prison in San Pedro.

'What do you mean, probably?'

'Briggs didn't know for sure, but he remembered the contractor's name was Lloyd Cunz. Briggs remembers because he liked the guy's work so much that he tried to hire him for another development he had goin', but Cunz turned him down. He was based in Palm Springs, he said, and they didn't want to take any more long-range jobs.'

'The contractor came all the way from Palm Springs?'

'Not just the contractor. He brought his crew: the carpenters, the cement people, plumbers, electricians, everybody. Three or four years later, Briggs tried to hire Cunz again and learned that he'd been indicted on racketeering and hijacking charges.'

Talley already had a sense of where this was going. Organised crime. He closed his phone and stared at the cul-de-sac. Walter Smith was almost certainly involved in organised crime. The Watchman was probably his partner, and the disks probably contained evidence that could put them away. Talley knew that when the Watchman's phoney FBI agents arrived, he would lose control of the scene, and that would put the people in the house in even greater jeopardy. The Watchman didn't care who died; he just wanted the disks.

Talley wanted the disks, too. He wanted to know what was on them. These people would never have taken Talley's family if the disks in Smith's house didn't pose a terrible threat to them. They feared those disks being discovered more than they feared the investigation that would come from having kidnapped Talley's family. That meant the disks named names.

Talley believed that he and his family would not survive the night. He was certain that as soon as the Watchman had the disks, he would murder all three of them. Talley wanted the disks first. He thought he knew how to get them.

He trotted into the cul-de-sac to join Maddox and Ellison at their car. 'He answer your calls yet?'

'Negative. Phone company says he's got it unplugged.'

'You guys have a PA in this car?'

'No. What're you thinking?'

Talley headed to the lone Bristo car that remained in the street, grabbed the mike, then flipped on the public-address system.

Maddox had followed him over, curious. 'What are you doing?'

'Sending a message.' Talley keyed the mike. 'This is Talley. I need you to call me. If it's safe, call me.'

Rooney's voice answered from the house. 'Screw you!'

Maddox said, 'What was that about being safe?'

Talley didn't answer. He tossed the microphone into the car, then crept to the far side of the cul-de-sac, where he sat on the kerb behind the patrol cars. He wanted the boy. He hoped that Thomas would understand that Talley had been asking him to call.

His phone rang almost at once.

It was Sarah, sounding excited. 'Chief, it's the little boy again.'

Talley's heart raced. If Smith couldn't tell him who had his family, maybe the disks could.

The boy sounded calm. 'I wasn't sure you were talking to me. Is my daddy OK?'

'He's in the hospital over in Canyon Country. What about you and your sister? Are you all right?'

'Yeah. They took her downstairs to cook.'

'How's your battery on that cellphone?'

'Ah, showing half a charge. I turn it off when I'm not using it.'

'Good. Can you plug it into a charger when you're not using it?'

'No. All the chargers are downstairs.'

'OK, Thomas. Your dad, was he working in his office today?'

'No. He was trying to finish something because a client was coming to pick it up.'

'Thomas, I need your help with something. It might be easy or it might be dangerous. If you think those guys in there could find out and hurt you, then I don't want you to do it, OK?'

'Sure!'

The boy was excited. He was a boy. He didn't understand risk.

'Your dad has a couple of disks. I'm not sure, but they're probably on his desk or in his briefcase. These disks are labelled Disk One and Disk Two. When you're downstairs in the office again, could you get to your dad's desk? Could you find those disks and try to see whose files they are?'

'I might be able to sneak into the office if they're not around. Then I could just swipe the disks and open them on my computer up here in my room.'

'I thought they locked you in your room.'

'They do, but I can get out.'

Talley listened as Thomas described being able to move through the crawl space in the eaves and attic, and emerge in different parts of the house through access hatches.

'Thomas, could you get to his office that way?'

'Not into his office, but I can get into the den. There's a service door in the wine cellar. It's right across from my dad's office.'

'That sounds too dangerous.'

'It won't be if they don't see me. Once I'm in the den, all I have to do is sneak across the entry and go to my dad's desk. That wouldn't take any time at all.'

Talley thought it through. He would have to get all three subjects away from that area of the house. He would have to blind the cameras in case one or all of the subjects were in the room with the monitors. 'If I could get Rooney and the others away from the office, do you think you could get the disks without being caught?'

'No problemo.'

'Could you do it in the dark?'

'I do stuff like that almost every night.'

'All right, son. Let's figure this out.'

TALLEY FOUND JORGENSON and brought him to the Department of Water and Power truck. The DWP technician was stretched across the bench seat of his truck, sleeping.

ROBERT CRAIS

Talley shook his foot. 'Can you cut the power to the house?'

The service tech rubbed his sleepy face. 'I could do that, yeah.'

'Not yet.' Talley left Jorgenson with the technician, then radioed Martin to have her meet him at the command van with Hicks and Maddox.

When Talley arrived, he did not tell them that he had spoken with Thomas again, nor the true reasons for everything he was about to do. 'We know that Rooney is sensitive to the perimeter. I want to cut the power to the house, then shake him up with a Starflash to make him start talking.' A Starflash was a shotgun-fired grenade that exploded like a string of powerful firecrackers. It was used to disorientate armed subjects during a breach.

Hicks crossed his arms. 'You're going to fire into the house with the gas in there?'

'No, outside. We need to get his attention. The last time I pushed the perimeter, we didn't have to call him because he called us.'

Martin glanced at Maddox. Maddox nodded. So did Hicks.

THOMAS LISTENED at his door. The hall was quiet. He edged back along the walls to his closet, and then into the crawl space.

When he reached the access hatch to the wine cellar, he listened again. After a few seconds, he slowly lifted the hatch. The wine cellar was empty and dark. Thomas clicked on his flashlight, wedged it in a wine rack, then turned round to dangle his feet and feel for footing. In a few moments he had reached the floor.

He eased open the door. The den beyond was bright with light. He could hear the TV in his father's office across the hall.

All Thomas had to do to reach the office was cross the den to the double doors, then run across the hall.

Thomas took out his cellphone and called Chief Talley.

TALLEY CHECKED his radio. 'Jorgenson?'

'Here, Chief.'

'Stand by.'

Talley was at the rear of Smith's property with a Sheriff's SWAT Tactical Team officer named Hobbs. Hobbs had a rifle fitted with a night-vision scope. Talley carried a shotgun fixed with the Starflash grenade.

'Let me see.' Talley took the rifle from Hobbs and focused the scope on the French doors. He had been peering over the top of the wall, waiting for Thomas to call. Jennifer and Krupchek were in the kitchen. He thought Kevin was in the family room and Dennis was probably watching the perimeter on the monitors.

Talley's phone rang. He handed the rifle back to Hobbs, then answered, his voice low. 'Talley.'

Thomas whispered back at him. 'Hi, Chief. I'm in the den.'

'OK, bud. You ready? Just like we said?'

'Yeah. I won't get caught.'

'If there's any chance—*any!*—you get back up to your room. Here we go.' Talley keyed his shoulder mike. 'Kill the lights.'

DENNIS WENT to the bedroom and put the suitcase on the bed. The notion came to him as he stared at the money. Cops are poor. Cops wanted to be rich like everyone else. Maybe he could split the loot with Talley, trade cash for safe passage to Mexico, work out a scam so that the other cops wouldn't know, something like pretending to swap the hostages for Talley so that the two of them could drive down to Tijuana together. He would even toss in Kevin and Mars; let 'em have someone to swing for the Chinaman. Everyone knew that cops made shit for a living.

Dennis decided to call Talley right away. He was halfway back to the office when the house died. The lights went out, the TV stopped, the background hum that fills all living homes vanished.

Kevin shouted, 'Dennis? What happened?'

'It's the cops!' Blind in the darkness, Dennis rushed forward, following the wall. He expected to hear the doors crashing open at any second, and knew his only chance was to reach the girl or her fat brother. 'Kevin! Mars! Get those kids!'

Then the back yard erupted. Explosions jumped and careened over the surface of the pool. Star-bright flashes lit the back yard like a Chinese New Year parade. The world was going to hell. Dennis threw himself behind the kitchen counter, waiting for it to end.

THOMAS PUSHED OUT of the wine cellar as soon as the lights went off, and scurried to the double doors. Dennis and Kevin were shouting, their voices coming from the family room. He got down on his hands and knees, and peeked through the doorway. Across the hall, his father's office flickered with light from the candles. Thomas leaned out to see if anyone was coming. The hall was empty.

He ran across the hall into his father's office. He knew that

ROBERT CRAIS

something loud was going to go off, so he tried to ignore all that. He concentrated on listening for footsteps.

Thomas went to the computer on his father's desk. The desk was scattered with papers, but he didn't see any disks. He checked the Zip drive. It was empty. He lifted the papers around the computer and keyboard, but he didn't see any disks there, either.

A series of explosions cut through the house like a giant string of firecrackers. Kevin shouted something. Thomas was scared that they were on their way. He ran to the door to go back into the den, but stopped at the hall, listening.

Thomas looked across the entry hall to the safety of the den, then glanced back at the desk. A picture flashed in his memory: Earlier on, his father had tried to talk Dennis into getting a lawyer and giving up; he had gone to his desk, placed the disks in a black case and put the case in the drawer. The disks were in the drawer!

Thomas went back to the desk.

TALLEY'S AMPLIFIED VOICE echoed from the back yard. 'It's time to talk, Dennis. Me and you. Face to face.'

Kevin scrambled into the kitchen on all fours, fast, like a cartoon. 'What are they doing? What's going on?'

Dennis didn't know. He was confused and suspicious, and then suddenly very afraid. 'Mars! Those bastards are trying to blindside us! See what they're doing in front!' Dennis grabbed the girl from Mars, who lurched to his feet and went down the hall.

THE CANDLELIGHT behind the desk was too dim to see into the drawer, so Thomas turned on his flashlight, cupping the lens to hide most of the light. The black leather case was in the top drawer.

It opened like a book. Each side had pockets to hold disks. Two disks were in the right pockets, labelled just as Chief Talley had described, Disk One and Disk Two. Thomas was closing the drawer when he heard footsteps coming fast down the hall.

Thomas turned off his flashlight, ducked under the desk and pulled himself into a ball, hugging his knees, trying not to breathe.

His father's desk sat on curvy legs that left a small gap between the desk and the floor. Thomas saw feet. He thought it was Mars, but he couldn't be sure. The feet went to the window.

Thomas heard the shutters snap open. Light from outside poured into the room. The shutters snapped closed.

Dennis shouted from the back of the house.

'What in hell's going on out there? What the hell are they doin'?'

The feet walked to the desk. Thomas tried to look away, but he couldn't. He watched the feet as if they were snakes.

'*Mars!*'

The feet turned and left. Thomas followed them with his ears, down the hall, away, gone. He scrambled from under the desk and went to the door. He peeked down the hall, then ran across to the den. He pushed into the wine cellar, climbed the racks and found the safety of the crawl space.

TALLEY KNEW that Rooney and the others would believe that Talley had launched a breach and one of them would probably run to the front of the house to see what the Sheriffs were doing. Talley had to keep their attention focused here at the back of the house.

He keyed the portable PA. 'We are *not* breaching the house, Dennis. We need to talk. Me and you. Face to face. I'm coming out to the pool.' He dropped the PA and heaved himself over the wall. He wanted to draw Rooney's attention away from the front of the house even if it meant offering himself up to do it.

Talley walked to the edge of the pool and raised his voice. 'I'm unarmed, and I'm coming alone.' He held his hands out from his sides, open palms forward, and walked towards the house along the side of the pool.

Dennis shouted from the house. 'You're friggin' crazy!'

'No, Dennis. I'm tired.' Talley walked closer. 'No one's going to hurt you. Not unless you hurt those kids.'

Talley stopped outside the French doors. He could see Dennis and Jennifer plainly now. Dennis held the girl with one hand, a pistol with the other. A shadow moved to Talley's left, deep in the family room, and Talley saw a slender figure. Kevin. On the other side of the kitchen, a hall disappeared into the house. Talley saw a flickering glow from a door. A large shape blocked the light, growing in the shadows. That would be Krupchek. Talley felt relief; wherever the boy was, they didn't have him. He had to keep them focused.

'I'm standing here, Dennis. Come out and let's talk.'

Talley heard them talking, Dennis calling Kevin into the kitchen. Dennis came to the French doors. He looked out past Talley, then tried to see the sides of the house.

'No one here but me, Dennis. You have my word.'

Dennis placed his gun on the floor, then pushed open the door and stepped out. 'You got a sniper out there, gonna shoot me?'

'If you tried to grab me, they probably would. Otherwise, no. We could have shot you from the wall if we wanted to do that.'

Dennis seemed to accept that. He stepped away from the door and joined Talley by the foot of the pool.

Talley could see Kevin still with the girl in the kitchen and Krupchek still in the hall. The boy was inside somewhere, getting the disks. Talley hoped it wouldn't take long. Talley said, 'We've been at this a long time now. What are you waiting for?'

'Would you be in a hurry to go to prison for the rest of your life?'

'I'd be doing everything I could to get the best deal possible. I'd let these people go, I'd cooperate, I'd let a lawyer do my talking. I'd be smart enough to realise that I'm surrounded by police officers and I'm not getting out of here except through their good graces.'

Dennis glanced back into the house. Finally, he faced Talley again and lowered his voice. 'How much would it be worth to you, getting me out of here? A hundred thousand dollars? You could drive me down to Mexico, just me and you, no one the wiser, just tell the others that was the deal we made. They got money in this house, Chief. More money than you've ever seen in your life. We could carve it up.'

Talley shook his head. 'You picked a bad house to hole up in, Dennis.' He wondered about Smith, what he did here in the safe, anonymous community of Bristo Camino, with so much cash and information in his house that this kid was willing to die for it and the men in the car were willing to kill for it.

'You tryin' to drive up the price? OK, three hundred. Three hundred thousand dollars. Could you ever earn that much? You can have Mars and Kevin. Make that part of the deal.'

'You don't know what you're dealing with. You can't buy your way out of this.'

'Everybody wants money! Everybody! I'm not giving this up!'

Talley stared at him, wondering how far to go. If Rooney quit now, walked out right now, Talley would have the disks. Once the Watchman's people arrived, Talley might not have the chance.

'This house isn't what you think it is. You believe some guy has this kind of cash just lying around in his house?'

'There's a million bucks in there, maybe *two*! I'll give you half!'

'The man you sent to the hospital, Walter Smith, he's a criminal.

He has partners, Dennis. This is their house, and they want it. The way I'm offering is the only way out for you.'

'Screw you, Talley. Just screw you. You think I'm an idiot.'

'I'm telling you the truth. Give up. Work with me here, and at least you'll have your life.'

Rooney sighed. 'And what's that worth?'

'Whatever you make of it.'

'I'll think about it and give you my answer tomorrow.'

Talley knew that Dennis was lying. Talley had a sense for when they would give up and when they wouldn't, and Rooney had hold of something he couldn't turn loose. 'Please, Dennis.'

'Get lost.' Rooney backed to the door, then stepped inside and pulled it closed. The darkness inside swallowed him like dirty water.

Talley turned back to the officers lining the wall and walked away, praying that Thomas had the disks and was safe. Rooney wasn't the only one holding on to something he couldn't turn loose.

Saturday, 12:04am. With the power off, Thomas didn't have to worry about being seen on the monitors. He pushed through the hatch into his closet and crossed the room to his computer. He took the computer and lugged it to the floor at the foot of his bed so that he wouldn't be seen by the camera when the power returned.

The lights came on without warning. Thomas worried that they would probably come upstairs to check on him, so he hurried to load the first disk. The file icon that appeared was unnamed. He double-clicked on the icon to open it. A list of corporate names appeared that Thomas didn't know anything about. He opened a random file, but saw only tables and numbers. Nothing that he saw made sense to him, but maybe Chief Talley would understand.

Thomas stopped to listen for squeaks. The hall was quiet.

He turned on his phone again, but this time the power indicator showed that he was down to almost a quarter of a charge.

Thomas pushed his redial button to call Chief Talley.

TALLEY CLIMBED BACK over the wall where Martin and Hicks were waiting for him. Martin was angry.

'That was really dumb. What do you think you accomplished?'

Talley hurried away without answering. He didn't want her around when Thomas called. He radioed Maddox to recount his conversation with Rooney as he walked round the side of the neighbour's

383

house. He left out that Rooney had told him about the cash in the house, as that would raise too many questions, and felt terrible about it. Maddox was depending on him, and Talley was lying by omission.

His phone rang as he reached the cul-de-sac. He hurried into a neighbouring drive, out of sight of the house, and stood by himself.

'I got 'em!'

'Good work, son. You're back in your room now, right? I need to know what's on those disks.'

'I got one open right now.'

'OK, tell me what you see.'

Thomas described a list of files named for companies that Talley didn't recognise. Then Thomas mentioned two more companies: Palm Springs Ventures and The Springs Winery. There was the Palm Springs connection: Smith's home had been built by a Palm Springs contractor. Talley had Thomas open the Palm Springs Ventures file, but it sounded like a balance sheet or some kind of profit-and-loss statement without identifying the individuals involved.

'OK. Open the other disk. Tell me what that one says.'

Even the few seconds that it took Thomas to change the disks seemed to take for ever, Talley sweating every moment of it that the boy would be discovered. But then Thomas read off file names and Talley knew that this was the one: Black, White, Up Money, Down Money, Transfers, Source, Cash Receipts, and others.

'The file named Black. Open that one.'

'It's more files.'

'Named what?'

'I think it's states. CA, AZ, NV, FL. Is NV Nevada?'

'Yeah, that's Nevada. Open California.'

Thomas described a long table that went on for pages listing names that Talley didn't recognise, along with dates and payments received. Talley grew antsy. This was taking too much time.

'Read off more of the file names.'

Thomas read off six or seven more names when Talley stopped him again.

'Open that one. Corporate Taxes.'

'Now there's more numbers, but I think they're years. Ninety-two, ninety-three, ninety-four, like that.'

'Open this year.'

'It's a tax form that my dad makes up to send to the government.'

'Up at the top, does it say whose tax it is, maybe a company name?'

'It says Family Enterprises.'

'Look for something like Officers or Executive Compensation, something like that.'

Thomas said, 'There's a place called Compensation to Officers, but there's only one guy listed.'

'Who?'

'Charles G. Benza.'

Talley stared at the ground. The cool night air suddenly felt close. Talley had been wrong. Walter Smith wasn't a mobster. The boy's father was Sonny Benza's accountant, and he had Benza's financial records. It was all right there in Smith's house, enough to put Benza away and his organisation out of business.

This was why people were willing to kidnap and murder. The men in the car were the mob. The head of the largest crime family on the West Coast had Jane and Amanda.

Thomas's voice suddenly came fast and thin. 'Someone's coming. I gotta go.' The line went dead.

Talley ran for his car. If the disks could put Benza away, so could Walter Smith. He radioed Metzger at the hospital as he ran.

THOMAS HEARD the nail being prised from his door. He jerked the computer's plug from the wall, then vaulted onto his bed, shoving the cellphone under the covers as the door opened. Kevin stepped inside, carrying a plate with two slices of pizza and a Diet Coke.

'I brought you something to eat.'

Kevin handed over the pizza and Coke. Thomas said, 'When are you leaving my house?'

'Never.' Kevin left without looking back and pulled the door closed. The nail was hammered back into the doorjamb. The floor squeaked as Kevin moved away.

Thomas once more made his way to the closet. He wanted to know what they were planning. He also wanted the gun.

Saturday, 12:02am. Marion Clewes cruised round the Canyon Country Hospital, finding the emergency-room entrance at the rear. Friday night, a little after midnight, and the place was virtually deserted. The Santa Clarita Valley must be a very nice place to live, he thought.

The small parking area outside the ER showed only three cars and a couple of ambulances, but four news vehicles were parked off to the side. Marion parked close to the entrance with the nose of his car facing the drive, then went into the hospital.

The newspeople were clumped together at the admissions desk, talking to a harassed woman in a white coat. Marion listened enough to gather that she was the senior emergency-room physician, Dr Reese, and that tests were currently being run on Walter Smith. Two nurses stood behind the admissions desk, watching with interest.

Marion went to a coffee machine in the waiting area, bought a cup of coffee and went back to the admissions room. A gate opened to a short hall, beyond which was a communal room with several beds partitioned by blue curtains, and a corridor with swing doors at the end. Marion waited at the gate until an orderly appeared, then smiled shyly. 'Excuse me. Dr Reese said someone would help me.'

The orderly glanced at Reese, who was still busy with the reporters across the room.

'I'm Walter Smith's next-door neighbour. They told me to pick up his clothes and personal effects.'

'That the guy who was the hostage?'

'Oh, yes. Isn't that terrible?'

'Man, the stuff that happens, huh?'

'I'm supposed to bring his things home.'

'OK, let me see what I can do.' Marion watched as the orderly disappeared into one of the doors further up the corridor, then he stepped through the gate and walked up the corridor just far enough so that the nurses at the admissions desk could no longer see him. He waited there until the orderly returned with a carrier bag.

'Here you go.'

Marion took the bag. He could feel shoes in the bottom. 'Listen, thank you. Is there another way out of here? I don't want to leave past the reporters. They were asking so many questions before.'

The orderly pointed to the doors at the end of the corridor. 'Through there, then left. That'll bring you out the front.'

'Thanks again.' Marion put the bag on the floor to go through Smith's things. The bag contained clothes, a wallet and a wristwatch. There were no disks. Mr Howell would be disappointed.

Marion tucked the bag under his arm and walked down the corridor past the communal room. The beds were empty. He found Smith in a room at the end of the passageway. Smith's left temple was covered in a bandage, and an oxygen cannula was clipped to his nose. Two nurses, one red-haired and one dark, were setting up monitor machines.

Marion found a quiet spot further down the corridor where a trolley was resting against the wall. He put the bag on the trolley, then put a syringe pack and a vial of a drug called lignocaine into the bag. Both the syringe and the lignocaine were Marion's, brought in from the car.

Marion worked inside the bag so no one could see. He tore open the syringe pack, twisted off the needle guard and pierced the top of the vial. He drew deep at the lignocaine, filling the syringe. When injected into a person with a normal healthy heart, lignocaine induced heart failure. Marion placed the syringe on top of Smith's clothes, then closed the bag and waited.

After a few minutes, the nurses left Smith's room.

Marion let himself into the room. He put the bag on the bed. Smith's eyes fluttered. Marion slapped him. 'Wake up.' Marion slapped him again. 'Walter?'

Smith's eyes opened, not quite making it all the way.

'Are the disks still in your house?'

Smith made a murmuring sound that Marion could not understand. Marion gripped his face and shook it violently. 'Speak to me, Walter. Have you told anyone who you are?'

Smith's eyes fluttered again, then dulled and once more closed.

Marion felt confident that he could report that the disks were still in the house and that Smith hadn't been able to speak since his release from the house. The people in Palm Springs would be pleased. They would also be pleased that Walter Smith was dead. Marion opened the bag and reached in for the syringe.

'What are you doing?' The red-haired nurse stood in the doorway. She stared at Marion, clearly suspicious, then came directly to the bed. 'You're not supposed to be in here.'

Marion smiled at her. His hands still in the bag, Marion let go of the syringe and lifted the clothes so that the syringe would fall to the bottom. 'I know. I came for his belongings, but I got the idea of leaving something from home, you know, like a good-luck piece.'

Marion took out the wallet and opened it. He took out a worn picture of Walter with his wife and children. He showed it to the nurse.

'Could I leave it? Please? I'm sure it will help him.'

The dark-haired nurse stepped through the door and went to one of the monitors. Marion closed the bag.

The red-haired nurse said, 'Is it OK if he leaves this picture? It belongs to Mr Smith.'

'No. It'll get lost and someone will bitch. That always happens.'

Marion put the picture into his pocket and smiled at the red-haired nurse. 'Well, thanks anyway.'

Marion heard the sirens as he walked back to the admissions room. The female police officer outside the entrance was talking into her radio. The sirens grew closer. She suddenly ran back into the hospital. Marion decided not to wait and went out to his car. Palm Springs was not going to like his report after all, but there was nothing to be done about it. Not yet.

Then two police cars arrived. Marion watched the officers run into the hospital, and then he phoned Glen Howell.

RUNNING FOR HIS CAR, Talley radioed Metzger at the hospital. He told her that there had been a threat to Smith's life, and to get outside Smith's door. He grabbed Jorgenson and Campbell from Mrs Peña's home and told them to follow him.

Talley rolled code three, full lights and siren. He knew that Benza's people would learn what he was doing, and that this might jeopardise his family, but he couldn't let them simply kill the man.

When they reached the hospital, Talley hurried out of his car to meet Jorgenson and Campbell. 'Let's get in there.'

As they entered the hospital, Talley glanced from face to face, from hands to bodies, hoping for a glimpse of a deep tan, a heavy Rolex watch, and for clothes similar to those worn by the men and woman he had seen in his parking lot. Everyone was a suspect.

The hospital security chief, an overweight man named Jobs, met them at the admissions desk with Klaus and Dr Reese. Talley asked that they speak somewhere more private, and followed them past the admissions desk, through a gate and round a corner into a corridor. Talley saw Metzger standing outside a door not far away. Talley went directly to her, telling Reese and the others to wait.

'Is everything OK?'

'Yeah. It's fine. What's going on?'

Talley stood in the doorway. Smith was alone in the room. Talley glanced back at Metzger. 'I'll be right back.'

Talley told Jorgenson and Campbell to wait with Metzger, then explained to the doctors. 'We have reason to believe that there could be an attempt made on Mr Smith's life. I'm going to post a guard outside his room and have police here on the premises.'

They were talking about it when Metzger called from her post.

'Hey. He's waking up.'

Klaus pushed past them and hurried into the room, Talley following. Smith's eyes were open and focused, though still vague. He mumbled something, then spoke again, more clearly. 'Where am I?'

Klaus said, 'My name is Klaus. I'm a doctor at Canyon Country Hospital. That's where you are. Do you know your name?'

'Smith. Walter Smith. Where are my children?'

Talley said, 'They're still in the house.'

Smith's eyes tracked vaguely over. Talley lifted his sweatshirt so that Smith could see his badge.

'I'm Jeff Talley, the Bristo chief of police. So far as we know, your children are OK. We're trying to get them out.'

'Thank you.' Smith's voice was soft and fading. He settled back, his eyes closed. Talley thought they were losing him again.

Klaus didn't like what he saw on the monitors. His face pulled into a pinched frown. 'I don't want him to overdo it.'

Talley brought Klaus aside and lowered his voice. 'I should have a word with him now.'

'I don't see as it would do any good. It will only upset him.'

Talley stared at Smith, knowing he could punch the right button because he could read Klaus as easily as he read a subject behind a barricade. 'He has a right to know, Doctor. You know he does. I'll only be a moment. Now, please.'

Klaus scowled, but he left.

'Smith.'

Smith opened his eyes, not quite as wide as before. Talley watched as they flagged closed. He bent close.

'I know who you are.'

The eyes opened again.

'Sonny Benza has my wife and daughter.'

Smith stared up at him, as blank as a plate, showing no surprise or shock, revealing nothing. But Talley knew. He could sense it.

'He wants his financial records. He's taken my wife and daughter to make sure I cooperate. I need your help, Smith. I need to know where he has them. I need to know how to get to him.'

Something wet dripped on Smith's shoulder. Talley's eyes blurred, and he realised that he was crying. 'Help me.'

Smith shook his head. 'I don't know what you're talking about.'

Klaus came back into the room. 'That's enough.'

'Let me speak to him a few more minutes.'

'I said, *That's enough.*'

Talley posted the guards, then left. He drove with the windows down, frustrated and angry. He pulled the Nokia from his pocket and set it on the seat. It rang.

Talley swerved to the shoulder of the road. He skidded to a stop and answered the call, the Watchman shouting before Talley spoke.

'You screwed up, you dumb cop, you screwed up *bad*!'

Talley was shouting back, '*No, YOU screwed up!* Do you think I'm going to let you just murder someone?!'

'*You wanna hear them scream?* That it? You want a blowtorch on your daughter's pretty face?!'

Talley punched the dashboard. 'You touch them, you harm one damn hair, and I'll go in that house right now, I'll get those disks. You want the *real* FBI to have 'em? I don't think you want that, you *bastard*! And I've got *Smith*! Don't you damn well forget that!'

When the Watchman spoke again, his voice was measured.

'I guess we each have something the other wants.'

Talley forced himself to be calm. 'You remember that.'

'All right. You have a guard on Smith. Fair enough. We'll deal with Smith when we deal with Smith. Right now we want our property.'

'Not one damn hair. One hair and you bastards are mine.'

'We're off that, Talley. Move on. You still have to make sure that I get those disks. If I don't, more than hair will be harmed.'

'So what's next?'

'My people are good to go. You know who I mean?'

'The FBI.'

'Six in two vans. If there's any screw-up, if you do anything other than what I tell you to do, you'll get your family back in the mail.'

'I'm doing what I can, goddammit. Tell me what you want.'

'Whatever they want you to do, you do it.'

'We can't have an assassination squad out here. The neighbourhood is full of professional police officers. They're not stupid.'

'I'm not stupid, either, Talley. My guys will behave in a professional manner. Use the Sheriffs for your perimeter, but have their tactical team stand down. My guy, the team leader, he'll cover that with the Sheriffs. They were in the area on a training mission. They called you, offered their assistance, and you accepted.'

Talley knew that Martin would never buy that. 'No one will believe that. Why would I accept with the Sheriffs already here?'

'Because the Feds told you that Walter Smith is part of their witness protection programme. My man will cover it with the Sheriffs when he gets there. He knows what to say so they'll go along. Now take care of my people and get them set up.'

The line went dead. Talley was left shaking and sweating. He got himself together. He drove back to the house.

Saturday, 12:03am. When Dennis went back into the house, Kevin started on him right away. 'What did he say? Did he offer a deal?'

The girl was on her hands and knees on the kitchen floor.

'Mars. Get her out of here. Take her back to her room.'

Dennis went to the office for the vodka, then brought it to the den. The lights came on as he dropped onto the couch.

Kevin stopped in the doorway. 'It's over, Dennis. We have to give up.'

'The hell it's over! That money is *mine*!'

Kevin stepped closer. 'You're going to get us killed for that money.'

Dennis raised the bottle. 'Then we might as well die rich.'

'No!' Kevin slapped the bottle from his hand, and then Dennis was off the couch. He shoved Kevin over the coffee table and followed him down. Dennis held Kevin with his left hand and punched with his right, hitting his brother again and again, as hard as he could. Kevin rolled into a ball, his face blotched red, sobbing.

Dennis climbed to his feet, 'That money is mine. I'm not leaving without it, Kevin. Get that in your head. *We're not giving up.*'

Kevin crawled away, whimpering like a beaten dog.

TALLEY PULLED HIS CAR to the kerb outside Mrs Peña's and went inside for a cup of black coffee, but returned to his car. He sat on the kerb with the Nokia and his own phone beside him. His radio popped at his waist.

'Chief, Cooper. I'm here at the south gate. We got some FBI guys asking for you. They say you're expecting them.'

'Let them in.' Talley walked up the street to the corner.

Two grey vans eased to the corner, four men in the lead van, two in the rear. Talley raised his hand. Both vans pulled to the kerb and cut their engines. The men inside had short haircuts and were wearing black tactical fatigues, standard issue for FBI tactical units.

The driver said, 'You Talley?'

'Yes.'

The man on the passenger side of the lead van got out and came round the nose of the van. 'OK, Chief, let me see some ID.'

Talley took out his wallet and showed the photo ID. When he was satisfied, he took out his own badge case and opened it for Talley.

'OK, here's mine. My name is Special Agent Jones.'

Talley inspected an FBI credential that identified the man as William F. Jones, Special Agent of the Federal Bureau of Investigation. It showed a photograph of Jones. It looked real.

'Every man in my group has the ID.'

He slapped the nose of the lead van, nodding at the driver. The doors of both vans opened. The remaining five men stepped out, moving to the rear of the second van. They strapped into armoured vests with FBI emblazoned on the back.

Jones said, 'In a few minutes your phone is going to ring. You know the phone I mean. So let's get some stuff straight before that.'

Talley was watching the men. They strapped on the vests, then snapped on new thigh guards with practised efficiency. Someone at the rear of the second van passed out black knitted masks, flash-bang grenades and helmets. Each man folded the mask twice and tucked it under his left shoulder strap where he could reach it easily later. They clipped the grenades to their harnesses without fumbling and tossed their helmets into the seats or balanced them atop the van. Talley knew the moves, because he had practised them himself when he worked SWAT Tactical. These men had done this before.

'You used to be a cop.'

'Don't worry about what I used to be.'

Talley looked at him. 'How can you people expect this to work? The Sheriffs have a full Crisis Response Team here. They're going to be pissed off and they're going to have questions.'

'I can handle the Sheriffs and anything else that comes up. I'm Special Agent Jones. Think of me that way and you won't screw up. I can lift my end, you got a wife and kid praying you can lift yours.'

Talley's head throbbed, but he managed a nod.

Jones turned so that they both faced the line of vehicles. 'Who's in charge there?'

'Martin. She's a captain.'

'You told her about us yet?'

'No. I didn't know what to say.'

'Good, that's better for us. The less time she has to ask questions, the better. Now, the man on the phone, you know who I mean, did he tell you how we're going to cover this?'

'Smith is in witness protection.'

'Right, Smith is in the programme so we have a proprietary interest. I'm in charge of a Special Operations Unit that was working
training exercises on the border when Washington learned what was
happening here. The DC office called you and asked for your cooperation. We owe Smith, we're obligated to protect him and his cover,
so you agreed. I'm going to explain all this to Captain Martin, and
you're going to sit there and nod. You got that?'

'What if Martin checks? What if she knows people in the LA office?'

'It's after midnight on a Friday night. Even if she calls the agent in
charge in Los Angeles and wakes him, he'll wait until tomorrow to
call DC, because none of these people, not one, will have any reason
to doubt us. We're not gonna be here that long.'

Jones handed Talley a white business card with the FBI seal
pressed into the left corner and a phone number with a Washington,
DC, area code.

'If she gets it into her head to call someone, tell her that this is the
guy back there who called you. She can talk to him until she's blue.'

Talley put the card in his pocket, wondering if the name on the
card was a real agent, and thought he probably was. Thinking that
scared him. It was like a warning: this is how much power we have.

Talley glanced at the men. 'What are you people going to do?'

'You and I are going to straighten this out with the Sheriffs. Two
of my people are going to reconnoitre the house, see what we have.
After that, we'll deploy in a secure position and wait for the man to
call. When he gives the word, we move. If something happens in the
house that provokes a launch beforehand, we'll do it. But we will
control the scene until we've recovered our target. After that, the
house is yours.'

'I won't be able to keep the others out. You know that. The
Sheriffs will come in, and I'm going, too.'

Jones met Talley's eyes and shook his head.

'Listen, man, if it helps you get through this, we don't want to kill
anyone, not even the three dicks who started this mess. We just want
the stuff in the house. But we know what's required when we breach
that house. We'll have to secure the scene before we can recover what
we want. We'll do that, Talley. We're professionals.'

The phone in Talley's pocket chirped. He pulled it out. It was the
Nokia. It chirped again.

'Answer it, Chief.'

Talley pressed the button to answer the call. 'Talley.'

'Is Mr Jones with you?'

'Yes, he's here.'

'Put him on.'

Talley passed the Nokia to Jones without a word. As Jones spoke, his eyes flicked nervously to the Sheriffs in the distance. Talley thought that he was probably scared. Any sane man would be scared, doing what he was doing. Talley wondered what the Watchman had on this man, or if Jones was doing it for money.

Jones ended the call and passed the phone back to Talley.

'What does he have on you?'

Jones stared at him, then looked away without answering.

'I know why I'm doing this. What does he have on you?'

Jones cinched down his vest, tighter than necessary, so tight the straps cut. 'You don't know shit.'

Jones started up the street. Talley followed him.

KEVIN'S EYE WAS SWELLING from the beating Dennis had given him. After the shootings, the running, the nightmare terror of the day, he knew what he had to do, and why. He was not willing to die with his brother; no matter their childhood and the horrors they had endured. Dennis was willing to die for money he couldn't have, and Kevin refused to die with him. He would take the girl and her brother, and the three of them would get the hell out.

Kevin stumbled into the little bathroom off the entry and splashed his face with water. Then he dried his face and went back to the den to see if Dennis was still there. He expected that Dennis and Mars would try to stop him from leaving, so he wanted to get the kids out of the house without being seen. Dennis's feet sprouted up over the end of the couch, flat on his back. Kevin peeked into the office, checking for Mars, but he didn't see him. He thought if he moved quickly enough it wouldn't matter.

Kevin hurried up the stairs. He knocked twice softly on the girl's door, pulled the nail from the door and let himself inside.

The girl was on her bed, her eyes open, the lights full on. She swung her feet out and stood as the door opened. 'What do you want?'

'Shh. Keep your voice down. We're going to get out of here.'

She seemed confused, her eyes flicking to the door, then back to him. 'Where are you taking me?'

'Not with them. I don't mean with Dennis and Mars. I'm taking you and your brother. We're going to leave them here.'

'They're letting us leave?'

'Mars and Dennis don't know I'm doing this. They would stop us, so we have to be careful. Now do you want to go or not?'

'I want to go!'

'Stay here. I'll get Thomas and come back for you. When the three of us are together, we'll go straight downstairs and out the front door. Do you have a white pillowcase?'

'We're going to walk out the door? Just like that?'

'Yes! We need a white flag so the cops don't shoot us.'

'All right, OK. I have a pillowcase.'

'Get it while I'm getting your brother. When I get back, don't say a word. Just follow me and try to be quiet. We're going to walk fast.'

Kevin eased the door open and peered into the hall. He heard voices and grew worried. If Mars and Dennis were in the office, they would see the three of them coming down the stairs.

Kevin pulled the door shut behind him and crept back along the hall to the stairwell, listening. When he reached the top of the stairs, he listened harder, then felt a well of relief. The voices were coming from the television. He turned back towards the boy's room. The floor creaked behind him. Kevin spun round.

Mars stood inches away, backlit by the light from the stairs. Kevin jerked backwards. They were screwed unless he could keep Mars away from the front door. He thought of the security room, as far from the front door as it was possible to get in this house.

'Jesus, Mars, you scared me. I was looking for you. Dennis wants you to watch those monitors back in the bedroom.'

Mars stepped closer, his pale face empty.

'I heard you with the girl, Kevin. You're going to leave.'

'I've had enough of this, Mars. We're trapped. It's over! If we stay, the cops will kill us. Don't you get that?'

Mars stared down at him, his pasty face thoughtful. Then he stepped aside. 'I get it, Kevin. That's OK. If you want to go, go.'

Kevin stared up at Mars, then turned and stepped into darkness.

AFTER TALLEY AND JONES had spoken with Martin, Jones moved his two vans to the mouth of the cul-de-sac. Talley returned to his car so that he could avoid the Sheriffs and his own men. When he and Jones had been in the command van with Martin, he couldn't bring himself to look at her. He had let Jones do the talking.

Martin climbed down from the command van, saw Talley in his

car and walked over. 'You gonna tell me what's going on?'

'What do you mean?'

'I'm not stupid.'

Talley didn't answer.

'All the phone calls. That scene in the ambulance between you and the doctor, wanting him to wake Smith. Charging off to the hospital. I had my intelligence officer call over there, Talley; if someone phoned in a death threat, it's news to everybody else. Now we got the FBI with this bullshit about Smith being in witness protection. What's going on, Chief? Who is Walter Smith?'

Talley glanced over. Her eyes were steady and cool, meeting his without guile. He liked her direct manner; she was probably a pretty good cop. The weight of the day suddenly pressed down on him with an intensity that left him numb. There were too many things to control and too many lies to tell. It was all too complicated, and he couldn't afford to mess this up. Like a juggler with a hundred balls in the air, he was going to drop one sooner or later and someone would die. He couldn't let that happen. He couldn't fail Amanda and Jane or the kids in that house or even Walter Smith.

'Do you know the name Sonny Benza?'

She searched his face, Talley thinking that she couldn't place the name, but then she did. 'That's the mob guy, right?'

'Smith works for him. Smith has something in that house that can put Benza away, and Benza wants it.'

'Jesus.'

Talley looked at her, and felt his eyes go wet. 'He has my wife and daughter.' He told her about the disks, the Watchman and Jones. He told her how he had played it, and how he intended to play it.

She listened without question or comment until he was finished, then stared at the two vans where Jones's people waited. 'You have to bring this to the Bureau. With what you have they could move on Benza right now, pull him straight out of bed and hang him by his thumbs. We breach into that house, get these disks he wants, and that's how you save your family.'

'It's not your family.'

She sighed. 'No, I guess not.'

'All I have is a voice on a phone, Martin. I don't know where they are, I don't know who has them. I don't give a damn about making a case. I just want my family.'

Martin stared at the two vans, and sighed again. 'I am not going to let murder happen out here, Talley. I can't do that.'

'Me neither.'

'Then what are you going to do?'

'I can't let those disks go into evidence. They're my only leverage.'

'What do you want from me?'

'Help me get those disks. I can't let Jones go into that house alone.'

'I'll do what I can. You keep me informed, Talley. I don't want to get shot in the back. I can't let my people get hurt, either.'

Talley's cellphone rang. It was Mikkelson, sounding strange.

'Chief, Dreyer and I are still out here at Krupchek's trailer with detectives from the Sheriff's Bureau. Krupchek isn't Krupchek. His real name is Bonnier. His mother's head is in the freezer.'

PART FOUR

Saturday, 12:52am. Alvin Marshall Bonnier, aged twenty-seven, also known as Mars Krupchek, was wanted in connection with four counts of homicide in Tigard, Oregon. The local authorities theorised the following chain of events based on witness interviews and forensic evidence. Bonnier, who lived alone with his mother at the time of the murders, abducted and raped his next-door neighbour, Helene Getty, aged seventeen, and disposed of her body in a nearby wood. Mrs Bonnier subsequently discovered Getty's clothing in her son's bedroom. She confronted her son, at which time Alvin stabbed his mother to death, then dismembered her body. Bonnier buried the limbs and torso in Mrs Bonnier's rose bed. Bonnier kept his mother's head in the refrigerator, but later transferred the head to the trunk of the family car. Twelve days later, an eighteen-year-old high-school senior named Anita Brooks hitched a ride with Bonnier after missing her bus. Instead of bringing her to school, Bonnier drove to a nearby lake, where he strangled her before branding her with cigarettes. Evidence gathered at the scene indicated that he had placed his mother's head on a nearby picnic table, so that she could watch the mutilation.

Talley listened to Mikkelson's recitation of the facts with a growing sense of urgency that Martin read in his expression.

'What in hell is happening?'

Talley raised his hand, telling her to wait. 'Mikki, they're positive that Bonnier and Krupchek are the same person?'

'That's affirm, Chief. The palm print he left in Kim's matched dead on, and the Sheriff's Homicide Bureau guys brought a copy of the warrants fax from Oregon. I saw the photo. It's Krupchek.'

'What's happening out there now?'

'The detectives here have locked down the scene to wait for an FBI team from the LA field office.'

Talley checked his watch. 'What's their ETA?'

'I dunno. You want me to check?'

'Yeah.' Talley filled in Martin while he waited for Mikkelson.

Mikkelson came back on the line. 'Chief? The Feds should be here within a couple of hours. You want us to wait?'

Talley told her to come back, then shut the phone. 'Great. I've got the Mafia outside and Freddy Krueger in the house.'

Martin watched him calmly. 'This changes things.'

'I *know*, Captain! I'm trying to save my wife and daughter, but I have to get those kids out of that house.' Talley left Martin at the command van and found Jones briefing his people at their vans.

Jones saw Talley approaching, and separated from the others. 'What's up, Chief?'

'We have a problem. One of the three subjects in the house—Krupchek—is wanted for multiple homicides in Oregon.'

Jones smiled tightly. 'You're kiddin' me.'

'I'm not. The *real* FBI are on their way. They'll visit Krupchek's trailer in Pearblossom, then they'll come here. By morning, this place is going to be covered with FBI, including a *real* FBI SWAT team.'

'We'll be gone by then. We're breaching the house as soon as I hear back from the man.'

'I want to go in now.'

Jones shook his head. 'Not until I get the call.'

'Listen to me. It's different now. This isn't just three guys holding a family hostage any more. Those kids are in there with a lunatic, Jones. He cut off his own mother's head and keeps it in the freezer.'

'We'll breach when I get the call. It won't be long.'

'Screw you.' Talley walked away. He decided that Rooney did not know that Krupchek was really Bonnier. Rooney's need to be seen as special would have forced him to drop hints of Bonnier's identity in hopes of impressing Talley, but he had not done that.

Talley decided that he couldn't wait any longer. He had to warn Rooney and Thomas, and he had to get those kids out of there.

DENNIS ROONEY HAD RUN out of ideas, and now he was thinking that maybe his parents and teachers had been right all along: he was stupid. He was a small-time loser, who would always be a loser, living on dreams. An urge to run with a bag of cash, sprinting through the shadows in a final lame attempt to get away, swept over him, but he believed the cops would kill him and he did not want to die. His eyes filled with tears of regret. Kevin was right. It was time to quit.

Dennis called Kevin. Kevin didn't answer. 'Mars!' Nothing.

Dennis made his way to the kitchen. It was wrapped in shadows, lit only by the glare from the police lights shining in through the French doors. He wanted a glass of water, and then he would call Talley. He thought he might be able to trade one of the kids for a conversation with an attorney, then see what kind of deal he could cut for himself before surrendering.

'Kevin, dammit, where are you?!' He had begged to surrender, and now that Dennis was ready, the wimp wasn't around. '*Mars!*'

The voice from the other side of the kitchen startled him. 'What are you doing, Dennis?'

Dennis wheeled round, squinting into the shadows. 'Where's Kevin? I need to see him.'

Dennis wanted to get things straight with Kevin before telling Mars. Part of him was afraid that Mars might try to stop him.

Mars took shape in the light. 'Kevin left.'

Dennis stared at Mars. 'Wait a minute. Are you telling me that he *left*, as in went out the door and surrendered to the cops?'

'I overheard him talking to the girl.'

'*Shit!* That *asshole!*' Dennis felt sick. If Kevin had surrendered and taken the kids with him, he had taken Dennis's last chance to cut a deal with Talley. 'Did he take those kids with him?'

'I don't know.'

'Mars! Get upstairs and see! If he did, we're screwed!'

Mars went for the stairs without another word.

THOMAS OVERHEARD DENNIS and Kevin fighting through the air-conditioning vent. Kevin wanted them to give up. Dennis wouldn't.

The shouting died quickly. Thomas waited for someone to come upstairs, but the hall remained silent. He decided that they were trying to sleep.

Thomas slipped back into his closet and returned to the crawl space. He worked his way across the house, stopping at the air vents to listen, but all he heard was the television playing in the den.

Thomas let himself down through the ceiling hatch into the laundry room, climbing down from the hot-water heater to the washing machine to the floor. It was dark, lit only by some dim light filtering from the kitchen through the pantry. He had to use his flashlight.

Just as he reached the floor he heard Dennis shouting for Kevin and Mars. Dennis was close. Thomas panicked. He started climbing back to the ceiling, but then Mars answered Dennis, and Thomas stopped. He strained to listen. Dennis was cursing Kevin; they weren't coming this way, they weren't looking for him.

Thomas hurried into the utility room. He cupped his hand over the flashlight and flicked it on again, just long enough to mark the spot in his mind where the gun box waited on the highest shelf. He rested the flashlight on the bench, then climbed onto the bench.

He went up onto his toes, stretching as tall as he could, and his hands found the gun box. Thomas pulled the box from the shelf, then climbed down from the bench and lifted out the gun.

Thomas was on his way back to the laundry room when his foot slipped from under him. He almost fell. He explored the floor with his foot and found something slippery and wet. He lifted his foot. His shoe came free with a tacky sound. A dark liquid like oil was spreading on the floor. He followed it with his light. It was coming from the broom closet. The oil was red.

Thomas stared at the closet door. He stepped across the red pool, gripped the knob and slowly pulled open the door.

Kevin fell out, collapsing in a lifeless heap at Thomas's feet, his dead arms thrown round Thomas's legs.

His throat was slashed, his head lolling on white bone; the horrible second smile was locked in silent laughter. His eyes were open.

Thomas screamed.

JENNIFER LISTENED at her door, hoping to hear Kevin return. He only had to go down the hall to reach Thomas, but he was taking so long that she feared Mars or Dennis had interfered.

The hall outside her door creaked. *Kevin!*

She heard the nail being pulled from the doorjamb.

The door swung open, and Mars stepped inside, tall, wide and massive as a bear. She jumped back so fast that she almost fell.

He said, 'Were you expecting someone else?'

She backed away from the door, wishing that Kevin would come back. 'I'm not expecting anyone except the police.'

Mars nodded agreeably.

'They'll be here soon. You probably don't have long to wait.'

Mars stepped into the room and pushed the door shut. He held the big nail that they used to wedge the door. She crossed her arms protectively over her breasts. 'What do you want?'

'Kevin left without you. He said to tell you he was sorry.'

'I don't know what you're talking about.'

Mars came closer. 'No? Well, it doesn't matter.'

Jennifer backed into her desk. She had gone as far as she could and now Mars was very close. He touched the nail to her chest.

'Don't touch me.'

Mars raked the nail slowly down between her breasts. Jennifer stared into his eyes, her vision blurred with tears. His eyes were black pools, their surface rippled by secret winds. He didn't watch the nail; she sensed that his pleasure came in seeing her fear. Jennifer slid her hand down her belly to her waistband, jerked the knife free and stabbed, striking out blindly, trying to force him away. The stiff short blade struck something hard. Mars grunted in surprised pain, as they both looked down. The knife was buried high on his chest in his left shoulder.

Jennifer pushed at him, screaming, trying to get away, but he didn't move. He grabbed her throat, squeezing hard, pressing his hips into hers to pin her to the desk.

He grabbed the knife with his free hand, whimpered, then pulled out the blade. A crimson flower blossomed from the wound.

THE SCREAM from the rear of the house cut through the alcohol, surprising Dennis more than startling him. It was high-pitched like a girl shrieking, followed by bumping, slamming noises that came from the far side of the kitchen near the garage. Dennis pulled out his gun, shouting. 'What the hell was that? Who is that?'

It couldn't be Mars, who had just left, or the two kids, who were both upstairs unless that chickenshit Kevin had taken them. Maybe Kevin had returned. 'Kev? Is that you!'

Dennis turned on his flashlight and swept the light beam across the kitchen. No one answered and nothing moved. He pushed the gun ahead of him and eased through the kitchen towards the garage.

Dennis stepped into the pantry, shining the light through into the laundry room. The floor was covered with a red stain that oozed towards him. Dennis saw his brother on the floor. It was hard to keep his balance. He stopped at the edge of the pool of blood and shone the light on his brother. He saw the open neck, the wide, staring eyes.

The fat boy and the girl could not have done this. Mars.

Dennis backed out of the pantry into the kitchen, then ran for the stairs. He took the stairs two at a time, intent only on finding Mars, killing him. Halfway up, he heard the girl scream.

Dennis slammed into the girl's door, shoving it open. Mars had the girl by her throat. Dennis aimed his gun. 'You're dead, you bastard.'

Mars calmly pulled the girl in front of him, blocking Dennis's aim. He lifted the girl by the neck and rushed forward, charging Dennis. Dennis hesitated only a heartbeat because he didn't want to shoot the girl, but that was too long. The girl crashed into him, the full force of Mars's weight behind her, knocking Dennis backwards into the hall. Then the girl was cast aside, Mars was on top of him, and Dennis saw a glint off the knife as it came down.

THOMAS COULDN'T MOVE fast enough. His only thought was to reach Jennifer. The two of them would run downstairs and out the door, and neither Mars nor Dennis could stop them. *He had the gun!*

Thomas heard Jennifer's door crash open as he squeezed through the hatch into her closet. Dennis was shouting at Mars. Mars was holding Jennifer. Thomas drew the gun from his trousers.

Then Mars pushed Jennifer into Dennis, and all three of them sprawled into the hall. Thomas crept into the room. Mars grunted as he stabbed Dennis over and over. Jennifer was crawling away.

'Jen! C'mon!' Thomas darted past Mars into the hall, and grabbed Jennifer's arm. He pulled her towards the stair. 'Run!'

The two of them stumbled away as Mars heaved to his feet. He was bigger, stronger, faster; Thomas knew that he would catch them.

Thomas whirled round and jerked up the pistol with both hands. 'I'll shoot you!'

Mars stopped. He was streaked with blood and breathing hard. Dennis bubbled like a fountain and moaned.

They backed away, Thomas trying to hold the gun steady.

Mars walked after them, matching them step for step.

They reached the landing. Jennifer started down the stairs.

Mars walked faster. 'I'm going to cut out your heart. But I'm going to cut out your sister's heart first, so you can watch.'

Thomas didn't want to shoot; he was scared to shoot, scared that it would be wrong even though he feared for his life, but Mars came on and he was too scared not to shoot, too scared of that awful knife and that Mars really would cut out his heart, and Jennifer's.

Thomas pulled the trigger. *Click!*

Mars stopped, frozen at the sharp sound.

Click! The gun didn't fire.

All the things that his father had showed him at the pistol range came flooding back. He gripped the slide hard and pulled back to load a bullet into the chamber, but the slide locked open and did not close. Thomas glanced down into the open action. The magazine was empty. The pistol was unloaded. *There were no bullets!*

When Thomas looked up again, Mars smiled.

Jennifer screamed, 'Run!'

Thomas threw the gun at Mars and ran, following Jennifer down the stairs. Jennifer reached the front door first, and clawed at the handle, but the door would not open.

'The deadbolt is locked! Where's the key?'

The key wasn't in the lock. Thomas knew with certain dread that it was probably upstairs in Dennis's bloody pocket.

Mars pounded down the stairs. They would never reach the French doors or garage before he caught them.

Jennifer grabbed Thomas's arm and pulled. 'This way! *Run!*'

She pulled him towards their parents' room. Thomas realised that she was taking him to the safest place in the house, but Mars was getting closer, right behind them. Thomas raced after his sister down the hall, through their parents' bedroom and into the security room. They slammed the steel door and threw the bolt in the same moment that Mars crashed into the other side of the door.

Thomas and Jennifer held each other, shaking and scared.

Thomas remembered the cellphone.

He clawed it out of his pocket and turned it on.

'Thomas! Look!' Jennifer was watching Mars on the monitors. He was in the entry by the front door. He picked up the two containers of gasoline, then walked through the house splashing gasoline on the walls. Jennifer said, 'Oh my God, he's going to burn us.'

Saturday, 2:16am. Mars turned off the remaining lights as he passed them. The entry hall turned black. The office followed, then the den.

Mars went to the kitchen first. He found matches in a jar by the range, then blew out the pilot lights. He splashed gasoline over the range top and gas line, then moved back towards the master bed-room, carefully pouring an unbroken trail of gasoline along the walls. He continued the trail into the bedroom. He splashed the bed and the walls and the security door. Then he took out the matches.

THOMAS DIALLED Talley's number and pressed the button to send the call. The phone died. 'The battery's low! You never charge it!'

Jennifer snatched the phone from him and prised off the battery. She rubbed the copper contacts hard on her shirtsleeve, then licked them before snapping the battery back onto the phone.

'What are you doing?'

'Thomas, I *live* on this phone. I know every trick in the book for making it work.'

Mars grinned at the monitors, then lit a match. He held it up to make sure they saw it. Then he brought it close to the door.

Jennifer pushed the power button. The phone chirped as it came to life, and this time it stayed on. She jammed the phone into Thomas's hands. 'Here! It's working!'

Thomas punched in Talley's number, then glanced up at the monitors. Mars was staring into the camera and Thomas saw his lips move. 'What's he saying?'

Jennifer grabbed Thomas and pulled him away from the door.

'He's saying goodbye.'

Mars tossed the match. The room erupted in flame.

WHEN TALLEY HEARD the first scream from the house, he moved down the line of patrol cars, listening hard. The house was silent. Then room by room, the lights went off.

Talley saw Martin approaching, excited. 'What's going on?'

Talley was starting to explain when they saw a dull orange glow move inside the house at the edges of the window shades.

His phone rang. It was Thomas.

'Mars killed Kevin and Dennis, and now he's burning the house! We're in the security room, me and Jennifer! We're trapped!'

The cell connection faltered and died.

Talley felt strangely distant from himself. He had no choice now; he would act to save these children. It didn't matter what the Watchman wanted, or Jones, or even if it put Jane and Amanda at risk. He pulled Martin by the arm, taking her with him as he ran along the street towards Jones, shouting instructions as they ran.

'Krupchek's torching the house! Get the fire truck up here!'

'What about Jones?'

'I'm getting him now. Tell your people to stand by; if Jones won't move, we'll go in without him!'

Martin fell behind to use her radio. Talley ran towards Jones.

'Krupchek's torching the house. We have to go in.'

Jones didn't believe him. 'We're waiting to hear from the man.'

Talley grabbed Jones's arm, and felt him stiffen. Behind them, the fire engine rumbled to life and swung round the corner.

'The house is *burning*! Krupchek has those kids trapped. We can't wait.'

'That's bullshit.'

'Look at it!' Talley shoved Jones towards the house.

Flames were visible in the den window. Police radios crackled as the perimeter guards reported the fire. Hicks and the Sheriff's tactical team trotted towards Martin.

Jones seemed frozen in place, anchored by his expectation of the Watchman's call. Talley jerked his arm again, pulling him round.

'I'm breaching that house, Jones. Are you coming or not?'

'They'll kill your family.'

'*Those kids are trapped!*'

Jones gripped his MP5.

Talley slipped his hand under his sweatshirt and touched the .45.

'What? You want to shoot it out with the chief of police here in the street? You think you'll get the disks that way?'

Jones glanced at the house again, then decided. 'All right, goddammit, but it's just us going into that house. We'll secure the structure, then retrieve the disks.'

They made their assault plan as they ran to the house.

MARS WANTED MUSIC. He went to the den, where he remembered a nice sound system. He tuned to a local hip-hop station, and cranked the speakers to distortion, then returned to the bedroom.

He checked the Chinaman's gun, saw that there were still plenty of bullets, then crouched at the far side of the room, far from the flames and below the smoke.

TWO MEN WOULD BREACH the front door, two the French doors; Talley and Jones would breach through a window to enter a guest bedroom next to the master. Once inside, Jones would radio the sixth man, who would shatter the sliding doors in the master bedroom to distract Krupchek from the bedroom door, which would be the point of ingress for the assault. All of them would carry fire extinguishers.

Talley borrowed a vest from one of the CHiPs, strapping it over his sweatshirt, then slung a fire extinguisher over his shoulder. The firemen ran out their hoses, remaining under cover until word would come down that the hostiles had been neutralised.

Jones set off for the house. Talley caught up with him at the corner of the house outside the guest bedroom window. They heard music, loud and throbbing within the burning house. The noise would cover their entrance. They pulled away the screen, then Jones used a crowbar to wedge open the window. He pushed aside the shade, then gave Talley a thumbs up, saying the room was clear. They lifted the fire extinguishers into the room, then they waited. They would not enter the house until the others were in position.

Jones glanced over his shoulder at Talley, and twirled his finger. They were spooling up, getting ready to launch.

Jones jabbed his finger at the window. 'Go!'

Jones went first, Talley giving him a boost up, then scrambling inside after him. The room was lit only by a low wall of flame that barred the door to the hall. The master bedroom door was only ten feet away. They turned on their flashlights, then met each other's eyes. Talley nodded. Jones keyed his mike. 'Now.'

Talley heard the sliding glass doors in the master bedroom shatter at the same time that the front door blew inwards off its hinges.

Two shots came from the master bedroom. Talley and Jones charged down the hall as a third shot cracked in the bedroom, then they were through the door. The room was an inferno. The man who had shattered the glass doors was down, writhing in agony. Talley glimpsed a flash of movement from his right and saw Krupchek heave up from behind a chair, pumping out shots even as Talley and Jones fired. Krupchek stumbled backwards, arms windmilling as he fell into the flames, thrashing and screaming. Jones fired into him and he was still.

They unstrapped their fire extinguishers as Jones's other men cleared through the door, covering the room with their weapons.

Jones pointed at the first two, then the fallen man.

'You and you, him, out to the van.'

Talley blasted gouts of CO_2 at the burning security door, and shouted for Jones to help. 'Jones! The kids are in here.'

Jones shoved the next man towards the door.

'The office is at the front of the house. Make sure the hall is clear.'

Jones and the last man joined Talley. Their CO_2 extinguishers hissed. The red walls turned black as the flames engulfing them died.

Talley banged at the door with his extinguisher. 'Thomas! It's me!'

The fire on the walls licked to life again, and Talley fogged the door as it opened. The boy and his sister stood back, wary of the heat. Jones grabbed Talley's arm.

'They're yours, Talley. We're getting the disks.'

Talley let them go. He blasted the walls around the door again to beat back the flames, then stepped through and took the boy's hand.

'We're going to move fast. Stay behind me.'

Talley hurried them along the hall, using the fire extinguisher whenever the flames crowded too close. He paused only long enough to switch his radio to the Bristo frequency, and called Mikkelson.

'Mikki! The kids are coming out the front. Take care of them.'

When they reached the entry, Talley could see into the office. Jones and his men were searching Smith's desk. Talley pulled Thomas aside out of their view. 'Are the disks still up in your room?'

'Yeah. With my computer.'

Talley pointed at Mikkelson waiting in the cul-de-sac, and pushed the kids through the door. 'Go to her. Go!'

Talley waited to see that both kids ran towards the cars, then slipped up the stairs. The air on the first floor was dense with smoke so thick that it choked the beam from his flashlight. He couldn't see more than a few feet. He worked his way along the wall and found Rooney lying outside the first door. Talley couldn't tell if he was dead or alive, and didn't take the time to check. He kicked Rooney's pistol away, then looked in the first room long enough to realise it belonged to Jennifer. The second room belonged to the boy. Talley found his computer on the floor at the far side of the bed. One disk sat on the floor, the other in a disk drive beside the keyboard.

'Talley!'

Talley jerked at the voice, then saw that Martin was standing in the doorway. Her helmet was cinched tight and her pistol was at her side.

'Did you find them?'

He joined her. 'Where's Jones?'

'They're tearing up the office. They haven't found the disks.'

'The boy had them in his room.' Talley showed her the disks and started for the stairs.

Martin brought up her gun. 'Give them to me.'

He was startled by her tone. 'What are you talking about?'

He glanced at the gun again, and knew that Benza owned her.

'Give me the disks, Talley. You'll get your family.'

He knew he wouldn't. He knew that once Benza was safe, anyone who knew anything about Smith's relationship to Sonny Benza would die. Once she had the disks she would kill him.

'What are you going to do, Martin? Tell them I was shot in the confusion? You going to blame Krupchek and Rooney?'

'If I have to.'

'How much are they paying you?'

'More than you'll ever know. Now give me the disks.'

The flames crept up the stairwell at the end of the hall.

Talley saw something moving in the smoke. A shadow lifted itself from the floor. 'Rooney's alive.'

Her eyes flicked once to the side, then came back to him. She didn't believe him. '*Give me the disks!*'

Dennis Rooney lurched into the light, eyes glassy and dripping with blood. He had found his gun.

'*Martin!*'

She turned, but not in time. Rooney fired before she could swing her gun to him. Something hard slapped Talley in the chest. The next bullet caught Martin in the thigh, and the third in the cheek beneath her right eye. Martin spun slowly into the smoke as Talley drew his weapon and fired.

Saturday, 2:41am. The heavy bullet from Talley's pistol bounced Dennis Rooney off the wall. Talley planted a knee in Rooney's chest and knocked away his gun, but this time Rooney was dead. Talley listened for the sound of Jones's team coming up the stairs, but he couldn't hear anything over the crackling sound of the fire.

He radioed Mikkelson. 'You got the kids?'

'Yes, sir. They're safe.'

'The FBI agents took out a wounded man. Three of them went to their van.'

'Ah, roger. We saw that.'

'Get Jorgenson and Cooper. Arrest them. Strip their radios and cellphones, cuff them, and don't let them talk to anyone.'

'Ah, arrest the FBI?'

'They're not FBI. Arrest them, Mikki. They are armed and

dangerous, so you watch your ass. Bring them to the jail, but do not—I repeat, do *not*—let them communicate with anyone: no phone calls, no press, no lawyers, nothing. Don't tell anyone about this. Understand?'

'Ah, sure, Chief.'

Everything now depended on speed. The Watchman might learn that his people were being arrested, but his information would be spotty and incomplete; he wouldn't know what had happened or why, so he wouldn't act against Jane and Amanda until he knew the details. Talley was counting on that.

He pushed the disks under his vest and ran to the stairwell. The smoke was a twisting orange haze. He crept down the stairs with his eyes on the office, then crossed to the door just as one of Jones's men stepped out. Talley aimed at his face, touching his own lips to motion the man quiet, then stripped his pistol and MP5. Talley handcuffed him and pushed him into the office. Jones was frantically searching the floor around the desk, his flashlight beam dim in the haze; the drawers had been pulled, their contents scattered. The second man was stripping books from the shelves. They both looked up when Talley pushed the first man to the floor.

Talley trained his gun on them. 'Hands on your heads, lace your fingers, turn round with your backs to me.'

Jones said, 'What the hell are you doing?'

The second man swung his MP5, but Talley squared him with a round, the heavy .45 punching through his vest.

Talley brought his gun back to Jones. 'Lace your fingers. *Now!*'

Jones raised his hands, then slowly turned.

'You're screwing up, Talley. They've got your family.'

Talley stripped the second man of his weapons, never taking his gun from Jones. He checked the pulse in the man's neck, then went to Jones. He took his pistol and MP5, tossed them to the side then ripped the power cord from Smith's computer. He forced Jones onto his belly, then pulled his hands behind his back.

'Move, and I'll kill you.' Talley planted his knee in the small of Jones's back, then tied his wrists. He wanted to get Jones out of the house, but he didn't want to do it on television. He keyed his radio.

'Mikki? Have the firemen move in, then roll your car to the back of the house on Flanders Road. Meet me there.'

Talley knew that the cameras would be trained on the firefighters. He wanted everyone's attention on the front of the house, not the rear. He didn't want the Watchman seeing this on TV.

Talley pushed Jones and the surviving man to the rear of the house. He changed his radio to the Sheriff's command frequency and told the officers on the back wall to kill their lights. The back yard plunged into darkness. Talley pushed the two men outside and hustled them to the wall. When the Sheriff's sergeant-supervisor saw that Talley had two FBI agents bound, he said, 'What the hell's going on?'

'Help me get these guys over.'

Mikkelson and Dreyer were climbing out of their car by the time Talley jumped to the ground.

The SWAT officers stared at Jones and the other man. Here they were, their vests emblazoned with a huge white FBI, cuffed and dragged over the wall. The sergeant again asked Talley what was happening.

'Martin's inside. The first floor. She's been shot.'

Talley got the response he wanted. The SWAT cops poured over the wall and rushed towards the house.

Talley shoved his prisoners towards Mikkelson's car, pushed the first man into the back seat, then shoved Jones against the fender.

'Where are they?'

'I don't know. I'm not part of that.'

'Then where is *he*?'

'I don't know.'

'What's his name?'

'It doesn't work like that, Talley. He's a voice on the phone.'

Talley searched Jones's pockets as he spoke, and found Jones's cell-phone. 'What's his number?'

'I don't know any more than you.'

Talley kneed him in the stomach, doubling Jones over.

Mikkelson and Dreyer squirmed uneasily. 'Ah, Chief . . .'

'These bastards have my family.'

Talley cocked the .45 and pressed it into Jones's cheek. 'We're talking about my wife and daughter. You think I won't kill you?'

'He calls me. Just like with you.'

Talley's head throbbed. He told himself to shoot the sonofabitch, put one in his shoulder joint and make him scream.

Mikkelson's voice came from far away. 'Chief?'

Talley lowered his gun. He wasn't like them.

Talley stared at Jones's phone, then dropped it to the street and crushed it. He had the Nokia, but if it rang, he would not answer it. If the Watchman placed the call, the Watchman would expect him to answer. Talley didn't want to do what the Watchman expected.

'Put him in a cell with the others.'

Walter Smith would know. They trusted Smith with their closest secrets. It had all come back to Smith again.

'Where are the kids?'

'Cooper has them with the paramedics. They're OK. We finally got the mother, Chief. She's flying back from Florida.'

'Tell Cooper to meet me at the hospital, and to bring the children.'

WHEN A STRING of dull pops snapped from the direction of the house, Ken Seymore recognised the sound: gunfire. He trotted to the nearest news van to find out what was happening. The tech there monitored a scanner tuned to the Sheriff's tactical frequency.

'You guys get anything on that?'

The tech waved him silent. He listened to the scanner with a bug in his ear, because their news director didn't want anyone else to hear.

'They called up the fire company. The goddamned house is on fire.'

'What was the shooting?'

The tech waved Seymore quiet again and tuned his receiver, working through the frequencies. 'The SWAT team went in. They got casualties. The kids are coming out.'

Seymore took out his phone.

THE LOCAL STATIONS resumed live coverage because of the fire, but the aerial shot was so murky that Glen Howell couldn't tell who was who or what was happening, just that everything was going to hell.

'You sure Jones's people got hit?'

'They said it was FBI, so it hadda be Jones's guys. We're getting this stuff off the scanner.'

'They get the disks?'

'I don't know. It's happening right now; no one's talking to us.'

Howell tried to stay calm. 'Is Jones still in the house?'

'I don't know.'

'Where's Talley?'

'I don't know.'

'You're paid to know, goddammit. That's why you're there.'

Howell broke the connection, then punched in Jones's number. A computer voice said that the user had turned off his phone. Howell called Martin. He let her phone ring and finally hung up. 'Shit!' He dialled Talley's number and listened to the Nokia ring twenty times. Then he snapped his phone shut so hard he thought he might have broken it.

TALLEY ROLLED code three all the way to the hospital. The parking lot was almost deserted; the remaining press camped by the emergency room entrance. Talley parked at the side of the hospital to avoid them, but got out of the car because sitting was difficult. He leaned against the door with his arms crossed, watching the street, then realised he was still wearing the bullet-resistant vest and the radio. He took them off and tossed them into the back seat. He found the Nokia, and dropped it onto the front seat.

The Nokia rang. Talley felt his chest tighten, and realised that he had stopped breathing. The phone ceased ringing as Cooper swung into the parking lot, then turned towards him.

Thomas and Jennifer got out of Cooper's car.

Jennifer said, 'Are we going to see our father?'

'That's right. Did Officer Cooper tell you about your mother? We spoke with her in Florida. She's flying back now.'

They beamed. Jennifer actually said, 'Yay.'

Talley put out his hand.

'We didn't really meet before. My name is Jeff Talley.'

'I'm Jennifer Smith. Thank you for what you did.'

She shook his hand firmly. Thomas shook his hand, too.

'It's good to finally meet you, Thomas. You were a big help. You were very brave. You both were.'

'Thank you, Chief. Is our daddy OK?'

'He's doing better. Let's go see him.'

Talley brought them through the side entrance. He held their hands, letting go only to show his badge to an orderly who led them to the emergency room. It was only a matter of time before word spread to the press that he had brought the children to their father. When the press knew, the Watchman would know.

A nurse that Talley recognised from before stopped them.

'You're the Chief, aren't you? May I help you?'

'I'm bringing the Smith children to see their father.'

'I'd better get Dr Reese.'

'Fine, you go get her. We'll be in the room.'

Talley found Smith's room without waiting. Smith was staring at the ceiling. He was still wired to the monitors.

Jennifer said, 'Daddy?'

Smith lifted his head enough to see, then his face registered surprise and elation. The kids ran and hugged their father. Talley waited in the doorway, giving them a moment, then entered and stood at the end of the bed. Jennifer cried, her face buried in her father's chest. The little boy wiped at his eyes and asked if it hurt.

Smith wrapped his arm round Jennifer and held Thomas's arm. He looked past them, met Talley's eyes, then hugged his children tighter. 'Thank God you're all right. You're all right, aren't you?'

Talley stepped up behind Jennifer. 'We reached your wife. She's in the air now.'

Smith met Talley's eyes again, then looked away.

Talley said, 'Your family is safe.'

Smith nodded, still not looking at him.

Talley squeezed Jennifer's shoulder. 'Could you guys wait in the hall for a second? I need to talk to your dad.'

Smith glanced up, then nodded to send his children to the corridor. Jennifer took Thomas's hand and led him outside.

Smith took a deep breath, let it out, then looked up. 'Thank you.'

'Those are good kids you got there. That little boy, Thomas, he's something else.'

Smith closed his eyes. Talley watched Smith, wondering if there was anything he could say to get this man to help him. He had negotiated with hundreds of subjects, and that was the game: Figure out what they needed to hear and say it; find their buttons and push them. All of that seemed beyond Talley now. He glanced over at Thomas and Jennifer standing in the corridor, and felt a pain so deep he thought it might break him. If he could just get Jane and Amanda back, he would never let them go.

He patted Smith's arm. 'I don't know what you've done in your life, but you'd better do right by those kids. You've got your family now, Smith. They're safe. Help me get mine.'

Smith blinked hard at the ceiling. He shook his head, then closed his eyes tight. He took another deep breath, then looked past Talley to his own children. 'Shit.' Smith's eyes were wet.

'Who has my family?'

'That would be Glen Howell. He was coming to the house today. He's Benza's man on the scene.'

Talley touched his wrist. 'Gold Rolex here? Dark tan?'

Smith nodded.

Talley had something now. 'OK, Smith. OK. Glen Howell. He's been calling me, but now I need to call him. How do I reach him?'

Smith gave him Howell's phone number.

Saturday, 3:09am. Talley doubled the guards on Smith and his children, then hurried back to his car. He closed his eyes and tried to find focus. He was a crisis negotiator; Howell was a subject; Amanda and Jane were hostages. He had done this before; he could do it again. It was just him and the phone. When his breathing was even and his shoulders relaxed, Talley got into the car. His task was to sound confident and controlled. His task was to assume control.

Talley punched Howell's number into the Nokia.

The Watchman answered on the second ring, sounding abrupt and irritated. 'What?'

Talley made his voice soft. 'Guess who.'

Howell recognised his voice. Talley heard it in the quality of the silence even before Howell answered.

'How'd you get this number?'

'Here are two words for you: Glen Howell.'

'Screw yourself.'

'I think Sonny Benza is going to screw *you*. I have his financial records. I have your SWAT team. I have Captain Martin. I have you. And I have Walter Smith.'

Howell's voice rose. 'I have your family. Don't forget that.'

Talley kept his voice even. He knew that if he remained calm, Howell would grow more frightened. Howell would suspect that Talley was up to something, and, by suspecting it, he would believe that it was true. 'I'll give you five minutes. Call Benza. Ask him if he wants to spend the rest of his life in prison.'

'I'll ask him how many times he wants me to screw your daughter.'

'Ask him if I can keep the money.' All Talley heard was the hiss of the cell connection. 'I have something else that belongs to you. I found some money in the house. Looks like almost a million dollars.'

Talley had learned from a hundred negotiations that all liars think everyone lies, all crooks think everyone is crooked. The strain in the silence was the sound of Howell trying to read Talley just as Talley was reading Howell. He would be scared and suspicious, but he would also want to believe. His belief was everything.

Howell answered slowly. 'What do you want, Talley?'

'How much money did I find?'

'One point two million.'

'I'll sell you a pass. My wife and daughter, and the money, for the disks. If you hurt them, the disks go straight to the FBI and I'll keep the money anyway.' Talley knew that Howell would never consider a straight-up trade, his family for the disks, because there was no reason for Talley to keep his word. But the money changed things.

Talley didn't wait for Howell to answer. 'I'll tell you how this is going to work. I'll bring the disks to the north entrance of the mall by the freeway. You bring my family. If they're OK, we'll trade. If I don't make it home tonight, my officers will still have Smith and your phoney FBI SWAT team.'

'You make it home, you'll cut them loose?'

'I'll cut them loose.'

'OK, Talley, I think we can do this. But not at the mall.'

'As long as it's not in the middle of nowhere.'

'The Comfort Inn west of Bristo.'

'I know it.'

'Be there in ten minutes. Someone will be waiting in the parking lot. One minute late, there won't be anyone there to find.'

Talley ended the call. The Comfort Inn was less than a mile away. He still had much to do.

GLEN HOWELL was shaking when he put down the phone. Talley had caught him off guard and jammed him into making a deal that might be a setup, but his job was to recover the disks. Howell picked up the house phone. Duane Manelli was sitting in a room two doors down with LJ Ruiz.

'I need you and LJ outside. Talley's coming here. I don't know if he's coming alone. Get outside and set up to watch the area.'

Howell hung up. He didn't want to make his next call, but he didn't have a choice about that, either. Making the next call scared him more than waiting for Talley. He dialled Sonny Benza.

Palm Springs, California

'Sonny? Sonny, wake up.'

Benza opened his eyes, and saw Phil Tuzee. Charles Salvetti was pacing by the desk, looking upset. Benza was stretched out on the couch, the three of them still in his office at four in the morning.

'Glen Howell's on the phone. We got a mess here. Look.'

Benza sat up and squinted at the television. Smith's house was in flames. 'Jesus. What happened?'

'It's a friggin' blood bath. Howell's team went in, and everything went to hell. Now they're pulling bodies out of the place.'

'Did we get the disks?'

'No, skipper. Talley has the disks.'

Salvetti called from the desk. 'C'mon. Howell's on the speaker. He says we don't have much time.'

Benza went to the phone, trying to control his anger. 'What the hell are you doing down there?'

Howell explained the situation. Benza saw himself driving Glen Howell to the desert and chopping him into sausage with a machete.

'Sonny?'

Benza's rage cleared. He saw Salvetti and Tuzee watching him. Sonny Benza was more frightened now than he had ever been in his life. Howell was still talking.

'He wants the money that Smith was holding for us, the one-point-two. He gets his family and the money, he says he'll give us the disks.'

Salvetti said, 'Wait a minute. Are you saying that this asshole wants to be paid off? He's *extorting* us?'

Tuzee shook his head, looking at Benza but speaking to Howell. 'It's a set-up. He's baiting you to get the wife.'

'What other choice do we have?'

Benza answered, softly. 'You don't have any other choice.'

Howell didn't answer for several seconds. 'I understand.'

'Hang on.'

Benza muted the phone. He was trying to figure out which way to jump. If Talley was setting up Howell, federal agents might already be poring over the disks and petitioning for warrants. Benza knew that he should warn New York, but the thought of it made his bowels clench.

'Phil, call the airport and have the jet prepped. Just in case.'

Tuzee went to the other phone.

Benza took the phone off mute. 'OK, Glen, listen: I don't care about the money. If I gotta lose the cash to buy some time, so be it.'

'That's what I figured.'

'If Talley is setting you up, we're screwed anyway. Get the disks, then get rid of him. If you don't get the disks, you're gonna have a problem, Glen. You understand that?'

'Our guys will still be in custody. He's not going to cut them free until after he has his family.'

'After Talley is dead, we'll take care of Smith and Jones and his people. Everyone has to die.'

'I understand.'

Benza ended the call, then went back to the couch.

Salvetti came over and sat next to him. 'This thing is goin' south, Sonny. We should warn New York. We let 'em know what's comin', old man Castellano might cut us some slack.'

Benza considered that, then shook his head. 'Screw New York. I'm not that anxious to die.'

'You sure about that, Sonny? We still got a few minutes here.'

'We lose those disks, the last thing I want is a conversation with that old man. Even prison looks good by comparison.'

'That old man has long arms. He'll reach us even in prison.'

Tuzee crossed his arms and shrugged. 'What the hell, we get those disks, we'll beat the Feds and Castellano will never know this happened. Things could still work out.'

Benza decided to pack. In case things didn't.

Santa Clarita, California

Saturday, 3:37am. Talley drove without lights. He pulled off the road 100 yards before the motel and left his car in the weeds, thankful for·the black sweatshirt he had pulled on earlier. He tied a roll of duct tape to a belt loop, then shoved a handful of plastic restraints into his pocket. He rubbed dirt on his face and hands to kill their shine, then drew his pistol and trotted towards the motel. The moon was up, bright like a blue pearl, giving him light.

Talley guessed that Howell would post observers to warn him if the police were approaching. He worked his way to the edge of the motel property and froze beside a spiky-leafed manzanita bush, searching the shadows at the edge of the light for some bit of movement or blackness that did not fit. The motel was a long two-storey barn surrounded by a parking lot. Talley worked his way round the perimeter of the grounds, moving outside the field of light, pausing every two paces to look and listen.

He spotted one observer sitting between the wheels of a truck. A few minutes later, he found the second man hunkered beneath a pepper tree. He looked for others, but only the two men were posted.

DUANE MANELLI lay belly-down in the dirt at the base of a pepper tree, watching LJ Ruiz move between the wheels of the eighteen-wheeler. They were hooked up by cellphone. If either saw an oncoming vehicle or anything suspicious, they could alert the other, and then Glen Howell. Manelli didn't like it that he could see movement.

He whispered into his phone. 'LJ, you in position?'

'Yeah, I'm here.'

'Settle in and stop moving around.'

'Screw yourself. I'm not moving.'

Manelli didn't respond. LJ had stopped moving, so Manelli let it go. Manelli settled into the dirt.

Ruiz said something, but Manelli didn't understand.

'Say again.'

Ruiz didn't answer.

'I didn't hear you, LJ. What'd you say?' Manelli heard the rocks crunch behind him, then his head exploded with rainbow light.

TALLEY BOUND MANELLI'S wrists behind the man's back with the plastic restraints. He secured Manelli's ankles the same way, then rolled the man over. Talley slapped Manelli's face. 'Wake up.'

Manelli's eyes fluttered. Talley waited until the eyes focused, then pressed the gun into Manelli's neck.

'You know who I am?'

'Talley.'

'Which room are they in?'

'They're not. Howell sent them away.'

Talley cursed. He didn't expect that Howell would have kept them with him, but he had hoped. 'All right. Where are they?'

'I don't know. Clewes took them.'

Talley had not heard that name before, Clewes, but it didn't matter. If Jane and Amanda were being held somewhere else, he would have to force Howell to bring them back.

'How many people does Howell have?'

'Five here at the motel, plus Clewes.'

'You and the asshole at the truck, leaves three inside?'

'That's right.'

Talley thought it through. Three against one. None of it mattered. He had no other choice. 'Which room?'

Manelli hesitated.

Talley pushed the .45 harder into Manelli's throat. 'Which room?'

Manelli sighed. 'One twenty-four.'

Talley covered Manelli's mouth with duct tape, then returned to the parking lot. He found the green Mustang on the far side of the motel, parked one place down from 124. A man was standing by it, smoking, which left two more men in the room. Talley saw a silver watch on his left arm; this man wasn't Howell. Talley worked his way as close to the Mustang as possible. The man was less than fifteen yards from him. When he turned away, Talley rushed forward.

The Mustang man started at the sound, but he was too late. Talley hit him hard on the side of the head, using the .45 as a club. The man staggered sideways. Talley grabbed him round the neck from behind in a choke hold, and pushed him towards the room. He didn't want the man unconscious; he wanted him as a shield.

Talley kicked the door next to the knob, busting the jamb, and shoved the Mustang man through, screaming his identification.

'*Police! You're under arrest!*' Talley didn't think they would shoot him until they had the disks. He was counting on that.

Glen Howell brought up a pistol as he dropped into a crouch, shouting at a man with a big head seated by the window. The man rolled out of his chair and also came up with a gun, aiming from the floor in a two-handed grip as Howell shouted not to fire.

'Don't shoot him! Don't shoot!'

Talley shifted his aim between the two men, making himself small behind the Mustang man. Talley shouted, 'Where's my family?'

Howell abruptly released his gun, letting it swing free on his finger. 'Just take it easy. We're here to do business. Do you have the disks?'

Talley shifted his aim to the man with the big head. 'You know I have the disks, you sonofabitch. Where's my family?'

Howell slowly stood, hands out, letting his gun hang. 'They're all right. Can I take a phone from my pocket?'

'They were supposed to be here.'

'Let me get the phone. You can talk to them, see they're OK.'

Howell took out a cellphone and pressed a number. Someone on the other end answered, and Howell told them to put the woman on.

He held out the phone. 'Here. Talk to her. She's all right.'

Talley jammed his gun under the Mustang man's jaw, and warned him not to move. Howell brought the phone over, holding it with two fingers. Talley took it with his free hand, and Howell stepped back.

'Jane?'

'Jeff! We're—' The line went dead.

'*Shit!*'

Howell shrugged, reasonably. 'You see? They're alive. Whether they stay that way depends on you.'

Talley tossed the phone back to Howell, then took out a single disk. 'One disk. You'll get the other when I have my girls. Not talk to them on the phone, but *have* them. You don't like it, tough.' He tossed the disk onto the bed.

He knew that Howell would be wondering if Talley had the second disk with him, thinking that if Talley had both disks, Howell could simply shoot him and take the disks and this would be over. But if Talley didn't have both disks, then Howell would be screwed. So Howell wouldn't shoot him. Not yet. And that gave Talley a chance to jam him into revealing Amanda and Jane.

Howell picked up the disk. 'I have to see if it's real.'

An IBM ThinkPad with a Zip drive attached was set up on the night table. Howell sat on the edge of the bed as he opened the disk, then grunted at the contents. 'All right. This is one. Where's the other?'

'First my girls. I have my girls, you get the disk.'

Talley waited as Howell considered his options. Talley already knew what he would decide. Talley had left Howell no other choice.

Howell picked up his phone and called Marion Clewes.

HOWELL SPOKE CLEARLY, never taking his eyes from Talley. 'Bring them. Stop the car outside the room, but don't get out. Don't hang up. I'll want to talk to you again.'

Howell lowered the phone. Clewes was parked behind a Mobil station down the street. He would be there in seconds.

'OK, Talley, they're on their way.'

Howell heard the car before he saw it. Clewes wheeled to a stop in the space next to the Mustang, the nose of his car framed dead centre in the open door. The woman, Jane, was in the passenger seat. The daughter was in the rear. They were both tied, their mouths taped.

Talley moved towards the door. 'Tell him to get out of the car.'

Howell raised the phone. 'Marion?'

Outside, Clewes lifted his own phone. 'Yes, sir?'

'Aim your gun at the woman's head.'

MARION HAD his orders. Just as Glen Howell's job was to recover the disks, Marion knew exactly what he was supposed to do and when he was supposed to do it. It was all about doing your job, being rewarded if you succeeded, being punished if you failed. Success or failure were defined by the disks.

Marion raised his gun to the mother's head. She trembled, and clenched her eyes. Behind her, in the back, the daughter moaned.

HOWELL KEPT the phone to his mouth, speaking to Talley but also the man in the car. 'Give me the second disk or he'll kill your wife.'

'*No!*' Talley jerked his gun to the man in the car but was scared that the angle of the windshield would deflect his shot. Talley jerked his aim back at Howell. 'I'll kill you, Howell! You'll never get the disk!'

'He'll kill your wife, but your daughter will still be alive. Are you listening to this, Marion?'

Talley saw the man behind the wheel nod. Talley shifted his aim again, back to the man in the car.

'I'll damn well kill you! Can you hear *that*, you sonofabitch?!'

The man in the car smiled.

Howell spoke reasonably. 'I'll still have your daughter. Your wife will be dead, but your daughter will be alive. But if you shoot me, then he'll kill your daughter, too. Do you want to lose both of them?'

Talley aimed at the man in the car again. His gun shook. If Talley shot at the man in the car, Howell or the man with the big head would shoot him, and then all of them would be dead.

Howell said, 'The negotiation is over, Talley. I won.'

Talley glanced at Howell. He measured the shots; first the man in the car, then Howell, lastly the man on the floor. He would have to make all three to save his family. He didn't think that he could.

Howell said, 'Drop your gun, and give me the second disk. Give me the disk or he'll put her brain on the window.'

Talley's eyes filled because he thought they would all die anyway, but he still had one small chance left. Talley dropped his gun.

The Mustang man jumped out of the way. Howell and the big-headed man charged forward. They scooped up Talley's gun and shoved him against the wall, pinning him like an insect to a board. Howell searched him even as Talley told him about the second disk.

'It's in my left front pocket.'

Talley felt numb. Defeated. Outside, the man behind the wheel climbed out of the car and came to the door. Talley watched Amanda and Jane in the car. Jane met his eye, and in that moment he felt buoyed by a tide of love that felt as if it could carry him away.

Howell loaded the disk into the ThinkPad.

Talley watched him open the disk, and took a grim pleasure in watching Howell's face darken and grow fierce.

'You sonofabitch. This isn't the second disk! It's blank!'

Talley felt strangely removed from this room and these people. He glanced at Jane again. He smiled at her, and then he turned back to Howell. 'I don't have the second disk any more. I gave it to the Sheriffs, and they're giving it to the FBI. Benza's over. You're over. There's nothing either of us can do.' Talley watched the disbelief float to the surface of Howell's face like a great slow bubble.

'You're lying.'

'I'm not lying. We're done here, Howell. Let us go. Let us go and save yourself the murder charge.'

Howell stood stiffly, like a mechanical man. He lumbered around the bed as if he was in shock, picked up his gun from the floor, and aimed it at Talley. 'Are you out of your mind?'

'I just want to take my family home.'

Howell shook his head as if he still couldn't believe that this was happening, and then he blinked numbly at the man in the door, the man who had been in the car. 'Kill every one of these people.'

The man in the door whom Howell had called Marion raised his gun and aimed it squarely at Talley's face. Marion was a small man, ordinary in appearance, the type of anonymous man who would be invisible in a mall and impossible for witnesses to describe. An Everyman; average height, average weight, brown, brown.

Talley stared into the black hole of the muzzle and braced for the bullet. 'I'm sorry, Jane.'

Marion shifted his gun hard to the side and fired. He adjusted his aim, and fired again, then again. The first bullet took Howell above the right eye, the second the Mustang man dead centre in the left eye, and the third caught the man with the big head in the temple.

Marion crossed the room to retrieve the one good disk, pocketed it, then went to the car. He helped Jane out, then opened the back door and helped Amanda. He walked round the car, climbed in behind the wheel, and drove away without another word.

Talley stumbled out of the room and ran to his wife. He hugged her with frantic desperation, then pulled his daughter close, squeezing them to him as the tears spilled down his face. He held them and knew then that he would never let them go, that he had lost them once and now had almost lost them this second time, lost them for ever, and that he could and would never allow that to happen again.

Palm Springs, California

Saturday, 4:36am. Sonny Benza didn't try to sleep after they got off the phone with Glen Howell. The three of them sat down to wait.

The phone rang, Tuzee answered. He punched on the speaker, saying, 'It's Ken Seymore. Ken, Sonny and Charlie are here. What do you have down there?'

'All of it's gone to shit. I'm still here at the development, but—'

Benza shouted over him. 'Do we have the disks or not?'

'No! They got the disks. Glen Howell and two more of our guys are dead. They got Manelli and Ruiz and I don't know who else. It's a goddamned catastrophe down here. I don't know what happened.'

'Who killed Howell? Talley?'

'I don't know! Yeah, I think it was Talley. I don't know. Man, I'm hearing all kinds of things.'

Sonny Benza closed his eyes. Just like that it was gone, everything was gone, three lowlifes break into a house and everything that he had worked for his entire life was about to end.

Tuzee said, 'You *sure* they got the disks?'

'Talley gave the disks to the Sheriffs. That much I know for sure. Then I don't know what happened. Glen got jammed up at the motel, they had a big firefight or somethin', and now the FBI just rolled up, the *real* FBI. What do you want me to do?'

Benza shook his head; there wasn't anything Ken Seymore or anyone else could do.

Tuzee said, 'Vanish. Anyone who isn't in custody, take off. You're done.'

The line went dead. Ken Seymore was gone.

Benza stood without a word and went to the great glass windows overlooking Palm Springs. He was going to miss the view.

Salvetti came up behind him. 'What do you want us to do, Boss?'

'How long do you figure we have before the Feds get here?'

Salvetti and Tuzee traded a shrug.

Tuzee said, 'Talley will tell them what's on the disks, then they'll probably talk to Smith. They'll get a warrant based on our alleged involvement with the killings and kidnaps in Bristo. Say they get a telephonic warrant and coordinate with the state cops out here through the substation . . . I'd say two hours.'

Benza sighed. 'OK, guys. I want to be in the air in an hour.'

Salvetti said, 'You gonna tell New York?'

Benza wouldn't tell New York. He was more frightened of their reaction than he was of battling the Feds. 'Screw 'em. Go get your families. Don't bother packing, we'll buy new when we get there. Meet me at the airport as soon as you can.'

The three of them stood mute for a time. Benza shook each man's hand. They were good and dear friends. He loved them both.

They hurried away. Benza went to wake his wife.

New York City

Saturday, 7:49am, Eastern time. Vic Castellano sat on his terrace overlooking the Upper West Side of Manhattan. He still wore the white terry-cloth bathrobe. He put down his coffee. 'I can tell by your expression it ain't good.'

Jamie Beldone had just come out to see him. 'It's not. The police have the disks. They have Benza's accountant. Once the Feds develop the information, we're going to have a fight on our hands.'

'But we'll survive it.'

Jamie nodded. 'We'll take a few shots, but we'll survive. Benza, that's something else.'

'That sonofabitch still hasn't had the decency to call.'

'It shows a lack of class.'

Castellano settled back in his chair. 'We'll survive, but because of this West Coast asshole we're exposed to serious heat from the federal prosecutor. This means we've got just cause to seek redress.'

'The other families will see it that way.'

'And since the Feds are going to put Benza out of business, no one can beef if we take care of it for them.'

'It's a fair trade.'

Castellano nodded. 'All in all, it's probably good for everyone that all this happened. We can send somebody out west, take over Benza's end of things, and cut ourselves a bigger piece of the pie.'

'What are you going to do, skipper?'

Castellano had known what he was going do for the past six hours. He had it all arranged. 'Jamie, I want to be sure about this. That guy Clewes, Marion Clewes, he's kinda flaky. I don't want to just take his word that Benza screwed up. I want to know for sure.'

'I'm sure, Vic. I double-checked. I just hung up with Phil Tuzee.'

Castellano felt better. He knew that Phil Tuzee wouldn't steer him wrong. 'That's good enough. Make the call and finish this.'

Palm Springs, California

Saturday, 4:53am, Pacific time. Benza trotted back through the house
to the garage. All he carried was a blue nylon gym bag with $100,000
in cash, and his .357. Anything else he needed he could buy when
they landed; Benza had over $30 million stashed in foreign accounts.

Benza hit the button to open the garage door. He tossed the nylon
bag into the back seat of his Mercedes, then slid behind the wheel.
He started the car, threw it into reverse, then hit the gas hard, back-
ing in a wide arc towards the front door. He was moving so fast that
he almost broadsided the nondescript sedan that blocked his path.

Flashes of light speckled the air around the sedan, exploding
Benza's rear window. The bullets knocked him into the steering
wheel, then sideways onto the seat. He tried to get the .357 out of his
bag, but he didn't have time. Someone pulled open the driver's-side
door and shot Sonny Benza in the head.

PART FIVE

Two weeks later. Sunday, 2:16pm. The fantasy was always the same:
On the days that Jeff Talley visited the avocado orchard, he imagined Brendan Malik playing in the trees. He saw the boy laughing as
he ran, then climbing into the branches. Brendan was always happy
and laughing in these daydreams, even with his skin mottled in death
and blood pulsing from his neck. Talley had never been able to imagine the boy any other way.

Jane said, 'What are you thinking?'

The two of them were slouched down in the front seat of his patrol
car, watching red-tailed hawks float above the trees. Amanda had
stayed in Los Angeles, but Jane had come up for the weekend.

'Brendan Malik. Remember? That boy.'

'I don't remember.'

Talley realised that he had never told her. He had not mentioned
Brendan Malik to anyone after that night he left the boy's house, not
even the police psychologist. 'I guess I never told you.'

'Who was he?'

'A victim in one of the negotiations. It's not important any more.'

Jane took his hand. She turned sideways so that she faced him. 'It's important if you're thinking about it.'

Talley considered that. 'He was a little boy, nine, ten, something like that. About Thomas's age. I think about him sometimes.'

Talley found himself telling her about the night with Brendan Malik, of holding the boy's hand, of staring into his eyes as the little boy died, of the overwhelming feelings of failure and shame.

Listening, she cried, and he cried, too.

'I was trying to see his face right now, but I can't. I don't know whether to feel happy or sad about that. You think that's bad?'

Jane squeezed his hand. 'I think it's good we're talking about these things. It's a sign that you're healing.'

Talley shrugged, then smiled at her. 'About damn time.'

Jane smiled. 'Did you find out about Thomas?'

'I tried, but they won't tell me anything. I guess it's best this way.'

Walter Smith and his family had entered the US Marshals' witness protection programme. They had simply vanished. Talley hoped that Thomas would one day contact him, but he didn't think it likely. It was safer that way.

Jane said, 'How much time before you have to get back?'

'I've got time. I'm the Chief.'

Jane smiled wider. 'Let's walk.'

They walked from sunlight to shade to sun. It was good to walk. It was peaceful. Talley had been away for a very long time, hiding inside himself, but now he was back. He was on the way back.

The orchard, as always, was as still as a church.

'I'm glad you're here, Jane.'

Jane squeezed his hand. Talley knew, then, that though a church was a place to bury the dead, it was also a place to celebrate the living. Their lives could begin again.

ROBERT CRAIS

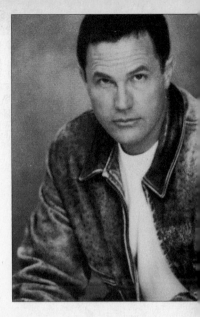

Robert Crais's *Hostage* is an intense read—a hard-edged crime novel that vividly conjures up the realities of hostage negotiation and crime-fighting in America today. It will come as no surprise to learn that Crais is very familiar with the the world in which the book's hero, Jeff Talley, moves. 'I come from a family of four generations of police officers and so I've heard a lot of cop stories,' he says. 'I know what policemen's lives are like and what the job does to a person. When I write about someone like Jeff Talley, the SWAT team negotiator in my latest book, it's based on some of the things I've heard over the years as well as on extensive research.'

Crais has been writing since he was in junior high school. In his early twenties he sold his first short story, but he remembers it being an uphill struggle. He received no less than 116 rejection letters before finally earning a fee of fifty dollars. From school he went on to study mechanical engineering, but writing remained his great love and, in 1987, his first novel, *The Monkey's Raincoat*, was published.

Nine books later, the size of Crais's fan club seems to have grown with every new publication. His novels starring the wisecracking private eye, Elvis Cole, earned him a devoted following; when he took a rest from Cole last year and published *Demolition Angel*, a gripping thriller about a female bomb-disposal expert, the book was a huge hit and placed Crais high on the best-seller lists.

The forty-eight-year-old author has also been highly successful as a scriptwriter, producing material for TV shows like *Hill Street Blues*, *Miami Vice* and *LA Law*. With film rights in *Hostage* already sold to MGM and Bruce Willis, his career is about to take another leap forward. From the days when he struggled to sell that first short story, the Louisiana-born author has come a long, long way, earning himself international acclaim.

ON THE STREET

WHERE YOU LIVE

MARY HIGGINS CLARK

From reading the diaries, he's come to know the killer's mind inside out. Already, he's copied the first two murders. Now he's looking for victim number three.

So, when fate brings the beautiful Emily Graham to his neighbourhood, it's just perfect. She is, without a doubt, his destiny, the key to his fulfilment.

Tuesday, March 20

He turned onto the boardwalk and felt the full impact of the stinging blast from the ocean. Observing the shifting clouds, he decided it wouldn't be surprising if they had a snow flurry later on, even though tomorrow was the first day of spring. It had been a long winter, and everyone said how much they were looking forward to the warm weather ahead. He wasn't.

He enjoyed Spring Lake best once late autumn set in. By then the summer people had closed their houses, not appearing even for weekends. He was chagrined, though, that with each passing year, more and more people were selling their winter homes and settling there permanently. They had decided it was worth the seventy-mile commute into New York so that they could begin and end the day in this quietly beautiful New Jersey seaside community.

Spring Lake, with its Victorian houses that appeared unchanged from the way they had been in the 1890s, was worth the inconvenience of the trip, they explained.

Spring Lake, with the fresh, bracing scent of the ocean always present, revived the soul, they agreed.

Spring Lake, with its two-mile boardwalk, where one could revel in the silvery magnificence of the Atlantic, was a treasure, they pointed out.

All of these people—the summer visitors, the permanent dwellers—shared so much, but none of them shared *his* secrets. He could stroll down Hayes Avenue and visualise Madeline Shapley as she had been in the late afternoon on September 7, 1891, seated on the wicker sofa on the wraparound porch of her home. She had been nineteen years old then, brown-eyed, with dark brown hair, sedately beautiful in her starched white linen dress.

Only he knew why she had had to die an hour later.

St Hilda Avenue, shaded with heavy oaks that had been mere saplings on August 5, 1893, when eighteen-year-old Letitia Gregg had failed to return home, brought other visions. She had been so frightened. Unlike Madeline, who had fought for her life, Letitia had begged for mercy.

The last one of the trio had been Ellen Swain, small and quiet, but far too inquisitive about the last hours of Letitia's life. And because of her curiosity, on March 31, 1896, she had followed her friend to the grave.

He knew every detail, every nuance of what had happened to her and to the others.

He had found the diary during a cold, rainy day in his fourteenth summer. Bored, he'd wandered into the old carriage house, which served as a garage. He climbed the rickety steps to the dusty loft and began rummaging through the boxes he found there.

The first one was filled with utterly useless odds and ends: rusty old lamps; faded, outdated clothing; pots and pans. All the sorts of items one shoves out of sight with the intention of fixing or giving away, and then forgets altogether.

Another box held thick albums, the pages crumbling, filled with pictures of stiffly posed, stern-faced people refusing to share their emotions with the camera. He came across a rotted leather binder that had been hidden in what looked like another photo album. He opened it and found it stuffed with pages, every one of them covered with writing.

The first entry was dated September 7, 1891. It began with the words *Madeline is dead by my hand.*

He had taken the diary and told no one about it. Over the years he'd read from it almost daily, until it became an integral part of his own memory. Along the way, he realised he had become one with the author, sharing his sense of supremacy over his victims, chuckling at his play-acting as he grieved with the grieving.

What began as a fascination gradually grew to an absolute obsession, a need to relive the diary writer's journey of death on his own.

Four and a half years ago he had taken the first life.

It was twenty-one-year-old Martha's fate that she had been present at the annual end-of-summer party her grandparents gave. The Lawrences were a prominent Spring Lake family. He was at the festive gathering and met her there. The next day, September 7, she left for a morning jog on the boardwalk. She never returned home.

Over four years later the investigation into her disappearance was still ongoing. At a recent gathering, the Monmouth County prosecutor had vowed there would be no diminution in the effort to learn the truth about what had happened to Martha.

I could tell you all about it, every detail, he said to himself, and I could tell you about Carla Harper too. Two and a half years ago he had been strolling past the Warren Hotel and noticed her coming down the steps. Like Madeline, as described in the diary, she had been wearing a white dress, sleeveless, revealing every inch of her slender young body. He began following her.

When she disappeared three days later, everyone believed Carla had been accosted on the trip home to Philadelphia. Not even the prosecutor, so determined to solve the mystery of Martha's disappearance, suspected that Carla had never left Spring Lake.

Now he could feel the need stirring within him—the need to complete his trio of present-day victims. The final anniversary was coming up, and he had yet to choose her.

The word in town was that Emily Graham, the purchaser of the Shapley house, as it was still known, was a descendant of the original owners. He had looked her up on the Internet. Thirty-two years old, divorced, a criminal defence attorney, she had come into money after she was given stock by the grateful owner of a fledgling dot-com company whom she'd successfully defended *pro bono publico*. When the stock went public and she was able to sell it, she made a fortune.

He learned that Graham had been stalked by the son of a murder victim after she had won an acquittal for the accused killer. The son, protesting his innocence, was now in a psychiatric facility. Interesting.

More interesting still, Emily bore a striking resemblance to the picture he'd seen of her great-great-great-aunt Madeline Shapley. She had the same wide brown eyes and long, full eyelashes. The same midnight-brown hair with hints of auburn. The same tall, slender body. Maybe *she* was the one destined to complete his special trio.

There was an orderliness, a rightness to the prospect that sent a shiver of pleasure through him.

EMILY GAVE A SIGH of relief as she passed the sign indicating she was now in Spring Lake. 'Made it!' she said aloud. 'Hallelujah.'

The drive from Albany, New York, had taken nearly eight hours. She had left in what was supposed to have been 'periods of light to moderate snow', but which had turned into a near blizzard that only tapered off as she exited Rockland County. Along the way, she had witnessed a terrifying skid. For a moment it had seemed as though two vehicles were destined for a head-on collision. It was avoided only because the driver of one car managed to regain control and turn right with less than a nanosecond to spare.

Kind of reminds me of my life the last couple of years, she had thought as she slowed down—constantly in the fast lane and sometimes almost getting clobbered. I needed a change of direction.

As her grandmother had put it, 'Emily, you take that job in New York. I'll feel more secure about you when you're living a couple of hundred miles away. A nasty ex-husband and a stalker at one time are a little too much on your plate for my taste.'

And then, being Gran, she continued, 'On the bright side, you never should have married Gary White. The fact that three years after you're divorced, he'd have the gall to try to sue you because you have money now only proves what I always thought about him.'

Remembering her grandmother's words, Emily smiled as she drove through the darkened streets. The houses, the majority of them restored Victorian, looked secure and serene. Tomorrow I'll officially own a home here, Emily mused. March 21. The equinox. Light and night equally divided. The world in balance.

She considered, then rejected, the impulse to drive by the house. There was still something unreal about the knowledge that in a matter of hours it would be hers. Even before she'd seen the house for the first time three months ago, it had been a vivid presence in her childhood imaginings—half real, half blended with fairy tales. Then when she stepped into it that first time, she had a feeling of coming home.

Enough driving for now, she decided. It was almost ten thirty. Check into the inn, she thought. A hot shower. Then, as Samuel Pepys wrote, 'And so to bed.'

When she'd first come to Spring Lake and impulsively put a deposit down on the house, she had stayed at the Candlelight Inn for a few days. She and the inn's owner, Carrie Roberts, had immediately hit it off. On the drive down, she'd phoned to say she'd be late, but Carrie had assured her that was no problem.

Turn right on Ocean Avenue, then four more blocks. A few moments later, with a grateful sigh, Emily turned off the ignition and reached in the back seat for the one suitcase she'd need overnight.

Carrie's greeting was warm and brief. 'You look exhausted, Emily. The bed's turned down. You said you'd stopped for dinner, so there's a Thermos of hot cocoa with a couple of biscuits on the night table. I'll see you in the morning.'

After a hot shower Emily sipped the cocoa and felt the stiffness in her muscles from the long drive begin to fade. Her cellphone rang. Guessing who it was, she picked it up.

'Hi, Emily.'

She smiled as she heard the worried-sounding voice of Eric Bailey, the shy genius who was the reason she was in Spring Lake now.

As she reassured him that she'd had a safe trip, she thought of the day she'd first met him, when he moved into the closet-sized office next to hers. The same age—their birthdays only a week apart—they'd become friendly, and she recognised that underneath his meek, little-boy-lost exterior, Eric had been gifted with massive intelligence.

One day, when she realised how depressed he seemed, she'd made him tell her the reason. It turned out that his fledgling dot-com company was being sued by a major software provider who knew he could not afford an expensive lawsuit. She took the case without asking for a fee and joked to herself that she would be papering the walls with the stock certificates Eric had promised her.

But she won the case for him. He made a public offering of the stock, which immediately rose in value. When her shares were worth $10 million, she sold them.

Now Eric's name was on a handsome new office building. Their friendship had continued, and he'd been a rock during the time she was being stalked. He even had a high-tech camera installed at her town house. The camera had caught the stalker on tape.

'Just wanted to see that you made it OK,' he said now.

They chatted for a few minutes and promised to talk again soon. When she put the cellphone down, Emily went to the window and opened it. A rush of cold, salty air made her gasp, but then she inhaled slowly. It's crazy, she thought, but at this moment it seems to me that all my life I've been missing the smell of the ocean.

She turned and walked to the door to be absolutely sure it was double-locked. Stop *doing* that, she snapped at herself. You already checked before you showered.

But in the year before the stalker was caught, she had begun to feel fearful and apprehensive. She remembered the first time she had come home and realised he'd been there. She had found a picture of herself propped up against the lamp on her bedside table—a photograph showing her standing in the kitchen in her nightgown. She had never seen the picture before. That day, she'd had the locks of the town house changed and a blind put on the window over the sink.

After that, there'd been a number of other incidents involving photographs—pictures taken of her at home, on the street, in the office. They would be in her mailbox, or stuck on the windscreen of her car or folded inside the morning newspaper that had been delivered to her doorstep. Attempts by the police to lift fingerprints from the items had been unsuccessful.

For over a year the police had been unable to apprehend the stalker. 'You've got people acquitted who were accused of vicious crimes,' Marty Browski, the senior detective, told her. 'It could be someone in a victim's family. It could be someone who knows you came into a lot of money and got fixated on you.'

And then the camera caught Ned Koehler—the son of a woman whose accused killer she had successfully defended—lurking outside her town house. He's off the streets now, Emily reassured herself. There's no need to worry about him any more. He'll get the care he needs. He was in a secure psychiatric facility in upstate New York, and this was Spring Lake, not Albany. She got into bed, pulled up the covers and reached for the light switch.

Across Ocean Avenue, standing on the beach in the shadows of the deserted boardwalk, a man watched as the room became dark. 'Sleep well, Emily,' he whispered, his voice gentle.

Wednesday, March 21

His briefcase underneath his arm, Will Stafford walked from the side door of his home to the converted carriage house, which, like most of those still existing in Spring Lake, now served as a garage. The snow had stopped some time during the night, and the wind had diminished. Even so, the first day of spring had a sharp bite.

A real estate attorney, he was meeting Emily Graham for breakfast at Who's on Third?—the whimsical Spring Lake corner café. From there they would go for a final walk-through of the house she was buying, then to his office for the closing.

As Will backed his Jeep down the driveway, he reflected that it had been a day not unlike this in late December when Emily Graham had first walked into his office. 'I just put down a deposit on a house,' she'd told him. 'I asked the broker to recommend a real estate lawyer. You're the one she favoured. Here's the binder.'

She was so fired up about the house that she didn't even introduce herself, Will remembered with a smile. He got her name from her signature on the binder—'Emily S. Graham'. There weren't too many attractive young women who could pay $2 million cash for a house.

He was ten minutes early, but she was already in the café, sipping coffee. One-upmanship, Will wondered, or is she compulsively early? Then he wondered if she could read his mind.

'I'm not usually the one holding down the fort,' she explained, 'but I'm so darn excited about closing on the house that I'm running ahead of the clock.'

At that first meeting in December, when he had learned that she'd only seen one house, he said, 'I don't like to talk myself out of a job, but, Ms Graham, you're telling me that you just saw the house for the first time? You didn't look at any others? This is your first time in Spring Lake? I suggest you think this over carefully.'

That was when she'd told him that the house had been in her family, that the middle initial in her name was for Shapley.

Emily gave her order to the waitress: grapefruit juice, a single scrambled egg, toast.

As Will Stafford studied the menu, she studied him, approving of what she saw. He was certainly an attractive man—a lean six-footer in his late thirties, with broad shoulders, sandy hair and dark blue eyes.

At their first meeting she had liked his combination of easy-going warmth and cautious concern. Not every lawyer would try to practically talk himself out of a job, she thought. Except for that one day in January when she had flown down in the morning and back to Albany in the afternoon, their communication had been by phone or mail.

The Kiernans, who were selling the house, had owned it only three years and had spent that entire time faithfully restoring it. They were in the final stage of the interior decoration when Wayne Kiernan was offered a prestigious position in London. On that hurried visit in January, Emily went through every room with them and bought the Victorian-era furniture and carpets. The property was spacious, and a contractor had just completed a poolside cabin and would be starting to excavate for a pool. Will Stafford had handled all the paperwork covering the various agreements.

He was a good listener, she decided, as she heard herself telling him now about having grown up in Chicago. 'My maternal grandmother lives in Albany. I went to Skidmore College in Saratoga Springs, which is a stone's throw away, and spent a lot of my free time with her. *Her* grandmother was the younger sister of Madeline Shapley, the nineteen-year-old who disappeared in 1891.'

Will noticed the shadow that came over Emily's face, but then she sighed and continued. 'Well, that was a long time ago.'

'A *very* long time,' Will agreed. 'Are you planning to move in immediately or use the house weekends, or what?'

Emily smiled. 'I plan to move in as soon as we pass title this morning. All the basic stuff that I need is there, including pots and pans and linen. The removal van from Albany will arrive later today with the relatively few things I'm bringing here.'

'Do you still have a home in Albany?'

'Yesterday was my last day there. I'm still settling my apartment in Manhattan, so I'll be back and forth between the apartment and this house until May 1st. That's when I start my new job at Todd, Scanlon, Klein and Todd. After that, I'll be a weekend-and-vacation kind of resident.'

'There's a great deal of curiosity in town about you,' Will cautioned. 'I want you to know that I'm not the one who leaked that you're a descendant of the Shapley family.'

The waitress was putting their plates on the table. Emily did not wait for her to leave before she said, 'Will, I'm not trying to keep that a secret. I mentioned it to the Kiernans and to Joan Scotti, the real estate agent. She told me that there are families whose ancestors were here at the time that my great-great-great-aunt disappeared. I'd be interested to know anything any of them have heard about her—other, of course, than the fact that she seemingly vanished from the face of the earth. They also know I'm divorced and that I'll be working in New York, so I have no guilty secrets.'

He looked amused. 'Somehow I don't visualise you as harbouring guilty secrets.'

Emily hoped her smile did not look forced. I *do* intend to keep to myself the fact that I've spent a fair amount of time in court this past year that had nothing to do with practising law, she thought. She had been a defendant in her ex-husband's suit, which claimed he was entitled to half the money she had made on the stock, and also had been on the witness stand testifying against the stalker.

'As for myself,' Stafford continued, 'you haven't asked, but I'm going to tell you anyway. I was born about an hour from here, in Princeton. My father was CEO of Lionel Pharmaceuticals in Manhattan. He and my mother split when I was a teenager. Since my father travelled so much, I moved with my mother to Denver and went to high school and then college there.'

He ate his last sausage, glanced at his watch, and signalled for the bill. 'It's nine thirty. Let's not keep the Kiernans waiting.'

After Will asked for the bill, he said, 'To finish the not very thrilling story of my life, I married right after law school. Within the year we both knew it was a mistake.'

'You're lucky,' Emily commented. 'My life would have been a lot easier if I had been that smart.'

'I moved back East and signed on with the legal department of Canon and Rhodes, a high-powered Manhattan real estate firm. It was a good job, but pretty demanding. I wanted a place for weekends and came looking down here, then bought an old house.'

'Why Spring Lake?'

'We used to stay at the Essex and Sussex Hotel for a couple of weeks every summer when I was a kid. It was a happy time.'

The waitress put the bill on the table. Will got out his wallet. 'Then twelve years ago I realised I liked living here and didn't like working in New York, so I opened this office. A lot of real estate work, both residential and commercial. And speaking of that, let's get going to the Kiernans'.' They got up together.

BUT THE KIERNANS had already left Spring Lake. Their lawyer explained he had power of attorney to execute the closing. Emily walked with him through every room, taking fresh delight in architectural details she had not fully appreciated before.

'Yes, I'm satisfied that everything I bought is here and the house is in perfect condition,' she told him. She tried to push back her impatience to get the deed transferred, to be in the house alone, to wander through the rooms, to rearrange the living-room furniture so that the couches faced each other at right angles to the fireplace.

She needed to put her own stamp on the house, to make it *hers*. She'd always thought of the town house in Albany as a stopgap place, although she had been in it three years—ever since she returned from a visit to her parents in Chicago a day early and found her husband in an intimate embrace with her closest friend, Barbara Lyons. She picked up her suitcases, got back into the car, and checked into a hotel. A week later she rented the town house.

The house she had lived in with Gary was owned by his wealthy family. It had never felt like hers. But walking through this house seemed to evoke sensory memory. 'I almost feel as though it's welcoming me,' she told Will Stafford.

'I think it might be. You should see the expression on your face. Ready to go to my office and sign the papers?'

THREE hours later Emily returned to the house and pulled into the driveway again. 'Home sweet home,' she said joyously as she got out of the car and opened the trunk to collect the groceries she'd purchased after the closing.

An area near the new cabin was being excavated for the pool. Three men were working on the site. After the walk-through she'd been introduced to Manny Dexter, the foreman. Now he caught her eye and waved.

The rumble of the excavator drowned out her footsteps as she hurried along the blue flagstone path to the back door. This I could do without, she thought, then reminded herself that the pool would be nice to have when her brothers and their families came to visit.

She was wearing one of her favourite outfits—a dark green winter-weight trouser suit and a white turtleneck sweater. Warm as they were, Emily shivered as she shifted the grocery bag from one arm to the other. She was putting the key into the door when Manny Dexter shouted frantically to the operator of the excavator, 'Turn that thing off! Stop digging! *There's a skeleton down there!*'

DETECTIVE TOMMY DUGGAN did not always agree with his boss, Elliot Osborne, the Monmouth County prosecutor. Tommy knew Osborne considered his unceasing investigation into the disappearance of Martha Lawrence an obsession that might succeed only in keeping her killer in a state of high alert.

'That is, unless the killer is a drive-through nut who grabbed her and dumped her body hundreds of miles from here,' Osborne would point out.

Tommy Duggan had been a detective for the last fifteen of his forty-two years. In that time, he'd married, fathered two sons, and watched his hairline go south while his waistline travelled east and west. With his round, good-humoured face and ready smile, he gave the impression of being an easygoing fellow who had never encountered a problem more serious than a flat tyre. In fact, he was a first-rate investigator. All his life he had lived in Avon by the Sea, a few miles from Spring Lake. As a college student, he had been a waiter at the Warren Hotel in Spring Lake. That was how he had come to know Martha Lawrence's grandparents, who regularly dined there.

Today, as he sat in his cubbyhole, he spent his short lunch break glancing once more through the Lawrence file. He stared at a picture of Martha that had been taken on the boardwalk in Spring Lake. She had been a beautiful twenty-one-year-old—with long blonde hair and a sunny and confident smile—who, when that picture was taken, should have had another fifty or sixty years of life. Instead she had had less than forty-eight hours.

Tommy shook his head and closed the file. He was convinced that by continuing to make the rounds of people in Spring Lake, he would eventually stumble upon some crucial bit of information previously overlooked that would lead him to the truth. As a result, he was a familiar figure to the neighbours of Martha's grandparents and to all the people who had been in contact with Martha in those last hours of her life.

Most of the guests who had attended the party at the Lawrence home the night before Martha disappeared were locals or summer residents who kept their homes open year-round and came down for weekends. Tommy always kept a copy of the guest list folded in his wallet. It wasn't a big effort for him to drive to Spring Lake and look up a couple of them just to chat.

And I'm working on my own time, he thought sourly as he observed the contents of the lunch bag his wife, Suzie, had packed for him: tuna on wholewheat bread. The doctor had told him to take off twenty pounds, and Suzie was hell-bent on making the weight loss happen by starving him to death.

Martha had last been seen jogging on the boardwalk at six thirty in the morning of September 7, four and a half years ago. As Tommy unenthusiastically bit into his sandwich, he made a decision.

As of 6.00am tomorrow, he was going to become one of the joggers on the Spring Lake boardwalk. It would help him to shed the twenty pounds, but there was something else. Like an itch he couldn't scratch, he was getting a feeling that sometimes came when he was working intensely on a homicide: He was closing in on the killer.

His phone rang. It was Elliot Osborne's secretary. 'Tommy, meet the boss down at his car right away.'

Osborne was just getting into the back seat when Tommy, puffing slightly, arrived at the reserved parking section. Osborne did not speak until the car pulled out and the driver turned on the siren.

'A skeleton has just been uncovered on Hayes Avenue in Spring Lake. Owner was excavating for a pool. There are remains of two people buried there, and from the look of it, one has been in the ground a lot longer than the other.'

AFTER MAKING THE 911 CALL, Emily ran outside and stood at the edge of the gaping hole looking down at what appeared to be a human skeleton. The body had been wrapped in heavy, clear plastic. Although the flesh had crumbled, the plastic had done a good job of keeping the bones intact.

When the first police car raced up the driveway, Emily returned to the house. She knew that the police would want to speak to her. The bag of food was on the kitchen counter, where she had dropped it in her rush to phone. With robotlike precision she put the groceries away and made a cup of tea.

A large window in the kitchen overlooked the grounds behind the house. Teacup in hand, Emily stood at it, observing the quiet efficiency with which the area around the excavation was being cordoned off. Police photographers arrived and began snapping pictures of the site. She knew it had to be a forensics expert who scrambled into the excavation, near the place where the skeleton was lying.

The doorbell rang.

A GRIM-FACED TOMMY DUGGAN stood next to Elliot Osborne on the porch and waited for the door to be opened. Both men were sure that the search for Martha Lawrence was over. The forensics chief had told them that the condition of the skeletal frame wrapped in plastic indicated it was that of a young adult. He refused to speculate on the loose human bones found near the skeleton until they were examined in the morgue.

Tommy glanced over his shoulder. 'There are people starting to gather out there. The Lawrences are sure to hear about this.'

'Dr O'Brien is going to rush the autopsy,' Osborne said crisply. 'He understands that everyone in Spring Lake is going to jump to the conclusion that it's Martha Lawrence.'

When the door opened, both men had their identification badges in hand.

'I'm Emily Graham. Please come in.'

They stepped into the hall, where the only piece of furniture was a quaint Victorian love seat. Emily invited them into the living room.

'We'd just like to ask you a few questions, Ms Graham,' Osborne said. 'I understand that you only closed on the house this morning. How long have you been coming to Spring Lake?'

To her own ears, her story of driving down for the first time three months ago and immediately buying the house sounded almost ludicrous. She chose her words carefully. 'I came to Spring Lake on an impulse because all my life I've been curious about it. My family built this house in 1875. They owned it until 1892, selling it after the older daughter, Madeline, disappeared in 1891. In looking up the town records to see where the house was, I found it was for sale. I saw it, loved it, and bought it.'

'I didn't realise this was the Shapley house,' Osborne said. 'We're expecting the remains will be those of a young woman who disappeared over four years ago while visiting her grandparents in Spring Lake.' With a brief shake of his hand he signalled to Duggan that now was not the time to mention the second set of remains.

Emily felt the colour drain from her face. 'A young woman disappeared over four years ago and is buried here?'

'It's a very sad day for this community,' Osborne said. 'I'm afraid we'll have to keep the scene under protection until they have finished processing it. As soon as it is, you'll be able to have your contractor resume digging for your pool.'

There isn't going to be a pool, Emily thought.

As they walked to the door, the bell pealed insistently.

The removal van from Albany had arrived.

WORD OF THE POLICE activity on Hayes Avenue spread through the town. Rumours of the discovery of human remains followed quickly. Everyone knew that the victim was going to be Martha Lawrence. Old friends gathered one by one in the home where Martha's grandparents lived. One friend took it upon herself to call Martha's parents in Philadelphia. Even before the official word came, George and Amanda Lawrence had set out for Spring Lake.

By six o'clock, as darkness settled over the East Coast, the pastor of St Catherine's Church accompanied the prosecutor to the Lawrence home. Martha's dental records exactly matched the impression Dr O'Brien, the medical examiner, had made during the autopsy. A few strands of what had been long blonde hair still clung to the back of the skull. They matched the strands the police had taken from Martha's hairbrush after her disappearance.

A sense of collective mourning settled on the town.

The police had decided to withhold, for the present, information about the second skeletal remains. They were also those of a young woman. The forensics chief estimated that they had been in the ground for over 100 years. In addition, it would not be revealed that the instrument of Martha's death had been a silver silk scarf with metallic beading, knotted tightly round her throat.

However, the most chilling fact the police were not ready to share was the revelation that, within her plastic shroud, Martha Lawrence had been buried with a finger bone of the century-old victim and that a sapphire ring still dangled from that bone.

NEITHER THE STATE-OF-THE-ART security system nor the presence of a policeman in the poolhouse to guard the crime scene could reassure Emily the first night in her new home. The bustle of the removal men, followed by the need to unpack, had distracted her in the afternoon. As far as was humanly possible, she tried to take her mind off the activity in the back yard.

At seven o'clock she made a salad, baked a potato, and grilled lamb chops. But even though she drew all the blinds, she still felt vulnerable. Several glasses of Chianti neither warmed nor relaxed her. She loved to cook, and friends had always commented that she could make even a simple meal seem special. Tonight she could barely taste what she was eating.

After she had tidied the kitchen, checked all the doors, and set the alarm, she climbed the stairs to the first floor. It was only nine o'clock, but all she wanted to do was to change into warm pyjamas and go to bed.

After Emily had changed, she hesitated. Had she bolted the front door? Annoyed at herself, she hurried out of the bedroom and down the landing. At the head of the stairs she flipped the switch that lit the hall chandelier, then hurried down the stairs.

Before she reached the front door, she saw the envelope that had been slipped under it. Please, God, not again, she thought as she bent down to pick it up. Don't let that business begin again.

She ripped open the envelope. It contained a snapshot of a woman at a window, the light behind her. For a moment Emily had to focus on it to realise she was the woman in the picture.

And then she knew. Last night. At the Candlelight Inn. When she'd opened the window, she had stood there, looking out. Someone on the beach had snapped her picture and had it developed, then slipped it under the door within the last hour. It hadn't been there when she went upstairs.

It was as though the person who had stalked her in Albany had followed her to Spring Lake! But that was impossible. Ned Koehler was in Gray Manor, a secure psychiatric facility in Albany.

The house phone had not yet been connected. Her cellphone was in the bedroom. Holding the picture, Emily ran to pick it up. Her fingers trembling, she dialled information.

'Welcome to local and national information—'

'Albany, New York. Gray Manor Hospital.'

A few moments later she was talking to the evening supervisor of the unit where Ned Koehler was confined. She identified herself.

'I know your name,' the supervisor said. 'You're the one he was stalking.'

'Is he out on a pass?'

'Koehler? Absolutely not, Ms Graham.'

'Is there a chance he managed to get out on his own?'

'I saw him at bed check less than an hour ago.'

A vivid image of Ned Koehler flashed through Emily's mind: a slight man in his early forties, balding, hesitant in speech and manner. In court he had wept silently throughout the trial. She had defended Joel Lake, who had been accused of murdering Ned's mother during a bungled robbery. When the jury had acquitted Lake, Koehler had gone berserk and lunged at her. He was screaming obscenities, Emily remembered, telling me I'd got a killer off. It had taken two sheriff's deputies to restrain him.

'How is he doing?' she asked.

'Singing the same old song—that he's innocent.' The supervisor's voice was reassuring. 'Ms Graham, it's not uncommon for stalking victims to feel apprehensive even after the stalker is under lock and key. Ned isn't going anywhere.'

When she replaced the receiver, Emily studied the picture. In it she was framed in the centre of the window—an easy target for someone with a gun instead of a camera, it occurred to her.

She called the police. The officer who took the call sent a car immediately. The cop was young, probably not more than twenty-two. She showed him the picture, told him about the stalker in Albany.

'My guess is that a smart-aleck kid who knows you had this problem is playing a practical joke,' he said soothingly. 'Have you got a couple of plastic bags you could give me?'

He held the snapshot and then the envelope at the corner as he dropped them into the bags. 'These will be checked for fingerprints,' he explained. 'I'll be on my way now.' She walked with him to the door. 'Tonight we'll be keeping a close watch on the front of the house, and we'll alert the officer in the back to keep his eyes open,' he told her. 'You'll be fine.'

Maybe, Emily thought as she bolted the door behind him.

CLAYTON AND RACHEL WILCOX had been guests of the Lawrences' the night before Martha disappeared. Since then, like all the other guests, they had been visited regularly by Detective Tommy Duggan.

Sixty-four years old, Rachel was handsome, with shoulder-length iron-grey hair. Tall, with impeccable carriage, she exuded authority. Her eyes, a greyish blue, had a perpetually stern expression.

Thirty years ago, when, as a shy, nearly forty-year-old assistant dean, Clayton had been courting her, he lovingly compared Rachel to a Viking. 'I can imagine you at a ship's helm, armed for battle, with the wind blowing through your hair,' he had whispered.

He now mentally referred to her as the Viking. The name, however, was no longer an endearment. Clayton lived in a constant state of high alert, ever anxious to avoid his wife's blistering wrath.

As they watched the eleven o'clock news broadcast on the discovery of Martha Lawrence's body, Clayton listened in suffering silence to Rachel's caustic comments.

'It's very sad, of course, but at least this should put an end to that detective coming round here and annoying us,' she said.

If anything, this will bring Duggan round *more* often, Clayton thought. A large man with a leonine head of shaggy grey hair and knowing eyes, he looked the academic he had been.

When twelve years ago, at the age of fifty-five, he had retired from the presidency of Enoch College, a small but prestigious institution in Ohio, he and Rachel had moved permanently to Spring Lake. He had first come to the town as a young boy, visiting an uncle who had moved there, and over the years he had come back for occasional visits. As a hobby, he had delved with enthusiasm into the history of the town and was now known as the unofficial local historian.

Rachel had never forgiven Clayton for an indiscretion with a fellow professor three years after their marriage. Later, the mistake that had caused him to retire abruptly from Enoch College, a place where she had enjoyed the lifestyle, had permanently embittered her.

As a picture of Martha Lawrence filled the TV screen, Clayton felt his hands go moist with fear. There had been someone else with long blonde hair and an exquisite body. Now that Martha's remains had been found, how intensely would the police probe into the backgrounds of the people who had been at the party that night?

'Martha Lawrence had been visiting her grandparents before returning to college,' the CBS anchorwoman was saying.

'I gave you my scarf to hold at the party,' Rachel complained for the millionth time. 'And naturally, you managed to lose it.'

Thursday, March 22

Ever since they began digging for the pool, he had known they might come across Martha's remains. He could only hope that the finger bone was still intact within the plastic shroud. But even if it wasn't, they were bound to find the ring.

Of course, it was too much to expect the medical examiner to realise that Martha and Madeline had died the same way—Martha with the scarf tightened round her neck, Madeline with the white linen sash torn from round her waist as she tried to flee.

He could recite that passage from the diary from memory:

It is curious that without a single gesture on my part, Madeline knew she had made a mistake in coming into the house. There was a nervous plucking at her skirt with those long, slender fingers, even though her facial expression did not change.

She watched as I locked the door.

'Why are you doing that?' she asked.

She must have seen something in my eyes. The muscles in her neck moved as she vainly tried to scream. She was too frightened to do anything but whisper, 'Please.'

She tried to run past me to the window, but I grabbed her sash and pulled it from her, then grasped it in two hands and wrapped it round her neck. At that, with remarkable strength she tried to punch and kick me. No longer a trembling lamb, she became a tigress fighting for her life.

Later I bathed and changed and called on her parents, who by then were deeply concerned as to her whereabouts.

There was a front-page picture of Martha in all the papers. Why not? It was newsworthy when the body of a beautiful young woman was found, especially when she was from a privileged family in an up-market and picturesque community. How much more newsworthy it would be if they announced that inside the plastic they had found a finger bone with a ring. If they had found it, he hoped they would realise that he had closed Martha's hand over it.

Her hand had still been warm and pliable.

Sisters in death, 105 years apart.

It had been announced that the prosecutor was holding a news conference at eleven. It was five to eleven now. He reached over and turned on the television set, then leaned back and chuckled in anticipation.

FIFTEEN MINUTES before the news conference, prosecutor Elliot Osborne briefed his aides on what he would and would not tell the press.

He would report the findings of the autopsy and that the cause of death was strangulation. He would not tell them a scarf had been the murder weapon or about the metallic beading that had edged it. He would say that the victim's body had been wrapped in thick layers of plastic that had kept the skeletal remains intact.

'Are you going to talk about the finger bone, sir? That's gonna really stir up a hornet's nest.' Pete Walsh had just been promoted to the rank of detective. He had been a police officer in Spring Lake for eight years before joining the prosecutor's office.

Walsh was smart and young and couldn't wait to get his two cents in, Tommy Duggan thought sourly. He and Osborne had been back here at dawn. They had gone over every detail of O'Brien's completed autopsy report. They didn't need Pete Walsh to tell them the media would have a field day with this one.

Osborne told Walsh to let him finish, then continued, 'In my statement I will reveal that Martha Lawrence was buried in contact with other human remains, and those remains are over a century old. Four and a half years ago, when Martha disappeared, the *Asbury Park Press* dug up the story about the disappearance of nineteen-year-old Madeline Shapley on September 7th, 1891. It is very likely that the media will jump to the conclusion that the finger bone found with Martha belonged to Madeline Shapley, since the remains are on the Shapley property.'

'Is it true that the new owner of that property is a descendant of the Shapleys?' Pete Walsh asked.

'That is true, yes.'

'Then can't you check her DNA against the finger bone?'

'If Ms Graham is willing, we can certainly do that. However, last night I ordered that all available records of Madeline Shapley's disappearance be examined and a search be made for any other cases of missing women in Spring Lake around that time. Our researchers found that two other young women had been listed as missing at around that same time. Letitia Gregg disappeared on August 5th, 1893. According to the police file, her parents feared that she might have gone swimming alone, which was why that case was never classified as suspicious. Three years later, on March 31st, 1896, Letitia's devoted friend Ellen Swain disappeared. She had been observed leaving a friend's home at dusk.' Osborne glanced at his watch. 'It's one minute to eleven. Let's go.'

The briefing room was packed. The questions thrown at Osborne were rapid and hard-hitting. The *New York Post* reporter said that the finding of the two skeletal remains on the same site could not be a bizarre coincidence.

'I agree,' Osborne said. 'The finger bone with the ring was deliberately placed inside the plastic with Martha's body.'

'*Where* inside the plastic?' the ABC reporter asked.

'Within Martha's hand.' Osborne held up a photo. 'This is an aerial shot of the crime scene.' He pointed to the excavation pit. 'Martha's killer dug a relatively shallow grave, but it might never have been found except for the pool excavation. Until a year ago a very large holly tree totally blocked that section of the back yard from the view of anyone in the house or on the street.'

The inevitable question came. 'Are you suggesting that this perhaps was a serial killing, tied into a murder in Spring Lake one hundred and ten years ago?'

'I'm suggesting nothing.'

'But both Martha Lawrence and Madeline Shapley disappeared on September 7th. How do you explain that?'

'I don't.'

'Do you think Martha's killer is a reincarnation?'

The prosecutor frowned. 'Absolutely *not*! No more questions.'

Osborne caught Tommy's eye as he exited the room. Tommy knew they were sharing the same thought: Martha Lawrence's death had just become a juicy headline story, and the only way to stop it was to find the killer.

The remnants of a scarf with metallic beading was the only clue they had with which to begin the search. That and the fact that whoever the killer was, he knew about a grave that had been dug on the Shapley property secretly over 100 years ago.

AT 9.00AM EMILY AWOKE from the uneasy sleep she'd fallen into. A shower helped to diffuse the sense of heaviness that was gripping her.

The body of the missing girl in the back yard . . .

The snapshot slipped under the door . . .

She headed downstairs to make coffee. Ever since her college days it had been her routine to shower, make coffee, then dress, with a cup of coffee nearby. She had always sworn she could feel lights go on in different sections of her brain as she sipped.

She could see that it was going to be a beautiful day. Rays of sunshine were streaming through the stained-glass window at the landing of the staircase.

In the kitchen, Emily waited for the coffee to brew. When it was ready, she poured a cup and took it upstairs. She dressed in jeans and a sweater, then twisted her hair into a knot and caught it with a comb.

She was making the bed when she heard the firm ring of the doorbell. The phone company was there to install new telephone lines.

By eleven the technicians were gone. Emily went into the study and turned on the television to catch the news.

'. . . century-old finger bone with a ring . . .'

When the programme ended, Emily turned off the TV. As the screen went black, she continued to stare at it, her mind a kaleidoscope of childhood memories—Gran telling the stories about Madeline over and over again. I always wanted to hear about her, Emily thought.

Gran's eyes would get a faraway look as she talked about her. 'Madeline was my grandmother's older sister, and she worshipped her. She would tell me how beautiful she was. Half the young men in Spring Lake were in love with her. They all made it their business to walk past the house, hoping to see her sitting on the porch. That last day, she was so excited. Her beau, Douglas Carter, had spoken to her father and received permission to propose to her. She expected him to bring her an engagement ring. Madeline showed my grandmother how she had changed her sixteenth-birthday ring from her left to her right hand so that she wouldn't have to take it off when Douglas came.'

Two years after Madeline disappeared, Douglas Carter had killed himself, Emily remembered.

She got up. How much more could her grandmother recall of the events she had been told about as a child? Like many very elderly people, her long-term memory had strengthened with age. Emily dialled her number and heard the phone picked up on the first ring.

'Tell me about the house,' her grandmother ordered after a quick greeting.

There was no easy way to tell her what had happened.

'A young woman who disappeared has been found there? Oh, Emily, how could that happen?'

'I don't know, but I want to find out. Gran, remember you told me that Madeline had had a ring on the day she disappeared?'

'She was expecting that Douglas Carter would bring her an engagement ring.'

'Didn't you say something about her wearing a ring that had been her sixteenth-birthday present?'

'Let me see. Oh, yes, I did, Em. It was a sapphire ring set with tiny diamonds. You're not trying to figure out what happened to Madeline after all these years?'

'You never know. Love you, Gran.'

Emily's next call was to the prosecutor's office. When she gave her name, she was put through immediately to Elliot Osborne.

'I watched the news,' she said. 'By any chance, was the ring you found a sapphire surrounded by small diamonds?'

'It was.'

'Was it on the ring finger of the right hand?'

There was a pause. 'How do you know that, Ms Graham?'

After she had hung up, Emily walked across the room, opened the door and stepped out onto the porch.

They had found Madeline's ring and finger bone with Martha Lawrence. The rest of Madeline's remains were found just inches below the plastic shroud. Was it possible after 110 years to learn what had happened to her? *Someone* found out where she was buried, Emily thought, and chose to bury Martha Lawrence with her.

IT WAS NEARLY NOON when Will Stafford called Emily. 'I went to New York right after your closing yesterday,' he said, 'and didn't know what was going on until I heard it on the news late last night. I'm so sorry for the Lawrences, and I'm sorry for you.'

It was gratifying to hear the concern in his voice. 'Did you see the interview with the prosecutor?' she asked.

'Yes, I did. Do you think that by any chance—'

She knew the question he was going to ask. 'Do I think that the ring they found in Martha Lawrence's hand belonged to Madeline Shapley? I know it did. I spoke to my grandmother, and she was able to describe the ring from what she'd heard about it.'

'Then all these years your great-great-great-aunt has been buried on the property.'

'It would seem so,' Emily said.

'Someone knew that, and put Martha's body with hers. But how would anyone have known where Madeline Shapley was buried?'

'If there is an answer to that, I intend to try to find it. Will, I'd like to meet the Lawrences. Do you know them?'

'Yes, I do. They used to entertain pretty frequently before Martha disappeared. I was often at their house.'

'Would you call and ask if they would allow you to bring me over for a short visit whenever they're up to it?'

'I'll get back to you,' he promised.

Twenty minutes later the voice of his secretary, Pat Glynn, came over the intercom. 'Mr Stafford, Natalie Frieze is here. She wants to see you for a few minutes.'

Just what I need, Will thought. Natalie was the second wife of Bob Frieze, a long-time Spring Lake resident. Nearly five years ago, Bob had retired from his brokerage firm and fulfilled a lifelong dream by opening an up-market restaurant, called The Seasoner.

Natalie was thirty-four. Bob was sixty-one, but clearly each had got what was wanted from the marriage. Bob had a trophy wife, and Natalie, a luxurious lifestyle. She also had a roving eye that sometimes settled on Will.

But today, when she came in, Natalie was not her normal flirtatious self. 'Will, it's so sad about Martha Lawrence,' she said, 'but is this going to stir up a hornet's nest? I'm worried sick.'

'With all due respect, you don't look worried sick. In fact, you look as though you just came back from a shoot for *Vogue*.'

She was wearing a three-quarter-length chocolate-brown leather coat with a sable collar and cuffs and matching leather slacks. Her long blonde hair hung straight past her shoulders. The even tan, which Will knew had been recently acquired in Palm Beach, accentuated her turquoise-blue eyes.

She ignored the compliment. 'Will, I came straight over to talk to you after I saw the news conference. Bob almost had a heart attack. He stayed to watch the prosecutor finish his statement before he left for the restaurant. He was so upset, I didn't even want him to drive.'

'What would make him so upset?'

'Well, *you* know how that Detective Duggan keeps coming round to talk to all of us who were at that party at the Lawrence house the night before Martha disappeared.'

'What are you getting at, Natalie?'

'It's obvious that Martha was murdered, and if people round here get the idea that one of us was responsible for her death, it's going to be pretty bad publicity.'

'*Publicity!* For God's sake, who's worried about publicity?'

'My *husband* is. Every nickel Bob owns is sunk into his fancy restaurant. Now his guts are all tied up in a knot. He has the idea that if there's a lot of attention aimed our way because we were at the party, it might hurt his business.'

Will had gone to the restaurant a few times. The decor was heavy-handed, the food average, and the prices much too steep. 'Natalie,' he said, 'I understand that Bob is under a lot of stress, but the idea that being at the Lawrence party would keep anyone away from his restaurant is really stetching the imagination.'

Natalie shrugged and grinned. 'I hope you're right. I feel better talking to you. Let's go and get some lunch.'

'I was going to send out for a sandwich.'

'No, you're not. We're going to eat at the Old Mill. Come on.'

When they were on the street, she tucked her hand under his arm. 'People may talk,' he suggested, smiling.

'Oh, so what? They all resent me anyhow. I told Bob we should have moved. This town is too small for me and his first wife.'

As he held the car door open for Natalie and she ducked her head to get in, sunbeams made her long blonde hair glisten. For some reason the prosecutor's statement raced through Will's mind: 'Strands of long blonde hair were found on the remains.'

Bob Frieze, like his wife, was known to have a roving eye. Especially for beautiful women with long blonde hair.

DR LILLIAN MADDEN, a prominent psychologist who used hypnosis regularly in her practice, firmly believed in reincarnation and would regress appropriate patients to previous lifetimes. She believed that emotional trauma suffered in other lives might be the source of emotional pain in present-day experience. Very much in demand on the speakers' circuit, she expounded a favourite premise—that the people we know in this life were probably people we knew in other lives.

A childless widow, with her home and office in Belmar, a town bordering Spring Lake, she had heard about the discovery of Martha Lawrence's body the night before and experienced the communal sorrow that afflicted the residents of all the nearby towns.

Her morning schedule of patients began at eight o'clock, an hour before her secretary, Joan Hodges, came in. It was noon before Dr Madden talked to Joan at her desk in the reception room.

'Any important messages?' Dr Madden asked.

Joan looked up. 'Oh, hello, Doctor. I don't know how important they are, but you're not going to like these messages,' she said bluntly. A forty-four-year-old grandmother, Joan was, in Lillian Madden's opinion, the perfect person to work in a psychologist's office. Breezy, matter-of-fact, unflappable, and naturally sympathetic, she had the gift of putting people at ease.

'What about them am I not going to like?' Lillian Madden asked mildly as she reached for the notes.

'The prosecutor held a news conference, and in this past hour you've received calls about it from three of the most sensational tabloids in the country. Let me tell you why.'

Lillian listened in startled silence as her secretary described the discovery of the ringed finger of another woman in Martha Lawrence's skeletal hand and the fact that Madeline Shapley, like Martha, had disappeared on September 7.

'Surely they don't think that Martha was Madeline reincarnated and destined for the same terrible death?' Lillian demanded.

'They didn't ask that,' Joan said grimly. 'They want to know if you think Madeline's killer is the one who's been reincarnated.'

AT TWO O'CLOCK Tommy Duggan got back to his office, trailed by Pete Walsh. After the press conference ended, a team from the prosecutor's office had begun poring over the Martha Lawrence file to see if anything had been overlooked.

Osborne had put Tommy in charge of the investigation and made Pete Walsh his assistant. Walsh and a research team had spent the night before at the hall of records in the courthouse going through the dusty archives, searching for material relating to the disappearance of Madeline Shapley in 1891.

Now Tommy Duggan looked at him with sympathy. Walsh's eyes were bloodshot, and his shoulders were drooping with fatigue. At thirty, even with a hairline that was already receding, he looked like a tired kid. 'Why don't you just go home, Pete?' Tommy said. 'You're asleep on your feet.'

'I'm fine. You talked about phone calls you wanted to make. I'll split them with you.'

Tommy shrugged. 'Have it your way. The morgue will release Martha's remains to the family later today. They've arranged for them to be taken to the crematorium. The immediate family will be there and will escort her ashes to the family mausoleum in St Catherine's cemetery. That information is not to be leaked to the public. The family wants it to be absolutely private.'

Pete nodded.

'By now the family will have announced to the press that a memorial Mass will be held for Martha on Saturday at St Catherine's.'

Tommy was sure that most, if not all, of the people who had been at the party the night before Martha vanished would be in attendance at the Mass. He had already told Pete that he wanted to get them under the same roof somewhere and then question them individually. Inconsistencies in their recollections could be straightened out much faster if they were together. Or perhaps *not* straightened out, he thought grimly.

Tommy pulled out the list of the guests who had been at the party.

'I'm going to call Will Stafford and ask if I can have everyone meet at his house after the memorial Mass. If I clear that with him, we'll start making phone calls.' He reached for the phone.

Stafford had just returned from lunch. 'Sure you can meet at my house,' he agreed, 'but you'd better schedule it a little later. The Lawrences are inviting friends back to their house for a buffet luncheon after the Mass. I'm sure most of the people who were at the party will be included in that.'

'Then I'll ask them to be at your place at three, Mr Stafford.'

I'd give a lot to be at that luncheon, Tommy thought. He nodded at Pete. 'Now that we have the place and the time, let's start making these calls. We're supposed to be at Emily Graham's house in an hour. We're going to try to sweet-talk her into letting that excavator dig up the rest of her yard.'

They began making the phone calls and reached everyone. With the exception of two elderly couples who could not possibly have been involved in Martha's death, all the other people who had been at the party were planning to attend the Mass on Saturday.

AT TWO FORTY-FIVE, Emily parked in front of the home of Clayton and Rachel Wilcox on Ludlam Avenue. Half an hour earlier she had called Will Stafford and asked him to suggest where she should begin her research into the disappearance of Madeline Shapley.

'Our own library on 3rd Avenue has excellent reference material,' he told her, 'but a good short cut might be to talk to Dr Clayton Wilcox. He's a retired college president and has become the town's unofficial historian. Let me give him a ring.'

He called her back fifteen minutes later. 'Go right over. I told Clayton what you wanted, and he's already putting together some material for you. Here's the address.'

And here I am, Emily thought as she got out of the car. She walked up the steps to the porch and rang the bell. A moment later the door opened. Even if no one had told her, she would have guessed that Dr Clayton Wilcox was an academic—the shaggy hair, the glasses perched on the end of his nose, the heavy-lidded eyes.

His voice was deep and the tone pleasant when he greeted her. 'Miss Graham, please come in.'

He took her coat, then led her down the hall, past the living room. 'When we decided to move to Spring Lake twelve years ago, my wife did the house hunting,' he explained as he waved her into a room where, except for the window, all four walls were lined floor to ceiling with bookshelves. 'My one criterion was that I have a true Victorian house, with one room that would provide ample space for my books, my desk, my couch and my chair.'

Emily smiled. 'Well, you got what you asked for.'

It was the kind of room she liked. The wine-coloured leather couch was deep and comfortable. Most of the books on the bookshelves appeared to be old. At least a dozen notebooks were crisscrossed around an open laptop computer on a large desk. Emily could see that the screen was lit.

'I've interrupted you,' she said. 'I'm sorry.'

'Not at all. My writing wasn't going well, and I looked forward to meeting you.'

He settled in the club chair. 'Will Stafford tells me that you are interested in learning about the history of Spring Lake. I've been listening to the news reports, so I know that your ancestor's remains were found along with those of poor Martha Lawrence.'

Emily nodded. 'Martha's murderer obviously knew Madeline had been buried there, but the question is, how could he know?'

'*He?* You're assuming the present-day killer is a man?'

'I think it's more than likely,' Emily said. 'But can I be sure? Of course not. Nor do I have any certainty about the killer over one hundred years ago. Madeline Shapley was my great-great-great-aunt. She was murdered when she was only nineteen. In a peculiar way, to our family she's not dead. She's unfinished business.'

Emily leaned forward. 'Dr Wilcox, there's a *connection* between the deaths of Martha Lawrence and Madeline Shapley, and when one of those murders is solved, it may be that the other one will be solved too. I believe that whoever learned that Madeline was buried in the grounds of her home also learned how and why she died.'

He nodded. 'It's possible there's a record somewhere. A written confession or a letter. But then you're suggesting that whoever found such a document not only concealed it but used the grave-site information in it when he committed his own crime.'

'I guess that *is* what I'm suggesting. And something else. I believe neither Madeline in 1891, nor Martha four and a half years ago, was the kind of young woman who would have gone off with a stranger. More likely, both of them let themselves get trapped by someone they trusted.'

'I think that's a big leap, Miss Graham.'

'Not necessarily, Dr Wilcox. I know Madeline's mother and sister were in the house when she vanished. It was a warm September day. The windows were open. They would have heard her if she had screamed.

'Martha Lawrence was jogging. It was early, but surely she wasn't the only jogger. There are houses overlooking the boardwalk. It would have been pretty daring, and pretty tough, to overcome her and drag her into a car without being observed.'

'You've done a good deal of thinking about this, haven't you, Miss Graham?'

'Please call me Emily. Yes, I guess I *have* done a good deal of thinking about it. It isn't hard to focus on the subject when a forensic team is sifting through my back yard for murder victims.' She stood up. 'I've taken enough of your time, and I must get back to meet a detective from the prosecutor's office.'

Wilcox hoisted himself to his feet. 'I've pulled out some books and articles about Spring Lake that might be helpful to you. There are also some copies of newspaper clippings from the 1890s.'

On the desk was a pile of books and papers. He opened the bottom drawer and pulled out a folded cloth bag with the words ENOCH COLLEGE BOOKSTORE printed across it.

'If you keep my books in this, they won't get separated,' he suggested. He gestured at the desktop. 'I'm writing a historical novel set in Spring Lake in 1876, the year the Monmouth Hotel was opened. It's my first attempt at fiction, and I find it quite a challenge.' He walked with her to the front door. 'Let's talk after you've had a chance to go through all these references. You may have questions.'

'You've been very kind,' she said as she shook his hand at the door. Emily did not know why she had a sudden feeling of discomfort, even claustrophobia. It's that house, she thought as she went down the steps. Except for his office, it's utterly cheerless.

She had glanced into the living room as she passed it. The upholstery and heavy curtains were the worst of the Victorian-era decor, she decided, everything heavy, dark, formal.

FROM THE WINDOW of his study, Clayton Wilcox watched Emily drive away. A most attractive young woman, he decided. He sat at the desk and pushed the ENTER key on the computer.

The screen saver disappeared, and the page he had been working on came into view. It concerned the frantic search for a young woman who had come to Spring Lake with her parents to attend the gala opening of the Monmouth Hotel in 1876.

Clayton Wilcox put his hands on the keyboard and began to type: 'His need was so great that even the unspeakable consequences of what he was about to do could not deter him.'

'I CAN'T DO IT any more,' Nick Todd said aloud as he stood looking out of the window of his corner office in the law firm of Todd, Scanlon, Klein and Todd, located on Park Avenue South in Manhattan.

The morning had been spent in the conference room working on the Hunter case. Hunter is scum, and he's going to get off scot-free, and I'll have helped to make that possible. The absolute certainty made Nick feel physically sick.

I don't want to hurt Dad, but I can't do it any more, he acknowledged to himself. I want to prosecute these creeps, not defend them. He heard the door of his office open. He turned round slowly. His father was framed in the doorway.

'Nick, I must have been out of my mind when I told Emily Graham she could wait until May 1st to start work. A case just came in that's tailor-made for her. I want you to go down to Spring Lake and tell her that we need her to be in here within the week.'

Emily Graham. An image of her floated through Nick's mind. Before they offered her the job, he and his father had gone up to Albany to observe her in court. She had been brilliant, getting an acquittal for a client who had been charged with criminally negligent homicide. Afterwards she'd had lunch with them. Nick remembered the eloquent praise his usually taciturn father had heaped on her.

They're as alike as two peas in a pod, he thought now. They were born to be criminal defence attorneys.

He'd been within inches of telling his father that he had to resign from the firm. I can wait a little longer, he decided. But once Emily Graham's on board, I'm out of here.

THE QUESTION to the prosecutor from the shrill reporter during the televised news conference delighted him: 'Do you think Martha's killer is a reincarnation?'

But then the prosecutor's brusque dismissal of the possibility affronted him.

I *am* reincarnated, he thought. We have become one. I shall prove it.

By late afternoon he had decided the way he would reveal the truth about himself. A simple postcard would be sufficient—a crude drawing, no better than what a child might send.

He would mail it on Saturday. On his way to church.

TOMMY DUGGAN and Pete Walsh were on the porch waiting for Emily when she arrived home.

Tommy brushed aside her apology for keeping them waiting. 'We're a little early, Ms Graham.' He introduced Pete, who promptly reached down and picked up the bag of books Clayton Wilcox had given Emily.

'You must be planning to do a lot of reading, Ms Graham,' Pete commented as she unlocked the door.

'I guess I am.'

They followed her into the hall. 'Let's talk in the kitchen,' she suggested. 'Maybe I can persuade you to join me in a cup of tea.'

Pete accepted. Tommy passed on the tea but could not resist helping himself to a couple of the chocolate-chip cookies she put out on a plate. They sat at the kitchen table. The big window afforded a stark view of the excavation site and the piles of earth around it.

'I see that the forensic team is gone,' Emily said. 'I hope that means you're through with the investigation here.'

'That's just what we want to discuss,' Tommy said. 'While the excavator is here, we'd like to have the rest of your yard dug up.'

'Surely you don't believe there are other bodies buried out there?' The shock in Emily's voice was unmistakable.

'Ms Graham, I know you watched the prosecutor on TV, because you phoned in about the ring that was found.'

'Yes.'

'Then you heard him say that after your—what is it?—great-great-great-aunt disappeared in 1891, two other young women vanished from Spring Lake.'

'Dear God, do you think they may be buried out there?'

'We'd like to find out,' Tommy said. 'The bones we found here underneath Martha's skeleton were in a relatively shallow grave. A few might have surfaced over the years. I think what happened is that somebody came across them at some point, maybe even found the finger bone with the ring, kept it, and, when he killed Martha, decided to bury her there with it.'

'No, Mr Duggan, I can't agree,' Emily said. 'It's too much for me to believe that someone found the bone, never told anyone about it, murdered Martha, then decided to bury her here.'

'How would you explain it?'

'I think whoever murdered Martha Lawrence knew *exactly* what happened in 1891 and has committed a copycat murder.'

'You're not into that reincarnation theory, I hope?'

'No, I'm not, but I do believe that Martha's killer knows a whole lot about Madeline Shapley's death.'

Tommy stood up. 'Ms Graham, this house has turned over ownership quite a few times during all those years. We're going to look up the records, find out who those owners were, and see if any of them are still around. Will you allow us to dig up your yard?'

'Yes, I will.' Her voice was resigned. 'And now I'm going to ask *you* something. Let me see the records about Madeline Shapley's disappearance and the disappearance of those other two young women in the 1890s.'

The two men looked at each other. 'We'd have to check, but I don't see a problem there,' Duggan told her.

She walked to the front door with them.

Back in the car, the detectives drove in silence for five minutes. Then Duggan said, 'Are you thinking the same thing I am, Pete?'

'Maybe.'

'That girl, Carla Harper, from Philadelphia? She disappeared two and a half years ago, in August.'

'Right. An eyewitness swears she saw her talking to a guy at a rest stop just outside Philadelphia. Claims they were driving separate cars, but when they left, he followed her. Then a couple of days later Harper's bag with apparently nothing missing was found in a wooded area not far from that rest stop. The case has been handled by the Philadelphia prosecutor.'

Tommy picked up the phone and called the office and asked to be put through to Len Green, one of the other detectives working closely on the case. 'Len, when did the second woman disappear in the 1890s?'

'Give me a minute.' There was a pause. 'August 5th, 1893.'

'When was Carla Harper reported missing?'

'Be right back to you.'

Tommy held the phone until he heard the words he'd been expecting to hear: 'August 5th.'

'We're on the way. See you in twenty minutes. Thanks, Len.'

They had to talk to the Philadelphia detective who had handled the case of Carla Harper. The fact that Madeline Shapley and Martha Lawrence had disappeared on September 7, even though separated by 105 years, might have been coincidental. The fact that then two young women had disappeared on August 5 in the same time frame could not be coincidental.

They *did* have a copycat killer on their hands in Spring Lake. 'You know what this means, Pete?' Tommy asked. 'It means that if this guy is following a pattern, he's going to target one more young woman, on March 31st.'

'*This* March 31st?'

'I don't know yet. In the 1890s the three women vanished several years apart.' He got back on the phone and called Len.

When Tommy had the information he wanted, he said, 'There was a difference of twenty-three months between the disappearances of the first two women in the 1890s. There was exactly that same number of months between the disappearance of Martha Lawrence and Carla Harper.' They were pulling into the parking lot at the prosecutor's office. 'If some woman vanishes next week on March 31st, the cycle will be complete. And to add to the fun, we may have a copycat stalker of Emily Graham on our hands too.'

AFTER THE DETECTIVES had left, Emily decided to prepare a pot of soup and have it for dinner.

The open pit in the back yard and the possibility that other bodies were buried there made her feel as if the scent of death were permeating the very air around her. Chicken soup does do something for the psyche, and right now, Emily admitted to herself, mine needs some help.

She went into the kitchen and drew the blinds, grateful to block out the dismal scene in the yard. Her hands worked independently, scraping carrots, cutting up celery and onions, reaching for seasonings. By the time she had turned on the flame under the pot, she had made a decision to call the Albany police and report what had happened last night.

She went into the study. She walked over to the desk, got the portable phone, and perched on the ottoman in front of the deep armchair. Her first call was to Detective Marty Browski in Albany. He had been the one who had collared Ned Koehler lurking outside her town house. Browski's response to what she told him was both astonishment and concern. 'My guess is that you've got a copycat. We'll look into it, Emily. Tell you what. I'll give the local police a call and alert them to the seriousness of the problem.'

Her next call was to her friend Eric Bailey. He was delighted to hear from her. 'Albany's not the same without you.'

She smiled. 'I miss you too,' she assured him. 'And I've got a favour to ask.'

'Good. Whatever you want, you've got it.'

'Eric, the security camera you put in the town house—you offered me one for Spring Lake. Can you send someone down to put it in?'

'I can send myself down. I want to see you anyhow, but the next few days are really busy. Is Monday OK?'

'Monday is fine,' she said, then replaced the receiver.

Emily spent the next three hours curled up in the big chair, absorbed in the books Wilcox had lent her. He had chosen well, she decided. She found herself pulled into an era of horse-drawn carriages, oil lamps, and stately summer 'cottages'.

At eight o'clock she went back into the kitchen and completed preparing dinner. She propped a book up on the table and read while she ate. *Reflections of a Girlhood* was the title. The author, Phyllis Gates, had summered in Spring Lake from the late 1880s to the mid-1890s. The book gave a vivid picture of the social life of those days— picnics and dances, events at the Monmouth Hotel, bathing in the ocean. What intrigued Emily most were the excerpts from a diary Phyllis Gates had kept during those years.

Emily had finished dinner. Her eyes were burning with fatigue and she was about to close the book for the night when she saw Madeline Shapley's name in a diary excerpt:

June 18, 1891. This afternoon we attended a festive luncheon at the Shapley home. It was to celebrate Madeline's nineteenth birthday. Twelve tables beautifully decorated with flowers from the garden had been placed on the porch. I sat at Madeline's table, as did Douglas Carter, who is so very much in love with her. We tease her about him.

In another 1891 excerpt the author wrote:

We had just closed our cottage and returned to Philadelphia, when we learned of Madeline's disappearance. Mother hurried back to Spring Lake to express her condolences and found the

family to be in a state of profound grief. Madeline's father con-
fided that he will remove his wife and family from the area.

Emily skimmed through the pages. An October 1893 entry caught
her eye:

Douglas Carter committed suicide. He had missed the early train
from New York on that tragic day and was forced to wait for a
later one. He became obsessed with the idea that had he been there
earlier, he might have saved her.
  My mother felt that it had been a mistake for Douglas's parents
not to move from their home, directly across the street from the
Shapleys. She felt that the melancholy that overcame Douglas
might have been avoided had he not sat hour after hour staring at
the porch of the Shapley home.

I knew Douglas Carter had committed suicide, Emily thought. I
didn't know he lived directly across the street. I wonder how sure they
were that he did, in fact, miss the train?

Friday, March 23

T he rumour had begun with a reporter's question to the prosecutor: 'Do you think Martha's killer is a reincarnation?'
  Dr Lillian Madden's phone started to ring without stopping
on Thursday afternoon. On Friday morning Joan Hodges, her secretary, had a stock answer, which she delivered crisply over and over
again: 'Dr Madden has deemed it inappropriate to discuss the subject of reincarnation in regard to the Spring Lake murder case.'
  At lunchtime on Friday, Joan had no problem discussing the matter with her boss. 'Dr Madden, look at what the newspapers are saying, and they're right. It was no coincidence that Martha Lawrence
and Madeline Shapley both disappeared on September 7th. And you
want to know the latest?'
  Pause now for dramatic effect, Lillian Madden thought wryly.
  'On August 5th, 1893, Letitia Gregg "failed to return home".'
Joan's eyes widened. 'There was a girl, Carla Harper, who spent the
weekend at the Warren Hotel two years ago, then just vanished into

thin air, also on August 5th. I remember reading about it. She checked out of the Warren and got into her car. Some woman swears she saw her near Philadelphia. But now, according to this paper, that eyewitness is starting to sound like Looney Tunes.'

Joan was holding a copy of the *National Daily*. The headline read SERIAL KILLER RETURNS FROM THE GRAVE. The story began:

Red-faced police are admitting that the eyewitness who claimed to have seen twenty-year-old Carla Harper at a rest stop not far from her home in Rosemont, Pennsylvania, may have been mistaken. They now admit it is entirely possible that Harper's bag was planted by her killer after the eyewitness account was widely published. The focus of the investigation is now centred in Spring Lake, New Jersey.

Joan's eyes bored into Lillian's face. 'Doctor, I don't think Carla Harper ever left Spring Lake. I think—and apparently lots of people think—that there was a serial killer in Spring Lake in the 1890s and that he's been reincarnated.'

'That's utter nonsense,' Lillian said brusquely. 'Reincarnation is a form of spiritual growth. A serial murderer from the 1890s would be paying for his transgressions now, not *repeating* them.'

With decisive steps, her entire posture telegraphing her disapproval of the tone of the conversation, Lillian went into her private office and closed the door. There she sank into her desk chair and massaged her temples with her index fingers. What was bothering her? What memory was trying to force itself into her conscious mind?

Lillian wondered if she could skip her lecture tonight. No, that wouldn't be fair to the students, she decided. In ten years she hadn't missed one session of the course in regression she gave every spring at Monmouth Community College. There were thirty students enrolled. The college was allowed to sell ten more single-session tickets for each lecture. Would some of those reporters who had been phoning find out about those tickets and be there tonight?

In the second half of the session it was her practice to ask for volunteers to be hypnotised and regressed. She made the decision to eliminate the hypnosis section tonight. During the last ten minutes she always took questions from the students and visitors. If reporters were there, she would have to respond to them.

Tonight's lecture was based on the observations of Ian Stevenson, a professor of psychology at the University of Virginia. He had tested the hypothesis that in order to identify two different life histories as belonging to the same person, there would have to be continuity of memories and/or personality traits. Lillian was painfully aware that Stevenson's findings could be interpreted as bolstering the theory about a reincarnated serial killer.

THAT EVENING, as Lillian Madden had expected, all the available guest passes for her lecture had been sold. She sensed that several people who had arrived early enough to get front-row seats might be from the media. They were carrying notebooks and recorders.

'My regular students understand that no recorders are permitted in this class,' she said, looking pointedly at one thirtyish woman.

Lillian took a moment to adjust her glasses. She did not want to appear nervous or ill at ease in front of the reporters. 'In the Middle East and Asia,' she began, 'there are thousands of cases where children under the age of eight will talk about a previous identity. They will recall in vivid detail the life they previously lived, including the names of members of their former families.'

She went on. 'Dr Stevenson's monumental research explores the possibility that images in a person's mind and physical modifications in that person's body may manifest themselves as characteristics in a newborn. Some people can choose their future parents, and rebirth tends to happen in a geographical area quite close to where the earlier incarnation led his life.'

After Lillian's lecture the questioning was heated. The thirtyish female reporter led off. 'Dr Madden,' she said, 'everything I heard you say tonight validates the idea that a serial killer who lived in the 1890s has been reincarnated. Do you think the present-day killer has images of what happened to the three women in the 1890s?'

Lillian paused before answering. 'Our research shows that memories of past lives cease to exist at about the age of eight. That is not to say that we may not experience a sense of familiarity with a person we have just met or a place we have visited for the first time. But that is not the same as vivid, recent images.'

There were other questions, and then the thirtyish reporter cut in. 'Doctor, don't you usually include hypnotising a few volunteers as part of your lecture?'

'That is correct. I have chosen not to do so tonight.'

'Will you explain how you go about regressing someone?'

'Certainly. Three or four people volunteer for the experiment. I speak, one at a time, with those who are clearly in a hypnotic state. I invite them to travel back in time. Then I pick dates at random and ask if a picture forms in their mind. Often the answer is no, and I keep going back until they have reached a previous incarnation.'

'Dr Madden, did you ever have anyone specifically ask to be regressed to the late 1800s?'

Lillian stared at the questioner, a heavyset man with brooding eyes. He had brought to the surface the memory that had been eluding her all day. It must have been four, five years ago that someone *had*, in fact, asked her that very question. He had been in her office, with an appointment, and told her that he was sure he had lived in Spring Lake at the end of the nineteenth century.

But then he resisted hypnosis. Indeed, he seemed almost frightened of it and left before the hour was up. She could see him clearly in her mind. But what was his name? What was it?

It will still be in my appointment books, she thought. I'll recognise it when I see it. She could hardly wait to get home.

In Albany, Marty Browski walked up the path to Gray Manor, the psychiatric hospital where Ned Koehler, the man who had been convicted of stalking Emily Graham, was being treated.

A short, trim, fifty-year-old with a stern face and deep-set eyes, Marty had made the trip across town from the precinct because he had to satisfy himself that Koehler was still where he belonged.

While there was no question that the man was dangerous, there had always been something about the case that bothered Marty. No question Ned Koehler had cut the telephone wires to shut down the alarm system in Graham's apartment and tried to enter it. Fortunately, the security camera her friend Eric Bailey had installed not only went on high-tech back-up but summoned the police and also took a picture of Koehler, knife in hand, jemmying the lock on the bedroom window. Koehler was screwy. Probably always had been on the edge; then the mother's death pushed him all the way over. He was right. Joel Lake, the bum whom Graham got acquitted, was the mother's killer.

And now Graham was the victim of another stalking episode, this one in Spring Lake. I've always wondered about her ex-husband, Browski thought, as he opened the main door of the hospital and went into the reception room. He found himself weighing the possibility that Gary Harding White might have been—and might still be—the stalker. Despite a privileged background, good looks, and a good education, Gary was getting a reputation as something of a con man. A womaniser too.

Marty checked in at reception. A few minutes later he was sitting at a table opposite Ned Koehler and Hal Davis, his lawyer. The door was closed, but a guard was watching through the window.

'How's it been going, Ned?' Browski asked in a friendly voice.

Tears welled in Koehler's eyes. 'I miss my mother.'

It was the reaction Browski expected. 'I know you do.'

'It was that woman lawyer's fault. *She* got him off. He should be in prison.'

'Ned, Joel Lake was in your building that night. He admitted he burglarised your apartment. But your mother was in the bathroom. He could hear the water running in the tub. She never saw him. He never saw her. Your mother was on the phone talking to her sister after Joel was seen leaving the building.'

'My aunt has no sense of time.'

'The jury thought she did.'

'That Graham woman twisted the jury around her little finger.'

Maybe she didn't twist the jury, Browski thought, but she *did* make them believe Joel's version.

'I hate Emily Graham, but I didn't follow her around or take pictures of her.'

'You were trying to break into her home that night. You were carrying a knife.'

'I was just going to scare her. I wanted to make her understand what my mother felt when she looked up and . . .' He started to cry. 'I miss my mother.'

Davis patted his client on the shoulder and stood up. 'Satisfied, Marty?' he asked Browski as he nodded to the guard to take Koehler back to his unit.

ON FRIDAY, Nick Todd invited his father, Walter, to have lunch with him at the Four Seasons. They walked together up Park Avenue to 52nd Street.

As usual, the restaurant was filled with recognisable faces: heads of studios, well-known authors and business tycoons—the typical mixture of the well known and well heeled. They stopped at several tables to greet friends. Nick winced hearing his father's proud introduction of him to a retired judge: 'My son and partner . . .'

But when they were seated in the Pool Room and had ordered a drink, Walter got right to the point. 'All right, Nick, what's up?'

It was misery for Nick to see the bleak pain that settled over his father's face as he heard his son's plans.

Finally Walter swallowed and said, 'So that's it. A pretty big decision, Nick. Even if you get a job in the US Attorney's office, it isn't going to pay you the kind of salary you make now.'

'I know, and don't think I'm so altruistic that I won't miss the big bucks.' He broke off a piece of roll and crumbled it.

'You do realise that being the arm of the law isn't all putting the bad guys away? You have to prosecute a lot of people you might wish you were defending.'

'That's something I'll have to face.'

The two men looked across the table at each other, mirror images distinguished only by thirty years of the inevitable toll of the ageing process.

The waiter came by with menus and recited the specials of the day. They ordered, and when he was out of earshot, Walter said, 'You're a damn good trial lawyer, Nick, the best. When you pull out, it will leave a mighty big hole in the firm.'

'I know it, but Emily Graham is going to fill the bill for you. My heart's just not in it. She has your passion for the job. When I go down to see her, I'll tell her that the workload is going to be heavier than she expected, at least for a while.'

'How soon do you want to leave?'

'As soon as Emily can take over my office. I'll move my stuff to one of the smaller ones in the transition phase.'

'Have you spoken to her?'

'Not yet. I'll go down to see her in the next day or two.'

Walter nodded. 'If she baulks about coming in before May 1st?'

'Then of course I'll wait it out.'

THE CLATTER of the excavator began promptly at eight on Friday morning. When Emily looked out of the kitchen window as she made coffee, she winced at the destruction of lawn and flowerbeds.

She went back upstairs to shower and dress, carrying her coffee. Forty minutes later she was settled in the study.

The book *Reflections of a Girlhood* remained a treasure trove of information. In a diary excerpt in 1893, the author, Phyllis Gates, referred to the fear that Letitia Gregg might have drowned:

Letitia loved to swim. August 5 was a warm and sultry day. She was alone in the house. Letitia's bathing costume was missing, which is the reason behind the belief that she went by herself to cool off with a dip in the ocean.

Following the disappearance of Madeline Shapley two years ago, the sadness throughout the community is palpable, and a sense of fear is apparent. Since Letitia's body has not washed up, there is always the possibility that she met with foul play.

I remember how we young people would gather on each other's porches, endlessly discussing what might have happened to Madeline and Letitia. The young men included Douglas Carter's cousin—Alan Carter—and Edgar Newman. I always sensed a bond of unspoken sorrow between these two young men, because Edgar had been very sweet on Letitia, and we all knew Alan had been smitten with Madeline, even though she was about to be engaged to Douglas when she disappeared. Another member of our group is Ellen Swain. She was Letitia's bosom friend and misses her dreadfully.

The final entry from the diary was written on April 4, 1896:

A most appalling tragedy. Last week Ellen Swain vanished in Spring Lake. She was walking home after visiting Mrs Carter. It is now believed that Letitia was not lost by drowning, but that all three of my friends met with foul play. Mother has cancelled our lease on the cottage we usually rent for the season. She said she will not put me at risk. We are planning to go to Newport this summer. But I shall miss Spring Lake very much.

Emily closed the book, stood up, and stretched. She was surprised to see it was nearly noon. A long walk on the boardwalk, she decided, then a sandwich in town on the way home.

Two hours later, when she returned home, there were two messages on the answering machine.

The first was from Will Stafford. 'Give me a ring, will you, Emily? I've got something to tell you.'

The second was from Nicholas Todd. 'I need to get together with you, Emily. Hope you can pencil me in for a visit some time on Saturday or Sunday. It's important I have a chance to go over some things with you. My direct line is 212-555-0857.'

Stafford was in his office. 'I spoke to Mrs Lawrence, Emily,' he said. 'She wants to meet you. She'd like you to join them for the luncheon after the memorial Mass. I told her you planned to attend.'

'That's very kind of her.'

'Why don't you let me pick you up about ten forty tomorrow morning, and we'll go to the service and to the Lawrences' together.'

'I'd like that. I'll be ready. Thanks.'

She dialled Nick Todd's number. He answered on the first ring. 'We've been following the news. Hope it hasn't been too upsetting.'

'Sad rather than upsetting,' she said. 'You left word you needed to see me? Has your father changed his mind about hiring me?'

His laugh was both spontaneous and reassuring. 'Nothing could be further from the truth. How's tomorrow lunch or dinner for you? Or is Sunday better?'

Emily considered. 'Sunday lunch would be better,' she said. 'I'll find out where to go and make a reservation.' She hung up.

At five thirty a member of the forensic team rang the bell. 'We're finished, Ms Graham. There's nothing else buried out there.'

Emily was surprised at her relief. She had been expecting the remains of Letitia Gregg and Ellen Swain to be unearthed.

The police officer said, 'Now maybe some of this talk about a reincarnated serial killer will die down.'

'I certainly hope so.' But why do I have a feeling it's only going to get worse? Emily thought as she thanked the police officer, then closed and locked the door against the encroaching darkness.

A SENSE OF DANGER surrounded him. It is similar to what I felt when Ellen Swain first began to link me to Letitia's death, he thought. At that time I moved swiftly.

It was rash and foolish of me to have consulted Dr Madden five years ago. What was I thinking? Of course I could not have allowed her to hypnotise me. Who knows what I might have divulged involuntarily when I opened my mind to her? It was simply the enticing possibility of being placed into my previous incarnation that tempted me to visit her. Will she remember that five years ago a client asked to be regressed to 1891?

It *is* possible, he decided with a chill.

Would she consider a conversation that took place in her office, client to psychologist, to be privileged? Maybe.

Or will she consider it her duty to call the police and say, 'Five years ago I was asked if I could regress a man from Spring Lake to the year 1891. He was very specific about the date. I explained that unless he had been incarnated at that time, it would not be possible.'

He could visualise Dr Madden, her intelligent eyes looking directly at him. She had been challenged by him but also curious.

Curiosity had been the reason Ellen Swain died, he reflected.

'Then,' Dr Madden might tell the police, 'I tried to put my patient into a hypnotic state. He became quite agitated and left my office abruptly. This may not be of great importance, but I felt I should pass this information on to you. His name is . . .'

Dr Madden must *not* be allowed to make that call! It was a risk he could not afford to take. Like Ellen Swain, she will soon learn that *any* knowledge of me is dangerous, he thought—even fatal.

Saturday, March 24

Will Stafford was in the kitchen, having scrambled eggs and sausages for breakfast. While he ate, he read the *New York Post*. Their writers had consulted a parapsychologist about the possibility that a serial killer from the late nineteenth century had been reincarnated. The parapsychologist said that he did not believe anyone came back with exactly the same personality—criminal or otherwise. Sometimes physical characteristics were carried through, he explained. Sometimes an inherent, almost mystical, talent arrives with the new person. Mozart, for example, was a genius at the age of three.

Another article raised the possibility that the murder of Madeline Shapley in 1891 might have been the deed of Jack the Ripper. The time frame was right. He had never been caught, but his brutal crimes had suddenly stopped in England, and there had always been a theory that he had migrated to New York.

Shaking his head, Will got up and carried his dishes to the sink. He looked into the refrigerator and checked he had a supply of cheese. This afternoon, when Detective Tommy Duggan got them all together here, it wouldn't be a social event, but Will would put out cheese and biscuits and offer everyone a glass of wine or a coffee.

He debated about asking Emily Graham to have dinner with him. He was escorting her to the church and then to the Lawrences' for the luncheon, but he wanted to have some one-on-one time with her.

Maybe he would offer to cook dinner here. Show off, he thought with a half-smile. On Thursday, at lunch, Natalie had joked that people begged for an invitation to his dinner table.

I *am* a hell of a good cook, he admitted to himself. No, make that a hell of a good chef!

He walked slowly up the stairs to dress for Martha Lawrence's memorial service.

WHEN RESTAURATEUR Bob Frieze returned home after an early-morning jog, he found his wife in the kitchen, eating her usual sparse breakfast: black coffee and a single slice of unbuttered toast.

'You're up early,' he commented.

'I heard you moving around and couldn't get back to sleep,' Natalie said. 'Honestly, Bob, you had a couple of nightmares last night. I had to wake you up. Do you remember that?'

Remember. The word that was beginning to frighten him. It had been happening again lately—those blank periods when he had not been able to account for a couple of hours, or even a whole afternoon. Like last night. He had started to drive home from the restaurant at eleven thirty. He didn't get home until one. Where had he been that extra hour?

These disturbing occurrences began when he was a teenager. First he started sleepwalking, then having periods when he would find time gaps in his activities and not be able to explain to himself where he'd been. He had never told anyone about it. He didn't want anyone to think of him as a nutcase.

The episodes had let up after college, then stopped completely. But for the last five years they had been happening again, and now they were becoming frequent.

He knew what was causing them: the restaurant—the most colossal mistake of his life. It was haemorrhaging money. It was the stress that was driving him into the blank periods again.

He hadn't told Natalie that three months ago he had put the restaurant up for sale. He knew she would have hounded him every day to see if anyone had shown interest.

The real estate agent had called yesterday afternoon. Dom Bonetti, who once ran the Fin and Claw, a four-star place in New Jersey, was bringing an offer to the table.

I'll be fine as soon as I sell it, Frieze promised himself.

'Do you intend to pour that coffee or just stand there holding the cup, Bobby?' Natalie's tone was amused.

'Pour it, I guess.'

He knew Natalie was getting sick of his moods, but for the most part she'd been uncomplaining. She looked gorgeous, even with her hair tousled around her shoulders and no make-up.

He leaned down and kissed the top of her head.

'Spontaneous gesture of affection. Something that's been lacking for a long time,' she said.

'I know. It's just that I've been under a lot of pressure.' He decided to tell her about the prospective offer. 'I've put The Seasoner up for sale. We may have a buyer.'

'Bobby, *fantastic*!' She jumped up and hugged him. 'Will you get your money back?'

'Most of it, even allowing for some bargaining on the price.' As he said these words, Frieze knew he was whistling in the dark.

'Then promise me once that's done, we'll move to Manhattan.'

'I promise.' I want to get out of here too, he thought. I *have* to get out of here.

'I think we should leave early for the memorial Mass. You didn't forget about that, did you?'

'Hardly.'

And after that, he thought, we go back to the Lawrence house, where I haven't been since that night I spent so much time talking to Martha. Then we go to Stafford's place to get grilled by Duggan about what we were doing the morning after the party.

He dreaded both sessions. The problem was, he remembered the party, but not what followed. Early that next morning he'd had one of his episodes. He hadn't come out of it until he found himself showering in the bathroom. His hands were grimy, and his jeans and T-shirt had patches of dirt on them, he remembered. He had planned to work in the garden that morning. It was his one hobby and always calmed him down.

I'm sure I worked in the garden that morning, he told himself, and that's certainly what I'm going to tell Duggan.

As HE HAD PROMISED, Will Stafford arrived at ten forty on Saturday morning to pick up Emily. He was wearing a dark blue suit, white shirt and subdued blue tie. She was waiting for him in the hall. It had been a stroke of luck that she had brought her new black and white hound's-tooth-check suit with her to Spring Lake, since most of the clothes she had here were casual.

'You look lovely,' Will said quietly. 'I just wish we were dressed up to go to a different kind of gathering.'

'So do I.'

He gestured towards the back yard. 'I see the contractor is filling in the hole. Are they satisfied there's nothing else to be found?'

'Yes, they are,' Emily said.

'That's good. We'd better be on our way.' As she picked up her bag and set the alarm, Will put his hand under her elbow. Emily realised it gave her a sense of emotional and physical security to feel it there.

It has been a rough few days, she thought. Maybe it's taken more out of me than I realised. It's even more than that, she decided as Will opened the door of the car and she slipped into the passenger seat. In a crazy way, I feel as if this memorial Mass isn't just for Martha Lawrence. *It's for Madeline too.*

As Will started the car, she told him how she felt, then added, 'I had been wrestling with the idea that to go to this Mass for a girl I never knew might seem voyeuristic. But now it seems different.'

'Different in what way?'

'I believe that heaven exists. I'd like to think that those two girls—who must have been so frightened in the last moments of their life, who were murdered a hundred years apart and their bodies dumped in my back yard—are still together now in a place of peace.'

'Where do you think their murderer is?' Will asked. 'And what will be his fate some day?'

Startled, Emily turned and stared at him. 'Will, surely you mean murderers! Two separate people.'

He laughed. 'Good God, Emily, I'm starting to sound like the nutty tabloid writers. Of course I mean *murderers.* Two. Plural. One long since dead, the other probably out there somewhere.'

They were silent for the few minutes it took them to drive round the lake. As St Catherine's Church came into view, they could see a steady stream of cars approaching. 'I wonder if Martha's murderer is in one of those cars, Will,' Emily said.

'If he is from Spring Lake, as the cops seem to think, I doubt very much that he'd have the nerve to stay away. It would be too conspicuous not to be here, grieving with the family.'

I wonder which of Madeline's friends, with blood on his hands, grieved with our family 110 years ago, Madeline thought.

AT ELEVEN O'CLOCK on Saturday morning Joan Hodges was on her way to the beauty salon to have her hair done, when the phone rang. It was Dr Madden's sister, Esther, phoning from Connecticut.

Her voice was troubled. 'Joan, I tried to call Lillian last night at about eleven thirty. When she didn't answer, I thought she might have gone out with friends after her class, but I've phoned twice this morning, and I still can't reach her.'

'Sometimes she turns off the phone. With all the pestering from the media over this murder investigation, she probably did just that. I'll go over and make sure everything's fine with her.' Joan tried to sound reassuring in spite of her own misgivings.

'I don't like to put you out.'

'You're not putting me out. It's a fifteen-minute drive.'

Her hair appointment completely forgotten, Joan drove as fast as she dared. The sinking feeling in her stomach and the lump in her throat betrayed the panic that she was trying to keep in check. Something was terribly wrong. She *knew* it.

As she pulled into the driveway of Dr Madden's house, Joan thought, Please, God, let her have gone for a long walk.

She approached the house and saw that the bedroom blinds were down and the newspaper was on the front porch. Her hands trembling now, she fumbled for the key to the office door. She knew that if Dr Madden had locked the connecting door from the office to the rest of the house, there was a spare key hidden in her desk.

She stepped into the small hallway and went into the reception room. Files had been pulled out of the filing cabinet, emptied and tossed aside, the contents strewn all over the floor.

Her legs resisting her attempt to run, Joan entered Dr Madden's office. The shriek that ripped from within her was only an agonised moan when it left her lips. The body of Dr Madden was slumped over her desk, her head turned to one side, her lips drawn apart, as if gasping for air. A cord was twisted tightly round her neck.

Joan did not remember running out of the office, down the porch steps, across the lawn to the pavement, screaming all the way. Her knees crumpled, and merciful darkness blotted out the gruesome image of her murdered friend and employer.

THEY ARE BEING simply magnificent, Emily thought. She and Will Stafford had just arrived at the Lawrence home, where an informal receiving line had formed in the spacious living room. Standing together, greeting the guests and accepting condolences, were Martha's grandparents, the senior Lawrences, silver-haired and straight-backed octogenarians; Martha's parents, George and Amanda Lawrence, a couple in their late fifties; and their other daughter, Christine, and Christine's husband.

The dignity and serenity with which they had conducted themselves during the memorial Mass had filled Emily with admiration. She and Will had been in a pew at a right angle to where the family was seated, and she had been able to see them clearly. Although tears had welled in their eyes, they had sat composed throughout the service. Christine had just had a baby and was sitting next to her parents with the infant, Martha's namesake, in her arms.

When one of Martha's friends broke down weeping as she eulogised her, Emily saw Amanda Lawrence reach over and take the baby from Christine. Amanda held the infant close. Emily watched Amanda taking comfort in her newborn granddaughter even as her murdered daughter was eulogised.

Now Will introduced her to them. They realised who she was immediately. 'This happened in your own family four generations ago,' Martha's father said. 'We only pray that whoever took our daughter's life will be brought to justice.'

'Ignoring the reincarnation nonsense, do you think that Martha's death may have been intended to copy what happened to Madeline Shapley?' Amanda asked.

'Yes, I do,' Emily said. 'And I even believe that a written confession or statement may exist that the present-day killer has found. I'm digging into old records and books, trying to piece together a picture of Madeline and her friends.'

George and Amanda Lawrence exchanged glances; then George turned to his parents. 'Mother, don't you have photograph albums and other memorabilia from your grandmother's time?'

'Oh, yes, dear. All packed away in that cabinet in the attic. My maternal grandmother, Julia Gordon, was very meticulous. She wrote captions under all the pictures, listing the date, place, event, and the names of the people, and she kept extensive diaries.'

Julia Gordon's name was sprinkled throughout the book *Reflections of a Girlhood.* She had been Madeline's contemporary.

'Would you consider letting me look through the contents of that cabinet?' Emily asked quietly. 'I believe we may learn something from the past that will help now.'

George Lawrence spoke without hesitation. 'We will do *anything* that will help in any way to expose our daughter's killer.'

'Emily.' Will pressed her arm and indicated the people waiting behind them to speak to the Lawrences.

'I can't hold you any longer,' Emily said hastily. 'May I call you tomorrow morning?'

'Will has the number. He'll give it to you.'

The buffet table was in the dining room. Tables and chairs had been set up on the long, enclosed back porch.

Plates in hand, Emily and Will went out onto the porch. 'Over here, Will,' a voice called. 'Join the other suspects.'

'That's Natalie Frieze,' Will said as they walked over.

Dr Wilcox was at the table and greeted Emily warmly. His wife, Rachel, was introduced, as were Bob and Natalie Frieze.

'Have you found the books helpful?' Dr Wilcox asked.

'Very much so.'

'I understand that you're a criminal defence attorney, Emily,' Natalie said.

'Yes, I am.'

'If someone in this room is indicted for Martha's murder, would you consider defending him?'

She likes to make waves, Emily realised, but she noticed that the atmosphere at the table changed instantly. Someone—or perhaps even everyone—is not finding that question amusing, she thought.

She tried to pass off the question lightly. 'Well, I *am* a member of the New Jersey Bar, but since I'm sure that won't happen, I don't think I'll look for a retainer here.'

Later Will introduced her to a number of people who were residents of the town. They chatted for a few minutes with John and Carolyn Taylor, Will's close friends.

Carolyn said, 'We're fourth-generation Spring Lake people. In fact, a distant cousin of mine, Phyllis Gates, wrote a book about life here in the 1880s and 1890s. She was very close to Madeline Shapley.'

Emily stared at her. 'I read her book cover to cover last night.'

'Phyllis died in the mid-1940s, when my mother was a teenager. Despite the age difference, they were very fond of each other. Phyllis used to take Mother on trips with her.'

'Did she ever talk to your mother about Madeline?'

'Yes, she did. In fact, Mom and I were on the phone this morning. We've been discussing everything that has happened here these last few days. Mom said that Phyllis didn't want to put it in her book, but she was always sure that it was Douglas Carter who killed Madeline. Wasn't he the fiancé, or have I got that wrong?'

TOMMY DUGGAN ATTENDED the Mass at St Catherine's with Pete Walsh. The entire time there he had been infuriated by the certainty that Martha's killer was somewhere in the church, though his expression remained composed and grave as he joined in the prayers being offered for her. Following the Mass, he had planned to go to his office until it was time to meet the group at Will Stafford's house, but when he and Pete got back to the car and checked their messages, he learned about the death of Dr Lillian Madden.

Fifteen minutes later he was at the crime scene, with Pete at his heels. The body was still there, the forensic team efficiently at work.

'They figure death occurred some time between ten and eleven last night,' Frank Willette, the Belmar police chief, told Tommy Duggan. 'It wasn't a burglary that went sour. There's jewellery and money in the bedroom, so whoever did this was only interested in finding something here in her office. The secretary, Joan Hodges, found her. She ran outside and collapsed in the street. She's being treated in there.' He nodded towards the open door that led to the living quarters on the other side of the hall. 'Why don't you talk to her?'

'I intend to.'

Joan Hodges was propped up on pillows on the bed in the guest bedroom, a medic from the ambulance team at her side.

'I do *not* want to go to the hospital,' she was saying as Duggan and Walsh entered the room. 'I'll be all right. It was just the shock of finding her . . .' Her voice trailed off, and tears began to run down her cheeks.'

A Belmar policeman was standing at the foot of the bed.

Tommy looked at the Belmar cop, whom he knew slightly. 'I've already talked to Ms Hodges,' the cop said. 'I guess you have some questions for her too.'

'I do.' Tommy pulled up a chair, sat down by the bed, and introduced himself. 'Joan, you saw the way the office records were thrown around. The killer was obviously looking for something, maybe even his own file. Can you think of any of the doctor's patients who might have threatened her?'

'I don't know of a single patient who would ever have wanted to harm Dr Madden,' she told Tommy. 'It's that serial killer. I *know* it is.

He's afraid that she figured out something about him.'

That makes sense *if* he'd been a patient of hers at some time, Tommy thought. 'Where else would a patient's name appear besides in his own file?'

'In the appointment books I keep and in the computer.'

Tommy stood up. 'Joan, we're going to find this guy. I promise.'

When he and Pete returned to the doctor's office, the body bag holding the remains of Lillian Madden was being carried out.

'We're finished here,' the head of the forensic team told them. 'I doubt that we have anything useful for you. My guess is that this guy was smart enough to wear gloves.'

'Whatever he was looking for in the files, he probably found,' Chief Willette said.

'Do you know if she often worked at night?' Pete asked.

'Dr Madden lectured last night at the community college. Looks like she came back from the college, then went straight to her office. She was obviously at her desk, working, when she was killed. Probably never heard the intruder.'

'How'd he enter?'

'Nothing forced. Maybe an unlocked window? We found three or four of them. The alarm was turned off.'

'He was a patient,' Tommy said positively. 'Maybe someone who said too much under hypnosis and was worried. Otherwise why go through the files? Joan Hodges said that if he *was* a patient, his name will be listed in the appointment books.'

'He tried to smash the computer,' Willette said.

Tommy nodded. He was not surprised. 'Unless the hard drive is broken, we may be able to bring the files up.'

An hour later a frustrated Tommy Duggan was certain of only one fact: the murderer of Lillian Madden had been a patient some time in the last five years. All the appointment books covering that time period were missing, both Dr Madden's personal copies and the ones Joan Hodges kept.

SINCE THE PHONE CALL from Emily Graham about the photograph that had been slipped under her door in Spring Lake, Albany detective Marty Browski had been deeply disturbed. He had been convinced that Ned Koehler was the stalker and that they'd caught him just in time, before he had a chance to kill Emily. But now he wasn't so sure.

On Saturday afternoon Marty talked it over with his wife, Janey, as they took a long walk in the park near their home. 'When we arrested Koehler, he was outside Emily Graham's town house. He claimed that he'd only planned to frighten her. He said he had no intention of going inside.'

'You believed him, Marty. Everyone did. He was convicted of stalking her,' Janey observed.

'He changed his story when I talked to him yesterday. He added to it, saying he wanted Emily to experience how frightened his mother was before *she* died.'

'Nice guy.'

'Janey, Ned Koehler supposedly arrived home and found his mother dead, the knife in her chest. He went crazy: picked her up, carried her body out of the apartment, yelling for help. Joel Lake had been in that apartment, had burglarised it. It's a miracle that Emily Graham got him acquitted of the murder charge.'

'As I remember, the jury believed Ruth Koehler's sister when she testified that she'd spoken to Ruth after Joel Lake was seen leaving that building.'

'I didn't think they'd buy that story at the time. Anyway, we collared Lake a couple of blocks away. He had the stuff he'd taken from the apartment on him. The fact that he had no bloodstains didn't mean anything, because the knife had been thrown at Ruth Koehler and caught her in the chest.'

'Fingerprints?' Janey asked.

'Joel Lake wore gloves during the burglary. But Ned Koehler compromised the crime scene by pulling the knife out of his mother's body and carrying her out of the apartment. We all bought his story that he had found her and become hysterical.'

'You had pegged Ned Koehler as a weirdo but also a grieving son who stalked the lawyer who got his mother's killer acquitted. Is the know-it-all detective about to face the fact that he might have rushed to an erroneous conclusion?'

Marty sighed. 'Janey, why didn't your mother teach you to respect your husband? Ned Koehler is a weirdo and a liar. After seeing him yesterday, I now believe he is his mother's murderer. And—'

'What else?' Janey asked.

'I also think that he may not be the stalker who was making Emily Graham's life hell. I think that whoever shoved a picture of her under her door the other night was the real stalker. Think about it. If somebody from around here followed her down to Spring Lake, found out where she was staying, took her picture, developed it, and shoved it under her door the next night while a policeman was on the premises—what does that say to you?'

'Obsession. Recklessness. Cunning.'

'Exactly.'

'So whoever stalked her up here didn't mind making the drive to Spring Lake,' Janey said. 'If you eliminate Ned Koehler, where do you start looking for him?'

'Maybe Joel Lake? He's slime. He got a light sentence for the burglary and was out on the streets when the stalking started. Then I'm taking a good look at Gary White.'

'Marty, Emily and Gary have been divorced for over three years! I heard he broke up with Barbara What's-her-name and is playing the field. He's just a minor-league Don Juan.'

'He sued Emily Graham for five million dollars, half of what she made when she sold her dot-com stock. Which, incidentally, was the smartest thing she ever did in her life,' Marty added. 'It's really taken a beating lately.'

They had just reached the T-junction in the park, where they always turned round and started back home. In an instinctive gesture they each reached for the other's hand.

'And your next stop is . . ?' Janey asked.

'To look at the files on Ruth Koehler's death, with the premise that her son, Ned, may well be the killer. To reopen the stalking case. And to warn Emily Graham.'

AT THREE O'CLOCK Will Stafford's living room was crowded with people. Chairs from the dining room had remedied the need for extra seating.

Tommy Duggan stood at the fireplace, the focal point of the room. 'I appreciate that you all were kind enough to join us,' he began, his tone conciliatory. 'The reason we are here together is that you were present at the party at the Lawrence home only hours before Martha disappeared. I have talked with all of you individually during these past four and a half years. My hope is that by bringing you together, something you noticed that night, then forgot, may surface in your minds. Perhaps Martha mentioned her plans for meeting someone later that night or the next day. What I'd like to do is take you into Will's study, one at a time, and ask you to give me the details of any conversation you had with Martha that night and any conversation you may have overheard her having with someone else.' He paused. 'I then want to go over with each one of you exactly where you were the next morning between the hours of six and nine.'

Tommy's eyes scanned the room for reactions. Bob Frieze's cheeks were turning a deep shade of crimson. He had claimed he'd been working in his flowerbeds that morning. His wife had been asleep. With the high hedges round his house, no one else would have been able to see him to verify his alibi.

Dr Wilcox hid behind a philosophical expression, as he had whenever Tommy had questioned him during the past four and a half years. He'd admitted to being out for a long walk that morning, but not on the boardwalk, just around town. Maybe. Maybe not.

Mrs Wilcox. Brunhild. I'd hate to get in *her* way, Tommy thought. She appears to be one tough cookie.

Will Stafford. Good-looking. A single guy. The women were attracted to him. Natalie Frieze had given him a mighty warm kiss when she came in. Had Martha Lawrence been attracted to him?

There were five other couples, each wife distinctly remembering that her husband never left the house early that morning. Would they lie rather than let their husbands come under suspicion?

Tommy and Pete had decided how they would conduct the sessions. Not quite good cop-bad cop, but Pete would sit behind the person being interviewed, the notes of all previous statements in his hand, and interrupt whenever he found a discrepancy. That technique always rattled anyone who was trying to conceal something.

Tommy had two questions to ask each of them. The first was, 'Do you remember any of the women at the party that night wearing a silver silk scarf with metallic beading on the edges?' The second, 'Have you ever been a patient of Dr Lillian Madden's?'

The first hour went slowly. Everyone stuck to the stories they'd told for the past four and a half years. Nobody knew anything about a scarf. Martha hadn't mentioned any plans she had for the next day. Nobody had seen her use a cellphone.

Then Rachel Wilcox came in, every inch of her formidable body conveying her outrage at the entire matter. Her answers to their questions were brusque. 'I spoke to Martha about graduate school, since I knew she was planning to attend. She was having second thoughts.'

'You never mentioned that to me before,' Tommy said.

'If every word that people exchanged at social events were weighed and measured, the world would drown in trivia,' Rachel told him. 'Is there anything more you require of me?'

'Do you know if anyone was wearing a silvery grey scarf with metallic beading that night?'

'*I* was wearing it. Has it been found?'

Tommy felt his palms begin to sweat. Was Clayton Wilcox stupid enough to use his wife's scarf to kill Martha? 'Mrs Wilcox, when were you aware that the scarf was missing?'

'It was warm that evening, so I took it off. I asked my husband to put it in his pocket and thought no more about it until the next afternoon, when I asked him to give it to me. He did not have it.'

'Did you or Dr Wilcox look for it?'

'He phoned the Lawrences to ask about it, but it wasn't there.'

'I see.' Leave it alone, Tommy told himself. Let's get *his* version. Banking on the probability that the news of the murder in Belmar had not yet reached the ears of these people, he asked, 'Mrs Wilcox, do you know a Dr Lillian Madden?'

'The name is familiar.'

'She is a psychologist who lives in Belmar.'

'She teaches a course on reincarnation at Monmouth County Community College, does she not?' asked Rachel.

'Yes, she does.'

'I cannot imagine a greater waste of time.'

When she left the study, Tommy and Pete exchanged glances. 'Get Wilcox in here before she has a chance to talk to him,' Duggan said.

'I'm already on my way.' Pete disappeared into the hallway that led to the living room.

The demeanour of Dr Clayton Wilcox, by all outward appearances, was measured and calm, but Tommy wondered if he was at last sniffing the scent he'd been trying to catch all day—*fear.*

'Sit down, Dr Wilcox,' Tommy said.

They asked him about any conversation he might have had with Martha Lawrence at the party.

'She knew my career was in academia, and she asked me if I was friendly with anyone at Tulane University Graduate School of Business in New Orleans, which is where she had enrolled.'

'And the next morning you went for a long walk but did *not* go on the boardwalk, nor did you run into Martha at any point?'

'I think I have answered that question repeatedly.'

'Dr Wilcox, did your wife lose a scarf the night of the party?'

'Yes, she did.'

Tommy watched as perspiration formed on the forehead of Dr Clayton Wilcox. 'Did your wife ask you to hold that scarf for her?'

Wilcox waited, then said deliberately, 'My wife's recollection is that she asked me to put the scarf in my pocket. My recollection is that she asked me to put it with her handbag, which was on a table in the hall. That is exactly what I did.'

'Then the next afternoon, when you both realised it was missing, did you call the Lawrence home to enquire about it?'

'No, I did not.'

Direct contradiction of his wife's statement, Tommy thought. 'Wouldn't it have been appropriate to ask the Lawrences?'

'Mr Duggan, by the time we realised the scarf was missing, we all knew that Martha had disappeared. Do you seriously believe I would ask that distraught family about a scarf at that time?'

'Did you tell your wife you enquired about it?'

'For the sake of peace I did tell her that, yes.'

'Dr Wilcox, did you personally know Dr Lillian Madden?'

'No, I did not.'

'Were you ever a patient of hers, or did you ever consult her?'

Wilcox seemed to hesitate. Then, the tension apparent in his voice, he said, 'No, I was never a patient, and I don't recall having met her.'

He's lying, Tommy thought.

NICHOLAS TODD PHONED Emily at nine fifteen on Sunday morning. 'We're still on for today, I hope?' he asked.

'Absolutely. The Old Mill serves a fabulous brunch, I'm told. I made a reservation for one o'clock.'

'Great. I'll be at your house by about twelve thirty if that's OK. Incidentally, I hope this wasn't too early to call. Did I wake you up?'

'I've already walked to church and back, and it's over a mile away. Does that answer your question?'

'You're showing off. Now run through the directions to your place for me.'

PROMPTLY AT TWELVE THIRTY Emily's doorbell rang. When she opened the door, she realised that since Nick's call on Friday, she had been looking forward to his visit. His smile was warm as he stepped inside. She was glad to see that he was casually dressed in a jacket, trousers and turtleneck sweater.

'It's good to see you, Emily. It's been at least a month.'

'Yes, it has. The last few weeks in Albany were really round-the-clock sessions, trying to wrap up everything. I was so weary for the last seventy miles of the drive here on Tuesday evening that I could hardly keep my eyes open.'

'And you certainly haven't had a restful time since.'

'That's putting it mildly. Want to take a quick look round?'

'Sure, but I have to tell you I'm already impressed. It's a wonderful house.'

After the tour they headed for the restaurant. At the Old Mill, their table overlooked a pond, where swans were gliding through the water. When the Bloody Marys they'd ordered were served, the waitress offered menus. 'We'll wait a few minutes,' Nick told her.

Since she had agreed to accept the position with the law firm, Emily had dined with Nick and Walter Todd three or four times, but never with Nick alone. Though his smile was warm, he seemed uncomfortable. Did it have anything to do with her, or was it a personal problem? She knew he wasn't married.

'I wish I could read your mind, Emily.' Nick's voice broke in on her reverie. 'You seem to be deep in thought.'

She decided to be candid. 'There's something about me that troubles you, and I wish you'd lay it out on the table. Do you *want* me in the firm? Do you think I'm right for the job?'

'Do I want you in the firm? Absolutely! I wish you'd start tomorrow, frankly. Which, incidentally, is why I'm here right now.' He began to tell her about his decision.

As he told her of his desire to leave the firm, Emily was dismayed to learn of Nick's plans. I was looking forward to working with him, she thought. 'Where will you apply for a job?' she asked.

'The US Attorney's office. That's where I'd really like to go. But my guess is that I'm not going to be able to sweet-talk you into starting at the office next week, am I?'

'I'm afraid not. Will your father be very upset?'

'He's probably hanging me in effigy right now because I'm leaving. When I report back to him that you'll be unavailable until May1st, you'll be right there beside me.'

'"We must indeed all hang together, or most assuredly . . ."' Emily smiled.

'"We shall all hang separately." Exactly.' Nick Todd picked up the menu. 'Business concluded. What's your choice?'

IT WAS NEARLY FOUR O'CLOCK when Nick dropped Emily off at home. He walked her to the porch and waited while she put her key in the door. 'You do have a good alarm system?' he asked.

'Absolutely. And tomorrow an old friend from Albany is going to install security cameras.'

Nick's eyebrows went up. 'After that stalker you had in Albany, I can understand why you'd want them.'

She opened the door. They saw it at the same time—an envelope on the floor of the hall, the flap side facing up.

'Looks as if someone left a note for you,' Nick said as he bent to pick it up.

'Pick it up by the corner. It may have fingerprints.' Emily did not recognise her own voice. It had come out as a strained whisper.

Nick looked at her sharply, but obeyed. As he stood up, the flap of the envelope flew open, and a photograph fell out. It was of Emily in church at the memorial Mass. Scrawled across the bottom were three words: 'Pray for yourself.'

Monday, March 26

I am eagerly looking forward to the activity that I know will ensue later today. I am very pleased that I made Emily Graham the recipient of my message.

Her mail should be delivered soon.

As I expected, there were questions about the scarf, but I'm sure that no one can prove who finally took possession of it that night.

Martha admired it. I heard her tell Rachel that it was very pretty.

I remember that at that very moment, the thought ran through my head that Martha had just chosen the instrument of her own death.

After all, a scarf, I thought, is not unlike the sash that squeezed the breath from Madeline's throat.

TOMMY HAD BEEN about to leave the office on Sunday when the call came in from Emily Graham. He and Pete rushed to Spring Lake and took the envelope and photograph from her.

On Monday morning, Tommy and Pete were in the prosecutor's office, filling their boss in on the events of the previous weekend.

Elliot Osborne had been in Washington since Friday evening.

Tommy briefed him on the Madden murder and his interrogation at Will Stafford's home of the guests at that final Lawrence party.

'It's Mrs Wilcox's scarf, and she was wearing it that night. She claims she asked her husband to put it in his pocket. He claims she asked him to put it next to her handbag.'

Osborne tapped the top of his desk with his index finger. 'That scarf appeared to be fairly long. It would have been pretty bulky to put in the pocket of a summer jacket.'

Tommy nodded. 'That's what I thought too. By the time it was used to strangle Martha, part of it had been cut off. But on the other hand, Wilcox lied to his wife about calling the Lawrences to ask if it had been found. His story is that by then Martha was missing, and he wasn't going to bother them about a scarf.'

'How much do we know about Wilcox?'

Pete Walsh pulled out his notes. 'Solid academic career. Ended up president of Enoch College. Retired early, twelve years ago. Used to come to Spring Lake for summer vacations when he was a kid, so settled here. Publishes regularly in academic journals. Since he moved here, he's done a lot of historical writing about New Jersey. He's considered something of the town historian in Spring Lake.'

'Which ties in with Emily Graham's theory that Martha's killer had access to records about the women who disappeared in the 1890s,' Tommy pointed out. 'I swear that guy was lying when he said he didn't know Dr Madden. I want to start digging a lot deeper with him. My bet is that there's dirt to be found.'

Tommy and Pete then filled in Osborne on the call they had received at four o'clock on Sunday afternoon from Emily Graham.

'She has guts,' Tommy said. 'White as a sheet, but composed when we got there. She thinks it's a copycat situation. I also talked to Marty Browski, the guy who handled her stalking case in Albany.'

'What does he think?' Osborne asked.

'He thinks that the wrong guy is doing time on this one. He's reopened the investigation and has two suspects: Emily Graham's exhusband and a slime she got off on a murder rap.'

'What do you think?'

'Best possible scenario: copycat,' Tommy said. 'A couple of teenagers found out that Emily was being stalked in Albany and are playing sicko games with her now. Worst possible scenario: the guy who killed Martha Lawrence is toying with Graham.'

'Which scenario do you buy?'

'Copycat. Dr Lillian Madden, the psychologist who was murdered in Belmar, was definitely tied to the Lawrence case. I'd stake everything that Martha's killer must have been Dr Madden's patient and couldn't take a chance on her talking to us about him. But I don't think he would be so dumb as to risk being seen hanging around Emily Graham's house. He has too much at stake.'

'Suppose Graham's original stalker is on the loose in Spring Lake? I'd say that if he's obsessed enough to come all the way down here from Albany, she's in extreme danger.'

Elliot Osborne's secretary's voice came over the intercom. 'I'm sorry to interrupt, but Ms Emily Graham is on the phone. She insists she must speak to Detective Duggan at once.'

Tommy picked up the phone. 'Duggan, Ms Graham.'

The prosecutor and Pete Walsh watched as the lines deepened on Duggan's face. 'We'll be right over.' He hung up and looked at Osborne. 'She received a troubling postcard in the morning mail.'

'The stalker? Another picture of herself?'

'No. This one is a drawing of two tombstones. The name on one is Carla Harper. The name on the other is Letitia Gregg. If this card is on the level, they're buried together in the back yard of 15 Ludlam Avenue in Spring Lake.'

ERIC BAILEY BEGAN Monday morning early, as a guest on the news hour of the local Albany television channel.

Slight of frame and barely medium height, with rumpled hair and frameless glasses that dominated his narrow face, he was unprepossessing in appearance and manner. When he spoke, his voice had a nervous, high-pitched quality.

The anchorman of the programme had not been happy to see Bailey's name on the list of guests. 'Whenever that guy is on, the loud clicking sound you hear is all the remote controls in Albany switching to another channel,' he complained.

'A lot of people around this area invested money in his company,' the financial editor snapped back. 'The stock's been on the skids for the last year and a half. Now Bailey claims he has new software that will revolutionise the computer industry. He may sound like a chipmunk, but what he has to say is worth hearing.'

'Thank you for the compliment. Thank you both.'

Eric Bailey had come onto the set quietly, without either man hearing him approach. Now, with a slight smile, as if enjoying their discomfort, he said, 'Perhaps I should wait in the greenroom until you're ready for me.'

THE SECURITY CAMERAS Eric Bailey was going to install around Emily's home were already packed in his van, so immediately after the television interview, he began the drive to Spring Lake.

He knew he had to be careful not to drive too fast. Anger combined with humiliation made him want to press the accelerator to the floor of the car, to weave in and out of traffic, terrifying the occupants of the vehicles he would cut up. Instilling fear was his answer to all the rejections in his life, to all the rebuffs, to all the ridicule.

He would find a way to punish the two who had rubbished him this morning. It just took a little quiet thinking, that's all.

Depending on traffic, he would be in Spring Lake between one and two. He knew the route fairly well by now. This would be his third round trip since Wednesday.

'I DIDN'T EXPECT to see you again so soon,' Emily told Tommy Duggan and Pete Walsh when she opened the door for them.

'We didn't expect to be back this soon,' Duggan replied as he observed her closely. 'How did you sleep last night?'

Emily shrugged. 'Meaning that you can tell I didn't sleep much last night. I'm afraid that photograph yesterday got to me. I am terribly frightened, I have to admit it.'

'Since you live alone, it would be much safer—'

She interrupted. 'I'm not moving out of the house.' She led the detectives into the study. 'The only mail that's been delivered since I've been here was addressed either to the Kiernans or to "Occupant",' she told them. Then she pointed to the postcard on the writing desk. 'But this is addressed specifically to me.'

It was a crude drawing of a house and the property surrounding it, the address '15 Ludlam Avenue' scrawled between the lines of what was meant to be a sidewalk. Two tombstones were depicted side by side at the extreme left-hand corner behind the house. Each bore a name. One was Letitia Gregg, the other Carla Harper.

Tommy took a plastic evidence bag from his pocket, picked up the postcard by the edges, and slipped it into the bag. 'Ms Graham, this may be someone's idea of a sick joke, but it also may be on the level. We've checked out 15 Ludlam Avenue. It's owned by an elderly widow who lives there alone. We're hoping that she'll be cooperative when we tell her about this, and will let us dig up her yard.'

'Do *you* think it's on the level?' Emily asked.

'After what we found there'—Tommy nodded in the direction of Emily's back yard—'I think that there's a very good chance that it is, yes. But until we know for certain, I'd appreciate if you don't say anything to anyone about it.'

Emily thought about Nick Todd. He had phoned after the mail came, but she hadn't told him about it. When they had found the photo on the hall floor after they had returned from brunch yesterday, he'd urged her to drive to Manhattan and stay in her apartment there. But she'd insisted that the cameras Eric was going to install were the best hope of finding out who was doing this to her.

Brave words, she thought, as she walked Tommy and Pete to the door and closed and locked it behind them, but the fact is, I'm scared to death.

Stop it! Emily ordered herself. Get busy! Call Dr Wilcox and ask if you can drop off his books. Then go to the museum and do some research. See if you can figure out where those people lived in the 1890s in relation to one another. There has to be a map of the town as it was then. I need some art supplies too. And I should be able to buy a Monopoly game somewhere—the small houses that are part of that game would be perfect for my needs.

On a sheet of cardboard she would draw a plan of the town as it had looked in the 1890s, put in the street names, then place the tiny houses on the properties where Madeline's friends had lived.

Then I'll get the history of the ownership of those properties since that time at the town clerk's office, Emily decided.

BOB FRIEZE was in The Seasoner's first-floor office, wearing his dark blue jacket and grey trousers. He looked at his watch. It was almost one o'clock. The potential buyer of the restaurant, Dominic Bonetti, was due any minute to discuss the sale over lunch.

The phone rang. It was the *maître d'*. 'Mr Bonetti is here. Shall I seat him at your table?'

'Yes. I'm on my way.'

He hurried downstairs. He felt his palms begin to sweat when he walked into the dining room to see that only six tables were occupied. Dominic Bonetti was waiting for him.

They did not begin discussing business until after they finished the grilled salmon, which had been dry and unappetising.

As espresso was served, Bonetti came to the point. 'You want out of this place. I want in. You've got a great location here.'

But then, in the next half-hour, Bob learned what The Seasoner did *not* have, which turned out to be almost everything.

The decor: 'I know you spent a fortune on it, but it's cold and uncomfortable. The layout of the kitchen is inefficient . . .'

The price Dominic Bonetti offered was half a million dollars less than the absolute bottom price Bob thought he could accept. 'That's your initial offer,' he said with a dismissive smile. 'I'll be happy to counter it.'

Bonetti's easy-going manner vanished. 'If I buy this place, I'm going to spend big bucks to make it look the way I want it,' he said quietly. 'I've given you my price. I won't consider a counteroffer.' He stood up. 'Think it over, Bob. It's actually a very fair price, considering what needs to be done.' He extended his hand. 'Let me know.'

After Bonetti left the dining room, the waiter appeared with a cellphone. 'Urgent call from Mrs Frieze, sir.'

To Bob's surprise Natalie said, 'I just heard that there's an excavator digging up the yard at 15 Ludlam Avenue. The rumour is that they're looking for the body of Carla Harper, that girl who disappeared two and a half years ago. Bob, isn't that the house your family lived in when you were growing up?'

'YOUR FATHER IS HERE to see you, Mr Stafford.' The voice of Will's secretary, Pat Glynn, sounded puzzled. It was almost as if she were saying, 'I didn't know your father was alive.'

'My father!' Angered and dismayed, Will threw down the pen he was holding. 'Send him in.'

The door opened slowly. The man who came in was a shadow of the one Will had seen a year ago. Since then his father had lost at least fifty pounds. His complexion was now waxy yellow, the cheekbones prominent under tightly drawn skin. The full head of greying sandy hair was now reduced to loose strands of dingy grey.

Will stood up. His voice rising, spitting out the words, he demanded, 'Can't you understand I want no part of you?'

'Will, I made mistakes. I admit it. I haven't got long. I wasn't there for you when you needed me, son. I want to make it up to you.'

'You can't. Now go, and don't come back.'

'I should have understood. You were an adolescent—'

'Shut up!' In two strides, Will was round his desk and in front of his father. His strong hands gripped the other man's thin, shaking shoulders. 'I paid for what someone else did. You didn't believe me. You could have afforded a team of lawyers to defend me properly. Instead you washed your hands of me, your only son. I don't need you coming here and destroying everything I've built up for the past twenty-three years. Just get out of here.'

Willard Stafford, Snr, nodded. His eyes moist, he turned towards the door. Then he stopped. 'I promise I won't be back. I wanted to see you face to face for the last time and ask your forgiveness. I know I failed you . . .' His words trailed off into silence.

Will did not respond.

His father sighed. 'It's just that reading about that girl whose body was found—'

'You have the nerve to come here and say *that* to me? Get out! Do you hear me! Get out!'

It did not matter to Will that he was shouting. It only mattered that he get control over his blinding rage before he put his hands around the scrawny throat of the man who had sired him, and squeezed it until the neck snapped.

NED KOEHLER'S LAWYER, Hal Davis, and Marty Browski were at Gray Manor in Albany on Monday afternoon. They waited together for Koehler to be brought into the conference room.

When the door opened, he was escorted to a seat by the guard. 'Ned's a little agitated today,' the guard said. 'I'm right outside if you need me.'

'Why are you doing this to me?' Koehler demanded of Marty.

'I just have a few questions,' Browski said soothingly. 'But I must specifically inform you that you are a suspect in the death of your mother, so anything you say can be used against you.' He rattled off the rest of the legal rights by rote.

'Ned, you don't have to answer any questions,' Davis said.

'Did your mother ever get angry at you, Ned?' Marty asked.

'My mother loved me. Very much.'

'I'm sure she did, but she used to get angry at you sometimes?'

'No. Never.'

'She was especially angry because you were so careless when you went out about pulling the door closed tight so that the lock would engage. Isn't that right?'

'I always locked that door when I went out.'

'Always? Joel Lake says the door wasn't even fully closed. That's why he went into your apartment. Isn't it a fact, Ned, that the week before your mother died, the same thing happened? Didn't she shout at you that someone could come in and put a knife through her? Your neighbours told me that's what she always said to you when you didn't make sure the lock had caught.'

'Ned, I don't want you to talk any more,' Davis urged.

Koehler's eyes had narrowed to slits. 'Leave me alone, Hal.'

'Ned, how do you know how frightened your mother was when she saw the knife and knew she was going to die?' Marty hammered the question at Koehler. 'Did she beg you not to hurt her? Did she say she was sorry for picking on you? She was sitting at the kitchen table. She had just realised the apartment had been burglarised. She must have been very angry. The knife was right there on that rack on the wall. Did she point to it and tell you that whoever came in could have used it on her and that it would have been your fault?'

Koehler buried his face in his hands. 'She said, "Don't, Ned. I'm sorry, Ned. Don't Ned, please." But it was too late. I didn't know I was holding the knife, and then it was in her chest.' Great racking sobs shook his body as he shouted, 'I'm sorry, Mommy! I'm sorry!'

ERIC BAILEY WAS WAITING on Emily's porch when she arrived home, back from delivering the books to Dr Wilcox, visiting the museum, and buying the supplies she needed.

He waved away her apologies. 'Don't worry. I made good time, but I am hungry. What have you got to eat?'

Inside, she got out sandwich fillings—ham and Swiss cheese, lettuce and tomatoes, and fresh Italian bread—and while she prepared lunch, he began to unpack the camera equipment.

They ate in the kitchen. 'I added some chicken soup to the menu,' she told him. 'I made it the other night.'

'This reminds me of when we were in those dumpy offices in Albany. I'd go down and get sandwiches from the deli, and you'd heat up your homemade soup.'

'It was fun,' Emily said.

'It was fun, and I wouldn't have had a company if you hadn't defended me against that lawsuit.'

'And *you* made *me* rich. Fair's fair. I can live the rest of my life without a financial care, thanks to you.'

'Any time you need taking care of . . .' Eric left the sentence unfinished as Emily smilingly shook her head.

'Why spoil a beautiful friendship?' she asked.

He scraped the last drop of soup from the bowl, then helped load the dishwasher.

'That's my job,' she protested.

'I like helping you.'

A few minutes later she closed the dishwasher with a decisive snap. 'OK. If you work at one end of the dining-room table, I'll set up at the other end.' She explained what she was planning to do with the copies of the maps and town records. 'I want to enter these people's lives. I want to see where Madeline's friends lived. I'm—'

The sudden ringing of the phone caused Emily to gasp and grab Eric's arm. She managed a shaky laugh as she ran to the study to answer the call.

It was Detective Browski. He did not waste time greeting her. 'Emily, your client in the Koehler case is a louse and a bum, but you may be glad to hear he's not a murderer. I just left Ned Koehler. Wait till you hear . . .'

Fifteen minutes later she returned to the dining room.

'That was quite a conversation,' Eric commented, his tone light. 'New boyfriend?'

'Detective Browski. You've met him. He's been saying nice things about you.'

'Let's hear. Don't leave out a detail.'

'According to him, you probably saved my life with the camera you installed that caught Ned Koehler.' Emily heard the quiver in her voice as she told Eric about Koehler's confession. 'He admitted today that although he hadn't been stalking me, he was planning to kill me. Marty said that in Koehler's twisted mind, Joel Lake, the guy I defended, caused his mother's death. He told Browski that if Joel hadn't burglarised the apartment, his mother would be alive today, that Joel was the real killer.'

'Pretty crazy logic, I would say,' Eric said. He began assembling the equipment needed to install the cameras.

'Crazy, but I'm sure he didn't mean to kill his mother, and I know he can't bear to think that he's the cause of her death. If Joel Lake had been found guilty, he would have been able to transfer his own guilt to him. Then I got Joel off, so *I* became the villain.'

'You're not a villain,' Eric said emphatically. 'What worries me is that from what you say, Browski is worried about this renewed stalker business. Who does he think is doing it?'

'He's checked out my ex. Gary has airtight alibis for Tuesday night and Saturday morning, when these last pictures were taken. Browski hasn't been able to locate Joel Lake yet.'

When Eric left at 7.00pm, the cameras were in place on all sides of the house. What he did not tell Emily was that he had installed others inside the house and attached a line-of-sight antenna on an attic window. Now, within a half-mile radius, with the television set in his van, he would be able to follow her movements and hear her conversations in her living room, kitchen and study.

As he left her with a friendly kiss on the cheek and began the return trip to Albany, he was already planning his next visit to Spring Lake. He smiled, thinking of how she had jumped when the phone rang. She was more unnerved than she wanted to admit.

Fear was the ultimate weapon of revenge. She had sold her stock at peak value. Shortly after that, other sell-offs had started, leading to a chain of them. Now his whole company was on the verge of bankruptcy. He could even forgive her for that if she had not rejected him as a man. 'If you will not love me, Emily,' he said aloud, 'you will live your life in fear, waiting for that moment when someone steps out of the dark and you can't get away.'

Tuesday, March 27

A replacement excavator was delivered to 15 Ludlam Avenue at eight o'clock on Tuesday morning, the first one having malfunctioned the day before. This time, the media were present, mingling with people standing on the sidewalk in quiet, sombre groups. Everyone knew the searchers had to be looking for another body. But whose? It had to be Carla Harper, that young girl who vanished two and a half years ago, they whispered among themselves.

At nine thirty, nearly an hour and a half after the excavation began, the onlookers saw the excavator abruptly stop digging and the forensic crew rush to look down into the hole.

'They've found something!' one person cried.

The arrival of the hearse from the morgue confirmed that human remains had been found. The prosecutor arrived in a squad car and promised to make a statement shortly.

Half an hour later Elliot Osborne stepped up to the microphones. He confirmed that a full skeleton wrapped in the same type of heavy plastic that had contained the remains of Martha Lawrence had been uncovered. A human skull and several loose bones had been found further down.

Osborne refused to answer the questions shouted at him, the loudest of which was, 'Doesn't this absolutely *prove* you have a reincarnated killer stalking this town?'

TOMMY DUGGAN and Pete Walsh had planned to follow the hearse from the crime scene to the morgue, but delayed to speak to Margo Thaler, the eighty-two-year-old present owner of the house.

Visibly upset, she was sitting in her living room, sipping tea.

'Mrs Thaler,' Tommy said soothingly, 'I'd just like to ask you a few questions. How long have you lived here?'

'Forty years. I'm the third owner of the house. I bought it from Robert Frieze, Senior. He owned it for thirty years.'

'Would he be the father of Robert Frieze, owner of The Seasoner?'

A look of disdain came over Margo Thaler's face. 'Yes, but Bob's nothing like his father. Divorced his lovely wife and married that Natalie woman! Then he opened that restaurant. My friends and I tried it once. High prices and bad food.'

Bob Frieze certainly doesn't have many fans in this town, Tommy thought as he began to do some arithmetic. Frieze was about sixty years old. Mrs Thaler had owned the house for the past forty years, and the Frieze family owned it for thirty years before that. That meant that Bob Frieze was born ten years after his father had bought the house, and lived in it for the first twenty years of his life.

'Mrs Thaler,' Tommy said, 'we believe that the skeleton will prove to be the remains of a young woman who disappeared about two years ago, probably on August 5th. It seems to me that you would have noticed if someone had dug up your yard.'

'I certainly *would* have noticed, yes.'

Which means that the remains had to have been kept somewhere else until they could safely be buried here, Tommy thought.

'Mrs Thaler, I was on the police force here for eight years,' Pete said.

She looked sharply at him. 'Oh, of course. Forgive me. I should have recognised you.'

'I seem to remember that it was your habit to leave for Florida in October and not return until May. Do you still do that?'

'Yes, I do.'

That explains it, Tommy thought. Whoever murdered Carla kept her body somewhere else, maybe in a freezer, until he could safely bury it here. 'You've been very cooperative and also very kind to let us talk to you now, Mrs Thaler,' he said. Then another question occurred to him. 'Do you happen to know how old this house is?'

'It was built in 1893.'

'Do you know who owned it then?'

'The Alan Carter family. They owned it for nearly forty years before selling it to Robert Frieze, Senior.'

DR O'BRIEN was finishing his examination of the remains when Tommy Duggan and Pete Walsh arrived at the morgue.

The sum of the findings was nearly identical to what they had heard on Thursday. The skeleton was that of a young female. The cause of death was strangulation.

'Look at this,' O'Brien said. With his gloved hands he held up threads of material. 'See those metal beads? This is a piece of the same scarf that we found round Martha Lawrence's neck.'

'You mean that when someone stole that scarf at the party— assuming that's what happened—he not only killed Martha with it, but cut it up so he could use it again?' Pete asked with disbelief.

'This killer is following the 1890s timetable,' Tommy said angrily. 'There may not even have been anything personal about killing either Martha Lawrence or'—he looked at the figure on the table—'Carla Harper, if this is her. The only reason they would have been chosen is that both Martha and Carla were around the age of the women who vanished in the 1890s.'

'A comparison of dental records will establish if this is Carla Harper.' Dr O'Brien adjusted his glasses. 'The separate skull we found had been in the ground much longer than the full skeleton. My estimate is it's been there at least one hundred years.'

'Carla Harper and Letitia Gregg,' Tommy said softly.

'Judging from the names printed on that postcard, it would seem likely,' Dr O'Brien agreed. 'There's something else here you'll be interested in.' He was holding up a small plastic bag. 'A pair of old-fashioned earrings. Garnets set in silver, with a pearl teardrop.'

'Where did you find them?' asked Tommy.

'Same as before. Folded in the hand of the skeleton. When in the 1890s did you say the third girl disappeared?'

'Ellen Swain disappeared on March 31st, thirty-one months and twenty-six days after Letitia Gregg vanished on August 5th. Carla Harper disappeared on August 5th. Thirty-one months and twenty-six days ago this Saturday, March 31st.' Tommy knew he was not so much responding to the question as thinking aloud.

'Madeline and Martha on September 7th, Letitia and Carla on August 5th, and now you have the next anniversary coming up this Saturday,' Dr O'Brien said slowly. 'Do you think that this killer plans to choose another victim and bury her with Ellen Swain?'

Tommy felt overwhelmingly weary. He knew that this question was exactly the one the media would ask. 'Dr O'Brien, I hope and pray that *isn't* the scenario, but I promise you that everyone connected with law enforcement in this area is going to act on the premise that a psycho is planning to choose and kill another young woman from this town four days from now.'

He had to talk again to Dr Clayton Wilcox, whose own wife admitted she gave him the scarf the night of the Lawrences' party.

Pete and I both sensed Wilcox was lying to us the other day at Will Stafford's house, Tommy told himself. Now it's time to sweat the truth out of him.

THEY HAVE BEGUN to believe in me, he realised. This morning the highlight of the *Today* show was an interview with Dr Nehru Patel, a prominent philosopher and writer on the subject of psychical research. He firmly believes that I am the reincarnation of the serial killer of the late nineteenth century!

What puzzles the good Dr Patel, as he explained to the interviewer, Katie Couric, is that I am acting against the laws of karma.

Patel said that some may choose to return near to where they had lived in a previous lifetime because they need to meet again people whom they knew in a previous incarnation. They wish to repay the karmic debts they may owe to these people. On the other hand, these karmic actions are supposed to be good, not evil, which was very puzzling. It is possible, he continued, that in a previous lifetime Martha Lawrence had been Madeline Shapley and Carla Harper had been Letitia Gregg.

That's not true, but it's an interesting concept.

Dr Patel was asked whether it is possible that Ellen Swain is now alive in a different body and that I have recognised her and will seek her out on Saturday.

Well, I have chosen my next victim. She is *not* Ellen, but she will sleep with Ellen.

And I have conceived of a novel plan to throw the police off the track. It is quite delicious and pleases me very much.

AT NINE O'CLOCK on Wednesday morning, George Lawrence phoned. 'Emily, my mother and I went through all those photograph albums and memorabilia she has stashed away. We culled anything that wasn't relevant. If it's all right with you, I'll drop off the rest of it in a half-hour or so.'

'That would be wonderful.' Emily was in the dining room, working on a model of the town at the time of the earlier murders. On her cardboard plan she had Monopoly houses in place, indicating where the Shapleys, the Carters, the Greggs and the Swains had lived.

When the doorbell rang, she crossed the hall and opened the door. George Lawrence entered with two heavy boxes. He carried them into the dining room and set them on the floor. 'You can go through them at your convenience,' he said. He looked round the room, taking in the street plan on the table.

'Let me show you what I'm trying to do here,' Emily offered.

George Lawrence bent attentively over the table as she showed how she was re-creating the layout of the town in the 1890s.

'This is your home?' he asked, touching the top of one.

'Yes.'

'And this is ours?'

'Yes.'

'What exactly are you trying to do?'

'Figure out how three young women could have vanished without a trace. I'm looking for a house of one of their friends—one of their male friends perhaps—where they might have been enticed inside.' Emily pointed. 'Here's the Shapley house, and here, right across the street, is the Carter house. Supposedly, Douglas missed the early train home the day Madeline vanished. But did he?'

'Surely that was checked out at the time?'

'I've been promised a look at the police records. I'll be very interested to see what they show. Visualise that day. Madeline was sitting on the porch, waiting for Douglas. Suppose Douglas suddenly appeared on his porch, and she ran down to greet him?'

'And he pulled her into the house, killed her, and hid her body until he could bury it in her own back yard?' George Lawrence looked sceptical. 'What would his motive be?'

'I don't know, and admittedly it *is* a far-fetched theory. On the other hand, I've found indications that his cousin Alan Carter was in love with Madeline as well. His family lived in the house on Ludlam Avenue where the bodies were found yesterday. Suppose *he* came by in a closed carriage and perhaps told Madeline that Douglas had been in an accident.'

'We heard about the discovery yesterday, of course. Now the Harper family has to face what we faced last week.' The stark pain George Lawrence was experiencing was evident to Emily. 'Well, I'm on my way. We're starting home this afternoon. Mother said to call her if you have any questions.'

As she closed the door behind him, the phone rang. It was Nick Todd.

'I would have called before,' he said, 'but I didn't want to become a nuisance to you.'

'Trust me, that's the last thing I'd ever consider you to be.'

'No more incidents with your stalker, I hope?'

'Not a one. And on Monday my friend Eric Bailey came down from Albany and installed security cameras round the outside of the house. The next time someone tries to slip something under the door, he'll soon see his own picture on a mug sheet.'

'And you turn your security system on when you're alone?'

It's not on now, Emily thought. 'Always at night.'

'It wouldn't be a bad idea to have it on during the day as well.'

'I guess it wouldn't. I intend to be careful, but I don't want to reach the point where I begin to feel as if whoever is doing this is winning.'

'Believe it or not, I do understand. The papers are full of what happened in Spring Lake yesterday. The stories say the police got an anonymous tip. Have you any idea where it came from?'

'From me,' she said, then had to explain about the postcard.

Nick said, 'Emily, do you think there is even a *slight* chance that this killer is also the guy who stalked you in Albany?'

'No, I don't. And neither does Detective Browski.'

Mentioning the name of the Albany policeman meant filling Nick in on Ned Koehler's confession. Then she told him about her project of re-creating the town layout to see if she could figure out who had murdered the three young women.

When the conversation ended, she had accepted Nick's invitation to have a return brunch at the Old Mill on Sunday. 'I only hope we won't be talking about another murder,' she said.

After they had said goodbye, Nick sat at his desk and thought, Emily, why are you so smart and still so dense? Has it never occurred to you that *you* might be targeted as the next victim?

TOMMY DUGGAN and Pete Walsh began the morning in Elliot Osborne's office.

Tommy had his notebook open. 'We now have a positive ID on the skeleton we found yesterday. The dental records confirm it to be the remains of Carla Harper. The section of scarf apparently used to strangle her is part of the same scarf that was used to strangle Martha Lawrence. The killer used one end on Martha and the centre piece on Carla. The third piece is missing.'

'Meaning that if the killer follows what seems to be his plan, he'll use the scarf again on Saturday.' Osborne frowned and tilted back his chair. 'No matter how many cops we have patrolling Spring Lake, we can't be on every street, in every back yard. How's the background check on Wilcox progressing?'

'So far there's nothing much more than we had before. However, we have learned that Wilcox abruptly resigned his presidency of Enoch College twelve years ago. At the time, he'd just had his contract renewed and had all kinds of plans for further expansion.'

'Any explanation?'

'Ill health was the official reason. Apparently, a serious heart condition. Got a big, tearful send-off. They named a building after him. But I'd bet the ranch that he has no more heart trouble than me or Pete. My guess is that either he was told to resign or resigned on his own because he had a big problem that he didn't want made public. Now our job is to squeeze out of him what it was.'

'We're seeing him at three,' Pete volunteered. 'We thought it would be a good idea to let him squirm a little while waiting for us.'

'It is a good idea.' Osborne made a move to get up, but Pete had more to say.

'Just to keep you posted, sir, I spent last evening going through the records of the police investigations about the disappearance of those three girls in the 1890s.'

'Did you find anything at all useful?'

'Not that I could see. It's like what's been happening now. The girls

502

seem to have vanished off the face of the earth.'

'You're giving a copy of those records to Emily Graham?'

Pete looked worried. 'I cleared it with the first assistant.'

'I know you did. I'm not in favour of records, even if they're over one hundred years old, being made available outside the usual channels, but if you've promised them to her, I'll let it happen.'

Osborne stood up—a signal that the meeting was over.

Duggan and Walsh also got to their feet. 'One piece of good news,' Tommy added as he headed to the door. 'Dr Madden's killer is better at strangling people than at whacking computers. Our research people were afraid the hard drive had been damaged, but they've been able to get it going. With any luck we'll retrieve Madden's files and maybe find out that a guest at the Lawrence party that night four and a half years ago also spent some of his time with a shrink who specialised in regression therapy.'

'BOB, WHERE DID you go last night?' asked Natalie Frieze.

'When I couldn't sleep, I went downstairs and read. I came up at about five, took a sleeping pill, and for once it worked.'

It was nearly noon. Bob Frieze had come downstairs to find Natalie sitting in the living room, waiting for him. He looked at his beautiful wife, taking in her shimmering blonde hair, her near-perfect features, her catlike turquoise eyes. Remembering how exciting he had once found her, he was amazed at how detached he now felt.

Natalie was wearing a tailored dark green trouser suit that he had never seen before. Obviously new. Obviously pricey. He wondered how she found room for it in her closet. 'You look very nice,' he observed. 'Are you going somewhere?'

'I have a lunch date.' Natalie got to her feet swiftly. 'Believe it or not, I'm not sleeping very well myself. I came down here at two this morning. You weren't here, Bobby. And your car was gone. Now, will you please explain to me where you were.'

She wouldn't tell me that unless it's true, Frieze thought frantically. I don't know where I was. 'Natalie, I was so tired, I forgot. I did go out for a spin. Wanted to get some fresh air and do some heavy thinking.' He groped for words. 'I've decided to take Bonetti's offer, even though he's low-balled me.'

Natalie walked over to him. 'When you were taking your spin last night to clear your head, you apparently thought that a drink would clear it more. A drink with a friend, I mean. Here's what I found in your pocket.' She tossed a piece of paper at him.

He read what was written on it: *Hi, handsome. My number is 555-1974. Don't forget to call. Peggy.*

'I don't know how that got there, Natalie,' he said.

'I do, Bobby. Someone named Peggy put it there. I have news for you. Get rid of that restaurant. Sell this house. And then figure out what you were worth the day I became your blushing bride. Because half of that is what I intend to take out of this marriage.'

'You're out of your mind, Natalie.'

'Am I? Bobby, I've been doing a lot of thinking about the night at the Lawrence party. You were wearing that boxy jacket. You could have hidden that scarf under it. And the next morning, when I got up, you were digging in the garden. Any chance you were getting rid of Martha's body until you could move it to the back yard of the Shapley house?'

'You can't believe that!'

'Maybe I can. And maybe I can't. You're a strange man, Bob. There are times when you look at me as if you don't know me. You have a way of disappearing without telling me where you're going. Maybe I should tell Detective Duggan that I've become concerned about your behaviour and, for your own sake as well as for the safety of the young women in this community, feel I have to report it.'

The veins in Frieze's forehead began to bulge. He grasped Natalie's wrist and tightened his grip on it till she cried out in pain. His face was flushed with rage. Between clenched teeth he spat out, 'You tell Duggan or anyone a story like that, and you'd better start being concerned for *yourself*! Got it?'

ON WEDNESDAY AFTERNOON Marty Browski called Emily to tell her that Joel Lake had been located. Lake's alibi checked out, and he was definitely not the stalker. Marty then asked if she had received any new photographs.

'No, not so far. The alarm system is state of the art, although I admit that in the middle of the night I think about how Ned Koehler disarmed the one in the town house. But I do feel that the cameras Eric Bailey put in are added security.'

Browski could hear the nervous tremor that occasionally surfaced in Emily's voice. He felt angry and frustrated that he was completely without a stalking suspect. He admitted to himself that he was also deathly afraid that Emily was in very real danger. 'Emily, last year we checked out as many of the people as possible who might have been upset at some of the not-guilty verdicts you got for your clients. They all seem to be clean. How about that building where you had your office? Was there anyone who might have had big eyes for you or become jealous after you came into all that money?'

'Marty, I have an idea,' she said. 'You know that Eric Bailey worked in the office next to mine for several years. Maybe he could come up with the name of someone in our building or even one of the deliverymen that he thought was a little strange. I know he'd be glad to talk to you. He calls every few days to make sure I'm OK.'

It would probably be another dead end, Marty thought, but you never know. 'I'll do that, Emily,' he said.

THE TELEVISION reception in the van parked six blocks away was excellent. Eric sat in the small chair he had placed in front of the TV set. Very good, Emily, he thought in silent approval. Thank you for the vote of confidence. I'd hoped to stay another day, but now I'll have to get back to see Mr Browski tomorrow. Too bad.

He had an excellent shot of Emily opening the door for George Lawrence, but it would be unwise to send it to her now.

'MR STAFFORD asked if you'd mind waiting for a few minutes, Mrs Frieze. He has to finish writing up a contract.'

Pat Glynn, Will's secretary, smiled nervously at Natalie Frieze. She's so glamorous, Pat thought. Every time she walks through that door, I feel as if everything about me is wrong.

'You look gorgeous, Mrs Frieze,' Pat said shyly.

Natalie was always amused by the awe she knew she inspired in Will's plain secretary, but realised that it gave her an unexpected lift to hear a compliment. 'It's good to hear a kind word, Pat.'

'Don't you feel well, Mrs Frieze?'

'Not really. My wrist is terribly sore.' She held up her arm, causing her sleeve to slide back and reveal an ugly purple bruise.

Will emerged from his office. 'Sorry to keep you waiting. What's with your wrist?'

Natalie kissed him. 'I'll tell you all about it over lunch. Let's go.'

As they went out, Will pulled the door closed behind them, but not before Pat Glynn heard Natalie say, 'Will, I was scared to death of Bobby this morning. I think he's going crazy.' She appeared to be on the verge of tears.

'Calm down,' he said sympathetically, as they got into his car. 'We'll talk over lunch.'

When they were seated and their orders had been taken, Will looked at Natalie. 'You do realise that Pat probably overheard what you said about Bob and that she is something of a gossip.'

Natalie shrugged and lit a cigarette. 'I really don't care. I've given five years of my life to Bob Frieze. Now he's not only going to hell in a handbasket financially, but he's getting weird.'

Will raised his eyebrows. 'Weird?'

'I'll give you an example. I know Bobby has told you that he's an insomniac and often reads half the night. Last night I went downstairs at two o'clock and looked into Bobby's study. There was no sign of him. I looked in the garage, and his car was gone. I don't know where he went, but this morning I found a note in his pocket from some woman, saying she wanted him to call her. When I confronted him about it, he was shocked. I honestly don't think he *remembered* meeting her! He tried to make some lame excuse, but I believe he may have blacked out. In fact, I think he's been having intervals of blacking out for some time.' Natalie's voice was rising.

'Best keep it down, Natalie,' Will suggested.

'I don't know if I want to,' she retorted, but then, her voice slightly lower, she went on. 'Will, I keep thinking back to that night at the Lawrences' party. Bobby was wearing that stupid boxy jacket he seems to think makes him look younger.'

'Are you suggesting that Bobby stole Rachel Wilcox's scarf?'

'I'm saying that when I went into the powder room, I noticed it on a side table, but when I came back, it was gone.'

'Did you see Bobby anywhere near it?'

Uncertainty flickered over her face. 'I'm pretty sure I did.'

'Why didn't you tell this to the police?'

'Because until the other night, nobody knew they were asking about the scarf. I'll just keep concentrating on trying to remember that night. Maybe more will come to me,' Natalie concluded.

'I HAVE SOME OTHER BOOKS you might be interested in seeing, Emily. May I drop them off in half an hour?' Dr Wilcox asked.

'I don't want to inconvenience you. I can pick them up.'

'It won't inconvenience me. I'm going out to do a few errands.'

When she'd replaced the receiver, Emily returned to the research materials she'd spread out in the dining room, to continue to try to trace and identify the 1890s serial killer. There were more Monopoly houses placed on the map she had sketched, all of them neatly marked with the names of people who had lived at that address at that time. The names of their daughters or sons appeared in the lists of those present at parties, picnics and dances attended by Madeline Shapley, Letitia Gregg, and Ellen Swain.

Emily opened one of the boxes George Lawrence had brought over and was thrilled to see that it contained diaries and letters written by his great-grandmother Julia Gordon. Fascinated, she immediately began to read some of the letters. As the collective personal stories began to unfold, she felt as if she were stepping back in time and actually sharing the world of the 1890s. Sometimes she found herself almost wishing she had lived then. Life in the 1890s seemed so much more sheltered.

Then Emily asked herself abruptly if she was crazy. Sheltered! she thought. Three friends who had confided in each other, who had shared gatherings and picnics and dances, died at the ages of nineteen, eighteen and twenty. That's not very sheltered.

Emily had intended to close off the dining room before Clayton Wilcox arrived, but she was so deeply absorbed in her reading that when the doorbell rang, she ran to answer it, forgetting to turn off the light or close the door.

The sight of Dr Clayton Wilcox's hulking figure standing on the porch caused a sensation of pure fright to rush through her. What is *happening* to me? she asked herself, as she stepped aside to let him in and murmured a greeting.

She had been hoping that he would hand her the bag of books and leave, but instead Wilcox walked past her and stood well inside the hall. 'It's got quite chilly,' he said pointedly.

'Of course.' Emily had no option but to close the door. She realised her palms were drenched with perspiration.

He was holding the bag of books and glancing round the hall. The entrance to the living room was to the right, revealing a room already filled with shadows. There was also an entrance to the dining room from the hall, and in that room the chandelier over the table illuminated the board with the Monopoly houses. It was plainly visible to Wilcox.

'I see you're working in the dining room,' he said. 'Why don't I put these books in there.'

Before she could find a way to stop him, he was in the dining room, had placed the Enoch College book bag on the floor, and was carefully studying the board. 'I could help you with this,' he offered. 'I don't know if I mentioned that I am attempting to write a historical novel set in Spring Lake in 1876?' He pointed to the house at 15 Ludlam Avenue that she had labelled with Alan Carter's name. 'You are correct. This is where the Carter family lived for many years, beginning in 1893. Before that, this was their home.' He picked a house out of the box and placed it directly behind her own home.

'Alan lived right behind this house?' Emily said in shock.

'At that time, the house was in the name of his maternal grandmother. The family lived with her. When she died, they sold her home and moved to Ludlam Avenue.'

'You *have* done a great deal of research on the town.' Emily's mouth was dry.

'Yes, I have. For my book. May I sit down, Emily?'

'Yes, of course.' She quickly decided she would not invite him into the living room. She did not want to go into that darkened area with him walking behind her. Instead she deliberately took the chair nearest the door to the hall.

He sat down and folded his arms. 'Emily, you are a criminal defence lawyer and from what I understand a very good one. I believe I have become the prime suspect in the deaths of Martha Lawrence and Carla Harper. I want you to represent me.'

'Have the police told you that you are a suspect, Dr Wilcox?'

'Not yet, but they will be able to build a substantial case against me. Let me tell you why.'

'Please don't, Dr Wilcox,' Emily interrupted. 'I must tell you that I could *never* represent you. I am a witness in any legal hearing involving Martha Lawrence. Don't forget I was here when her body—or, I should say, skeleton—was discovered. So please don't tell me anything that I might be asked to repeat under oath. Since I can't be your lawyer, there would be no attorney-client privilege.'

He nodded. 'That had not occurred to me.' He got up slowly. 'Then, of course, I won't share with you any more of the great difficulty I am facing.' His face became suddenly haunted. 'If only one could undo a moment of weakness,' he said quietly as he got up from his chair.

Emily shrank back as he passed her. To her relief, he went directly to the front door and opened it. Then he paused. 'I think you should bolt the doors these next few nights, Emily,' he warned.

Thursday, March 29

One can feel the increasing apprehension of the residents of Spring Lake. The police patrol the streets more frequently. One seldom sees a woman alone.

In two days my task will be finished. I shall again return to a normal state and live out the remainder of my life in peace.

But I shall continue to write of everything that is occurring. In it, as in the other diary, the who and what and why and when will be made clear.

Maybe some day a fourteen-year-old boy will again find the diary—the two diaries—and want to relive the cycle. When that happens, I will know that I have returned to Spring Lake for the third time.

WHEN MARTY BROWSKI got to his office on Thursday morning, he saw that at seven o'clock on Wednesday evening Eric Bailey had returned his phone call in which he had requested an appointment.

Marty dialled Bailey's number. When his secretary answered, Marty was put through to him immediately.

'Sorry to have missed you yesterday,' Eric said pleasantly. 'I played hooky. I took an afternoon off to brush up on my golf game.' He readily agreed to a meeting. 'This morning if you want. I happen to be free at eleven o'clock.'

Marty had met Bailey face to face only once, but he had seen his picture in the newspapers from time to time. He was a local celebrity—Albany's miniversion of Bill Gates.

Bailey's office was located just outside the Albany city limits. A long drive led to a handsome two-storey red-brick structure with floor-to-ceiling tinted windows. Marty pulled into the parking lot.

Inside, the receptionist's desk was in the centre of reception. Expensive red leather sofas and chairs were placed around Persian carpets in defined seating areas. Paintings that looked to be of very fine quality were hanging on the walls.

The receptionist was expecting him. 'Mr Bailey's suite is on the first floor. Turn right and go to the end,' she directed.

Browski climbed up the winding staircase. As he walked down the long corridor on the first floor, he glanced into the offices he was passing. Many seemed to be empty. He had heard rumours that Bailey's dot-com was losing money, that the technology that had made the company a hot stock had been surpassed.

The carved mahogany double door at the end of the corridor signalled that he had arrived at Eric Bailey's private domain. Marty slowly pushed open the door.

'Come in, Mr Browski,' a voice called. As he stepped inside, a sleek, stylish woman of about forty got up from behind her desk. Introducing herself as Louise Cauldwell, Mr Bailey's personal assistant, she ushered Marty into the private office.

Eric was standing at the front window and turned when he heard them approaching. 'Detective Browski, it's good to see you again.'

'Good to see you too, Mr Bailey.'

Eric gestured towards the couch and chairs by the bank of windows overlooking the rear of the property.

Marty settled on the butter-soft leather couch. 'This is a beautiful office in a beautiful building, Mr Bailey,' he said sincerely.

A smile flickered across Eric's lips, then disappeared. 'Did you ever see my *old* office? It was the one next to Emily's.'

'I saw Emily's office a few times. Fairly small but pleasant.'

'My former workplace was a third of that size.'

'Then you must have had my present digs before I inherited them, Mr Bailey.'

This time Bailey's smile seemed real. 'I visited Emily in her new home on Monday. I installed cameras there for her.'

'Yes, she told me,' Marty said.

'I'm terribly concerned that this stalker seems to have followed her to Spring Lake. Or do you think he's a copycat?'

'I don't know,' Marty said. 'But I can tell you this. Any stalker is a potential time bomb. If this is the same guy who hounded her up here, he's getting ready to put a match to the powder keg.'

Marty leaned over and showed Eric the photograph of Emily in St Catherine's Church on Saturday morning. 'That guy was nervy enough to follow Emily into the memorial Mass for the murder victim who had been found buried in Emily's back yard.'

'I've been puzzling over that,' Eric said. 'To me it suggests that the stalker may be somebody she has never met. Even in a crowded church you can get a glimpse of a familiar face. I think that argues for a copycat stalker.'

'You may be right,' Marty admitted unwillingly. 'But if you are, it means we may be dealing with two stalkers, not one. The reason I wanted to see you, Eric, is to ask you to concentrate on the people in the building where you and Emily had offices. Can you think of anyone who might have become obsessed with her? It could be one of the maintenance staff or a deliveryman, or it could be some nice, amiable, nondescript guy who has a wife and kids.'

'Don't forget, I've been out of that building for three years,' Eric warned. 'Emily closed her office there for good only last week. But I'll certainly try to rack my brains.'

'Something else. Is there any other device you can install that will help to further ensure Emily's safety when she's alone in her home?'

'I wish there were. My only suggestions would be to have panic buttons installed in every room.'

'Well, too bad she hasn't got a boyfriend to take care of her, preferably one who's a linebacker for the Giants.'

Marty expected Bailey to agree with him. Then he saw the change in his face—an expression of pain and anger. This guy's in love with Emily, Marty thought. Oh, brother.

'You're a busy man. I am not going to take any more of your time,' Marty said, standing up.

But you're going to start taking a *lot* of mine, he thought as he said goodbye and started back down the long corridor to the staircase. I may be wrong, but all of a sudden I think that Eric Bailey may be the guy we're looking for.

But wait a minute. Surely Eric Bailey would never take a chance on going into the church last Saturday? Emily would have seen him.

'THERE IS NOTHING on Wilcox we can dig up at Enoch College,' Tommy Duggan snapped as he put down the phone. 'Not a hint of any scandal. The investigator spoke to people who were on the board of trustees when Wilcox resigned. Every one of them was indignant at the suggestion that Wilcox had been forced out.'

'Then why did he resign so suddenly?' Pete Walsh asked. 'Want to know what I think? I think Wilcox might have faked a heart condition because he had something hanging over his head and didn't want the college to be involved if it became public. The people there may not know the actual reason he resigned.'

They were in Tommy's office, where they had been waiting for the call from their investigator in Cleveland. Now that it had come, they got up and headed for the car. They were going to stop at Emily Graham's house with the copies of the 1890s police reports, then have another talk with Dr Clayton Wilcox.

'Maybe Wilcox didn't have his hand in the till there,' Pete said. 'Suppose it's the other way round. Why don't we look at his income tax records for the year he resigned from Enoch and see if he liquidated any assets?'

'It might be worth a try,' Tommy said, as they walked through the parking lot to the car.

On the way to Emily Graham's house, he placed another phone call to the investigator in Cleveland.

'To what do I owe the pleasure of your visit?' Bob Frieze asked as he joined Natalie at his table at The Seasoner. He had been both surprised and displeased to receive a call from the *maître d'*, informing him that his wife had joined him for lunch.

'Neutral territory,' Natalie said quietly. 'You look terrible. After you did this to me'—she indicated her bruised wrist—'I slept in the guest room last night, with the door locked. I see you didn't make it home at all. Maybe you were with Peggy.'

'I stayed here last night and slept on the couch in my office. I thought after yesterday's scene it might be a good idea to have a cooling-off period.'

Natalie shrugged. 'Neutral territory. Cooling-off period. Listen, we're both saying the same thing. We're sick of each other, and quite frankly, I'm physically afraid of you.'

'That's ridiculous!'

'Is it?' She opened her bag and took out a cigarette.

'You can't smoke in here. You know that. When did you start again? You've been off cigarettes since right after we got married, and that's nearly five years ago.'

'To be precise, I promised you I'd give them up right after Labor Day that summer four and a half years ago. I've always missed them. No need to miss them now.'

As she ground out the cigarette in the serving plate, Natalie was seized with a sudden awareness. That's what I've been trying to remember, she thought. The last time I smoked prior to yesterday was at that party the Lawrences gave for Martha. That was September 6. I went out on the front porch because, of course, you weren't allowed to smoke in that house.

He had something in his hand and was walking to the car.

'What's the matter with you?' Bob snapped. 'You look as though you've seen a ghost.'

'Let's skip lunch. I thought I owed it to you to tell you face to face that I'm leaving you. I'm going home to pack now. My friend Connie's letting me use her apartment in the city until I find a place. I told you yesterday what I want for a settlement.'

'There's no way any judge will give you that ridiculous amount. Get real, Natalie.'

'*You* get real, Bobby,' she snapped. 'You *find* a way to make it happen!' She pushed her chair back and almost ran to the door.

The *maître d'* waited a tactful few minutes before approaching the table. 'Would you like to order now, sir?' he asked.

Bob Frieze looked up at him blankly. Then, without responding, he got up and walked out of the restaurant.

THE MAP on the dining-room table was dotted with a dozen more tiny houses. All roads lead to Rome, Emily thought, but it still doesn't make sense. There *has* to be another answer.

The photo albums George Lawrence had brought over with the rest of the memorabilia were putting faces to the names. Emily had found one group picture with the names of the participants inscribed on the back. It was faded and too small to see the faces clearly, so when the detectives came by later, she planned to ask them if the lab could make an enlarged copy, with the features enhanced.

It was a large group. All three victims—Madeline, Letitia and Ellen—were listed on the back of the photo as being present in it, as were both Douglas and Alan Carter and some of their parents, including Richard Carter.

The back of her house and the back of the house where Alan Carter had lived at the time of the murders faced each other. The holly tree that had sheltered the grave had been practically at the border of the two properties.

Douglas Carter had lived directly across Hayes Avenue.

In reviewing what she'd learned about Letitia Gregg, she decided that the young woman may well have been planning to have a swim when she disappeared. Her bathing dress was missing when she vanished. Her house had been on Hayes Avenue, between 2nd and 3rd. She would have had to pass the homes of both Alan and Douglas Carter to get to the beach. Had she been waylaid along the way?

But Douglas Carter committed suicide *before* Letitia disappeared.

Alan Carter's family later bought the property where Letitia's body was buried. There seemed to be many connections.

Ellen Swain, however, did not fit into that scenario. She lived in one of the houses on the lake.

Emily was still pondering the map when Detectives Duggan and Walsh arrived. She gave them the group picture, which they promised to take care of for her. 'Our guys are good,' Duggan told Emily.

Walsh was studying the cardboard map. 'Nice job,' he said admiringly. 'You getting anywhere with this?'

'Maybe,' Emily said.

'Ms Graham, is there anything you're finding that may be useful in giving us something to work with?' Tommy asked.

'No,' Emily said honestly. 'Not yet.'

AFTER THE DETECTIVES left, Emily settled into the comfortable club chair in the study and began to read the police reports, starting with the first page of the file on Madeline Shapley:

Sept. 7, 1891: Alarmed phone call received from Mr Louis Shapley of 100 Hayes Avenue, Spring Lake, at 7.30pm, reporting that his nineteen-year-old daughter, Madeline, is missing.

Sept. 8, 1891: Foul play is suspected in the mysterious disappearance. Mother and younger sister had been at home. Under Mrs Kathleen Shapley's supervision eleven-year-old Catherine Shapley had been taking a piano lesson with teacher, Miss Johanna Story. Theorised that the sound of the piano may have kept any cry Miss Shapley may have uttered from being heard.

Sept. 22, 1891: Mr Douglas Carter was questioned again in the disappearance of his fiancée. Mr Carter continues to claim that he missed the train he had intended to take from Manhattan by moments and was obliged to wait two hours for the next one. The later train was quite crowded, and Mr Carter states he did not recognise anyone on board. The conductor on the train doesn't remember having punched his ticket.

The ringing of the phone came as an intrusion. It was Will.

'I've been wanting to call you,' he said, 'but it's been an awfully busy week. Look, would you like to have dinner tonight?'

'I would love to,' Emily said sincerely.

'Seven o'clock good for you?'

'It's fine.'

'See you then.'

Emily hung up and then, realising how stiff she felt from sitting so long, did a few quick stretches to limber up.

The camera noiselessly recorded her every move.

JOAN HODGES HAD SPENT the last four days trying to put the patients' files back in order. It was a tedious task. The killer had done a thorough job of trashing the records—clinical information and Dr Madden's notes had been totally scattered and mixed.

On Thursday a police technician came back with the rebuilt computer. 'That guy did his best to wreck this one,' he said, 'but you got lucky. He didn't get to the hard drive.'

'That means all the records can be retrieved?' Joan asked.

'Yes, it does. Detective Duggan wants you to look for one name right away—Dr Clayton Wilcox.'

Joan was at the computer, her fingers flying. His file came up on the screen. She reported triumphantly, 'He was a patient for a brief time in September four and a half years ago and again in August two and a half years ago. He came in the evening, so I never met him.'

The police technician was on his cellphone. 'I have some information Duggan needs to have immediately,' he snapped.

AFTER THEY LEFT EMILY, Tommy Duggan and Pete Walsh went directly to the home of Dr Clayton Wilcox. Their interview with him was frustrating and unsatisfactory. Wilcox stuck to his story about laying the scarf next to his wife's handbag. When asked about Dr Madden, he *did* recall that some years ago he had been experiencing mild depression and might have consulted her.

'How long ago was that, Dr Wilcox?' Duggan asked.

'It's quite a while ago. I'm really not sure.'

The only satisfaction the policemen were able to extract from the meeting was the fact that Wilcox was visibly coming apart at the seams. His eyes were sunken. When he talked, he kept folding and unfolding his hands. Beads of perspiration kept forming on his forehead, even though the temperature in his study was cool.

'If nothing else, he's getting rattled,' Tommy told Pete afterwards.

Then, at four o'clock, two things happened almost simultaneously. The technician phoned from Dr Madden's office and gave them the dates Dr Wilcox had consulted the psychologist.

'He saw her a few weeks after Martha Lawrence vanished and three weeks after Carla Harper vanished,' Tommy repeated, his tone both incredulous and exhilarated. 'And he claims he didn't remember! The guy's a world-class liar.'

'He told us he saw her for a mild case of depression. If he *did* strangle those girls, it's no wonder he was depressed,' Pete Walsh said sarcastically.

The second serving of manna from heaven came in the form of a phone call from the investigator in Ohio.

'I have a connection at the brokerage firm where Wilcox has his portfolio,' he said. 'It would cost the guy his job if it were known, but he looked up the Wilcox file. Twelve years ago, when Wilcox retired, he took a one-hundred-thousand-dollar loan against his stocks. He took it in the form of a cashier's cheque made out to himself. However, the cheque was deposited in a bank in Ann Arbor, Michigan, in a new account opened by one Gina Fielding. On the bottom of the cheque someone wrote, "Antique desk and bureau".'

'Is Gina Fielding a bona fide antiques dealer?' Tommy asked.

'Gina Fielding was a junior at Enoch College and dropped out of school abruptly just before Wilcox resigned.'

'Where is she now?'

'We're tracing her. She moved to Chicago, got married, then divorced. We'll locate her in the next day or two.'

Tommy hung up the phone and looked at Pete with grim satisfaction. 'We may have our smoking gun,' he said. 'Tomorrow morning we arrange to see the eminent former president of Enoch College.'

Friday, March 30

When Emily woke up on Friday morning and looked at the clock, she was surprised to see that it was already eight fifteen. Shows what a couple of glasses of wine will do to relax you, she thought, as she pushed back the covers.

But the long, dreamless sleep did make her feel a lot more refreshed than she had been feeling all week. And it had been a very pleasant evening. Will Stafford is a nice guy, she reflected.

He had arrived to pick her up almost half an hour early. I still hadn't put on lipstick or jewellery, Emily thought. She had left him in the study, watching the news.

This morning, as she slipped into white jeans and a red-and-white-checked cotton shirt, she thought how funny it was that an outsider's impression of other people's lives can be so different from what actually is going on in them.

Like Will, Emily thought as she made the bed. From what he told me the day I closed on the house, I'd have thought that his life was always pretty much OK and free of hardship.

Over dinner, however, Will had opened up about himself, and a different picture had emerged. 'I'm an only child,' he told her, 'raised in Princeton, and I moved with my mother to Denver after my parents split. After the divorce my father married his secretary, the first of three more wives.' Will's eyes filled with sadness when he said, 'My mother was heartbroken after that. He broke her spirit.'

There was so much raw pain in his face when he talked of that time, Emily thought.

She went down the stairs and walked towards the kitchen, stopping in the dining room to pick up a book from the Lawrence collection of memorabilia. It was a diary kept by Julia Gordon after her marriage. Over toast and grapefruit Emily opened it and began to read. In one of the early entries Julia wrote:

Poor Mrs Carter continues to decline. She will never recover from the loss of Douglas. We all visit her frequently and bring flowers to brighten her room or a sweet to tempt her appetite, but nothing seems to help. She talks constantly about Douglas. 'My only son,' she sobs when we try to console her.

It's very sad how life has turned out for Mrs Carter. She was blessed with great beauty and substantial wealth. But crippling rheumatism set in shortly after Douglas was born. She has been a semi-invalid for years and now never leaves her bed.

Mother Lawrence feels that for a long time, in an attempt to alleviate her pain, the doctors have been prescribing daily doses of laudanum that seem far too strong. Now Mrs Carter is in a sedated state that gives her no opportunity to take an interest in life. Instead the only outlet to her grief is to shed copious tears.

Emily closed the book after reading that entry. Suppose Douglas actually had been on the early train, arrived home, and Madeline had run across the street to greet him. If something had gone wrong

517

between Madeline and Douglas, would Mrs Carter, upstairs, sedated by laudanum, be aware that a tragedy was unfolding downstairs?

Or had Madeline left the porch and walked into her own back yard and found Alan Carter outside in *his* back yard? He was in love with her and probably aware that she was about to receive his cousin's engagement ring. He might have made a pass at her, Emily reflected, and then became enraged when she rebuffed him.

Either possibility was intriguing. As Emily went into the dining room to return the diary to the collection of Lawrence memorabilia, a new thought occurred to her. Did Douglas Carter *really* commit suicide, or was he murdered because he began to suspect the truth?

ON FRIDAY MORNING, BOB Frieze was woken by the ring of the telephone on the night table beside his bed. He opened his eyes and groped for the phone. His greeting was gruff.

'Bob, this is Connie. I expected Natalie to be here last night. She never showed up. Is she there? Is everything all right?'

Frieze pulled himself up. He was lying on top of the bed. Natalie, he thought, his mind still foggy.

'Bob, what's going on?' Irritation was apparent in Connie's voice, but he detected something else as well. There was fear.

Fear? Natalie had probably told Connie about their fight. He was sure of it. Had she told Connie about her bruised wrist too?

He tried to think. Natalie told me she was leaving. She was going home to pack. She was going to stay at Connie's apartment in New York. She never got there? It was morning now. I've lost almost a day, Bob thought. How long exactly have I been out?

He said, 'Connie, I saw Natalie at the restaurant yesterday. She told me she was going home to pack and was planning to go to New York to your apartment. I haven't seen her since.'

'*Did* she pack? Are her bags there? What about her car?'

'Hang on.' Bob stumbled to his feet, realising that he had a massive hangover. I don't normally drink much, he thought. How did this happen?

He opened her walk-in closet. Natalie's largest suitcase was open on the shelf. Bob looked into it and saw that it was half filled.

Afraid of what he might find, he stumbled into the guest bedroom, remembering that was where Natalie had told him she had spent Wednesday night. The bed was made, but when he looked into the bathroom, he saw that her cosmetics were all still on the shelf.

He ran downstairs into the kitchen and opened the door to the garage. Her car was parked inside. Where is she? he wondered.

Back in the bedroom, he picked up the phone. 'Looks like Natalie changed her mind, Connie. All her stuff is here.'

'So where is Natalie?'

'I don't know. We had a disagreement on Wednesday. She's been sleeping in the guest room. I got home late last night and went straight to bed. I'm sure she's fine. Natalie can be careless about calling people when she makes a sudden change of plans.'

The click in his ear told Bob that his wife's best friend had hung up on him. She was going to call the police. That certainty hit him with the impact of a gun firing in his face. What should he do?

Act normal, he decided. Where have I been since yesterday noon? he asked himself. His mind was a complete blank.

When a police officer rang his doorbell thirty minutes later, Frieze was prepared for him. He was calm, but explained he was becoming concerned. 'With all that has been going on in town this last week, I am beginning to be deeply worried about my wife's disappearance. I can't bear the thought that anything might have happened to her.'

Even to his own ears that statement did not ring true.

FOR THE PAST two and a half hours Emily had been alternating between the old police reports and the Lawrence memorabilia.

Julia Gordon had kept yearly diaries. She had not made daily entries, but she did write in the books frequently. I could enjoy reading every word, Emily thought, and I will if the Lawrences let me keep them long enough. But for now, I need to find information in them that ties in directly to those disappearances of Madeline and her friends and to Douglas's death. With a start, she realised she no longer thought of his death as a suicide, but considered him a victim of the same person who had killed the three young women.

Ellen Swain vanished on March 31, 1896.

Of course, Emily thought, Julia must have written about that. She went through the diaries and found the one for that year.

Before she started reading it, however, there was something else she wanted to do. She opened the door that led from the study to the porch, went outside, and looked across the street at Douglas Carter's house. It was a turn-of-the-century Victorian home, complete with wraparound porch. If Madeline was sitting here and Douglas or Alan beckoned to her . . .

Emily wanted to verify in her mind that the scenario she had come up with earlier was possible. She walked round on the porch to the back of the house and went down the steps into the yard. She walked the length of the yard to the boxwoods that defined the end of her property, where the remains of the two victims had been found. The massive holly tree with its heavy, low branches would have made it impossible for anyone in the house to know if Alan Carter had seen Madeline come out, and then either deliberately or accidentally harmed her. The sound of Madeline's sister taking her piano lesson would have covered any outcry.

But even if it happened this way, Emily asked herself, how does that tie any of these murders to the present?

She went back inside, picked up the 1896 diary, and looked for entries dated after March 31. On April 1, 1896, Julia had written:

My hand shakes as I write this. Ellen has disappeared. Yesterday she stopped to see Mrs Carter, who has told the police that Ellen seemed to be in a state of excitement. Mrs Carter was resting in a lounge chair at the window of her bedroom and saw Ellen leave the house and walk down Hayes Avenue on her way home. That was the last she saw of her.

Emily turned the next pages quickly. An entry dated three months later read:

Mrs Carter has been called to her heavenly home this morning. We are all so saddened, yet feel that for her this is a great blessing. She has been released from pain and grief and is now reunited with her beloved son, Douglas. Her last days were spent with her mind in a state of confusion. Mr Carter has endured with grace his wife's long illness and the loss of his son. We all hope the future will be kinder to him.

What about him—the husband and father? Emily wondered. There isn't very much at all written about him. Obviously, he and Mrs Carter weren't attending the parties and festivities. From the few references to him, she had learned his name was Richard.

She kept turning the pages, looking for more references to anyone named Carter. There were many more references to Ellen Swain for the rest of 1896 but nothing that Emily could spot about either Richard or Alan Carter.

The first entry in the 1897 diary had been made on January 5:

This afternoon we attended the wedding of Mr Richard Carter to Lavinia Rowe. It was a quiet affair due to the fact that the late Mrs Carter is not yet deceased a year. However, no one begrudges Mr Carter his happiness. He is a strikingly handsome man and still only in his forties. He met Lavinia when she was visiting her cousin, Beth Dietrich. Lavinia is a most attractive girl, poised and mature. At twenty-three she is half Mr Carter's age, but we have all seen many May and December romances and some of them very successful.

TOMMY DUGGAN and Pete Walsh arrived at the Frieze home to find a highly agitated Bob Frieze sitting on a couch in his living room, speaking with a local police officer.

'My wife and I have been eager to move to Manhattan,' he was saying. 'I have just sold my restaurant and will put this house on the market immediately. She was offered the use of a friend's apartment and planned to go there yesterday. I don't know why she changed her mind. Natalie is impulsive. For all I know, she got on a plane to Palm Beach. She has dozens of friends there.'

'Can you tell if any of her warm-weather clothes are missing?' the police officer asked.

'My wife has more clothes than the Queen of Sheba. If Natalie got on a plane to Palm Beach, she would think nothing of going with the clothes on her back and, when she got there, spending a couple of hours shopping with credit card in hand.'

'Do you mind if I take a look round, Mr Frieze?'

'Go ahead. I have nothing to hide.'

Tommy knew that Frieze had seen him and Walsh when they came into the room, but he had not bothered to acknowledge them. Now Tommy moved into the seat the police officer had just abandoned. 'Did you happen to go jogging this morning, Mr Frieze?'

Did I? Bob asked himself. I had my sweats on. When did I change into them? Last night? Did I follow Natalie home when she left the restaurant? Did we have another fight?

He stood up. 'Mr Duggan, I am sick and tired of your accusatory manner. I will no longer submit to questioning by you or anyone else. I intend to start phoning friends in Palm Beach to see if any of them have seen my wife.' He paused. 'However, Mr Duggan, my first call will be to my lawyer. Any further questions you have for me should be addressed to him.'

JOAN HODGES was going through the computer files and making lists of all Dr Madden's patients for the past five years. A police technician had been assigned to help her reassemble the patient files that had been scattered about the office.

The accelerated pace of the activity had been requested by Tommy Duggan. If the file of Dr Clayton Wilcox remained missing, he reasoned, it would point to the strong possibility that he had been the killer. Joan had already been able to ascertain that no one else on the list Duggan had given her to check had been one of Dr Madden's patients.

She came across a name with a Spring Lake address and frowned. She read the name and couldn't place him. He could have been one of the evening patients; she never did meet most of them. But wait a minute, she thought. Is he the one who came only once, about four years ago?

I got a glimpse of him getting into his car when I came back that evening to pick up my glasses, which I had left here. I remember him, she thought, because he seemed to be upset. The doctor said he left abruptly. She handed me a one-hundred-dollar bill that she said he'd thrown on her desk. I asked her if she wanted me to bill him for the rest of her fee, but she said to forget it.

I'd better pass his name along to Detective Duggan immediately, she decided as she picked up the phone.

Douglas Carter of 101 Hayes Avenue, Spring Lake.

TOMMY DUGGAN and Pete Walsh were in the prosecutor's office, where they had just given Elliot Osborne a run-down of their findings in the disappearance of Natalie Frieze. 'So the husband told us she's probably in Palm Beach, and now he won't talk to us except through his lawyer,' Tommy concluded.

'What's the likelihood that she'll turn up in Palm Beach?' Osborne asked.

'We're checking the airlines to see if she flew out on any of them.'

'The husband invited you to look round the house?'

'The Spring Lake cop went through it. No sign of any struggle. It looks as if she was in the middle of packing, then left.'

'We'll have to wait and see if she shows up,' Osborne said. 'As an adult, she has the right to pick up and go whenever she wants. You say her car was in the garage? Somebody must have picked her up. Is there a boyfriend in the picture?'

'None that we're aware of,' Walsh said.

'Then for the moment we have to just wait and see,' Osborne said. 'What's the matter, Duggan? You don't look happy.'

'I'm wondering if somebody has anticipated the 31st by a couple of days,' Tommy said flatly.

For a long moment there was silence. Then Osborne asked, 'Why do you think that?'

'Because she fits the pattern. She's thirty-four, not twenty or twenty-one, but like Martha Lawrence and Carla Harper, she's a beautiful woman.' Duggan shrugged. 'Anyway, I've got a bad feeling about Natalie Frieze. Plus I don't like the husband. Frieze has a weak, unsubstantiated alibi for where he was when Martha Lawrence disappeared. Claims he was working on his flower beds.'

Walsh nodded. 'He lived the first twenty years of his life in the house where the remains of Carla Harper and possibly Letitia Gregg were found. And now his wife is missing.'

'We'd better get to Dr Wilcox,' Tommy suggested. 'He's coming in at three o'clock.'

'What have you got?' Osborne asked.

Tommy leaned forward in his chair. 'He was willing to come. He knows he doesn't have to. When he gets here, I'll emphasise that he's free to leave at any time. As long as he's fully aware of that, we don't have to warn him of his legal rights, and frankly, I'd rather not have to. He may button up if we do.'

'What's your take on him?' Osborne asked.

'He's hiding a lot, and we *know* he's a liar. Those are two big handicaps in my book.'

CLAYTON WILCOX arrived promptly at three o'clock. Duggan and Walsh escorted him to an interrogation room, where the only furniture was a table and several chairs, and invited him to sit down. They assured him that he was not in any way being detained and that he was free to leave.

Tommy began. 'Dr Wilcox, in looking at your background, I'm surprised to see that you retired from Enoch College at the age of fifty-five. Yet you had just signed a new five-year contract.'

'My health would not permit me to carry on my duties. Believe me, the role of president of a small but prestigious institution requires a great deal of energy as well as time.'

'What is the nature of your ill health, Dr Wilcox?'

'A serious heart condition.'

'Do you have regular check-ups?'

'My health has been stable of late. Retirement has removed a great deal of stress from my life.'

'When was the last time you went to a doctor?'

'I'm not sure.'

'You weren't sure about whether or not you ever had an appointment with Dr Madden. Do you still claim that?'

'I may have had an appointment or two.'

'Or nine or ten. We *have* the records.' Tommy proceeded carefully in conducting the interrogation. He could tell that Wilcox was becoming rattled, but he didn't want him to get up and leave. 'Doctor, does the name Gina Fielding mean anything to you?'

Wilcox paled as he leaned back in the chair. 'I'm not sure.'

'You gave a one-hundred-thousand-dollar cheque to her twelve years ago, just at the time you retired. You marked the cheque "Antique desk and bureau". Does that refresh your memory?'

'I collect antiques from many sources.'

'Miss Fielding must be pretty smart. She was only twenty years old at the time and a junior at Enoch College. Isn't that right?'

There was a long pause. Wilcox looked directly at Tommy, then moved his gaze to Pete.

'You are quite right. Twelve years ago Gina Fielding was a twenty-year-old junior at Enoch College. A very worldly twenty-year-old, I might add. She worked in my office. A consensual relationship developed between us, which of course was inappropriate and potentially scandalous. She was a scholarship student from a low-income family. I began giving her spending money.'

Wilcox reached for the glass of water they had put on the table for him. 'Eventually I came to my senses and told her that the relationship would have to end, but she threatened a lawsuit against me and the college for sexual harassment. She was prepared to swear that I had threatened to have her scholarship taken away if she did not have a relationship with me. The price of her silence was one hundred thousand dollars. I paid. I also resigned my presidency because I did not trust her, and if she broke her word and sued the college, I knew there would be much less media interest were I no longer the president.'

'Where is Gina Fielding now, Doctor?'

'I have no idea where she lives.'

I believe him, Tommy thought. But that still doesn't let him off the hook, as far as I'm concerned. If anything, it's proof that he's attracted to young women; besides, it's still his wife's scarf that is the murder weapon. And he still doesn't have an alibi for the morning of Martha Lawrence's disappearance.

After the interrogation Tommy and Pete went back to Tommy's office, where the message from Joan Hodges was waiting for them. 'Douglas Carter!' Tommy exclaimed. 'The guy's been dead for over one hundred years!'

ERIC BAILEY PLANNED to drive down to Spring Lake on Saturday and get there by midafternoon. He'd park the van in an inconspicuous spot near the boardwalk. There were plenty of parking spaces on Ocean Avenue, and no one would pay attention to an old navy-blue van.

Faced with an empty evening ahead, Eric felt himself growing impatient. He had so much on his mind, so much to deal with in the days ahead. Next week the company's stock would be downgraded to junk. Everything he had would have to be sold.

He was engulfed in this nightmare because of Emily Graham. She had started the selling trend on his company's stock. She had not put a penny of her own into the company, but had made $10 million because of his genius. She had then rejected his offer of love with a dismissive smile. And she was set for life.

He understood that soon it would not be enough to make her fearful. There was another step he would be forced to take.

Saturday, March 31

E mily spent a restless night filled with vague dreams. She awoke from one of them with tears in her eyes and no memory of what had brought them on. It was only seven o'clock, and she hoped she could fall back asleep.

It was difficult, though; she had so much on her mind. She had the tantalising feeling that she was very close to finding the link between the past and the present, and being able to make the connection between the two sets of murders.

Detective Duggan had called the day before and told her that the photo lab would have the enlargement of the group picture for her by late today. She was looking forward to seeing it. Getting that photo would be like finally meeting people that she'd heard a lot about.

The clouds were heavy and grey, and the overcast morning meant that the room was in semidarkness. Emily closed her eyes. It was eight thirty when she woke again, this time feeling more cheerful.

It was a state of mind that lasted only an hour. When the mail was delivered, in it was a plain envelope with her name printed in childish letters. Her throat closed. She had seen that printing on the postcard with the tombstone drawings that had come only a few days ago. With trembling fingers she ripped open the envelope and pulled out the postcard inside it.

She turned it over and saw a drawing of two tombstones. The names on them were Natalie Frieze and Ellen Swain. They were placed in a wooded area adjacent to a house. The address printed across the bottom of the card was 320 Seaford Avenue.

Shaking so violently that she misdialled twice, Emily phoned Tommy Duggan.

ONCE AGAIN, TAPES marked CRIME SCENE went up on the property of a Spring Lake homeowner.

The spacious property was composed of two building lots. The house and garden were on the left, while the area to the right was unchanged from its natural wooded state.

It was there, in the shadow of a cluster of sycamore trees, that the body of Natalie Frieze, encased in heavy plastic, was found.

For area residents, the events that followed had the feeling of déjà vu. The media flocked to the scene in large vans with antennas. The neighbours gathered on the sidewalk and on the closed-off road.

After receiving Emily's phone call, Tommy Duggan and Pete Walsh had alerted the Spring Lake police. They soon received confirmation that the postcard was not a hoax. The difference was that this time the remains had not been interred.

'Wonder why he didn't bury her?' Pete asked soberly, as once more they watched the forensic team perform the grim task of examining and photographing the victim.

Before Tommy could reply, a squad car pulled up to the site. A pale and shaken Bob Frieze emerged from the back seat, spotted Duggan, and rushed to him. 'Is it Natalie?' he demanded.

Tommy nodded. He had no intention of offering even perfunctory sympathy to the man who might well be the murderer.

Duggan and Walsh followed the hearse conveying Natalie's body to the medical examiner's office.

'She's been dead between thirty-six and forty hours,' Dr O'Brien told them. 'I can narrow it down more when I do the autopsy. Cause of death appears to be strangulation.' He looked at Duggan. 'Are you going to dig for the remains of the March 31st, 1896, victim now?'

Tommy nodded. 'We'll probably find her there.'

'Why didn't the killer wait until the thirty-first to kill her?' the medical examiner asked. 'That would have followed his pattern of matching the dates on which the earlier victims died.'

'I think he wanted to be sure he got her when he had the opportunity,' Tommy said. 'And with so much security in town he couldn't take the chance of digging a grave. His need was to have her *discovered* today, the 31st'.

'There's one more factor you'd better consider,' the ME told him. 'Natalie Frieze was strangled by the same kind of cord the killer used on Dr Madden. The third piece of the scarf that was used on the Lawrence and Harper women is still out there.'

'If that's the case,' Tommy said, 'it may not be over yet.'

WHEN EMILY PICKED UP the phone, she was not sorry to hear Nick Todd's voice.

'I've been listening to the radio,' he said.

'It's so awful,' Emily told him. 'Just a few days ago I sat with Natalie at the luncheon the Lawrences gave after the memorial Mass. It's just impossible to think that now she is dead—murdered!'

Nick caught the distress in Emily's voice. He was in his SoHo apartment and had been planning to catch a movie, followed by dinner at his favourite pasta restaurant in the Village. 'What are you up to tonight?' he asked, trying to sound casual.

'Absolutely nothing. I want to finish reading the old diaries I've been loaned and then rejoin the twenty-first century.'

'How's the project going?'

'I may be kidding myself, but I'm seeing a pattern to all those deaths, and it's horrific. Did I tell you that Douglas Carter, the man Madeline was engaged to, killed himself?'

'No, you didn't.'

'Nick, he was found with a shotgun beside him. He had been

depressed over Madeline's disappearance, but he was also young, good-looking, with family money and a promising future on Wall Street. Everything that's written about him in all the diaries is positive, and nothing points specifically to his being suicidal. His mother was sick, and he was very close to her. He must have known that his death would destroy her. Just think—how would your mother feel if something happened to you?'

'She'd never forgive me,' Nick said wryly. 'But how would your mother feel if something happened to you?'

'She wouldn't like it, of course.'

'Then until your stalker and this killer are apprehended, keep your doors locked and the alarm on when you're there alone.'

He confirmed that he would pick her up at twelve thirty on Sunday for brunch. But when he hung up, he found he was too restless to go to a movie. Instead he phoned and made a reservation at the Breakers Hotel, then got into his car and drove to Spring Lake.

MARTY BROWSKI went into the office on Saturday evening to try to clear his desk, looking forward to a few hours without interruption. But after only a few minutes there, he decided he might as well have stayed at home. He simply could not concentrate. All of his attention was focused on only one person: Eric Bailey.

The financial page of the morning newspapers stated that Bailey's dot-com company would be forced into bankruptcy and that the misleading statements of its founder about new product developments were a matter of great concern to the director of the New York Stock Exchange. Bailey might even be facing criminal charges.

He fits the profile of a stalker so well, he could have posed for it, Browski thought.

Suddenly Marty thought of something. He got the licence numbers of Eric's van and Mercedes convertible, called E-ZPass, the electronic toll-collection company, and asked them to check the numbers against their records. E-ZPass confirmed his hunch: the van had been on the Garden State Parkway this afternoon, and at five o'clock it had turned off at exit 98.

He's in Spring Lake, Marty thought as he picked up the phone to dial the police there.

'We'll keep an eye on her house,' the desk sergeant promised. 'The town is crowded with media and with curiosity seekers doing a drive-through, but I promise you, if that van is here, we'll find it.'

EMILY'S PLEASURE on hearing Marty Browski's voice changed to shock when she realised why he was calling.

'That is absolutely impossible,' she said.

'No, it isn't, Emily,' Marty said firmly. 'Now listen. The local police are going to keep the house under surveillance.'

'How are they going to do *that*?'

'They'll drive by your house every fifteen minutes. If Eric calls and wants to see you, put him off. *Don't open the door for him.* Keep your alarm on the "instant" setting. The Spring Lake cops are looking for Bailey. Now check those locks!'

'I will.' When she hung up, Emily went from room to room, testing the doors to the porch, then the front and back doors. She pushed INSTANT and ON and watched the signal on the alarm box switch from green to a flashing red.

Eric, she thought. Friend, buddy. He was here on Monday, installing the cameras, acting so worried about me, and all the while . . .

Betrayal. Hypocrisy. Putting in security cameras and laughing at me while he was doing it. 'I hope when they find that wacko, they throw the book at him,' she said aloud, not knowing that at that very moment, Eric Bailey was parked in his van six blocks away, watching her on his television screen.

'ONLY YOU WON'T be around when they do throw the book at me,' Eric responded aloud.

The shock of being found out and of Marty telling Emily that he was the stalker stunned Eric. I've been so careful, he thought, looking at the box that contained the woman's coat, dress and wig he had worn to St Catherine's Church on Saturday and thinking of all the disguises he had used to get close to Emily in the past without being detected.

And now the police were looking for him and no doubt soon would arrest him. He would be sent to prison. His company would collapse in bankruptcy. The people who had praised him so lavishly would turn on him like dogs.

He focused on the screen again and leaned forward. Emily had gone back to the dining room and was on her knees going through the box of books.

But on the split screen he could see that the handle of the door leading from the porch to the study was turning. I know she has the alarm on, he thought. Someone must have tampered with it!

A figure wearing a ski mask and a dark sweatsuit stepped into the study, got behind the club chair in which Emily always sat, and dropped to his knees. As Eric watched, the masked man took a piece of material from his pocket and pulled it taut.

Emily came back into the study carrying a book, settled down in the club chair, and began to read.

The intruder did not move.

'He's *enjoying* this,' Eric whispered to himself. 'He doesn't want it to be over too soon. I understand. I understand.'

TOMMY DUGGAN AND PETE WALSH were still in the office at eight thirty on Saturday evening. Bob Frieze had steadfastly refused to answer any questions about his whereabouts on Thursday afternoon and evening, and now, claiming chest pains, he had been admitted to the Monmouth Hospital for observation.

'He's stalling until he can get a story together that will hold up in court,' Tommy told Pete. 'There are three ways this could play out. One is Frieze is the serial killer and is responsible for the deaths of Martha Lawrence, Carla Harper, Dr Madden, and his wife, Natalie. Two is he may have killed his wife but *not* the others. The third possibility is that he is innocent of all these deaths.'

'You're worried that the third piece of scarf is missing,' Pete said.

'You bet I am. Why do I have a feeling that Natalie Frieze's murder was a ploy to trick us into thinking that the killer had completed the cycle? Which means that another young woman may die in Spring Lake tonight. But who? No one has been reported missing. Let's call it a day, we can't accomplish anything more here.'

They started to leave, when Pete said, 'Wait a minute,' and pointed to an envelope on Tommy's desk. 'We never did drop this enlarged photo at Emily Graham's, like we promised.'

'Take it with you, and run it over tomorrow.'

As Pete picked up the envelope, the phone rang. It was the Spring Lake police, relaying the message that Emily's stalker had been identified and was believed to be somewhere in town.

On hearing the news, Tommy said, 'On second thoughts, maybe we'll drop that photo off tonight.'

EMILY HAD HER CELLPHONE in her pocket, a habit she had developed since the picture of her in church was slipped under the door last Sunday. She reached for it now, hoping that her grandmother hadn't turned in early. She had been reading the final diary of Julia Gordon, and she had a question about it she hoped her grandmother could help answer.

She had read earlier that Richard Carter's second wife gave birth to a baby girl in 1900. In relation to that, an entry in 1911 puzzled her. In it Julia had written:

> *Lavinia writes that she is very happy to be home in Denver. After a year her little daughter has quite recovered from the loss of her father and is flourishing. Lavinia herself confesses to being tremendously relieved. In fact she was rather astonishingly frank when she took pen to paper. She writes that Douglas had a deep well of coldness within him, and at times she was quite frightened of him. She feels that it was a blessing that his death released her from that marriage and has given her child a chance to grow up in a more congenial and warm atmosphere.*

Emily snapped open the cellphone. Her grandmother answered with a quick hello.

'Gran,' Emily said, 'I have something I have to read to you because it simply doesn't make sense.'

'All right, dear.'

Emily explained the entry and read it to her. 'Why would she refer to him as Douglas when his name was Richard?'

'Oh, I can tell you that. His name was Douglas Richard, but in those days it was common to call a man by his middle name if he had the same name as his father. Madeline's fiancé was Douglas Richard the Third. I understand the father was a very handsome man.'

'He was a handsome man with an invalid wife, and she had the money. Gran, you've been a great help. I'll call you tomorrow.'

Emily clicked off the phone. 'It *wasn't* young Douglas who was the killer,' she said aloud. 'It wasn't his cousin Alan either. It was his *father*. And when he died, his wife and daughter moved to Denver.'

Denver! Suddenly she saw the connection.

'Will Stafford was raised in Denver! His mother lived in Denver!' she said aloud.

Emily suddenly felt a shadowy presence hovering over her and froze in stunned terror as she heard a voice whisper in her ear.

'That's right, Emily,' Will said. 'I was raised in Denver.'

Before she could make a move, Emily's arms were pinned to her sides. A rope was looped round her chest, holding her to the back of the chair. With lightning-swift efficiency Stafford was on his knees before her, tying her feet and legs.

Make him *talk* to you, an inner voice whispered. Keep him talking! The police *do* have the house under surveillance. Maybe they'll ring the bell, and when they don't get an answer, they'll force their way in.

He stood up. Pulled the ski mask off his face. Unzipped his jacket. Stepped out of the sweatsuit.

Underneath his outer layer of clothing Will was wearing a very old-fashioned high-collared shirt and string tie. The wide lapels of his turn-of-the-century dark blue suit accentuated his stiffly starched white shirt. His hair was combed in an uncharacteristic side parting and brushed tightly across the top of his head. He had painted a narrow moustache above his upper lip.

'May I introduce myself, Miss Graham?' he asked with a short, formal bow. 'I am Douglas Richard Carter.'

Don't panic, Emily warned herself. It's all over if you panic. The longer you can stay alive, the better chance you have that the police will check on you. 'I am very pleased to meet you,' she said, struggling to mask her terror.

'You do know, of course, that you must die? Ellen Swain has been waiting for you to join her in her grave.'

His voice was different too, Emily thought. The words are more precise, clipped almost. It sounds as if he has a slight British accent. Reason with him, she ordered herself fiercely.

'But Natalie Frieze is with Ellen,' she managed to say.

'Natalie was never meant to be with Ellen. It was always you. Ellen is interred near the lake. The drawing I sent showing Natalie's tombstone next to Ellen's was meant to mislead. They are not together. But you will sleep with Ellen soon.'

He bent down and caressed Emily's cheeks. 'You remind me of Madeline. You, with your beauty and youth and vitality. Can you understand what it was like for me to look across the street and see my son with you and to know that I was condemned to live my life with an ailing woman whose sole attraction was her wealth?'

'But surely you loved your son and wanted him to be happy?'

'Surely I would not allow someone as exquisite as Madeline to be in his arms while I sat at the bedside of a confused invalid.'

There was a flash of light from a passing police car. 'Our police in Spring Lake do their best to secure our safety,' Will said as he reached into his pocket and brought out a piece of silvery material edged with metal beading. 'Since they have just checked this house, we will have at least a few minutes more.'

THE SPRING LAKE POLICE squad car was cruising along Ocean Avenue. 'There it is!' Officer Phil Reap said to his partner, pointing to a dark blue van parked in a spot facing the boardwalk.

They pulled into the space beside it and rapped on the front window. 'There's light coming from the back,' Phil said. He rapped again, harder. 'Police, open up!' he called.

Inside, Eric was watching the screen in rapt fascination. He pressed the remote button that unlocked the doors. 'Come in,' he said. 'I'm right here. I've been expecting you. But please let me finish watching my show.'

Reap and his partner slid open the door and saw the TV. This guy must be a nut, Reap thought as he glanced at the screen. For an instant he thought he was watching a horror movie.

'He's going to kill her,' Eric said. 'Be quiet. He's talking to her.'

The two officers stood immobile, transfixed by the realisation of what was unfolding in front of them and by the calmness of the voice that came through the speaker.

'In my current incarnation I had only expected to repeat the pattern of the past,' Stafford was saying, 'but it was not to be.'

'Why Natalie?' Emily asked, fighting for time.

'I am sorry about Natalie. The night of the Lawrence party she had stepped onto the porch to have a final cigarette before she gave them up for good. From that vantage point she may have seen me carrying the scarf to the car. When she started smoking again at our luncheon last Wednesday, I could sense that she was starting to remember. She had become a danger. I could not allow her to live. But don't worry. Her death was mercifully swift. It will be for you too, Emily. I promise.'

Astounded, Officer Reap realised suddenly that he was about to see a murder committed.

'When I was fourteen, my mother and I came to Spring Lake. A sentimental journey for her. We walked past the house where her mother—my grandmother—had been born.'

'Oh, God, that's Will Stafford and Emily Graham! Stay here with him!' Reap shouted to the other officer as he leapt out of the van and broke into a run.

'The woman who lived in my great-grandfather's house invited us in. I became bored and started rummaging around in the loft of the carriage house. I found his old diary. I was *meant* to find it, you see, because I am Douglas Richard Carter.'

Don't let me be too late, Reap prayed as he got into the squad car. As he raced to 100 Hayes Avenue, he radioed for back-up.

NICK TODD DECIDED that for his own peace of mind he would drive past Emily's house to reassure himself that all was well inside. He was just approaching it when a police car came racing down the street from the other direction and pulled into the driveway.

With a sense of dread Nick pulled in behind the police car and quickly jumped out. 'Has anything happened to Emily?' he demanded. Please, please, don't let anything happen to her, he begged silently.

'We hope not,' Reap said tersely.

THE POLICE WILL DRIVE by again, Emily promised herself. But then, if they didn't see him come in, what good is that? she reasoned. He's managed to get away with the murders of Martha, Carla, Natalie and probably others. I'm next. Oh, dear God, *I want to live!*

'Tell me about the diaries,' she said. 'You have kept a record of everything, haven't you? You must have written down every detail of the way everything happened, of your emotions at the time, of the reactions of the families of the girls.'

'Exactly.' He seemed pleased that she understood. 'When I was sixteen, I began following my great-grandfather's example. I overpowered a young woman, but before I could complete my mission, her screams were heard. I spent three years in juvenile detention.

'It is time, Emily—time for you to join lovely Madeline, time for you to rest with Ellen.'

Emily stared at the tattered shreds of cloth in his hands. He's enjoying himself, she thought. Make him keep answering questions. He wants to brag.

'When I am with Ellen, will it be over?' she asked.

He was behind her now, gently wrapping the remnant of scarf round her neck.

'I wish that could be true, but alas, there is at least one more. Dr Madden's secretary, unfortunately, caught a glimpse of me the night I visited Dr Madden. In time she might remember me. Like Natalie

Frieze, she poses an unacceptable risk.' He leaned forward and brushed her cheek with his lips. 'I kissed Madeline as I tightened her sash,' he whispered.

TOMMY DUGGAN and Pete Walsh arrived at Emily's house just in time to see Officer Reap running up the steps to the porch, followed by another man.

Reap quickly reported what he had seen on the monitor in Eric Bailey's van.

'Forget the front door. Take one of the porch doors,' Duggan shouted. He and Walsh, followed by Nick, ran to the left. Reaching the door to the study, the three men looked in the window and saw the scarf being tightened round Emily's neck.

Tommy knew that in another few seconds it would be too late. He drew his pistol and fired through the glass.

The impact of the bullet caused Will to jerk back, then crumple to the floor, the remains of the scarf that had snuffed out the lives of Martha Lawrence and Carla Harper still clutched in his hand.

Sunday, April 1

O n Sunday morning Tommy Duggan and Pete Walsh joined Emily and Nick in the breakfast room of the Breakers Hotel. 'You were right, Emily,' Tommy said. 'There was a complete written record of what his great-grandfather did. In addition, Stafford kept his own journal and wrote the details down in the same clinical fashion his great-grandfather did.'

He continued. 'We got a search warrant for Stafford's house, and we found Douglas Carter's original diary, as well as the one Stafford kept. I stayed up all night reading it. It was exactly the way you had figured it. Douglas Carter's wife was out of it with the amount of laudanum she was taking. And maybe he was feeding her more. He writes in his journal that he had beckoned Madeline over to his house, saying that his wife was having a seizure. When he tried to kiss her, she began to struggle, and he knew he'd be ruined if she talked.'

'I find it hard to think that it was Will Stafford's great-grandfather who did this,' Emily said. It was like being touched by fingers from the grave. I still feel so frightened, she thought. Will I ever feel safe again?

'Douglas Carter was nearly fifty years old when his second wife, Lavinia, gave birth in 1900 to a girl. They named her Margaret. After Douglas died in 1910, Lavinia and Margaret moved away to Denver. Margaret married in 1935. Her daughter was Will's mother.'

'He told me that he found that diary by chance when he and his mother were visiting Spring Lake and stopped at the house where his great-grandparents lived,' Emily said.

'It seems to me,' Nick said, 'that the seeds of corruption were in him then. A normal kid would have been horrified and would have shown the journal to an adult.'

Listening to the discussion, Emily felt as though she were still in a kind of dreamworld. The night Will had taken her to dinner, he had obviously arrived early so that he could remove the sensor from the alarm system for the door that led into the study. He must have taken the key for that door from the ring the Kiernans gave him to enter the house before the closing.

Last night, after his body had been removed and the forensic team was sifting for evidence, Nick told her to pack an overnight bag and took her to the Breakers, where he was registered.

'Once again my home is a crime scene,' she told him.

'It won't be after this,' he assured her. 'It's all over now.'

But even in the safety of the Breakers, Emily woke at 3.00am, startled, frightened, sure that she had heard footsteps in the corridor. Then the certainty of Nick's presence in the next room had been enough to make the trembling stop, to allow sleep to claim her.

'Did Douglas Richard Carter kill his son?' Emily asked.

'His diary isn't really clear on that point,' Duggan answered. 'He says that Douglas had a gun, and he struggled with him. After it went off, he managed to make it look like a suicide. I wouldn't be surprised if Douglas had figured out what his father had done and confronted him. Who knows?'

'What about Letitia and Ellen?'

'Letitia was on her way to the beach,' Pete said. 'She had brought a bouquet of flowers from her garden for Mrs Carter, and Carter happened to be home. Again his advances were rebuffed, and again he killed a young woman.'

Tommy shook his head. 'The diary makes for pretty nasty reading. Ellen Swain was visiting Mrs Carter and began to ask questions, apparently having come to suspect that Carter was the cause of her two friends' disappearances. She never got out of the house that day, although given his wife's befuddled state, it was easy enough for Carter to convince the poor woman that she had seen Ellen leave.' Tommy frowned. 'He's very specific about where he buried Ellen. We're going to try to find her remains and put them in her family's plot. She died trying to find out what happened to her friend Letitia. So in a way it's especially fitting that the two family plots are side by side in the cemetery.'

'*I* was supposed to be buried with Ellen,' Emily said. 'That was his plan for me.'

She felt Nick Todd's arm round her shoulders. This morning he had knocked on her bedroom door with a cup of coffee for her in his hand. 'I'm an early bird,' he explained. 'This is one of the things you'll miss at the office, because if I get the job I think I'm going to get, I'll be downtown. I invited my dad to have lunch with me at the cafeteria at the US Attorney's office. You can come too. Better still, you can come down *without* him.'

I'll be there, she thought. You bet I will.

Pete had just finished a double order of scrambled eggs, sausage, and bacon. 'Your study is being cleaned right now, Emily. I think from now on you'll find peace in your home.'

Tommy's breakfast had been just orange juice, black coffee and a banana. 'I have to be on my way.'

'Before you go,' Emily said quickly, 'what about Dr Wilcox and Bob Frieze?'

'I think Dr Wilcox is one relieved guy,' Tommy said. 'It's now out in the open that he got too cosy with a student years ago.'

'What was his wife's reaction?'

'My guess is that the public humiliation will finish the marriage. She *did* know why he resigned the college presidency, and I guess she's been throwing it at him on a regular basis. Actually, I think he's relieved about everything. He *did* tell me that he thinks his novel is good. Who knows? The guy may end up with a whole new career.' Tommy was pushing back his chair. 'As for Bob Frieze, he can thank Natalie that he's in the clear. She gave him a piece of paper she'd found in his pocket, with a phone number and the name Peggy, asking him to call her. Our guys checked her out. Frieze was in the habit of dropping into some bar in Morristown. Claims he didn't remember any of it, but obviously he didn't waste time during his blackouts.

Peggy's pretty cute. Between Peggy's testimony and Will Stafford's diaries, Frieze is in the clear.'

Tommy stood up. 'Some final information. Stafford accosted Martha after she left the boardwalk. Drove up to her and told her he was having chest pains. Asked her to drive him home. She knew him and fell for it, of course. He forced Carla to ride with him when she was on the way to her car after leaving the Warren Hotel. Then he went back and got her car later. Nice guy, huh?' He turned to go. 'Enjoy the rest of your breakfast, folks. We're off.'

After they had left, Emily was silent for a long moment. 'Nick, the reason Tommy Duggan came to my house last night was to deliver an enlarged photograph. I looked at it this morning.'

'What did you find?'

'The police lab did a magnificent job of enlarging the photograph. The faces are very clear now, and I can match them with all the names that are on the back of the original—Madeline and Letitia and Ellen and Phyllis and Julia. And the men: George and Edgar and young Douglas and even Douglas Carter, Senior, or Will Stafford, as we knew him in the present.'

'Emily,' Nick protested, 'you *can't* mean that you believe he really was reincarnated.'

She looked at him, her eyes pleading for understanding. 'Nick, Will Stafford was the image of his great-grandfather as he appeared in that picture, but . . .'

'What is it, Emily?'

'I found that picture in the Lawrence family memorabilia. It's a million to one Will never saw it.'

His hand, reassuring and firm, was over hers.

'Nick,' Emily whispered, 'in that picture, Douglas Carter was holding what appeared to be a woman's scarf with metal beading.'

MARY HIGGINS CLARK

When Mary Higgins Clark, America's queen of suspense, bought a summer home in Spring Lake, New Jersey, she had no idea it would provide the inspiration for her twenty-fourth novel. But as the renovation work began, she discovered that the deceased owner's maiden name had been Eleanor Higgins, and it set her thinking. 'I am Mary Eleanor Higgins Clark. Absolutely no relation. But I began to wonder what would happen if, by coincidence, a woman bought her great-great-grandmother's house . . .' One thought led to another, and before long Mary Higgins Clark had her plot worked out and had decided that Spring Lake would be the setting for her novel. 'As it turned out, the house triggered the book and the book paid for the house!'

While carrying out her research she was particularly pleased to incorporate two personal interests into the storyline: her love of history and her enjoyment of diaries. 'I found old newspapers and old memoirs, and that made it so much more interesting to do the 1890s. I sometimes wish I had been born then.' *On the Street Where You Live* is about a 19th-century serial killer who seems to have returned to life. 'I don't believe in reincarnation,' the author says, 'but I do believe that somehow psychic coincidences could happen.'

While Mary Higgins Clark enjoys spending time in Spring Lake, and in her other homes in Manhattan and on Cape Cod, she does most of her writing at her main residence in Saddle River, New Jersey, where she lives with her second husband, retired financier John Coheeney. They now have nine grown-up offspring and fifteen grandchildren between them.

ACKNOWLEDGMENTS AND PICTURE CREDITS: *Jackdaws:* pages 6–8: illustration by John Jinks. *The Smoke Jumper:* pages 146–147: Gettyone Stone; fire: FPG; page 148: The Image Bank; page 289: © David Middleton. *Hostage:* pages 290–292: Gettyone Stone. *On The Street Where You Live:* pages 428–430: illustration by Ericka O'Rourke. Page 539: © Bernard Vidal.

DUSTJACKET CREDITS: Spine from top: John Jinks, Gettyone Stone, FPG, Image Bank, Gettyone Stone, Ericka O'Rourke. Back jacket: Photograph of Nicholas Evans © David Middleton.

Printed by Maury Imprimeur SA, Malesherbes, France
Bound by Reliures Brun SA, Malesherbes, France

216AL